THE WORLD
THAT DEATH MADE

Borgo Press/Wildside Books by LLOYD BIGGLE, JR.

THE WORLD THAT DEATH MADE

A SCIENCE FICTION NOVEL

LLOYD BIGGLE, JR.
& KENNETH LLOYD BIGGLE

THE BORGO PRESS
MMXIII

THE WORLD THAT DEATH MADE

FIRST EDITION

Published by Wildside Press LLC

www.wildsidebooks.com

DEDICATION

To the loyal fans of Lloyd Biggle, Jr.,
with thanks—*klb*

Special thanks to Michelle Zdrojewski Leeson, for
her careful reading of the manuscript—*klb/dbe*

CONTENTS

CHAPTER ONE 9

CHAPTER TWO. .19

CHAPTER THREE 31

CHAPTER FOUR .44

CHAPTER FIVE. .52

CHAPTER SIX. 71

CHAPTER SEVEN 87

CHAPTER EIGHT. 107

CHAPTER NINE 127

CHAPTER TEN 142

CHAPTER ELEVEN. 160

CHAPTER TWELVE 170

CHAPTER THIRTEEN 186

CHAPTER FOURTEEN 199

CHAPTER FIFTEEN 215

CHAPTER SIXTEEN 235

CHAPTER SEVENTEEN 256

CHAPTER EIGHTEEN 280

CHAPTER NINETEEN 294

CHAPTER TWENTY 313

CHAPTER TWENTY-ONE 330

CHAPTER TWENTY-TWO 344

CHAPTER TWENTY-THREE 362

CHAPTER TWENTY-FOUR 381

CHAPTER TWENTY-FIVE 406

CHAPTER TWENTY-SIX 430

CHAPTER TWENTY-SEVEN 449

CHAPTER TWENTY-EIGHT 463

CHAPTER TWENTY-NINE 476

CHAPTER THIRTY 491

CHAPTER THIRTY-ONE 507

CHAPTER THIRTY-TWO 520

CHAPTER THIRTY-THREE 536

CHAPTER THIRTY-FOUR 548

CHAPTER THIRTY-FIVE 561

CHAPTER THIRTY-SIX 577

CHAPTER THIRTY-SEVEN 595

CHAPTER THIRTY-EIGHT 609

CHAPTER THIRTY-NINE 621

ABOUT THE AUTHOR 628

CHAPTER ONE

In the beginning there was agony.

First came pounding pain: blunt strokes of a relentless bludgeon that slowly ground Caland's brain cells to a pasty slime. When finally the brutal throbbing diminished, a searing rapier of pain probed with fiery slashes, isolating, cauterizing each quivering nerve. Caland's hands tore at his scalp, attempting to peel it open, to rip vents for the churning anguish within, and his body twisted and heaved, tensing with each scalding incision.

As the pain slowly eased, he slid helplessly into the third stage of his purgatory, the nightmare. He stood on the bank of a small stream. The land about him was devastated—trees, shrubs, buildings were flattened as by a wrathful cosmic fist. The screaming wind whipped sheets of rain across the tortured countryside, but the steep-banked stream contained no water. It was filled with the dead, with hideously bloated bodies limply awaiting some cataclysmic expectoration that would mercifully wash them into oblivion. The dead eyes stared at Caland, and the death mouths screamed at him, and the limp hands shaped their woeful supplication. He attempted to turn away, to blind himself, to clap his own hands to his ears; and the eyes continued to stare, and mouths to scream, and the hands to beseech pathetically.

The first slow seepage of consciousness cooled his senses and abruptly calmed the storm that was ravaging his mind. His exhausted mental processes, debris-cluttered and wind-torn, took refuge in a paralyzing numbness. Brilliant, blinding points of light surged across his retinas, tracing a grotesque web of brightness against a heaving backdrop of purplish velvet: the after image of besotted universes in convulsion.

The wind's anguished moan was muted by sudden, thunderous pulsations that racked his skull as pain's bludgeon returned: drumbeats of the spheres; hollow thuds on a rent fabric of time; seed worlds rattling in a galactic gourd; hysterically thumping heartbeats of the pantheistic god in labor.

He opened his eyes.

Instantly he closed them again. He often saw multiple images when he regained consciousness, but the six faces hovering above his bed were a preposterous redundancy. He clutched his head as a new wave of pounding agony engulfed him. The lights flashed, the drumbeats echoed, and pain twisted his limbs into knots of aching muscle. Finally he was able to relax and open his eyes again.

The massed faces above him still numbered six, all staring formidably. He fluttered his eyelids in a vain attempt to resolve them or blink them into oblivion.

"Jarv Caland?" a strident fem voice demanded.

Caland focused his bleary vision and discovered that the faces were not identical. He sat up in alarm and looked about him perplexedly. The unadorned, scantily furnished cubicle could only belong to a cheap gen hote or to a hospital, and the six hulking figures gathered about his bed did not look like doctors. They were dressed identically in hooded slick suits of drab gray, and he could not distinguish fems from the mals unless one spoke.

"Rynaif Security Proctors," the fem voice said. "Come along."

"Where am I?" Caland asked.

The faces drew back and exchanged glances. "Rynaif."

Caland fingered his scalp and applied gentle pressure, though he knew that this would not help. As the pain slowly faded, he looked about him again. "Is this a hote?"

"Rynaif Hote Central," the fem voice said. "Come along."

"All right," Caland said.

He pushed aside the thin vibrator blanket that covered him. His clothing had been draped over the two cubes that were standard hote furnishings. The proctors handed the garments to him, steadied him when he tried to stand, and assisted him in poking arms and legs into the correct openings. When he had donned the clothing, he stumbled to the nearest cube and anxiously inspected its interior.

It contained his traveling case. Caland opened it. It had been packed with care—far more care than he ever expended on it—and the contents had not been disturbed. He must have stripped off his clothing and fallen into bed the moment he arrived. Or perhaps someone had put him to bed.

The clothing rack under his bed contained his cloak. "Do I need cover?" Caland asked.

"It's a fair-weather day," the fem proctor said. "Warm. You'll feel better outside. Come along."

"All right," Caland said again.

One of the proctors took a firm grip on his arm. The gesture could have been meant kindly, for Caland obviously needed assistance, but it made him feel like a prisoner. Another proctor opened the door, and Caland forced his feet forward. After a few uncertain steps along the corridor, he stubbornly shook off the supporting hand. Headache still pounding, he permitted himself to be swept along with the proctors.

They loaded him into their vehicle, a lumbering, multi-windowed van that ran on rollers and seemed more suitable for the tundra than for errands about a metropolis. And Rynaif City was a metropolis—crowded, bustling, noisy, its streets dim chasms between towers. The streets were crammed with vehicular traffic, and pedestrians crossed them on overhead walkways.

At the government circle, the van swung into a spiraling vehicle entrance and rumbled to a halt in a cavernous service room at the base of one of the towers. Only three of the proctors dismounted with Caland, and by the time they reached the L, his escort was reduced to the fem proctor who had first spoken to him. They thrust skyward on a blast of air. Their capsule debouched on the seventy-fourth level, and the proctor firmly guided him along the corridor and into an office. She announced their arrival to a buzzing, light flashing monitor, nudged him forward without waiting for a response, and escorted him into a Presence.

It was a type of bureaucrat that Caland had been meeting all of his life, all across the galaxy. He was pompous, self-important, obnoxious. He wore a daysuit of flashing green stripes, and taut across his obscenely bloated middle was a chain that displayed the citations and memorabilia of a long career of sordid manipulations.

The fem proctor indicated a chair to Caland and got him seated. "Jarv Caland," she announced. "He seems to have had a night." She did not deign to pronounce the official's name and rank.

The repulsive individual eyed Caland with sour disapproval. "A night, eh? Or perhaps a sennite?"

"You aren't so pretty yourself," Caland observed mildly.

The official squirmed indignantly and pointed an accusing finger. "Mal Caland. Have you ever visited the world of Cenaru?"

He accented the second syllable. Caland repeated the word twice, rearranging the accents. "Not consciously," he answered.

"Mal Caland, this is a serious interrogation. Are you in the habit of visiting worlds unconsciously?"

"Unfortunately, I am," Caland said.

The official scowled. "Have you ever visited the world of Olyndyt?"

"Not consciously," Caland said. He clutched his head, which had begun to ache sharply.

"A sennite wouldn't be enough," the official drawled. "He must have made a term of it."

Caland leaned back in his chair. "I'm suffering from

eyestrain," he said, still keeping his voice mild. "Your daysuit blinds me."

The official's scowl deepened, with purple overtones. "Have you ever visited the world of Skarlont?"

"The name sounds familiar," Caland conceded. "But there are so many worlds with similar names."

"Mal Caland." The finger jabbed at him menacingly. "We are not playing games. I have asked you a simple question. Have you ever visited the world of Skarlont?"

"Not consciously."

The official thumped his desk. "Mal Caland. An Intragalactic study commission has been set up to determine the cause of identical catastrophes on three widely-separated worlds. The commission has discovered that you were the only—repeat, the *only*—individual who was present on all three worlds during the period of time under investigation. In each instance your visit coincided with the catastrophe. The commission has traced you from one end of the galaxy to the other, despite your sly meanderings, and with our assistance, it finally has cornered you. I have been instructed to interrogate you relentlessly. I have every intention of doing that. You can make the ordeal easier for both of us if you will give these questions your serious attention and answer them tersely and honestly. What do you have to say to that?"

Caland straightened up and asked with polite interest. "What sort of catastrophes?"

"Quakes, tidal waves, volcanic action. Surely that won't be news to you. You were present on each of the three worlds when it happened."

Caland sat wonderingly, "An Intragalactic commission is investigating the cause of quakes, tidal waves, and volcanic action?"

"The commission's purpose is to determine *who* caused them."

Caland absently ruffled his hair and then fingered his scalp. His headache had lessened somewhat. He tried to focus his thoughts on the official's last pronouncement.

"How would anyone go about causing a quake? Or a tidal wave? Or a volcanic action?"

"That's what the commission wants me to ask you. What is your background, Mal Caland? Your profession. Your occupation. Your education."

"I'm a dramatic impersonator."

"An actor!" The official snorted. "What did you act in?"

"Mostly theatricals, but in times of need I accepted any role I could find."

"Then you are not a scientist?"

Caland shook his head.

"Have you ever studied science?"

"Nothing beyond first level rudiments."

"Concerning your visits to the worlds of Cenaru, Olyndyt, and Skarlont—"

Caland was searching his pockets. He brought out a dirty, multiple folded paper, flipped it open, and passed it to the official without looking at it. The official accepted it distastefully, as though he feared to soil his fingers. He glanced at it, glanced again at Caland, and sat back to read.

Caland knew it by heart. He not only memorized it; he had studied and pondered the meaning of every word:

POLYSCIENCE INSTITUTE
Folamnin

TO WHO IT MAY CONCERN: In the independent fiefdom of Makliaf, this world, on the date 487/22.6/14 Galactic, Jarv Caland was killed in a vehicular accident. His head was crushed. When his body was brought to this institute for emergency treatment, both cerebral and cardiac action had ceased. The institute's medical staff revived him, and its neurological research team removed pieces of his crushed skull from his brain and surgically repaired and rebuilt it. The crushed portion of his skull was replaced with a cap fashioned of special alloy. The institute's neurological scientists have dedicated their lives to brain research and rank among the most skilled in the galaxy, but even under their care, Caland's survival as a functioning human must be considered miraculous. His fortunate endowment of good health and above normal bodily stamina should enable him to enjoy a life of reasonable duration. However, because of the severe brain damage he suffered, he may be subject to disabling headaches, sensory malfunctions, and intermittent periods of blackout or unconsciousness, sometimes of long duration. He may also lapse into amnesia at unpredictable intervals.

A seal was embossed over the scribbled signature that followed.

The official grunted and handed the paper to the fem proctor. "Register this and make a copy for the commission."

She strode away with it.

The official carefully laced his fingers together and studied them. "Now as I understand it, you are subject to prolonged blackouts and periods of amnesia. Since you say that you have no recollection of visits to the worlds of Cenaru, Olyndyt, and Skarlont, and since passenger rosters clearly show that you did, in fact, visit those places and were there when the catastrophes occurred, I conclude that during these blackouts or periods of amnesia, you are able to travel from world to world and function normally, even though you have no knowledge of where you've been or what you've been doing when the blackout or amnesia ends."

"Then you understand more than I do," Caland said. "I only know that there are long blanks in my memory, and even when conscious I often have very little awareness of what is going on about me because of my frequent and severe headaches. I have one now."

The official unlaced his fingers and scrutinized those of each hand in turn, as though counting them. "But you have traveled without any recollection of it afterward?"

"I can't even make that claim of my own knowledge. I've awakened in a lot of places when I had no recollection of how I got there or why."

"And you are you financing all of this travel that you don't remember taking? Travel is expensive."

Caland smiled. The mal was not a fool. He wondered why bureaucrats who were not fools persisted in acting foolish. "Have you checked my name through Credit Centrex?" he asked.

The official stared at him. Then he turned abruptly and punched a question on his desk comp. He was a long time reading the answer. When the screen finally went dark, his expression had altered perceptibly.

He said, "Indeed, sir—"

Caland silenced him with a wave of his hand. "When I regained consciousness this morning, I didn't know what world I was on. My last distinct memory was of supping in a small restaurant near the spaceport on the world of Gmemaria. Because your proctors gave me no time to orientate myself, I still don't know the date or the time of day. And of course I don't know how I got here. I don't know how I get to any of the places where I wake up, or what I've been doing in the meantime. It's possible that I visited those three worlds while blacked out. It's also possible that my name has been doing a lot more traveling than I have, on a forged passport."

The official nodded thoughtfully. "Has it ever happened that records said you were somewhere else at a time when you weren't blacked out?"

"I haven't seen all the records that exist, and I often have difficulty in remembering anything at all. I'm dead, you see. I've been dead. There's no doubt at all about that. I took the trouble of investigating myself, after I left the institute, because I'd lost a huge chunk of memory. I had to find out who I was and what I was doing on the world of Folamnin. My skull was crushed in the accident and I died. The Institute employees that pulled me from the wreck were positive that I was dead. My head was smashed flat. They didn't take me to the Institute for emergency treatment. They were looking for a doctor to officially pronounce me dead. I'm not really convinced that I'm alive now. I have to persuade myself, and regardless of what that certificate says about my health and longevity, I know that such life as I have left is highly precarious."

The fem proctor returned and handed the embossed paper to Caland. He thanked her and got to his feet.

"What makes the commission think that quakes and tidal waves and volcanic action on three different worlds might have a human cause?" Caland asked.

"My dear Caland!" The official was being ingratiatingly tolerant. "Tidal waves are caused by quakes. In the pertinent instance, so was the volcanic action. And quakes are predictable. On any world that has a geophysical bureau, not one quake in ten thousand happens unexpectedly. When three, of considerable severity, occur inexplicably within a short time on three different worlds in the same sector, the scientists become curious."

"I wish them the pleasure of their curiosity," Caland said. "I don't understand how a quake could have anything but a natural cause. Since my accident, there's so much that I don't understand. Please convey my regrets to the commission. I have no knowledge of any kind that could possibly assist it."

"I shall. I convey to you the commission's thanks for your cooperation."

The fem proctor returned him to the lower level. She now seemed to regard him sympathetically. "Would you like transportation to your hote?" She asked.

"No thank you," Caland said. He smiled wistfully. "I'd rather walk. It's a useful way of convincing myself that I'm where I am. Would you tell me how to find it?"

Following her instructions, he strolled along an elevated pedestrian walk above a crowded, narrow street severely encroached upon by tall buildings. Eventually the street debouched into a throughfare with vehicular traffic on either side of a broad, ground level pedestrian mall. It was called the Avenue of Fountains, and it extended for a very long way through the heart of Rynaif City. Founts of every conceivable design dotted it in artful disarrangement. Benches were scattered about, most of them unoccupied. So bustling were the citizens of Rynaif City that few of them found the time for sitting and looking at fountains. They viewed their lovely mall as an obstacle to be crossed on the way to somewhere else.

Caland dropped onto one of the benches and stared unseeing at the nearest convoluted arrangement of water spouts. Natives hurried past him in spirited conversation or silent concentration. Leisurely strolling tourists stood with their backs to him, watching the fountains. None of them wasted more than a passing glance on Jarv Caland, a shabby, alien-looking figure who had nothing to do but occupy a bench while a city's vast day population streamed past him purposefully.

No one was paying the slightest attention to Caland; and yet—someone was watching. He knew that another's eyes followed him everywhere, and often he had a physical awareness of them. He sensed them now, while he sat in total isolation at the vortex of a teeming metropolis.

The city's churning sounds and smells and sights impinged upon him. Its life swarmed about him. Of all those animate specks of implied humanity, only Jarv Caland had no knowledge of where he had been, or why he had come there, or where he might go when he left. He was a wanderer in darkness, blind—except when a rare flash of consciousness illuminated his surroundings—and he felt very much alone in the universe.

"Who am I where am I why am I?" he muttered.

He knew that fate had rendered him uniquely and terrifyingly different. He did not know if this were because he had been dead, or because his mind was possessed by someone else.

CHAPTER TWO

The Rynaif Hote Central was a stately old building whose interior had been tastelessly renovated into impersonal cubicles and whose exterior had been disfigured by the pedestrial walkway that gave access to its second level. Caland passed through the cramped, cheaply furnished reception hall, returned the scowl flashed at him by the desk super, and paused at the L while he tried to remember his room number.

An appetizing aroma of food enveloped him. Every gen hote offered a food service, usually abominable. The Rynaif Hote Central called its establishment the Speedery Eatery, and its open doorway beckoned to Caland. He forgot his diminishing headache in a sudden, compelling awareness of hunger. He had no way of knowing how long it had been since he had eaten.

He drifted toward the doorway in the wake of another hote guest. When he reached it, he recoiled in dismay.

The room was crowded. Caland's need for food unfortunately coincided with Rynaif City's midday pause, and all of the individual tables were occupied. Latecomers were being seated at long group tables at the far end of the room.

Caland turned away. He shrank from close contact with strangers, and he could not eat comfortably when he felt himself ringed by insolently staring eyes that seemed intent on stripping his secret from him.

He re-crossed the reception hall and then turned back. He was more than hungry—he was famished. He meekly obeyed the restaurant super's gesture toward one of the long tables.

To his surprise, the food was delicious—a savory, deep-dish blending of meats and vegetables. He attacked it ravenously. Not until he had blunted his hunger somewhat did he look about him.

Most of his fellow diners, of both sexes, wore the brightly-colored one-piece day suits that were common work or leisure costumes on many worlds. Caland had the sensation of being adrift in a sea of garish, clashing colors. His own rough, drab, two-piece suit seemed embarrassingly conspicuous. He began to eat faster.

Then a large party of mals and fems suddenly entered together, setting off a flurry of activity. They formed a group—all wore suits of the same dilute shade of blue. The restaurant super, fluttering about excitedly, escorted them to a reserved table at the end of the row.

But someone had miscounted. One member of the group, a pathetic, lost-looking little mal of a type that always would finish last in life, came scurrying after the others and found all of the places taken. He looked about forlornly. The restaurant super surveyed the room with a glance and pointed at Caland. The little mal approached timidly.

Caland half got to his feet before he realized that the objective was not himself but the vacant chair beside him. The little mal seated himself apologetically; a server brought food. Caland returned his attention to his own meal.

But someone was watching him. He looked up apprehensively and met the rude stare of a stout, red-faced fem who was seated across the table. "You in the dark lounge suit. You look sick."

Faces turned toward Caland. He managed a polite smile and said quietly, "I'm a stranger here. Is there some ordinance against looking sick?"

The fem glared. Her mal companion, equally stout but with a nicely tanned complexion, nudged her and said, "Hush. Maybe he's just unhappy."

"He shouldn't bring unhappiness to din with him," the fem

said sullenly. "I always say—if you insist on pushing dark clouds about, you shouldn't be surprised if you get rained on."

Caland resumed eating. Others at the table had lost interest, but the fem across from him continued to stare. "Where are you from?" she demanded.

"A hundred worlds," Caland said lightly. "En route to a hundred more."

"How unfortunate," the fem said. "Nothing more pathetic than a person who doesn't have a world he can call home."

"But think of the enormous advantage it is to be able to call any world home," Caland said.

The fem pondered this turn of thought for a moment, scowling. "I don't believe it. It isn't possible."

The little mal who was seated beside Caland spoke for the first time. Predictably, his voice was high-pitched and squeaky. "I think it would be sad not to have a world of one's own."

"Sad," the fem agreed. "Deplorable."

"But I envy people who've done a lot of traveling," the little mal went on. "This is my first trip away from home. I find it confusing." He turned to Caland. "Have you really seen a hundred worlds?"

"At least," Caland said.

"That's wonderful. And sad."

"The Almighty never intended humans to be gallivanting about like that," the fem said.

"Why would He go to the trouble of making all those worlds if He didn't want anyone to see them?" Caland asked.

A riposte to this unexpected doctrine was beyond the fem's capacity. She subsided; Caland quickly finished eating. He pushed aside the crumbling mess that constituted dessert cake at the Speedery Eatery and politely took leave of his table companions before the fem could speak again. When he reached the doorway, he looked back. The fem was inflicting unwelcome attention on another diner, but the little mal was staring after him.

Again Caland paused at the L while he desperately attempted

to remember his room number. Finally he had to ask the desk super. This was the pattern of his life: fighting his way back to consciousness in a hote room on a world he had to identify in order to learn that he'd never heard of it; eating a meal now and then when he remembered that he was hungry; finding a park to sit in while coaxing his headache to subside; devoting most of his hours of consciousness to dredging his shattered memory.

Who am I where am I why am I?

Every gen hote room was an inevitable replica of the last he'd occupied: the narrow, hard bed with underslung clothing racks; the two massive cubes that served for chairs and storage, one with a reclining support; and, opposite the entrance, an inner door leading into a cramped sanitary sanctum that reeked of disinfectant.

Caland seated himself on the bed and emptied his pockets. This was the one ritual in his life, and he performed it with meticulous regularity. He had few belongings, and he owned nothing except what he carried with him. The odds and ends that he shook from his pockets rarely varied, but he sifted them over and over, searching for a clue to who he was and where he was and why he was—especially why he was—but he never found one. Sometimes he wrote notes to himself, but always, when he regained consciousness, the notes were missing.

This time he found the usual small wad of currency; the three keys, blackened with corrosion—he could not remember what they were for, but he felt uneasy about discarding them; his passport, in the name of Jarv Caland, dotted with smudges imparted to it by registration comps on a long succession of unremembered worlds; and a metallic strip that registered one reserved passage from the world of Rynaif to the world of Barlomal.

The space reservation interested him the most. He'd often found such reservations in his pocket. This one perhaps meant that Barlomal was his next destination but not necessarily that it was the world where he would next regain consciousness. He had never heard of it before, and he knew that he might never hear of it again.

He counted the money carefully. Money was a puzzle that loomed hugely in his threadbare existence. It was true that space travel was expensive. His tortuous wandering from one end of the galaxy to the other must have cost a fortune—must have cost *someone* a fortune. Although he belonged to one of the galaxy's wealthiest families, he had been estranged from it for years. He'd been so impoverished when he left the Institute that the staff had taken up a collection to outfit him. He'd earned no money since then.

But he always had ample funds for his frugal mode of living. Whenever he emerged from a mental blackout, he found himself with a new supply of currency. In addition, there were the paid reservations for space travel. He had no recollection of making them and no intention of using them. He also had no notion of where the money for them could have come from. He vehemently rejected the idea that he was somehow acquiring this wealth on his own initiative, either legally or illegally. He'd never possessed acumen for financial acquisitiveness when conscious, and he could not believe that he was somehow exercising one when unconscious. Someone was giving him money, and over a period of time, the total sum had been enormous. Why? And for what purpose?

Resignedly he returned the items to his pocket.

Something scratched at his door. It sounded like the pleading of a small animal, but the hote did not allow pets. He decided to ignore it.

Then it happened again, and this time it sounded like a signal of despair from a person too timid to knock. As Caland released the latch, the little mal who'd sat beside him in the eatery burst into the room.

He halted confusedly as Caland closed the door. "Excuse me, but I thought—I wondered—"

"Come in," Caland said indifferently. "Since you are." He did not really mind talking with individuals. It was crowds that disconcerted him. It was bad enough to have an unseen pair of eyes watching him when he was alone.

"I'm sorry to bother you," the little mal said. He sounded more than sorry—he sounded miserably remorseful. His pale eyes pleaded with Caland. "I thought you might be able to help me."

Caland regarded him with astonishment. "Help you?" he said incredulously. He had been obsessed with his own broken life for so long that he could not comprehend a situation in which he might be of assistance to someone else.

"I'm Wes Fulm," the little man said. "From the world of Mort."

"Jarv Caland," Caland told him. "From everywhere."

They touched hands politely.

"Have you ever been to Mort?" The little mal asked eagerly.

"No." Caland said, trying to sound regretful. "No I haven't. At least, I don't think I have. I don't think I've ever heard of it. So I'm really not from everywhere, am I?"

Fulm seemed to not have heard him. He was trembling, either from excitement or fright. He backed up to one of the cubes, perched uneasily on the edge, and brushed perspiration from his forehead.

If an omnipotent deity ever decided to typecast the human race, Caland thought, a character such as this one could serve as the archetypal clerk. His deeply wrinkled forehead merged with his gleaming oval of bald head. His hands were tiny and soft; his voice fawning and apologetic; his thin, ageless face mild and deprecating. His eyes, which bulged with artificial lenses, probably embodied all of the vision problems of the universe. Their color matched that of his absurdly washed-out blue uniform. He had been destined from birth to become adjunct to a desk. Unfortunately, the more competent clerks kept getting promoted into positions that had nothing to do with clerking. Caland's father had been fond of attributing most of the problems of the universe to clerks who had been unwisely elevated beyond their abilities.

Fulm echoed his thought. "I'm not used to this sort of thing. I know I'm doing it badly."

He looked so pathetically bewildered that Caland felt a surge of sympathy. He seated himself on the other cube and said gently, "But you haven't told me how I can help you."

"You said you'd traveled a lot. I thought maybe you could tell me how to find a prober."

Caland was caught with his mouth open and nothing to say. He could only stare at the little mal with unabashed incredulity. In the absence of an interworld police force, probers were the agency that kept galactic crime in check. Their exploits were justly celebrated in fact and fiction, but who they were, and how they functioned, were among the galaxy's better-kept secrets. Apart from the rumors that circulated after their more spectacular probes, Caland knew nothing at all about them.

"Probers snoop out injustices on their own," he pointed out. "Probably very few people would know how to get in touch with one, and I doubt that they have time to interest themselves in anything but the most important kind of interworld problems. What do you want a prober for?"

"I'm being followed."

"Indeed." Caland studied him skeptically. "You mean—right now you're being followed?"

The little mal nodded.

"How do you know?"

"It's the same person!" Fulm protested. "Right behind me! Wherever I go!"

"If you know who's following you, there shouldn't be any problem," Caland said thoughtfully. His attitude toward Fulm had changed abruptly to one of grudging respect. He had long been convinced that someone followed him wherever he went, but he'd never been able to identify the person.

"But I don't know who it is or why he's following me," Fulm protested. He added abjectly, "I'm wasting your time. If you're busy—"

Caland couldn't remember the last time that he'd been busy. Certainly he had nothing else to do on this day except to resume the futile dredging of his memory. "Tell me about it," he said.

"From the beginning"

Fulm leaned forward eagerly. The pale blue uniform fit him so badly that it emphasized his grotesqueness, but any clothing not cut precisely to his measurements would have fit badly.

"Mort is a beautiful world," he said. His hands, upraised in emphasis, made his coat gape and revealed a pale, hairless chest. "But the name means 'death,' so people make jokes about it. The only city on Mort is called 'Paradise,' and people make jokes about that, too. It's unfair."

"I'm sure it is," Caland said.

Fulm was gaining confidence. "Tourists come to Mort," he went on defensively. "There are two lovely tourist hotes, and the tourists come there, and they sit around looking at the beautiful beach and making jokes about death."

"We were talking about your need for a prober," Caland suggested.

Fulm flushed and turned his gaze to the floor. "I'm doing this badly. I'm not used to such things. Dom said—" He broke off.

"Who is Dom?" Caland asked.

"A mal on Mort. I discussed this trouble with him. You have to understand Mort in order to understand what's happening." He dropped his voice. "There's sabotage. To Mort's tin production."

"Does the world of Mort have enemies?"

"No!"

"Competitors?"

"None," Fulm said firmly.

"It certainly is an unusual world," Caland observed. He tried to sound perplexed rather than sarcastic. "If Mort has no enemies and no competitors, who could profit from the sabotage, Mal Fulm?"

"No one. That's what's so bewildering about it."

"What's your position on Mort?"

"I'm a member of the Council of Supervisors of Pak Enterprises," Fulm said proudly. "But the council is not involved. I mean—we discussed the sabotage without being able to decide what to do. The council frequently has difficulty in deciding on a course of action. I discussed the situation with Dom, who has a unique position on Mort, and he thought that the sabotage might be one phase of a larger conspiracy."

"How far away is Mort?" Caland asked.

"It's more than a hundred light years."

"If sabotage on Mort resulted in your being followed on a world that's more than a hundred light years away, the conspiracy certainly is a large one," Caland conceded. He continued to study Fulm perplexedly. He had never encountered a more harmless-looking specimen. It was difficult to imagine how this little mal could pose a threat to anyone or anything. "Why did you come to—" For a moment he could not remember where he was. "—to Rynaif?"

"Pak Enterprises sent me for twenty days of training."

"What sort of training? Is there anything about it that might attract hostile curiosity?"

"Nothing," Fulm said fervently. "I'm only an accountant learning a new comp method along with forty-nine other accountants."

"Does Pak Enterprises have labor problems? The person with the best opportunity and skill and knowledge for sabotage is an employee."

"No." Fulm shook his head. "Impossible. If you knew our world, you wouldn't suggest that. It's a wonderful place to live and work. We have excellent jobs—living quarters provided—no workers in the galaxy have finer benefits—the city of Paradise really is one. No."

Caland asked slowly, "Would it be possible for an employee to become acquainted with a visitor to Mort—a tourist, for example—who would pay him liberally to perform acts of sabotage?"

"It would be *most* disloyal!" Fulm exclaimed indignantly.

"Of course. But loyalty always carries a price tag. If disloyalty is far more profitable than loyalty, and if the risk is minimal—the person responsible hasn't been caught, has he?"

"I'm not used to this kind of thing," Fulm muttered.

"It's an evil universe. You haven't seen much of it, and I've seen too much." There was nothing that Caland could do for the little mal, and he began to wonder how he could extricate himself from the absurd situation without hurting Fulm's feelings. They sat facing each other, and the silence became awkward.

"This person who is following you," Caland said finally. "Did you ever see him on Mort?"

Fulm shook his head.

"How long has he been following you?"

"Just today. But *someone* has been following me ever since I arrived here. Twelve days ago."

"How many people knew you were coming here?"

"That was *news!*" Fulm protested. "It was in the company announcements! Why would anyone follow me?"

"The quickest way to learn that would be to twist this person's toe and ask him." Caland said. Resignedly he got to his feet, reminding himself again that there was nothing pressing about his futile search for his memory. "Since this seems to be a civilized planet, it probably has laws that discourage toe twisting in public, or even in private. Do you have free time right now?"

Fulm nodded.

"I want you to go out and act like a tourist. Wander about leisurely, gawk at things; buy presents for your family. When you get tired, come back to the hote. You're staying here, right?"

Fulm nodded again.

"Come back here when you get tired. But take your time, don't do anything impulsively, and don't look behind you. If anyone is following you, make it as easy for him as possible. I'm going to follow him. I'll look you up later today and—maybe—tell you who he is and where he comes from. Once you know that, you may be able to figure out why he's following you."

Fulm obediently got to his feet.

A short time later, Caland was third in a ridiculous procession along the Avenue of Fountains. Fulm followed instructions perfectly. He stopped at each fountain and gawked, and Caland had the irritating apprehension that he might be overdoing it.

But the character following him was not a type who would notice subtleties. Even Caland, whose limited knowledge was derived from a role he'd once played on the stage, could not fail to observe a total absence of technique. When Fulm stopped to gawk, the mal following him didn't even pretend to be looking at another fountain. The impudent transparency of the thing made the situation ludicrous. If a vital reason existed for spying on the harmless creature, why was the work being done by a rank amateur?

Fulm continued to wander among the fountains, conspicuously followed. Caland, who had the advantage of knowing that Fulm was unlikely to alter his leisurely pace, dropped back and found a seat for himself on one of the many vacant benches.

Immediately he made an incredible discovery. Either Fulm had two mals following him, or the first of the two was also being followed. A bony apparition of an old mal—Caland assumed that it was a mal—came tottering along the mall matching the paces of the other two mals precisely. Black garments enveloped him except for his face and hands, and Caland received an impression of skin shrunken to bones, of a sharply protruding nose, of watery eyes that blinked repeatedly into the softly stirring breeze.

"Another amateur!" Caland muttered disgustedly. "He couldn't have dressed more conspicuously if he were trying to attract attention to himself!"

The scene's absurdity was heightened by the fact that the Avenue of Fountains was so sparsely populated at that moment. The far end of the mall, which Fulm's minuscule figure was now approaching, was completely deserted. The considerably larger, plump figure of the first mal following him was virtually tromping on his heels in maintaining a close contact that could have been justified in a crowd only. The shrouded black apparition was far behind them but following just as persistently.

"And I make three," Caland said bitterly. "The city's proctors ought to arrest us for parading without a permit."

Resignedly he rejoined the procession, but he did not hurry. He knew that he could close the distance rapidly once he saw which turning Fulm would take. The mall ended in a plaza at the foot of one of the towering buildings, and Fulm hesitated there. The mal following close behind him hesitated at the same time. The black figure, still trailing at a distance, took another step and then waivered uncertainly.

At that instant the first two men vanished in a blinding explosion that sent a column of flame skyward but produced very little heat and almost no blast.

The black figure wheeled and raced off with surprising speed, darting into a side turning. Caland, along with a few passersby, started on a run toward the site of the explosion, but Caland quickly veered off in pursuit of the old mal. He knew that there was nothing he could do for Fulm, and he thought he still might salvage something from this bungled adventure if he could identify one of the two spies.

The narrow side street had a ground-level pedestrian walk, and Caland saw the black figure far ahead of him, still moving quickly. Caland lengthened his stride. Then the old mal vanished into another turning, and although Caland dashed after him frantically, and finally hired a passing 'cab to cruise the entire area, he never saw him again.

Caland returned to his hote and did something he should have done terms—or years—before. He asked the desk super for a message blank and wrote out a spacegram: "Trouble. Please send immediately name reliable searcher this sector. Jarv, Rynaif City Hote Central."

CHAPTER THREE

In the beginning there was agony.

Caland clutched his head, tensing as each new wave of pain washed over him; and the bludgeon pounded, and the rapier seared, and finally the nightmare's dungeon of horrors erupted.

The muffled black figure raced along the street far ahead of him, and Caland ran desperately in pursuit. The street stretched endlessly; heavy traffic whirred past; Caland ran faster and faster, ran until his breath came in panting sobs, and still he could not overtake him. Suddenly the black figure vanished. Caland ran on, legs churning furiously. This turning—or the next? But there was no turning. Caland's lungs were bursting, but he continued to run.

Then the blinding points of light flashed, and explosive pulsations rocked and deafened him. His mind retched spasmodically as a chill, cutting wind swept through it. In its wake came the slow, uncertain seepage of consciousness.

Tentatively he opened his eyes.

He closed them instantly. Seated near his bed was an apparition far more spectacular than the one he'd just been chasing in his nightmare. Slowly Caland opened his eyes again.

A large, massively fat mal with an enormous clout of silvery hair and a face pleated with wrinkles was seated beside his bed. His coiffure was the more startling because it crowned a mountain of pale pink, that being the color of his stylish day suit. His chins—several of them—flashed friendly grins at Caland.

"Finally awake, eh?"

Caland sat up and swung his legs over the side of the bed. His surroundings, except for his visitor, were unexceptional. Gen hotes usually decorated their sterile cubicles in pastels; this one had indulged in garish tones of yellow and green. The furnishings never deviated: the bed, with its built-in clothing racks; the two duo-service cubes for sitting and storage; the narrow door that led to a cramped sanitary sanctum. Caland noted with irrational irritation that his pink-clad visitor had made himself comfortable on the cube with the reclining support.

"I might as well post an 'Open to the Public' sign on my door," Caland grumbled. "Don't tell me you're a Rynaif Security Proctor."

The chins continued to grin at Caland. "Spare me that," the mal said. "I'm not a proctor, and this world isn't Rynaif. Don't you remember me?"

Caland studied him resentfully. He did not need to be reminded of his memory failures. Often he could not even remember what it was that he'd been trying to remember, or why. "No. Am I supposed to remember you?"

"It would speed matters considerably if you did," the mal said good-naturedly. "However, if you don't, you don't. Do you remember asking for a searcher?"

Caland shook his head.

"I quote a spacegram you sent recently from the world of Rynaif: 'Trouble. Please send immediately. Name reliable searcher this sector. Jarv, Rynaif City Hote Central.' Do you remember sending that?"

Caland shook his head.

"In veriest fact, that was the fourth time you'd asked for a searcher in the last four terms."

"How do you happen to know that?"

The grins broadened. "I'm Regelz Arlu." The head bowed slightly. The pink mountain below gathered itself as though tensing for an eruption and then subsided. "I'm the searcher you asked for."

"I don't remember asking for a searcher, and I'm certain I

didn't ask for you."

"I'd received ample warning that you'd be unreasonably skeptical," Arlu said. The chins assumed a serious droop. "You were the last time we met, and it placed an unfortunately frigid atmosphere around a discussion that should have been fraught with congeniality. Sure you don't remember?"

"Positive."

"Pity. However, this time I'm armed. I was instructed that whenever your suspicions got out of hand, I should remind you that Uncle Orp sent me."

Caland got to his feet. "Oh, well. If you know that—"

He began to pull on his clothing, which was draped over the unoccupied cube.

"I was worried that you might not remember Uncle Orp," Arlu said. "You've forgotten so much, and you forget so easily. Some private password?"

"That's what I called him when we were kids. I'm his cousin."

Arlu chuckled. "And now he's Orluf Prylon, a big name in a galactic law partnership, and he hopes that no one remembers the sins of his childhood except you. He informed me that any time you're willing to admit that you're in trouble; it won't be just a little trouble. My instructions are to do whatever is necessary to get you out of it."

"How'd you find me?"

The chins flashed their grins. "Which time? I searched you, of course. Searched your name. Why not? That's my profession. The first time, I found you on the world of Gwarner. You were somewhat less cooperative than I'd hoped and a whole lot more suspicious than seemed reasonable. All I was able to do was confirm that you really were Jarv Caland and make arrangements to meet again the next day. That night you boarded a ship for Kloff. I had business on Gwarner and couldn't follow you. Sure you don't remember?"

Caland did not answer. He had finished dressing, and he emptied the contents of his pockets onto the bed. Two metallic reservation strips fluttered free, and he snatched them.

One was a paid space reservation, world of Aravia to the world of Mort, passage for one. The other confirmed a prepaid room reservation at Mort's Paradise View Hostelry. Caland fingered his keys, glanced at his passport, and confirmed that the wad of currency now was in Aravian script.

"This world is Aravia?" he asked.

Arlu nodded. "I've been searching your name ever since I saw you on Gwarner and keeping track of your meanderings. When I found you listed on an Aravia-bound ship, I thought perhaps you were coming here to see me. Obviously you weren't. Why *did* you come to Aravia?"

Caland kicked the unoccupied cube into position and dropped onto it. He clutched his head for a moment as a wave of pain left him gasping. "Sorry," he muttered. The pain faded, and he opened his eyes and straightened up. "Until this moment, I never heard of Aravia. I don't know why I came here. I don't know why I go anywhere."

Arlu nodded complacently. "It isn't necessary to explain that. I told you I've been searching your name. When a person says he's in trouble, any search concerning him has to start with the proctors on the various worlds he's visited. I have a copy of your medical certificate and the report that the Rynaif Security Proctors filed with that idiotic intergalactic study commission. You've been wandering from one end of the galaxy to the other, doing most of your traveling while blacked out, and you don't know where you've been or what might have happened while you were there. That was what you told the Rynaif proctors. They considered it a medical problem and therefore several light years removed from their field of expertise. They were skeptical, but they felt obliged to believe you because your name is Caland. Do you have anything different to tell me?"

Caland shook his head.

"The proctors were adversaries. I'm on your side. Nothing different?"

"Nothing."

"About your memory. You do remember the Rynaif Security

Proctors. When you first opened your eyes, you said—"

Caland said slowly, "I remember the faces bent over me when I woke up. Six faces. I thought my vision was impaired. They all wore the same clothing, and the faces all looked alike. One of them said they were Rynaif Security Proctors. They took me—somewhere. In a vehicle. I remember the vehicle, because it was an odd thing for a city transport. They escorted me, politely but firmly, and I climbed in." He gestured. "Blankness."

Arlu nodded. "Don't strain yourself. I doubt that a mind will remember more when it's squeezed. I've learned a few things about you since we met on Gwarner. Let's talk and see if we can turn up anything else. Have you ever collected a medical opinion from anyone except this Polyscience Institute?"

Caland shook his head. "I can't remember. Sometimes when I first wake up, everything is blank. Then things begin to come back to me." He got to his feet. "Perhaps if I walked around a bit—"

Arlu had cocked his head. The chins were frowning.

"I often feel the urge to get outside when I regain consciousness," Caland said apologetically. "It seems to cool my head. That probably doesn't make sense to you, but it's true."

Arlu's chins flashed their grin. "Do that. Walk around, eat something, admire the beauties of Aravianna, which is Aravia's capital city. I'll look you up first thing this afternoon. Agreed?"

He got to his feet with surprising agility and waddled away. When Caland followed after him, only a few minutes later, he had completely disappeared. Caland found this disconcerting. Arlu had seemed as immobile as a navigational landmark, and just as conspicuous.

Emerging from the hote, Caland found himself in a crowded, bustling, noisy metropolis, its streets dim chasms between towers. It was a pungent echo of all of the other crowded, bustling, noisy metropolises of which faint memories lurked in his subconscious to provoke the unsettling sensation that he'd been here before. Such cities were the hallmark of worlds with middle-aged settlements. Young worlds did not have the problem of arranging huge populations in cities; old worlds had been forced to solve the problem. The middle-aged worlds were still nourishing the delusion that the problem would eventually solve itself, and this was the result.

Somewhere among the multiple veneers of ugliness, Caland knew there would be a park. There always was a park. Humans could not despoil in good conscience unless they preserved a few centimeters for every thousand kilometers they laid waste to.

Caland found it a mere three blocks from his hote. It was a narrow sward of green misplaced among tall, windowless buildings. Like most city parks, it was blighted by a scattered population consisting of the elderly, the diseased, and the indolent: social misfits and outcasts without occupation or ambition or future. Caland felt at one with them. A mal who blacked out unexpectedly for days at a time could not be entrusted with any kind of employment, and he could not trust himself to think of the future.

He seated himself on a bench, and slowly, very slowly, he turned his mind on itself and explored the extent of his memory loss. Great chunks had been ripped away, first by the surgeon's knife and then by frequent periods of blackout. Those tattered shreds that survived to seep back into his consciousness from time to time were, more often than not, random flashes that seemed too distorted or indistinct to be comprehended.

Two elderly fems were seated on benches nearby. While Caland sifted the dregs of his memory, they silently contemplated the nothings of their futures. The three of them neither spoke nor looked at each other for more than an hour.

Then a younger fem walked slowly through the park and seated herself on the bench opposite Caland. She had the brisk, conservative air of a successful business fem on her midday pause. Her clothing, her artfully tossed coiffure, and her sleek, dark complexion looked like the expensively coordinated products of the same stylish salon. She achieved a matter-of-fact elegance without being either handsome or pretty. Her presence there seemed so odd that Caland misinterpreted her motives. The third time she sent a calculating glance in his direction, he apprehensively got to his feet and walked away.

But probably he had been wrong. When he looked back, he saw her in conversation with one of the elderly fems.

When he finally returned to his hote room, he found Arlu waiting for him. The searcher was comfortably extended on the cube with the reclining back, and he did not change his position except to nod to Caland.

"How's the memory?" he asked.

"I managed to collect a few items," Caland said. "Probably it won't be enough for you, but it was almost too much for me."

Arlu nodded sympathetically. "Yes, I can understand that."

Caland seated himself. "You said my spacegram used the word, 'trouble.' If I'm in trouble, by which I mean outside trouble, I don't remember a thing about it. And I don't see how a searcher could possibly help me with my subjective problems."

Arlu nodded again. "Yes. As I see it, the most important thing—the basic thing—is this: whatever it is that you've had to contend with, you've been trying to do it on your own. You're not alone any longer. It'll maybe take some time for you to grasp that and begin to trust me, but this is the turning point. From now on, I'll give you as much support as you need. Let's see what you've remembered. Have you been examined by a doctor since you left the Institute?"

"Doctors," Caland said slowly. "I don't remember how many. Several. Maybe a lot. They weren't able to get good brain scans because of this metal dish I have over my skull. It's some peculiar alloy. All they can tell me is that my brain is a mess. There's a complicated web of metal in it, as though it were wired together, and they think that in putting it back together, the Institute's specialists repaired broken connections with fine wires. They tell me I ought to be grateful to be alive and functioning as well as I am. It seems that I've been the beneficiary of a miracle. It was a billion-billion to one that whatever they did wouldn't work and I drew the lucky number. As far as I'm concerned, I'm considerably less than alive, and I'm not grateful for how well I function when I'm blacked out. Conscious, I'm as much a mess as my brain is."

"Mmm." Arlu brought his index fingers together and tapped the tips slowly, one against the other.

"One doctor suggested that the accident left me with a kind of duo-functioning brain," Caland went on. "I'm two brains in one body, he said. They function in turn, and neither is aware of the other."

"Mmm." Arlu scowled. "But you haven't bought that?"

"I've tried writing notes to myself—messages that an outsider couldn't make sense of, but which my other self would. My other self never answered. Very inconsiderate of it, don't you think? The self that I am now is exceedingly and urgently concerned about my other self, and it seems strange that my other self wouldn't be just as concerned about this self. If you can follow that."

"Mmm. I'll have to start looking into all of this. Unfortunately, a proper search will have to cover a lot of space, and that'll take time."

"I ought to warn you," Caland said. "My monerating is one of the best in the galaxy, but there's no substance in it. It's my family's rating. I haven't been in touch for years. I became an actor, you see, and Calands with moneratings don't become actors."

Arlu's chins flashed their grins. "They threw you out?"

"No, because I had the good sense to leave before they got around to it."

"Interesting, but not relevant. Your Uncle Orp sent me a blank credit memo. Does he owe you something?"

"No one owes me anything, and I don't accept charity."

"Please." Arlu raised his hand. "Don't deprive me of my commission and a fascinating case. We can sort out the sordid financial considerations afterward. I take it that you've found no clues at all to substantiate this theory of another self. Is there anything to refute it?"

"Yes. The money. I always wake up well-supplied with money. Sometimes there are paid reservations, too, but they're just evidence of more money. How would my other self be able to acquire all of that wealth while wandering from place to place? Would brain damage make half of my duo-functioning brain a financial wizard? I certainly wasn't one before the accident."

"Mmm." Arlu was tapping his index fingers together. "What do you really believe?"

"I believe that someone is controlling me. It works like this. When I regain consciousness—on a world I've never heard of—I have money in my pocket and maybe a space reservation to another world I've never heard of. The reservation has a departure date a few days to a sennite in the future. Naturally I have no desire to use it, but I also have no desire to stay where I am. Whoever is controlling me has left me no choice. There's never enough money for passage to anywhere else. There's just enough to keep me comfortably until the departure date."

He paused. Arlu waited expectantly and finally said, "And?"

"I know that I'm helpless, but I'm damned if I'll make things easy for whoever's doing it. I refuse to travel to a world I don't want to visit merely because I have a reservation I don't remember buying. I'm determined not to go."

"And?"

"I go anyway. A few hours before my ship lifts, I lose consciousness. When I next wake up, I'm in a gen hote on the world of my reservation, or maybe two or three worlds further on. With money in my pocket. Sometimes but not always with another reservation. Obviously, if I won't do what's wanted, I can be made to do it while I'm blacked out."

Arlu had left off tapping his fingers. "It would seem so. In veriest fact, it would seem so. Then what you're really afraid of is what else this someone may have made you do when you were blacked out. Have you any idea as to how this person is controlling you?"

Caland shook his head. "The metal in my brain must have

something to do with it. Even so, I can't understand how I'm controlled from a distance. Someone must be watching me closely. Otherwise, how could I be made to behave normally enough to avoid social miscues and minor legal infractions and otherwise keep from attracting unwelcome attention to myself? Someone has to be watching me. For more than a year I've been trying to identify him, and I can't do it. That's what I'd like to have you do—identify the person who's following me and controlling me."

"Mmm. What then?"

"I'm going to kill him."

"Mmm." The chins flashed a grin. "I understand how you feel, but there are several better solutions. Anyway, if you notice someone following you from now on, please don't commit murder. It may be one of my people. Don't worry about it, don't pay any attention to it. From now on, you'll have a guardian. We'll quickly find out whether you're engaging in irregular activities while blacked out. If anyone else is following you, we'll quickly find that out, too."

They sat in silence for a time, with Arlu studiously contemplating his index fingers. "This Polyscience Institute," he said finally. "Its doctors put the metal in your head. Have you thought of going back there and asking what's blacking you out?"

"How could I? I only go where someone wants me to go. Besides, there's the matter of money. I never have enough for passage to the next world, let alone a trek across the galaxy."

"Who paid your surgery and medical costs at the Institute?"

"No one. The Institute did."

"Charity patient?"

"The Institute charged according to one's ability to pay, and I was an impoverished actor. But I don't think it accepts charity cases. My fellow patients seemed to be extremely wealthy. I wasn't charity—I was an interesting experiment. For all I know, I'm a celebrated medical case, and my treatment enhances the Institute's galactic reputation and brought it an avalanche of wealthy brain patients. If it's made a profit on me in that way, I have no resentment. It didn't charge me anything, and the staff was very kind.

"I'll have to give this Institute a careful look, as a matter of routine, but I can't see any logical reason for it to chase you across the galaxy playing tricks with your brain. It could have performed as many tricks as it liked while you were a patient and saved the fortune in space travel." He fell silent for a time. "Hard to figure how the worlds of Cenaru, Olyndyt, and Skarlont could come into this," he said finally, "but I'm assuming that they must. I refuse to write off your presence on all three worlds as a coincidence. I've learned, through bitter experience, that coincidence on a galactic scale doesn't exist."

"I must have been there if the records say I was, but I don't remember any of the worlds. Did they really experience catastrophes?"

"According to the report of that intergalactic study commission, someone on Cenaru was doing a forestry survey shortly before the quake there. Aerial fotes were taken with various filters. One of them caught something in a forest that clearly ought not to be there—a steel tower, hidden in the trees and cleverly camouflaged. It was the camouflage that gave it away. In a filtered fote, it screamed for attention. The forestry bureau investigated and found the tower erected over a shaft of concrete sunk some considerable distance into the ground. Embedded in the shaft was a copper cylinder more than a meter in diameter. The bureau assumed that it belonged to some other governmental department and started an investigation to find out who was trespassing in its forest. Before it could learn anything, the quake happened. The entire area was devastated. Forest leveled. Massive upheaval of ground. Tower vanished."

"Someone caused a quake by building a tower?" Caland asked incredulously.

"I don't know. Nor does anyone. The quake was a fact. So was the tower. On Olyndyt, the quakes and subsequent volcanic and tidal wave action completely obliterated a good-sized island. The only thing remaining is an underwater volcano, still active.

Thousands of people died. After the tragedy, a fem who had visited the island shortly before the catastrophe remembered seeing steel towers there. There were three of them, she thinks, and they formed a triangle that included most of the island. She assumed that they had something to do with communications. No one issued authorization to erect them, and no one knows who did it, or what they were for. No resident of the island survived, and the commission hasn't been able to find any more witnesses."

"On Skarlont, a large continental area was wracked by quakes and tidal waves. No one remembers seeing any towers before the quakes, but the remnants of an unexplained tower were found afterward.

"No one thought that you caused the quakes. The commission is trying to find people who may have seen one of the mysterious towers and noticed persons who seemed to be associated with it. No scientist or engineer can suggest any legitimate function for the towers, and by coincidence, which I don't believe in, their presence approximated the area on each world where the damage centered. Do you remember anything at all about towers, anywhere?"

Caland shook his head, slowly.

"Whether or not they had anything to do with the catastrophes, you can be certain that worlds all across the galaxy will now be watching diligently for unauthorized towers. You may hear from the commission again. When it gets frustrated over not finding out anything, it's bound to come back to the fact that you were present in all three places at the critical times. That does rather put a strain on coincidence. What's the date on your space reservation to Mort?"

Caland found it in his pocket and stared incomprehensibly at the row of numbers. "It must be a local date."

Arlu glanced and nodded. "Four days hence. Very well. And you've never heard of the world of Mort?"

Caland hesitated. "Maybe in a nightmare."

"Before you're finished with this, your nightmares may turn

out to be highly important. Very well. We'll be watching you carefully. If you actually travel to Mort, we'll soon find out—"

Caland was shaking his head. "I'm going to Mort. Myself. I'm going to use this space reservation and also the hote reservation. I want to look for a person who's controlling me. In a big city, or even a big hote, it's hard to figure out who it might be. I'd have a better chance on a spaceship. Even if I travel voluntarily, he'll have to come along and keep an eye on me, won't he?"

"It's much more certain that he'd have to come along if you were blacked out."

"Maybe. But I want this one trip while I'm conscious and look for him."

"Very well. But from now on, my people will be watching. You won't have to look for the person who's controlling you. If he's there, we'll find him."

"I'm going to look," Caland said stubbornly.

Arlu smiled. "He'll probably conceal himself expertly. Odd that you're going to Mort. It's a sole proprietor planet. I could invent several theories about why you're traveling around the galaxy, but none of them would explain a visit to Mort."

"What's a sole proprietor planet?" Caland asked.

"One man owns it."

"The whole world? Just one man?" Caland thought for a moment. "What does that have to do with me?"

"Perhaps nothing," Arlu conceded. "But I thought I'd mention it. I'm sure we'll find out when you get there."

CHAPTER FOUR

Most spaceship passengers viewed the metal latticework that projected from walls and ceilings of passageways as an *outré* design that for some obscure reason was much favored in outer space architecture. The effect of dim, interwoven shadows cast by black metal strands that were affixed three centimeters from the luminescent white background was pleasant enough to be imitated in landside installations where it had no relevance whatsoever. Only the more knowledgeable passengers were aware of its functional reality: ship's gravity units did fail, and when that occurred, hand motive power became the most effective and sometimes the sole means of inboard transportation—but only when the hands had something to grip.

Jarv Caland had found another use for the latticework. One could round a corner at normal stride, take a firm hold on it, and in the same motion twist back and peer through the strands to see whether one was being followed.

He remained convinced that someone spied on him—intermittently, if not constantly. Throughout the voyage he had been surreptitiously, attempting to surprise someone in the act. The fact that he did not succeed only convinced him that the person he was trying to catch was more skilled in spying than Caland was in catching spies.

He had discussed the problem with Arlu before he left Aravia. The searcher reluctantly decided against accompanying Caland. He did not want to give anyone cause to link their names together, not even on a spaceship passenger list. Arlu promised that Caland would be very capably watched by an assistant, and he would have preferred Caland leave the spy catching to a professional. When Caland persisted, Arlu advised him to look for the unexceptional, the disarmingly ordinary. Caland's inclination was to seek out the unusual, the irregular, the odd action or remark that did not fit. He had tried both approaches and gleaned nothing at all, not even a hint of a suspicion. This left him disappointed but not discouraged. He always took a circuitous route to his stayroom so as to be able to perform his anti-spying maneuver several times.

On this, the last day of his voyage, Caland followed his usual zigzag route in returning from the lavish meal that the ship's salon called a break. He turned one more corner and tensely gripped the latticework. Then he relaxed and meekly continued along the passageway.

Approaching in the opposite direction was the weirdest individual Caland had ever met off the stage. He was tall and grotesquely thin. His face was a mass of shaggy hair, and the hair on the top of his head hung below his shoulders. He wore a brightly colored but filthy wrap about his torso, his waist was bare, and his baggy lower garment, equally bright-colored and dirty, had legs that fastened in some manner about the ankles. His shoes were strips of cloth that secured his bare feet to large pads. On his head, he wore a ridiculous peaked hat with a broad drooping brim.

Caland nodded politely and murmured something unintelligible as they passed. He caught a side glimpse of a monstrously hooked nose and bushy eyebrows. Caland took two more steps before he turned and stared. Zoological parks excepted, he could not remember ever encountering such a hairy specimen or one so overtly animal-like. The woven metal lattice that surrounded him suddenly took on aspects of a cage.

A few meters along the passageway, Caland came to an open door. He glanced into the exposed stayroom as he passed, and what he saw there brought him to a momentary halt. The room was populated with creatures similar to the one he'd just met.

Three fems and two mals, each displaying highly individual combinations of shagginess and filth and ludicrous clothing, sprawled on the floor, talking loudly and eating with gusto. The food consisted of containers and packages of cheap snacks of the unnourishing variety commonly sold in spaceports.

Caland walked on. At the far end of the passageway, he entered his own stayroom and dropped onto the heavily cushioned couch that was his station for liftoffs and landings.

He was wondering what connection the zoological specimens might have with him. Thus far, all of the passengers he had met had been, in Arlu's words, disarmingly ordinary. They were as conventional as wealthy vacationists could be. As the scion of a wealthy family, Caland had associated with the same kind of boring millionaires for the first twenty years of his life, and he found these examples to be totally and consistently commonplace.

And none of them had demonstrated more than a casual, polite interest in him. There were no suggestive actions or revealing glances except from the fems, when their husbands weren't around, and Caland found nothing out of the ordinary about that. He surprised no one watching him from across a room, nor did anyone rush to occupy a vacant chair at the next table when Caland seated himself in the salon. Neither did anyone cup an ear to hear what some stodgy businesser was telling him about quarterly sales increases.

The zoological specimens were the first passengers he'd seen who were in any way out of the ordinary, and they were outrageously so. Surely a spy would not make himself so flagrantly conspicuous; or might such a disguise be chosen because no one would suspect it? Caland thought long about the zoological specimens.

The message screen flashed a bulletin:

PORT IN 83 MINUTES. LOUNGE
CLOSES TWENTY MINUTES BEFORE LANDING.

It was a polite nudge aimed at stampeding passengers out of their stayrooms for a last drink. It also provided Caland with a final opportunity for a close scrutiny of his fellow travelers. He got to his feet resignedly and started for the lounge.

The stayroom door he'd looked into was now closed. Caland met the steward at the end of the passageway. He stopped and asked, with a jerk of his thumb, "What species of animal are those creatures?"

The steward asked anxiously, "Have they been disturbing you?"

"Not at all," Caland assured him. "I just wondered who or what they are. Their grooming and attire seem a bit abnormal."

The steward snickered. "They're for the Valley. We get a few now and then, coming or going. They always book waiting space—take anything that isn't sold when the ship lifts. And then they carry their own food and take a second discount for passage without a table."

"What's the Valley?" Caland asked.

"The Valley on Mort," the steward said as though that explained everything. "They never grat, and sometimes they leave a frightful mess. But they occupy unbooked space, so the company accepts them." He absolved himself of responsibility with a vague gesture and moved on.

Caland spent the next hour in the lounge listening to portly businessers expound hedonistic philosophies to other portly businessers. The wives of those who'd unwisely brought them along on this pilgrimage to hedonism had been left in their stayrooms to do the packing.

The passenger seated next to Caland asked him, "Have you ever been to Mort?"

Caland shook his head.

"Quite a place," the passenger said with a smile. "Quite a place."

"You there," one of the hedonistic philosophers called to Caland. "I don't remember your name—"

"Jarv," Caland said. Businesser tourists always used first

names.

"You're young enough, and pretty enough—"

The businesser laughed and applauded.

"—pretty enough to render important services to all of us. If you could arrange to keep our wives occupied while we follow our natural inclinations elsewhere—"

"Have mercy on the young mal," another businesser interposed. "There's only one of him. If he could arrange to keep just one of our wives occupied—"

"How about one at a time?"

"But which one at what time?"

"We could draw for it."

"Nonsense. With the stuff that's available at the Dolls' House, why would he want to—"

"Maybe he could use some extra money."

"If he spends much time at the Doll's House, he'll need it."

The message screen flashed another bulletin.

MORT TOUCHDOWN IN 60 MINUTES.

One of the philosophers got to his feet and raised a goblet. "In an hour we'll be in Paradise!"

Laughter swept the table. It heightened when another tourist proposed a death toast. Caland did not like jests about death, though he had to admit that these were extenuating circumstances. When the name of a planet has a root woven through a host of languages, ancient and modern, in a massive vocabulary of words relating to death, when its only city is called Paradise, when its inhabitants are widely known as Morticians, there will be death jokes. The combination was irresistible comical to the tourists. The gags they thought they invented—"As soon as we meet Death, we'll be in Paradise!"—no doubt were clichés that were created anew on each successive vacation cruise. The previous day, in the salon, a fat fem spooning her second serving of dessert had giggled, "I'm eating my way to Death," and everyone at the table had been convulsed. "My wife has been nagging me to Death for years, so I thought I might as well bring her along," was a specimen of the bright repartee from the lounge. Caland was happy not to be a citizen of Mort.

He excused himself, finally, and returned to his stayroom. Not only had he failed to identify the person watching him, but he had not even been able to single out Regelz Arlu's assistant or assistants. He felt chagrinned. He was thinking again, perplexedly, about the zoological specimens, when the world of Mort loomed largely on the viewing screen and the warning for descent sounded.

The ship touched ground. Caland gathered up his personal effects, all of which fitted into his one traveling case, and moved toward the exit ramp.

Sparkling views of mountains and alluring seashores had filled the screen during their descent. When finally they emerged from the ship, Caland's grumbling fellow tourists were voluble in their disappointment. The single large gray terminal building was a rectangular lump, and the Port was not even automated. Passengers had to walk fifty meters to the arrival entrance or board an electrobus. The tourists gathered into a compact, rebellious group and stood looking disdainfully from the gaudy blue vehicle to the squat, unattractive building and the bleak, treeless landscape.

Caland thought the place impressive. Considering that not more than two or three passenger ships called at Mort in a sennite, the facilities surprised him. The lovely mountains had not vanished; they were only screened by the looming hull of the ship. The sea could not be seen from the Port, but all of the tourist blurbs about Mort, conspicuously displayed in the ship's lounge, touted hote rooms with a bay view, so it could be no further away than their destination.

But pampered millionaires who came to Mort to laugh at death and—according to individual bents—pursue hedonisms did not expect to do their chasing on foot.

Then the six revoltingly clothed and coiffured figures the steward had said were "for the Valley" descended the ramp.

They passed by the complaining tourists without a glance and strode briskly toward the terminal building. They carried bundles and packages and bags in addition to back pouches supported by heavy straps.

Caland followed them at a discreet distance. If these six had been watching him throughout the trip—so expertly that he did not become aware of their existence until the final day—he deserved a turn at watching them.

Tourist worlds rarely complicated the formalities of arrival or departure for their visitors. The six young people "for the Valley" instantly made themselves a sensational exception. They took possession of all three customs stations, objected to any inspection of luggage or personal effects, refused to furnish destinations, and gave answers that were so patently false that the clerks were reduced to quivering rage. A super charged out of an office, took in the developing state of chaos with a glance, and bellowed for reinforcements. Eventually the six were herded off for private examination.

When Caland's turn finally came, the perspiring clerk perfunctorily inspected his passport; glanced with respect at the hote reservation strip clipped to it, and exclaimed, "Ah! You'll be staying at the View." He bowed deeply. "Welcome to Mort. Sorry about the delay."

Traveling case unopened, Caland was conferred the freedom of a world by a wave of the clerk's hand. He turned his case over to yet another clerk, whose badge read, "Hote Transport." Then he found a seat for himself in a remote corner of the vaulted terminal room where his fellow passengers were unlikely to notice him.

He gave them his final scrutiny. A few of them headed for the terminal's lounge, which bore the unfortunate name, "The Gate to Paradise." Others browsed briefly through the displays of merchandise in the shops that lined one side of the room and advertised everything that an unimaginative tourist could desire, from exotic gourmet snacks to leisure clothing in fashions that seemed as revolting to Caland as the garments worn by those "for the Valley."

Most of the tourists moved directly toward exits, intent only on transportation to their destinations. Caland watched unobtrusively until the waiting lines were reduced to zero.

Finally the six "for the Valley" emerged from their ordeal on inspection and interrogation. One of them had been detected in an attempt at smuggling. A clerk was holding a small, furry creature, obviously the pet of one of the young fems. She was weeping; the three mals were storming threats; the super was again bellowing for reinforcements.

Caland had seen enough. The spy who adopted a conspicuous guise in order to be overlooked would not dare to be that conspicuous. He still was convinced that he was being watched, but he had no notion as to who was doing it, or why, or how.

He turned his back on the turmoil that centered around those "for the Valley" and strode toward the sole proprietor world called Mort.

CHAPTER FIVE

In the beginning there was agony.

Caland's hands clutched and flailed as he struggled to ward off the bludgeon, to turn aside the rapier. The pain subsided, finally, and he lay in the huddled weariness of total exhaustion. Then the nightmare engulfed him.

The pursuit was almost upon him. He ran frantically across a sward of strangely tinted grass to seek shelter among the tall hedges of a formal garden. The long shadow of his prison still lay heavily upon him; ahead, just beyond the garden, a looming, beckoning forest offered safety.

The thick hedges were neatly trimmed but impenetrable. The wide, graveled paths debouched upon intersections where flower beds were drawn up in stiffly formal array or hideous statuary stood in massed ranks about starkly ugly fountains— monuments to the death of art. Caland trotted forward, rejoicing in the exhilarating reality of freedom. The protective forest loomed closer.

And then, as he took one frantic turn after another, the forest seemed to recede. A chilling realization seized him: these innocent, well-kept alleys were a maze, and he was trapped. He heard the hurrying footsteps of pursuit close behind him, and he began to run. He crashed through flower beds, he knocked over statues, he hurled himself futilely at the hedge barriers, battering and kicking and tearing.

Exhaustion overwhelmed him. He slowed his pace, defeated, humiliated. The trap closed with an almost audible click as his pursuers surrounded him. With the limping, uncertain tread of the vanquished, he slowly moved into the circle of flashing lights and heaving pulsations. A sudden, chill wind left him gasping. He hunched his shoulders against it; not until he opened his eyes was he aware of returning to consciousness.

He pushed himself to a sitting position and looked about him with astonishment.

Who am I where am I why am I?

He closed his eyes and opened them again on a world gone completely askew. He felt as befuddled as a pain-wracked head left it possible to be. It was commonplace for him not to know who or where he was, but at least he knew what sort of place he was supposed to wake up in. This should have been a cubicle in a cheap gen hote, with his clothing draped over one of the two inevitable cubes, with the faintly luminous, windowless walls arranged closely about him, with the sharp odor of disinfectant emanating from the partially opened door of the sanitary sanctum.

Thus it always was. Thus it should have been. He had *never* regained consciousness except in the cubicle of a gen hote.

He was stunned. Again he closed his eyes and slowly opened them on a cramped room that looked as though the combined afflictions of war, pestilence, and decay had passed through it. The solitary window was a rectangular gap, most of its framing long since rotted away. The walls had been shredded by time and the whimsy of previous occupants, and their holes were as revealing of the building's structure as an engineering drawing. The room's one piece of furniture was the multiple-patched water bed Caland was sitting on. It almost filled the room, and it was covered only by the enormous sleeping bag on which Caland had been lying. In one wall was an open doorway leading into a room that looked like the mirror image of this one.

Each new impression added to his bafflement. His shoddy surroundings should have been filthy, but they were not. Incongruously, the place seemed almost antiseptically clean. The worn, stained, cracked, and gaping floorboards had been scrubbed to an occasional streak of whiteness, and what survived of the inner walls still contained damp blotches from a recent cleaning.

Caland swung his legs over the side of the bed and tried to stand. Then he sank backward, clutching his head, as the agony began to pound anew. It was several minutes before he could make his way, with two faltering steps, to the window.

It afforded him only a ragged glimpse of an excessively dilapidated building next door, viewed through rampantly growing shrubbery and the drooping, leaf-clotted limbs of nearby trees.

Caland pressed his fists against his eyes. "Unreal!" He murmured.

Who am I where am I why am I?

His eyes fell on the clothing that was piled in one corner as though flung there. He gathered it up and seated himself on the bed again while he went through the pockets. The small wad of money was strange, crinkly coupons of unfamiliar monetary units. There was no other clue at all. He pushed the currency back into his pocket and pondered the rough work garments. He could not ever remember ever wearing such clothing. If it were his, there should have been something else in the pockets, but he could not remember what it was that he missed.

Slowly he donned the clothing, which fit him with rough approximation. His shoes had been tossed into another corner. He retrieved them and summoned his resolution to face the open doorway.

Again he looked about him in astonishment. He saw a scarred table roughly fashioned of wood, and two dented and scratched metal chairs. On the table stood an odd-looking device that he could not identify. The manufacturer's label called it a vibrator stove. Two long shelves contained packages of dehydrated foods; battered pans, mugs, and eating accoutrements; a box of candles.

Caland turned his attention to the window, which, like that of the first room, was a gaping hole in a rotting frame. This one looked out onto a weed- and shrub- and junk-cluttered gap between property frontages that probably had been intended as a street. The only mark of passage was a meandering footpath that approximated its center.

Dazedly Caland moved one of the chairs to the window and seated himself. "Unreal!" he murmured again.

He did not know where he was. He did not know who he was.

He frowned, straining his memory, and suddenly he recalled his name. He experienced a ridiculous satisfaction in knowing that he was not nameless. He was Caland. "But who is Caland?" he asked himself.

Again he concentrated fiercely, attempting to force the memory barrier, but in the end he only knew that he was Caland. He also had remembered that he could not remember—that it was in no way unusual for him to wake up not knowing who or where he was. Eventually some shreds of recollection would return to him, either by slow seepage or in an unexpected rush.

His surroundings disturbed him more than his lack of memory. They were totally inexplicable, and he did not know what to do about it. In a gen hote, he could borrow a space schedule from the desk super, and in a matter of seconds he would know the world he was on and its relationship to a hundred other worlds. There were numerous clues as to time and place that could be picked up around an urban hote. In these utterly strange surroundings, there were none. He would have to ask someone, and he hated to ask. People did not react in friendly fashion when one said to them, "Excuse me, but—could you tell me what world this is?"

From somewhere nearby he could hear, faintly, the crash of breakers, and he could identify the cool, tangy freshness of sea air in an onshore wind. "So it's a planet with an ocean," he mused. That wasn't much to go on in identifying a world, but it was a start.

Then he added bewilderedly, "But where is everyone?"

Trees and bushes obscured their outlines, but he could see that the overgrown right-of-way in front of him was lined with decrepit buildings. If all of them were divided into small living units like the one he found himself in, this community should be a moldy hive packed with humanity, but he saw no one at all. "Maybe they only emerge when the sun vanishes," he told himself, not convincingly.

The first appearance was dramatic enough. A young fem bobbed into view from the house on Caland's right, skipped lightly over some of the discards that cluttered the unused street, and took the central path eastward. Her costume looked like underwear arranged on top of scanty outer garments. She'd had her head shaved except for a fuzzy question mark that ornamented the top of her skull. She was barefoot. Only her ample bust distinguished her as feminine.

Caland watched her passage incredulously.

She was followed shortly by a young mal with identical dress and coiffure except that his skull ornament was a fuzzy exclamation mark. His masculinity was evident only in his flat chest. Caland found himself speculating as to whether the mal might be a young fem of slight stature, or whether the young fem had been a mal with a contrived figure. He had the dizzying sensation of having been dropped into an environment where anything was probable.

Neither of the two had glanced in Caland's direction. He did not know whether that fact should please him or alarm him.

A middle-aged mal and fem materialized from an invisible pathway in the tangle of shrubs and trees between two buildings opposite Caland. They carefully picked their ways through the scattered junk and disappeared into another invisible pathway. They were headed to the beach for a swim; they wore soiled towels carelessly draped about themselves and nothing else.

Several family groups of swimmers followed them as the afternoon waned and dusk came on. The children burst from the tangled vegetation with yelps of excitement, swinging about their heads the towels they were supposed to be wearing. The parents followed more sedately. Other residents began to drift eastward in single file along the narrow, meandering path. Caland heard footsteps overhead. They paced back and forth briefly and then descended a staircase. The persons responsible must have exited from the other side of the house, because Caland never saw them.

He studied each passerby with intense interest, alert for a gesture, a signal, a surreptitious glance, but none of them betrayed the slightest awareness of him.

And yet—the eyes were watching him. He sensed it.

As the dusk slowly ripened into darkness, Caland suddenly realized that he had not yet seen a light. He remembered the box of candles on the shelf by the food, and he asked himself if such a primitive existence were possible, even on a backward world. He recognized the candles only because he had seen them in theatricals with historic settings.

It startled him that he remembered that. "I'm Caland," he told himself wonderingly, "and I'm an actor. Or I was an actor. And I've seen candles used in theatricals. Where?"

But the thread of recollection had snapped.

He left his window for an uneasy search of his immediate surroundings. The second of his two rooms opened into a central hallway that ran straight through the decrepit old building from the front entrance to the rear. All of the doors that opened off of the hallway were closed except one, which exposed the building's damp and medicinal-smelling sanctum. Caland several times paced the length of the hallway to stare into the impending night from each entrance. His perplexity increased. He knew of no world in the galaxy where established communities existed without transportation or communication, and he'd seen no sign of either. The community did not even have electricity!

His perplexity gave way to fright. He knew—though he could not remember why—that no world could ever be more to Jarv Caland than a way stop en route to another way stop. But he had to know where he was.

Beyond the rear entrance was a small clearing, thickly surrounded by a mass of shrubs and trees. As Caland's panic became overwhelming, he leaped into the night and found shelter there.

He crouched in a tangle of vegetation. Voices approached and receded as traffic toward the beach moved along a nearby path. He could faintly hear waves breaking—not the deep, rhythmic pounding of an open sea colliding with the shore, but the gentle smacking of waves from some sheltered inlet. He could hear the shouts of the bathers and of those gamboling on the beach. When he finally shifted his position, he could see the leaping flames of beach fires, and occasionally he caught the irresistible aroma of cooking food. He sniffed hungrily. He had no way of knowing when he'd eaten last and felt famished.

Cautiously he pushed through the bushes to the open beach beyond. The long stretch of white sand gleamed silvery in the light of the beach fires. Those dotted the beach at irregular intervals for more than a kilometer, and they were not the modest affairs of flammable synthetics that Caland was familiar with. These were fires such as he'd never experienced—great, leaping masses of flame fed by huge chunks of log. Fire pits were marked off with circles of stones; surrounding them at a comfortable distance were wider circles of small boulders that served as seats for the revelers.

Most of the seats were occupied. Scattered shouts could still be heard beyond the faintly phosphorescent line where the waves met the beach, but many of the swimmers already had joined the non-swimmers around the fires. A few of them were nude; some carelessly wrapped themselves in soggy towels. Songs from adjoining fires blended in hideous cacophony. Nude children pursued revels of their own as they raced along the beach or chased one another between the fires, screaming merrily.

Such uninhibited public behavior was totally alien to Caland, and for a time he could only stare at it uncomprehendingly.

But he was the alien here, the outsider. He pointed his way through a gap between the fires until he reached the lapping waves. Then he turned and walked slowly along the water's edge. He cringed at the thought of intruding on these merrymakers, but he had to know where he was. His mind fumbled with words, phrasing and rephrasing, searching for a way to ask without provoking curiosity or attracting attention to himself. He skirted the fires as widely as possible in the hope of encountering a solitary bather.

The massed faces around the fires repelled him. The tossing flames highlighted them grotesquely, and he surreptitiously studied each group he passed with the fascination of horror: faces conversing animatedly, faces radiant with laughter, faces listening, faces contentedly eating.

None of them sent as much as a casual glance in his direction. The contrast between bright fire light and surrounding darkness seemed to have rendered him invisible.

"Who's this?" a clear voice called suddenly.

Caland came to a startling halt.

A chubby youth draped in a wet towel was peering at him uncertainly. "Someone new, isn't it? Come and join us." He grinned and pointed at the vacant rock beside him.

His openly friendly manner and Caland's compulsion to know where he was overcame his impulse to flee. He timidly edged forward and accepted the proffered seat with a nod. The stone's hard, irregular surface was as uncomfortable as it had looked.

The youth grinned again. "People call me Moppy." He brushed water from a shock of sopping hair that stood upright. "I wonder why."

Caland said uncertainly, "I'm Caland."

Moppy turned to the girl beside him. "Sippy?" he nudged her. She was also draped in a towel, and her wet hair was considerably shorter than his. "Sippy, he says he's Caland. Shall we call him Cal?"

She turned a pert smile on Caland. She was very young and too thin to be pretty, but there was an attractive vivacity in her fire-flushed face. "Let's," she said. "'O, Cal."

"Cal you are," Moppy said, with the ceremonious air of one performing a christening. "In the Valley, it isn't your name that counts, it's what people call you. How do you waste your time?"

"Waste—time?" Caland echoed doubtfully.

"What's your bit? What pushes you?"

The girl giggled at Caland's bafflement. "He means what do you do. Moppy and I write. When we feel like it. When we can afford paper. We've got artists here, and musicians, and dancers, and all kinds of writers. No one really works at it except a few of the artists—they now and then can sell something to the tourists. Most of us don't make any money, so it's considered a way to waste time. Everyone ought to have a way to waste time. Do you?"

"Waste time," Caland repeated again. "I am—I was—an actor, but I never thought of it as a way to waste time."

Sippy shook her head. "It isn't. At least—you can't waste time that way in the Valley. There's no place to act. Do you ever write plays?"

"Write plays," Caland repeated. "Yes, I write—I've written—plays." He hesitated, wondering whether he'd experienced another seepage of memory or imagined it. "Yes," he went on soberly. "I've written plays. I've had them produced. But I never considered the writing a waste of time. I wrote them to make money."

"Oh, that's all right," Sippy said. "All of us write to make money, but it never seems to happen that way. Writing plays should be as good a way to waste time as any."

She turned her attention to an older woman seated on the next rock, and Caland began looking about him perplexedly. He'd hoped to learn something of his surroundings—to find out where the ocean was and what body of water was lapping the beach—but the night shrouded everything, and the massive fire made it difficult to see beyond its periphery. Where was he?

Caland began glancing behind him and trying to trace the shore line. Moppy thought he was watching the next fire, where a feast was in progress. "You picked an impoverished rabble," he chuckled. "None of us has any food, tonight, but these cheapies are good for a lot of laughs. They're all sprung except Sippy and me."

"Sprung?" Caland echoed.

The bushy-bearded, heavy-set man on the other side of Caland had been listening to the conversation with evident amusement. "The only reason Sippy and Moppy aren't sprung is because they started out with the genetic endowment of idiots," he said good-naturedly. He had a round, plump face that radiated good humor. He was a non-swimmer; the comfortable protrusion of fat around his middle was superficially disguised by patched, baggy clothing that was smeared with a spectrum of paint stains.

"I'm Sam the Artist," he said.

"Cal," Caland said and touched hands with him.

"Of course I'm not really an artist," Sam the Artist went on. "And my name isn't Sam. For some stupid reason people started calling me that, and then they had to call me Sam the Artist to distinguish me from the other Sams in the Valley. Actually, I'm a painter. Interior decorator variety. I'm a highly skilled painter of rooms, only I'd rather not. Meet the others."

He introduced Caland to a husky, middle-aged mal named Willen Blens; to an older mal who was an artist of some sort named Sig; to a fat, elderly fem named Thalm; to a good-looking young couple in their twenties, Duggal and Huggal; to a plump, attractive-looking fem of about thirty named Tel. The swimmers, Duggal, Huggal, and Sig, wore towels. Blens wore ragged shorts; Thalm, shorts and a ludicrously brief halter around her massive breasts. Tel wore a simple dress of a dark brown, coarsely knit material. Caland, in his rough, all-enveloping work garb, would have felt overdressed had it not been for the supporting presence of Sam the Artist.

Thalm leered at Caland and announced that she was a retired inmate of the Dolls' House. "Involuntarily retired," she wheezed, continuing to leer. "Any time I'm needed, I'm still available."

"Now, Thalm," Sam the Artist said, shaking a finger. "You know the rules. No soliciting on the beach."

"Screet! All the other girls are wagging it at him. Just because I got the nerve to speak up—"

Duggal leaned over and whispered something to her. She giggled shrilly, and Caland returned his embarrassed attention to Sam the Artist.

He asked, "Is it possible to waste much time painting rooms here? My quarters don't look as though they've been painted since the house was built."

Sam the Artist's laughter was convulsive. When his ample stomach had stopped shaking, he said, "But look at the potential! Consider how many rooms need painting. Except for the fact that no one has money to spend for decorating, I have a lifetime of work ahead of me."

"Is there any work for you?" Caland asked politely.

"Very little, fortunately. Just enough to keep me going. Once in a while the girls in the Houses of Fame get tired of their rooms, and I do a quick morning job for them, complete decoration in a couple of hours with instant-dry paints so they don't lose business. And I paint the interiors of the Fig Stump and the Burned Wafer and the Road to Hell every two or three years. Occasionally I do a small job over in Paradise, and a couple of times I've helped out with a big job at Pak Enterprises when someone was in a hurry. I've worked in Pakovich's mansion. It adds up to more work than I'd like, but not quite as much as I need."

Caland had been desperately seeking information about his surroundings, but this was more than he could assimilate. "Houses of—Fame?" he repeated.

"That's what we call the whore houses. The Dolls' House and Yda's. Why not? They're very high-class, and they're certainly the best known houses on the world of Mort. I heard you say you're an actor."

It slipped past Caland so fast that he almost missed it. Now he knew where he was—on the world of Mort, in a place called the Valley. He could not remember ever having heard of Mort, and he didn't know where it was located, but the space coordinates were easy to come by when one knew what to look up.

"I *was* an actor," he said. "I might as well start calling myself something else. There seem to be fewer acting jobs here than painting jobs."

"True. Very true," Sam the Artist agreed. Then he leaned back, closed his eyes, and declaimed stentoriously.

> *"All the galaxy's a stage*
> *Dimly lit by a universe of suns;*
> *And we poor actors vainly shape our egos*
> *Into fanciful images of God*
> *While we fumble every cue*
> *Except the last."*

Caland beamed at him. The memory seepage had become a flood. *"The Jester of the Four Suns,"* he said reverently. "That was my first principal, if a leading role in an almost empty amateur theater can be called a principal. But I'll never forget it."

He got to his feet.

> *"The distant sun swallowed a comet*
> *And belched.*
> *'Nova!' screamed the sage.*
> *'The touch of God's breath,' intoned the priest.*
> *'My stomach feels the same way,' sobbed the jester."*

He seated himself again, squirming to find a comfortable position on the hard seat, and Sam the Artist applauded delightedly.

"Bravo!" Sam exclaimed. "You have the voice. And the intonation. Pity we haven't got a theater here. It might be fun. It might be a good way for a lot of people to waste time. We rarely get any actors, but that's only because we haven't got a theater."

"All you have to do is announce a play. A plague of actors will follow."

Sam the Artist laughed merrily. "They'd be a worse pollutant than the fertilizer factory, eh? You're probably right. Anyone in a dozen sectors who wanted to waste time acting would head to Mort. The Valley is one of the few places left in the galaxy where one can waste time without becoming the subject of warped governmental concern."

"The government of Mort pretends that the Valley doesn't exist."

Caland glanced around the circle of threadbare fireside companions. He had never seen a shabbier group of candidates for a governmental sustenance list. He lowered his voice. "No governmental aid at all? Then how do these people exist? They have to eat. They have to pay rent, even if not much. Now and then they must need other things, even if not often. How can an economy function in a place where everyone is wasting time?"

"Not everyone," Sam the Artist protested. "We've got our entrepreneurs, big and little, and a lot of the Valley people work regularly, even if not long. Almost anyone who can get one will take a temporary job once in a while for food money. But it's true that only a few of us earn very much, and many of us don't earn anything. As to how people live—"

He broke off and leaped to his feet. "Look!" he exclaimed, pointing. "The Great Watcher is entertaining."

Caland stood up, as did the others. A few small beach fires burned at the distant head of the bay. Further along the shore, two tall buildings were ablaze with light. A short distance inland could be seen the suffused glow of a town or small city. Suspended high above that, and seeming to hover over it, was a brilliant triangle of illumination.

"Ah, zwingy!" Sippy exclaimed.

"That's where Pakovich lives," Sam the Artist said. "He's the stodge that owns the world of Mort. Think of that—owning a world. He's got a big mansion high up on the side of a mountain so he can look down and tell himself he's lord of all he surveys, and his special hobby is night flowers. He imports them from all over the galaxy. He has an enormous garden of them. Whenever he entertains, he illuminates the garden, and all of those huge blooms think it's day and start closing and the guests go, 'Ahhhhh!' to show how thrilled they are by the exciting action.

Owning a world must be a frightful bore."

They sat down again, and Caland admitted that world owner-ship was something he had never aspired to.

"You asked how the Valley economy functions," Sam the Artist said. "It's complicated, but a real life example might help you to understand it. Yesterday morning, Mucks Groilan woke up with a wet face. As soon as he was sufficiently awake, he deduced that his roof was leaking. It takes a container of sealant to fix a roof effectively enough to make the water leak into someone else's room, and sealant is expensive. A container costs five chits here in the Valley and six or seven over at Pakovich's Mercantile Mart, which the people of Paradise call Merc Mart and which we call the Mercenary Mart. Mucks had one chit, which he'd hoped to use for food. So he set out to borrow five. First he called on a good friend of his named Hashface, who runs a little 'up' eatery over on the Prom. We don't have good or bad eateries, they're all bad, but at least you have a choice between eating standing up or eating sitting down. Hashface's is an 'up.' Mucks said to Hashface, 'Can you lend me five? My roof leaks.' This is proper Valley mooching etiquette, telling your chosen philanthropist what you're borrowing money for. He may think he needs it himself, and you have to convince him that your need is more urgent than his. But you'd better be truthful. If you lie just once and get caught, you'll never be able to borrow again from anyone. Hashface knew that a leaky roof is a curse that almost never fixes itself, but he didn't have five spare chits. He said, 'I'll see what I can do for you.' So he started asking people, and since he wasn't borrowing for himself, he just said he had a friend with a need. All of the people he asked were as broke as he was, but some of them began trying to borrow five chits from their friends for Hashface to lend to someone in need, and of course Mucks was trying to borrow from everyone he met, and by noon almost the entire Valley population either was looking for someone who could lend those five chits or avoiding the people who were trying to borrow them. Finally someone asked the Reverend—he's a chap who wastes time with religion—and the Reverend said he'd see what he could do. And the next person he met was Mucks Groilan."

Moppy was listening attentively. Sippy had lost interest. She'd removed her towel and was indifferently holding it closer to the fire to dry. Caland self-consciously averted his eyes.

"In the meantime," Sam the Artist went on, "Mucks had decided there weren't five spare chits in the entire Valley, and—not wanting to wake up with a wet face the next morning—he pawned his cimbalom. This was no great sacrifice. Most of its strings were missing, and he'd never been able to play it anyway. He got ten chits for it. Five of them went for the sealant. No sooner did he get his roof fixed than the Reverend came along wanting to borrow five chits for a friend of a friend who needed them urgently. Since the Reverend is a real up person, and since Mucks now has five spare chits, he lent them to him. The Reverend turned them over to whoever had asked him, and eventually the money got to Hashface. The next time Mucks happened by, Hashface flagged him and gave him the five chits. So Mucks will eat well for the next sennite, but he still doesn't know that he borrowed his own money. And that's how the Valley economy works."

"You borrow from yourself?" Caland asked bewilderedly.

"No, no!" Sam the Artist waved a protesting hand. "That isn't the lesson at all. Mucks borrowing from himself was a fluke of circumstance. The Valley survives economically because everyone owes everyone else the same five chits."

Caland got slowly to his feet. The sea breeze had turned cooler, and the fire was burning down, but the glow of warmth surrounded him—the warmth of good fellowship, of a generous friendliness, freely given. After years of loneliness, of being a wandering stranger even to himself, he was experiencing an emotional thaw. He beamed upon his new friends, and they beamed back at him.

He fumbled in his pocket and produced the wad of strange currency he had found there earlier: flimsy, brightly colored coupons. It meant nothing to him; there would be more the next time he regained consciousness. "It is money, isn't it?" he asked doubtfully.

"Schlock printing of the realm," Sam the Artist said, cheerfully. "Not very artistic, but it's all we've got."

Caland let some of the coupons fall to the ground. With exclamations, Moppy and the nude Sippy began to gather them up for him. Caland counted as the slips of crinkly paper were handed back. "Ten, fifteen, nineteen, twenty-two chits." Everyone around the fire was watching him intently. "I need five to lend, so I can work my way into the Valley's economic system." He pocketed a five-chit coupon and bowed to Sam the Artist, who grinned and nodded. "And I should keep something to eat on. What do I need to eat on?"

"How much and for how long?" Sam the Artist asked. "A chit a day will feed you, though not lavishly. If you do your own cooking, that is. If you patronize the eateries—"

Caland had pocketed another five chits. "This leaves me with twelve wholly unnecessary chits. Let's have a party. Is there any place where one can buy food at this time of night?"

"That's another economic truth about the Valley," Sam the Artist said solemnly. "No business establishment is ever closed to a customer who has twelve chits in cash."

The matter was quickly settled. Huggal, who had been doing just that to Duggal, emphatically, ever since Caland joined the group, abruptly released him. Sippy donned her towel. The two young couples dashed off to buy food, and Willen Blens went for more logs. Caland wondered where the logs came from but decided not to ask. He'd had enough economic lectures for one evening. He discussed drama with Sam the Artist while listening to desultory conversation around the fire and watching the sporadic traffic along the beach. It was getting late; families with children were saying farewells and marching their protesting offspring off into the darkness. Caland looked about him uneasily. He had the sensation that someone was watching him.

Finally the young couples returned with the food.

Minutes later, chunks of meat were sizzling and tubers were baking. Duggal and Moppy quickly concocted dough with Mort's sea water—which they described as having a superabundance of culinary and nutritional virtues—and coarse flour, and they stuffed it with vegetables, mushrooms, and shredded meat. They wrapped this around the long sticks upon which the chunks of meat were skewered. A ceramic jug containing a fiery kind of cider slowly made the circuit with each person taking a portion described as one slop.

People at the adjoining fires were staring enviously. Caland thought it strange—considering the Valley's peculiar economy and obvious poverty—that their group hadn't been mobbed. He mentioned this to Sam the Artist.

"Valley etiquette again," Sam said. "A fire belongs to the person who brought the first logs and lit them. That was Blens. The rest of us are here because we were invited. Others might stop to chat for a moment, but they won't join a fire group unless asked by someone who already belongs. And now that you've furnished the food, none of us would ask anyone else to share it because it's yours. When you introduce food at a fire, you're expected to be generous with everyone there, but no outsiders will try to wedge unless you invite them yourself. It's the only way we keep our chaos organized. It wouldn't be possible to live here if every hungry person graved the moment anyone had anything to eat."

"I can understand that," Caland said. "But some of the people at the other fires might be *really* hungry."

"Probably a lot of them are really hungry," Sam the Artist said. "But I see where you're headed, and I can tell you in advance that there's not enough food here to feed the whole Valley."

"I'm hungry myself," Caland said. "I can't remember when I ate last, but I couldn't claim to be starving. Have we got enough to feed a few more people?"

Sam the Artist contemplated the cooking food. "This is quite a feast you've laid out for us. Four or five more, I'd say.

Considering that some of us have already eaten well today, make that five or six. If you want them."

"Let's invite six people who are really hungry."

"Your choice," Sam the Artist said, gesturing at the long line of fires.

"But I don't know anyone. Why don't you ask them?"

Sam the Artist turned to the fem Tel, who was watching them with interest from across the fire while she held one of the long skewer sticks.

"Tel. Go find us six really hungry people."

"Sure," Tel said. She handed the stick to Moppy and strode away. She had lustrous, long, dark hair and a handsome profile, and her easy, swinging stride suggested to Caland that his first impression had been wrong. Her body was more muscular than plump.

He turned and found Sam the Artist looking at him with amusement. "Right," Sam said. "And some of these idiots chase the young girls. Unfortunately, when girls get to be Tel's age, they prefer to do their own chasing. Tel pursues a good-looking youngster named Gary Dwand, who is madly in love with a girl named Melana. This is the kind of proposition that leaves everyone frustrated. Half the men in the Valley are madly in love with Melana, but as far as anyone has found out, she neither pursues nor lets herself be pursued. My theory is that human relations are going to be totally irrational, everywhere, as long as there are two sexes. One thing I ought to caution you about. The Valley has a reputation for licentiousness. People bathe nude, relations between the sexes are as informal as people care to make them, or as formal, and all the whores on Mort who admit it live here. But this really is a highly moral community. The people are no more licentious than people anywhere else. Their reputation comes from the fact that they refuse to waste time and effort in pretending not to be."

Tel returned with a motley assortment of people: a ragged, elderly mal; a thin, hungry-looking, middle-aged couple; a wildly unkempt mal of uncertain age; and two young girls.

"None of them has had a good meal for days," she told Caland.

"Please join us," Caland said. "Eat well."

Under Sam the Artist's tutelage, he was ripping chunks of bread from the long loaves. These would serve as plates for the pieces of meat. A moment later the feast began, and all of those present—even the ones who already had eaten that day—consumed food as though famished. Caland wondered if it were the Valley's theory of nutrition: eat as much as you can whenever you can, because tomorrow you'll probably starve.

He had the warm, persistent glow of one celebrating a long-dreamed-of homecoming. He got to his feet and raised the jug high above his head. "To the Valley," he announced. "I think I'm going to like it."

It was unlike any other place in the galaxy. He couldn't remember very many places, but he felt certain that this one was unique, and his presence here made less sense with each passing moment.

There was only one possible explanation. Someone had made a mistake.

The jug went around the fire from mouth to mouth, and eventually it returned to Caland carrying everyone's felicitations. Caland got to his feet again. He raised the jug and took a generous slop.

Then he dropped it. It struck the sand with a *whap*; Sam the Artist's quick hands kept it from tipping over. Caland stood staring bewilderedly at his own upraised hands.

Someone had made a mistake. Now it was being corrected. His body suddenly went rigid. He teetered back and forth, muscles twitching. He was incapable of speech, incapable of any kind of an appeal for help. He knew that he would fall, and he could only hope that he would miss the fire. Then the tidal wave of pain swept over him, and he spun into blackness.

CHAPTER SIX

In the beginning there was agony.

Caland lay tensed and writhing while the pain cycle ran its grim course. Finally, resignedly, he sank into his nightmare.

He stood in a small clearing surrounded by mammoth trees whose arching branches formed a thick canopy high overhead. A slender metal tower thrust upward and disappeared into the foliage.

A storm was raging. Thunder crackled about him, brilliant flashes of lightning sketched a tracery of illumination even in the depths of the forest, giant branches creaked and moaned in a punishing wind, rain dripped from the whipping leaves.

Then the earth heaved, and trees and tower were tossed about as though by the shake of an impatient deity's head.

Caland stirred and opened his eyes.

Who am I where am I why am I?

What he saw startled him more than the cataclysmic upheaval that had terminated his nightmare. He was in the same room in which he'd last awakened.

He closed his eyes, opened them again. His memory was less ravaged than usual, and down its dim recesses marched a procession of images of previous awakenings, always in cheap gen hotes, always on strange worlds, always with himself in bed and disrobed as though someone had put him there.

This time he lay in the same patched water bed in the same decrepit room he'd last awakened in, and only his shoes had been removed. Had he ever before regained consciousness twice on the same world? He could not remember.

He slipped on his shoes and moved unsteadily to the open doorway. A fem sat by the wood table with her head resting on her arms, sound asleep. His astonishment was intensified by the fact that he recognized her. Her name was Tel, and he'd met her at the beach fire. He remembered the beach fire. On the table in front of her was an edged board. Something had been sculpted on it in moist sand—her method of wasting time, he supposed, and then he marveled that he'd remembered that. The sculpture was a vaguely familiar human face, and he puzzled over it for a moment before it occurred to him that it might be himself, slightly distorted by a nose that had dried out and crumbled.

Tel's sturdy figure looked robust, rather than voluptuous, but there was a genuine beauty, a quiet serenity about her relaxed slumber. She was wearing the same dark, coarsely woven dress she'd worn on the beach. He clutched his head as the pain returned. When the spasm had passed, he stepped past Tel to the hall doorway. He stood there for a moment and studied her doubtfully. Was she friend or enemy? Guardian or jailer?

Agony continued to wash over him sporadically, though the intensity was slowly subsiding. As frequently happened when he regained consciousness, he felt an overwhelming need to get outside, to escape, as though all of the uncertainties that confronted him, along with the nightmare and the pounding agony and the searing flashes of light and pain, were furnishings of the room in which he found himself. He wanted to walk through the door and leave them behind him like discarded clothing.

Softly he tiptoed away.

Dusk lurked in heavily shaded places along the overgrown street that ran in front of the building. The night people were emerging, singly and in pairs. All of them were strangers to Caland. One gave him a casual nod; the others passed him indifferently.

He turned westward and walked with a slow, unsteady pace toward the sound of the ocean, pausing with bowed head and closed eyes when a new spasm of pain seized him. The surf became louder as he approached it, but the tangled vegetation at the end of the street kept it from his view until the path took a last, sharp turn and ended at the beach.

There Caland halted abruptly and started to turn back. Two large boulders at the rear of the beach were framed by the encroaching tangle of shrubs. They were waist high, with bulging, irregular contours. On one of them, a mal was seated.

He was small and wiry in stature, and his much-patched work clothing seemed more bizarre than the weird costumes of the night people. The fresh splotches of dirt and grease suggested that he actually had performed work in it. He wore a skull cap with a long, tinted visor, and his darkened face and hands and squinting eyes were their own evidence of years in the sun and wind. Caland could not decide whether he was a young man prematurely aged by a hard life or an old man whose superb physical condition made him look middle-aged.

Obviously he relished solitude. One who sat alone watching the endless rhythms and perpetual counterpoints of the ocean had to be as private a person as Caland, with his own agonies and enigmas to contend with, and Caland forbore to intrude.

Suddenly the mal looked up, nodded at Caland, and returned his attention to the ocean. The gesture emboldened Caland to hunch himself onto the unoccupied boulder.

But he did not speak. This mal was willing to share his ocean with Caland, but he would keep his inner turmoil to himself, and he'd expect Caland to do the same.

The sun's burnished disk hung low on the horizon, and beneath it the waves rolled shoreward with a slow, regular, crashing beat. Caland found hypnotic restfulness in their powerful thrust toward the land and the foaming rush on their withdrawal. He selected a line of gray water and watched its frothing progress as it coursed inexorably toward him, rearing higher and higher, shedding flecks of foam on the whipping breeze, and finally crashed onto the silvery sand in a shower of spray. Probing fingers of water searched the steeply inclined beach to the limit of their momentum and then subsided. The magnificent inevitability made Caland think of perpetual motion or of infinity. As he contemplated the relentless shoreward reach that began thousands of kilometers away on the open ocean, his mind seemed on the verge of expanding and taking wing.

Reality intruded a painful awareness of his hard, lumpy seat. He kicked the rock irritably, squirmed into a more comfortable position, and returned his attention to the waves. For how many millennia had they pounded futilely on this narrow beach? Like his own vain attempts to breach his memory barrier, they always crashed short of their objective and trickled away ineffectually. Occasionally one stretched a trifle higher or crashed a trifle harder and seemed about to flow further up the beach and illuminate something, but its momentum quickly soaked into the sand and was lost.

He abandoned the pounding surf and began to look about him. On his immediate right, a tapering spur of land pointed northward to an opening where a bay met the ocean. At its tip, a concrete pillar anchored a cable that supported a net across the mouth of the bay. This extended to a long, narrow island in the bay's mouth, where clouds of strange-looking flying creatures congregated. From the north tip of the island, another net with supporting cable stretched to the bay's opposite lip. Caland speculated briefly on the possible usefulness of nets that closed off an entire bay and could think of none. At least the geography of his position finally had been made clear to him. The beach fires and the swimming took place on the bay side of the Valley, and the city of Paradise lay at the bay's distant head.

The sun dipped lower. Suddenly, as it touched the water, the entire gray surface took on a magnificent, coppery sheen. Caland heard a sharp intake of breath from the mal seated nearby. He turned for a moment and saw him staring raptly at an ocean that now flowed like molten metal.

The moment of magic passed quickly. The sun sank lower; the awesome loveliness was fractured by heaving waves, and its fragments were quickly dissipated. In the space of a few heartbeats, a fiery beauty had spanned the horizon and been abruptly extinguished by a gray, rocking ocean that already had begun to corrode slowly into blackness.

The mal turned to Caland and offered his hand. "I'm Bar."

"I'm Cal," Caland said, touching hands with him.

"I don't often see anyone here in the evening," Bar said. "Most people prefer the bay beach."

"Maybe it's because the water's quieter over there."

"Too quiet," Bar said scornfully. "It's like a wild animal that's been tamed. It may be pretty, but it's not the same animal. Those shallow little waves run on all the time, like a person who has nothing to say and can't stop talking. The ocean, now—it doesn't talk as fast, but there's depth to it. It expresses things one can take ahold of and ponder. It's the real animal."

He gesticulated with his right arm and hand; his left arm was held stiffly, close to his body.

Tel spoke abruptly into Caland's ear. "So here you are."

He had not heard her approach. Her face was flushed as though she'd been running. "Don't ever do that again," she told Caland sternly.

"Do what?"

"Walk off on your own."

"Why not?" Caland asked, genuinely puzzled.

"We'll talk about it later. 'O, Bar."

"Evening," Bar said politely.

"Bar is the Valley's leading citizen," Tel told Caland. "He's our number one entrepreneur and civic booster, but when he sits here by the ocean, he tends to get moody. Did you arrive in time to enjoy the sunset?"

Caland nodded. "It was magnificent."

"On a clear night, it always is. It's one of Mort's most celebrated events, though the *Galactic Almanac* still claims that Mort got its name—which means 'death'—from the fact that its oceans periodically turn to blood as the creatures living there slaughter each other. It's true that Mort has more than its share of voracious sea creatures, but they don't bleed red, or even copper. That legend must have been started by Mort's sunsets. Probably it gives Pakovich's tourist bureau fits. How'd you happen to come out here?"

"No special reason. I wanted to walk."

Bar slid down the boulder. "Come to din tomorrow," he said to Caland. "You too, Tel. When the klaxon sounds." He grinned—which transformed his gloomy countenance—and walked away before Caland could answer.

"Now you're a social success," Tel said. "Still feel like walking?"

He fell in behind her, and they started back along the path. There was a transcendent grace and rhythm to her walk, and he watched the sway of her hips as hypnotically as he'd watched the enigmatic beat of the ocean waves.

The sound of voices distracted him. Bar was strolling through the deepening dusk far ahead of them, and shadows were converging on him. One at a time they accosted him and, after a brief contact, faded away to be replaced by another shadow, and through it all Bar moved along steadily without breaking stride.

Caland rubbed his eyes fretfully. It was too dark, and Bar was too far away for him to make out what was happening. Then Bar turned off, vanishing into one of the paths that were hidden by the thick vegetation between buildings.

Tel moved ahead with firm strides, and Caland, still feeling a bit unsteady, began to have difficulty in keeping up. His problems intensified when she turned into a side path. The going became much rougher. An occasional branch from a tree or bush snapped back from her passage, and Caland had to protect himself with an extended arm. Soon he was perspiring.

Abruptly they emerged in another street, and overgrown space with a meandering central path like the one in front of Caland's apartment.

"This is Junk Vista Avenue," Tel said. "Your house is on Bay Unview Boulevard.

"Bay *Un*view—"

"It used to be Bay View Boulevard, and then the trees and

shrubs got so overgrown that it was impossible to see the bay, so the name was changed. There are five east-west streets in the Valley: Bay Unview Boulevard, Junk Vista Avenue, and then the Valley Promenade, which is called the Prom. A lot of people think that's where the action is." There was a note of scorn in her voice. "Actually, it's where the money action is. All the commercial establishments are located on the east half of the Prom. It's also where the tourists congregate. South of the Prom is Primrose Lane, and then Fishstink Alley, which is the street nearest Pakovich's fertilizer factory. Whatever else Valley people may be, they're realists."

They had crossed Junk Vista Avenue and moved into another overgrown path, and Tel, now only dimly visible, slowed her pace so he could keep up with her. They emerged in a cleared area behind a row of buildings. A well-worn path led through a narrow gap to the Prom.

Caland recoiled. Beyond that gap was a street thronging with people. He hung back in dismay even when Tel turned and beckoned to him. Finally he willed himself to join her.

They stood between two buildings out of the traffic flow. The street was dim, with only three widely-spaced overhead electric lights. The shops were lit just as feebly, and in some of them he saw candles flickering. One establishment further along the street had huge candles burning in lanterns by its entrance. For a time he puzzled over the use of candles when electricity was available.

He asked Tel about it.

"Candles are cheaper," she said, "and the tourists think they're romantic. Some of the tourists have never seen candles. They drool over the charming atmosphere."

Passersby drifted along in gusts and eddies, and even in the dim light the tourists were easy to pick out. Many of them wore expensive but revoltingly colored and designed lounge dress. Occasionally a Valley resident conveyed a group of tourists, acting as informal guide—and working for grats, Tel said. Clouds of shabbily-dressed Vals—Tel's term for Valley people—

hung about the other tourists. They were paras, passing out leaf-lets, offering something for sale, begging. Their voices ranged from the suavely persuasive to the brashly wheedling.

Caland felt revolted. He was humanity and he was being violated.

A male voice called, "Tel—have you seen Melana?"

"Not tonight, Gary," Tel called back.

A tall, husky man in a neat work suit came striding past, and Tel hailed him and introduced him to Caland: Chan Worntling, an enforcer for the Doll's House.

"Gary is off again," Tel told him.

"Is he?"

"Have *you* seen Melana?"

"Saw her at her usual time, which is a bit before sunset. She walked out to the gate and took the 'bus." He paused. "Sdissler tagged after her almost to the gate."

"It figures."

Worntling gave them a grin and a wave of his hand and moved on. He veered aside to shine a light into the face of a young fem who was swaying her hips provocatively at a tourist. She greeted him profanely. He replied in kind and headed on down the Prom.

"What's an enforcer?" Caland asked Tel.

"An order keeper. Originally the enforcers limited their activ-ities to the Houses of Fame. That didn't help with the disorder outside, which was giving the Valley a bad name. So they were promoted to the status of unofficial proctors. There are six of them, three from the Dolls' House and three from Yda's. Any one of them is capable of inflicting as much order as most situ-ations call for, and they have the full support of anyone sober enough to recognize them."

"Unreal!" Caland murmured. He was not thinking of the scene before him, though that seemed unusual enough, but about his presence here. He said to Tel, "Is the Valley really as strange as it looks?"

"It is and it isn't," Tel said seriously. "Certain kinds of problems are people problems, and you get them wherever you have people. You can't get away from them unless you're away from people. But the Valley definitely is different. You'll find good things here that don't exist anywhere else."

"And bad things?"

Tel thought a moment. "I think most of the bad things here aren't as bad as things elsewhere. Not nearly as bad. But don't confuse the Prom with the Valley. The real Valley is what you saw on the beach the other night. Would you like to go back?"

Caland nodded, and turned away. He had a new perplexity to contemplate. She had said, "...on the beach the other night." He'd thought it had been the previous night. He wondered how long he'd been unconscious.

* * * * * * *

They drifted down the long line of beach fires until a voice hailed them. Sam the Artist waved a hand. "Join us?" he called.

It was a small group, and there were several unoccupied rocks. Caland and Tel seated themselves, and Sam the Artist performed introductions. A gaunt, solemn-looking mal who managed to appear formally dressed in shabby black work clothing was the Reverend. Four of the others, three middle-aged fems and a mal, seemed to be pleasant nonentities who were drifting easily through life, Valley fashion. The fifth was a fem in her late teens who eyed Caland with undisguised calcu-lation.

"Don't mind Cleo," Sam the Artist said. "She's a mal-eater, but sooner or later she spits them out again, more or less intact. She performs an invaluable function here. If a pregnant woman wants to know the sex of her unborn child without expensive testing, all she has to do is walk past Cleo. If it's a boy, Cleo reacts."

The young fem giggled and fluttered her lashes at Caland. She had been swimming, and she wore only a very inadequate towel. She radiated exuberant, glowing youth, but to Caland's jaundiced eye she already had a sadly faded look. Her hair style seemed to vacillate between blonde and dark; her complexion hovered blotchingly between suntan and peeling pallor; her manner, for all of her overt aggressiveness, concealed a pathetic uncertainty. She was the ruthless pursuer whose goal in life was to be pursued. She would never achieve it. He'd often seen the type among actors of both sexes: a personality attuned to easy small victories and—perhaps for that reason—demolished in all of life's major battles.

"We've been looking for you," the Reverend said to Tel. He had a pleasant, deep, resonant voice. "In fact, we were worried. Someone saw Cal wandering about by himself. But Mucks said the two of you were headed for the Prom and everything seemed regulated."

"Nicely regulated—I think," Tel said.

Caland felt both embarrassed and resentful; but the night was wonderfully pleasant, and the leaping flames quickly soothed and relaxed him. He stretched out his legs and sniffed the odor of cooking food that came from the next fire, wondering when he'd eaten last. How long ago had it been, that "other night" on the beach?

One of the fems asked the Reverend a question that Caland did not catch; the Reverend reflected for a moment and began a lengthy reply about the difficulty finite humans had in understanding an infinite deity. The others listened attentively, though Caland was certain that few of them understood what the Reverend was saying.

During the next lull in the conversation, he said to Sam the Artist, "What are the nets for?"

Sam's good natured, bristly face puckered with perplexity. "Nets?"

"Across the mouth of the bay."

"They're to keep Mort's ocean life from harassing the citizens of Paradise and the guests at the tourist hotes," Sam said. "Or maybe they're to keep the human population from harassing the ocean life, since no human has ever been attacked or even inconvenienced by anything living in Mort's oceans. Admittedly, the ocean creatures are gruesome in appearance and possessed of unmentionably voracious social habits. Pakovich had the nets installed when he built the tourist hotes."

"Let us pray for our good sibling Pakovich before all the billion-billion deities of the billion-billion religions," the Reverend intoned good-naturedly.

"Why?" Sam the Artist demanded. "What's he done to need that many prayers?"

Again Caland sniffed deeply at the odor of cooking food. He said absently, "That was a good party last night."

Sam the Artist looked quickly at Tel.

"Or whenever it was," Caland persisted. "Wasn't it last night?"

Tel patted his arm. "We'll talk about it later."

"Whenever it was, it was a good party," Caland said. "If I knew anyone I could borrow from, we could have another."

He was feeling sufficiently famished to really believe that his last meal had happened days before. Unfortunately, the essential ingredient of the Valley's nightly beach ritual was talk, rather than eating, and on this night few of the fires had food.

Sam the Artist's face suddenly was transfixed with horrified surmise. He said to Tel, in a low voice, "Hasn't he eaten since he woke up?"

Tel shook her head.

"Why didn't you feed him?"

"I didn't have a chance."

Sam mournfully turned a pocket inside out. "I'd be proud to lend you money for a party if I knew where I could borrow some on short notice," he said to Caland. "That's the problem with Valley economics. When everyone subsists by owing everyone else the same five chits, sometimes you have to wait in line for your turn to use them."

Caland stood up abruptly. "I just remembered," he said, searching his pockets. "I held back five chits to lend, to put myself into the Valley economic system, and I also kept five for food."

He produced the two five-chit coupons and handed them to Sam the Artist. "Glad to be able to lend these to you," he said.

"Thanks, but to what purpose?"

"So you can lend them to me."

Sam clutched his bulging stomach and rocked with laughter. When he finally regained control of himself, he ceremoniously lent Caland his own ten chits. Cleo overheard the conversation and offered to go for food.

"No," Sam the Artist said firmly. "You tend to bring too many mals back with you. It's Cal's money, so he does the inviting. If you try floating wedgers at us, we'll exempt you."

The Reverend and the middle-aged mal went together and thereafter the night took on a glow of contentment and camaraderie such as Caland could not remember experiencing since his early days in the theater. It did not even seem remarkable to him that he could remember his early days in the theater.

Meat was sizzling, tubers and the strange clumps of stuffed dough were baking, and the fems were breaking chunks from the long loaves of bread. The jug had circulated enough times for Caland to feel drowsily elevated.

He took one more slop, handed the jug to Sam the Artist, and announced, "I once was an actor."

"I know," Tel said. "You told us the other night."

"But I just remembered!" Caland protested.

He slid forward off the rock and found a position against its hard surface that enabled him to lean back comfortably. His feet and legs soon became uncomfortably warm, but he subsided there, drowsily soaking up the heat and listening to the others talk.

"I have a theory about the origin of the universe," Sam the Artist said suddenly.

They had invited six really hungry people to share their feast, and as these and the others watched and smelled and handled the food they were about to eat, it was certain that none of them had the slightest interest in anyone's speculative sifting of the cosmos. It also was certain that none of them possessed sufficient energy to engage Sam in verbal combat and steer the conversation elsewhere. The food was passed around, and all of them settled back and munched contentedly while Sam the Artist expounded the universe.

"Once upon a time there was a great big ball of dough that God's mother was going to use for a raisin cake," he began oracularly. "Now, God, who was just a snotty kid at the time, was fond of raisins, and the ball of dough, which was uncounted light years in diameter, had quadrillions and quintillions of raisins in it—to the quintillionth power. When God's mother baked, she wanted it to last. God tried to figure out how to get at those raisins. Finally he started that big ball of dough spinning, and it began to thin out and spread out until it was a quintillion, quintillion times its original size, meaning that it was a kind of thin mist with those raisins scattered about everywhere and beginning to spin themselves, and God was ready to start grabbing them. He'd already glommed a handful or two when his ma came back and caught him at it. She was mad as hell, but being divine, she didn't just wade in and lambast him, as an ordinary mother would have. She thought it over for a moment, and then she changed all those raisins into suns. God burned his hands so badly that he forgot all about raisins for a few trillion eons, and by that time he was almost grown up."

Caland was drunkenly rocking back and forth while he chewed on chunks of meat that were surprisingly tender after their open fire sizzling. He suddenly became aware that Tel was pushing the jug at him. He'd already had more than enough, but he took another slop and handed it along. His mind was on Sam the Artist's fable. "Makes sense to me," he announced, wondering why his voice sounded so strange to him. "The Christians have Jesus, who is also God and the Son of God, which has never made sense to me. They show pictures of him with his hands wounded, which likewise has never made sense. But I see, now, that his hands weren't wounded at all. They were burned."

"About that, I wouldn't know," Sam the Artist said. "But I do know that God, with his burned hands, couldn't do much for a long, long time, so whenever he felt like it he amused himself with that whirling film of mist and all those new suns made of raisins. And that was the origin of the universe and its history right down to the present. God still does a little meddling from time to time, but it's all mental. He mostly keeps hands off, because he has scar tissue from those burns, and if he were to wade in and fuss the way the owner of a universe would like, he'd probably burn himself again."

The Reverend cleared his throat. "Deism is an extremely old doctrine. It denies that God preoccupies himself with the affairs of humans. Presumably he has other and better things to do. Mechanism, another very old doctrine, was an attempt to explain everything through mechanical laws, which can postulate a universe in which there is no God, or one in which God handed down the laws and then sat back—with his burned hands, according to Sam—to watch them work. On the other hand, Rationalism—"

"Are you serious?" Sam the Artist demanded.

"Certainly. These are very old philosophical doctrines. Rationalism—"

"I don't want to hear about Rationalism," Sam the Artist said. "The one religious doctrine that stands as the foundation for all other religions is this: you can't have any fun at all with religion without someone going and making a theology of it."

The jug circulated until it had been emptied, one slop at a time. Another took its place. The talk continued. Caland, his hunger satiated, felt his eyelids drooping. Suddenly he was jerked into drowsy consciousness, and he became aware that the fire had burned down and Tel was helping him to his feet.

"Bed!" she said.

"Be merciful!" Sam the Artist pleaded. "Cal is in no condition for bed."

"I know it's too much to expect politeness from you," Tel told him sternly, "but as a matter of principle, you ought to try to avoid stupidity."

"You shouldn't go about inflicting principles on people at this time of night," Sam grinned. "Let's all of us see Cal to bed."

A laughingly, contentedly surfeited crowd escorted Caland and Tel to the rear door of Caland's dwelling. Sam the Artist, his voice a bit unsteady from his self-appointed task of draining any jug that they encountered on their trek down the line of beach fires, solemnly recited Anloy's famous good-night soliloquy from *Tales of a Comet*. Caland, by dint of intense mental effort, managed a drunken response with Holantifz's "Salute to the Dawn," from the *Equivocal Equinox*. He and Tel slipped into the house to the accompaniment of much applause and a few inebriated cheers.

As Tel helped Caland along the hallway, it suddenly occurred to him that this highly attractive woman actually was taking him to bed. "Wait!" he protested desperately. "I had an accident. My head was smashed. I was killed. And ever since then—"

"Never mind," she said. "We'll talk about it in the morning. Right now you're going to bed."

She left him at the house's one sanctum. When he emerged, she was waiting for him. She had a candle burning on the table in the outer room. She gently but firmly stripped his clothing from him and helped him into the sleeping bag.

He spoke from the depths of his drunken confusion. "What am I doing here?"

"A lot of us would like to know that," she said. "Someone's coming to see you tomorrow. Maybe he can figure it out."

"Someone I know?"

"That's one of the things he wants to find out."

It was more than a puzzle; it was a conundrum, and Caland did not feel equal to it. He relaxed and fell asleep almost immediately.

Sometime during the night he awoke. The room was totally dark, and Tel lay beside him, her warm body pressed against his, her arm firmly about him. He struggled for a moment, and, when the arm did not relax, he began to talk about his accident.

"Don't be silly," she said, holding him tighter. "If your mind slips into the wrong gear, you may try to walk off. I'm going to make damned certain that you're still here in the morning. Then we'll meet your friend and think up all the questions we can and see whether any of them have answers."

Caland lay awake for a long time pondering the anomaly of this attractive fem, a total stranger, suddenly sharing his bed. Fems had been sexually attracted to him all of his life, but that fact suddenly became meaningless when his accident and brain surgery left him totally impotent. Since then, he had shunned fems. He shrank from the explanations he would have to furnish when faced with an overt sexual contact.

He had shunned everyone since his accident. With his ravaged memory and his periods of blackout, any kind of human contact must inevitably involve him in explanations.

And now there was Tel. He could not understand why she was protecting him, any more than he could comprehend how he had come to this strange place; but he felt comfortably secure for the first time since that remote moment when he awoke in a hospital with his mind askew and began to wonder who and where and why he was and whether it mattered to anyone— least of all himself.

CHAPTER SEVEN

Caland was following three mals along a wide pedestrian mall. The mall was dotted with excessively ornate fountains, each different, each with its own convoluted display of water-spouting sculpture and gadgetry, but Caland had no time for studying fountains. His attention was fixed on the three mals. Two of them were far ahead of him and were nearing the end of the mall. The third, a shrouded black figure, hovered far behind like a specter looking for someone to haunt.

Suddenly the first two figures vanished in a searing explosion. The black shape raced away with Caland in pursuit.

Caland stirred himself and opened his eyes.

He lurched to a sitting position and stared about him dazedly. He was experiencing no agony—none at all. His mind was clear, and even retained some memory. The room, the water bed, the sleeping bag that still held the impression of Tel's body—all were familiar.

He remained motionless, savoring these fragile connections with a recent past and puzzling over the strange sounds and odors that assailed him. There were stairs somewhere nearby, and feet clumped up and down. Voices sounded faintly in the room above. The odors were indefinable and wholly beyond his comprehension.

Tel's voice called, "Awake, finally?"

He abandoned his attempt to decipher some kind of meaning from the patternless cracks and holes in the room's ceiling. She stood in the doorway smiling at him.

"Your break is waiting for you," she said.

She vanished. He swung his feet to the floor and sorted out the pile of clothing that lay beside the bed, marveling that his hands and legs were steady and that his head did not ache. He dressed himself and took a long, steady step to the doorway and paused to marvel at that, too.

Tel had his break on the table: a thick gruel prepared from a blend of dehydrated cereals, and a drink made from the fried and powdered fruit of a native planet.

"It's the traditional Valley break," she explained cheerfully. "Yuck and glop. The glop is the gruel. What you have here might be called basic glop, because I didn't try to fancy it up. Some cooks consider glop a challenge, and they add herbs and spices, or various kinds of sweets, or fruits in season, or even meat and vegetables. Most of us can't afford such trimmings, and few of us would want to break with such a heavy meal anyway. So we keep it basic. Yuck is the standard Valley drink, and no one has figured out how to make it taste any better than just barely tolerable. But it's always with us, and you might as well get used to it."

Caland seated himself unenthusiastically and set about sampling the yuck and the glop. The gruel was neither solid enough to chew nor liquefied enough to drink. He mouthed it distastefully while his tongue searched in vain for a flavor, any flavor. Finally he swallowed it and took a sip of the yuck.

He winced. The drink was an unappetizing-looking gray liquid, steaming hot, pungently strong, and bitter enough to bring tears.

"This is the traditional Valley break?" He asked incredulously when he had stopped coughing.

"It's cheap, filling, and nourishing," Tel said. "It keeps one going until the next meal—whenever the next meal may be."

"I believe you," Caland said fervently. "Probably it makes some people swear off eating altogether."

"Eat!" Tel said sternly. "You're a Val, now. Resign yourself to a daily break of yuck and glop."

Caland managed to consume a modest serving of glop, and by the time he finished the mug of yuck, which the glop made necessary, the drink seemed halfway palatable. Tel sat watching him soberly, but he had the impression that she was trying not to laugh. She wore the same dark, knitted dress she'd been wearing as long as he'd known her, but now her long hair was plaited into loops on either side of her head. It changed her appearance startlingly.

"What are you staring at?" She demanded.

"You. I like your hair that way. I like your eyes. I never realized that they were so black."

"You never looked at them before," she said matter-of-factly. "How's the memory this morning?"

"I won't know until I've tried to remember something."

She seemed interested. "Is it that uncertain? Sometimes you remember more than other times, but you don't know which it will be until you try?"

He nodded.

"And it started with your accident?"

He nodded again. "I died, you see, and ever since then—"

"If you died, how does it happen that you're alive now? What makes you think that you died?"

"I did. I know I did."

"If you can't remember, how can you remember that?"

Caland frowned stubbornly. He knew that there was something to remember about his death, something he had remembered before, but the substance of it hovered tantalizingly beyond his reach.

Tel refilled his mug and offered more glop. When he refused, she put it aside without comment. He sat staring into the mug, searching for his reflection, or for a wisp of memory, in the liquid's dull, dirty surface.

Finally Tel got to her feet. "Are you ready? It's time to go."

"Go where?"

"To meet this friend of yours. And other people." She smiled sympathetically. "This may be a bit of an ordeal for you. If it weren't important, we wouldn't bother you. Ready?" Caland was suddenly aware of a sloshing outside the door. Tel opened it on a flood of water. A youth in a long robe was wielding a mop in the hallway beyond. He looked up and grinned at them.

"Don't wash us away, Zooie," Tel said sternly.

She introduced Caland, and Zooie carefully dried one hand on his robe and touched hands with him.

"Houses are as dirty as people let them be," Zooie said cheerfully. "It's a natural law. We try to keep this one clean. We take turns with the mopping. I'll let you know when you're due." Except for the flopping robe, he might have been an elder image of the youth Moppy, whom Caland had met on the beach. He had tucked up the bottom of his much patched garment to keep it out of the water, and he was barefooted.

"It's been a long time since I mopped anything," Caland said.

"It don't take practice," Zooie told him confidently. "Just patience." He splashed more water from a leaky bucket and wielded the mop again.

Tel took a firm grip on Caland's arm, as though she were afraid that he might become enamored of the mop and insist on a lesson, and guided him away.

They walked a route similar to that of the previous evening: east on the meandering path that bisected Bay Unview Boulevard, and then a turn into one of the overgrown paths that took them southward toward the Prom. It was Caland's first look at the Valley by full daylight, and what he could glimpse of the buildings through the rampant growth of trees and shrubs perplexed him. They sprawled tentatively in all directions and presented aspects of imminent collapse.

"They started out as large vacation homes," Tel explained. "They've had one addition after another inflicted on them, each shoddier than the decaying original. While they bulged externally, they shrank internally. The rooms have been subdivided over and over."

"They're storehouses for people," Tel went on. "Some rooms have private access from the outside. Some are without windows and can be reached only through other rooms. Often they're shared by as many people as can be crammed into them. You're unusual in having an apartment all to yourself."

If she wondered how he had managed that, she said nothing. Neither did Caland, though he, too, wondered how he had managed it.

They crossed Junk Vista Avenue and plunged again into the tangle of an overgrown path. Along the way, she talked to him about some of the people he was going to meet. Eventually they emerged in an open space behind three large brick buildings, and Tel halted and waited for him to catch up.

"On the left is the Dolls' House," she said, pointing to a large three-story building. "The curtains are worth studying. Each of the girls tries to be flamboyantly original and at the same time reflect her own personality. Directly ahead is the Fig Stump, one of the Valley's two high-class restaurants." It was a two-story building with an outside stairway in the rear. "And on the right," she said, indicating a sprawling, one-story building, "is the Road to Hell, the Valley's one respectable gambling establishment."

Caland said wonderingly, "The part of the Prom you showed me last night looked so run-down!" These buildings were old, but they had been meticulously maintained.

"With a few exceptions, the entire Valley is run-down," Tel said. "These are three of the exceptions. Yda's, and the other restaurant, the Burned Wafer, are two more. They're on the opposite side of the Prom. The exceptions tell you where the big money is—Houses of Fame, the restaurants, and the gambling hall."

They mounted the outside stairway at the rear of the central building and entered a large but cozy room, exquisitely furnished. There were several comfortable chairs, carpets, electric lights, shelves of data chips, a viewing screen, and an enormous table with sturdy wood chairs drawn up around it.

"This is the only place in the Valley where one can hold a meeting both comfortably and privately," Tel said.

The interior door opened. A mal younger than Caland grinned at them, said, "Morning, Tel," and placed a tray on the table: mugs, dishes, servers, a steaming carafe. He wore a robe and slippers, and through the door he'd left open, a baby could be heard crying.

Tel introduced him: Alz Hernl, who, with his father Hran, ran the Fig Stump.

He smiled shyly at Caland. "Call if you need anything," he told Tel and slipped quietly out.

Caland glanced at the contents of the tray and blanched. Yuck and glop.

"Try it," Tel suggested. "The Fig Stump's glop ought to be different. Maybe even a gourmet dish."

Caland grimly shook his head.

Sam the Artist poked his bristly face through the outside door. "Food!" he exclaimed. He slouched over to the table. He was wearing the same paint-stained clothing, and he looked as slovenly as Caland remembered him—and just as exuberantly cheerful. The Reverend came next, lank, clean-shaven, still looking neatly dressed in his rough black work garments.

The Reverend asked Caland how he felt; his quietly sympathetic manner instantly conveyed a genuine concern. Then he told them, with contagious delight, about a blind child, a neighbor of his, whom he had only that morning taught to spell a word with block letters.

Calta Drawning arrived next—large, voluptuous, with alluring streaks of pink and blue in her blonde hair. The startled Caland had the impression of a fem bursting into the room and out of her dress. The sheer gown that strained—unsuccessfully—to cover her magnificent proportions would have been illegal in public places on any world he could remember. Tel had sketched Calta's career for Caland: street whore on Aravia at the age of twelve, she had risen to the top of her profession through natural talent and brilliant business ability. Now she was either the proprietor or the manager of the Dolls' House, business hierarchies in the Valley being difficult to delineate.

Calta greeted Caland heartily and scrutinized him with a matter-of-factness that he never before experienced from a strange fem. "Better wipe his face, dearie," she told Tel, while she caressed his several day's growth of beard with the back of her hand. "You don't want him looking as shaggy as Sam. Why don't you feed him? He's undernourished."

"He can't be!" Tel protested. "He stuffed himself on the beach last night, and he had a break before we left this morning."

"It takes more than a meal or two, dearie," Calta said. "He has the look of a mal who's neglected his stomach for years. He needs to be seduced into eating."

"But not in public, Calta," Sam the Artist cautioned.

Calta clucked her tongue reprovingly and went to the inner door. She whistled; Alz responded promptly. She whispered something to him, and he returned a short time later with a platter piled with iced and stuffed break sweets.

"Better not," Tel cautioned Caland. "They're irresistible, and they're addictive, and they're expensive. One shouldn't acquire habits one can't afford."

Caland felt tempted, but the yuck he'd drank made him desist. He feared that a sudden ingestion of sweets would cause stomach convulsions. Calta scrutinized him again and whistled for Alz a second time. Soon Caland was contentedly sipping a delicious blend of fruit juices.

Sam the Artist poured himself another mug of yuck and reached for a sweet, simperingly informing Calta that a break in her glowing presence was one of the universe's highest aesthetic pleasures, exceeded only by the delight he would experience if he'd also passed the night in her company.

"I'm sorry I can't return the compliment, dearie," she drawled. "How you maintain that belly while living on nothing in the Valley is a mystery second only to the one involving our friend Cal. How do you do it?"

"I can't imagine," Sam mumbled, grinning, his mouth stuffed with pastry, and he reached for another sweet.

The Reverend began a discussion of the doctrinal philosophies of various religions on the subject of gastronomical indulgence.

"I don't know anything about that," Calta said, "but I'll tell you this much: A restaurant like the Fig Stump next door to a whore house ruins a lot more girls than the customers do. Some of them have the expense of a complete new wardrobe twice a year, and they have to retire at thirty—not because they're prematurely aged, but because they're too fat."

"Is Bar coming?" Tel asked.

"Probably not," Calta said. "This isn't his kind of problem."

Yda, the proprietor of the rival House of Fame, entered quietly, and Caland's immediate impression was that anyone trying to imagine Calta Drawning's opposite would have invented her. She was red-haired, tiny, delicately formed. The statuesque Calta was good-natured, friendly, jovially vulgar. Calta did everything in a grand style that matched her physique. Yda had the air of inflicting high society on a gathering just by entering the room. It was said that she could swear like a spacer without using a word of profanity.

The two were the friendliest of business rivals whenever there was a common cause that they could get their claws into. When there wasn't one, they used their claws on each other. On this morning the nature of the occasion hadn't yet been fully defined, and they circled each other like a pair of amorous spine pups who knew that even their most affectionate moments would involve thorny entanglements.

"Where's the windbag?" Yda demanded.

"She just walked in," Calta said icily. She turned to Caland. "Your friend is an old friend of ours, but Yda doesn't care for him. Once ten years ago he asked her if her figure was artificial, and she's never forgiven him."

Tel and Sam the Artist both chuckled. Artificial modification of any part of the petite Yda's figure would have constituted gross distortion.

"That's a question he's never had to ask you," Yda snapped. "No one could acquire that much bloat naturally."

The sound of footsteps arriving at the interior door averted impending bloodshed. The door opened.

Caland stared. A blinding mass of bright orange stood there, topped with a silver halo. A multiple-chinned face produced a row of smiles. The total effect was so unlikely that without firm links to reality—Sam the Artist's earthly presence, Tel, the faint aroma of yuck from the carafe—Caland would have suspected another nightmare.

Then he realized that he was the only one watching the newcomer. Everyone else in the room was staring at him and waiting for some kind of reaction. This was more bewildering than the incongruously fat figure in orange that confronted him.

"Don't you know me?" the pleated chins demanded.

"No," Caland said irritably. "Have we met before?"

"Several times."

"You must have been wearing a different suit," Caland said dryly. "That one I would remember."

The chins seemed to multiply as the grin broadened. "No you wouldn't. That's our problem. One of them. It's frustrating to have a client who forgets from one meeting to the next that I'm working for him, but we'll have to cope. I'm Regelz Arlu. I'm a searcher. You asked for one, and your Uncle Orp sent me. Do you remember your Uncle Orp?"

Caland rubbed his forehead fretfully. "Uncle—"

"Never mind. It'll come back to you. Our immediate problem isn't the past so much as the present."

He scowled at the heavy wood chairs and finally helped himself to a comfortable lounger in the corner, activating the reclining support and leaning back comfortably.

"Would you show these people your medical identification card?"

Caland scowled. He hated to be asked to remember. "What kind of card—"

Arlu sat up abruptly, his eyes wide with astonishment. "You mean you no longer have it? It wasn't in your pocket when you regained consciousness?"

Caland shook his head.

Arlu sank back into his chair. "That's interesting. That's extremely interesting. Do you have our passport? No?" He meditated for a moment; the others waited silently.

"Very well," he said finally. "You told me a great deal about yourself at our past meetings—enough to keep years of search going. I came here today because I wanted to check the state of your memory for myself, and also because I want you to know that all of these people are your friends. You can rely on them absolutely." He turned to Tel. "Show him the Valley, so he can find his way about. Make certain that he meets all of the right people, and see that they know about him. The only other thing we can do right now is find out whether he recognizes anyone. All of you will have to be on the alert for that. If it happens, I want to know immediately."

"Would you tell me what this is all about?" Caland asked.

The chins had stopped smiling. "I wish I knew," Arlu said seriously.

"It's an extremely complicated mystery, and thus far I have no answers at all. Just questions. Tell me this. When did you first hear of the world of Mort?"

"When I regained consciousness here, I didn't know where I was," Caland said slowly. "It always happens that way, but this time I wasn't in a gen hote, and I didn't know how to find out. I walked along the beach hoping I'd think of a way to ask someone. Then I met Sam and Tel and some others, and in the conversation someone—I think it was Sam—mentioned Mort. I'd never heard of it before. I still don't know precisely where it is."

"Mmmm." Arlu sat tapping his index fingers together. "Don't strain yourself, but I would like to have you think very carefully for a moment. Are you certain you'd never heard of Mort?"

Caland closed his eyes. "I'm certain," he said finally. "Unless you count nightmares. I may have heard it mentioned in a dream."

"Mmmm." The fingers were taping again. "When you dream, what do you dream about?

"Terrible dreams."

He turned to Tel. "Find out what you can about his dreams. Make note of any flashes of memory he has. Anything at all may turn out to be important, and it'll probably come when least expected. But don't pressure him. Just take what comes naturally. His mind is a very unusual case."

"I feel like a pawn in someone's cosmic game of chess," Caland said disgustedly.

Arlu cocked his head at him. "Not a pawn. You definitely aren't a pawn. And it's not a game that you have any personal interest in, though someone certainly has been moving you about the board. I don't think you have the status of king or queen, but you're much more important than a pawn."

"Reggie Arlu hasn't changed one iota in twenty years," Calta said caustically. "He has the kind of mind that makes a mystery out of a trip to the sanctum."

"That's what he gets paid for, darling," Yda said. "Manufacturing mysteries." She turned to Arlu. "Can't you unbend just once and let us know what's going on?"

Arlu got to his feet. "I don't know what's going on," he said irritably. "There's a considerable conspiracy, and it seems to involve most of the galaxy, but I have no idea who is doing the conspiring, or for what purpose. I don't know where the thing is going to focus, or when. I don't know what Mort has to do with it. This world may be headed for an indescribable catastrophe, or its role may be comparable to that of an electrobus stop where a few people get on or off. I simply don't know, and I don't understand what Cal has to do with it or it to him." He sighed. "A lot of very peculiar things are happening. I'm working as fast as I can, but a trail that zigzags across the galaxy requires a lot of searching."

He started for the door.

Tel called after him, "I meant to tell you. Cal has a morbid feeling that he was killed in an accident. He seems certain about it."

Arlu turned and nodded. "That's one of our many problems. It's true."

He left, closing the door quietly.

"Well!" Yda exclaimed. "If it wasn't already a mystery, he's certainly lived up to his profession by making it one." She said to Caland, "If you ever think you're in trouble, come to Calta or me. We'll take care of it. Bring him around, Tel, so everyone can meet him."

The meeting dissolved quickly. Caland and Tel descended the outside staircase, and Tel said, "You ought to see the Prom by daylight. That's as good a place as any to start meeting people. We'll go down to the entrance and make the grand tour."

A rickety, two-meter-high board fence marked the eastern boundary of the Valley, and just inside it was a strip of cleared land some ten meters wide that had been a street when the Valley was young. More recently, effort had been made to convert it into a park. There was a playground for young children, a cramped game field, scraggly flower beds, and a few sagging benches. Young mothers were watching their children at play, and a few elderly people were enjoying the sun. The costumes, for all ages, ranged from the threadbare to the improbable.

"Why is it called the Valley?" Caland asked. "Everything I've seen has been flat."

"It started as a real estate promotion," Tel said. "A speculator named Dombrily, who must have been a super salesman, conned a lot of people into investing in a cultural center for Mort. He was going to make Mort a paradise of the arts, with theater, concerts, opera, and such stuff. He actually managed to buy a couple of square kilometers of Mort outright. When he decamped with the treasury, it turned out that the Valley property was registered in the name of his son, and the son has managed to hold onto it. It once was a high-class vacation community, and wealthy people from nearby worlds leased land here and built homes. Eventually the rich got bored with the place and moved elsewhere, and the Valley has been in decline ever since. In the eyes of the present owner of Mort, it's an appalling slum and a haven for social misfits, and its chief business is in catering to the vices and whims of Mort's tourists, who unfortunately have a lot of vices and whims to be catered to."

"If he feels that way about it, why does he tolerate the place?" Caland asked.

"He can't help himself. Once he threatened to cut off services, and the Valley countered by threatening to dump its sewage into the bay—which would have blighted the town of Paradise and the tourist hotes. He hadn't any answer to that, so he tried to isolate the Valley and limit access to it. He even restricted the delivery of food. The case got into the interworld courts, which imposed restraints on him. Now he's in a fix. He has to treat the Valley like an independent country. Any action he takes against it is likely to snap back on him in the form of damage assessments. So he sits up there on his mountain and sulks about it. The fact that the Valley is the one thing that makes his tourist hotes profitable probably adds to his resentment. The only retaliation he's been able to get away with is his fertilizer factory. He built that as close to the Valley as possible."

"Does it bother people?"

"Not at all. It converts Mort's sea creatures to fertilizer, and they have their own special chemistry. When the wind does blow this way, the smell is spicy and rather attractive. It's even rumored to have an aphrodisiacal quality. Some of the tourists who visit the Valley are really trying to smell the fertilizer factory."

A paved highway approached the Valley from the east and looped southward just outside the Valley entrance. The Prom extended its makeshift pavement across the cleared land to the two posts that were the only surviving evidence of a gate that long since had weathered away. Just beyond it, in a deeply rutted turning loop, the strangest vehicle that Caland had ever seen was discharging a few Vals and a number of tourists. The Vals looked bored; the tourists, flamboyantly dressed creatures of both sexes, seemed keen for a glimpse of the Valley's reputed licentiousness and a sniff of the fertilizer factory.

The 'bus was a converted electrotruck with a long body resembling an improvised shack. Its sides were veneered with salvage from packing cases, and its high, peaked roof was thatched with a brittle native grass. The seats were wood benches. On the side was a neatly stenciled sign, "Valley Transportation Company." Beneath it someone had hand drawn the number 4.

Caland took a deep breath. "Who concocted that?"

"It's Bar's work," Tel said. "Baris Bronlan. The man you were watching the sunset with. Years ago he bought some worn-out trucks from Pak Enterprises. Worthless trucks, the Pak people thought. But Bar is a mechanical genius, and he cannibalized the worst specimens for parts and converted the best to electro-busses and 'cabs. Now he has a monopoly of public transportation on Mort."

"And Pakovich lets him? Why doesn't Pak Enterprises set up its own transportation company?"

"If Pakovich did that, he'd have to transport people to and from the Valley, and that would constitute public admission that the Valley exists."

"He sounds like a rather petty individual."

"He'd call it being a mal of principle."

They joined the 'bus's passengers and strolled along the Valley Prominade and into the Valley of Mort, the Valley of Death.

Two parallel rows of rickety, decayed, dilapidated, and sometimes makeshift buildings faced each other across the narrow street. Substantial frame structures of two or even three stories had once stood there, but the decades of neglect had disintegrated them into teetering shacks. Some had collapsed completely, and rough shelters had been erected on their vacated sites.

There were no pedestrian walkways. The street was cluttered with litter and awash with unlikely odors and even less likely specimens of humanity. It had been paved with anything available that was flat on one side and seemed durable: chunks of concrete, salvaged brick, stone, iron castings. The people who thronged it were as variegated as contrary eddies of galactic transportation could make them. Overdressed multimillionaire tourists brushed against impoverished teenagers—and said, "Excuse me."

Retired crafters of both sexes, young and old, rubbed elbows with ne'er-do-wells who had never held a job. The tourists wore the arrogantly condescending air of social and material success; the Valley residents encompassed a kaleidoscope of types, but their hallmark was failure. They were unsuccessful artists, unsuccessful writers, unsuccessful businessers, unsuccessful artisans, all destined to fail one more time on the Valley's Prom. Many of them were simply unsuccessful at life. Even the vibrant young girls who occasionally prostituted themselves were already failures despite the tourists' lavish fees. They would never graduate to the affluent security of Yda's or the Dolls' House, which scorned local talent and imported carefully selected girls from neighboring worlds.

What fascinated Caland the most about the Valley was that none of this seemed to matter.

The business establishments were as diversified as their potential customers. There were clutter shops that bought and sold second- or third- or tenth-hand merchandise of all kinds. There were expensive "in" shops that offered the latest in styles and knickknacks to wealthy tourists. There were improbable "it" shops that tried to meet the demand of Valley residents for cheap merchandise of every kind—"if anyone has it, we do," or, "You need it, we have it." There were numerous pawn shops. There were garment stores at every level of price and quality and style from cheap remnants and secons and 'fects to a glittering shop in a well-maintained and recently painted lavender building that offered only the most exotic and expensive imports. The eateries ranged from narrow stand-up counters to small, cramped, sit-down establishments with more tables than their dimensions could accommodate. They featured names like Jinj's Poison and Hef's Place, the latter boasting of the Valley's most putrid putrebun. The confectionary stores were interspersed with handicraft shops and shabby art galleries. There was one meat market, in a white, sparkling clean building, that served as the Valley's outlet for the Pak Enterprises meat packing plant, dairy, and cheese factory. There were several food stores with fresh native produce as well as packages of dehydrates. Tents erected between buildings offered gambling and games of chance.

The tang of sea air acted as a universal solvent for the Valley's blended odors: of cooking food, of exotic sweets and spices, of strange-looking fruits, of confections manufactured on the premises, of handmade soaps and candles and perfumes, and probably of the fertilizer factory as well. Its location was pinned to the horizon by an occasionally glimpsed tall chimney, and its musky effluent should have been tainting the southwest breeze.

Caland was startled to see a familiar name on a large, well-maintained red and white striped building: Olgi's Cloy Shop. He knew he'd seen it before, but he could not remember where.

"Confectionaries and ices," Tel said. "They're famous. You can buy them as luxury items on a number of worlds, and they're the only Valley product that Pakovich permits to be sold in Paradise and at the space port—by popular demand. Even the tourist hotes display the candies and serve the ices in their salons. All of it is made right here, from secret recipes—or so Olgi says. Olgi's and Bar's Valley Transportation Company are our biggest employers."

Across the Prom was the Shell House. Only the lower meter of corrugated surface remained of the enormous replica of a shell that had been constructed atop the low building at some time in its dingy past, but shells were still the firm's principal business. The oddity was that no life on Mort had ever evolved a shell. The firm imported attractive, oddly-shaped specimens from other worlds, and offered them to tourists at prices so exorbitant that the purchasers assumed that they were acquiring rare local specimens. The shop also sold replicas of Mort's more hideous sea creatures. These were casts that had been painted luridly by local artists. Studying them, Caland decided that the artists were spoofing the tourists while at the same time indulging their surrealistic fantasies.

Valley Handicrafts occupied a makeshift shelter between two teetering buildings and offered all manner of things made by Valley residents—from knit garments to bric-a-brac. A shabby store with a sale on cheap shoes advertised, "One size— 'Doesn't fit'." Next door was a shop specializing in individually designed and hand-made fem apparel of a quality and price that certainly put the garments beyond the reach of most residents of Mort.

"Who buys them?" Caland asked.

Tel shrugged. "A few tourists. A few wives of Pakovich's executives who of course pretend that they imported them from Aravia. All of the girls at Yda's and the Dolls' House."

A large, two-story frame building in a fair state of repair was set back a short distance from the street, and the small plaza under its balcony was filled with overflow tables from the lounge and eatery located on the first level. Its sign read, "Valley Hote," and its lounge boasted, "We Never Close." It was headquarters for the girls who competed with the more celebrated Houses of Fame, and several of them were drinking with tourists.

There was a tiny, one-story building that at one time had been fronted by a large glass display window. The glass had long since gone the way of most of Valley glass; no shards or splinters remained. A coarsely woven mat could be unrolled for protection against the weather. Inside the window sat an enormously old, enormously fat fem. She looked as though she had been there longer than the Valley, which had grown up around her and then decayed.

She was a seer. She read ears. There were other Valley seers who read palms or used external devices, but this one read ears.

And she was blind. When she had a customer, she traced each convolution with infinitely sensitive fingers while whispering her tale of past frustrations and future good fortune.

At a ceramics shop, fascinated tourists were gathered around the pottery wheels. Several accepted the invitation to "put a hand in" and then were permitted to buy the pieces they'd helped to create. They could watch them glazed and fired in a crystal-fronted kiln.

Midway along the Prom were the substantial brick edifices of the Houses of Fame, the restaurants, and the gambling hall. Yda's and the Burned Wafer were on the south side; the Dolls' House, the Fig Stump, and the Road to Hell faced them. The Houses of Fame seemed to be challenging each other, though the buildings looked exactly alike except for the fact that the Dolls' House had balconies with iron railings at the upper windows facing the Prom.

They moved along steadily, despite the jostling of the crowd, and the panorama continued to unfold, but Caland's curiosity had been satiated. He was able to pass the Road to Hell without a glance at the glittering gambling machines. Instead, he dropped back a pace so he could watch Tel.

She swung along easily, head turning from side to side, hands gesturing as she pointed things out to Caland. He had been wondering what this innocently bawdy, tawdry place could possibly have to do with a galactic conspiracy, or—more to the point—what it could have to do with him. Now it was occurring to him that Tel might be more of a misfit than he was. At least he qualified as a social outcast; she obviously didn't. She seemed as poised and capable as any millionaire businesser. Her robustly handsome body made the slender Valley fems look debilitated; her simple attractive garb accentuated the silliness of the fem tourists. He enjoyed watching her, but he had to keep turning his head so she wouldn't catch him at it.

A long gap between buildings opened up a short distance beyond the Road to Hell. A board fence, inset several meters, paralleled the Prom, and the street's improvised paving had been extended back to the fence to form a long, narrow plaza sprinkled with benches where passersby could rest their feet, or consume their putrebun and yuck, or talk with friends. The sign on a wide gate read, "Valley Transportation Company."

Caland absently raised his eyes. Then he came to an astonished halt and exclaimed, "What's that?"

To the rear of the Valley Transportation Company, a gleaming silhouette rose above the trees.

Two mal tourists had stopped to look at it. One of them said to Caland, "Some nut is pretending to build a spaceship in his back yard."

"It's a very realistic pretense," Caland observed. "It almost looks as though he's succeeded.

"Don't be silly," the tourist said. "These old buildings are as likely to fly as that thing. The guy also claims he's going to design his own engine and run it on baking soda, whatever that is. He's completely sprung."

The tourists moved on. Caland asked Tel, "Who's building it?"

"Bar," she said. "Baris Bronlan. Didn't I tell you he's a genius?"

"He certainly does beautiful work," Caland said.

The graceful, tapering hull was breathtakingly lovely—an object for aesthetic contemplation. The smooth, polished surface looked flawless. Caland wondered if it were Bar's method of wasting time, as Tel sculpted moist sand and others painted or wrote.

Then a muffled black figure brushed by Caland, stepping out of a dimly remembered nightmare, and Caland discarded the spaceship as one brushes aside a cobweb. He caught no more than an oblique glimpse of the face—sharply protruding nose, watery eyes, skin shrunken to bones—before the figure passed from nightmare to reality and tottered away to lose itself in the eddying Prom traffic.

Tel was watching him with interest. "Did you recognize someone?"

"I don't know," Caland muttered.

"Who was it?"

"The old mal in black."

"You've seen him before?"

"Perhaps in a nightmare."

"Mal Arlu said dreams may be extremely important. Tell me about it."

They found an unoccupied bench by the Valley Transportation Company fence, and Caland tersely described his vague recollection of trailing a black figure along a pedestrian mall with fountains, and then, when it ran off following the explosion, of futilely chasing after it. "But none of it makes sense," he added. "What was I doing there? Why would I be paying attention at all to him?"

"The Avenue of Fountains is famous," Tel said thoughtfully. "It's in Rynaif City, which is the capital of the world of Rynaif. That was a very potent nightmare, my friend, and we can quickly find out whether it had any basis in reality. If an explosion really occurred on the Avenue of Fountains, there had to be a public investigation."

"Who is he?"

"The character in black? His name is Dombrily. We call him Dom. He's the son of the promoter who bought the Valley. He owns this place. Every square centimeter of it."

CHAPTER EIGHT

Midway between the Valley entrance and the ocean, the Prom's dilapidated business establishments gave way to dilapidated dwellings. At that precise point the makeshift pavement terminated abruptly, as though no one cared to extend it a millimeter past the last stop for truck deliveries. Just beyond, accessible only by a pathway through high, encroaching weeds, was a shack with a weathered sign: "RENTAL CE."

"There's someone I want you to meet," Tel said.

She guided him along the path and over the creaking threshold.

At first glance the room inside appeared to be empty. On one wall, pinned to an enormous bulletin board, were slips of paper that carried handwritten descriptions of "Space for Rent." Most of the locations were precisely that—a corner of a room, an outside shelter. Under the heading, "To Lease," was posted a description of a single apartment, with a required deposit and a term rent payable in advance.

A tall counter divided the room. Behind it were a desk and a long table, both piled with records. It seemed unreal to Caland than anything at all could be vibrant with dust in such a humid climate, but the old records gave him that impression.

Filling the wall behind the desk was an enormous street plan of the Valley. It showed every habitable niche, down to the hovels that were mere ground shelters covered with sod. These latter filled the few vacant lots in the Valley, and the map identified them as "cemeteries." Attached to the map were hundreds or thousands of slips of paper indicating who lived where. The place was more than a rental office; it also was a census bureau.

The mal at the desk was aged, yellowed, and dusty, like his records. The only other person in the room, a shabbily dressed young mal with a vast mop of blond hair, leaned his patched elbows on the counter while he waited, tapping one foot impatiently, for the old mal's attention. When Caland and Tel entered, he glanced in their direction once blankly, as though to warn them that the line formed behind him.

Finally the old mal looked up at him blearily.

"I'd like to see the apartment that's for lease," the young mal said.

"If you're that particular, you won't like it." The old mal flipped a page in his ledger and resumed drawing figures with an arthritic claw of a hand.

He looked up again. "You got the chits?"

"If I want the place," the young mal said, "I've got the chits."

The old man approached the counter with a bent shuffle. Everything about him drooped: his scraggly hair, his eyelids, his dirty clothing. He produced a receipt book from under the counter and filled a page with cramped writing. He turned toward the young mal. "Apartments are so rare there aren't any. That one on the board has been empty for two terms. It may be empty for two more, or someone may walk in and grab it while you're thinking about it. When it's gone, there aren't any more. You pay your deposit and a term's rent now, and I'll have someone take you to see it. If you don't like it, bring your receipt back, and I'll refund your money. See—I wrote that here. Any time up to midday tomorrow, you can have your money back."

"All right," the young mal said. From his pocket he took a bundle of chits and counted out the amount. The old mal's drooping eyelids opened wide as he watched, and he purred his thanks as he swept the pile of money into one hand. His head bobbed a mocking little bow. It was a ceremonious gesture—acknowledgement that anyone with chits for a deposit and a term rent in advance was a person of distinction in that office.

"Your name?" he asked.

The young mal hesitated.

"Call yourself anything you like," the old mal chuckled. "It won't be stranger or sillier than some of the names I already got. But I have to have a name."

"Nalce," the young mal said, and spelled it. "Is that enough?"

"Plenty. But now that I have it, don't you forget what it was."

He handed over the receipt.

"Does it have a set lock, or is there any key?" Nalce asked.

The old mal grinned at him. "There's maybe a few locks in the Valley that still work. Places handling a lot of money, like the Road to Hell, and the whore houses, and the restaurants, and Olgi's, and a few others, they maybe have safe boxes or even safe rooms. No one else has anything worth stealing, and thieves couldn't last long here anyway. Vals live so close together that someone would notice, and things would be made very unpleasant for the thief. He'd have to leave Mort or sign up for one of Sdissler's stinking labor details. You don't need a lock on your apartment. If it's privacy you want, just put a big 'M' on your door. Means you're meditating. Nobody'll even knock. Your neighbors may think you've got a fem there, but in the Valley, that's a legitimate form of meditation." He cackled. "People here will borrow you to death, but they won't steal from you. They won't dare."

He raised a section of the counter and went to the door. He peered at the flow of pedestrians for a moment, and then he bellowed, "Hairy!"

A moment later a gangly youth strode into the room. He wore shorts and nothing else. The visible portions of his body were totally devoid of hair. His head had been wiped cleanly. His eyebrows were plucked. He had no hair on his chest or under his arms.

His face lit up when he saw Caland. "I've been looking for you. Was the apartment all right?"

Caland sputtered uncertainly. "Ah—yes. It was—all right."

"You have some change coming. The bed didn't cost as much

as I expected." He handed Caland a wad of chits.

He waved away Caland's bewildered thanks and bounded to the counter, where he listened to the old mal's instructions. He was off before the flow of words had quite finished, snatching the description of the apartment from the rental board and motioning to Nalce to follow him.

Not until they had left did the old mal turn toward Tel and Caland.

"'O, Tel. 'O, Mal Caland. Enjoying the Valley?"

Caland managed to reply that he was enjoying it very much.

"Making friends, too, eh?" The old mal cackled and winked at Tel. "Thought you would. Good-looking fellow like you couldn't wander around the Valley long without getting snatched. Giving up your room, Tel?"

"Nope. Just dropped by to pay my rent. Thought I'd better do it while I have it."

The old mal's grin broadened. "Always the best time. No doubt whatever about that. The time to pay rent is when you got it." He accepted the crumpled chits that Tel pushed at him and wrote her a receipt.

"See you next time, Gus," Tel said.

"Drop in any time. Renters with money are always welcome."

They moved slowly back along the Prom, and Tel began introducing Caland to passersby and even taking him into shops to meet their proprietors: a coarse, bosomy fem who ran a place called Head Styles—it offered coiffures in a spectrum of colors and shapes, and, if a person preferred to strip his or her head to its bare scalp and start over, it also bought human hair; a nondescript little mal with a horde of children who sold cheap clothing; the grossly fat owner of an up eatery whose stomach was evidence enough of where his profits went. At the Dolls' House and at Yda's, she took Caland inside through rear entrances and introduced him to as many enforcers and girls as were available. All of the enforcers were modeled on Chan Worntling: formidably tall and hefty. The girls, with their elegant figures, their artistically made-up faces and their resplendently styled daysuits and frocks, seemed as artificial as both establishments' tinseled furnishings.

A short distance further on, they met Sam the Artist. "What's the add?" he asked.

"A lot of routine zeros and one 'Wow!'" Tel said.

"Interesting."

"I think so. You take over, and I'll pass the word." She turned to Caland. "Stay with Sam until I get back."

She hurried away.

Sam the Artist scrutinized Caland. "What's Tel been doing to you? You look as though you'd just finished your fifth fence lap."

"What's a fence lap?"

"Distance along the fence from the ocean to the bay. It's said to be a very invigorating run, but I couldn't name a single Valley resident who's actually done it."

"I'd rather not try. I'm not even used to walking."

"Whatever else can be said about the Valley, it certainly does change people's habits. For the better, I think. You live here, you do a lot of walking."

Caland nodded. "I can't remember when I walked so much. I also can't remember the last time I slept in a room from which I couldn't communicate with any of a billion or more people at the touch of a button. Of course I never used the button, because I never knew anyone on any of those worlds, but it was there. Before I came here, I couldn't have imagined a place where transportation and telation were so primitive."

"Civilization," Sam the Artist said, "is nothing more than the accumulation of the superfluous. If you start peeling away inessentials, you eventually end up with a place something like this. The problem is to filter out the corruptive influences while retaining basic values. It's so hard to get people to agree on what constitutes a value. I can remember a time when—"

His voice flowed on, describing some droll recollection, but Caland had stopped listening because his mind refused to accept words. They were walking along slowly, in a flowing, shifting crowd of Vals and tourists, and suddenly he noticed, moving in the opposite direction, the most beautiful girl he had ever seen. She was small—not as tiny as Yda, but noticeably below average height. Her features were perfect, her brown hair only moderately long but unadorned and flowing, her figure beautifully molded by a simple conservative gown. It was as though she knew instinctively that the outlandish styles and colors and affectations of either Vals or tourists would have distracted from her beauty. Wearing subdued colors, banal clothing, a simple coiffure, and no artificialities of any kind, she looked ultra-stylish.

Caland stared until the small form was hidden in the crowd, not realizing that he had come to a stop and was disrupting the Prom's traffic. When finally he stirred himself, Sam the Artist's ample stomach was shaking with soundless laughter.

They walked on, and when Sam could control his voice, he said, "Well, now you've seen her. You don't have to tell me what you think."

"Who is she?"

"That's Melana. The Valley's mystery girl. If you fall in love with her, don't expect condolences from anyone. All of the fems resent her, and all of your rivals, meaning most of the mals in the Valley, will resent you. Because she's not available. *Why* she's not available is maybe a considerable riddle. She's taking art lessons and researching a book, and if she's ever displayed the slightest interest in mals, no one has noticed it. She seems to be a thoroughly nice kid, and it isn't her fault she's so damned beautiful. She plays it down as much as she can, but mals chase her anyway."

The Prom had become so crowded that it was difficult for the two of them to walk abreast. Sam drew him into Nello's, a little down eatery. They edged their way across the cramped room and claimed an empty table in the corner.

"Yuck?" Sam the Artist asked.

"I couldn't."

Sam nodded sympathetically. "Takes time to get used to it."

He left Caland alone at the table and returned a moment later with a mug of yuck for himself and one of a fruit-flavored drink for Caland.

"It's a synthetic," he said. "Not many people like it. Nello bought some on Aravia hoping it'd catch on here, but he's almost the only person in the Valley who pretends to like it. What do you think?"

Caland took a sip. "It's worse than the yuck, but in a different way."

"As some great philosopher said, it's really the difference that makes the difference." Sam raised his mug in a mock salute.

Caland risked another sip before he pushed the mug aside. "If Melana is capable of even a halfway pretense at acting, she can earn a fortune on the stage."

Sam the Artist choked on a gulp of yuck. He wiped his eyes and said, "You too? Quite a few people think they know how Melana could earn a fortune if she'd let them peddle her body one way or another. Rich tourists are always trying to buy her. That foul excrement Sdissler is blatant about it. It wouldn't surprise me if Calta and Yda have put in bids. Several Valley mals have offered marriage to her, which of course is another form of purchase."

"Who's Sdissler?" Caland asked.

"You'll know him when you meet him by the pool of slime he'll be wading in. He makes money by exploiting people. He has a genius for it. He can figure out a way to exploit anyone. Most Valley residents run out of money sooner or later, and when they do, Sdissler is waiting. Usually he exercises a kind of smirking patience, but with Melana he's trying to rush things. Like all the others who are trying to talk her into earning a fortune with her body, he doesn't mention that it would be his fortune, not hers. I don't think anyone has offered her the stage, yet. What angle did you have in mind?"

It was Caland's turn to grin. "Sam, I was an actor for—for years. I can't remember much, but I'm sure about that. For years. Beautiful fems are no novelty in the acting profession. Too many of them use beauty as a substitute for talent and a screen for gross defects of character. You quickly learn that beauty is as superficial as clothing. It's all right to enjoy the esthetic experience, but you'd better find out what the package contains before you start entering bids. Where'd Melana come from?"

"No one knows. No one knows anything at all about her past. She seems to have plenty of money. She has one of the few nice apartments in the Valley, and she pays her rent regularly. People like Sdissler are waiting for the money to run out, but that may be wistful thinking. For all anyone knows, she may come from a family rich enough to buy out Pakovich."

"Is she really studying art and writing a book?"

"Going through the motions, at least. She attends classes that Pakovich's pet artists give at the Art Bazaar."

"Art—Bazaar?" Caland echoed blankly.

"Some years ago, Pakovich got piqued because Valley artists were doing very well selling paintings of Mort to the tourists. It's his world, and he figured no one should be allowed to paint it without his consent. So he set up his own art colony in competition. There's a bazaar that displays and sells paintings by the colony's artists. The artists also give lessons to anyone who can afford them. They say Melana maybe has some talent, but it'll never come to anything because she doesn't work seriously enough. The book thing is much more mysterious. She spends most of her evenings at the Paradise Library doing research."

"What kind of book?"

"No one knows. She's friendly enough, in a distant way, but she isn't really close to anyone in the Valley, and she never talks about herself. That's what Sdissler bases his hopes on. We have people who beg brazenly, whether they need it or not, and we have people who'll accept help if it's offered, and all the stages in between. We also have proud ones who refuse to impose on anyone. They think it would be bad manners to tell their troubles to others or to ask for help and degrading to accept it. Melana would be one of the proud ones. If she ever runs out of money, she'll be in deep trouble, and Sdissler will be waiting. In the meantime, she keeps outside the entangled Valley cliques, fields every proposition with a shy, innocent smile that's rimmed with an iron negative, talks about art and literature with anyone who's willing, avoids all Valley activities, and is adroitly evasive whenever anyone asks a personal question. That's Melana. Enjoy your esthetic experience and let it go at that. She's not for sale at any price, and she doesn't give samples. At first people thought she was a dratted Pakovich spy. He sends us one now and then—usually good-looking mals who try to be pals with everyone and date all the ugly fems while pumping them for information. They label themselves in about an hour. Melana just didn't qualify. She wasn't curious enough."

Tel joined them carrying her own mug of yuck. She gave Caland's mug a puzzled glance, sniffed at it, and wrinkled her nose.

She'd changed her dress. Now she wore a similar garment that was dark blue. She'd been hurrying, and her face was flushed. Caland studied her appreciatively and contrasted the appeal of her ripened beauty with Melana's.

She frowned at him. "What's the matter? What have you two been chewing?"

"We saw Melana in the Prom," Sam the Artist said. "I've been telling Cal all about her.

"That didn't take long."

"I've been trying to convince him that there's no hope for him. We don't need any more Gary Dwands doing a 'Have you seen Melana?' routine." Sam turned to Caland. "Gary is a bright boy, good-looking, talented, doing well, has a good future—he's the Valley Transportation Company manager—and all he's offering Melana is love and marriage and devotion. Almost any Valley girl without attachment would jump at that, but not Melana. Makes you wonder. I think she's too smart and has too much common sense to fall for Sdissler's line. I wonder what it is that makes her snub Gary."

"That's easy," Tel said. "She's in love with someone else."

"Who?" Sam demanded.

"It doesn't have to be someone in the Valley. It can be a person of either sex—close at hand or worlds away—alive, dead, or missing. You mals are much too myopic." She sipped her yuck and then turned to Caland. "You need a change of clothing. As long as you have money—"

"Money?" Caland said in surprise.

"The money Hairy gave you. It doesn't matter if it isn't enough. You haven't been here long enough to burn your credit. We'll have time to do some shopping before the klaxon."

Sam the Artist drained his mug. "Good touch. I'll see you at Bar's."

He scrambled to his feet, raised a hand in farewell, and inched his way out through the clutter of tables, chairs, and people.

"You've been checking my memory, haven't you?" Caland said to Tel. "Don't you think I'd be of more help if you let me know what's going on?"

"There are contrary opinions about that," she said frankly. "One holds that we should try to jar your memory into functioning by confronting you with things you should remember. The other maintains that we'll never find out whether you really remember anything if we tell it to you first. There's also the possibility that the stress of trying to remember might turn your memory off permanently. Even the doctors Arlu has consulted can't agree."

"Look," Caland said. "If being confronted with things I can't remember bothered me, I'd have blown my mind years ago. It happens every time I regain consciousness. I never know where I am or how I got there, but I know I couldn't travel from one world to another without knowing my destination, and making a space reservation, and taking passage, and landing and going through customs, and all the rest. I've never been able to remember any of that. I must have heard of Mort before I came here. I must have arrived at the Mort space terminal and found transportation from there to the Valley, and walked down the Prom as far as the rental office, and paid a deposit and a term's rent on an apartment. Someone had to show me the apartment.

Was it Hairy?"

Tel nodded. "He did more than that. You hired him to clean the place thoroughly, and disinfect and vermin-proof it, and buy the furnishings, and lay in a stock of food and other necessities. He returned the money that was left over."

"What about the other people?"

"You bought the clothes you're wearing from Marto, who runs that clothing shop. You told him someone was following you and you wanted to give him the slip, so Marto took you out the back way, and Birtal, who runs Head Styles, cut your hair and restyled it to change your appearance."

"I wonder who was following me and whether it worked," Caland mused.

"Arlu had sent word that you might show up here. He asked a few of us to be on the lookout for you and give you help if you needed any. He gave us a good description of you, but of course we weren't aware that you'd disguised yourself. No one recognized you until you started talking about acting at the beach fire. When your mind suddenly stripped gears, we decided to look after you until you got your mental furnishings organized. Then you frightened us by lapsing into a coma and staying there for two days. Let's get your clothing and talk about it later."

She threaded her way through the crowded eatery with surprising agility, and Caland followed her resignedly. It no longer frustrated him that there were no answers. However much he strained and prodded his memory, there never were any answers, and he expected none. Sometimes he turned up an unexpected cache of information, but that was not the same thing. *Who am I where am I why am I?*

* * * * * * *

Baris Bronlan lived in a shack on the lot directly behind that occupied by the Valley Transportation Company. Its setting was mountainous, but the mountains were prodigious piles of junk comprising every imaginable kind of metallic or plastic discard.

These arose starkly amidst a luxurious growth of weeds and shrubs, and encroaching trees partially obscured their lower slopes.

"This is where Junk Vista got its name," Tel said. "Bar's predecessor was one of the galaxy's great scavengers. Every scrap of discard from the city of Paradise and Pak Enterprises passed through his fingers, and he threw very little away. When he died, Bar took the place over, and he's been sifting through piles ever since, separating the contents into other piles. What's really incredible about Bar's spaceship is that he built all of it out of discards."

The ship loomed incongruously above the junk mountains. Bronlan was still at work on it when his din guests, summoned by the midday honk of the fertilizer factory's strident klaxon, began to converge on him. He sat in the ship's hatch, legs dangling, a small, shabby figure whose outlines were distorted by the odd hat and the stiffly held left arm. He was making calculations on a piece of slate that hung from a loop of cord. He called an occasional total down to a mournful-faced, bald-headed mal who sat on the ground below and punched Bronlan's figures into a poc comp.

Finally Bronlan pushed the slate aside and descended a rickety wood ladder. "Got a total?" he asked.

The mal with the poc comp punched one more button and announced the result. Bronlan nodded and turned for a last, satisfying scrutiny of his spaceship's silhouette.

"I think baking soda will work," he said.

"What's baking soda?" the mal with the poc comp asked.

Bronlan smiled mysteriously. "A chemical."

He turned to greet Tel and Caland, warmly but shyly touching hands with them.

"Time to eat," he announced. His inward-turning smile was beatific.

Others were arriving: Sam the Artist, the Reverend, and a man of spectacularly ragged appearance even for the Valley. The latter cheerfully introduced himself as Louie Laggie, a scav.

"A scavenger," Tel explained to Caland. "In the Valley we all scavenge a bit, by necessity, but Louie makes a career of it."

"But there's no money in it," Louie Laggie said cheerfully. "It's my way of wasting time."

Din with Baris Bronlan was an established ritual. Near the spaceship was a large fire pit with a grill fashioned of metal discards. Sam the Artist and the mal with the poc comp, whose name was Kren Krent, began building a charcoal fire there. Others strolled off to the shack that was Bronlan's home. They brought back a platter of meat chunks, a bag of tubers that Bronlan had grown himself in a flourishing garden between the junk piles, several long loaves of Valley bread, and a jug. Tel arranged the chunks of meat on the grill. Others coated the tubers with mud and rolled them into the coals. Then each guest went to the nearest junk pile and took whatever came to hand that might serve to sit on. These makeshift seats were arranged about the grill wherever a patch of shade looked inviting. Guests continued to arrive. By the time the jug began to circulate, there were a dozen people present, all of whom belonged to one or the other of two groups: those whose company Bronlan enjoyed, and those who needed a meal.

While the guests talked and took slops from the jug, Bronlan turned the chunks of meat with a long-handled fork, keeping them close to the heat where they would char to his favorite degree of crunchiness. Bronlan himself spoke very little, but he had a remarkable talent for listening. His eyes flitted from face to face, seeking out the listeners, rather than the talkers. He was more interested in the reactions than in what was being said.

Finally he began to transfer the meat to chunks of bread and pass them around.

Sam the Artist accepted his serving with thanks, bit off a mouthful, and chewed solemnly. He diluted it with a slop of cider before he swallowed. "Ackie says he saw Pakovich yesterday," he announced. "He says the Great Watcher was standing there in the Merc Mart's food canteen looking about him and scowling just the way you'd expect a god to smile when he'd dropped in to inspect things and wasn't pleased with what he'd found. Pakovich takes life too damned seriously. I don't mind him insisting on everyone toeing the mark, but I resent it when he insists on drawing that mark himself."

"If you owned a world, you'd take life seriously," Tel said.

"I would not!" Sam replied heatedly. "Taking life seriously means wasting time and effort and money on fertilizer factories and power plants. I'd concentrate on enjoying myself."

"But that's what Pakovich is doing," the Reverend protested. "To you, enjoying life is a party with plenty of food and a jug that never empties. To Pakovich, it's fertilizer factories. You'd resent his trying to impose his vision of happiness on you, and he'd be just as resentful of your trying to impose your parties and jugs on him. Didn't someone say, 'If a mal asks for directions, give them to him, but don't tell him when to beat his donkey'?"

"What does the donkey have to do with it?" Louie Laggie demanded.

"Pakovich is an ass," Sam the Artist said. "The Reverend has a brilliant talent for unconscious innuendo."

"What's a donkey?" Kren Krent asked.

"Pakovich is," Sam the Artist said.

"No. Really." Krent waved his hands in protest. "I've heard donkeys mentioned, but I've never seen one. What's so disreputable about donkeys?"

"Anything that can be likened to a Pakovich is disreputable," Sam the Artist said.

"Pakovich tries to snoop around without anyone recognizing him," Louie Laggie said. "Like God does in some religions."

"Which is blasphemy," the Reverend said with a smile. "God does not snoop. He *knows*."

Louis Laggie ignored him. He was still grappling with the notion of an anonymous Pakovich. "I'll bet he gets mistook for a tourist. He'd be silly-dressed the way tourists are."

"But I've never seen Pakovich, either," Kren Krent said. "How can I compare a Pakovich I've never seen to a donkey

I've never seen?"

"The only way to see Pakovich is to hang out in Paradise and pray for a visitation," Sam the Artist said. "He's never set foot in the Valley, and he never will."

Bronlan began raking the tubers from the coals. He tested each one with his fork, tossed back the ones that hadn't cooked enough, and distributed the others. Finally he helped himself to bread and meat and sat back to listen. An outsider would have taken the small, dark figure in dirty clothing for a lackey called in to help with the cooking.

Caland considered him incomparably more interesting than anything that could be said about Pakovich. Tel had related something of Bronlan's history.

He had worked for Pak Enterprises when he was young, and Pak Enterprises had considered him a technician of enormous promise. Then he got his arm crushed in a freak accident. Pakovich, in one of his rare fits of generosity, awarded him a full pension for life. Bronlan continued to live in his company house in Paradise, and he devoted all of his time to his scavenging instincts and his passion for building things. The accumulated discards quickly made his yard a massive excrescence on an otherwise tidy neighborhood, and to Pakovich's finicky mind, an outrage. Some of the mechanical marvels that Bronlan contrived with his discards were duly reported to Pakovich, who began to wonder if the medical reports on Bronlan's disability had been greatly exaggerated. Pakovich sent spies to watch Bronlan at work and fote him, and Bronlan, in deep resentment, moved to the Valley and took his junk and his mechanical marvels, and his pension with him. There he founded the Valley Transportation Company with discards that Pak Enterprises unwisely sold to him. Now Bronlan was a wealthy mal—or he would be if he weren't feeding so many of the Valley's indigents. Pakovich still had to pay him his pension, and Bronlan magnified the insult by giving that away, too. If the owner of Mort ever died of apoplexy, it would be while thinking of Baris Bronlan.

The Vals regarded him with awe and circulated legendary tales of his philanthropy and his inventive genius, but Bronlan was indifferent to praise as he was to wealth. Although he cared nothing about being called a genius, he immensely enjoyed being one because of the things it enabled him to do. He could build anything, repair anything, and design anything. Every industrialist tourist who encountered him went away dazzled by the scope of his talents. Bronlan could have put together interworld combines and designed machines that would have changed the course of civilization and gained for him money and power beyond the dreams of even the galaxy's Pakoviches, but he preferred to live in the Valley, pointed out to tourists as a crackpot who was trying to build a spaceship in his back yard and run it on baking soda. He remained where he was because the Valley gave him the freedom to be precisely what he wanted to be.

It was said that he passed the long hours of darkness sitting alone in his shack and consuming enormous amounts of alcohol. It also was said that he was a total abstainer. Fems sometimes were attracted by his grave courtesy and especially by his sad eyes, and, missing a subtle twinkle there, they concluded that he was mourning tragic love. Mals always noticed the twinkle; they thought he was mourning a tragic marriage. All agreed on one thing: no one was close to him. In the teeming Valley, he actually achieved something like solitude.

According to Tel, Bronlan considered life a monstrous joke on everyone, tolerable only when one had the freedom to do what one chose with it. He fervently believed that humans should be encouraged to follow their natural bents to whatever extent their talent made possible or their stupidity made necessary. People sought him out to pour their troubles into his sensitive hands, and he listened to them with great solemnity, his face eloquent with sympathy; only those who knew him well suspected that he was inwardly contorted with glee.

Caland watched him with fascination. He had never met anyone like him.

Louie Laggie, still brooding about Pakovich, followed a slop of cider with a mouthful of food and spoke around it while wiping a greasy hand on his ragged trousers. "Maybe owning a world really is a worrisome business. Maybe that's why Pakovich takes life so seriously. Pity we can't invite him here once a sennite so he could forget his troubles and have a good time."

"But he wouldn't come," the Reverend said. "If he did, he wouldn't enjoy the Valley any more than you would enjoy one of his posh parties. Anyway, it isn't the world he owns that makes him take life too seriously. It's the two kilometers he doesn't own."

"That," Sam the Artist said, "is a profound observation. Tell a mal that a fem belongs to him completely except for her navel, which he is forbidden to touch, and he'll spend hours contemplating the navel. The Valley is the navel of Mort, and Pakovich doesn't own it. I don't know whether he spends hours contemplating it, but I'm betting that it's on his mind a lot."

"I resent this display of masculine stupidity," Tel said. "You can't compare Pakovich's behavior with things like that. He's unique. Tell a fem a mal belongs to her except for his left ear, and she may or may not spend hours contemplating the ear, but she certainly won't spit in it. Pakovich doesn't contemplate anything."

"Right," Louie Laggie said. "And whether he sees the Valley as an ear or a navel, he keeps trying to think it's an asshole."

Bronlan was distributing the remainder of the tubers. While he chipped the mud from them, his eyes continued to flit from face to face, but he no longer seemed to be wearing a suppressed smile. When the laughter had subsided, he spoke.

"We got to do something about Pakovich."

"Sure," Sam the Artist said with a grin. "What?"

"A little while ago I was watching the Valley kids playing around that old house they use for a school. They should be attending school in Paradise, where there are plenty of teachers, and readers they can take home, and a whole library full of data chips, and a playground, and all the rest of it. And they should have a midday meal right at school, the way Paradise kids do. Hot food. Most of our kids probably don't get anything at all to eat midday."

"Agreed," the Reverend said quietly. "But all of that takes money, and the Valley hasn't got any."

"Pakovich is the problem," Bronlan said. "Him a multi-billionaire, and he can sit up there in his mansion and look down on hungry people without having his own appetite affected. There are too many hungry people in the Valley. We've got to do something about Pakovich."

"Maybe his son will do better," Louie Laggie said.

"What sort of a person is the son?" Caland asked.

"Quiet," Sam the Artist said. "Probably he grew up that way because his father never let him get a word in. He might have been a decent sort if he'd been brought up in a different family."

"No one really knows what sort of a person he is," the Reverend said. "His father has never let him do anything on his own. Right now he's the Paradise super. Runs the city. Does a good job, they say, very conscientious, and works long hours. But he couldn't change anything if he wanted to. His father won't let him."

"When he inherits from his father, maybe he'll do things differently," Louie Laggie said.

Sam the Artist shook his head. "Not a chance. I can see what's coming. Pakovich is ambitious, and being rich isn't enough for him. What he'd really like to be is king, with divine right and all that stuff. Of course he could crown himself any time he wanted to—there's no one on Mort who could keep him from calling himself anything he likes—but that wouldn't satisfy him. He doesn't just want to be called king, he wants to *be* king, and for that he has a fatal handicap. He's a slob and the son of a space pirate, and high society on Aravia would laugh itself silly. So he doesn't dare call himself king.

"But his son, now—the poor guy is also an Alexander Pakovich, but he's been to the university on Aravia, which gave him an indifferent education but managed to teach him manners, and he knows all about navigating high society. Now his father has pulled strings and probably entered an outrageously high bid and got the son engaged to an impoverished Aravian princess. The old mal can't call himself king, but his son is going to be a legitimate prince, even if only by marriage, and his grandchildren will be born royal. That's what Pakovich is after. Slob he may be, but his descendants are going to be bona fide royalty with a genuine royal pedigree, and eventually one of them will be able to call himself king without being laughed at. Pakovich will go down in history as the founder of a dynasty. With all of that on his mind, you can understand why he isn't much concerned about whether school kids in the Valley have a hot lunch." Sam raised the jug. "Here's to King Pakovich, I hope not."

The last servings of meat and bread were offered and gratefully received. The tubers were eaten. The jug made its final circuits. Most of the guests would have enjoyed spending the afternoon there, talking and passing the jug, but their host had serious work to do. Even before they reluctantly began to drift away, Bronlan was on his way up the ladder, and the faithful Kren Krent had positioned himself below with the poc comp.

Caland and Tel carried the platter, fork, and jug back to Bronlan's shack. Like most Valley buildings, the low structure was overgrown with vegetation, and its rotting boards and sagging condition made it seem in danger of imminent collapse. It contained a large living room, where Bronlan slept on a worn-out couch; a small kitchen with an unpartitioned sanctum in the corner. Tel said that Bronlan's friends called it a sanctum with an unpartitioned kitchen. Despite the house's run-down condition, the fact that it had electricity and the living space it provided for one person made it seem palatial by Valley standards.

Tel rinsed out the jug and gave the platter and fork a thorough washing. "And now," she announced, "we're going to clean this place. Bar ought to have it done regularly, but he spends so little time here that he doesn't realize how dirty it gets. Let's fetch some tools."

Caland, returning a short time later armed with mop, broom, and bucket, bewilderedly asked himself again what he was doing in Mort's Valley, this most unlikely of unlikely places for a mal whose mind was possessed by someone else.

He was beginning to feel stronger. Also, as time passed since his last seizure, he felt more alert mentally.

But the eyes were still watching him, and he was more intent than ever on finding out who was tampering with his mind. He no longer asked himself who he was and why he was and where he was; now his mind shaped a single unfathomable question: Why am I *here*?

CHAPTER NINE

They enjoyed a long, festive evening at a beach fire, where the artist Sigley Varno—whom everyone called Sig—threw a lavish party with the proceeds of a picture sale, a rare event for a Valley artist. While a parade of Vals crowded about the fire and ate contentedly, Sig sat with the Reverend, Sam the Artist, Caland, and Tel, and described his early career with affectionate nostalgia. He'd been a brilliant young artist who somehow took every wrong turn and ended up a Valley hack.

"I wonder," he mused, "if success would have made me any happier than I am now. If I could live my youth over again—"

"If you could teleport yourself through space," Sam the Artist chortled. "If you could levitate Pakovich's garbage dump. If you could go back in time. If Pakovich ever gave a free sample of anything. These are the most implausible thoughts human language is capable of expressing. If cider jugs were electro-busses, our traffic would be far more congested than it is."

"But those thoughts aren't implausible," the Reverend said. "Bar Pakovich and the cider jugs, it's been known for centuries that the others are theoretically possible."

Sam the Artist's face was indignant with incredulity. "You're fogging us!"

"Not at all. It's true."

"Teleportation is theoretically possible?"

"A scientist named Odan developed the mathematical formulas more than a century ago."

"Levitation?"

"Certainly. I don't recall the name of that scientist, but I've studied the formulas."

"Time travel?"

"Certainly. More than three hundred years ago, a brilliant mathematical physicist named Zareent proved that it was theoretically possible. About the same time, another scientist named Fremanz proved mathematically that systematic telepathy was possible."

"How do you happen to know these things?" Sam the Artist demanded.

"I once was a student of mathematical physics."

"I still think you're fogging us. How'd you come to make the move from mathematical physics to religion?"

Louie Laggie was eavesdropping while he chewed contentedly on a chunk of meat-stuffed bread. "Is there a difference?" he asked with a puckish grin.

"There are profound similarities," the Reverend said. "Both religion and science seek ultimate answers, but only religion has the courage to consider ultimate questions. So I abandoned mathematical physics. So, incidentally, did Zareent. He was laughed out of his profession, which was a great pity. He defended himself by publishing his theory—a mathematical masterpiece."

"Did he switch to religion, too?" Sam the Artist asked.

"In an oblique way he did, and it may have cost him his life. He offered to remove the word 'theoretical' from his proof of time travel. He proposed to restore to life one of the martyred saints of the Later Pristine Church. He had the notion that he could use the saint's bones for temporal leverage. Unfortunately, the saint's followers caught him in the act of looting the sacred tomb."

"Didn't the saint's followers want him restored?" Caland asked.

"Not by Zareent. Zareent wanted to confront them with the old reprobate in the flesh—alive and screeting, as he put it—so as to shatter their religious delusions and enable them to lead healthier, happier, and more productive lives. It was a splendid example of the misapplication of mathematical principles to things not capable of measurement. The saint's followers responded with a misapplication of their religious principles. They demonstrated their love and charity by attempting to assassinate Zareent. Some historians think they succeeded. In any case, he was never heard from again. It's a great pity. He was indeed a brilliant scientist. I once spent several terms in attempting to understand his time travel theory. There were eleven steps, I remember, and I never mastered the fourth. The moral—"

"Please!" Sam the Artist said. "No morals tonight. I haven't the stomach for them." He rubbed his bulging abdomen. "Why didn't the Later Pristine Church retaliate by recruiting—who was it who proved that telepathy was possible?"

"Systematic telepathy," the Reverend corrected. "We've long known that telepathy happens, but it's a random thing, totally uncontrolled. Fremanz proved mathematically that systematic telepathy was possible."

"Why didn't the saint's followers call him in to communicate with the saint and settle the dispute that way?"

"Communication with the dead is not telepathy," the Reverend said patiently. "As far as I know, no one has tried to apply mathematical physics to necromancy. If you're interested—"

"No, thank you," Sam the Artist said. "I'd be afraid to let myself be interested in a thing like that. Someone might come along and tell me more than I wanted to know. And demonstrate it mathematically. I'm sorry I brought up the subject. Now my dreams will be disturbed by Zareent robbing the saint's tomb, and Fremanz communicating with the dead, and Odan levitating Pakovich's dump, and—"

"Odan worked with teleportation."

"Teleporting the dump, then."

"That would be levitation."

"Not in my dreams, it wouldn't," Sam the Artist said.

Life in Mort's Valley already had fallen into a pattern,

and it amused Caland to see the Valley's vaunted freedom so constricted by custom and habit. They remained at the beach fire as long as the cider jugs circulated. They slept. The break that Tel served the next morning was identical to that of the day before, with yuck and glop. Then the bald-headed Hairy arrived with a message, but that, too, seemed part of the Valley routine. The ubiquitous Hairy constituted a one-mal Valley communications system.

Again, they mounted the outside stairs to the room above the Fig Stump. Regelz Arlu was waiting for them. On this day he was a mountain of pale lavender, and he'd already taken possession of the room's reclining chair. He greeted them with an unceremonious wave of the hand.

"Sit down. I haven't much time. *We* haven't much time. Have you recovered any memories about coming to Mort?"

Caland shook his head. "None."

"How about dreams?"

"Dreams don't usually happen with a label telling you what world they're supposed to be on," Caland said irritably.

"True enough. Now listen. As far as the world of Mort is concerned, you're an ordinary tourist. You arrived with a shipload of tourists, you had a prepaid reservation at the Paradise View Hostelry, you went there directly from the space port, and you stayed there for three nights. For all the hote staff knows, you're still staying there."

"It can't be a very observant staff," Caland said. "I've been here—how many days has it been?"

Tel counted on her fingers. "I think this is the fifth day since you moved here."

"Listen." Arlu was tapping his index fingers together. "It isn't unusual for guests to take their meals away from the hote. Some of them are so impressed with the Valley's restaurants that they come here every day. Or maybe they're impressed with other things and use the food as a pretext. It also isn't unusual for guests to be out all night or even for them to sleep in hote rooms officially registered to someone else." He paused. "You didn't check out when you left, and no one at your hote has any idea that you've been missing. So I want you to go back there."

Caland gazed at him in consternation. He had begun to feel restless among the Valley's whimsical inhabitants and impatient to get on with his search for the person controlling him—but he wanted to conduct that search from the Valley, not from a sterile tourist hote. He enjoyed listening to characters like Sam the Artist, and he enjoyed the total lack of cant and formality among Valley residents. He looked forward to the rambling talk around a beach fire or even to another leisurely mug of yuck at a down eatery. He could not remember the last time he'd had anything at all to look forward to, and now Arlu wanted to send him away.

His stark dismay produced a broad, multiple-chinned grin from Arlu. "It'll only be for a couple of days. Then you can come back to the Valley and relax."

"Is it really necessary?" Caland said.

The grins reshaped themselves into a scowl. "It's maybe a chance to learn something, but it has to be done right now. Today. If you go back immediately, you should be able to slip into the hote routine without causing comment. That's important. This ploy won't be effective unless your fellow guests don't realize that you've been away."

"Let's go, then," Caland said resignedly. He got to his feet.

"Sit down and listen," Arlu said. "You've got to know a few things. The hote staff considers you a rather retiring guest, though you did socialize a bit. You were seen on the veranda talking casually with your fellow guests, never more than one at a time, and you ate in the hote salon—but only when a private table was available. You walked in the hote gardens by yourself. Once you went for a walk in the direction of the Art Bazaar, but you didn't actually visit the bazaar—though my searcher is probably the only one who knows that. You visited the Valley twice, the first time in the company of another hote guest, a vintage fem."

"The devil he did!" Tel exclaimed.

"Your traveling case, personal effects, and clothing are still in your room," Arlu went on. "I brought a suit for you. I want you to put it on and return to your hote like any other weary guest who's been having a fling in the Valley. You may have a few embarrassing moments. For one thing, you have a different hair style. Guests who ordinarily would have a vague recollection of you now may not recognize you at all. Anyone who seems curious about it has been paying careful attention to you, but they aren't likely to say anything. If people do recognize you, you may have a sticky problem when they refer to incidents that you've forgotten, but don't worry about it. I want to know who they are and what they say. The only person you spent enough time with to establish complicated recollections was that vintage fem. Fem Wobbons is the name. Mean anything to you? No? I suggest that you avoid her."

"I shall," Caland said fervently.

"What if he blacks out and wanders off?" Tel asked.

"It'll be your job to see that he doesn't. You're coming along."

"Hold everything!" Tel waved both hands in protest. "If I go near one of Pakovich's palaces, they'll throw me out."

"You'll have to go down to one of those obnoxious tourists shops on the Prom and get yourself a suitably revolting casual wardrobe," Arlu said. "Also a traveling case to put it in."

"Who—or what—am I supposed to be?"

"You're a very proper millionaire's daughter who came to Mort to visit friends and liked it well enough to prolong your visit. You don't feel like imposing on your friends any longer, so you're moving to the View. I've made your reservation, and I have a complete identity set ready for you. You'll have the room next to Cal's. All you have to do is walk in and claim it."

"What if they check with Port Customs to make certain that this fake millionaire's daughter really arrived here?"

"Tsk. For a certified heiress who's already paid in advance? Why would they bother? Why would they care? What I want you to do is watch for reactions to Cal. And what I want Cal to do is look for familiar faces. I don't care whether he remembers someone from a dream, or a psychic revelation, or a hunch, or any other way. If a face looks even vaguely familiar, I want to know about it immediately."

"All right," Caland said. "I'll go, but I won't enjoy it." Arlu wagged a finger. "There's one thing both of you should be prepared for. Cal's name is Caland. That may not mean anything to the average citizen in this sector, but if anyone takes the trouble to run it through Credit Centrex, it'll light up the place. Cal's father is one of the wealthiest men in the galaxy, and Cal rides on his father's rating. There are a lot of small millionaires at the hote, and that's a type that tends to recognize the names of large billionaires. Don't be surprised if someone reacts to your name. Will you be able to handle it?"

"I'll act in my own distinctively modest manner," Caland said. "Is that really who I am?"

Arlu stared. "Have you forgotten that?"

"I remember it now. I'm not sure that I would have before you mentioned it."

"When I talked with you on Aravia, you told me all about it," Arlu said, dabbing at his forehead with a lavender-tinted tissue. "This is a complicated case."

"I wondered why you were doing all this searching in behalf of an impoverished nobody," Caland said. "At the moment, my true assets are whatever Tel is holding for me."

"Which is nothing, actually," Tel said. "We spent the whole bundle for clothing. We not only spent it, we ran you two chits into debt."

"I'll notify Credit Centrex to deduct it from his rating," Arlu said dryly. "Now you know the situation. Let's get moving."

He handed a wad of chits to Tel, and she hurried off to outfit herself. As soon as she'd gone, Arlu opened a package. "Your suit," he told Caland. "Put it on."

Caland fingered the soft material and whistled. "I was wearing stuff like this?"

"You bought it at my suggestion on Aravia so you wouldn't look scruffy among your fellow millionaires. Here are some chits—you'll be an unconvincing millionaire without money. Now get dressed. And wipe your face. Even in that suit, you can't walk into the Paradise View with a slovenly growth of whiskers without causing comment."

* * * * * * *

They boarded a Valley Transportation Company electrocab, which was actually a miniature 'bus with three wood benches in its squat, wide interior. Their initial destination was the space port, but first came a lovely drive along Paradise Bay. Caland, who had been living only a few meters from the water's edge, had never seen it by daylight.

It possessed a unique, breathtaking beauty. The waters were a swirling tumult of ever-changing colors, and the bright sails of the boats that dotted it added more vivid hues to the churning pastel shades of the water.

"Mort's scenic charms are almost equal to the extravagant claims of Pakovich's tourist bureau." Tel observed finally.

But Caland had already abandoned the bay to enjoy another revelation of beauty: Tel, in her ridiculous tourist outfit.

She'd selected a lounge suit in pale yellow, and not even the silliness of the flapping trousers could distract from the way the color deliciously offset the darkness of her deeply tanned body and the rich cascade of her black hair. Caland began asking her questions about various Valley people as an excuse to keep looking at her.

The highway followed the bay for seven kilometers. Then came the city of Paradise, a strange community of identical, circular, cement houses. The two tourist hotes loomed ahead on the left. Closer, facing the bay was the sprawling community park. They passed the Mercantile Mart, a long row of shops and stores, and beyond it they glimpsed the Government Mall, which bisected the city and contained service and governmental offices, the schools, and the medical center. Finally they were in open country again, and the distant bulge on the horizon was the upper contour of a parked spaceship.

At the terminal building, Arlu told the 'cab driver to wait for them. They moved slowly through the public rooms, which—since there were no recent or pending arrivals or departures—were almost deserted. Finally they entered a lounge, which bore a predictable title: The Gate to Paradise. Arlu placed an order, and the server brought their drinks.

The tall, chilled goblets were filled with a liquid that swirled with color like Paradise Bay. Caland took a sip and choked. The liquid was syrupy in texture and nauseatingly sweet.

"What is it?" he demanded.

"'Nectar of Paradise.' It's a Mort specialty—liquor blended with juices of native fruits. It's said to be Pakovich's favorite drink."

"I'm sorry to hear that," Caland said. "All the other bad things about Pakovich I've been able to excuse, but this—"

Arlu said impatiently, "Well?" The tour of the building had been directed at testing Caland's memory or jogging it, or both, and Arlu had ordered him not to talk until it was over.

"Nothing." Caland said.

"Not even in a dream?"

Caland shook his head.

"My hunch is that your dreams are really memories. From now on, be sure you describe all of them to Tel, in as much detail as you can remember."

"There's something I'd like to know," Caland said. "It must have been my second visit to the Valley when I tried to disguise myself because someone was following me. Who was it?"

"It wasn't my searcher," Arlu said. "I'll guarantee that you didn't see him, and he didn't notice anyone else. He lost you when that shop owner obligingly slipped you through his back door, and he lost you a second time when you sneaked away to the Valley apartment you'd rented—you went out the hote's service entrance and cut through Pakovich's formal gardens and the city park to the Merc Mart and took a 'bus. He traced you later."

"The Vals who remember Cal didn't notice anyone following him," Tel said. "But of course no one was paying any attention to him."

They lingered on for a time, in the casual manner of tourists, but they talked little. Arlu had wrapped himself in the puzzle of Caland's memory, and he was morosely contemplating his drink. Caland was still occupied with studying Tel, who found it amusing and retaliated by studying him. She had scorned the large floppy tourist hat that came with her lounge suit. Caland tried to coax her into putting it on—he would have enjoyed seeing her dark hair further offset by that splash of yellow—but she refused. He resolved to buy her a yellow headband at the earliest opportunity.

"All right," Arlu said finally. "This is what we'll do."

He told them.

He was staying at the neighboring Paradise Vista Inn, and they rode there together in the 'cab. Tel continued on to the Paradise View Hostelry with her traveling case; she was to register and wait for Caland in her room. He sat for a time on the Paradise Vista Inn's wide veranda, sipping another of the insufferable Paradise drinks and watching the shifting colors of the bay. Arlu occupied a comfortable reclining chair a short distance away and pretended not to know him.

Finally Arlu caught his eye and nodded. Caland got to his feet resignedly and strolled along the broad, beach-side walk that connected the two hotes. He did not look back, but he knew that Arlu would follow him at a distance and see him safely into the building.

He met no one who seemed to know him. He crossed the Paradise View Hostelry's veranda and walked uncertainly through the palatial reception hall. The desk super looked up at him unseeingly and returned his gaze to the papers he was sorting. Caland had one moment of confusion when he couldn't locate the L. Eventually he found it and ascended to his floor. A moment later he was safe in the grotesque luxury of a room that seemed more of a fantasy than the fantastic Valley. Tel joined him immediately.

"Any adventures?" she asked.

"None, except that I had trouble finding the L."

"Interesting. It's obvious that the setting didn't stir your memory. I don't think Mal Arlu realizes even now how complicated this problem really is. I'd feel sorry for him if he weren't so obviously enjoying himself."

They sat for a time on Caland's private balcony. The sea breeze that stroked them was invigorating; the beauty of Paradise Bay was enhanced by the lofty view. Below them was the gleaming white sand of the hotes' long private beach, blighted only by the scattering of overweight sunbathers. A sailboat pier marked off one boundary of the hotes' grounds. Boats were coming and going; a cluster of tourists stood on the pier waiting for a sail around the bay. The scene was worth painting, and several artists had set up easels on the beach and were doing so.

Delightful as the panorama was, Caland soon abandoned it to concentrate on dredging something from the murky depths of his memory. Everything had been so totally strange to him that he felt certain that Arlu's experiment would garner nothing at all.

"There's still time for a late din," Tel said. Her light tones sounded a relentless call to duty, and Caland gave up his fruitless introspection.

They entered the hote salon separately and were seated at different tables. The salon super, solemnly performing a Paradise View ritual, introduced the guests at the table to each other. His voice faltered when he reached Caland, and Caland politely supplied his own name. It provoked no noticeable response among his fellow diners. He still had not recognized anyone, and he had not met anyone who professed to know him. The few unattached fems at his table, whose ages were scattered between maturity and infinity, all showed noticeable interest in him, but they were at least as interested in the other unattached mals. One of them, plump and effusive, made motherly comments on Caland's pallid complexion and asked whether he had been ill.

Caland modestly confessed that he was convalescing from injuries received in an accident, whereupon she immediately became coy and informed him, "Fortunately, we guests have our own physician. He just arrived yesterday." She indicated the diner seated on Caland's right. "He's modest about his distinction, but he's really *Doctor* Gormaz."

Caland relaxed. The fem was already in full pursuit of the doctor, and she was making use of Caland in the sly manner of one attempting to sneak a new pawn into a game already underway. Caland would not have minded if he could have been left free to watch Tel, who was dazzling both the unattached and the obviously attached mals at her table on the far side of the room.

Unfortunately, Caland's position placed him in the center of the conversation. Doctor Gormaz was a plump, pompous-looking elderly man with a strange excess of facial hair that did not quite succeed in forming a beard. He leaned across Caland and addressed the woman with mock sternness. "Really, Mathild. It isn't polite to poke fun at a person who's been ill." He said apologetically to Caland, "Mathild will have her little joke. It's true that I'm a doctor, but it's a D.S.A.—a Doctor of Applied Science. My specialty is sociology. I hope no one ever confronts me with a medical emergency.

His bulging lenses gave his eyes a hypnotic quality that seemed quite out of place in his good-natured face. The two tufts of hair atop his gleaming head stood like wilting horns. He wore his untidy, wrinkled clothing in a grand manner that implied that he was above sartorial considerations. Oddly enough, his voice boomed hoarsely.

"Stran Gormaz," he said, extending his hand.

"Jarv Caland," Caland said, touching hands with him.

"Are you enjoying Mort?" Gormaz asked politely.

"More than I expected," Caland answered noncommittally. He was trying to watch Tel without turning his head.

"If you're looking for unspoiled beauty, you'll find some,"

Gormaz said, "provided that you don't ask the natives for directions. To the good citizens of Mort, beauty begins and ends with their municipal park. The city of Paradise has a grossly misleading name."

Their fellow diners seemed unable to decide whether the proper response to this remark was laughter or a sagacious nod of the head. They decided to ignore it, and talk turned to idle tourist chatter interspersed with the inevitable death-world jokes. Doctor Gormaz took no interest in it. He concentrated on his food, eating slowly and with great deliberation.

Caland continued to watch Tel—he was beginning to feel jealous of the tourist seated beside her. Suddenly she caught his eyes and scowled, and it occurred to him that he ought to display some semblance of tourist curiosity. He turned to Doctor Gormaz and asked, "What brings a social scientist to Mort?"

"I study societies," Gormaz said. "I'm working on a theory of social structures."

"Congratulations," Caland said gravely. "But—on Mort?"

Mathild giggled. "Tell him about Mort, Doctor. It's so exciting!"

Gormaz winced, as did Caland; but the doctor, having made the scientist's typical assumption that a polite conversational question indicated a deeply repressed thirst for knowledge, brought silence to their table with a sweeping gesture.

"There are two possible bases for a definitive study of structures," his booming voice proclaimed. "The microcosm and the macrocosm. Since there is no social structure in being that equates to the macrocosm, it is necessary to find one that perfectly equates to the microcosm: a social structure maximally controlled with minimal variants. The supreme essence of a social structure."

"Is there such a thing?" Caland asked politely.

"Mort. Did you know that the world is owned by one mal?"

Caland nodded politely.

"There's only one such world left in the galaxy. Did you know that? Think of what it implies! Think of the experiments one could conduct! Mort could be an invaluable laboratory in which to research the basic principles of human society."

"And it isn't?"

"Unfortunately, no. The owner prefers to run it as a business venture. It's controlled for profit. I didn't know that until I arrived here. I fear that my trip has been wasted."

"Now, doctor," Mathild pouted. "Don't we tourists make an interesting social structure?"

"Fascinating," Gormaz said, eyes twinkling, "but a shade too amorphous for systematic study."

He returned his attention to his food. Mathild continued to pout. Conversation around the table reverted to sailing, to the colors of the bay, to the probable menus for the next day's meals. Caland listened while watching Tel. He heard the Valley mentioned once, in a hushed conversation between two mals.

The meal came to an end. Doctor Gormaz wandered off with Mathild in pursuit. Caland, knowing that Tel would be close behind him whatever he did, drifted along with the group of tourists and found himself on the veranda. The others joined in a scramble for advantageously placed chairs near the hote entrance. Caland was unaccustomed to heavy midday meals, and he felt like walking. He strolled along the veranda, looking about him curiously. He had spent several days at this hote. Presumably he had walked here before and even sat here talking with his fellow guests, but everything looked strange to him.

The hote was proud of its veranda. In its literature, of which Caland had seen several specimens in his room, the veranda was called the longest in the universe. This was rank tourist bureau hyperbole, but Caland already had noticed that it was an extremely long veranda. It was, in fact, unending. The building curved convexly along a concave curve in the shore of Paradise Bay, and the veranda extended completely around it. Chairs were arranged in conversational groupings near its outer railing, with ample space left behind them for the traffic of any addicted promenaders among the guests. In well-established tourist tradition, those athletic individuals would emerge in the cool of the morning to indulge in a wearisomely repetitive orgy of veranda circuits, keeping meticulous count so that they could inflict their totals on spouses, friends, eating companions, or total strangers during the remainder of the day.

By the time Caland began his stroll, the athletes had faded with the rising temperature. Their places were taken by sightseers who were content to view the world of Mort without leaving their hote. Caland, once he noted that Tel had emerged from the hote and was surreptitiously watching him, decided to join them.

He drifted along slowly. A richly comical array of tourists languished in chairs by the veranda railing, and Caland found them as entertaining as the hote's spectacular view of the bay. The revoltingly blended colors of their vacation clothing challenged and clashed with the delicate tints of the churning waters. Caland had quickened his pace and was just approaching the veranda's first turning when he came to an abrupt halt.

There was a momentary flurry of confusion as the plump couple who had been following on his heels apologized for bumping him. Caland apologized for stopping so suddenly, and then all three of them apologized to those behind them for blocking the passageway. Further apologies were launched at random, all accompanied by affable smiles. Caland made his escape, claimed an empty chair, casually changed its angle with a kick of his foot, and sank into it.

Against all of his expectations, he suddenly had encountered a familiar face.

CHAPTER TEN

Caland had positioned his chair so that he could watch the mal without turning his head. He was able to sit looking out at the bay with the subject of his interest in handsome profile, and a great chunk of memory came leaping at him out of the past.

He was a Caland, and a kaleidoscope of his early life paraded before him and slowed to a stop when this mal made an entrance. Caland had been no more than fifteen years old at the time, but the incident was etched indelibly on his memory—even on his accident-shattered memory—because his father had made dramatic use of the occasion to further Caland's education. Caland could not remember the mal's name, but he recognized his face instantly.

His father had a business caller—prosperous-looking, suave, articulate, charming. Caland was invited to hear the mal's remarkable sales pitch. An astute investment in some property or other would increase ten-fold in a year and two-hundred-fold in five. The caller was so eloquently persuasive that Caland gave him a fifteen-year-old's rarest gift: his open-mouthed, rapt attention. His father coolly asked questions, took notes, and then told the mal to return in a sennite.

"What do you think?" he asked Caland afterward.

"Do it!" Caland exclaimed.

His father shook his head. "Never invest without investigating. Only a swindler makes promises like that."

And so it turned out. The mal had left the planet before the sennite expired, taking with him substantial sums of money that others had invested without investigating.

"Sometimes the most profitable investment is the one you don't make," Caland's father said afterward. "Remember that."

Caland had remembered, and he also had remembered the mal.

A server hurried up with a tall goblet on a tray, deftly unfolded a holder from the arm of the mal's chair, and placed the goblet ceremoniously. "Anything else, Mal Felroy?" he asked. He pocketed a hefty grat and scurried away.

Caland continued to gaze vacantly at Paradise Bay. He saw the mal calling himself Felroy sip his drink, purse his lips with satisfaction, and return the goblet to the holder. On that long ago afternoon in Caland's father's study, his name certainly had not been Felroy. Probably he changed his name as often as his stylish day suit. Otherwise, the ensuing years had altered him very little. He'd gained some weight, but it was the easy portliness that only wealth and success and good living could bestow. He was well-appearing and richly but conservatively dressed. His ready smile marked him as the most congenial of companions, and fems of a certain age would find his graying profile fascinating. He'd be a favorite of servers and the life of any sup party that had the good fortune to entertain him.

On this day, his manner was that of a mal who had dined well, and who intended, eventually, to sup well; in the meantime, once his digestive processes were properly activated, he was prepared to accept graciously whatever titillations the world of Mort chose to offer him. He presented the classic profile of a mal at ease with himself and the universe. Wherever he went, the hote lackeys would have him coded I.T.—the universal designation for "Ideal Tourist"—within moments of his arrival.

"And perhaps he is," Caland told himself. "Even criminals vacation now and then. Or so I've been told. The law of averages would send one to Mort occasionally. Surely this mal's presence has nothing to do with me."

But he feared, instinctively, that it had. Arlu believed that coincidence was absolutely dependent on time and distance—

that there could be no such thing as a galactic coincidence. Caland did not understand that, but his ordinary common sense warned him that this coincidence was one that should be examined warily. He forced himself into the relaxed guise of a tourist and continued to watch.

Tel had settled into a chair a few meters away. Occasionally she sent a perplexed glance in Caland's direction. He ignored her.

After an appropriate period of digestive meditation, Felroy drained his goblet, pushed his sturdy form erect, and resumed the grand veranda tour that he'd interrupted just short of its first turning. The moment he disappeared around the corner, Caland followed him.

The swing to the left magically transformed the sea view into one of a formal garden smeared with riotously colored flowers. Hedge-lined paths converged on sculpture-cluttered fountains. Hideous flying creatures—Caland recognized them as the same that congregated on the spit of land in the mouth of Paradise Bay—were coming and going from the dome-shaped roof of a screened gazebo that the hote management probably called a garden house. To the alien eye, there was nothing to attract the ugly, membrane-winged beasts. They neither fed there nor nested. They simply landed on the curving metal-covered dome with a clatter of multiple feet, slowly slipped and slithered down the steep incline to the edge, and fell off. Then they flapped away, squawking stridently.

A passing tourist noted Caland's apparent interest. "Yodel birds," he remarked with a grin. This seemed to pose more questions than it answered, but Caland—watching Felroy out of the corner of his eye—nodded politely.

Beyond the park stood the rival tourist hote where Arlu was staying, the Paradise Vista Inn—if two hotes with the same ownership and management could be called rivals. The Vista was almost as tall as the View, but, because of its blunt, squarish contours, it looked squat by comparison. Its veranda, which extended only along the bay side of the building, offered little competition to the longest veranda in the universe.

Felroy, walking with heavy deliberation, had vanished around the next turning, and Caland hurried after him. As he turned the corner, he saw Tel following determinedly, but he did not signal. There were other tourists just behind her.

To the east, behind the two hotes, stretched an attractive private park that was equipped for various outdoor games and recreations. None of them was in use. Veranda walking was the ultimate exercise for most of Mort's tourists. Beyond the park loomed the mottled contours of a lovely highland that bore a curiously unromantic name, the Tin Mountains.

The side veranda had been sparsely populated; the rear veranda was deserted except for a few strollers who were leaving it as quickly as possible. Felroy continued to move along purposefully, and Caland lengthened his stride. When Felroy turned the next corner, Caland was a mere three meters behind him.

Caland approached the corner cautiously, peered around it, and then moved to the railing and selected a chair that was out of sight of the north veranda but perfectly placed for eavesdropping. As he seated himself, he saw Tel drop into a chair a short distance away. She no longer looked perplexed. She was glaring at him, but Caland was too intent on Felroy's doings to send her a reassuring glance. He leaned to one side, cupped a hand to his ear in a manner that would suggest that he was napping, and listened.

Just around the corner, Felroy was still exchanging greetings with a stout, ruddy mal his own age while he eased himself into a neighboring chair. The chair scraped.

"Every day on this beautiful world seems to be a nice day," Felroy said gallantly, returning a cliché for one Caland had missed.

That was for the benefit of some passing tourists. As soon as they were beyond hearing, the two men began to speak in undertones. Caland had to strain his hearing to the utmost. Even so, he was astonished that an old hand like Felroy would exchange confidentialities so close to the convenient corner.

"Hear from Hip?"

"May take a while," Felroy said, keeping his voice on the same level. "May be complicated."

"I suppose."

"Personally, I doubt that he'll find the ghost of an angle," Felroy went on. "Pity. Nice world. A lot could be made of it. Look at the stupid names they've inflicted on it. Paradise View. Paradise Vista. Tin Mountains. Paradise Annex—no wonder the natives twist that one to 'Attic'! Did you get any occupancy figures?"

"Just for the hote. Forty-one per cent this week. Unusually good week, the desk super said. Sickening, isn't it?"

Caland stretched his neck to peer around the corner. Two more complacent conspirators had never forgathered anywhere.

"Check on Pakovich?"

"Uh huh," Felroy said.

"As expected?"

"Spoiled brat that grew up to be a spoiled adult. Sits there in his aerie gazing out over his world, makes an occasional pronouncement, now and then dictates a law, and once in a while stirs himself for a token inspection of something or other. Knows only what he's told and understands none of it. Usual story of a lazy ignoramus inheriting."

Caland eased himself back into his chair as more strollers approached. The conversation stopped abruptly the moment they turned the corner. After a brief lull, punctuated by fading inanities from the passersby, it began again.

"Pity. To have this laid in one's lap and not know what to do with it—"

"He must occasionally get some good advice," Felroy said. "It's just that he doesn't know how to carry anything out. The fertilizer factory was an astute move, but it could sell a hundred or a thousand times what it produces. Pakovich built the most up-to-date plant modern technology could design, but he tries to supply it with a rickety fishing fleet."

"I heard he only built it to raise a stink over in the Valley. Literally."

"I suppose that's possible. The Valley rankles. Pakovich has two pet peeves, the Valley and someone named Bronlan. Bronlan is one of the few substantial citizens the Valley has, and I couldn't find out what Pakovich has against him. Some ancient feud, I take it. Where was I? Pakovich doesn't know how to run things. Find anything for us in the Valley?"

"Nothing. There's money to be made there, but there'd have to be a huge expansion of the tourist trade, which would take time and money and a lot of promoting. If we owned the hotes, I'd say it would be a sound investment, but I can't see building up Pakovich's tourist business in order to make a little fallout money."

"My conclusion exactly," Felroy said. "I think we're finished with the preliminaries, but we'll have to wait until we hear from Hip."

"Right. If he finds an angle, all bets are off. We can settle in and go to work right away. Otherwise—"

"The mines and plants and farms and their labor forces," Felroy said.

"How'll Pakovich react? He's not dependent on the income, he's got no stockholders to answer to, and it won't hurt him personally if he loses customers."

"He'll fight," Felroy said confidently. "And then he'll pay. The longer he fights, the more he'll pay. Money doesn't matter to him. The point is that the world is *his*."

"Ah!"

"And he'll pay well to keep it that way."

"Think we can maneuver him into a contract?"

"Don't know. Contract or one-shot, it's ripe and waiting to be plucked. The really surprising thing is that someone didn't beat us to it."

"Who'll we get?"

"Prency Tate. It's made to order for him. The world is ripe, but we don't want to bungle the plucking."

"Unless Hip turns up something."

"I don't expect that to happen. Alexander Pakovich is a fool, but Old Mort, his father, was as sharp as they come. Mort wasn't the type to leave loose ends. In anything. You'll see. He'll have his ownership tied down in all the relevant interworld courts and recognized by every world in this part of the galaxy that matters. That's probably why no one got there ahead of us. Old Mort was a character. Named the world after himself because 'Mort' has a double meaning and it tickled him to have people read it the wrong way. He collected 'death world' jokes, and he liked to make them up himself. He's responsible for calling Mort's inhabitants, 'Morticians.' Anyone trying to pluck Old Mort was likely to get skinned good. The only one who ever succeeded was Dombrily, the character who talked Mort into selling outright the land that's now called the Valley."

Caland suddenly realized that Tel had company. The mal who had sat next to her at dinner had tracked her down. Caland revisited the impulse to scowl at her and turned his thoughts again to the coincidence of this encounter with Felroy.

The conversation continued. "Did you know him?"

"Old Mort?" Felroy chuckled. "I knew him slightly. He used to visit Aravia once a year. I was just a youngster, then."

"How'd he happen to get clear title to a world?"

Felroy chuckled again. "Know that kids' card game, 'Take the World'? That's what Mort did. He took it. He stole, he extorted, and he embezzled. He schemed and cheated and lied and defrauded. Won one of the polar caps in a crooked poker game. Had a friend named Steinhort who was lost in a space disaster. Mort befriended the widow, bought food for her children, and found her a decent place to live and a job. She repaid him by selling him, for a modest price, some fake jewelry, some stock certificates that were phony, and a deed to a continent—which was beyond price. Mort picked up two more continents in a bar when a drunken space captain was trying to borrow money for a drink. Mort bought him one drink for each continent. All that time no one thought the deeds were worth anything. Mort collected them like pieces of a puzzle, and when the set was complete, he put them all together and registered them as the world of Mort. It wasn't until much later that the richest tin deposits in the galaxy were discovered here."

"Quite the old scoundrel, eh?"

"Old Mort? Absolutely not! Mort was the galaxy's one infallibly honest man. As a matter of principle, he never was an iota more mendacious than those he was dealing with. Remember— no one believed that this world was worth anything. Every time Mort acquired a piece of it, the other party always thought he'd done Mort in. I'm glad I never ran up against him. Alexander must take after his mother." There was a long pause. "Nothing to do now but wait until we hear from Hip," Felroy said finally.

"It may be just as well if he doesn't find anything. If we can't possibly take the place over, we won't have to be careful about breaking things."

"Right," Felroy agreed. "Prency enjoys a good fight, and Pakovich will give him one. And the harder Pakovich fights, the more he'll pay. It'll take Prency just about a hundred days to convert Pakovich's paradise into an opposite something that he won't like at all."

A chair scraped. Felroy was getting to his feet. "I'll let you know the moment I hear from Hip," he said.

His footsteps faded. Caland remained where he was for several minutes. Then he casually strolled around the corner, walked a short distance past the plumply recumbent form of the co-conspirator, and selected a chair for himself. He sat gazing out across another formal garden toward a sprawling, strangely asymmetrical building. After a moment of reflection, he identified it as the Art Bazaar. The high-peaked roofs beyond, each with a row of skylights, would be the art colony. The whole complex was officially called the Paradise Annex, but Caland hadn't known that the locals referred to it as the Attic.

Tel walked past with her new acquaintance hovering at her side, and the two of them took chairs at the distant end of the veranda. Caland pretended to pay no attention to them. When a server hurried past, Caland stopped him, and—with grim nonchalance—he ordered a Nectar of Paradise.

He still had not looked toward the co-conspirator, but now he sent a glance in that direction—not curious, not friendly, just a blank look upon which that paunchy individual could place any interpretation he chose.

He chose to place none at all. His own eyes were fixed meditatively upon some unidentified distant object, and if Caland's features meant anything to him, his face betrayed no ripple of recognition.

Caland resignedly waited for his drink. When finally it arrived, he sipped it with a demonstrative appreciation that ranked among his more difficult feats of acting. He much preferred the Valley's yuck.

When he finished, he got leisurely to his feet and left. If the co-conspirator had been feeling lonely, or loquacious, or in the mood for a bit of harmless talk, Caland might possibly have learned something; but his taciturnity hardly mattered. It would be easy to identify him, after which Arlu could search him as thoroughly as he pleased.

As Caland passed Tel and her escort, he nodded and murmured a polite greeting. Her frown instinctively transformed itself into a look of alarm until he winked at her. She'd had a startled apprehension that his mind had stripped gears again.

He walked on. When he rounded the corner of the veranda to the bay side, he found that Felroy had been captured by a predatory widow. Caland knew the type painfully well. This specimen was long and lank, and her bones had a lethal-looking sharpness. Curious to see how Felroy would handle himself under extreme duress, Caland secured a nearby chair and listened.

The fem was wagging a finger at Felroy. "Ah, ha! You can't keep secrets from me. So you finally succumbed!"

"Succumbed to what, Fem Wobbons?" Felroy asked politely.

Caland's sudden intake of breath must have been audible, but no one seemed to notice. He stared at Felroy's companion incredulously. Was *this* the vintage fem with whom he'd visited the Valley? He hadn't a shred of a recollection of either her or the event.

"The Valley!" she exclaimed triumphantly, as though echoing Caland's thought. "I know you went there!"

Felroy's innocence seemed genuine. "Went there yesterday afternoon. Came back yesterday afternoon."

The finger wagged again. "Naughty, naughty!"

"Why? It's only another tourist stop. This world doesn't have many."

"Don't try to tell me that vale of iniquity is only another tourist stop!"

"But it is," Felroy persisted. "Like the hydroelectric plant and the fertilizer factory and the Art Bazaar. The Valley doesn't smell any worse than the others do. It's no more interesting, either."

"Ha!"

"Do you really think it is?" Felroy asked politely, feigning surprise.

Fem Wobbon's face turned a pastel pink that matched one of the swirls in the bay. "I'm sure I don't know."

Caland, who was unwilling to accept the possibility that he had gone anywhere at all in this creature's company, had been watching the scene with increasing incredulity. Now he relaxed. If the mere thought of visiting the Valley made her blush, he must have escorted some other fem Wobbons. Perhaps she had a daughter; or—since Arlu had said "vintage fem"—a sister.

"But you ought to know," Felroy said. "There're no esoteric secrets about the Valley. Why is everyone so reluctant to mention it? I've seen far worse places no more than a stroll or a short ride from the space port of any world I've visited, including yours. The Valley had a couple of extremely attractive restaurants. I has an early sup at one of them, the Burned Wafer, and it was absolutely first-rate—a most pleasant change from the bland food these two hotes offer. Then there are the overly promoted Houses of Fame—"

"*Ill* fame!" Fem Wobbons hissed.

"Fame," Felroy insisted firmly. "Everyone calls them that. Why not? They're certainly the best-known edifices on Mort. I didn't visit them because I knew they couldn't possibly live up to their advertisements. Apart from the restaurants and the Houses of Fame, the only establishment in the Valley that looks faintly sanitary and respectable is a large gambling arena."

"Respectable!"

"*Looks* respectable," Felroy corrected. "Otherwise, the Valley has only one section of badly paved street, there are no pedestrian walks, and the whole community is an unending disaster area of ramshackle shops selling every possible variety of bad merchandise at inflated prices, and little eating places that look as though they were licensed to spread disease, and dwellings that would collapse if they didn't crowd so many people into them. The inhabitants are mostly unshaven and uncombed and unwashed and unemployed and in outrageous states of dress or undress. Especially unwashed, despite the fact that the Valley's beach is a continuation of this one and just as lovely. Valley residents look rather pathetic, but it wouldn't surprise me if they're just pretending to be naughty for the benefit of the tourists."

"The inhabitants certainly are pathetic," Fem Wobbons said angrily. "The whole Valley lives on the illicit earning of its young fems."

Felroy frowned. "But is prostitution actually illegal there?"

"I'm sure I don't know."

"Those earnings can't be called illicit if no laws are violated," Felroy said.

"They're certainly morally illicit!"

Felroy got to his feet. "The Valley is a rather dull and untidy vale of iniquity. Really, it is. If I were you, I'd stop worrying about it and go see the fertilizer plant. Your home world has far worse places. Or better, depending on the viewpoint. However, if you insist on experiencing the Valley yourself, I'd be honored to take you there to sup. The restaurants really are excellent."

Fem Wobbons drew herself up indignantly.

"Otherwise," Felroy went on, "I wouldn't waste energy in

being resentful about it. Fems who fuss over a 'vale of iniquity' are only trying to conceal their jealousy of the fems who inhabit it. But I assure you—you need have no fear whatsoever of finding any of those young fems in competition with you, about anything."

He gave her a nod and a half bow and left her perplexedly grappling with a compliment that seemed dangerously likely to turn out to be an insult. Caland watched Felroy admiringly until he disappeared into the reception hall.

Moving on, Caland found a seat apart from the languishing tourists and summoned a server. After a few whispered words, the server loped away. He was gone for just the length of time a mal in a hurry required to circle the building.

"The name is Gilrod Emson, Mal Caland," the server announced.

"Are you certain?"

"That's the name of the guest who's sitting at the east end of the north veranda."

"And—what's Mal Felroy's first name?"

"It's Mal Fellington Felroy."

"Splendid," Caland said, passing him a generous grat.

"If you ever need any more information—"

"If I need any, I'll come to you," Caland promised.

Tel had escaped from her escort. She was watching Caland warily from a chair near the entrance. Caland strolled in that direction, nodding politely at his fellow guests. As he passed her, he called a cheerful invitation to those lounging nearby. "Anyone for the Art Bazaar?"

There was no response, though Fem Wobbons looked up at him stonily. Caland smiled vaguely, shrugged to register suitable disappointment, and set out for the Art Bazaar. He descended the hote's sweeping flight of steps and selected a cobbled walk that seemed to point in the right direction.

When he had placed an outburst of colorful shrubbery between himself and the veranda, he paused and waited. Tel arrived a short time later. She affected a casual walk, but she was in frantic pursuit.

"What was that all about?" she demanded. "Did you recognize someone?"

They walked slowly toward the Art Bazaar, and Caland told her about the conversation he'd overheard.

"That memory of yours has odd twists to it," Tel said. "You can't recollect what happened a sennite ago, but you dredge up ancient events at the flick of an eyelash."

"I don't see how this could possibly have anything to do with me," Caland said. "I suppose it's conceivable that an innocent place like Mort could suddenly become a vortex of galactic conspiracies. According to an expert like Felroy, the world is long overdue. But I refuse to believe that it's happening right now just because I arrived here."

"Fortunately, you don't have to believe. That's Arlu's problem. We'll tell him what you found out and let him do the worrying. Is there anything else?"

"I've been thinking what an attractive tourist you make. You could have your pick of the mals in the dining room. Didn't you like the one you caught?"

"I threw it back. If it's a mal I'm after, I won't start my search at the Paradise View Hostelry. Where are you going?"

"I announced publically that I was going to the Art Bazaar, so I think I'd better go there."

He would have preferred to return to the Valley. It was obvious to him that Arlu's ploy was not working. Despite that doleful forty-one per cent occupancy figure, several hundred guests were living at the Paradise View in a resort atmosphere of casual camaraderie. If Caland had mingled with them for several days, some of them should have remembered him sufficiently well to give him a passing smile of recognition, disguise or no disguise. The explanation was simple enough: even in a resort hote, Jarv Caland had led the life of a recluse. That was in no way surprising; ever since the accident, he'd been a recluse. The one thing he could not understand was how any vintage fem—be it Fem Wobbons or a sister—had managed to attach herself to him for a trip to the Valley.

The Art Bazaar was a vast, ungainly building where paintings from Mort's official art colony were displayed and sold. The large main room was cluttered with representations of Paradise Bay. Side rooms offered groupings of other scenes of Mort, and the alcoves were devoted to the works of the individual artists. Caland and Tel wandered among the paintings for a time, keeping far enough apart to maintain the fiction that they were not together in case any of their fellow tourists decided belatedly to follow them.

They had the entire bazaar to themselves except for the two turbaned artists who seemed to be nominally in charge. Neither one of them paid the slightest attention to Tel and Caland. One, in a remote corner, was painting from sketches. The other, who was seated at the reception desk, kept his eyes on the screen of a book reader.

Mort's multicolored bay, its mountains, its beautifully mottled vegetation, and its untamed ocean furnished striking art subjects, but Caland had no urge to look at paintings when he could enjoy the originals. The displays of works by individual artists, especially the portraits, were much more appealing to him.

He completed his rapid circuit of the building and met Tel at the entrance. "Seen enough?" he asked.

The artist at the reception desk looked up at them. "New arrivals?"

Caland nodded.

"Enjoying Pakovich's paradise?"

"I have the feeling that I should be looking at it instead of the paintings."

The artist chuckled. His tall, gaunt figure was further elongated by his flappy, padded artist's turban. Tel asked him, "Why do you wear that thing inside?"

"Tradition," the artist said. He took the turban off and twirled it on a finger. "Without it I'm not an artist. Or so most tourists think."

"Do artists wear turbans when there are no tourists about?"

"Of course. A lot of artists wouldn't think they were artists without turbans. The rest of us are so accustomed to them that we feel naked without them. They're traditional, and tradition is the glue that holds the universe together. Especially the tourist world."

"Don't you get tired painting scenes of Mort?" Caland asked.

"Of course. It's a commercial sideline. A nuisance, but profitable. Tourists like to buy paintings of something they've seen. Also, our noble patron would murmur that we weren't promoting his world if he chanced to breeze through here without finding the place packed with views of Mort."

Caland turned and looked at the rows of paintings on easels and the vast, richly finished room that contained them. The Art Bazaar and the colony of artists were unlikely establishments for the world of Mort, and Pakovich, from all that Caland had heard about him, seemed to be an improbable sponsor for such institutions. "Is your noble patron an art lover?" he asked.

"Pakovich?" The artist snorted. "He's a snob. Worse, he's a pipsqueak of a snob. If he weren't rich, he'd be an unperson. Know why he started this bazaar? A lot of artists live in the Valley, and some of them were doing well with Mort landscapes. Pakovich has a phobia about the Valley, because it's the one speck on this world that he doesn't own, so he went to the trouble and expense of establishing an art colony just to undercut the Valley artists. Of course the colony has been a nice windfall for a lot of us—we get a three-year fellowship, and all we have to do is turn out a few scenes of Mort, and the Bazaar handles the sale of our paintings. It gives us the security to work and study and experiment, and it's produced some fine artists, but it was a shoddy thing for Pakovich to do. He's a pipsqueak of a snob."

"Do you know him?" Tel asked.

The artist's gesture of disgust sent his turban sailing across the room. "He may patronize artists, but he doesn't associate with them. I've seen him from a distance, which was close enough. Once when he wanted a mural painted in his mansion's dining room, a friend of mine worked twenty-one hours a day, slept among his paint containers the other five, and had his meals between brush strokes. If the Pakoviches of this universe want something, they want it *now*. Most of my friend's work was done with Pakovich leaning over his shoulder. The jerk had nothing else to do. Listen!" He banged on the desk with his fist. "Know what that pipsqueak does every morning? My friend saw it. Pakovich has a servant that runs the mansion for him, and this servant is always totally dressed—totally, understand? The super costume that gets worn to fancy state dinners on worlds that have normal governments. So every morning the servant waits on Pakovich at breakfast—the servant in total dress and Pakovich sitting there in his pajamas! My friend saw it several times."

"Does Pakovich know anything at all about art?" Caland asked.

"He doesn't know anything at all about anything."

The artist returned his attention to his book, and Caland and Tel left. Caland was wondering how a pipsqueak of a snob was going to fare in the coming encounter with Felroy, Emson, and Prency Tate.

Just outside the door, Fem Wobbons descended on them—tall, angular, grotesquely dressed. Her shimmering two-piece suit was designed to cling, but she had no figure for it to cling to. Her flopping tourist's hat had slipped to the back of her head, and her locks of lavender tinted hair were wildly askew. She stood for a moment glaring from Caland to Tel, face flushed with anger, nostrils dilated.

Then she pointed a trembling finger. "You scoundrel!" she hissed. "You told me—you said an accident impaired—left you unable to—you scoundrel! You *lied* to me! And now I find you running about with a Valley tart!"

"Fem Wobbons!" Caland spoke with a calmness that amazed him. "I have seen many low persons attempting to put on the airs of high society, but none of them were as low as you, or as preposterous. To retail in public matters told to you in a private conversation is worse than deplorable. You are a gross person. Do you know what your fellow guests would think of you if they knew that your fine public indignation about the Valley is a mere cover-up for your nocturnal excursions there in pursuit of young mals?"

Fem Wobbons's face had gone white. She stammered, "Oh, I'm sorry, I had no idea—"

And rushed away.

Tel had her hand clapped to her mouth. When she could contain it no longer, she burst into laughter. "Ah, my dear," she sputtered, wiping her eyes. "Fem Wobbons has recognized your name. I'll guarantee it. More than that—she's also looked up your monerating, and I'll guarantee that, too. She knows all about your background. When you mentioned her putting on the airs of high society, she suddenly remembered that you *are* high society. When you called her a gross person, it was as though you'd said, 'I'll tell my father on you.' You didn't have to threaten blackmail. She'd already collapsed. Why did you demolish her so completely? She called me a Valley tart, and didn't let me get a word in."

"I wonder what happened on that Valley excursion," Caland mused.

"You must know. You just told her. She enticed you to the Valley and tried to seduce you. She must have been brazenly aggressive about it. You didn't confide in me that much even when I actually got you in bed."

"But why would I go anywhere at all with her?" Caland demanded.

"Blame your innate good manners," Tel said. "Probably she asked you to do something—take her to sup, accompany her to the evening dance in the lounge, some harmless thing like that. You'd be much too polite to bluntly decline, so you'd think of an excuse. 'Sorry, Fem Wobbons, but I plan to sup in the Valley this evening.' That's you, clutching at a straw. 'How exciting, Mal Caland. Wouldn't you take me with you?' That's the straw turning into a noose. For a naively polite young mal like you, there was no way out of it."

"I still don't understand. How could she dare to wax so indignantly about the Valley in public when she's having private flings there?"

"You're just too innocent to understand these things," Tel said. "An invitation to go slumming with that suave, worldly, but socially contemptible character Fellington Felroy had to be treated like the insult it was. An opportunity to accompany the scion of one of the galaxy's first families anywhere at all was something to be snatched at. It must have happened that way. I won't try to describe the attempted seduction, though. I'm only sorry I wasn't there to see it. Aren't you overlooking the most intriguing part of Fem Wobbons's outburst?"

"What was that?"

"She called me—a respectable millionaire's daughter, mind you—she called me a Valley tart. Which means that she must have recognized me. And that means that she must spend more time in the Valley than anyone realizes, or that she has connections there, or both. And *that* is much more interesting than your scoop about Fellington Felroy."

CHAPTER ELEVEN

They separated, and Tel returned to the hote as though she'd been strolling in one of the formal gardens. Caland gave her time to get settled on the veranda before he walked back along the Annex path. In front of the hote he encountered Doctor Gormaz, just back from sailing with an excited crowd of tourists.

"Been sightseeing?"

"Art Bazaar."

Gormaz grimaced. "I saw it yesterday. A thousand and one views of the same natural beauty are not a thousand and one times as lovely as one view, and none of them compare with the original. The owner of the world of Mort isn't aware of that."

"He does seem to have his prejudices," Caland said. "I suppose if one owns a world and has unlimited wealth, in time it might become difficult to distinguish between whims and principles."

Gormaz grimaced again. "That's very good. 'Distinguish between whims and principles.' No, I don't suppose Pakovich could do that. Would you like to meet him?"

"Meet Pakovich?" The notion seemed ridiculous to Caland. Pakovich was a remote figure in a lofty mansion, probably secured by fences and watch animals and armed guards. Caland had no desire at all to meet him, and he saw no reason why Pakovich would want to meet Jarv Caland.

"I came here with the idea of setting up a sociological laboratory," Gormaz said. "The location seemed ideal. It still does, except for Pakovich. The success of my project would be directly dependent upon his continued good will. I can't make a decision one way or the other until I've appraised the mal personally. I'd much appreciate it if you would accompany me."

Caland experienced a rueful flash of insight into his entrapment by Fem Wobbons. There really was no polite way to refuse. He said, "If it wouldn't be intruding—"

Doctor Gormaz favored him with a smile. "You're a modest person, Mal Caland, and I commend you for it. You underrate yourself. In contrast, I know exactly who and what I am. When I request an appointment with Alexander Pakovich, I will *not* do so in the names of Doctor Stran Gormaz and Mal Jarv Caland. I shall do so in the names of Mal Jarv Caland and his associate, Doctor Stran Gormaz. Pakovich won't have heard of either of us, so he'll tell his secretary to investigate. The moment the secretary sees your monerating, he'll grant the appointment on his own initiative. It is your presence, Mal Caland, which will enable me to make a personal appraisal of Alexander Pakovich. I'm most grateful that you are willing to come along. Without you, I wouldn't be able to get near him. I hope that doesn't offend you."

"It's a burden I've had to bear all of my life. How did you happen to know who I am?"

"I come from your part of the galaxy, Mal Caland. I have served on fund-raising committees for several universities, and dossiers of the idiosyncrasies of the galaxy's leading philanthropists are the most valuable resource of such committees. Your father always fulfilled our expectations admirably. For every cause I served, he requested further information. He then sent lists of specific questions, and he followed that with a polite refusal. We knew that he gave away millions, and we never divined just where our causes were deficient. But—yes, I instantly recognized the name Jarv Caland. If you'll excuse me, I'll go and request the appointment. For tomorrow morning, I think. Is that convenient? I'll leave word for you as soon as I receive a response."

Gormaz hurried away, his tufts of unruly hair bouncing with each stride as though making distress signals. He was an amusing-looking little mal, and that fact probably had deceived a lot of people. He impressed Caland as highly intelligent, practical, and intensely serious. If the notion of a sociological laboratory sounded silly, it would be better not to let Doctor Gormaz know that one thought so.

Caland had a problem of his own to think about. He'd remembered belatedly that Tel was supposed to be keeping an eye on him. There was no possible way that he could bend Gormaz's invitation to include her.

He needed to talk with her. He paused at her chair on the veranda, murmured a pleasantry about the weather, and whispered, "Lounge."

He walked away.

To his dismay, he found the guests' lounge crowded. The group that had come in from sailing with Doctor Gormaz had gathered in the center of the room, Gormaz with them, to discuss the experience. All of the tables seemed to be taken. Caland's gaze swept around the room, swept back again, suddenly stopped.

He'd seen a familiar face, and it was fixed on him intently.

Unlike Fellington Felroy's, it was a face he'd encountered recently, but he could not remember where. The fem was probably in her mid-thirties, plain-looking, with short, straight dark hair. She wore a conservative day suit, and she looked so severely businesslike amidst the flamboyantly costumed tourists that his instinct told him she couldn't possibly be a hote guest. Either she was an employee taking a job break, or she was there on business.

It seemed that her business was with Caland. She got to her feet and started toward him purposefully. Caland turned to meet her.

Suddenly Fem Wobbons stood in his way. "Mal Caland, I wish to apologize. When I saw you with that—that—"

"I happened to encounter another guest of this hote at the

bazaar," Caland said icily. "She's extremely knowledgeable about art. She's a sculptor herself. It's to her you should apologize."

"I know," Fem Wobbons said miserably. "I know you weren't with her. I saw you return alone. I'm sorry. And about the Valley—"

"Perhaps it would be best if neither of us mentioned it again," Caland suggested gravely. He turned away.

"Yes. Yes, of course. Thank you," she said in a fading voice.

The unknown fem was no longer in the room. Tel had reached the doorway and was looking about for him, too late either to see her or to catch Fem Wobbons's dramatic scene. Caland passed her on the way out, whispered resignedly, "Veranda."

He had the frustrated feeling that things were piling up faster than his mind could deal with them. This was no time for a muttered exchange of confidences in a crowded room. He wanted a thorough discussion, and he wanted to see Arlu. When Tel appeared, he strode boldly to meet her.

He bowed ceremoniously. "Would you do me the great honor of visiting the Valley with me?"

"Are you sprung?" She whispered angrily.

"Certainly not."

"Then what do you think you're doing?"

"Acting like a tourist."

She began to laugh. "Damned if you're not. Let's go."

"Tell Arlu. I want to talk with him."

While Tel was relaying the message, Caland asked the desk super to com a 'cab for them. They swept across the veranda and down the steps, and Caland handed Tel into the odd-looking vehicle while a hundred guests stared curiously and Fem Wobbons watched with icy disapproval. He had the idiotic feeling that he was escaping.

* * * * * * *

That night Caland lay on the sculptured softness of the

Paradise View Hostelry bed and tried to sleep. His body resented the billowy mattress, his stomach was in open revolt against the Fig Stump's richly enticing food, and he sensed that the invisible eyes were gloating over his discomfort. He tried to relax in Tel's warm embrace and contemplate the deep mystery of her quiet breathing: the undulation of the universe, miraculously focused into something called life.

Twice his twisting awakened her, and she sleepily asked him what was wrong. He made a muttered, drowsy response, and she quickly dozed off again.

At the Fig Stump, Alz Hernl had greeted them with astonished delight and placed them in a secluded alcove. When Arlu arrived a short time later, Alz served them himself—not from the menu, but with dishes prepared only for special customers. They savored meat-filled noodles with spleshna sauce from Zlonif, a vegetable soufflé from Krifnora, yakavnis made with imported kress from Barlonol, and a special ice from Olgi's concocted with the juice of a rare native fruit that had to be smuggled into the Valley because Pakovich tried to restrict the entire supply to his own two hotes—which of course did not know what to do with it. Alz Hernl enlivened the meal by bringing them vintage wines from Rynaif to sample, and he joined them occasionally and took delight in discussing food with Arlu, whom he treated as a fellow connoisseur.

The mere recollection of it caused upheaval in Caland's churning stomach.

Alz worked the Fig Stump's magic on them, and they had eaten their way into what could only be termed a condition of internal beatitude. Caland wished that the Reverend had been there to share it with them. He would have enjoyed watching poised asceticism laid siege to by shameless gastronomy.

While they ate, Caland described the day's experiences. Arlu's chins, when they were spared the rippling motion of chewing, beamed smiles at Caland.

"It's been a good day," Arlu said. "Cal doesn't seem to have taken any harm from his experiences, and we've certainly gained a parcel of new data and illuminated some problems. Question is which of them are our problems. Your old acquaintance Felroy would seem to belong to Pakovich. His only importance to us is in the way he stimulated Cal's memory."

He meditated for a few minutes, one hand resting caressingly upon his ample and recently filled stomach and the other idly pawing at his mass of silver hair.

"Well, then," he said finally. "Pakovich. We'll file that one for consideration. When you see him tomorrow, if you see him, consider whether he'd be likely to believe it if you told him that devastating labor troubles are on the way. We won't mention it—yet—but it would be useful to know how he reacts to things.

"Then I'm to go with Gormaz?"

"Wouldn't be polite not to, now that you've let him use your name."

"Without Tel?"

"Mmmm. It's a bit late to be trying to include her. I'll make a few arrangements, and it'll be all right. I suppose I'll have to take a look at Doctor Gormaz's background, but if he only arrived here yesterday, he certainly wasn't tampering with Cal's mind several days ago. Did he mention where he came from? No? I'll do a quick search on him. With Fem Wobbons, we have the opposite problem. She's practically a permanent resident of the Paradise View Hostelry—been there for almost nine terms. Anything that happened to Cal during that time wasn't her doing. It's thought that she acquired her wealth recently, probably by inheritance. Her fellow guests consider her a vulgarly common fem, and her pursuit of young mals is notorious. There's no evidence that she's ever caught one, though. She's chasing her lost youth, or something, and I had her labeled as a silly, rather pathetic fem but basically harmless. If she actually has connections with the Valley, I'll have to search her."

"She knew me, but it was the way a tourist recognizes a native she's passed on the street several times," Tel said. "She has all the Valley fems classified as tarts, and all the mals as shiftless parasites living on the proceeds of the fems' sordid labor, or that sort of thing. She's not living here in disguise, if that's what you were wondering about, but she's a frequent visitor. I'll guarantee that."

Arlu sighed. "I'll look into it. I'm most intrigued by Cal's mystery fem, but there's nothing at all we can do about that until she shows herself again." There was another long pause while he caressed his stomach and pawed at his hair. "I don't think we've finished our run yet," he said finally. "Once you've made your excursion with Doctor Gormaz, Cal, stop roaming around. I want you on display and conspicuously available so all of your fellow guests can have a look at you and you at them. You haven't been exposed to more than a third of them."

"We ought to give the mystery fem another crack at him," Tel said.

Arlu nodded. "If he's on display and available, she'll find him, and if she doesn't find him, then we'll know that she's changed her mind."

"I suppose I should have asked a server about her," Caland said. "But she slipped away before I could do anything at all. Fem Wobbons—"

"Never mind," Tel said consolingly. "Tomorrow's another day. You'll meet the Great Watcher, and I'll go sailing. I have three invitations. I want to see what the Valley looks like from the bay."

"And then I'll make myself conspicuously available. I'm not looking forward to any of it." He especially did not like the idea of Tel going sailing while he wasted a morning with Doctor Gormaz and Pakovich.

"One more day at the hote should finish the job," Arlu said. "Now you two had better get back there."

The 'cab stopped at the Fig Stump's door, as it had on their arrival, and they slipped into it quickly so Tel's silly tourist costume would not cause comment among their friends. At the hote they nonchalantly walked the gamut of stares from the veranda; at least Fem Wobbons was not present.

The message light was on in Caland's room. On the screen

was a terse note from Doctor Gormaz: "Pakovich available at nine. Will you break with me at eight?"

Caland messaged his assent, and they went to bed. Tel dozed off at once, leaving Caland to his stifled contemplation of the vast bed's luxurious discomfort and his gorged abdomen. Eventually he fell asleep, and a scratching on his hote door awakened him.

It was the frightened little mal from Mort, and Caland even remembered his name, Wes Fulm. Fulm thought it wasn't fair that people make jokes about Mort's name, and he also thought he was being followed. Caland dutifully trailed after him along Rynaif's Avenue of Fountains, and Fulm met his flaming destiny with a bulky unknown mal on his heels and a shrouded black figure following far behind. This latter was Dom, who owned Mort's Valley, and his link with Fulm and his presence on Rynaif had never been explained. Caland wondered whether he'd asked Arlu about it. His nightmares were becoming confused with reality or reality with his nightmares. He chased after Dom's racing, flapping figure, turned a corner, and abruptly found himself in a queue.

Directly ahead were six revoltingly clothed and shaggy young people, three mals and three fems. They were arguing with officials. A super charged out of an office, arms waving. The six were herded away and Caland's turn came.

Six Rynaif Security Proctors closed on him and escorted him away. A repulsive official pointed an accusing finger. "Mal Caland, have you ever visited the world of Cenaru?"

"Never," Caland protested. "I've never been away from home. Besides, I'm dead."

The official scowled. "Have you ever visited the world of Olyndyt?"

"Never. I couldn't have. I'm dead."

"Have you ever visited the world of Skarlont?"

"I have seen the dead piled high," Caland confessed brokenly. "I have seen buildings toppled and heard screams and walked a street awash with blood and shredded flesh and brains more mutilated than mine. But I have never been away from home.

Ask my father; his name is Caland, too, and his monerating is even better than mine. And I'm dead—you must remember that."

"Ah!" The official exclaimed. "You have a reservation at the Paradise View Hostelry. Why didn't you say so?" He got to his feet and bowed deeply. "Welcome to Mort. Exit that way, please."

Caland took his traveling case and headed for a corridor leading out of the vaulted space terminal. Almost at once it took a sharp turning, and he found himself surrounded by the metal latticework that ornamented spaceship passageways. He followed a zigzag route, and it amazed him that he could perform the deft anti-spy maneuver while carrying a traveling case but he managed it. He had to do it. He knew that someone was following. He began taking panicky glances behind him as he hurried along the empty passageway. Another turning, another maneuver. And another. He broke into a run, the follower was on his heels, he was suddenly gripped from behind. He struggled, flailed out—.

"It's all right," Tel was saying. "It's all right."

He sat on the edge of the vast, super-luxurious bed and tried to control his trembling. He was perspiring; his heart was pounding. He willed himself to relax and could not.

"That must have been some nightmare," Tel observed.

"Yes." He stared at her intently, waiting to see whether she were real, whether her figure would dissolve into that of a Rynaif Security Proctor. She stretched out a hand and touched his face. The unexpected caress made him shiver.

"Are you?" he asked.

"Am I what?"

"Real?"

She folded him into her arms, cradling his head against the wonderful softness of her breasts. Still he could not relax.

He said, "Tel, have you ever seen six people—three couples, the mals with long hair and long untrimmed beards, and the fems young-looking, very thin, with hair longer than yours?

They all wear peculiar hats—"

His voice wandered on and on as he described clothing, shoes, the musical instrument, the back pouches, the small contraband animal.

"It must have been an exceptionally vivid dream," she said. "Do you mean—have I ever seen characters like that in the Valley?"

"Yes."

"No, I haven't, and if they'd ever showed up there, I couldn't have missed them. Valley people don't go in for contrived costumes and clothing fads. They can't afford them. They have to make do with what comes to hand. Hairiness we have plenty of, as you've noticed, but not the rest of it. I can't remember even one character who matches your description."

Caland's mind was performing gyrations. If the six "for the Valley" had never arrived there, perhaps they had been following him. Because his destination had not been the Valley when he arrived on Mort. They could have changed their clothing, trimmed their hair, and presented themselves at the Paradise View Hostelry looking like silly tourists.

Tel was becoming alarmed. She caressed his face again and asked, "What is it? What's bothering you?"

"I'm beginning to remember," Caland said.

CHAPTER TWELVE

Doctor Stran Gormaz seemed offensively bright and alert when Caland met him in the hote's salon for their break. He already had ordered a lavish break for two, and he greeted Caland effusively and heaped a platter for him. Caland, still feeling woozy after his unsettling nightmare and a bad night's sleep, regarded him with ill-concealed resentment.

"No, please," he protested. "I supped extremely well, and—"

"In the Valley?" Gormaz interrupted.

"Yes."

"Which restaurant?"

"The Fig Stump."

"How is it?"

"Superb. Magnificent. Incomparable."

Gormaz nodded. "I've heard they're both very good. I must try them before I leave. A tourist hote is a most inappropriate base for launching a scientific project. I'm running behind schedule. In fact, I'm making very little progress. Normally I would work through the local university, but here my credentials are meaningless." He gestured disgustedly. "There's a sociological puzzle about this place that I haven't been able to fathom. A resort hote seems to attract a certain type of unattached fem. It also attracts a certain type of unattached mal. The mal goes chasing off to the Valley's Houses of Fame. The fem pursues other guests who are only asking to be left alone. Now—why can't those two types make each other happy?" He fixed his hypnotic gaze intently on Caland. "But it never seems to work out that way. Sometimes I think we sociologists should abandon theory entirely and occupy ourselves with the solution of practical problems like that one."

"I wish you would," Caland said, with feeling.

"You too, eh?" Gormaz fingered his untidy growth of facial hair. "This character named Mathild—but you've met her." He shook his head and chewed meditatively. His two tufts of hair looked even more wilted this morning—perhaps in testimony to yesterday's pursuit and flight.

"Is Pakovich the type to be receptive to the idea of a sociological laboratory?" Caland asked.

"That's precisely what I have to find out. Some people are instantly receptive to new ideas. Some can be reasoned and persuaded. Some resist thinking about anything at all. To mention only three categories. I have to find out which one Pakovich belongs to. He's only one factor in several that I must consider, but he's the most important one, and it'd be silly for me to invest time here without appraising him personally. All I want is a close look at him and an idea of how he reacts to things. Is there anything you're interested in discussing with him?" His hoarse, booming voice filled the salon and attracted stares from the handful of guests who were enjoying an early break.

"Nothing," Caland said. "I'll leave the whole interview to you. A man who owns a world arouses a certain curiosity, and I'll be interested in meeting him, but I'll be more interested in enjoying the view from his mansion. It ought to be spectacular."

"What do you know about Pakovich?"

"Except for gossip, nothing at all."

"Gossip has it uses. I've been gleaning a lot of it. Pakovich is sixty-four years old. His wife has been dead for fifteen years. Apparently there's never been a breath of scandal connecting him with another fem, either before or after he became a widower. His only child, a son, is in his late twenties and seems to get along well with his father. The name Alexander Pakovich the Second seems like a horrible burden to inflict on a child, but he's adapted to it. He's working his way into the upper echelon of Pak Enterprises management with a kind of plodding competence. So Pakovich not only owns a world, but he has a son who is a modest credit to him and with whom he has a satisfying family relationship."

"He seems to be a mal without problems," Caland observed.

Gormaz nodded. "His health is good. He has all the wealth he could desire, and its numerical dimensions are irrelevant—he can magnify it by ten, or by a hundred, or by a thousand, any time he chooses. He hasn't even begun to exploit the resources of this world. He's the legendary mortal who has everything, and he's done the legend one better by having a world to keep it on. So the question is—what's bothering him? Why isn't that enough?"

Caland feigned surprised interest.

"The man owns a world," Doctor Gormaz went on. "Along with his enormous wealth, he has enormous power, and he finds it gratifying to possess and satisfying to wield. On this world, he's very close to divinity. He rewards the deserving and sternly inflicts punishment on transgressors. If he makes a mistake, and he does occasionally, he corrects it with generous magnanimity. The only check on his power is his own conscience. He has everything, he can do whatever he wants, his health is good, his family relationship is far better than that achieved by most mals—so what's bothering him?"

Caland had the answer, thanks to Sam the Artist. Pakovich might be close to divinity on Mort, but in high society on Aravia he was a slob and the son of a space pirate. He did not belong. The Aravian nabobs would do business with him, they would let their servants work him for grats, and they would flatter him if it seemed profitable to do so, but they wouldn't *invite* him. Pakovich sat up there in his mountainside retreat, lord of all he surveyed, and brooded about that.

This was why Pakovich had so eagerly granted an interview to two interlopers, one of whom was named Caland. Because Caland belonged. He might be the wreck of a man and a renegade from a disreputable profession, but the status Pakovich could never attain was his by birthright. If Caland went to Aravia, high society would invite him to every ripple it made. It would attempt to inflict its unmarried daughters on him, even if they were unwilling, and since he was a Caland, probably they wouldn't be. Pakovich envied that and respected it. There was no mystery at all about what was bothering him, but evidently Doctor Gormaz hadn't heard about the son's betrothal to an Aravian princess. The only thing that puzzled Caland was how the son of a Pakovich had managed to get himself accepted. She must be an extremely impoverished noblefem.

Gormaz continued to eat voraciously. Caland, his stomach still queasy from Fig Stump food and his bad night, played the finicky eater, tasting and rejecting. The flood of recollections he was experiencing unsettled him as much as his rebellious stomach. His childhood, his youth, his acting career were memories on the march, but as usual they came to a quivering halt at the barrier his accident had inflicted upon him.

"Sure you don't want to eat more?" Gormaz asked.

Caland shook his head.

Gormaz swallowed the last mouthful. "They serve a good break here. The other meals are insipid. You don't want any more? Then let's go."

They boarded an electrocab in front of the hote. The driver's neatly trimmed beard was familiar to Caland; he had seen him in the Valley. The 'cab was another cut-down monstrosity with one striking difference: the benches actually had padding on them.

The moment they were underway, Dr. Gormaz resumed his meditation about Pakovich. "The man has a conscience," he said. "He tries, and sometimes he even succeeds. On the other hand, his employees call him a snooping bastard. He held up one employee's promotion because his lawn needed trimming. Pakovich sits up there in his mansion with some kind of telescope and watches everything that goes on in the city of Paradise. If an employee puts his trash bags in the wrong place, or leaves a door unrepaired, down comes a memo from on high. Pakovich is said to have a map showing who lives in every house in Paradise, and what the employee's job is, and what shift he works. The employees claim that he checks kitchen lights before the morning shifters leave for the mines. If a light doesn't go on at a certain time, Pakovich figures the worker's wife is lying in bed and letting him go off to work without a break. Down comes another memo. Pak Enterprises workers toe the line. If they don't, they get passed over for promotions and raises."

Caland, still occupied with his stirrings of memory, simulated polite attention by asking a question. "Is he stingy?"

Gormaz pondered the question. "No. I don't think anyone would call him that. Many say he's an open, generous mal, highly concerned about doing the right thing for his employees and their families. But he's very cautious and extremely thrifty. He likes to get his money's worth, and he hates to waste money."

They were passing through Paradise, which for all of its trim neatness looked depressingly regimented. All of the well-kept plots were landscaped in the same uninspired manner, with the same kinds of shrubs and trees placed in identical locations. The round, white cement dwellings looked bleakly alike, as did the wide paved streets.

"But the dwellings aren't quite identical," Doctor Gormaz said. "They come in four different sizes, arranged by neighborhoods. The higher the position and the longer the employee's seniority, the larger his house. For those on the management level, there are fairly lavish villas in the suburbs. Pakovich has his rewards well organized. One thing is certain—the people have ambivalent attitudes toward Pakovich, but all of them love Mort. It *is* a beautiful world, it's an ideal place to raise children—the Paradise school is excellent—and compared with other corporation towns, this one is very good indeed. But I think the people would be much happier if God looked the other way now and then."

They put the city of Paradise behind them, and the road began to climb.

"I mentioned to an old-timer that Pakovich always tries to do the right thing," Doctor Gormaz said. "He agreed. But he thought it a great pity that Pakovich usually is too stupid to know what the right thing is. 'He was dumb as a kid and didn't get any smarter with age.' Probably that's as much as I need to know about him, but I'll have to see him anyway."

For a short distance they followed a broad highway that connected all of the Pak Enterprises: the mines, the hydro-electric plant, farms, dairy, packing plant, forest industries. Behind them, the highway looped around the city of Paradise and became the Bay Road that passed the Valley on its way to the fertilizer plant and Fish Town, the residence of the fishers and the plant's employees. Ahead of them, and northeast of the city of Paradise, the highway divided. The broad branch led to the mines and the ore processing establishments. The other, a narrow but excellently surfaced and maintained road, pointed steeply upward.

They took the narrow road, and their 'cab's electric motor sharpened its whirr to a high-pitched whine under the strain of the steep ascent. The road made great ascending loops across the face of the mountainside, and the lovely land below slowly dropped away from them. Finally they came to a gate, gave their names to a dignified, uniformed, white-haired attendant—who seemed to be unarmed—and moved along a drive that curved among lavishly landscaped lawns and gardens. They coasted to a stop before the mansion's pillared portico. Caland and Doctor Gormaz negotiated the high step to the ground, and the 'cab driver whirred the vehicle over to a parking allotment on the far side of the drive.

Caland turned to study the building. For a private dwelling, it seemed enormous, and its structure was unique among Mort buildings. Pakovich had used native woods for his palace, oblit-erating their colors and grains with a gleaming white chemical sealant.

The totally dressed butler—tall, gaunt, depressingly solemn—opened the door for them as they approached. He admitted them with ceremony and placed them in a vast reception room that bristled with the most bizarre collection of antiques Caland had ever seen. Doctor Gormaz, obviously not one to be intimidated by ceremony or surroundings, moved about the room with pursed lips, occasionally shaking his head over one of the more grotesque furnishings.

Neither was Caland intimidated. He had grown up in a larger mansion, furnished impeccably, and totally dressed butlers were not a novelty item to him. He savored the memory of it, reflecting that Pakovich's potential wealth was probably unequaled in the galaxy, but Caland's father certainly controlled far more monetary credits—though both were on a financial level where rank had become meaningless. On any other level, Pakovich held no rank whatsoever. There had been several Pakoviches among his father's business associates, all of them social misfits who—like Pakovich—did not belong, and all of them possessed the same deplorably bad taste. Caland thought he knew how Pakovich's mind worked.

Before Caland could decide which of the twenty or so uncomfortable chairs he wanted to occupy, the butler returned. He bowed formally and invited them to follow him.

Alexander Pakovich received them in an elongated plastic bubble that served as the veranda. He padded forward to greet them, smiling broadly—short, stocky, hair graying around the fringes, figure beginning to take on the contours of fat. He was superbly and uncouthly at ease—sandals on his feet, expensive lounge suit casually cut and violently patterned and colored. He touched hands with both of them and offered them their choice of a cluster of comfortable lounge chairs.

"Mal Caland," he murmured. His voice was just high enough pitched to sound abnormal. "The world of Mort is indeed honored to have you as its guest. And—er—Doctor Gormaz, also."

The doctor bowed solemnly and shot Caland an amused glance. Then he stepped to the edge of the veranda and looked out. Caland joined him.

"What a magnificent view!" Caland exclaimed.

He meant it. Mort's occupied stretch of coast lay below him in vibrant color: the city of Paradise, the hotes, the Annex with its bazaar and art colony. Off to the south, where the bay curved back to meet the ocean, the decaying structures that constituted the Valley were dark smudges partially concealed by strangely different tints of vegetation. Just beyond, on the ocean, was the fertilizer factory. The brightly painted fishing boats at its broad piers were sparkling lines on the dancing water. South of the factory was the small fish town community, a second conglomeration of concrete hives. Colored sails dotted Paradise Bay. The view was in every respect spectacular.

Probably this veranda and its sweeping panorama offered more insight into Pakovich's soul than even a hypnostudy could achieve. At daybreak, the little coastal plain would lay purpled with the dawn's expectations, and lights would show in many of the trim, circular houses below as the people of Paradise— Pakovich's people—struggled to wakefulness. Paradise Bay, which sparkled with swirling, multi-colored radiance under the sun, would be a tirelessly undulating dark cloak for unimagined secrets. The scene would evolve slowly, minute by minute, as the day unfolded from glint of dawn to full-blown light of noon; then would come the slow reversal until night posted its scattered artificial lights as sentries awaiting a new daybreak. Such a view easily could give a mal a diurnal illusion of divinity, especially if it were reinforced by the fact that he literally was the master of all that he surveyed. Each morning Pakovich could stand on this veranda and look upon his work and find it good.

Then he could step to his breakfast table in his pajamas and have his godliness underscored by the attentive service of a totally dressed butler. No wonder Pakovich resented the slights from Aravian high society and brooded about them.

As Caland turned away, he noted the binoculars on a nearby table. It was true that Pakovich snooped. Few people, living in that mansion with time on their hands, could have resisted the temptation.

"A magnificent view of a magnificent world," Caland said. "We tourists have been enjoying it immensely, but not as much as you do, I'm sure."

Gormaz added his own effusive appreciation. Pakovich beamed at them and again indicated the chairs, and the three of them sat down.

"What brings you to Mort?" Pakovich asked.

He addressed the question to Caland, but the smiling Doctor Gormaz quickly interposed his own answer. "As Mal Caland remarked, we're tourists. I suppose you could say that Mort brings us to Mort."

Pakovich's own smile broadened. He turned again to Caland; but Caland already had performed his obeisance to propriety. He was leaving the conversation to Doctor Gormaz.

The two mals formed an amusing contrast. They were the same general shape—short, sturdy in stature, rotund. Probably they were about the same age, though Gormaz looked younger. But Gormaz seemed muscular where Pakovich conveyed an impression of flabbiness. The sociologist bristled with energy. He had work to do, and he was impatient to get on with it. Pakovich had nothing to do. Whatever else might be said for the role of deity, it totally destroyed ambition. What was there for a god to dream about?

"We really have no excuse at all for imposing on you," Gormaz said. "We were merely curious."

"Curious?" Pakovich ruminated as though the word were new to him. He managed to convey the impression that he had never been curious about anything.

Gormaz gestured at the magnificent sweep of view, still visible from their chairs. "You have a splendid world. Its potential is nothing less than colossal. Why do you use so little of it?"

Pakovich gazed at him perplexedly.

"Your world is famous," Gormaz said, "but for the wrong reasons. It ought to be famous for what it is. Paradise. Instead, it's famous for what it's not. Death. All because the word Mort has that fluke double meaning. Don't the death jokes bother you?"

"They amused my father," Pakovich said. "I grew up with them. I learned to ignore them."

"I heard a new one last evening," Gormaz said. "It came from a tourist who'd decided to cut short his visit here. He said, 'On a death world, the only activity is dying'."

Pakovich stiffened. His plump grin shifted gears and became a scowl. "What are you two selling?" he demanded.

Gormaz met his gaze sternly. "Mal Pakovich," he said. "Mal Caland's home and all of his business interests are a long, long way from here, and—as much as he admires your world—when he leaves, it's unlikely that he'll ever be able to return. If he had anything at all to sell you, he has employees who can handle that function very capably. As for me, I'm a scholar. I convey nothing but ideas, and I accept no payment for them."

Pakovich's scowl had faded. His expression acknowledged a just admonishment for a breach of good manners, but he continued to eye them warily.

"As I said," Gormaz went on, "we called on you because we were curious. Your splendid hotes, so well designed, so efficiently run, are always more than half-empty. This beautiful world has a reputation that is both unfortunate and undeserved. Something should be done to counter it. You need some civic boosting."

Pakovich's expression implied that he lumped civic boosting with epidemics, natural catastrophes, and the discovery of new tin deposits on Aravia.

"The problem with this world," Gormaz went on, "is that nothing ever happens here."

Pakovich turned for a long look at the breathtaking view. "That," he announced with a smug smile, "is one of the best things about Mort. Tourists who want to get away from it all don't go where things happen."

Gormaz shook his head. "You're wrong. Getting away from it all doesn't mean going where nothing happens. It means going where something different happens. Look. Your hotes have a splendid view of a remarkably beautiful bay, with a lovely beach, but even the most spectacular scenic beauties pall when they confront one hour after hour and day after day. A few days of that, and your tourists take to staying inside and getting drunk. No doubt that's good for the lounge business, but they could get drunk somewhere else just as easily and without paying resort prices. By the time they get home, they have that worked out for themselves. Resort owners tell me that the ideal customer is one who returns year after year. Too many of your tourists will never come back. Worse, they'll go home and say that a death world is a great vacation place for anyone who's already dead. The Valley thrives because so many of Mort's tourists get bored. They begin to wonder whether the place lives up to its reputation. It doesn't, but after a few days on a world where nothing happens, it seems to."

Pakovich was flushing angrily.

"The money they spend in the Valley doesn't help you," Gormaz said, "and the fact that they only go there because they're bored doesn't help Mort. You need a program of promotion that will bring streams of tourists to Mort, and keep them happy here, and bring them back again next year."

Pakovich asked icily, "What kind of promotion?"

"A *program* of promotion that would have something going on every day in the year. Tourists could ignore it and sit on the beach or the veranda if they wanted to, but when they tired of that there'd be something else to do. Know what yesterday's entertainment consisted of? I took a long electrobus ride."

"What kind of thing going on every day?" Pakovich's voice had taken on a menacing tone.

"You need a year-around schedule, so a tourist could say, 'Ah—the Tin Festival was great. I'll see it again next year, but I'll plan my vacation to overlap with the Paradise Golf Tournament, so I can take that in, too'."

"Tin Festival?" Pakovich echoed dazedly. "Golf Tournament?"

"Or the Paradise Bazaar," Gormaz went on. "Fill Paradise

Park with tents. Carnival kind of show. Then there'd be the Paradise Beauty Pageant. Or the Paradise Flower Show—all the exotic blooms of a world on display. Or a special event, 'Days and Nights of Paradise,' timed to coincide with the harvest of the native fruit. Then you could use the motto, 'All the fruit you can eat, whenever you want it, free of charge'."

Pakovich winced. "Anything that's free is expensive to someone, and too frequently it's expensive to me. Where are you going to get golf players for a tournament and fems and mals for a beauty pageant? The Employees' Association talked about building a golf course years ago, but there weren't enough interested people to form a committee."

"Import the golfers," Doctor Gormaz said cheerfully. "Import professionals, that is, and make amateurs welcome. People interested in golf will time their vacations so they can watch the tournament or take part in it. They'll even pay for the privilege. If you offer prizes, handsome young mals and fems will come long distances for a beauty competition, but you have plenty of local talent. What you need is something happening all the time. Live theater, concerts, opera—"

"No!" Pakovich rasped.

"Tourists would come in streams."

"No! I don't want streams of tourists mucking up my world. My hotes show a good profit as it is, and I don't need more. I don't even need that. This was a nicer world when there weren't any tourists."

Gormaz started to speak, and Pakovich silenced him with an arrogant gesture. This was God on His native hearth, and He was in no mood to tolerate arguments. He was not even amenable to spirited discussion.

Except that no one could have envisioned Pakovich as God or even as King. He was a plump little mal of no more than average intelligence who hated to make discussions and who was accustomed to having his own way—always.

"To hold a golf tournament," Pakovich said, "I'd have to build a golf course. I don't want to own a golf course. Once the tournament was over, I'd have to use it myself to get any good out of it, and I don't want to play golf. To hold a beauty pageant and make it a success, I'd have to spend millions for publicity. I don't want Mort to have that kind of publicity. For live theater and concerts and the like, I'd have to build a theater and hire actors and musicians. I don't want any. People can enjoy all those things somewhere else. I like Mort the way it is, and I want the kind of tourists who like it the way it is."

He scrambled to his feet. Now he was trying to simulate a God of Thunder dismissing unwanted guests, but since one of them was named Caland, he had to be polite about it. "I'm glad you think Mort is beautiful, and I hope you enjoy your electrobus rides. *But don't try to change my world.*"

Caland and Gormaz exchanged glances. They got up slowly. "I'm only sorry that more tourists aren't enjoying it, Mal Pakovich," Caland said.

"My sentiments exactly," Gormaz murmured.

They took a few steps toward the door, where the butler's formidable totally dressed figure had materialized magically and stood waiting to escort them out.

"Not even a Tin Festival?"

"I'll think about it," Pakovich said, "but I don't think I'm going to like it."

Doctor Gormaz nodded. He spoke a polite, "Good morning," the two of them nodded pleasantly at Pakovich's muttered response, and they followed the butler. Pakovich's final, growled sentence chased them on their way. *"Leave my world alone."*

Gormaz and Caland did not speak until their 'cab had started its whirring, meandering route down the mountain. The driver put the vehicle in over, converting his motor to generator and charging his batteries on the descent. The result was a penetrating, high-pitched whine that blanketed their conversation.

Doctor Gormaz leaned close to Caland and asked, "What do you think of him?"

"Obviously, he'll never be one of the doers of the universe," Caland said. "He's content to leave things as they are, especially when he likes them that way and a change would cost money. His attitude is that the doers of the universe may leave a few impressive monuments, but they also cause a lot of unnecessary turmoil and unsettle a lot of lives."

"He never acts," Gormaz said. "He reacts. He only built his resort hotes to compete with the modest resort business the Valley once had."

"Perhaps he would act if his world were threatened." Caland said, thinking of Fellington Felroy.

Gormaz shook his head. "That would be a reaction."

"Did you get what you wanted?"

"Not what I wanted. What I had to have. It definitely wasn't what I wanted." He paused. "The situation is far worse than I expected. I'm very much afraid—but do you mind our stopping at the Government Mall for a few minutes?"

Caland minded very much. He wanted to get back to the hote, and put himself on conspicuous display, and get the ordeal over with. He assented because he had no choice, and Gormaz promised that it wouldn't take long.

"Have you met a fellow guest of ours named Fellington Felroy?" Caland asked.

"Not that I recollect. Why?"

"I heard him talking about Pakovich. His opinion is similar to yours, except that he thinks one shouldn't underestimate how fiercely Pakovich could react."

Doctor Gormaz shrugged. "A blind mal could react fiercely, but his choice of responses would be limited. If he tried to exceed those limitations, he'd fall."

"True enough," Caland agreed.

Pakovich was blind. He would refuse to believe in the possibility of a conspiracy until it erupted in his face. And then he would fight, fiercely, with no consideration at all for his limitations.

They threaded their way through the city of Paradise to the Government Mall, a sprawling complex of buildings solidly and massively constructed of concrete slabs. At the administrative building, Doctor Gormaz strode purposefully to the Paradise Super's office and sent in their names: two visitors to Mort requesting an interview with Alexander Pakovich the Second. Caland noted with amusement that the doctor listed his own name first. Alexander the Second would be far less conversant with moneratings than his father, but he might be impressed with Gormaz's title.

Alexander the Second received them immediately. He was a good-looking young mal of slight build with a narrow, sensitive face. His sandy hair already seemed to be thinning on top. His voice was pleasant. He wore casual dress, but he did so naturally and unassumingly. He neither looked nor acted like his father.

"What can I do for you?" he asked politely.

Gormaz explained. He was vacationing on Mort, and, as a scholar of social structures, he frequently combined business with pleasure. He wanted permission to consult Mort's official archives, which were housed in the Paradise library, and he had discovered that non-residents of Paradise were not permitted to use the library.

"There must be some mistake," the younger Pakovich said perplexedly. "Tourists are routinely granted the same library privileges as residents. The question seldom comes up, because few tourists are interested, but that has been the official policy ever since the tourist hotes were built. Do you mean that the library refused to serve you?"

"Not directly," Doctor Gormaz said. "It was my secretary who was refused. Of course that amounts to a refusal of myself. I've hired a secretary to work for me during my stay here. It's a very competent young mal who lives in the Valley."

"Ah!" Pakovich the Second nodded slowly. "I see. That would explain it. No Valley resident has any kind of library privilege." He thought for a moment. "If he's your secretary, and he's only requesting to use the library as a necessary function of his employment by you, then of course he wouldn't be exercising the privilege for himself." He paused again. "It *is* a problem. If you will leave the pertinent information with my secretary, I'll see what I can do for you."

"Thank you very much," Gormaz said.

They took their leave of him, passed through the outer office without speaking to the secretary, and returned to their 'cab.

"It's much worse than I expected," Gormaz said as they whirred their way back to the hote. "That youngster will never stand up to his father in anything. He can't even make a simple decision like that without studying the law according to the senior Pakovich and probably making an official request for an exception. I'm afraid I'll have to abandon my idea of placing a laboratory on this planet. Too bad. It *is* a beautiful place."

The remark sounded chillingly similar to something Fellington Felroy had said. Caland wondered if those studying a planet had much the same attitude toward their subject as those looting a planet.

He said nothing, because he had a problem of his own to meditate. He had never met Alexander Pakovich the Second, but he had seen him before. He was certain of it. He had recognized him at once.

CHAPTER THIRTEEN

They slept in the Valley that night, ending what Tel called their durance luxurious.

Caland first had to place himself on conspicuous display. Nothing happened. From mid-morning until mid-afternoon, without pause for din—Caland's stomach was attempting to cope with Doctor Gormaz's break on top of the lavish Fig Stump sup—he cultivated accessibility. He sat on the veranda near the entrance watching the bay; he sat in the lounge with an untouched Nectar of Paradise in front of him and smiled receptively at each and every passerby; he walked slowly through the hote's public rooms, detouring into unoccupied corners in case anyone wanted to approach him privately. The only person who gave him more than a passing glance was Fem Wobbons, who rewarded his ostentatious solitude with an archly sly smile whenever she walked by.

Finally Tel dropped a whispered instruction as she passed him. He strolled over to the Art Bazaar with her following circuitously. There, at the last moment, they had a nibble. A plump mal tourist—a carbon copy of fifty or two hundred other plump mal tourists Caland had seen that day, emerged from the bazaar, started to walk past Caland, hesitated, turned on him in evident surprise.

"Why—it's Jarv! I wondered what had happened to you. Did you find your way to the Dolls' House?"

Caland hoped his disconcertedness did not show. "Of course," he said. "To Yda's, too."

The plump tourist chuckled. "Of course you did. You look it. Better get some rest!"

Still chuckling, he moved on.

The moment he'd passed beyond a screen of shrubbery, Tel pounced. She handed Caland over to a 'cab driver named Knack and hurried after the plump tourist. Knack drove Caland directly to the Valley, where Sam the Artist claimed him and took him to the room above the Fig Stump. Tel arrived, and then Arlu and the Reverend; and Yda—sumptuously attired in a clinging afternoon gown—looked in to see how Caland had held up under the ordeal of a couple of days' association with tourists.

Arlu was resplendent in a checkered black and white suit that gave him the aspect of a monstrous optical illusion. Yda hooted when she saw him. "Look at that! With Arlu, seeing is never believing!"

Arlu's chins fluttered a grin. "You're looking well, Yda. If only you'd dress more stylishly, like Tel—"

"Screet!" Tel rasped. She looked down at her gaudy tourist clothing. "I wanted to change first. Let's get on with it."

Sam the Artist cleared his throat ruminatively. "I think Tel looks entrancing. If I had my choice—"

"You don't," Tel said. She turned to Arlu. "What have you found out?"

"A few bits," Arlu said. "We already knew that Dombrily was on Rynaif when Cal was there, but the Wesfulm thing was a complete surprise. He was a Pak Enterprises accountant. He went to attend an institute on Rynaif and disappeared there. No one on either Mort or Rynaif professes to know what happened to him. He dined, he was seen to leave his hote, and he never returned. Rynaif authorities are baffled."

"How'd you come up with that so fast?" Sam the Artist demanded.

"Chan Worntling got it from the security people at Pak Enterprises. The Valley's enforcers keep in touch with them. Cooperation on certain levels benefits everyone, and a few of Pakovich's employees aren't idiots. I can add one more bit myself. There really was a mysterious explosion in Rynaif City. I don't recall the exact date, but it'll certainly check, since everything else does. It caused a stir, but the Rynaif Proctors dismissed it as a natural phenomenon. No damage to persons or property."

Caland leaned forward. "Two mals disappeared in it," he said stubbornly.

"Ah, well. A natural phenomenon can be turned over to the scientists and forgotten. Crimes are very bad publicity and have to be searched. As long as no human debris was found, the proctors aren't going to strain their imaginations to cause trouble for themselves. They especially aren't going out of the way to find evidence of an attempt on the life of a specific person. That would open up all manner of complicated searches. As for Wes Fulm's story, Pak Enterprises has indeed been beset with sabotage problems. It's a widely known secret that no one dares to mention. Machines inexplicably break down or go out of adjustment, and by some peculiar coincidence, it's always a malfunction that disrupts ore shipments."

"What does that have to do with Cal?" Yda asked.

"Tangled threads," Arlu mused. "Tangled threads. But we can begin to maybe pick out a few knots. Cal's adventure with Wes Fulm took place on Rynaif. Mort's principal customer is the world of Aravia, which is highly dependent on Mort for tin. Any failure of Mort's tin production, due to sabotage or whatever, would have serious repercussions on Aravia. The chief beneficiary would be the world of Rynaif, which is Aravia's major industrial rival. These are murky doings, and no casual search is going to penetrate them. Dombrily certainly knows something about it. He was in touch with Fulm, who visited him in the Valley. He was on Rynaif when the explosion happened. Dombrily says he's never been to Rynaif and didn't know Fulm. In veriest fact, it does make one wonder what happened that would cause him to lie so elaborately."

"You didn't answer the question," Sam the Artist said.

"What's Cal have to do with all that murkiness?"

"Cal is the storm center. He's the eye of the hurricane. Wherever he goes, inexplicable things happen. An innocent little accountant speaks to him on Rynaif and gets blown up. Worlds he casually visits are wracked by quakes, tidal waves, and volcanic action. He can't call at a peaceful world like Mort without sharing his hote with a couple of interworld con men. Sabotage happens, and we find links to Cal. The real oddity is that all of this trouble happens only to other people. He passes through it untouched."

"That's a nasty thing to say about a mal who was killed in an accident," Tel said.

"Indeed it is. Because the accident was real, and so were Cal's sufferings—were and are. Cal really does wear a metal bowl under his scalp, and his brain is wired together in what must have been one of the most fantastic neurosurgical performances in history. There's some connection with him, and we've got to find out what it is. The problem is made infinitely more complicated by the havoc inflicted on his memory." He turned to Caland. "Wes Fulm actually asked for a prober?"

Caland nodded.

"Incredible. For sabotage in a mining establishment. Did he suspect that another world might be involved?"

"Definitely not," Caland said. "That idea never would have occurred to him."

"There've been a lot of fanciful stories about probers," Tel said. "Timid types like Fulm often are vivid readers of adventure literature. The stories show probers fighting for justice and bringing infamy down to a crashing defeat—just the stuff that would appeal to him."

"He certainly thought that the sabotage was infamy," Caland agreed. "He described it in even stronger terms. He said employee sabotage would be most disloyal."

Sam the Artist was frowning furiously and absently tugging at his beard. "Cal talked with Fulm on Rynaif. Fulm died in an explosion. Cal came to Mort. Is any of that cause and effect?"

"The veriest question," Arlu murmured. "Absolutely the veriest. If we knew the answer to that, we'd have half the mystery. That strange encounter with Fulm would seem to be accidental, but what other connection can we find between Cal and the world of Mort? Fellington Felroy is a figure out of Cal's remote past. He'd been on Mort for more than a sennite when Cal arrived. Surely we can write him off as a coincidence. Then we have this mysterious fem whom Cal recognized on Mort because he'd seen her before. That seems intriguing, but he easily could have seen her at the Paradise View when he first arrived on Mort."

Caland closed his eyes. "It was in a park. Or a park-like place. She sat down across the Promenade from me. But I can't remember enough to say where it was."

"Then it could have been on Mort?"

"I suppose, though I don't remember seeing a place on Mort that was anything like that. It's hard to remember when reality gets mixed up with nightmares. Dreams distort and rearrange things, and I end up not knowing which was which."

"Either way, there's not much we can do about this unless you see the fem again or remember something else. So we have Fellington Felroy, an obvious coincidence. We have a mystery fem who can't be classified until we know more about her. And we have Wes Fulm, whose contact with Cal maybe resulted only because they accidently sat beside each other at din." He turned to Caland. "Can you add to this list? Did you recognize anyone at all while you were on display?"

"I only recognized people I saw for the first time yesterday. Fem Wobbons. Doctor Gormaz. A silly fem named Mathild. A whole lot of guests whose faces were vaguely familiar. I suppose it's possible that I saw some of them on my first stay at the hote, but I still haven't remembered anything about that." He paused. "There *was* someone I recognized, but he wasn't at the hote. It was Alexander Pakovich the Second. I recognized him at once. I've seen him somewhere, but I can't remember when or where."

It caused a stir. Arlu left his recliner with a snap and leaned forward. "He hasn't been away from Mort for terms, has he?" he asked Tel.

"Not since he returned from Aravia. And I doubt that he's ever been out of this sector."

"So Cal must have seen him at the hote. His job takes him there occasionally. But why would Cal remember him so distinctly?" Arlu sighed and sank back against the recliner. "Probably means nothing at all, but I'll have to search it. Anything else?"

"Just as we were leaving, a tourist spoke to him," Tel said.

Faces turned toward Caland. He shook his head. "I don't remember him. He must have been on the ship with me."

"He was," Tel said. "His name is Weflan Krann."

"In the ship's lounge, there was a lot of talk about hedonism and the Houses of Fame," Caland said. "I remember a blur of faces, but I couldn't say whether his was one of them. He must have been there, because he called me 'Jarv.' That was how I introduced myself."

Arlu raised his hands despairingly. "Probably nothing. He saw you there and remembered you. I'll have to search him, of course. Well." He sighed again. "I'm trying to reconstruct Cal's route across the galaxy. Thus far, one interesting thing stands out. The only *long* visits he made to any worlds were those to Cenaru, Olyndyt, and Skarlont. He remained on each of those worlds for several terms. Any new memories about Cenaru, Olyndyt, and Skarlont, Cal?"

Caland closed his eyes and pressed his fists against his forehead. "No. The catastrophes are mixed up with nightmares, and I don't know what happened there or how much of it is real.

"What about towers?"

"Maybe. Maybe a glimpse. But I don't know if that's because I remember or because you told me about them."

Mmmm." Arlu absently tapped his index fingers together. "It's a dilemma, and I don't see any way to avoid it." He turned to the others. "We have a considerable problem, you know. Cal made long visits to those three worlds, and catastrophes struck them. Now he's making a long visit to Mort. Question is, does that mean—"

"Nonsense!" Tel exploded. "Cal is making a long visit to the Valley, at least, because we placed him under restraint when he was being made to leave. If we hadn't, he might have left Mort by now."

"Maybe," Arlu conceded. "You may be right."

Sam the Artist nudged the Reverend and said lightly, "Too bad we don't have Odan's mathematical formulas. We could send Cal back in time for another look at things, and we'd have this mess straightened out in short order."

Arlu scowled. "Who is Odan?"

"It's a joke," Sam the Artist said. "The Reverend gave us a glimpse of his sinful past—he was studying mathematical physics, of all things, and he was telling us about some great mathematicians who proved mathematically that it's possible to do almost anything. Travel through time, or levitate, or teleport, or communicate mentally."

"Odan," the Reverend said, "worked out the formulas for teleportation. Zareent was the mathematician of time travel."

"I see," Arlu said. "You say someone proved it possible to communicate mentally?"

"Fremanz was the mathematician of systematic telepathy," the Reverend said.

"I see. How recent was this?"

"Maybe three hundred years ago."

"But those scientists could have had followers or founded schools?"

"I suppose they could have. If they did, their followers never advance the masters' work, or it would have been referenced."

"I see." Arlu had resumed tapping his index fingers. "I'm thinking about those towers. That suggests communication. I'm wondering if the towers could have been intended to send thought waves to Cal through that metal in his head."

"Surely that would be an awkward way to communicate," the Reverend said. "So much easier to give him an inexpensive receiver and use electromagnetic waves."

"That depends on the motive," Arlu said. "My hunch is that the motive in this case is not merely complicated but convoluted. The objective wouldn't have been to communicate, but to control a person through signals to his brain. What if Cal were only an experimental model, and the next step would be to control the brains of people who don't have the metal? Ultimately, to control the thinking and actions of an entire population? If that sounds far-fetched, tell me something about Cal that isn't far-fetched. Who did you say this mathematician of telepathy was?"

"Fremanz," the Reverend said.

Arlu made a note. "Something else to search."

"But the danger still would have to come from the towers," Sam the Artist said. "And how does telepathy work in with quakes and volcanoes and tidal waves?"

"And," the Reverend added, "there aren't any towers on Mort."

"We don't know that," Arlu said. "Mort has millions and millions of square kilometers of forests. It'd be easy to hide a few towers from Pakovich's blundering administrators."

"There aren't any towers around here," Sam the Artist persisted. "Towers in the other hemisphere may constitute a threat to Mort, but they wouldn't harm Mort's human population. Even Pakovich's administrators aren't so inept that they would overlook a strange tower on their doorstep, and no one's going to smuggle a tower into the Valley unnoticed."

Caland was seated by a window. He turned and looked out. "But someone has," he said.

All of them stared at him.

"I'm looking at it now," Caland said.

They all crowded around him, even Arlu. And directly before them loomed a tower—the gleaming, silver silhouette of Baris Bronlan's spaceship.

* * * * * * *

That evening Cal and Tel went swimming in the ocean. Baris Bronlan, perched on his boulder to watch the sunset, remained long after his usual time of departure to enjoy the spectacle of humans swimming in his adored, untamed ocean. Caland, who was unaccustomed to nude bathing, felt self-conscious. Tel obviously did not. She tied her long hair into a loose knot, and her sturdy body made its own poetry as she dove, laughing, into the powerful, crashing waves.

Afterward Caland donned the new clothing he had bought— short-length pants the Vals called stubs and a shoulder wrap— and they sat on the beach to rest. Baris Bronlan slipped away into the gathering darkness, and the shadowy figures began to converge on him as he left the beach.

"Who are they?" Caland asked.

"Paras," Tel said indifferently. "Beggars. Every evening Bar gives away a pocketful of chits, one to a customer, first come, first served."

"Doesn't he resent being plagued by beggars?"

"Why should he? If they weren't hungry, they wouldn't beg."

"How many of them try to feed their hunger by working?"

"Bar would say it's important that they be free to work or not work. The right to choose is precious and must be defended."

"That's all very well for philosophy," Caland said slowly. "But it's contrary to human nature. Given a choice between working and not working, half the human race would choose not to work."

"I don't agree," Tel said. "That may be true on worlds where governmental handouts corrupt everyone. In the Valley, those who choose not to work—whether it's because they don't want to, or they can't, or they've simply given up on life—also choose everything that goes with not working: living in squalor, bad diet, getting along without essentials, being hungry enough to beg. It's a part of the choice, just as those who choose to work have to accept the regimentation of their lives, and enslave-ment to time schedules, and boring tasks, and subservience to others. In compensation, they receive an income to spend as they choose. Most humans, given a choice, prefer living in comfortable cells, like those dwellings in Paradise, and paying the price in work and in the loss of time they might otherwise enjoy wasting in order to have the income. The others gather in places like the Valley. Look. Haven't you been feeding hungry people on the beach at night?"

"Yes—"

"You didn't ask why they weren't working. You just asked whether they were hungry. That's all Bar is doing."

Caland was not convinced, but he was in no position to argue. He had existed on anonymous handouts for years.

"It couldn't be Bar," Tel said suddenly. She was referring back to the scene by the Fig Stump window when she and the others had stared in shocked silence at the camouflaged tower Baris Bronlan had erected in the Valley. Everyone present had exploded into protests. Caland had no comment for them, and he made none now. He was not filing an accusation; he was attempting to deal with a fact. The spaceship was a fact.

After the protests had subsided, Caland ventured a question. What about the possibility of someone else using Bronlan's ship for whatever the towers had been used for?

They still wouldn't consider it. In the end, Caland resolved—privately—to ask Bronlan about that possibility himself and see how he reacted. Certainly none of the others would undertake it, and he thought it should be done.

His thoughts returned to Bronlan's cloud of paras. His own two-day ordeal was over, and the effects of the Fig Stump sup and Doctor Gormaz's break had long since faded. He was beginning to feel hungry.

And he had no money. Both he and Tel had returned to Arlu the chits left over from their hote adventure. Never since his accident had Caland had the slightest concern for money. He always regained consciousness with more than enough to satisfy his modest needs. Now he was worse than broke. He was two chits in debt, and there was a looming question of where his next term's rent would come from.

And there was the matter of eating. "Are you hungry?" he asked Tel.

"A little."

"I haven't any money."

"I know. Neither have I. But we won't starve. There's plenty of yuck and glop at the apartment."

Caland shuddered,

"Or we could try a beach fire. We might be lucky enough to draw one with food."

"Or unlucky enough not to," Caland said. He got to his feet.

"Where are you going?" Tel asked.

"To the Prom," Caland said.

They stood in the shadows near the light at the east end of the Prom, the light closest to the gate. As the tourists arrived, Vals swarmed around them. Caland watched with interest. He suddenly had a whole new perspective on the subject of begging. Handled properly, it would not be a way to avoid work. It would *be* work, and he had to fashion a new career for himself or end up starving and sleeping in any shelter the Valley shrubbery could provide.

He muttered to Tel, "Wait here."

Nervously he approached a group of tourists who had just descended from the Valley electrobus. He had to fight the urge to walk past them to the 'bus or to turn and run; but the moment he began to speak, all of his apprehension dropped away. He was an actor. Suddenly his shattered career had been resurrected and he had another role to play.

He played it to the supreme limit of his ability. He quickly caught the correct intonation, the dramatic pauses, the inflection that implied deep humiliation and ravaging hunger. He went from one group of tourists to another, hand timidly outstretched, his entire body drooping with defeat, his manner artfully supplicatory. It was like a walk-on role in a long run—a role with a few simple lines and unlimited scope of improvisation. One tourist made a scathing remark about able-bodied mals refusing to work. Caland politely invited him to feel the metal in his head, which had been wired together after an accident. The response was a handful of chits.

One fem halted and stared at him. "Aren't you staying at the Paradise View?"

Caland kept his voice humble. "Indeed I am. This is how I pay my hote bill."

Her companions howled with laughter and showered chits on Caland.

Once having started, he found it difficult to stop. Finally Tel reached out of the shadows and drew him away.

"I was beginning to feel embarrassed for you," she muttered. "Your pockets are bulging."

"How long was I at it?"

"Thirty, forty minutes."

"It seemed like hours."

They slipped into a dim corner of a down eatery, and Tel counted his take. "I don't believe it," she exclaimed when she had totaled it a second time. "A hundred and twenty-seven chits? That just isn't possible. You have a very unusual talent."

"It's an act. I'm an actor."

"So it is and so you are. I'd forgotten. Even so, to find this much latent generosity in a crowd of tourists—"

"Generosity has nothing to do with it. Millionaires like to get their money's worth even when it's a handout. They paid for the performance."

"Some performance! A hundred and twenty-seven chits!"

"A handful of chits is nothing to people who are that wealthy. But they do like to get their money's worth."

"You ought to know. I still say you have a very unusual talent."

"It's the groveling expression on my face. What are we going to do with it?"

"With the money?" She laughed her deep, rich laugh. "I never thought I'd hear anyone in the Valley wondering what to do with money. Do you realize that you could wallow in luxury here by working an hour a sennite? Assuming that you'd always be this successful."

"I'd be more successful. I'd improve with practice."

"The hell you would. This much money, for that much effort, isn't even believable. As for what to do with it—"

"Pay my clothing bill," Caland said.

"Are you sure you want to? It would be a historic first. You only contracted that debt a couple of days ago. No one *ever* pays off a bill that quickly. It isn't done. It might ruin your credit forever."

They paid the clothing bill. Caland took out ten chits for a beach party. He agreed that the disposal of the remaining hundred and fifteen chits could wait until morning.

They joined a small fire group and had their party, inviting a few special guests who were really hungry. The meat sizzled, the jug circulated, and Caland, still not accustomed to alcohol, became quietly elevated and had the sensation of floating euphorically over the celebration until Tel firmly collected him and took him home to bed. He snuggled into her warm embrace wondering if he were about to achieve something he had thought lost to him forever—happiness—and he fell asleep without wondering why he was there.

CHAPTER FOURTEEN

Caland awoke in darkness. He had experienced a deep, dreamless sleep, and—more important—a dreamless awakening. He stretched out comfortably, savoring the Valley night, luxuriating in it. The old building emitted its spontaneous creaks; distant laughter reached him from the members of a late beach party who were wending their separate ways back toward the Prom; Tel's warmth and healthy body aroma enveloped him; the bedroom's familiar, sweet scent of decay permeated everything; all formed strands of the tightly woven cloak of security that surrounded him, relaxing, deeply satisfying. He sensed its presence like a tangible thing that he could stroke with the separate fingers of his hands.

He stirred, finally, swung his feet to the edge of the bed.

Tel was instantly alert. "What's the matter?"

"It's morning."

"Are you sprung? You can't have morning without a sunrise. It's a natural law."

"Morning is a state of mind," Caland said. "I feel like walking."

"Screet!"

Grumbling sleepily, she dressed herself and trailed behind him.

As they stumbled toward the path in front of the house, a shadowy figure intercepted them. The three of them came to a simultaneous, startled halt.

It was Baris Bronlan. He greeted them with the special

warmth he seemed to reserve for those who enjoyed his beloved ocean. "Going to see it?" he asked. "It has a different look in the morning."

"Everything has a different look when it's too dark to see," Tel said caustically.

Caland had been more interested in walking than in watching the ocean, but he was agreeable. He turned toward the beach.

Bronlan hesitated. "You ought to see the Prom at dawn," he said.

"What's there to see?" Caland asked.

"You ought to see it. This is a good time."

Tel groaned and dug Caland with her elbow; but to him, at that moment, seeing the Prom at dawn seemed exactly the right thing to do.

"Let's go see it," he said.

Bronlan led the way, guiding them along meandering, vegetation-cluttered paths that were rapidly becoming familiar to Caland. They crossed Junk Vista Avenue, circled around his shack, and wove their way past the mountains of junk and the tall, dark silhouette of the spaceship to the Valley Transportation Company lot. In the first faint wash of dawn, the scattering of vehicles in various stages of assembly or disassembly looked like debris from a gigantic game of jackstraws. Closer to the Prom were rows of electrocabs, electrobusses, and electrotrucks, all of them restructured fantastically by imaginative tinkering and resourceful scrounging. At one side was a miscellany of large machines that were unidentifiable because of missing parts or their thick camouflage of rust.

At the front of the lot, beside the shack that served as company office and also as his living quarters, the youthful, good-looking Gary Dwand was capably getting two electrobusses, three electrocabs, and an electrotruck underway. Neither he nor the drivers paid any attention to them. Bronlan led them to the wood fence that ran along the Prom.

Missing boards left occasional gaps in the fence. Bronlan pointed to one of them. "Look," he said.

In the slowly enlarging dawn, indistinct figures moved along the cluttered street, plotting zigzag routes from discard to discard and pausing frequently to fumble in the rubbish. These were Valley residents who were so destitute and friendless that they were forced to sift the Valley's impoverished litter for scraps of food or a mouthful of drink. They emerged in darkness so that they could begin their search the moment the light enabled them to stir the refuse meaningfully, and now they were ransacking the night's leavings: a jug with a few potable drops; a scrap of crust from a putrebun; a fruit core or a bit of ungnawed rind.

Watching them, Caland reflected that the Valley's social structure might be amorphous, but dregs still logically settled to the bottom. These were the lowest of the lowly, the most wretched of the unfortunate, the dregs of the dregs.

"The proud ones," he said slowly, remembering what Sam the Artist had said about Melana.

Bronlan was not watching the street. His gaze was intent on Caland. "In a place like this," he said grimly, "almost anyone is willing to share his last mouthful of food, but there are always those who are too shy, or too proud, or too stubborn to beg or ask for a loan. So I come most mornings and try to keep track of who they are, and then I try to see that they're included in a beach sup now and then, or that they're given a bit of work to do if they're able. But it can't look like charity. They wouldn't like that." There was a fierce sincerity in his voice. "It's hard looking after so many. What you've been doing on the beach at night—that's a help. Some of those people would be out here this morning if you hadn't fed them last night."

"How did you find out about that?"

"I hear things," Bronlan said. His smile illuminated his face in the dawn's half-light.

He turned again to the gap in the fence. Then he stiffened. He said softly, "Do you know what a snake is?"

"I've seen descriptions," Caland said.

"Some religions have a paradise that was blighted by a snake. Our paradise has something worse. Look!"

The mal plodding slowly along the center of the Prom should have been a tourist. He wore a daysuit of resplendent purple with green trim, in the most elegant of formal cuts. Its natural habitat would have been the overly ornate lounge at Paradise View Hostelry, except that the color combination was in such bad taste that even the tourists would have laughed at it. On the Valley's Prom, it simply looked preposterous. The mal was of average height, but his girth generously tripled the average. He was on the threshold of old age and probably would have been pleased to hear his years referred to as "indeterminate."

He affected familiarity with some of the scavengers as he minced along, but his manner made it a trifle too obvious that he would not have stooped for a ten-chit coupon if one of them had touched it first.

"Sdissler," Bronlan muttered. "He's a scavenger, too, but he scavenges people."

"How does he do that?"

"He runs an employment agency."

"In the Valley?" Caland exclaimed. He regarded Bronlan with amusement. He remembered hearing scathing comments about Sdissler, but he hadn't suspected that the mal's activities took that channel. "What's wrong with offering jobs?"

"Nothing—for those that want to work and aren't particular about what they work at. But even then they ought to get a fair rate of pay."

"What sort of jobs?"

"All of the dirty jobs on Mort. The back-breaking jobs. The dangerous jobs. Sdissler has a contract with Pakovich for picking up garbage and trash in Paradise and Fish Town and for all the Pak Enterprises. He runs the world dump. If Pak Enterprises has jobs so filthy or so rough that its own workers won't do them, it calls on Sdissler. People in Paradise call him for petty little house chores they don't feel like doing themselves—cleaning, fixing, moving. Sdissler can offer you work for a morning, or a day or two, or a term. If you want to work and don't mind what he offers, that's all right. But he'll try to catch you when you're hungry and sign you up for six terms in a forest labor camp or a couple of terms on the garbage trucks. He's sneaking dirty about it too. He collects at both ends—steep fees from the ones who need labor, and as much as he can wring out of the ones who take the jobs."

Caland had nothing to say.

"People ought to be free," Bronlan went on. "Free to work or not to work. Free to work at what they want to work at."

"That way, a lot of nasty work wouldn't get done," Caland said.

"Then let it not be done. If it's got to be done, pay enough so someone will want to do it. But leave people free to choose. The worst thing is what Sdissler does to the girls. When he finds a young fem out scavenging, he knows she's starving, and he tries to talk her into prostitution. He's got his own suite of rooms at the Valley Hote, and he keeps girls there and pimps for them."

"That seems to be a rather crowded profession in the Valley," Caland observed.

"In the Valley, every profession is crowded. The girls at Yda's and the Dolls' House—they're different. With them, it really is a profession. They're in it because they want to be. They can look after themselves, and Yda and Calta treat them well, and pay them well, and make them plan for the future. These young fems Sdissler picks up, they're only in it because they're hungry, and they feel disgraced. It shouldn't be allowed. And Sdissler cheats them."

"What can be done about it?" Caland asked.

"Feed them now and then when you can. That's all. If they weren't hungry, they wouldn't fall for Sdissler's line. And Sdissler is just another stooge of Pakovich's. It's all Pakovich's fault."

Bronlan turned away. "I got to do something about Pakovich," he muttered.

He moved over to talk with Gary Dwand and the drivers: a small, insignificant-looking figure with an awkwardly-held stiff arm. No stranger would recognize him as a mal of immense ability and the establishment's owner.

Caland experienced a sudden feeling of guilt. He'd forgotten his resolution to ask Bronlan about the possible misuse of his spaceship. But the others had been right. Bronlan never would knowingly take part in a scheme that threatened the Valley. Never.

Tel gripped Caland's arm firmly. "Come on," she said. "That's enough gloom for one morning. It's time you tried a putrebun. And meet Hef."

* * * * * * *

Hef's Place advertised, "The Valley's Must Putrid Putrebun." The glowing, gaudy sign had been designed and painted free of charge by Valley artists as a tribute to the mal they considered the galaxy's greatest cook. It adorned a little stand-up eatery that occupied a three-meter crack between buildings. The roof was of salvaged canvas, waterproofed after a fashion with sealant Hef had scraped from discarded cans. The floor was dirt. There were no tables, no chairs, not even a shelf for customers to rest food or elbows on. Hef worked and perspired behind a makeshift counter of stacked boxes. His stove was an open charcoal fire; his utensils, several large iron kettles; his larder, the stacked boxes.

Hefnan Troule had two restaurants fail because of fickle customers who could not distinguish food from provender. Two more failed because creditors from the first two failures sued for reimbursement at awkward times. Hef arrived in the Valley a broken man trailing clouds of bankruptcy. After a restful hiatus sustained entirely by handouts, he established Hef's Place.

The Valley staple known as the putrebun consisted of an extremely thick stew of meat and vegetables packed into a large roll. It seemed to offer very little scope for a cook's talents. The ingredients and their approximate proportions had been standardized by custom and economics long before Hef arrived in the Valley. The price, one chit for putrebun and yuck, also was traditional. The putrebun could not be made smaller without loss of business or larger without risk of bankruptcy. Some slight variation was achieved in the liquidity of the stew, and eateries were known for their splashy or dry putrebuns.

Hef's approach was one no other putrebun chef had thought of. He concerned himself with the concoction's flavor. He began experimenting with native herbs, and his putrebun took on a unique, pungent flavor. He then proceeded to marinate the meat with various brines until he found one that pleased him. When he finished, the Valley staple had been transformed into a gourmet experience. Customers crowded the narrow gap between buildings whenever Hef's Place was open, and it almost always was. When Caland and Tel arrived there, shortly after dawn, they had to wait in line.

After Caland's first, memorable bite of a Hef putrebun, he turned to Tel in astonishment and demanded, "Why doesn't he open a larger place?"

"He's failed four times," Tel said. "He can't fail where he is now."

"Is he making money?"

"Just enough to survive. But he's making a lot of people happy. The true chef is an artist. To Hef, the spectacle of ecstatic customers eating his food is as rewarding as an actor's experience of an ecstatic audience."

"Is he happy?"

"I think he is."

Caland had no more than a brief glimpse of Troule while they bought their food: tall, cadaverous, wearing an incongruously white smock, his thin red face perspiring from the heat of his crude stove, he beamed benevolently at each customer as he served him. Within the confined space behind his stack of boxes, he was a bustling dynamo. He darted away frequently to tend to the next batch of simmering putrebuns, fill in the kettle behind him, or to serve customers in the shops on either side of him, who clamored for attention from glassless windows that looked down on him from just under his improvised roof. Then he returned to his station, filled another putrebun with an expert scoop, wrapped it in a rubbery leaf from a native plant, and happily passed it to the next customer. Another expert scoop filled a mug of yuck—and Hef's yuck, also, had a faintly herbal aroma. Hef pocketed the inevitable chit and turned his beaming gaze on the next in line.

"Happiness can come in strange guises," Tel said.

The rubbery leaves served as all-purpose napkins. When they had finished eating, they added them to the Prom's debris and set their empty mugs against the nearest building. These were of cheap ceramic with the word "Hef's" engraved on them. A Valley character named Soapy had invented a business for himself based on these mugs. He collected them regularly, washed them, and returned them to the eateries identified on them. The cost was less than that of disposable mugs, which would have had to be imported.

Caland and Tel walked slowly to the east end of the Prom and then turned back. At that hour of the morning the street was crowded with Vals; the flood of tourists had not yet begun. There was a congestion of traffic up ahead, and they saw several girls leaning from the balcony of the Dolls' House to watch a street fight. They looked elegant even in dishabille, as did the girls watching from windows at Yda's across the street. Yda's did not have balconies. All were shouting encouragement to one or the other of the combatants. A few people had formed a circle to watch the fight, but most of the pedestrians weren't interested enough to turn their heads. Fights were not uncommon in the Valley. One of the enforcers was looking on, content to make certain that the fight did not get out of hand.

A whirring electrocab, its ludicrous, high body rocking above the foot traffic, moved along slowly, nudging people aside. It edged around the fight and swung up to the Dolls' House, where it halted with just room enough for its door to swing open. The passenger, a flamboyantly dressed tourist, stepped almost directly from the vehicle to the front door, and the 'cab moved on to the Valley Transportation Company lot where there was room to turn around.

Thalm, the retired doll, drifted past them in an eddy of Vals headed in the opposite direction and waved enthusiastically. Then Sam the Artist and the Reverend captured them and took off to a down eatery and another mug of the inevitable yuck. A short time later Moppy and Sippy joined them. Caland found himself staring at them. He'd never seen them with clothes on. At the nightly beach parties, they wore towels or nothing at all. Caland considered their ragged, ineptly patched stubs and wrappers and wondered if their beach attire might be due to the fact that they had so little else to wear.

He turned his attention to the Prom, where the flow of traffic at that early hour seemed astonishing.

"How many people live in the Valley?" he asked.

Sam the Artist responded with his deep, reverberating chuckle. "No one knows."

"*Someone* must know," Caland protested.

Sam the Artist shook his head. "No. No one."

"What about Gus, at the Rental Office? He has everyone's name posted on the map."

"Gus can tell you how many *renters* there are in the Valley. But even Gus couldn't guess at the number of sub-renters."

The Reverend interrupted Caland's dazed protest.

"Supposing a newcomer to the Valley were to say to you, 'I'll give you two chits a sennite if you'll let me sleep in your kitchen.' If you were destitute and hungry, that'd sound like a lot of money. Probably you'd take it, and you'd be a sub-renter. If it worked out, you might add one or two or three more. If you could collect regularly, you'd be able to eat and even save something toward your rent. But the Rental Office records would show only one person at your address, the renter. That's why Gus has no idea what the Valley population is. The same thing goes on all over the Valley, even in the cemeteries."

"Hasn't anyone tried to guess the population?"

The Reverend smiled. "Of course. Everyone tries to guess. My guess is about fifteen thousand."

Caland looked out at the Prom. The street was crowded, but—fifteen thousand? "Where *is* everyone?" he asked.

The Reverend gestured vaguely. "People sleep in shifts. If you went over to the beach, you'd find it just as crowded as it was last night. Some people prefer to swim during the day. Some do their Prom-walking during the day and others prefer darkness. It all works out except during bad weather. Conditions get rather crowded when everyone is trying to come in out of the rain. Most Valley squabbles happen during bad weather."

"What do fifteen thousand people live on when so many of them are wasting time? The tourists? Could the Valley survive without the tourists?"

Sam the Artist answered. "Definitely not. Tourist money trickles all through the Valley from top to bottom. The Houses of Fame, the restaurants, the Road to Hell, the expensive shops that cater to the tourists—all of those places hire Valley people to do their cleaning, and run errands, and hand out advertising blurbs, and provide extra help during rush periods, and a thousand and one other things. The girls in the Houses of Fame pay to have clothing cleaned and repaired and altered. The Valley Transportation Company has a big payroll. So does Olgi, and both hire a lot of part-time help so as to spread the money among as many people as possible. Apart from the businesses, some Valley residents can do quite well for themselves just hustling the tourists, as you've found out for yourself."

"If it weren't for the tourists," the Reverend said, "all we'd have would be Sdissler. He keeps a lot of people working, though not for much. Pakovich may loathe the Valley, but his world would be a stinking mess without Vals to keep it clean. And then we have people living here on pensions or on regular incomes from parents or relatives or even long-suffering spouses who remain at home and work. I know of two couples who live quite comfortably on payments received regularly from his wife and her husband. Not Moppy and Sippy, though."

"We should be so lucky!" Moppy muttered.

"All of that doesn't seem like much money for fifteen thousand people," Caland observed.

"That's true," Sam the Artist agreed. "That's profoundly true. Which is why so many Valley people don't eat regularly. Analyze it any way you like, but you can't get away from one central fact. The Valley's in an economic stranglehold because of Pakovich. It always has been, and it always will be."

"It would please Pakovich to know that you think so," the Reverend said. "My own opinion—"

They did not hear the Reverend's opinion. Hairy came squeezing through the cramped little room, a cheerful grin on his totally hairless countenance. He reached Tel first and stooped to whisper into her ear.

She nodded. Hairy, still grinning, edged his way out again.

"Someone should investigate Hairy's knack for finding people," Tel said. "He spends his waking hours touring the Valley, and he must remember infallibly where he last saw everyone and which direction everyone was moving in." She turned to Caland. "You're summoned. You'll have to complete your study of Valley economics some other time." Caland obediently got to his feet. Tel turned to Sam the Artist. "Dal Eddyer wants to see Cal. Would you take him?"

Sam the Artist arched his bushy eyebrows. "Indeed. Sure, I'll take him. Where'll you be?"

"I'll be along."

The others decided to leave with them, so they made their way in single file to the door and separated on the Prom. Sam guided Caland around to the rear entrance of the Road to Hell, of which Dal Eddyer was the proprietor.

"Do many Valley people gamble?" Caland asked.

"Sure. They don't gamble much, because not many of them have much to gamble with, and they mostly look for less expensive plays than the Road to Hell offers, but of course they gamble. The Road to Hell is mostly for tourists."

"Is it possible to win?"

"Sure. If no one won, the customers would get discouraged. A lot of people win little, and this encourages the big losers to go on losing. The big winner, of course, is the house. That's the golden rule of gambling. The game is always working for the mal who owns it. Are you maybe thinking of having a blast yourself?"

"I wouldn't even consider it," Caland said. "I never win anything. I was curious about the economics of gambling establishments in a place where people have so little money."

"It's the tourists who have the money. The Vals are all spending the same five chits—remember? Some buy food. Some gamble. It just about keeps a few crack-in-the-wall games afloat."

The rear door of the Road to Hell was opened by Dal Eddyer's wife, Monelle, a pleasant, middle-aged fem. She invited them into a very compact, neatly furnished apartment at the rear of the enormous building. Eddyer joined them almost at once—a plump, balding man about sixty. There was a good-natured sadness in his peering expression. He greeted Sam with a friendly smile and looked enquiringly at Caland.

"This is our friend Cal," Sam the Artist said. "Hairy said you wanted him."

"Ah. Then you're Jarv Caland?"

Caland nodded.

"Can you prove that?"

Caland thought for a moment, frowning. Since his medical card and passport had disappeared, he had no identification at all. "No," he said.

"Come to the office, please." Eddyer turned to Sam the Artist. "If you don't mind, Sam. This is private business."

Sam waved them away with a grin, and the puzzled Caland followed Eddyer.

Caland had caught a few passing glimpses of the Road to Hell's interior from the Prom. The glittering gambling machines and the strange noises they made were artfully designed to arouse curiosity, but he had experienced none. He was not curious now, though the noises were reverberating in the large room just beyond, accompanied by the cheers and groans of the players.

Eddyer guided him to a tiny private office that contained only a cluttered desk and two chairs. Eddyer seated himself at the desk, and Caland took the other chair and waited.

Eddyer picked up a paper and scowled at it. "You match your description fairly well. You're supposed to have a scar on your left arm just above the elbow. Have you?"

Caland raised his wrapper. Eddyer glanced at his arm and nodded.

"And one on your left ankle." Eddyer stooped over and examined his bare leg.

"And now—a rather extensive scar in your scalp, concealed by your hair. May I look?"

He got to his feet and examined Caland's head with care.

"Very well." He sank back into his chair. "Since you are new here, you may not know that I function as the Valley's bank. I do a modest amount of business in handling funds transferred to Valley residents from other worlds, and I also handle funds for Valley businesses. This transaction concerning you is a bit unusual, but it isn't the least unusual for me to have unusual requests. The situation is this: I've been instructed anonymously to pay your rent for you one term at a time as it falls due. I've already notified the Rental Office. I've also been instructed to pay you a living allowance of twenty chits per sennite. There's only one condition for all of this."

Caland had been listening incredulously. He cocked his head and waited.

Eddyer seemed embarrassed. "No conspicuous behavior, and that includes begging from tourists. Actually, with your rent paid and a generous allowance for expenses, you shouldn't need to, but that's the condition. Now, then—we're rather primitive in the Valley. I need your signature on this card and on this receipt. I need your thumb impressions. Then I'll pay you your first sennite's allowance. Before you leave, I want the cashiers to meet you." He talked on as he placed the card and a slip of paper in front of Caland.

Caland pushed his chair back and got to his feet. His mind

and emotions had been caged for so long that his sudden surge of anger exhilarated him. "I wouldn't dream of accepting a handout from anyone so impoverished that he can only offer twenty chits per sennite," he said.

Eddyer stared at him, open-mouthed.

"I can better that in ten minutes of begging. And while the tourists frequently are critical of my mode of living, they don't attempt to place conditions on the money they give to me."

He nodded politely and marched out.

Back in the living quarters, Caland found that Monelle Eddyer had already served the inevitable mug of yuck to Sam the Artist and was about to do the same for Tel, who had just arrived.

"Finished already?" Sam asked in surprise.

"Finished," Caland agreed.

His anger still burned, but he saw no reason to take it out on the Eddyers. He graciously accepted a mug of yuck, pretending that he'd developed an appetite for it instead of grudging tolerance, and he talked comfortably about his impressions of the Valley. Dal Eddyer joined them, and he stood in the doorway and now and then sent a bewildered glance in Caland's direction.

When they rose to leave, Caland thanked them for the promptness and consideration he'd shown. Once outside, Tel turned and looked at him curiously.

"That must have been an experience. I thought you were going to explode any minute."

"Really? I thought I was being very relaxed about it."

"When you suddenly become talkative, I know something is wrong. When your face is flushed and your hand on a mug of yuck gets white, as though you're trying to crush it—what happened?"

"Some kind of benefactor has offered to pay my rent and hand me an allowance of twenty chits per sennite."

Sam the Artist turned on him in astonishment. "Cal—you're rich!"

"There's a condition attached. In the future I'm to avoid conspicuous behavior, especially as concerns begging from tourists. I told Eddyer my conspicuously acquired money totals far more than twenty chits per sennite and has no restrictions on it. I wanted to send word to my generous benefactor to take his kind offer and eat it, but I was being polite."

Sam was shocked into silence.

Tel was convulsive with laughter. "I doubt it," she said, wiping her eyes. "I doubt that you were being polite. This is lovely. Your friend Arlu will be elated—I think. He's on his way here now, but we have time for a bit of din first. Sam looks as though he needs it."

"I need something," Sam the Artist said. "Let's go spend some of Cal's conspicuously acquired money."

Arlu *was* elated. On this day he was attired in a color he himself described as "sunburst pink," and both it and his chins shook with delight. "That's what I needed," he exclaimed happily. "That's precisely what I had to know. The person who controls Cal's mind is still on Mort, and he plans to stay here for a while. Eddyer did say your rent was to be paid each term as it falls due? That's suggestive. Now we know positively that the person we're interested in is here, and he is watching Cal closely or having him watched. Brilliant! I should have thought of it myself. How'd you happen to go begging?"

"I was hungry," Caland said.

"Is there any chance that Eddyer might slip some information about the payer?" Arlu asked Tel.

She shook her head. "His business depends on his integrity. If he knew anything, he wouldn't tell. But he didn't mind telling me that he doesn't know. He just said the arrangement for remittances was handled very adroitly."

"I'll bet it was." Arlu clapped Caland warmly on the shoulder. "All right, my friend. You've given me the raw material. I'll take it from here. Your job now is to rebuild your health and think about making a new life for yourself. Relax. Enjoy the Valley. But don't try to forget the past completely—anything you happen to remember is likely to be useful."

Caland and Tel waved the jubilant Arlu on his way.

And Caland wondered whether Arlu really expected him to relax and concentrate on the future now that they had proof that there was someone near at hand, watching closely, who could take possession of Caland's mind whenever he felt like it.

CHAPTER FIFTEEN

They swam at the ocean beach, and afterward, while Caland dozed, Tel moistened a pile of sand and fashioned an enormous enlarged dirt art model of his head. He was awake when she finished. She gave his features a searching look, scrutinized her model for a moment, and then kicked it into oblivion.

"What would you like to do now?" she asked.

He had enjoyed watching her hands skillfully shape the moist sand, but the image had disturbed him. "Why don't you make something else?" he suggested.

"Screet!"

He studied her for a moment. Her hair was still tied in the knot she affected when swimming, and her face had a startlingly youthful appearance with her hair pulled back. "What's your name?" he asked.

"Have they been tampering with your mind again?" she asked anxiously.

"I mean—what's your real name?"

"I'm Telis Zahnly. Or so my parents fervently believed. What would you like to do?"

"I don't know."

"You're free," she said, smiling. "Arlu gave you your freedom. You can do anything you like. What will it be?"

"Nothing."

"Where would you like to do it?"

They walked back to the Prom and found themselves a vacant table in Nello's.

Nello, the fat, jolly proprietor, ran the little down eatery like a public club. Whatever he had to offer was laid out on a long counter: the inevitable steaming crocks of yuck, along with the cheapest variety of rolls, crackers, cheese and meat spreads, and confections. Prices were posted. Customers helped themselves and dropped money into a box if they had any, and no one bothered with change. Somehow it all worked out. The convivial Nello presided over a large rear table in an atmosphere of hospitality and good fellowship.

Caland poured two mugs of yuck, grossly overpaid with a chit coupon, and joined Tel. A short time later Louie Laggie, the scav, saw them from the Prom and came to talk. He was carrying a large plastic gear wheel with several teeth missing.

"Found it over at the fertilizer factory," he said cheerfully. "It's a gift for Bar. Maybe he can melt it down and make something of it. Good plastic is expensive on Mort."

"Then why did the fertilizer factory throw it away?" Caland asked.

Laggie laughed scornfully. His tanned, deeply wrinkled face looked as though he himself had been weathering away on a junk pile, and his clothing was even more threadbare than Caland remembered it. He was one of the Valley's innumerable failures; paradoxically, he seemed to have succeeded at it.

"Pakovich's managers are idiots," he said. "They don't know anything about salvage. They throw away valuable stuff all the time. Then they get angry if someone tries to scav it. Have you seen the fence?"

"The Valley fence?" Caland asked.

"The fertilizer factory fence. It's of woven metal, four meters high with a top barrier, and it surrounds the place on the land side. As though Pakovich kept something there that needs protecting. Maybe he thinks the Vals are going to sneak in some night and eat his fertilizer."

"In that case, how did you scav the gear?" Caland asked.

"Ah!" Laggie gave him a sly grin. "I got a technique. You come with me sometime, I'll show you."

Tel had untied her swimming knot, and she was gently untangling snarls in her long hair. She seemed oblivious to her surroundings, but Caland already had learned that she missed absolutely nothing of what went on about her.

Sigley Varno, the artist, happened along next, followed by the young couple, Duggal and Huggal. Then Sam the Artist arrived and expansively bought yuck for everyone along with a mixed platter of what he called accessories. He was celebrating the completion of a small painting job at the Dolls' House, and his clothing had acquired several fresh smears of pale lavender. Others joined them, and their party overflowed to surrounding tables as fast as these became available. Nello flitted over from time to time, exchanged wisecracks with Sam the Artist, and then retreated to his customary headquarters.

Caland listened to the conversation and absently watched the passersby on the Prom. His thoughts were still fixed on the massive model of his head that Tel had fashioned from moist sand. He had said nothing at the time, but the magnified image had shaken him. It set him thinking of the quantity of metal that his scalp concealed. Arlu and others were efficiently looking into the mysterious events that surrounded him. They had assumed the responsibility for him as well as his problems, but that did not confer freedom. His bondage to the weight of metal in his head was permanent.

Melana walked past. The fleeting glimpse of startling beauty among the dowdy tourists and scruffy Vals halted conversation and turned heads. As the clamor of talk welled up again, Sam the Artist caught Caland's eye and grinned at him.

Her sudden appearance jolted Caland's memory. He asked thoughtfully, "How does it happen that Melana can research her book at the Paradise Library when they wouldn't let Doctor Gormaz's fictitious secretary into the place?"

Sam hadn't heard about the fictitious secretary, and Caland had to describe Doctor Gormaz's conversation with Alexander Pakovich the Second.

"There's no secret about the library being off limits to Vals,"

Sam said. "That's been the rule as long as anyone can remember. Everything on Mort is off limits to us except the space port, the Merc Mart, the Paradise Medical Clinic, and the world cemetery. One place is as mercenary as the other, except that the cemetery is free. The only Val Pakovich doesn't resent is a dead one. In a long-ago legal battle between Pakovich and Dombrily, Pakovich was ordered by an interworld court to make medical care available to Valley residents. He gets around the order by charging fees that no one in the Valley can afford. As far as how Melana manages to use the library, that's only one of many mysteries about her."

Tel turned with a jerk. "Nonsense! There's no mystery about that."

"Why would they let her into the library and not Doctor Gormaz's secretary?" Caland asked.

"Doctor Gormaz wasn't interested in using the library," Tel said. "He wanted to know how much authority the younger Pakovich wields. He invented a case the regulations wouldn't cover, and he quickly got his answer. Alexander the Second has no authority at all. He has to refer every piddling exception to Alexander the First. Right?"

"Right," Caland agreed.

"If Gormaz had wanted to use the library, he would have done what Melana did: ask Alexander the First. When there's a decision to be made, you ask the person who's going to decide. Melana went directly to Pakovich and presented him with letters of recommendation from a university professor and an Aravian duke. The duke's letter alone would have been enough. Add the facts that she's sensationally beautiful and she wanted to study something or other about the history of Mort, and how could Pakovich refuse her? He instantly dictated a directive making all facilities available to her and ordering library employees to give her every assistance. He never thought to ask where she was going to live. Now she has a strangely perverted impression of Pakovich. She thinks he's amusing but also rather nice."

Sam the Artist snorted.

A group of tourists passed by in a swirl of clashing colors leaving a familiar, high-pitched giggle in its wake: Mathild, afflicting her unwelcome attention on Doctor Gormaz. A moment later, a solitary tourist—tall, lank, angular, her face concealed by a light hood—flitted past Caland's line of vision and brought him to instant alertness. It had to be Fem Wobbons. He turned inquiringly to Tel and found her scowling at the Prom. She really didn't miss a thing.

Hairy bobbed out of the throng like a float popping to the surface. He slowed his pace, sent a long, searching glance through the eatery as though memorizing its population, and moved on. The Reverend followed on his heels. Sam the Artist waved a hand and went for more yuck.

They made room for another chair, and the Reverend stretched his long legs under their table and smiled benignly at them.

"What's steaming?" Sam the Artist asked.

"Virtually nothing," the Reverend said, "except that there seems to be an unusually large number of tourists about today."

"Maybe we should ask the hotes if Pakovich has evicted anyone," Sam the Artist said.

Conversation turned to Caland's new career as a para. The Vals who had witnessed his debut had been as awed by his performance as by its proceeds, and their story was being repeated all over the Valley.

"Did you ever earn that much money for an hour of regular acting?" Sam the Artist asked.

Caland had to perform an intricate interworld monetary conversion before he could answer. "Yes," he said. "But not often. I rarely was a principal. I wasn't a great actor, but I was competent, and I loved doing it."

"I'm considering whether to emulate Cal's success," Sam the Artist said. "Do you think I could beg for my widowed mother who's dying of malnutrition?"

"Of course you could." Tel said. "Any tourist who looks at you will know you've been stealing your mother's food."

Caland was still feeling disturbed about the massive model

of his head. He asked the Reverend hesitantly, "Is an artificial brain mathematically possible?"

The Reverend answered matter-of-factly. "Of course."

"According to mathematical physics, everything is mathematically possible," Sam the Artist said. He bowed to the Reverend. "On a theoretical basis, of course."

The Reverend smiled unresentfully. "It's a healthy attitude. Better that than using science to prove that everything is impossible. Some scientists have done that. Many of the things we take for granted were once considered scientifically impossible. Space travel, for example. I'd much rather believe the scientist who considers everything possible. Because it's just possible that everything *is* possible." He turned to Caland. "An artificial brain is probably the subject of a thousand experiments right now, and thinking machines of varying capacities have been in use for centuries. But a fully functioning artificial brain is still too elaborate for today's technology, and a partially functioning one is still far too bulky to put in anyone's head. An artificial brain is theoretically possible, but probably it'll never be achieved because it's so much easier and more efficient to make real brains simply by making more people."

Tel had turned her attention to the passing tourists. She said softly to Caland, "What *am* I going to do with that unspeakable wardrobe? It's the one type of clothing that has no resale value."

"Save it for your next foray into high society," Caland suggested.

"I never realized what it would be like," Tel said solemnly. "From time to time I've thought about how nice it would be to have a lot of money, but that's not the same thing as being rich and associating with rich people. How could you stand it?"

"I couldn't stand it. I left."

"So you did. No better evidence of sterling character could be offered. Did you have qualms about running out on all that money?"

"No. None at all. But that probably was because I'd never been without money. If you've always been wealthy, you can't imagine what it's like to be impoverished. I didn't give a thought to what I was leaving. I was too intent on what I wanted to gain."

The impromptu gathering was breaking up. Louie Laggie picked up his broken gear and departed. The Reverend and Sam the Artist went off together; a Val named Awkie—for awkward—had been seen using candles in a dangerous, almost incendiary manner on the previous night, and their chore was to deliver the Valley's equivalent of a stern official warning. Duggal and Huggal drifted away. Sigley Varno, who had been drawing caricatures of passing tourists, folded his sketchbook.

"Are you ready to do nothing somewhere else?" Tel asked.

"I want to talk with Bar," Caland said. "About his spaceship."

She gazed at him blankly. "His spaceship? You mean—but it couldn't be Bar. It absolutely couldn't be. Surely you know him well enough to know that. He'd react violently if anyone or anything threatened the Valley."

"The question is whether the ship could be used without his knowing it. Someone has to talk to him about it, and since the rest of you won't—"

"All right. Let's go."

They edged their way out to the Prom.

Caland had begun to experience misgivings. "It'd be easier to talk with him if I knew him better," he said.

"If you knew him better, it would be impossible."

They drifted westward with the crowd. Some of the bemused, tittering, squirming tourists were trying to avoid being brushed by passing Vals, but most reacted to the Prom's crush good-naturedly and accepted accidental contacts as an exotic experience. Caland and Tel turned off at the little plaza by the Valley Transportation Company, acknowledged waves from Moppy and Sippy, and slipped through the gate. Tel led the way along the narrow path that wound past Bronlan's mountains of junk.

Baris Bronlan was entertaining royalty. He was proudly exhibiting his spaceship to two space captains.

Spacers were common Valley visitors—so common that Vals who were interested enough to take notice knew more about arriving and departing ships than did anyone else on Mort except the control personnel at the Port. Spacers with a layover always visited the Valley, and many had close friends among the Vals. A few called the Valley home and kept a wife—or a husband—and a family there.

But space captains normally visited the Valley only as tourists.

The smiling Bronlan performed introductions. Captain Akonif, a short, husky, elderly man with elongated, pale eyes, a good-humored face, and the typical spacer's sallow complexion, commanded a ship that made a scheduled ore run between Aravia and Mort. Like most spacers, he avoided the sun as others would a torrential rain. He had taken refuge in a patch of shade. He was a long-time friend of Bronlan's, and he stood listening with a grin while Bronlan expounded his spaceship to the other captain.

Captain Willox was a newcomer. He was Akonif's opposite, tall and surly. He acknowledged the introductions with a curt nod and resumed his conversation. His expression was one of scornful skepticism.

"You mean," he blurted, "you're going to build the engines yourself?"

Bronlan, wearing his usual rough work clothing and his cap with the eyeshade, looked like an amused imp. His eyes twinkled. "Of course. Why not?"

"And you're going to run them on baking soda, whatever that is?"

"Baking soda and other things."

"Ridiculous!"

"Why?" Bronlan asked imperturbably. "Baking soda has atoms."

"So has spit. Why don't you run the ship on spit?"

"Could be done," Bronlan said, still unperturbed. "Put the right things with it, it could be done." His face assumed a faraway look as though he actually were contemplating a gigantic voyage in a ship propelled by spit.

"I suppose if you stripped the atoms efficiently, anything at all would move this crate in outer space, even though slowly." The captain's voice dripped scorn. "But you're talking about lifting off a planet, and there's a vast difference between bucking gravity to get into space and achieving a minimal useful thrust after you're there. Baking soda wouldn't even stir the dust around here—and there's a lot of dust."

Bronlan flashed a smile. "I'll invite you to the liftoff."

"I wouldn't come," Willox said. "It'd be a waste of time. Atomic propulsion is almost a lost art, but there're still a few people around who know something about it. If you insist on using it, you ought to consult one of them." He turned to Captain Akonif. "Shall we go? There's a girl at Yda's I'd like to see more of."

Akonif winked at Bronlan. "I'll look in on you tomorrow."

The two captains walked off together. Willox's irritated voice floated back to them. "Of course he's amazingly talented. Splendid piece of work, that contraption. Did he really build all of it from discards? Incredible! Great pity he's sprung. Baking soda! Why doesn't he use yodel bird guano?"

Bronlan turned to Caland and Tel and grinned broadly. "I considered that. Guano, I mean. But baking soda will be more effective."

Caland plunged blindly. "Bar, could your spaceship be used as a communications tower?"

"Any tall structure could be used as a communications tower," Bronlan said. "In cities, tall buildings are used. All you have to do is mount the equipment."

"Would it be possible for anyone to make use of it like that without your knowing about it?"

"No," Bronlan said.

"Even if the equipment were small?"

"I'd notice."

"What if it could be used that way without any equipment?"

Bronlan looked at him perplexedly. "What could it be used for without any equipment?"

"That's the problem," Caland said. "We don't know."

He described the catastrophes that had occurred on three distant worlds and the possible involvement of mysterious towers. Even as he spoke, the explanation sounded preposterous to him. He finished in an embarrassed rush.

But Bronlan was not resentful. He seemed immensely interested. "About my ship," he said. "I don't think anyone could run wires in here without leaving any trace. Either I'd see them, or I'd see where they were buried. Anyway, if someone tried to march through the Valley stringing or burying wires, people would notice and ask about it long before he got this far. Question is whether the ship could focus or amplify some kind of broadcast beam. I'll have to think about that. It might depend on the distance of the beam's source. If Pakovich were to rig something on one of the mountains—"

"I don't think it would be Pakovich," Caland said.

"Might if it were guaranteed to wipe out the Valley."

They left him sitting in the shade, arms about his knees, meditating. Before they were out of hearing, he called after them, "If you find out anything more about those towers, let me know."

"At least he didn't explode," Tel said as they threaded their way across Junk Vista Avenue. "Are you convinced now?"

Caland had no answer. Bronlan's reaction had seemed innocent enough, but he would have reacted the same way if he were guilty. He would have stalled and tried to find out how much they knew. And that was exactly what he had done.

They headed in the direction of the bay beach, which Caland wanted to see by daylight. When they stepped through the last barrier of bushes and onto the gleaming white sand, he was instantly convinced that the population of the Valley really was fifteen thousand. From the Valley boundary, where the wood fence came to a decaying termination at the edge of the beach, to the curving spit of land at the mouth of the bay, the beach teemed with people. There were swimmers and sunbathers, artists and dirt artists, children playing delightedly, elders snoozing under makeshift sunshades, young adults cavorting, and people of all ages talking or doing nothing. The colorful sail boats from the tourist hotes tacked close to shore so their passengers could take in the awesome spectacle of two full kilometers of nudity.

"Strange that Pakovich allows that," Caland said.

"Why shouldn't he?" Tel asked. "It's good business. Why do you think sailing is so popular with the tourists? Before Bar founded the Valley Transportation Company, the boats were the only way the tourists could visit the Valley except by walking. There was a makeshift pier down by the fence, and the boats landed their passengers there and went back for another load. But the transportation was unreliable and sometimes even a little dangerous. Tourists often got stranded here when the winds were fickle or when it stormed. Naturally Pakovich wouldn't tolerate the idea of power boats on his lovely bay. Alexander Pakovich is a mal of high principles. The boat service collapsed when Bar started running regular scheduled 'buses and made 'cabs available on call."

Tel selected a pile of sand to work on, and Caland helped her to moisten it with water brought from the bay in cupped hands. Then he lay on the beach and sunned himself while she fashioned a gigantic replica of one of Mort's ugly sea creatures. The startlingly realistic, leering, mouthless face quickly took shape under her skilled fingers. The long, tapering body followed, with gapping, toothed mouths along the lower belly.

Caland dozed off. When he awoke, the creature was fully formed in all of its resplendent hideousness from bulging head to multiple-forked tail, and Tel, working with exquisite skill and patience, was shaping its back into a representation of pebbly scales.

Hairy came crunching along the sand moving with long strides from group to group, his bald features glistening in the bright sunlight. As he approached them, he called, "Have you seen the Reverend?"

Tel waived him over to her and whispered something. Hairy's hairless brows arched; he nodded and crunched away.

Tel returned to her sculpture, and Caland closed his eyes again and enjoyed the sun.

"Enough!" Tel said suddenly. "You'll burn yourself. Get back in the shade."

"I feel hungry."

"What would you like to eat?"

"One of Hef's putrebuns. They're addictive."

"Can you wait until I finish this?"

She was surrounding the grotesque creature with a delicate network of tendrils, all of them poised to sweep prey into the hideous mouths. "What will be different when it's finished?" Caland asked.

Tel laughed deeply and gave the sculpture a kick. "All right. After modeling you I thought I could go on to greater things. Next time I'll do something simple like a tree louse."

Instead of heading into one of the paths that led toward the Prom, she walked off along the beach. Caland trailed after her. A group of children at play in the shallow water gleefully splashed at them.

"For a community of fifteen thousand, there don't seem to be many children," Caland observed when he caught up to Tel.

"As a percentage of the population, there aren't," Tel said. "So many of the Vals are middle-aged and older. But there are several hundred, and their education is the Valley's most severe problem."

They passed a young mal who was lolling in the shade at the edge of the beach. He looked up at them; Caland nodded politely and got a barely perceptible nod in return. Tel finally found a path that appealed to her and they turned southward.

When they reached Bay Unview Boulevard, Tel whispered, "Don't look back. Did you recognize him?"

It took Caland a moment to focus his thoughts. "You mean— that mal with the blond hair? He did look vaguely familiar, but he didn't seem to know me, and I can't remember—"

"*Don't look back*! He's been following us since we left the Prom."

"Why would anyone—?"

"Good question. Remember the first day when we went to the Rental Office?"

Caland thought for a moment. "Nalce!" he exclaimed. "The one who rented the apartment."

"Keep your voice down. Have you seen him since then?"

"Not that I recall."

"I'd like to know what he's been doing."

Caland felt totally chagrinned—angry, frustrated, humiliated. He'd known for so long that someone was following him. He'd tried every trick he could think of to identify the person with no success at all. Now Tel had casually picked Nalce out of the beach crowd.

"Don't look back," she said again.

They bought putrebuns at Hef's Place and walked slowly along the Prom, eating, sipping their yuck, and watching the late afternoon influx of tourists. There really did seem to be an unusual number of them.

"Perhaps the hotes have surpassed that forty-one per cent occupancy figure," Caland suggested.

"Or perhaps the forty-one per cent all got bored at once," Tel said.

Doctor Gormaz passed them with a group of tourists that had just emerged from the Burned Wafer. Caland recognized several of them; their glances washed over him and classified him with the Valley's other disgustingly unwashed inhabitants. Gormaz's eyes rested longer on Tel before they flicked away. His hoarse voice boomed out as he began to expound something to his companions.

Then Caland saw Nalce moving toward them. He studied him with interest, but he saw nothing about him that seemed untypical. The mop of unruly blond hair had acquired a balancing fringe around the bottom of his face since Caland first saw him in the Rental Office, as though Nalce didn't really want a beard but liked the idea of saving the cost of a wipe. He did not even glance at them as he passed.

"Screet!" Tel muttered. "Someone should be following him by now."

Then Sam the Artist pushed out of the throng and strode briskly along in Nalce's wake. He winked at them and hurried on without breaking his stride. They finished their putrebuns and yuck and left their mugs on the window ledge of Olgi's Cloy Shop.

"What are you thinking about?" Tel asked suddenly.

"Money," Caland said.

"Standard Valley preoccupation. Except that the people who think about money usually are those who don't have any. You're rich. You have more than a hundred chits and you just turned down an allowance."

"I need lots of money," Caland said. "Not just hundreds. Thousands."

"Going to buy the Valley?"

"Look," Caland said. He pulled her out of the eddying crowd into a gap between two sagging buildings. "The person who's controlling my mind is here on Mort. I want to find him."

"Arlu is doing the searching. Evidently he has plenty of money for it."

"Blast Arlu. What do I know about Arlu? I want to do my own searching and make my own decisions. If I'm being followed here in the Valley, I want my own searchers working on it. I don't want people who should be working for me reporting to Arlu, who'll tell me what he pleases or nothing at all. I need lots of money."

He felt angry. Intrigue and mystery continued to surround him even in the Valley, but others had taken charge of it. As the Vals would have said, it was regulated; but he was tired of being regulated by others. He wanted to do his own regulating. His mind felt ready to burst its metal restraints and soar.

Tel was looking at him gravely. "Ever since your accident, you haven't been able to do anything at all except react to things done to you. If you suddenly feel like making someone else react, that's a very good sign."

"I'm going to beg again tonight," he said. "I'll need some props. And some makeup."

She raised her eyebrows, but all she said was, "Let's see what we can scav."

Louie Laggie provided the ragged clothing Caland needed. Sig, the artist, lent him tubes of color compound that could serve as makeup. They wandered through clutter shops picking up odds and ends that suggested a theatrical use to Caland. Tel remembered seeing a battered old metal crutch on one of Baris Bronlan's junk piles, and on their way back to the apartment they asked the puzzled Bronlan to lend it to them. The most difficult prop to acquire was a mirror. Hairy finally produced a small one and steadfastly refused to tell where he'd gotten it.

Caland went to work on himself while Tel perched on the edge of one of the battered chairs and watched—first with amused interest and then with admiration. One deft touch at a time transformed him into a lame, disfigured, toothless old mal. He gave one cheek a twist of paralysis, made his right eyelid droop, and painted the slash of a hideous scar across his forehead. He had to call on long-unused muscles to achieve an arthritic distortion of a hand, a maniacal sneer, the hunch of a deformed shoulder. The ragged clothing, the crutch, and a dirty rag wrapped around his head completed the costume. The little mirror could not adequately capture the total effect, but Tel gave it her whole-hearted approval.

The rehearsal came next. Caland made Tel play the part of the haughty tourist while he squatted on the floor and reviled her with chaff.

"If it weren't for one thing, you'd remind me of the mother of my children," he proclaimed in a high-pitched whine. "You're the wrong sex."

She burst into laughter.

"One thing I don't like about a fat fem," he shrilled. "It's so easy for them to keep a mal at a distance. I came to the Valley to be with the tourists—I prefer to associate with people who dress like I do. I used to work at the Doll's House, but the customers complained that I was losing my figure. Now I'm a talent scout for the Fig Stump. I look for tourists with small stomachs—they eat less. I haven't been able to find any."

"It's wonderful," Tel said, wiping her eyes.

"Not really, but it may seem so to the tourists. They haven't had any entertainment since they arrived here except each other's death jokes."

"Will they pay to be insulted?"

"The insults are only the beginning. I need something else."

He stretched out on the water mattress and mentally composed a monologue about life in the Valley.

At dusk, Sam the Artist and the Reverend assisted him—a helpless old cripple—to his chosen position. Caland was less concerned with appearances than for properly feeling his way into the role he was creating. He settled himself in the center of the Prom under the first street light, where he could ambush the crowds of tourists arriving just after dark to sup at the restaurants and enjoy an exciting evening of gambling at the Road to Hell. The theme of his raillery was a simple one—he was an old roué who wanted one last fling at the Dolls' House, but the girls insisted on charging him double. The Valley was a hard place for an old cripple to live, he told the tourists—having to be carried all the way to the ocean every time he needed to use the sanctum, having to chew yuck without any teeth, having young girls chasing after him when he couldn't run, having so many beautiful tourists around to arouse his desires. "The fems, too," he added.

The tourists formed a circle about him and howled.

He described the hazards of a cripple's life in a community where all the good-looking fems lived upstairs. He described the staple Valley diet of yuck and glop—with feeling, out of his personal experience—and made it sound dreadful, asking how a mal was expected to keep awake at night on such feeble nourishment. He described Pakovich's agents, who sneaked into the Valley regularly and tried to kidnap him to work on the garbage 'trucks. He chaffed the tourists mercilessly, and they rocked with laughter and showered chits into the filthy hat that lay on the street beside him.

Finally they moved on. Tel picked up the money, and Sam and the Reverend helped Caland, still limping his part, along the Prom to Nello's.

"Can you drink yuck without spoiling your makeup?" Sam the Artist asked anxiously.

"It doesn't matter," Caland said. "I couldn't manage another performance. My muscles are refusing to function. So is my rear—that dratted Prom pavement leaves bruises."

Tel handed him a cloth, and he began wiping the makeup from his face. The Reverend, with all of the solemnity of one presiding at a ritual, helped him with the places he missed. Sam returned with the mugs of yuck and eased himself into a chair.

Tel was counting the money. "Three hundred and twelve," she said.

"Chits?" Sam the Artist exclaimed.

"I earned it," Caland said.

"You did," Tel agreed.

"All the same, I didn't realize how utterly bored the tourists are. How many of them were there? About thirty?"

"A few less than that," Tel said.

"Then it averages out to about twelve chits apiece, which isn't much."

"Some paid more. There are seven twenty-chit coupons."

"That's nothing to a tourist," Caland said. "At the hote, they use twenty-chit coupons for grats. Even so, I didn't think they'd pay that well for a few minutes of entertainment."

"Was Nalce around?" Sam the Artist asked.

"Didn't see him," the Reverend said. "Maybe Cal's disguise confused him."

Tel shook her head. "He followed us for a short time after we left the beach, and then he seemed to lose interest. I think maybe he was temporarily substituting for someone who's a lot more skilled."

They finished their yuck. The Reverend, on being assured

that Caland was through playing the cripple for that evening, went off to hold one of his periodic religious services at the end of the Prom. "But the tourists don't shower money on me," he said with a wistful smile. "They don't even stop to listen."

Sam the Artist pushed his mug aside. "Coming to the beach?"

Tel looked at Caland inquiringly.

"I feel awful tired," Caland said.

He'd had an active day in addition to the stress of preparing a strenuous performance, and worrying about it, and finally bringing it off. His unused muscles were still aching. He felt both pained and exhausted.

Tel shook her head at Sam

"Give Sam fifteen chits," Caland said. "He can have a big party and invite all the hungry people he can find."

Sam flashed his puckish grin. "With pleasure. There's nothing I enjoy more than throwing a party with someone else's money."

Tel was frowning at the milling crowd on the Prom. Another 'busload of tourists had arrived; there were many newcomers among them, and they disrupted the flow of traffic by stopping to gawk every few meters. A familiar figure separated from them and bounded into Nello's.

It was Hairy, and he edged his way purposefully toward their table.

"Dal Eddyer wants to see you," he told Caland. "As soon as you can."

Caland straightened up resentfully. "I've already seen him."

"He wants to see you again."

"But why?" Caland demanded. "I haven't anything different to say."

"Maybe he has," Tel said. She told Hairy, "All right. He'll see him."

"Silly waste of time," Caland protested. "Why go through that again?"

"Hush," Tel said. "Dal Eddyer is an up person. It isn't his fault that his business is handling money. Someone has to do it. Hear what he has to say and tell him no politely."

The Road to Hell was bouncing with activity. It sounded as though all of the gambling machines were in use, each with its own group of players, and the choruses of whoops and cheers and groans drowned out the clicks and chirps and whistles and chimes and roars of the machines. Eddyer was busy; Caland and Tel passed the time in polite conversation with Monelle Eddyer until he finally appeared and beckoned to Caland. Caland followed him to the tiny office, where he got Caland seated and shut the door on the blast of sound from the gambling rooms. If Caland's ragged clothing piqued his curiosity, he showed no sign of it.

"It's like this," Eddyer said, and Caland listened noncommittally while Eddyer told him how it was. Caland's rent was to be paid; arrangements already had been made. In addition, Caland was to receive an allowance of a hundred chits per sennite.

Eddyer presented the signature card. "Sign here, please."

Caland sat back and regarded him with studied disbelief. "No restriction?"

"None."

"No mention of begging?"

"None."

Caland reflected. "It's still not what I'd call generous. I can do better than this on the Prom in a few minutes. Much better."

"That's your business entirely. It has nothing to do with this. As far as I'm concerned, the rent and the hundred chits per sennite are a gift. But I have to have your signature and prints as a proper receipt for the payment."

Caland reflected again. Then he signed his name and surrendered his prints. Eddyer counted out a hundred chits, and then introduced him to the Road to Hell's two cashiers so they would know him when he came in each sennite for his allowance.

"I decided," Caland said to Tel afterward, "that if anyone was willing to enrich the Valley economy by one hundred chits per sennite, for whatever reason, he ought to be encouraged. I also like the idea of using a criminal's own money to bring him to justice."

Tel laughed heartily. "The Reverend says great truths don't require the support of logic, but those two certainly have it. Are you going to go on begging?"

"Of course. I still need a lot of money."

"Still want to go to bed?"

He nodded. "I'm really tired."

He also wanted to draw the comforting darkness about him and think. Money, and the knowledge that he still had talent that people would pay to enjoy, gave him an exhilarating sense of freedom, but he knew that it was illusory. He had someone watching him everywhere he went for an unknown purpose, and he had friends guarding him diligently at all times so that his body could not be abducted even if his mind were stolen.

It was a strange sort of freedom, but for the moment he was willing to settle for it because he was enjoying another, much more important freedom: the freedom from brain-seizing nightmares. He hadn't had a really painful one since that first night in the Valley, and that was something to be savored as they threaded their way back to the apartment and sleep.

CHAPTER SIXTEEN

Time flowed in the Valley, and Caland, though deeply preoccupied with his own problems, could not avoid drifting with it.
Elsewhere life moved in jerks—a spurt, a halt, a disconnected
sideways lurch, an altercation. Valley time coursed like a lazily
flowing river that meandered without purpose from Prom to
beach to—when exhaustion set in—the apartment for sleeping.

Sporadically the rains came. When the wind blew offshore,
solitary, brooding, humped clouds floated in from the ocean.
Often their passing was marked by a drizzle so light that it did
not interfere with the nightly celebrations around the beach
fires or the gawking clusters of tourists on the Prom. But occasionally there came a larger cloud, of formidable blackness,
bringing with it a sheet of water that instantly drenched anyone
or anything caught in the open.

Fate nodded fickly on the Prom merchants when the rains fell.
A heavy storm could bring prosperity or disaster. Those located
in quarters with sound roofs sometimes were fortunate enough
to have a crowd of tourists impulsively seek shelter there. Shops
not otherwise patronized by tourists maintained special displays
of merchandise against the happy possibility of a brief invasion
by captive, wealthy passersby. While the tourists waited impatiently for the rain to let up, their boredom inevitably set them
prowling among the displays. A few token purchases meant
temporary affluence to the small Prom merchant. Sometimes
the tourists found an odd item that mysteriously captured their
fancies and started a fad, and for days afterward, others would

trickle into the shop seeking more of the same.

The poorer merchants, in flimsy shelters, lost all of their customers during a heavy rain—even the Vals scrambled for cover. Often they suffered damage to their goods as well. But the impact, whether prosperous or ruinous, was fleeting. The rains passed quickly, leaving a soggy environment that was quickly tracked onto the well-drained Prom as Vals walked about with muddy sand clinging to mocs or bare feet. The newly affluent paid some of their debts; those who had suffered damage borrowed money for new stock; and Valley time slipped back into its unperturbed flow.

As Tel remarked, a nice thing about the Valley was that neither success nor failure mattered much. There was plenty of time to try things, and there also was plenty of time to try them over again or to try something else.

Despite the constant influx of tourists and the egress of Vals pursuing errands in Paradise or at the Port, the Valley fostered an illusion of self-sufficiency as though it were a world unto itself mysteriously surrounded by a fantasy called Mort. Spaceships descending at the Port or at the various Pak Enterprises could easily be seen from the Valley. Several times a sennite, an enormous cargo ship seemed to hover over the Valley as it slowly settled to the landing block behind the fertilizer factory. It discharged supplies and equipment, took on a full load of fertilizer, and lifted again in a matter of hours. None of these events seemed in any way related to life in the Valley, and none of the Vals paid the slightest attention to them.

Caland's thoughts were on money: how many searchers to hire, how to recruit and train them, what his payroll would be, how much it would cost if his own private search had to be extended to other worlds. He lost track of days, and when a sennite had expired, Dal Eddyer had to send Hairy to remind him to pick up his allowance. By that time the hundred chits had faded to insignificance. His strength and stamina were slowly returning to him, and he was able to polish his begging act and repeat it several times each evening. One record night he took in almost two thousand chits.

He devoted some time to carefully observing the techniques of his competitors. Some of their ploys were brilliant. A wiry little mal named Deve would select a group of tourists the moment they got off the 'bus and bombard them with his Valley lecture. "This is an upside-down community," he would tell them finally. "If you want to know what the Valley really looks like, you've got to walk on your hands."

Good-natured banter would follow, with the inevitable challenge, and Deve would deftly kick his feet into the air, and walk off on his hands surrounded by laughing, joshing tourists. Fifteen or twenty meters along the Prom he would collapse ignominiously, and the tourists would hoot their disdain and wander off.

"Idiot!" Caland muttered when he first saw the performance.

He changed his mind when he saw Deve counting his chits afterward. The little acrobat performed only two or three times a sennite and supported himself in style.

Caland's observations set him to working out new routines that would further inflate his own take. He continued to expend all of his energy on his evening performances, returning to apartment and bed immediately afterward, until one night he saw Baris Bronlan watching his act curiously while pressed amidst the audience of tourists. The sight twitched his conscience and turned his thoughts from the art and science of begging to those proud ones who preferred starvation and scaving the Prom at dawn to a para's self-inflicted humiliation. While money piled up in the special account he'd opened with Dal Eddyer, he had not been making his fair contribution toward feeding the hungry.

"Let's have a special beach fire of our own," he suggested to Tel later.

Tel flashed her warm smile. "Just the two of us? People will think we're perverted."

"Couldn't we have a party for just some really hungry people?"

"Most of them won't be at the beach. They can't stand it. If they don't luck onto a fire with food, they have to sit there all evening smelling it and watching someone else eat."

"Wouldn't Bar know whom to ask?"

"Let's see if we can find him."

They picked up the ubiquitous Hairy along the way, and they found Bronlan already in bed. Bronlan did indeed have an encyclopedic memory of those he'd seen scaving recently, but he knew very few of them by name and none by address. Many were living in concealed nests in the thick Valley vegetation. Bronlan described them to Hairy, who promised to do what he could while Caland and Tel got the fire going.

Because tending the fire and buying and cooking the food for a crowd of hungry people would be more work than two of them could manage, they recruited Moppy, Sippy, and a friend of theirs, a lubberly-looking fem called Baby, to help them. It was a lovely Valley night, with the long, sinuous line of beach fires stretching the entire two-kilometer length of the shining beach. Children raced about exuberantly, swimmers splashed and shouted, and the beach reverberated with song and laughter.

Into that atmosphere of hearty fellowship and good cheer, the proud ones ventured with almost excruciating timidity. Caland had expected them to be very young or very old, but they were of all ages, and they included two couples with young children. Under Hairy's patient prodding, small groups of them drifted along the beach toward the fire site Caland had chosen. Baby went to welcome them, and Hairy turned back to assemble another group.

In the end there were almost thirty of them, and Caland and Tel and their assistants worked frantically to prepare the huge quantities of food required. It was a subdued party with none of the repartee Caland had enjoyed around other beach fires. These unfortunates hypnotically fixed their attention on the sizzling food in silent anticipation of the moment when they could also occupy their mouths with it.

The single exception was a beefy, deeply-bronzed mal who contrasted starkly with the scrawny Vals about him. At first he watched quietly, like the others; but when Caland and Tel began passing out food, he grinned at Caland and said, "Quite a turnout this. A Caland putting food into mouths instead of taking it out."

Caland hardly heard him. His strength and stamina were returning, but his stint as a beggar left him totally exhausted, and he was intent on getting everyone served, on safely conveying chunks of bread with their sizzling bits of meat into every outstretched hand.

Tel reacted instantly. "Do I hear one of the guests complaining?"

"Not complaining," the beefy mal said easily. "Expressing my gratitude and amazement. It isn't often that one sees a billionaire giving anything away without first putting his hand into someone's pocket."

Tel looked him over carefully. "Who invited you?"

The mal hesitated before he answered, a bit uneasily, "The same bald mal who invited everyone."

"Then consider yourself lucky and enjoy your food. If you want to know who financed this party, tourists did. Cal did a para stint on the Prom this evening, and this is how he chose to spend the money."

There were no more outbursts, but when Hairy came by to see how the party was going, Tel motioned to him and whispered a question. Hairy looked the beefy mal over very carefully and shook his head.

"Do *you* recognize him?" Tel asked Caland softly.

"No. I don't think so."

Sam the Artist came by later and Tel held another whispered conference. Then she said to Caland, "Are you sure you don't recognize him?"

"I'm never sure that I don't. Sometimes I'm sure that I do. What's wrong?"

"Nothing—maybe. After Nalce stopped following us that day, he had a long talk with this character. We're wondering if he was reporting."

A subdued party was precisely the kind that Caland needed. Despite the unwelcome intrusion, he dozed off on the beach and had to be helped home to bed by Tel.

"You're working too hard," she said sternly. "I know you're getting stronger, but that doesn't help if you keep trying to do more. Was that the kind of party you wanted?"

"Yes, but—who was he?"

"Your rude guest? I don't know. We'll try to find out in the morning."

"How much money do I have?"

"Almost twenty thousand chits," Tel said. "If you're thinking of setting a record—"

"I'm thinking that it's time I started my own searching."

In the morning they took their break at a little eatery they'd never patronized before—it was so obscure that it was still nameless, which meant that it gave them a measure of privacy—and Hairy brought Louie Laggie to them. Laggie was Caland's first choice as a searcher—or watcher, which was what they wanted him to do. Watch and listen. Vals like Sam the Artist and the Reverend were personages. They had their own regular activities and self-assumed responsibilities, and they moved in regular orbits. They attracted attention and crowds of friends wherever they went. Except on a temporary emergency basis, they were useless for the kind of work Caland had in mind. But for years Louie Laggie had spent his waking hours snooping around everywhere, and anyone seeing him knew that it was only a scav at work and paid no more attention to him.

"Fifteen chits a sennite," Tel suggested.

"Wow!" Louie exclaimed. "For that, I'd be willing to hide under Pakovich's bed."

"If you're able to recruit a team of scavs like yourself and properly supervise them, I'll make it twenty," Caland said. "But I want people who can keep their mouths shut. It's supposed to be impossible to keep a secret in the Valley, but I want this one kept. No one is to know about your watching but us."

"Leave it to me," Louie Laggie said.

He went off with Hairy to find the beefy intruder of the previous night's beach party. Hairy was the one other person who had to know what was going on. It was impossible to organize anything at all in the Valley without Hairy.

But Hairy was completely reliable. He knew more Valley secrets than Dal Eddyer—and kept them.

Caland and Tel moved on to Nello's, where they found the Reverend and Sam the Artist at their favorite corner table arguing about religion. Sam welcomed them with his usual bushy grin and offered them yuck and an O loaf, a long loaf of sweet bread twisted into a circle. They broke off chunks and dunked them in the yuck, and Sam and the Reverend resumed their argument.

"I'm trying to convince him that he should establish a Valley church," Sam said. "The next store that's vacant, he should snap it up. It'd serve several useful purposes. It'd save someone from the temptation to start a new business and go bankrupt. It'd give his congregation a headquarters and an identity. It'd also give the Valley a public meeting place it has long needed. But he thinks his followers ought to have their devotion tested regularly by being forced to worship in the rain. Now I ask you." He appealed to Caland and Tel. "Why would a minister, or a pastor, or a priest, or whatever the Reverend fancies himself in this incarnation—why would he be opposed to having a church?"

"Churches—whether the term refers to a building for public worship or the religious organization that uses it—churches aren't essential to the practice of religion," the Reverend said. "On the most religious world I've ever encountered, churches are outlawed."

"How is it possible to legislate against the practice of religion?" Sam the Artist demanded.

"Not religion," the Reverend said. "Just churches. Places of worship and the organizations that occupy them. They tend to evolve according to their own peculiar genetics, and as they grow and become powerful, their concern for religion becomes incidental. They make use of religion to accomplish their secular aims. In the name of the Deity, they issue manifestos that would require the entire human race to live, work, believe, and worship in the manner their own narrow doctrine prescribes. Their consuming objective becomes the exercise of power— politically, economically, psychologically, sociologically—first over their own members and then over everyone. If they can't achieve that end through manipulations, legal or illegal, they resort to war. Churches are the authors of much of the misery suffered by humans throughout history. The world I mentioned, which is called Dlird Z, was determined to avoid that. So—no churches. This in no way interferes with the worship of what-ever God one prefers in whatever way one prefers, and espe-cially it doesn't prevent anyone from living according to the highest standards of religious ethics."

"None of those bad things are likely to happen in the Valley," Sam the Artist said.

"Of course not. My objection to a Valley church is that churches are symbols, and symbols tend to replace the things they're symbols of. If one worships and believes under the strict control of a church's dogma, one ends by worshipping the church and its dogma. Also churches tend to become store-houses—places where people keep their religion. The members may diligently call there at regular intervals and check out their beliefs for a time—damp and a little moldy—and air them, but then they pack them away again and go off to lead lives that are totally bereft of religion." Smiling, the Reverend turned to Caland and Tel. "Disputation is said to add savor to one's break, but I don't know whether religious disputation qualifies. How's the Valley's foremost para feeling this morning?"

"Full of ideas," Tel said. "But not about churches. He had me up at dawn to practice a new routine on me."

"Yes," the Reverend said meditatively. "Yes, indeed. I'm full of ideas myself and not about churches. I've been reflecting on what you said about begging being a form of acting. Would it be possible to teach others how to do it?"

Caland said slowly, "You mean—establish a school for

paras?"

"Something like that. Except that it would be a community project to raise money for things the Valley needs. School dins, maybe. Jobs for hungry people. There are simple things we could hire them to do, like clean up the Prom—which needs it—and we could pay them for it."

Caland hesitated. His mind was on Louie Laggie and an expanding force of searchers that would ultimately track down the fiend who'd been tampering with his mind. A school for paras would be a distraction. It easily could become a time-consuming hindrance.

But he could not in good conscience ignore the proud Vals who would not beg but would work if there was any. He thought about Baris Bronlan, and he was about to answer that he would do what he could when Sam the Artist cleared his throat ostentatiously—the warning signal for a proclamation.

"Let's consider a couple of practical matters before you start counting all the money this is going to take in. For one thing, there's no question of taking control of the Valley's begging business and organizing it for charity, no matter how worthy the charity may be. We have Vals who have been supporting themselves for years by begging or by working the tourists for grats. They're not as effective as Cal, but it's a living for them."

"There wasn't any thought of asking them to stop," the Reverend protested.

"Whether you ask them or not, you're bound to cut into their business if you launch crowds of trained paras at the tourists. I don't know how much money tourists are prepared to hand out in the Valley each day, but it's got to be finite. The more paras, the smaller each one's take. If ours are trained to put on a better act, they'll grab proportionally larger shares, and I can foresee trouble."

"Just a moment," Tel said. "Cal has an enormous take each night. Have any of the others claimed that he's cutting them out?"

"Not that I've heard of, but there's only one of him."

"I wasn't thinking in terms of crowds of paras," the Reverend said. "Just a few well-trained people with talent."

"Then you should consider this: once you've trained a group of people to beg for all of your cherished civic betterment projects, what's to prevent them from cutting loose and using the techniques you've taught them to beg for themselves?"

"We'd give you the job of making certain that none of them get out of line," Tel murmured.

Sam the Artist snorted.

"It must be tried," the Reverend said. "If a conflict develops, surely it can be resolved amicably. What have we to lose? There are so many needs in the Valley," he went on pensively, "and even a little buys so much. If Cal's students only gain a few hundred chits where he collects a thousand, a hundred would still buy a hot din each noon for a lot of children."

"When does this school of yours open for business?" Sam the Artist asked. "It seems to me—"

He broke off. Tel had leaped to her feet with an exclamation. She stood staring out at the Prom, and Sam and the Reverend twisted in their chairs to see what she was looking at.

"Sippy," she said. "With Nalce. Hand in hand." She sat down again. "What do you make of that?"

Sam the Artist shrugged massively. "One more fickle fem on a tear. That's what I make of it."

"I did hear that there'd been a disagreement," the Reverend said. "A rather loud one, in fact. Sippy and Moppy were sharing a shelter in one of the cemeteries, and they woke up the place."

"And Sippy walked out," Tel said. "Obviously."

"Yes. But the report I heard didn't suggest that it was permanent."

"I think you can take it that way. But why Nalce?"

"You're young," Sam the Artist grinned. "I've reached a point where I'm too wise to ask myself questions like that."

"Have *you* heard anything?"

Sam shook his head. "We checked Nalce in at his apartment and assumed that he'd gone to bed. It's impossible to keep effective watch in the dark."

Cal and the Reverend returned to the subject of a school for paras. Caland explained, choosing his words carefully, that a really successful para would have to develop and perfect his own unique approach—one suited to his personality and talent—and this could not be taught in school. It would require individual coaching. The first requirement would be a list of candidates for screening. The Reverend promised to produce one.

Caland and Tel moved on to the bay beach, where they saw Nalce and Sippy sunning themselves amidst a crowd of sunbathers. Caland turned away with a scowl. If he hadn't been tardy in launching his own team of watchers, he wouldn't have to speculate about what had happened the previous night. He'd know.

"Shall we try the ocean beach?" he asked Tel.

She pursed her lips thoughtfully. "First let's see if anything develops here."

She found a pile of sand and began fashioning a bigger and better sea monster. Caland helped her to bring water, pausing between trips to enjoy the changing tints of the bay and the darting blobs of color that were the tourist sail boats. The only thing that developed was a visit from the fat retired prostitute, Thalm. She staggered along drunkenly, weaving her way among the sprawled sunbathers until she stumbled over Tel's sculpture. She looked up at Caland and blinked bewilderedly. "It's you, dearie. Why'd you trip me?"

Before he could protest his innocence, she turned to Tel. "And you. Been wondering how you two were getting along. No lover's quarrels yet?"

Probably everyone in the Valley now took Caland and Tel's relationship for granted. When a mal and a fem had been insep-arable companions for sennites, speculation about them ceased; but Thalm was intent on probing strata untouched by ordinary gossip. She gathered her legs under her, smoothed down her flopping dress, and leered again, "No lovers' quarrels?"

"What would we quarrel about?" Tel asked with a smile.

"Any of a million, million things. Lovers always get their priorities mixed. Which is more important—love or a break? You'd better agree quickly on that, or Cal will be sulking."

"He wouldn't dare to be that stupid," Tel said. "He's only got to express himself. As long as I get both, I don't care what order they come in."

"It's all very well to talk like that," Thalm said reprovingly, "but it's a mistake to generalize about mals, dearie. Fems who say mals are all alike are too stupid to see the differences."

Caland roused himself. "Are you saying all mals are different?" he asked, affecting an innocent, wide-eyed amazement.

"In certain ways," Thalm giggled. "In certain ways. The differences are in the similarities."

"You'd better explain that," Tel said.

Thalm nodded sagely. "You're just the right age to understand. These young fems, they have an idea of what a mal should be, and they want every mal to be like that. The most foolish ones, they think every mal *is* like that. Fems my age, they can't afford to worry about the differences, they have to take what they can get. You're just the right age—you should be able to understand the differences and make the most of them."

On the crowded bay beach, no conversation spoken above a whisper was private. Nearby sunbathers shook off their somnolence and rose up on elbows, grinning, to take in the developing scene. Children interrupted their frenzied rushes to look on curiously. Players of Zexit, a strange game pursued on a diagram drawn in the sand, paused to watch and listen.

"Let's have that again about the differences being in the similarities," Tel suggested.

"The differences are in the ways mals are alike."

"I still don't grab the add."

Thalm looked at Tel disgustedly. "You can't be *that* naïve. You see, all mals have—"

Caland interrupted quickly. "I don't think this a suitable subject for public conversation, even in the Valley."

Thalm giggled again. "Anyway, all mals have one, but no two are alike. Don't you see? The differences are in the similarities."

"In that case, the differences between fems are also in their similarities," Caland said.

Thalm beamed at him. "Now you're growing. When a fem says any mal will do, she's thinking of the similarities. When she says only one mal will do, she's thinking of the ways his similarities are different."

"I never realized that human relationships could be so complicated."

"That's because there are so many ways the similarities can be different." Thalm pushed herself to her feet, waved a good-by, and huffed off along the beach. Shouts of laughter pursued her.

"And if a mal and a fem can't think of any differences," Tel said, "there'll always be a few meddlers around who can invent some."

She resumed work on her dirt art. Caland removed his stubs and stretched out in the sun. Already his sun-darkened skin resembled Tel's, and he luxuriated in the warmth that enveloped him. Never in his life could he remember having been contented, but it seemed to him that what he was experiencing now could be something remarkably like contentment if only the entangled vibrations of mystery would stop jangling around him.

* * * * * * *

Time flowed and Caland continued to flow with it. Tel convinced him that this was essential. He was the bait upon which the trap must eventually snap shut, and the trap would miss its quarry utterly if the bait persisted in wandering off on hunts of its own. Louie Laggie's growing team of scavs must do the watching; Caland must flow with the Valley time to provide a predictable orbit for the watchers.

He did his best to assume the role of conspicuous, unsuspecting bait—even when, emerging from sunbathing somno-lence, he opened his eyes and met those of Nalce, who was watching him intently while pretending to be a looker at a nearby Zexit game. He heard occasionally from Arlu, but the searcher could only report that he had nothing to report—a search that spanned a galaxy took time, as he seemed overly fond of explaining—and to ask whether Caland had had any more nightmares or recognized anyone or anything.

"He's as baffled as the rest of us," Tel remarked after one of these brief meetings.

Several days after Caland launched his own team of watchers, Louie Laggie sought them out on the beach to ask their opinion of a putrebun. A friend of his, a Val named Thinso—oddly enough because she was so thin—had opened a new eatery, and Louie had loyally purchased a few samples. Caland's reaction was decidedly negative, and Tel opined that no one would dare to sell a putrebun that was so totally inedible. Louie must have scaved them.

But the buns weren't why Louie had come looking for them. He wanted to report. Nalce had circulated widely through the Valley, but until he'd taken up with Sippy, he'd made no friends. He kept to himself and remained politely aloof to friendly overtures. Usually Valley newcomers, even the solitary types, melted quickly under the pressure of living in close contact with so many open, gregarious people, but Nalce hadn't. Nothing else very singular had been noted about him. He had no inter-ests that anyone could comment on.

But his neighbors were beginning to consider him peculiar. "He wastes time without doing anything," Louie Laggie said. "In the Valley, that's perverted behavior."

"Granst?" Tel asked. Granst was the beefy mal who had wedged at the beach party.

"No further contacts. Maybe Sippy could tell us something if she would, but she refuses to discuss her mal. That's why I wanted to see you. I can cover all the exits on both houses, but it would take two more people, per house, to make certain that one or both of them don't sneak out side windows. Do we really want to pay people to sit there in the dark all night?"

Caland looked at Tel and nodded. "We'll need them eventually," he said. "Better put them to work now and let them get some experience."

Louie grinned and shuffled off along the beach, pausing to distribute his remaining putrebuns along the way. His ploy in arranging a meeting pleased Caland, but the failure to find out anything about Nalce and Granst was disappointing.

Later, when Sam the Artist happened by, Cal tried to get at the puzzle from another angle. "Why did Moppy and Sippy break up?" he asked.

Sam the Artist's chest heaved and subsided—his method of understanding the futility of trying to understand human frailties. "As the Reverend would say, there is very little mathematical exactitude in human relationships. Their intimate friendship, which had flowered amicably for at least seven terms, came to an abrupt halt over a mug of yuck."

"Say that again," Tel demanded.

"It's the solemn truth. They had an argument about yuck. In the middle of the night, no less. It ended only when Sippy stalked away in a rage. If she hadn't happened to meet Nalce, she might have walked herself into a better temper and returned. Since she didn't, she didn't. But perhaps she would have been too late in any case, because Moppy didn't languish for long. Sippy's friend Baby, who occupied the shelter next door, was awakened along with everyone in the area. She tried to restore peace or at least to establish an armed truce. When Sippy walked out, Moppy and Baby decided it would be silly for both of them to sleep in the cold when they could so easily keep each other warm. It's as simple as that."

"The hell it is," Tel said. "How could anyone possibly work up a fight over yuck?"

"They were arguing about which Valley eatery serves the best. Silly but true. At least Euphemina is pleased about what happened."

Tel and Caland looked at each other. "It's a schizophrenic universe," Tel said, "and it keeps giving me the feeling that the people I'm listening to aren't saying what I'm hearing. Who— or what—is Euphemina?"

"Moppy's new girl. Everyone calls her Baby, but her real name is Euphemina. It's awkward for her that Sippy was her best friend—in fact, her only friend. The gossips are trying to make out that she's a traitor, but she's too happy to notice."

"There," Tel said. "The answer to all human problems. Being too happy to notice."

Valley time flowed, from apartment to Prom to beach to apartment, with the same landmarks cropping up periodically: Gary Dwand wandering aimlessly about and asking everyone, "Have you seen Melana?" Melana, a vision of poised beauty, boarding the Valley 'bus for the Paradise Library and an evening of research; Baris Bronlan quietly listening to the conversation of a strange assortment of guests at one of his din parties or raptly watching the spectacular Mort sunset; Sdissler scavenging the scavs at dawn on the Prom.

In the fourth sennite of Caland's Valley residence, Sdissler— who was no one's confidant and hence had not heard about Caland's spectacular career as a Prom para—succumbed to mercenary curiosity about Caland's financial status. He bearded him on the Prom in broad daylight while a crowd of interested Vals looked on.

Caland became aware of his presence when he heard his name pronounced like a proclamation. "Mal—ah—Cal."

With his obscene obesity, his preposterous dress, and his fatuous pomposity, Sdissler looked like a caricature of human excesses. He was wearing a brilliant daysuit ornamented with green trim, and his sagging, purplish jowls formed a blotch on his shirt front. It intrigued Caland that Regelz Arlu could wear such colors with spectacular effect, while Dedris Sdissler looked like something that even a bad artist would have wiped away the moment he perpetrated it.

"Mal—ah—Cal," Sdissler said again. "It may be that I can

be of service to you."

"I can't imagine how," Caland murmured politely. Tel, who had swung around belligerently and seemed poised to pummel Sdissler from behind if he made the slightest misstep, snickered.

"We both understand...ah, um...that employment requiring... um...executive capability...ah, um...is exceedingly difficult to discover in a place like this, but—"

"We do indeed understand that," Caland interrupted. "If my Valley Enterprises organization turns up an opening requiring such a capability, I'll keep you in mind."

He nodded solemnly and turned away. Tel managed to contain her hilarity for almost six strides before she burst into shrieks of laughter. Behind them the Vals were hooting while Sdissler's broad form shuffled away with an air of obtuse puzzlement.

"You said something remarkable," Tel observed when she could speak again.

"That in itself would be remarkable."

"I'm serious. You said 'Valley Enterprises.' What a lovely counter to Pakovich's Pak Enterprises. It's just what the Valley needs. I'll suggest it to the Reverend."

Cal nodded absently. His own enterprises were enjoying mixed success. He'd continued to expand and sharpen his para act, and his audiences were growing. Sam the Artist made the interesting discovery that many tourists visiting the Valley for the first time were coming to see Caland on the recommendation of friends. He also discovered that many of those watching Caland had seen him before and were enjoying his performance a second, third, or even fourth time. The average take had passed fifteen hundred chits each night, and Caland thought he could level off at two thousand.

If that enterprise was doing well, the Reverend's para school was a disaster. The Reverend looked for bright, eager people with acting ability—people who could enter into the roles Caland devised for them and perhaps even gain the competence to perform little skits and plays. He thought the tourists would be certain to pay generously for such honestly contrived entertainment. What he got were bright, eager people with no ability at all but with a burning ambition to be—another Cal. They had seen him perform and all of them wanted to be toothless old reprobates who snarled brilliant witticisms and insults. Even the fems. Further, they could not comprehend the years of experience and the thought and work that had gone into Caland's act. They expected the tourists to rain chits on them if they donned costume and makeup. Caland's suggestions as to other roles were followed reluctantly, and even the tourists ridiculed the results.

The disappointment had begun with Caland's first student, Moppy, who combined a total lack of acting ability with a voice that was just sufficiently high-pitched to sound ridiculous. Caland liked Moppy, and he had hoped that a modest success as a para would compensate for his loss of Sippy—Caland hadn't taken the new liaison with Baby seriously. The first lesson was the last. Moppy, like those who followed him, wanted to be another Cal.

Several days after the encounter with Sdissler, Caland was still brooding on his series of failures while he and Tel sipped yuck in Nello's; but his mind dwelt more heavily on the failure of his new watchers. Granst had moved out of the Valley, though he continued to visit it frequently. He was living in the small hote Pakovich maintained at the space port for spacers with layovers and the scattering of non-tourist visitors to Mort. Nalce's behavior remained peculiar, but he seemed to have abandoned interest in Caland.

"The problem with that kind of search," Tel said, "is that you don't know that there's anything to find. So it's silly to be disappointed when you don't find it."

"Do we call Louie's people off?"

"Definitely not. It's silly to be disappointed when you don't find anything, but it's also silly to give up too soon. Nalce and his friends are up to something, and we might as well keep on them until we find out what it is. Louie and his scavs seem to be functioning well. Speaking of scavs—"

Sdissler was walking past—a now familiar, bloated, ridiculously dressed figure. Vals hooted at him; he elevated his nose several degrees and ignored them. Caland looked at him absently. Then, as a whirl of facts and impressions suddenly snapped into clear focus, he stirred himself and leaned forward.

"There's something wrong," he announced.

"There's always something wrong in the Valley," Tel said complacently.

"There's something wrong about Sdissler. He's not real."

"Vals have known that for years." Tel turned and abruptly stared at Caland. "Don't tell me you've suddenly recognized him!"

"Yes. I mean—I recognize his type. He's an actor. I should have seen that before. He's acting a part, and he's doing it superbly well."

"Pity he didn't choose a more attractive one," Tel said. She leaned forward. "Look here. Are you saying—flat out—that Sdissler is a phony?"

"Why else would he be acting a part? He's created a ridiculous character, and he's going to great lengths to keep up the performance. What do you know about him?"

Tel waved a hand. Chan Worntling, the Doll's House enforcer, was passing by. He returned Tel's wave, and a moment later he joined them.

"Cal was asking about Sdissler's background," Tel said. "Know anything about him?"

"Very little about him before he came to Mort," Worntling said. "Too much after he arrived here. I heard that he met Pakovich on Aravia. Who he was, or what he was doing there, I have no idea. Pakovich was complaining about the problem of getting people to do his dirty work, and Sdissler offered to take it off his hands. That's the story. Rumor has it that Pakovich loathes him, but he puts up with him because Sdissler keeps costs down and gets the work done efficiently."

"But who actually does the work?" Caland persisted.

"He imports labor, and he hires as many Vals as he can,"

Worntling said.

"But everyone in the Valley loathes him, too," Caland said thoughtfully. "No newcomer could be here a day without being warned about him. How could he recruit labor under those circumstances? How many Vals actually work for him?"

"Most of them," Worntling said. "Most of the mals, anyway. From garbage 'trucks and all kinds of clean-up details to the forest labor camps. If you want work for a day or a week or a year and don't care what you do or how little you're paid, Sdissler has a job for you. He'll also provide a bed and meals if you need them, and are willing to let him deduct more than they're worth from your pay. The beds are said to be comfortable. Reports on the meals vary. Why the sudden interest in Sdissler? Surely you don't need a job!"

"Cal thinks Sdissler is up to something," Tel said.

Worntling shrugged. "If he is, he's been up to it for a long, long time. Why hasn't anything happened? What could happen?"

After he left them, Tel said thoughtfully to Caland, "You were right. We need to conduct our own searches with our own watchers. Sdissler has been here for so long that he's part of the landscape. An unsavory part, like his garbage trucks, and people pay no more attention to the one than the others. Arlu would never consent to waste time and money searching him. What could he have to do with you? He didn't even take note of your existence until a few days ago, and then he approached you the way he approaches all newcomers."

"Do you agree that we should have him watched?"

"Of course. The thing is—you're a part of the plan, and that plan now includes Mort, and anything off about Mort may turn out to have something to do with you. Certainly we'll have to have him watched."

Relaxed in the bedroom's softly enfolding darkness that night, drowsily teetering on the verge of sleep, Caland watched Sdissler mince along the Prom in a half-dream that seemed more like an awakening. Tel's lips, caressing the back of his neck, asking sleepily, "How long has it been since your accident? Can you remember?"

Caland reflected. "I suppose I could figure out an answer to that, but it probably wouldn't be accurate. There are so many blanks in my memory. I can't even remember whether there was a date on that medical card, and I'm sure I once knew it by heart. Arlu should know."

"It must be several years," Tel suggested.

"It must be," Caland agreed.

"And your sex life ended with the accident?"

Caland said lamely, "You see, my brain was smashed—"

Tel's warm body shook with laughter. "Until I met you, I didn't know there was any connection."

"Neither did I until it happened."

"Nerve damage," Tel said meditatively. "Naïve young girl that I am, I thought there was something involuntary about it. I'm wondering whether the problem might be mental rather than physiological. Of course you had what the doctors would call a massive trauma of the brain itself, but even so—" She was silent for a moment, and then she snuggled closer to Caland. "It just may be that this is something that could be worked out."

But it couldn't, or it took more working out than she could manage at the first attempt, and eventually they both slept.

CHAPTER SEVENTEEN

Time flowed, and Caland, who for so long had been threading one strange world after another onto the dreary skein of his
existence, should have found the sameness of its pattern, Prom
to beach to apartment, delicious. He did not. He worried about
the watches on Nalce and Sdissler and about the total failure of
the Reverend's para school. He seemed to be making no progress in any direction.

Louie Laggie had recruited a dozen scavs whom he could
call on as needed. These were mals and fems of assorted ages,
and they held certain traits in common. All were nondescriptly
familiar figures—not only in the Valley, but also in Paradise and
at Pak Enterprises installations, where they pottered endlessly
through refuse heaps. All possessed the same resourcefulness
that Louie Laggie demonstrated in worming his way through
Pakovich's many impenetrable fences. All possessed a fierce
loyalty to their benefactor. Louie kept scrupulous accounts and
submitted a payroll to Tel each sennite. The payments to individual scavs for their hours of watching seemed pathetically
small to Caland, but to the scavs they were a bonanza.

The watch on Nalce had turned ticklish. Arlu had placed Sam
the Artist in charge of his Valley searches, and Sam proved to be
a desultory searcher. For days his watch on Nalce was perfunctory; and then, with a bustle of too obvious activity, Sam would
have three people following Nalce everywhere he went. Louie
Laggie's scavs had to weave their own watch around that without
either Sam or Nalce detecting them. They not only succeeded;

they were enjoying the challenge, and Louie switched watchers on an intricate schedule that only he could understand.

The watch on Sdissler scored a sensational success on its second day. One of the scavs succeeded in following Sdissler to the Gate to Paradise lounge at the Port, where Sdissler held a long conversation in the darkest corner of that fashionably dim establishment with a mal easily identified as a tourist. The inexperienced scav, who was entirely on his own, made a brilliant decision. When the meeting broke up, he followed the tourist instead of Sdissler. At the Paradise Vista he quickly identified the tourist as one Weflan Krann, who had been on Mort for some time and who had acquired a reputation for his peculiar tastes. Krann eschewed such popular tourist activities as swimming and sail boating, and he was known to have made only one cursory visit to the Valley. On the other hand, he signed up for every available tourist tour of Mort's power plant, its fertilizer factory, its mines, its farms, its winery, its dairy, its cheese factory, its bakery, its meat packing plant. Suddenly they had a link between Sdissler and Caland, even though a tenuous one; and the supposedly innocuous Krann, who had traveled to Mort with Caland, and remembered him well enough to speak to him later, would have to be scrutinized by Arlu's searchers in Paradise.

They resolved not to tell Arlu about the link with Sdissler, however. For the moment that was theirs—to make of what they could.

"What really is so horrible about these forest labor camps I keep hearing about?" Caland asked. "And if they're that bad, why doesn't everyone simply walk out? Even if the recruits have signed contracts, neither Sdissler nor Pakovich could possibly enforce them."

"There are several camps," Tel said. "Some of them are hundreds of kilometers away. There's no transportation except Pakovich's flying freight platforms. There aren't any roads. Once you get there, you stay until your contract expires. Or longer if they really want you."

"What does the labor force do?"

"It labors in places that are too rough for machines. It's part of a continuing geological and forestry survey. Pakovich still has no notion of how wealthy his world is. This is his gesture at finding out. He really doesn't care, but he thinks he ought to take a peek now and then."

"If every Val is forewarned about these camps, where does Sdissler get his labor?"

"He imports it," Tel said.

"I don't believe that. Pakovich is supposed to tolerate Sdissler because he keeps costs down and gets the work done. But Sdissler can't keep costs down by hiring garbage collectors and forest laborers on other worlds and paying their transportation to Mort. What sort of decrepit specimens is he importing?"

"We only see the ones on the garbage details," Tel said. "Except for the Vals, they're all young and in good physical condition."

"But does he hire Vals for that?"

"Of course. Any Val who needs money badly enough to work long hours at short pay can have work any time he wants it—for however long he wants it. It's an established Valley tradition."

"That doesn't make sense either," Caland said. "How could anyone operate efficiently on that basis? Sdissler wouldn't know from one day to the next how much labor force he'd have or whether he'd have one. What about the girls he keeps at the Valley Hote?"

"The ones he has now are imported. It's rumored that he has a list of Valley girls for whom he occasionally makes deals with tourists, but if it's true, the girls don't brag about it."

"Do you know any Vals who've actually worked in these forest labor camps?"

"Of course. A number of them have. Kren Krent, for one. He still talks about it, and no one who heard him would want to have anything to do with Sdissler for any reason."

"I'd like to hear him myself," Caland said.

They found Krent engaged in a game of Zexit on the bay

beach. When they finally succeeded in prying him away, he told his tale of horror with gusto. He and two other Vals had signed on for a term at a forest labor camp shortly after their arrival in the Valley. They were hungry, and Sdissler promised plenty of good food. The pay was trivial, but at the moment it was food that interested them. What they got was lousy food, very little of it, and back-breaking, finger-tearing labor from dawn to dark. On the third day they refused to work. The Super returned them to the Valley, where Sdissler made them sign a forfeiture in return for a release from their contracts. They got paid nothing, they were fed almost nothing, and they were elated to be out of it. The other workers? They were from other worlds, and they hadn't seemed to mind the food and the work.

Tel compiled a list, and they got much the same story from other Vals who had been to the labor camps. Vals who had worked on the garbage 'trucks, picking up garbage and trash in the Valley and in Paradise and Fish Town and at the various Pak Enterprises, told a different story. It was hard, monotonous work for poor pay, and the hours were long; but it was sure pay and a sure job whenever anyone wanted one. Any time one of them needed money badly enough, he sought out Sdissler, and Sdissler signed him up for whatever time he wanted. Sdissler also recruited workers for special jobs, and for these, since many of them were urgent, he had to pay better rates. The Vals much preferred working the delivery details that unloaded provisions for Valley merchants or freight from the space port. Sdissler had nothing to do with these jobs. They also were hard work, but the pay was decent.

Caland and Tel were unable to find any girls who admitted to working for Sdissler.

"So what's the add?" Tel asked finally.

"I still say Sdissler's a fraud, but I couldn't guess why he would bother or how there could be any money in it."

"You're saying his attempt to hire Vals is an act, his pursuit of Melana is an act, and the character he's established here is a phony. But the only reason for an act would be to keep people's attention from what he's really doing, and what he's really doing is Mort's dirty work. He runs the world dump, he collects garbage, and he sees that tedious or filthy chores no one else wants to do are taken care of. If he stopped for a sennite, the world would begin to stink."

"All of that may be part of his act," Caland said. "Obviously, whatever he's trying to cover up isn't being done in Paradise or in the Valley. Is there any way we could get a good look at those forest camps?

"What happened to them is a part of Sdissler's act, too. Hire a few Vals now and then, make the pay so low and the work so rough that they'll warn everyone else off, and then import labor. If Sdissler really wanted to hire Vals, he'd have a different act—pay reasonably, offer decent working conditions, and make the work no more obnoxious than absolutely necessary. He'd also have a different reputation. Decent pay and working conditions ought to cost him less than importing labor. So how could we get a look at those camps?"

"I'm asking myself why I never thought of this," Tel said. "I suppose it's because no one pays attention to garbage, and none of the reports on the camps suggested that they were anything except what they were supposed to be. I have only the vaguest idea where they are."

"Where does Sdissler live?"

"At the Valley Hote," Tel said. "He has a sleeping room and an office there. He also has a tiny office over in the Paradise Government Mall."

"Seems straightforward enough."

"Immensely so. Everything about Sdissler always has been transparently straightforward. I suppose you'd say that's part of his act."

"It would be," Caland agreed.

"If it's an act, we'll soon catch him at it," Tel said grimly.

Arlu had been called away on business. When he returned, he held several conferences on the subject of strangers. The discussions were fraught with complexities. Wave after wave of strangers inundated the Valley daily. The problem was to delineate the one, or the two, or the several who might have an invisible connection with Caland.

"Tourists who seem to go places ordinary tourists wouldn't go," Arlu said for the tenth time in the manner of a professor reciting philosophical truths. He was clad in a chartreuse daysuit, and he made a most flamboyant oracle. "Non-tourists whose dress sets them apart. Anyone poking about where a stranger wouldn't. Anyone whose questions can't be accounted for by normal curiosity. Anyone asking about Cal."

Sam the Artist began to read through his list again. It consisted of fragmentary descriptions accompanied by dates and places, and most of the facts were embellished with question marks. Sam was too impulsive and too impatient to make a good searcher, and there were too many other things he preferred to waste time at. Arlu's disappointment in his findings was obvious.

None of the items on the list had meant anything to Caland the first he heard them, and he stopped listening. On the second reading his memory jerked him to attention with a click that seemed almost audible. "Read that again," he told Sam.

"Average height, slight build, narrow face, thin sandy hair, maybe bald on top but wearing a hat, clothing shabby in an artificial way—probably castoffs that once were good quality stuff. Seen at least four times, always after dark, always away from the Prom, always by accident when someone unexpectedly caught him in a light. Sounds downright suspicious, doesn't it?"

"But never seen anywhere near Cal," the Reverend pointed out.

"It sounds," Caland said slowly, "like Alexander the Second."

The silence was thunderous. Sam the Artist said quietly after a long pause, "Damned if it doesn't. But why would Alexander the Second be visiting the Valley in disguise or however?"

"*That* doesn't pose any problems," Arlu said. "He might have a favorite girl at the Dolls' House. Calta?"

"Absolutely not," Calta said. "Guaranteed."

"Or at Yda's?" Arlu persisted. Yda was not present.

"No. Also guaranteed. Yda would have told me."

"Would he disguise himself that elaborately to visit the Fig Stump?" the Reverend wondered.

"Excuse my contrariness," Tel said. "None of this is relevant. He's only been seen away from the Prom. No Yda's. No Dolls' House. No Fig Stump. No Burned Wafer. No girl at the Valley Hote. Since it's always night, no sunsets on the ocean beach. That also makes it unlikely that he comes here to admire Bar's spaceship. Unless you want to argue that he just happened to be walking from the fertilizer factory to Paradise by way of the Valley, this has got to mean that he's meeting someone, secretly, away from the Prom. Now, figure that out."

"But he's never been seen anywhere near Cal," the Reverend pointed out again.

Arlu turned to Caland. "You recognized him. Could you have seen him in the Valley?"

"I simply don't know," Caland said.

"Mmmm. Something more to search. Well then. Keep looking, and I'll go over my lists again." Arlu was conducting a search of his own concerning visitors to Mort whose stays at the tourist hotes or at the small space port hote overlapped certain crucial dates.

"What about that tourist that accosted Cal?" the Reverend asked. "Weflan Krann, wasn't it?"

Arlu snorted. "I've never encountered such a dull subject. He does nothing but take Pakovich's official tours. He visited the Valley just once and complained that the Fig Stump food was too rich. I'm going to write him off."

"Don't write him off," Tel said. "Cal has a hunch about him."

"If you say so," Arlu said. "But it can't be much of a hunch. Krann certainly has no interest in the Valley—or, by extension, in Cal. He's too dull to be anything but genuine."

"What about Zareent and his telepathic broadcasting towers?" Sam the Artist asked puckishly.

The Reverend protested. "Zareent was time travel. Fremanz

worked with telepathy."

Arlu drowned him out with another snort. "No respectable scientist has ever heard of him. At least none is willing to admit it. If he left followers, they were in hiding and stayed there."

"That leaves us with Nalce," Sam the Artist said. "He makes no sense whatsoever. He follows Cal; he loses interest completely; he suddenly follows him again."

The Reverend began solemnly, "Perhaps if I tried to talk with Sippy again—"

"I've talked with her," Sam the Artist said. "She parted with Nalce three days ago. All she knows is that he's a very strange mal. He seemed normal enough at first, but he never talked to her. He rarely said anything at all to anybody, and he was always sneaking off without telling her where he was going. That wasn't her idea of togetherness."

"Try this proposition," Tel remarked absently. "Alexander the Second visits the Valley to confer with Nalce."

Again the silence was thunderous, but only until Arlu lurched to his feet in disgust. "Why would he, when Nalce could so much more inconspicuously visit him? In veriest fact—I've never accumulated so many details that add up to so little."

"Is there anything new about Wes Fulm?" Caland asked. He had the feeling that the little mal ought to be on his conscience—a feeling difficult to reconcile with the fact that he remembered him so vaguely.

"Denials," Arlu said grimly. "Denials from Pak Enterprises and the world of Rynaif that there was anything unusual about his presence there. Denials from the proctors that anything unusual happened to him. Denials from Dombrily that he was anywhere near Rynaif. I suppose I ought to include your denial that his contact with you was anything but accidental. That's the way this search has gone—all of it."

He left for a sumptuous din downstairs in the Fig Stump, and Tel and Caland went down the outside staircase and circled around to the Prom, where they were confronted by Sdissler—a grossly large rainbow apparition in the most ornate daysuit

Caland had ever seen. Rumors that Caland was working a daily para stint had finally reached Sdissler, but not, apparently, accompanied by details about his success. Having noted that Caland was able-bodied, and having received this positive evidence of his impoverishment, the human scavenger dropped his line about an executive position and bluntly tried to recruit Caland for a few terms in a labor camp. Caland countered by trying to recruit Sdissler for the Reverend's nonexistent contingent of paras. A memorable scene ensued—one that was talked about for days by those who happened to witness it. It ended with Caland inviting Sdissler to report that evening for an audition.

"But change your clothes," Caland said. "Tourists almost never give money to paras wearing ruffles."

Caland and Tel walked away, leaving a thoroughly befuddled Sdissler staring after them.

"I especially liked it when you offered to show him how working for the Reverend furthered the cause of suffering humanity, whereas working for Sdissler only furthered the wealth of an insufferable Pakovich," Tel remarked. "That was a nice touch."

"What *is* he doing at those dratted forest labor camps?" Caland muttered.

They drifted from Prom to beach, where they encountered the usual spectacle of a crowd of Vals who had abandoned their swimming and sunbathing and Zexit games and time-wasting to form a circle and watch something. A familiar voice reached them mouthing familiar words. They exchanged startled glances and pushed through the circle to see what was happening.

Moppy sprawled on the sand, makeshift crutch lying nearby, makeshift hat open beside him with no money in it. He was mimicking Caland's para routine, and he had it memorized. In his impossibly thin voice, he recounted all of the jokes Caland had long since tired of while he delivered all of Caland's grimaces and leers and gestures with astonishing exactitude.

Except for the voice, it was a credible performance, but it also was pathetic. Where Caland received applause and a shower of money, Moppy would have gleaned only jeers and ridicule.

Suddenly Moppy saw them. He broke off his tirade and cringed like a scav about to be kicked.

"Splendid performance, Moppy," Caland said. "Come along. I want to talk to you."

Tel looked at him questioningly, but she turned without a word and followed him. Moppy trailed after them, still cringing.

Caland led him all the way to the spit that narrowed the bay mouth and then around to the total privacy of the ocean beach. Tel continued to glance curiously at him from time to time as they stepped over sunbathers and circled Zexit games, but she said nothing. She sensed some unusual purpose in this maneuver, and she was content to let him unfold it for her.

She perched on one of the two boulders, and Caland leaned against the other. Moppy faced them in stark panic.

"I'm curious about something, Moppy," he said. "Now watch me closely. I'm a tourist, and I just got off the Valley 'bus."

He was a fat tourist. He waddled. He spoke out of the side of his mouth, with grimaces. He performed silly gestures. After a few paces of that, he turned to Moppy.

"You're me," he said. "Do it."

Moppy's face relaxed. Then he grinned and did it.

Both of them watched him in amazement.

"He's a gargling genius!" Tel breathed.

"A natural mimic," Caland agreed.

He was more than that. He was a living caricature. His fat man was Caland's caught by a sardonic artist, with the waddle, the grimaces, the gestures all distorted to the level of art.

"And I have a lot to learn about teaching," Caland said aloud. He had overlooked a natural talent that needed no instruction because he was determinedly looking for mechanical details that he could coach.

Moppy dropped the characterization and rejoined them. Caland studied him as though he were seeing him for the first time. In a sense he was.

"It'll have to be done in the daytime," Caland said slowly. "The light's not good enough at night."

"If you say so," Tel said agreeably. "What are you talking about?"

Baby dashed into view from the bay beach, her tubby body heaving with exertion and emotion. She'd left her lover lolling on the beach and returned to learn that he'd been marched away by those terribly important people, Tel and Cal, and she couldn't imagine what trouble he could have got himself into in her brief absence. She took in the situation at a glance—no trouble, something very good was happening—and she beamed with delighted incomprehension.

"We'll need a few props," Caland said. "Let's go find them."

He concentrated on headgear, searching the used clothing shops for an assortment of the more revolting types. These were stuffed into a bag that Baby carried, and they went down to the 'bus stop to launch Moppy's artistic career as a para.

The first 'bus did not supply a suitable subject. Caland discussed each mal tourist as he dismounted, pointing out the things Moppy would have to look for and how they could be used most effectively. With the next 'bus they scored immediately. The third passenger to dismount was an obnoxious, overbearing personality who had to be well-despised by the other tourists. Baby pawed through the bag for a hat similar to the one the chosen victim was wearing, and Caland sent Moppy into action with a gentle push.

The selection of the subject was critically important; the act itself was simple enough. Moppy affixed himself to the heels of his victim and mimicked him until he was caught. He silently caricatured every posture, every movement, every facial expression, mercilessly delineated his victim's most despised mannerisms in grandiose exaggeration. They were almost to the Dolls' House when the victim, puzzled by repeated outbursts of sniggers and repressed laughter, turned and found himself grimacing into his own grimace. The tourists whooped their laughter; the handouts were lavish by anyone's standard. Moppy, grinning delightedly, handed Tel sixty-four chits, as she subsequently discovered, and announced himself ready to do it again.

They sent for the Reverend, and all four of them retired to Nello's to discuss business. Tel suggested that Moppy should have a regular allowance—one that would keep a Valley couple comfortable—and the remainder of his take should be paid into a Valley Enterprises account with Dal Eddyer.

Moppy demurred. He didn't need the money. "Not right now, anyway," he said cheerfully as Caland and Tel and the Reverend stared at him. If he needed it later, he would ask for it. In the meantime, he knew all about the dins for children and the beach parties for hungry people, and he wanted to help.

"I wouldn't have thought of doing something like this all by myself." he said. "And it's fun!"

They sat down on a rickety bench in the small park by the Valley gate to wait for the next 'bus, and Baby retired to a nearby bench to sort the hats and arrange them so she could find the most suitable one quickly. Caland discussed Moppy's performance with him and made a few suggestions.

"You'll soon pick up the knack of doing what will bring you the biggest handouts," he said. "Your audiences will be small— just whatever number of tourists happens to accompany your victim—and that limits your total take. You'll do well, but I ought to warn you that there's no future in it except as a Valley para." He didn't want Moppy suffering the delusion that his ability to mimic for a tiny audience would lead to a theatrical career.

Moppy grinned. "I've got no worries about the future. Young people have a lot of futures ahead of them. That's why the Valley looks so different when you're young."

"Different how?" Caland asked.

"The future doesn't mean the same thing to old people. Most of them, they've failed over and over until they've used up all of their futures except one. All they can look forward to is dying. There's nowhere else for them to go that they're able to go, and nothing else left for them to do that they're able to do. When you're young, you're just beginning your life, and have plenty of time. People say that the young people in the Valley have run away from life, but isn't true. It's just that our families, and our friends, and some silly thing called 'authority,' were trying to push us into choosing a future before we were ready for it. I think a lot of those old people failed because they got pushed into the wrong futures, things they didn't want or weren't able to handle or just weren't ready for. It's like launching a space-ship before it's completely built. Maybe what's left to be done can be finished after the journey begins, but if any emergency comes up in the meantime, there'll be trouble. It's the same way with lives. We young people are marking time here until we're ready, and when we are, we'll launch ourselves. And then it'll take more than an emergency to do us in."

Baby had stopped shuffling hats and was listening to him raptly.

"So I don't even think about the future," Moppy went on. "I know there'll be a lot of it, and no matter what it is, I know it can't happen to me any faster than a minute at a time. Or any slower. The future's just another present that we haven't got to yet."

They watched Moppy work all afternoon. Caland coached him between performances, emphasizing the importance of choosing the right subject, in a group of the right size, and not wasting his effort on a performance with no audience or with a victim so colorless that the caricature wouldn't be recognized. Moppy earned more than three hundred chits on his first after-noon, and he and Baby were exuberant.

On the following morning, Moppy's confident view of the future seemed to have evaporated. He came lopping along the beach with a look of intense worry on his face. He circled the small group of admirers who were watching Tel fashion a relief tableau of Caland and Sdissler locked in debate, and dropped down beside Caland, who was sunning himself a short distance away.

He asked, in a hushed, conspiratorial tone, "Cal—have you

been to college?"

"Briefly, a long, long time ago," Caland said. "I enrolled in a dramatics course, and when my father found out about it, he cut off my allowance and ordered me home."

"Was your father rich?"

"Was and is," Caland said cheerfully. "Except that he's no longer my father. He told me so when I announced that I was going to be an actor. I saved him the trouble of exempting me from home by going unasked."

Moppy pondered this information so gravely, and for such a length of time, that Caland sat up and regarded him with concern.

"Calta suggested that I talk with you," Moppy said finally. "She thought you'd probably been to college. We've got a big problem with Phem."

Tel was taking a rest from her dirt art, and she'd quietly joined them. "I don't know what's happening," she complained. "Suddenly the Valley's full of strangers and I don't know anyone. Who's Fem? Or is it Fem Who?"

"That's Euphemina," Moppy said. "We decided it was silly to keep calling her Baby, and anyway she doesn't like it. So now she's Phem. P-H-E-M. About this problem—Phem has a rich father."

"It can happen to anyone," Caland said sympathetically, and Tel gurgled peculiarly.

"She ran away from home, you see, and she's afraid her father will make her go back. She's only fifteen."

"Does Pakovich return runaways to their parents?" Caland asked Tel.

"Not from the Valley, he doesn't. He doesn't have any kind of jurisdiction in the Valley."

"No one has any kind of jurisdiction in the Valley," Caland said confidently. "You can tell Phem she has nothing to worry about."

Moppy frowned. "But what if her father sent someone after her?"

"You mean—someone might abduct her?"

Moppy nodded.

"I very much doubt," Tel interposed dryly, "that anyone could be dragged screaming along the Prom without a lot of people taking a personal interest in the matter. Well-ordered communities don't permit that sort of thing. Tell Phem to relax. No one is going to abduct her. Anyway, her father'll never find out where she is unless she tells him."

"That's the problem," Moppy said. "She did tell him."

"Why did she do a silly thing like that?" Tel demanded.

"He's so rich, you see, and she got tired never having any money, so she wrote and told him she was going to college, and she asked for an allowance, and now he wants to know all about the college."

"That's the way fathers are," Caland said. "If they're paying for an education, they think they should have something to say about where it's at and what it consists of. Otherwise, end of allowance."

Moppy nodded sadly. "That's what we're worried about. It's such a beautiful allowance, and we'd planned on doing all kinds of nice things with it. Old Fem Wristil had been sleeping on the floor, and we got a comfortable bed for her. And we're feeding some people who'd been hungry for a long time." He eyed Caland reproachfully. "We didn't just stuff a feast into them and then send them back to starve; we started giving them regular meals. Yda helped us choose the food—she used to be a nurse. And we wanted to save up for special things. Like old Mal Llabal—we thought it would be nice to send him to Aravia for an artificial arm."

"Llabal has both arms missing," Tel said.

"Well—artificial arms are expensive, and we didn't think we could afford two. But one would be useful to him, wouldn't it?"

"It would be fantastically useful," Caland said. "How does he manage now?"

"He's very good at using his feet, but we thought it would be nice if he had just one arm." Moppy paused to meditate wistfully. "Anyway, there are so many things one can do with money. Phem's father started spacing her this nice allowance as soon as he got her letter, and we had everything planned about how to spend it, but now her father wants to know all about the college."

"I can foresee an early termination to this allowance," Tel said.

Moppy nodded sadly. "We hoped someone who'd been to college would be able to tell her what to say. If she could just keep the allowance coming for a few terms, there are lots of things we could do."

"College is expensive," Caland said. "How is Phem supposed to have got into this nonexistent institution?"

"She won a subvent for her tuition."

"But she needs an allowance for living expenses. Reasonable enough. What's she supposed to be studying?"

"That's what her father asked her. That's why we thought someone who'd been to college could help."

"It's a lot more complicated than that," Caland said. "Phem's course of study will have to make sense to someone who knows her. What's she interested in?"

"You mean—other than mals?"

"As far as I know, there is no college that offers girls a course in mals. No college has ever considered that necessary. Certain aspects of mals get studied, like physiology and biology and psychology. Beyond that, girls specializing in mals usually are self-taught."

"When you have some free time," Tel said, "I'll tell you all about mals specializing in girls. Is this a recent interest for Phem?"

"Not recent, no. But she didn't have much chance for it at home."

"In any case, it would hardly do to tell Phem's father that his daughter has enrolled in a higher education course in mals," Caland pointed out.

Moppy grinned. "He'd stop the allowance instantly. That's

why we need help."

"But it has to be something believable to her father. In other words, she must be studying some acceptable subject that her parents won't consider utterly beyond her intellectual capabilities, and it also has to be something that isn't ludicrously incompatible with her interests and inclinations."

"What does that mean?" Moppy demanded.

"It means he's showing off because he's been to college," Tel suggested.

"It means we have a problem," Caland said. "Maybe it would be best if we talked to Phem and studied her father's letter."

"I'll bring her," Moppy promised. He leaped to his feet and dashed away.

Tel was looking skeptically at Caland. "Do you really think you can produce a letter that will keep the old mal paying?"

"I don't know."

"You don't seem to have had much luck with your own father. On the other hand, maybe your experience will be helpful."

"Not in this respect. I never tried to collect anything from my father. I never would. But this seems to fall into the category of noble causes. All those lovely things they could do with the money. Old Llabal absolutely must have his artificial arm, so I'll have to produce a plausible-sounding letter. If I can manage the right touch, maybe he'll get two arms. What puzzles me is this fervent philanthropy. I never would have suspected it of Moppy."

"The same thing puzzles a lot of people about you. Did you think it couldn't happen to anyone else?"

"I've never thought about it at all."

"Most Vals are decent but thoroughly normal. Meaning that they're as generous as they can afford to be while thinking of themselves first. It's an inborn defense mechanism. Why do you suppose Phem ran away?"

"You've seen her," Caland said. "She's fat, untidy, and moderately ugly. If her main interest always has been mals, that's because no mal before Moppy ever showed the slightest interest in her."

"That's no answer. Why did she run away?"

"She's the daughter of a wealthy father," Caland said impatiently. "She's also fat, untidy, and moderately ugly. Probably her intelligence is a bit subnormal. Why do you think her father was so elated when he thought she'd actually got into a college that he instantly forgave her and started sending an allowance? All of her life, her parents have been trying to make her the attractive, intelligent daughter they think they deserve. When a girl is unattractive and a bit stupid, and knows it, that's a horrible burden to carry. So she ran away. She invented the mals."

"Do you suppose the philanthropy kick was her idea?"

"She certainly didn't inherit it from her father, if that's what you're suggesting," Caland said. "The girl seems happy here, Tel, and she wasn't happy at home, so we should help her. But this isn't going to be easy. I can't think of any traditional course of study that doesn't require *some* intelligence."

"Then you'll have to invent one. Here they come."

Moppy had acquired a following. With him were Phem, Sam the Artist, and the Valley's mystery fem, Melana. Caland watched them approach and pondered the contrasts: Phem—blubbery, unattractive, sloppily dressed in ragged stubs and wrapper; Melana—poised, self-confident, exquisitely clothed in a simple white daysuit, radiantly beautiful. Then there was Moppy—bare to the waist, his chubby body deeply tanned; and Sam the Artist—clothed in his usual paint-spattered worksuit that stretched tautly over his bulging middle.

Melana seated herself beside Tel, with whom she was familiar, and nodded politely at Caland, whom she had not met. Moppy sprawled on the sand, and Phem, looking frantic with worry, knelt beside him.

"Melana has been to college," Moppy said. "Maybe she can help us."

"Really? What college?" Caland asked.

"University of Aravia," Melana said with a smile. "But I didn't graduate. It's a typical Valley biography, isn't it?" Her liltingly musical voice added another dimension to her beauty.

"A Valley platitude," Sam the Artist said. "Vals are betrothed but don't marry, attend school but don't graduate, make investments that don't mature, expect money that doesn't arrive, land jobs for which it turns out there is no pay, and constantly make great plans that come to nothing. The only thing that is consistently carried to full term in the Valley is pregnancy."

Caland turned his attention to Phem. "As I understand your problem, we have to convince your father that you're attending college in Mort's Valley. If he's ever seen the place, or even heard of it, this will be impossible."

Phem nervously began biting a fingernail. It was Moppy that answered. "He hasn't, or he wouldn't have spaced that first allowance payment."

"Then it's a question of deciding what course of study Phem is best suited to," Caland said. "Phem, what would you like to study in college?"

Phem looked at him blankly.

"Medicine? Do you have any yearning to be a doctor?"

"I wouldn't like that at all," Phem said. "Doctors have to go to school for years."

"We're not going to send you to school," Caland said patiently. "We're only going to pretend you're going to school. But maybe you have a point. If you dislike school that much, your father would have basis for suspicion if we put you in a medical program. Scientist?"

"Same problem," Moppy said. "She wouldn't like sitting in classes and studying."

"That makes it difficult to choose a college curriculum for her."

"There are business and professional programs," Melana suggested. "Nursing, fashion designing, journalism, sales promotion, business management—"

"Better stay away from business courses," Sam the Artist said. "They'd please her father, but there's always the risk that he'd try to put her to work."

Phem giggled. "I don't want to work."

"She likes to sew," Moppy said. "She's been altering clothes for people. Is there a college course in sewing?"

"Not that I ever heard of," Caland said.

They sat in silence for a few moments with Phem and Moppy looking on expectantly and the others exchanging blank looks.

"She could study art," Sam the Artist suggested finally. "That doesn't strain the intellect, and very few people work at it."

"Her father might react the way my father reacted to drama," Caland said. "Certainly art would be far down on his list of suitable subjects. As long as we're inventing, we might as well try to invent something that would please him."

"He wouldn't let me take art in school," Phem said. "He made me take mathematics."

"There. Did you like mathematics?"

"I hated it."

Caland turned to Melana. "What do you think?"

She shook her head. "Dead end. They don't make colleges that would offer her kind of curriculum."

"Then we'll have to invent the college, too." Caland said. He turned to Sam the Artist. "Is there anyone in the Valley capable of a bit of expert forgery?"

"Several people," Sam the Artist said. "What did you have in mind?"

"We need some official stationary for Valley University—a nice letterhead on quality paper, with matching envelope. Several of each in case a follow-up letter is necessary. And we need someone capable of producing voice-writer print. Will you give us your father's name and address, Phem?"

Phem produced the spacegram she had received from her father. It sounded brutally terse. The news Phem had sent was welcome. He and her mother applauded the fact that she was finally applying herself to something worthwhile. He asked for details about the college and her course of study. "Your allowance will be continued as long as I receive regular and satisfactory reports on your progress," he concluded.

The name and address looked vaguely familiar to Caland.

Partley hrv' Dasshlam
Galaxia Trading Interchange
Terminal Tower, Port of Wwilladcz Central
Wwilladcz 248/c19/487M

He studied it for a moment, straining against his memory barrier. Then he smiled at Tel. "Have you ever heard it said that it's a small universe?"

Tel stared at Caland in sudden surmise. "Do you know him?"

"No, but I know the firm, and the name is familiar. And that makes it virtually certain that he's heard of me—or of my family."

"Do I have to write the letter myself?" Phem asked. "I don't write good."

"I'll write it," Caland said with a smile. "You are now a formally matriculated student in Mort's Valley University, and I'm the—"He turned to Melana. "Give me a fancy title."

"Chancellor," Melana suggested.

"Something a bit more restricted than that."

"Academic Chancellor."

"Splendid. We'll make it 'First Academic Chancellor.' No one in the Galaxy's business community will dare to start an argument with a Caland who wears the title, 'First Academic Chancellor.' Neither will anyone dare admit to not knowing what it means. Find me a piece of paper, Sam, and I'll write the letter."

"What do you take me for?" Sam asked indignantly. "A writer?"

Tel was brushing aside the dry surface sand beside her. When she had exposed a meter of damp substratum, she smoothed the surface and reached for a stick she had used in her sculpture. "I have a feeling that this masterpiece is going to require several drafts," she said. "I'll inscribe it while Cal dictates. While we're working on it, Moppy can look for a piece of paper."

"I may have something I've only used one side of," Moppy said.

He went off cheerfully, and Tel sat waiting with stick poised. "Dictate," she said.

"Address to the Honorable Partley hrv' Dasshalm—"

"All right—we've got that on the spacegram.

"'Esteemed Mal Dasshalm—'"

"Screet!"

"All parents of the students of Valley University are esteemed. 'Esteemed Mal Dasshalm. Your daughter, Euphemina, has informed us of your desire for information concerning our institution. We are an informal university—'"

"No one could possibly dispute that," Sam the Artist observed.

"A well-mannered critic waits until a work of art has grown wings before trying to clip them," Caland said sternly. "'We are an informal university, dedicated to soundly progressive educational principles. Our achievements are but slightly known outside this sector—'"

Sam the Artist blew his nose loudly.

"'—because we have never felt the need to publicize them. Only last year we celebrated twenty-five years of educational achievement, and we have far more applicants than we can accommodate. Our students are selected through severely competitive examinations, and the generosity of our benefactors makes it possible to subvent tuition to all of them. Each student's curriculum is individually designed to meet his or her interests and educational objective. In the present academic pentameron, Euphemina is studying—'"

Caland paused to look at Melana. "What the hell *would* she be studying?"

Melana shook her head. "I don't know. But carry on, it sounds overwhelming."

"'—The History of Interstellar Trade; Commercial Opportunities in the Fine Arts; Occupational Class Structures in Galactic Sociology; and The Philosophy of Economics. In addition, she is of course required to participate fully in our programs fostering the mental and physical well-being of our students. Her present standing is Theta Plus (Commendatory). If you require further information, please address the request to me. I am—' Space for signature. 'Jarv Caland, First Academic Chancellor, at your service.'"

"Tremendous!" Melana breathed.

Sam the Artist blew his nose again. "A commendatory, meaning Theta Plus, effort. What kind of an individually designed curriculum could you offer me?"

"Food chemistry, with emphasis on the digestive processes that transform vegetable and animal matter into human fat," Tel said.

Phem was gazing blankly at Caland. "But what does it mean?"

"Nothing at all," Caland said.

"And that," Sam the Artist proclaimed, "is the unalloyed beauty of the thing. A letter that meant something wouldn't work. I move that we change Cal's name. The Valley has a Reverend. Now it also has its Chancellor. Agreed?"

"Not by me," Caland said. "The moment I sign the letter, I'm resigning."

"Will he believe it?" Tel asked.

"He will," Caland said firmly. "He can't question it without admitting that he doesn't understand it, and he'll never do that. And if he has any doubts at all, the name 'Caland' will settle them. This is the first time since I left home that I've attempted to exploit my name, but I think this one exception is justified. Now, if Sam can produce the stationary, and if someone can perform a reasonable facsimile of voice-writing, Phem will be able to do all of those nice things with her allowance."

The beaming Phem shyly thanked him.

Moppy returned with a scrap of paper that had been used on only one side, and Tel made a copy of the letter. Sam went off with it to find a cooperative forger. The rest of them remained on the beach watching the sedate maneuvers of the sailboats and talking about what a lovely thing it would be if the Valley really had a university.

But Caland had little to say. He had turned his thoughts to Sdissler and the forest labor camps. He also had noticed that the figure reclining in the shade a short distance from them was Nalce. Caland's every move was still being watched alertly.

CHAPTER EIGHTEEN

Walking along the crowded Prom with Tel, Caland met, headed in the opposite direction, a spectacular incongruity: Doctor Stran Gormaz strolling elbow to elbow with the spectral black figure of Dom. The withered, bony, tottering apparition towered over the short, pudgy, bouncing sociologist. The two of them were engrossed in conversation, with Gormaz's hoarse booming tones alternating with Dom's dry, pipping voice that crackled like old paper. Gormaz's gesticulations were a menace to traffic, and he wagged his scraggly beard like a signal flag and kept his tufts of hair flopping.

Caland and Tel halted and looked after the receding figures.

"You said Gormaz was a sociologist," Tel said.

"So he did. Repeatedly."

"Dom was something like that in his youth. Before he inherited the Valley." She thought for a moment. "It was some kind of '-ologist,' and I think he was a teacher. But maybe it was an '-onomist.'"

The mismatched pair disappeared into a cloud of tourists. Caland turned away wondering again why Dom persisted in denying that he'd been on Rynaif. Arlu had showed him the evidence—spaceship records, note records, an attestation from Rynaif immigration officials. Dom sneered and proclaimed the universe a liar.

"It seems odd that Dom would take up with your Doctor Gormaz even if he once was a sociologist," Tel observed. "Dom isn't given to making friends."

"It's odder that Gormaz should take up with him. It's even odder that Gormaz is still here. He decided to leave Mort the day he saw Pakovich."

They looked in at Nello's and found Sam the Artist and the Reverend discussing the latest Valley scandal. As with so many past Valley scandals, this one involved the young fem Cleo. The previous night she had brazenly seduced another fem's mal at a beach fire, and the two miscreants had been found merging a few meters away while children raced past and passersby stepped over them. Public merging was considered outrageous misconduct, and Valley society forbade it as effectively as it was able to forbid anything, and tried to take punitive action when it occurred.

"A few more steps and they could have crawled under a bush," Sam the Artist said disgustedly.

"What are you going to do about it?" Tel asked.

"I don't know," the Reverend said. "It's happened so many times with Cleo that we haven't got anything left to try."

"Maybe we can have Cal write a letter to her father," Sam the Artist suggested. "Tell him she's been exempted from the Valley University for prudery."

Neither Caland nor Tel had any interest in Cleo's fate, so they wished the judgment committee luck and left it to its deliberations.

"Hungry?" Cal asked.

Tel nodded.

"Hef's?"

They were passing the Valley Transportation Company yard when Baris Bronlan hailed them. "Come to din," he said.

Tel obediently turned toward the gate. Caland followed her with resignation. He would have preferred Hef's place. Bronlan's genius at building spaceships from discards did not extend to his cooking. Also, Caland liked Hef. He'd had no contact of any kind with the shy, inarticulate cook except over putrebuns and yuck, which the perspiring Hef was passing across his box counter to Caland, but Caland liked him.

Captain Akonif was visiting Bronlan. Pak Enterprises had suffered another equipment malfunction, and the captain's ore ship was grounded until repairs could be made to the loading machinery.

"Equipment malfunction, nonsense," the captain growled. "It's sabotage. It keeps happening, and Pakovich refuses to do anything about it. If this continues there'll be a tin shortage on Aravia, and Aravia can't tolerate that. It can't afford to. It'll have to look for other sources. Higher prices are better than uncertain supply."

He was still grumbling about Pakovich's mismanagement of his mining business when the klaxon sounded. Bronlan's other guests began to drift timidly into the clearing about the spaceship. They came to rest like flotsam that some vast, stagnant water had discarded, and the presence of each of them hinted at distant social convulsions, just as flotsam on an ocean beach told a tale of marine catastrophes. All of them were strangers to Caland, but Tel seemed to know them well. An elderly couple, Min and Mac, were thin almost to the point of malnutrition, with pure white hair and saintly smiles. Two young lovers of sixteen were so overwhelmed by each other's presence that they clung together constantly and answered in monosyllables that they mouthed in unison. Their personalities were as fused as their persons; no one knew who they were individually, so they were referred to as the Pair. Their thinness could have been due to the fact that they were too absorbed in each other to remember to eat. Other guests were a neat, slender, elderly fem named Zata; a bankrupt Prom merchant named Baggy whose mismatched clothing was made up of unsalable remnants from his stock; and a mixed trio of nondescripts of indeterminate age.

Caland and Tel assisted with the cooking; Min and Mac watched their every move with smiles that concealed their hunger; the Pair watched with each other and occasionally exchanged whispers; the others listened to the conversation Captain Akonif was holding with Bronlan.

"Willox still thinks this notion about using baking soda for fuel is idiotic," the captain said.

Bronlan's eyes twinkled. "It would be—for him."

"Do you really think it will work?"

"I know it will."

"But you won't prove anything if it does. You'll have a method of propulsion that's centuries out of date."

"I'll prove that it'll work," Bronlan answered indifferently.

"Damn it, mal, with your ability you could be discovering new things that could make you rich."

Bronlan shrugged. "What's rich? Except for money, it's nothing."

"You could buy the materials you need to work with. You wouldn't have to salvage them from junk heaps."

"A junk heap is a challenge," Bronlan said.

"You don't want to be rich?"

"Pakovich is rich. He can't even run a mining business."

"That's right. He can't."

"The reason is because he's not interested in mining," Bronlan said. "He's interested in money."

Captain took a long slop from the jug and wiped his face. "Do you mean people with money never accomplish anything?"

"They don't," Bronlan said. "But sometimes their money does if they're able to use any of it unselfishly."

The food was ready. Caland passed around the chunks of bread, and Bronlan served the meat while Tel raked out the baked tubers. The elderly couple began to eat ravenously, but within minutes their pace had slowed. They contemplated each mouthful regretfully as they approached satiety. The young couple amused themselves with pushing bits of food into each other's mouths and playfully trying to bite each other's fingers.

The captain ate with good appetite. His mind had been switched back to Pakovich, and he complained again and at length about the iniquity of having to leave his ship parked because the loading equipment wouldn't work. "On top of that, I have to come out here and listen to a lecture on baking soda. I won't believe you can lift a mug of yuck with your baking soda until I see it done."

Bronlan got to his feet. "Come on," he said.

"What for?" the captain demanded.

"To see it done."

Bronlan strode off toward his shack. The captain hesitated and then hurried to catch up. Tel and Caland exchanged glances and trailed after them. They followed a vehicle path that threaded its way between junk heaps and led directly to the large double doors of Bronlan's machine shop. On the cluttered workbench, clamped securely into a vise, was a strange-looking object.

It was strange-looking to Caland and Tel. Captain Akonif recognized it immediately and pronounced it a model of a once well-known but now totally obsolete spaceship engine.

But some if its features were strange even to the captain. He bent over it and traced a bulge on one side with a curious finger. "What's this?"

"Acceleration chamber," Bronlan said. "Steps up the power."

"Is that so?" The captain circled the model, squinting closely at it from different angles. Finally he said politely, "You really ought to buy your metal for a job like this. The cost wouldn't be worth gargling over. You've recrafted each piece beautifully, but can't disguise the fact that every one of them originated in a junk heap. That's why the thing looks so weird. It's hard to decide whether the strangeness is due to originality of design, or to the fact that all of the parts originally were intended to be something else."

It looked totally strange to Caland; but Caland had never before seen an atomic engine in its naked crudeness with no spaceship wrapped around it. He studied it curiously. It was small enough to enfold in his two hands, and—if Bronlan had loosened the vise's grip—Caland certainly could have picked it up and tossed it as far as the nearest junk heap, where it looked as though it belonged. Bronlan had not been concerned with appearances, so the various parts retained whatever finish they had displayed in their previous incarnations: a side was smooth; a bulge displayed a tinted ripple; another side had a grimy roughness; a humped end held a mirror-like polish. Caland wondered how many hours, over how many years, Bronlan had lavished in the lovingly tedious construction of this gadget.

"Why don't you build a modern engine?" the captain demanded.

"There'd be no fun in that. Modern engines don't run—they just move ships. The old models are a lot more interesting."

"You're going to build a full-scale model out of salvaged metal?"

"Of course. The whole ship's built out of salvaged materials. Why should the engine be different?"

"And—it'll run on baking soda?"

"And other things," Bronlan said with his shy smile.

"Does the model run?"

"Quite well, yes."

As Bronlan bent over with the obvious intention of starting it, the captain asked, "Where'd you get the atomic core?"

Bronlan looked up in surprise. "Salvage, of course."

"They let you walk in and pick up a nuke core? Even a salvage core is worth—"

"Piece of one," Bronlan said. "One shattered, and I glommed a piece of it. I wouldn't exactly say they let me—they didn't know it and never missed it. Don't need much for a little engine like this."

"When you build your full scale model, I suppose you'll walk in and glom a bigger piece."

Bronlan grinned. "The rest of the pieces are still there. They might have a salvage value in other places, but on Mort no one knows what to do with them. Those stupid supers Pakovich has running the Port will be happy to give them away to get rid of them."

The captain snorted. "All right. Let's see this thing run."

Bronlan bent over the model engine. The rest of them, including the captain, took apprehensive steps backward— Caland and Tel because they did not know what to expect; the captain because he did. An engine built from scrap, with a bit of salvage atomic core, using baking soda and other things for fuel, could have blown up without surprising any of them.

Bronlan opened a fuel well, and scraped a bit of white paste into it. Then he stepped back with folded arms and stood waiting.

"How do you ignite it?" the captain asked.

"It ignites itself and then it burns until the fuel's exhausted."

"You expect to lift a ship with an ignition system like that? It's no system at all!"

"This is only a model," Bronlan said imperturbably. "An ignition system is hard to build in miniature."

"But if you don't try it out on the model, how will you know it'll work when you—"

The tiny engine suddenly blasted them with sound. Immediately the bench pivoted as the engine's force swung one end of it in an arc. The four of them leaped to hold it in place.

Their combined strength was not enough. The captain shouted something; Caland saw his lips move but heard nothing. The vibration rattled the floor they were standing on and shook the work bench so violently that they had difficulty in hanging onto it. They were forced backward in a spiraling circle, moving ever closer to the wall, and Caland doubted that the rickety building's structure could hold the now violently rocking bench. When the wall went, the roof would collapse on them.

The engine cut off as abruptly as it had started.

"I gave it a bigger dose of fuel than I intended," Bronlan said. "I guess I ought to start measuring it."

The captain, who was energetically mopping his flushed face with a shaking hand, nodded gravely. "Fair amount of thrust you're getting."

"It'll improve when I get my carburetor finished."

"Carburetor? On an atomic thrust engine?"

"It'll use the ship's waste air. That's got atoms, too."

"I suppose so. Oxygen—"

"No. The nitrogen."

"If you improve this thing very much," the captain said, "you won't need to build a full-scale model. This one just lifted with us hanging onto the bench."

Bronlan was as indifferent to compliments as he was to criticism. "When I get it working the way I want, I'll build some instrumentation to measure the thrust."

"Where are you going to take your ship when you get it into space?" the captain asked.

"Not far. Maybe Aravia. I've always thought I'd like to see Aravia again."

"With an old-fashioned engine like this it'll take *terms*."

"I got plenty of time."

"How soon do you plan to make this trip?"

Bronlan gestured vaguely with his stiff arm. "When the ship's ready. And when I'm ready."

"I think," Captain Akonif said, "I'd like to sample that jug again."

After they'd finished eating, Caland and Tel remained behind to tidy up for Bronlan, and it developed that Bronlan had something on his mind other than their company when he invited them to din.

"About that forest labor camp," he said.

The nearest camp was some seventy-five kilometers north of Paradise, and it was the only camp accessible by road—although for long stretches the road was more a rumor than a reality. They had told Bronlan they wanted a very private look at that camp. He asked no questions; he simply nodded and said he would see what could be done. Now he had a suggestion.

Occasionally, Pakovich's air freight platforms were all in use on runs to the camps that were accessible only by air. When that happened, Sdissler hired Bronlan to haul supplies to the one camp that could be reached by road. Bronlan had been asked to make a run that day.

"But I got to thinking," he said. "If you two went up there today, people might start wondering why Cal missed his para act tonight. So I told Sdissler I wouldn't have a 'truck free until midnight. It'll have the load there early tomorrow morning, which suits him. If you two want to ride along, you can hop out just before the 'truck reaches camp and spend the morning looking around. The 'truck will have to leave as soon as it's unloaded. Otherwise Sdissler's people might get curious. But it can park under cover as soon as it's well out of hearing and wait for you. You should be able to get back in time for Cal to perform tomorrow night."

He added, "This is the best way. I could send you up there any time, but if a 'cab or 'truck were spotted from the air, or if the camp people were to hear a motor when one wasn't expected, it would cause comment. They might send out a search party. This way no one will suspect anything, and you can have a good look. You'll have to walk a bit when you're finished, but—" He grinned. "It'll be downhill all the way."

"Sounds great," Caland said. "We'll do it."

When they left Bronlan, Caland suddenly wanted to explore the Valley. He'd seen surprisingly little of it except for the Prom and the routes to and from the beaches. This time they walked east and west, slowly following one Valley street after another from the fence to the ocean. They covered Bay Unview Boulevard and Junk Vista Avenue; and then, skipping the Prom, they walked the lengths of Primrose Lane and Fishstink Alley.

Caland was surprised to find so many distinctively different neighborhoods within the Valley's constricted area. On the Bay side of Bay Unview Boulevard, the buildings had been the luxury homes of owners who were prideful of the bay view they offered. Before the blight set in and the houses began to bulge with improvised additions, each had possessed its private garden and grounds to ornament the sweeping view down to the bay. On the opposite side of the boulevard, the buildings were smaller and crammed closer together. On Junk Vista Avenue—except for the gap occupied by Bronlan's towering junk piles and the gleaming spaceship—the crowding became congestion.

South of the Prom a reversal took place. Primrose Lane was crammed with small dwellings, though there were a few vacant lots cluttered with the mounds of ground shelters, the Valley's cemeteries for the living. On Fishstink Alley, which in the days before the fertilizer factory and the fences must have been an appealing suburb with rolling open country just behind it, the houses again became larger and more widely spaced. Near the ocean were a few veritable mansions that, like the buildings on Bay Unview Boulevard, had been expanded into motley human hives.

There was one exception. The most imposing mansion of all was unblemished by additions and in a fair state of repair. Even its spacious grounds showed signs of recent, if superficial, care. It stood out so starkly that Caland came to an amazed halt and stared. The once handsome old structure was cluttered with ancient affectations like balconies, a multiple-peaked roof, and windows patterned in colored glass or plastic mosaics with functional shutters. The place deserved to be a museum.

"What is it?" Caland exclaimed.

"That's Dom's house."

"Ah! A fit residence for the Valley's owner."

"Evidently his father thought so. His father built it."

"I hope he doesn't live there alone."

"But he does. Periodically he hires someone to clean the place, and those who have worked there say he's maintained it exactly as it was when his father was alive: silver and crystal polished, knickknacks dusted, carpets fluffed, and hospitality rooms and all of the guest rooms ready for entertaining. But he hasn't had guests in anyone's memory, and no one is allowed inside except the few people who work for him."

"Has it occurred to anyone that Dom is very much like Pakovich?"

Tel nodded. "He's just as narrow in his outlook. Each of them owns a world outright. Pakovich's happens to be larger."

"There must have been a lovely view to the south before the fertilizer factory was built," Caland observed.

"South and West," Tel said. "There once was a sweeping view down to the ocean, with landscaped gardens. Then Dombrily's business ventures began to fail, and he had to raise money any way he could, so he leased the grounds and let himself be hemmed in by other buildings. Sad, isn't it?"

They walked along the edge of Dom's garden to the Valley fence, better preserved here than near the east gate. A meter beyond it, and towering over it, were shiny strands of an elaborate metal fence that guarded the fertilizer factory. Its top angled out as though defying anyone to climb it.

As they turned back, a hoarse, booming voice floated down to them from the screened veranda that ran the entire width of the rear of Dom's mansion. Doctor Stran Gormaz and Dom were seated side by side in luxurious recliners, goblets at their elbows. They were deep in a technical discussion, and terms like "social trichotomy," and "urban world sub structured parochialism," were tossed up from the flood of unintelligible jargon.

"The '-ology' must have been sociology," Tel said.

"Not necessarily. I've heard specialists in different fields conversing. Each has to pretend to understand the other's terminology."

"In that case they deserve each other."

At the east end of Primrose Lane, beside the diminutive strip of park, they looked in at the Valley school house. It was literally a house, and all of the rooms of its two stories and attic were crammed with children. In spite of the crowding, the volunteer teachers and students seemed to be enjoying themselves. Each room had a wall painted black upon which teachers and students wrote and drew lessons with soft stones. This primitive arrangement represented almost the only equipment the teachers had.

"Are the teachers paid?" Caland asked.

Tel shook her head. "Unfortunately, no. But it's an exemplary way to waste time."

In the school playground that had been fashioned at the end of the park, a young mother was rehearsing three tiny girls in Caland's latest para inspiration. They were clothed in long, elaborately ornamented gowns patterned on an example Caland had seen displayed in one of the specialty shops. The children were being trained to welcome tourists to the Valley with songs and dances.

They were charming, and both Caland and Tel felt certain that the tourists would be unable to resist them. They congratulated the mother, who was glowing with pride. "We'll start this afternoon," she promised.

Caland and Tel circled back to approach the Prom from the west. As they strolled along, Tel said suddenly, "The Reverend needs a business manager. He's too busy with other things to supervise a whole troop of para acts. Unless you want to take on the job yourself."

"Thank you, no," Caland said. "I'm not sure that this project is a wise thing, but since the Reverend wants it, I'll get it launched for him. After that, I want no part of it."

Moppy already was a Valley favorite—tourists came looking for him. Caland had two more acts he was about to launch. In addition to the children, there was a pretty Valley fem called Hoppy who had only one leg. Hoppy was one of the proud ones. She had never tried to beg for herself, but she readily consented to work for a Valley Enterprises Fund that would benefit everyone. Her "act" would be a simple one. She had only to present herself on crutches, smiling, and say, "Please—for a new leg." If it worked, Caland planned to place old Llabal at the gate to beg for new arms. He was meditating a different sort of act for Mac, the elderly mal he'd met at din. The sweet old mal's innate dignity would enable him to carry a part with ease if he could learn the lines.

"Someone has to be there whenever these acts are working to make certain everything goes right and everyone behaves," Tel said. "The Reverend also needs someone to take charge of the money, keep the books, and manage the payroll."

"Who?" Caland asked.

"Zata," Tel said.

"The fem we just met at Bar's? Could she do it?"

"She ran a large business on Aravia for an absentee owner. Ran it expertly for years. Then the owner took to speculating, looted the firm's treasury and also its pension fund, and left it bankrupt. She couldn't find another job—she's past retirement age. She used the last of her savings to buy a passage to Mort."

"You're right," Caland said. "This is getting to be a business, and I don't know anything about running a business."

"Neither do I. Neither does the Reverend."

"Let's try her."

"When you feel like sitting down again, I'll send Hairy for her."

The west end of the Prom provided a horizontal version of what they had already experienced vertically. The houses were large in the ocean suburbs and became smaller and more congested as they approached the business section, finally merging with the claptrap commercial structures.

They found a table at the rear of Nello's, and Tel summoned Hairy with the wave of her hand the next time he happened by.

"Zata," she told him. "Right away."

"Also Mac," Caland said.

Hairy cocked his head.

"Elderly mal, white-haired—"

Hairy nodded and loped away.

"What do you want with Mac?" Tel asked.

"I've thought of an act for him. Except that he won't have an act—he can be himself. I'll teach him a line about saving up for a last fling, and then at the end the 'last fling' will be something innocuous, like hot yuck at bedtime."

"Tourists will go for that?"

"Some of them will. I don't expect a huge success for any of these acts. But then—I didn't expect one from Moppy, and he's doing very well."

They sipped their yuck and watched the passing Prom traffic. A Val fem strolled by with a brilliant red flower in her hair, and Caland said thoughtfully, "There aren't many flowers in the Valley, are there?"

She shook her head. "I suppose the other stuff grew faster and higher and choked them out."

"Why is the Valley's vegetation so different? From Pakovich's veranda it looks like a place on a map that someone marked out with a different color."

"That's because the vacationers who first lived here brought in plants from their own worlds. Native shrubs and trees got crowded out or were removed. There's a big advantage—Mort's native fauna doesn't care for alien flora. That's why we have so few insects and vermin to plague us."

"Would it be possible to grow flowers?"

"I don't see why not if anyone took the trouble to clear some land and care for them."

"The flowers in the park look sickly."

"No one takes care of them."

"If it were possible to grow flowers, the Reverend could hire people to make garlands of them, and the children could sell them to the tourists."

They sipped their yuck again and watched the Prom traffic. Tel said finally, "This project really does need a business manager."

CHAPTER NINETEEN

With an all-night ride ahead of them, Caland would have preferred to sleep for a few hours after his para stint; but Tel thought that they should make themselves as conspicuous as possible. They joined a beach fire, and Caland made himself overly conspicuous through the happy idea of heating cider. There were vehement protests that he would break the jug or poison the whole group, but Caland persisted—he had paid for the cider—and eventually the leaping flames brought the liquid to a boil.

They had to send for mugs because the jug was much too hot to pass around for individual slops. Then the liquid had to cool in mugs before it could be tasted. When finally they were able to drink it, they found it delicious, but by that time they were almost too thirsty to care.

A tall, gaunt, red-haired fem called Flappy was hovering about their fire group. She wore a long, drab gown that was much too large for her, and she looked like a specter in search of someone to haunt. She existed in her own special limbo among the Vals, and each night she drifted from fire to fire, listening and making occasional strident comments. Because she never sat down and never accepted food, she could not be accused of that cardinal Valley sin, wedging. When possible the Vals ignored her.

Now she announced shrilly, "It is wisely written that food should never be hotter than normal temperature of the lips."

The Reverend straightened up like a soldier hearing a call to battle. "Wisely written by whom?" he demanded.

"Wisely written in the Vivendi Cause," Flappy said glibly. "It is the Gospel of the Shining Way."

"Nonsense!" the Reverend said disgustedly. "That claptrap couldn't possibly be scriptural."

"It's more than that," Flappy proclaimed serenely. "It's divine. It's the Book of Hit. The saint wrote it at God's dictation."

The Reverend heaved a sigh. "So much nonsense purports to come directly from God. I much prefer a scriptural passage from an author who admits to having written it himself."

Flappy drew herself up to her full height, which seemed formidable when she loomed over a seated fire group. "Just what do you mean?" she demanded coldly.

"There is no human, there never has been a human, with sufficient wisdom and moral restraint to receive word directly from God and pass it along unchanged," the Reverend said. "The temptation to editorialize is irresistible. As a result, any text alleged to be handed down from the Almighty has been riddled with misguided deletions and then with even more unfortunate additions because the individual intended by God only as a messenger has seized upon a unique opportunity to package up the carpings of a lifetime and blame them on some unfortunate deity. That's why I prefer the utterances of those saints who have the integrity to accept responsibility for what they say."

Sam the Artist abruptly wondered what idiotic thing Pakovich had been up to lately. No one could think of anything that hadn't occurred countless times before, and Sam admitted later that he'd only mentioned Pakovich because the name was a magic word that instantly diverted any Valley conversation away from a controversial subject.

Eventually the group discussion broke up into individual conversations, and Sam the Artist said quietly to Tel and Caland, "Chan Worntling tells me you think there's something peculiar about Sdissler."

"'Peculiar' is a mild word to apply to anything that flamboyant," Tel said.

Sam frowned. "You know what I mean. Funny business beyond his peculiarities. I was just interested that you'd noticed it."

"You've noticed it, too?" Caland exclaimed.

"It came to my attention some time ago. That is, if you're referring to his manipulations at the Port." He paused and scrutinized them in turn. "You've found another kind of funny business?"

"What about the Port?" Tel demanded.

"He imports people for his labor details, but they always register for the Valley. Virtually none of them show up here, ever. Since Sdissler is Pakovich's pet, there's no reason why imports couldn't declare themselves as his employees, but they never do. They're always for the Valley. I call that funny business. What's yours?"

"Cal thinks Sdissler's presence in the Valley is an act," Tel said.

"Could be," Sam mused. "It easily could be. His real office is over in the Government Mall. He's considered part of the Paradise City Government because he keeps the place clean. He runs the world dump to Pakovich's complete satisfaction, and he keeps the garbage 'trucks on schedule. Before Sdissler, no one succeeded in doing either of those things—or so I'm told. Now you tell me why he'd want to register his imported labor force for the Valley."

"Where do the laborers live?" Caland asked.

"He has barracks at the world dump and another over by the mines. I've never thought to ask what else he's got."

"No one has thought to ask because no one has had much interest in garbage," Tel said. "We're thinking it's time someone got interested."

Caland was forcefully prevented from heating another jug of cider, and the fireside talk gradually diminished as, a few at a time, their companions drifted off to bed. For appearances' sake, Caland and Tel entered the rear door of the house where they lived. They walked straight through the building and out of the front door on their way to the Valley Transportation Company lot. Bronlan was waiting for them beside one of his massive electrotrucks.

Bronlan handed a package to Tel. "Got everything. Should be enough."

"What is it?" Caland asked.

"Food, stupid," Tel said peevishly. "We won't be back until late tomorrow afternoon."

"I put some extra padding on that seat," Bronlan said with a chuckle. "It's a rough trip. Knack will look after you."

Knack, whom Caland already had met driving a 'cab, greeted them with a grin from the 'cab's dimly lit interior. "It isn't far," he said, "but it's a tedious trip. Can't go fast. Part of the way I can't even go slow."

They climbed in, and after a smooth run through Paradise and to the end of the north road's pavement, they bounced and jolted their way through the night. In a few places the road was soft, and the 'truck spewed clouds of sand as it clawed its way forward. Caland found sleep impossible. He was tossed forward, sideways, or backward—sometimes in succession— and he tried to relax with his eyes closed and think.

For a time he thought about the world of Mort and the assembly of abnormalities gathered there. Sdissler was an anomaly. So was the alleged tourist Weflan Krann. Caland was a monstrous anomaly. They had been brought together by someone's malicious design.

Caland doubted that Sdissler was the person responsible. Sdissler was no more than an agent, just as Caland was only a tool and the world of Mort the chosen arena of the movement. Weflan Krann had to be another agent. Nalce would only be an agent of an agent. Someone had spun a fiendishly complicated web, and it could only be attacked one strand—or one agent—at a time.

But at least Caland was attacking. He actually was doing something for himself, and he took immense satisfaction in each lurch and jolt that shook him as the 'truck rocked its way forward along the hint of a road that its lights picked out. That road was now climbing slowly but steadily.

Tel actually slept. "Pure mind and unruffled conscience," she explained when Knack finally awoke her by bringing the 'truck to a halt.

The thin light of pre-dawn morning scarcely touched the faint tracks they had been following. Beneath the trees that pressed close on either side, the night was still impenetrable.

"It's five, six kilometers to the last ridge," Knack said. "This is where I'll park the truck and wait for you. Bar thought I ought to come this far. It shouldn't be a bad walk."

Tel blinked sleepily and looked about her. "You mean we're almost there?"

"Almost," Knack said cheerfully. "I'll slow down so you can jump out just before I top the ridge. I don't want to stop—don't want to excite anyone's curiosity. From the top of the ridge you'll see the camp in the valley. Got binoculars?"

Caland cursed himself for a fool. To come so far and to have overlooked the most rudimentary preparations—

"Take these," Knack said. "Got hot drinks in that package? You'll need them. It's chilly up here until mid-morning. If you two want to be back at the Valley by late afternoon, better start down about noon. The ride back will be faster. It's easier to keep track of the road in daylight, and it's downhill, and the 'truck will have a lighter load."

He put the vehicle in motion.

As they approached the top of the ridge, he nudged Tel, who nudged Caland. They jumped out and slammed the door behind them, and the 'truck eased over the crest and started down into the valley without a ripple in the steady purr of its electric motor.

It was a triumphant moment for Caland when he and Tel reached the edge of the trees and looked down into the valley for their first glimpse of a notorious labor camp. From that point their spying expedition was anticlimactic all the way. They had a choice view of the camp, they were able to see much of what went on there, and when they wanted a closer look at anything, they could edge their way down into the valley along one of the many tongues of forest that extended there. But they saw nothing that looked even faintly anomalous.

The camp was new. Once an area had been stripped of the desired information, Sdissler moved his operation several kilometers northward along an ever-extending road and built a new encampment. The mals at work were young and healthy-looking, and they seemed superbly competent. There was a topographical team at work. Another crew worked along a survey line with a peculiar, power-driven machine, and most of the morning passed before Caland and Tel divined that the machine was taking soil cores. The occasional, distant crash of a falling tree marked the progress of a forestry crew. Other activities could not be identified from a distance, but the impression was one of a well-organized, capable force at work. If some of the work was hard, the mals performing it needed no slave driver to keep them occupied. The food—from the whiffs that reached Caland and Tel when the encampment assembled for break—was very good indeed.

They watched until noon, and when they made their way back down the uneven road to the place where Knack was waiting, all they could say for certain was Sdissler wasn't preparing any noticeable peculiarities in that particular camp.

"Get what you wanted?" Knack asked.

"Unfortunately—no," Caland said glumly.

Knack nodded sympathetically. He was a robust young mal with a short beard, and he looked much more comfortable driving the giant truck than he had with the misshapen cab. "It works out that way sometimes," he said. "Bar says he once disassembled an engine twenty-seven times, and put it back together twenty-seven times, before he spotted what was wrong with it."

"I hope," Tel said, "that this won't take twenty-seven times."

They were back at the Valley in time for a late-afternoon din, and Caland did his evening performance on schedule but with far less than his usual zest. Afterward it was beach—just briefly, to walk a length of the line of fires and greet friends—and bed.

* * * * * * *

Valley time flowed, but as the long, circular days drifted by, Caland increasingly thought of himself as a countercurrent attempting to break free. Stretched drowsily in the sun, lolling by a beach fire, seated at Nello's listening to Sam the Artist and the Reverend expound rival philosophies, lying awake in the darkness with Tel's arms gently caressing him, Caland found it difficult to maintain a detached point of view of himself as bait in an overwhelming mystery.

Valley trivialities kept intruding. The Reverend's para project was much on his mind and on his conscience. He had no argument against the worthy projects the Reverend wanted to finance—how could anyone take a stand against hot dins for schoolchildren?—but he wondered whether the most worthwhile objective really justified training children to beg or founding a new Valley economy upon a stratum of paras.

He could have rebelled had it not been for Zata. She proved to be a peerless businesser with a brisk efficiency and an instant grasp of what had to be done. Caland's role was reduced to the contribution of occasional insights and suggestions. Once he had explained to Zata what he was trying to accomplish, she was able to coach the acts and spot flaws in their performances. They quickly evolved a system: Caland created new para acts as inspiration moved him. Once he got them started, he turned them over to Zata. She managed the Reverend's entire project.

And Tel managed Caland. He hoped fervently that she was as contented with the situation as he was. He performed his own para act several times each evening, and the concentrated effort still left him tense and exhausted. He worked at it as hard as he'd ever worked at a serious theatrical role. Afterward, seated by a beach fire, taking an occasional slop of cider while listening to the bright chatter, he slowly relaxed until his mind could turn again to the mystery of himself.

He tried to ignore the innumerable small crises that rippled through the Valley and seemed to provide everyone living there with welcome diversion. It required deft navigation for him to keep himself clear of the domestic squabbles and reconciliations, the occasional fight on the beach or the Prom, the bankruptcy in the business community that was inevitably followed by the floating of a new concern to occupy the vacant space, and the high level conferences concerning Cleo's most recent act of flagrant misconduct, but he managed it.

Occasionally a larger crisis could not be ignored, as when a school child broke his leg during play and a playmate instantly ran to fetch Caland—eloquent testimony as to the stature he had achieved among the Vals. An older and wiser youngster went for Yda, the ex-nurse, and she had things all regulated by the time Caland and Tel arrived. She had set the broken bone and immobilized the child's leg, and she was seated beside him, an utterly incongruous figure in her stylish, rainbow-tinted gown, gazing into the small, pinched, white face with a raptly maternal expression. She was completely oblivious to stains left by the grubby hands that clutched at her pleadingly.

"Hospital?" Caland suggested.

Yda shook her head. "He'll be all right. I've injected him, and I've sent for a fracture wrap. He'll be back at play in a couple of hours. With a stiff leg, of course."

"Is he in pain?"

"Not much, but it hurt him like hell when it happened. He'll forget all of that as soon as he realizes that he's going to be a hero for a few days."

"The Valley needs a medical clinic," Caland said.

"Sure. It also needs a housing administrator, a whole corps of dietitians, a couple of building inspectors, and its own power and waste disposal plants."

Caland had been expecting a different kind of crisis. The Reverend's para acts now totaled seven, the Valley Enterprises account was growing by leaps, and its payroll—consisting of Zata and the paras Caland had trained—already was a significant Valley economic factor. But Caland had seen the regular Valley paras watching disapprovingly while Zata skillfully sent her own force into action. It was only a matter of time before they revolted, and Caland was in no way surprised when the Reverend sought him out where he and Tel were resting in the secluded quiet of the ocean beach.

"Something's come up," the Reverend said apologetically. "Sam's waiting for us at Nello's. Stupid thing, really, but it has to be dealt with immediately. If you can spare the time?"

There were many calls on the Reverend's time, and he wouldn't have come looking for them himself if the crisis weren't a real one. Caland nodded understandingly, and the three of them walked back to the Prom.

Sam the Artist was not waiting at Nello's; he also had gone looking for Caland and Tel. When they finally met, they found most of the Prom's down eateries much too crowded for a private conference. In desperation they claimed a table in a place called the Slop House. The fact that this particular eatery was half empty at that hour told its own tale of splintery seats and watered yuck. Sam the Artist brought mugs for them, and they sampled the yuck with appropriate expressions of distaste and settled back to listen to the Reverend.

"It really is a stupid crisis," he said. "Unfortunately, we can't ignore it. Dom's heard about our Valley Enterprises fund and the free dins for the school children. So he's decided to raise the rent we pay for the school building."

"Who's been paying the rent?" Caland asked.

"Everyone who can spare anything chips in. The Houses of Fame, the restaurants, the Road to Hell—they put up most of the money. It's a tidy sum, rent for a whole house, because we have to pay Dom something comparable to what he could charge by renting the rooms individually. But now he thinks he should have what he could charge if he subdivided the rooms and built some additions. The scoundrel. It's nothing to him whether the kids have a school or not."

"That's interesting," Caland said. "Not too long ago Tel and I were discussing the way Dom is similar to Pakovich."

"They're both asses," Sam the Artist said vehemently. "We can't do anything about that. Question is what to do about the school rent."

"What would be the chance of trading the school building for the Rental Office?" Caland asked.

The three responses came almost simultaneously.

"Since Dom owns both of them—" the Reverend began.

"Do we hold school in the Rental Office, or the Rental Office in the school?" Sam the Artist demanded.

"Are you sprung?" Tel asked anxiously.

"What I had in mind," Caland said, "was tearing down the Rental Office and putting up a new building that would use the land more efficiently. On the end facing the Prom, there'd be a kind of community building. You could give Dom space for his Rental Office, and there'd be room for a medical clinic and other community service organizations. The back would house the school. Valley lots are enormously deep, and most of the vacant land is overgrown and wasted. There's plenty of room back there for playgrounds, or for expanding the school if that ever becomes necessary. Maybe you could include an auditorium, both for the school and for indoor meetings. It's what the Valley needs to become a community."

"Will you let the Reverend's church meet in the auditorium?" Sam the Artist asked.

"I don't have a church," the Reverend said irritably. "And I don't want a church."

"Surely a public meeting room won't corrupt your congregation's religious principles!"

"Let's get this auditorium built before we start moving things into it," Tel said dryly. "The first question is whether Dom will consent to this."

"He'll consent," Caland said. "But be sure to get a perpetual free lease on the land as long as it's used for community purposes."

"You don't even know the old villain," Sam the Artist protested. "How can you be so certain?"

"If he won't consent, you can call a tenant's strike. Have you thought about how totally helpless Dom would be in the face of any kind of organized opposition? He couldn't possibly evict anyone. He couldn't collect any rents at all. I'm surprised that you didn't think of it years ago. How does Dom handle delinquent rents now?"

"He rents the space to someone else," Tel said.

"And the tenants fight it out?"

"Something like that. But if the other party has a valid receipt, there's really no fight. Valley etiquette says that the person paying for space is entitled to it, and other Vals would support that."

"Valley etiquette wouldn't enter into it if everyone refused to pay," Caland said. "A similar technique could be applied to Pakovich. The world of Mort is just as vulnerable as the Valley. It doesn't even have a force of proctors."

Sam the Artist's hairy face assumed a beatific smile. "It was a fortunate day for the forces of law and order when our friend Cal was born honest."

"No billionaire's son is born honest," Tel said. "It requires divine intervention. As long as the employees are loyal, Mort doesn't need proctors. Pak Enterprises can keep the employees in hand, and the employees can handle the tourists. The only full-time employee Dom has is old Gus."

"Give him an ultimatum," Caland said. "Free rent for the school from now on, and a permanent free lease on land for the new building. Otherwise, no more rent from anyone."

"It's a fitting response to his threat to raise the rent," the Reverend agreed. "What do I say if he asks when the new building will be finished? It's a fair question. I know my paras are bringing in a tidy income by Valley standards, but—a community building? What would it cost? And who would build it?"

"That's not my problem," Caland said. "I'm an ex-actor, not an architect. I'll do this, though—how much money is in my account, Tel?"

"About seventy thousand chits," Tel said.

Caland thought a moment. He needed a reserve for his own payroll, which was growing. "I'll transfer fifty thousand to your Valley Enterprises account for the new building, and I'll give another fifty thousand as soon as I have it. Beyond that, it's your problem."

"That's magnificent!" the Reverend exclaimed. "But—community building and school house? How would we do it? The Valley has enormous resources of unskilled labor, but who would do the planning and buy the materials and tell the labor what to do?"

"Morlef might know," Tel said.

"Who's that?" Sam the Artist asked.

"Retired worker, he calls himself, but his work had something to do with building."

Sam the Artist nodded. "Worth a try. I'll talk to him."

"And I," the Reverend said, "will talk to Dom. Over the years I have held many conversations with him, and this will be the first time I've ever enjoyed one."

Caland and Tel elected to go with Sam the Artist. At the north end of the strip of park, separated from the bay beach by a thick hedge of trees and bushes, some elderly Vals had built a tiny recreational center for themselves. They had a shelter, a thatched roof constructed on poles, to keep the rain off them, and at one end was a fire pit where logs burned on chill days. There were benches and chairs with seats of woven branches and leaf-stuffed bags for cushions. Some forty elderly Vals, mals and fems, had gathered to talk, to play various kinds of games, or just to nap or meditate among friends. The little center represented a pathetically courageous attempt to ameliorate those Valley hardships that would seem so trivial to the young and so burdensome to the elderly.

They found Morlef watching a game of Zexit. He was a giant

of a man—powerfully built with massive hands and massive muscles. His shaggy long hair and beard were pure white, but his eyes were bright, and his manner was anything but enfeebled. He greeted them with grave courtesy and readily consented to be led away for a yuck and conversation.

They took him to Nello's, and Caland brought the mugs of yuck and an O loaf to the table. Morlef sampled the bread, nodded appreciatively, and took a deep draught of yuck. He set the mug down carefully and asked with a twinkle, "What do the young want of the old?"

"Information," Sam the Artist said. "Would it be possible to build a building in the Valley?"

"What sort of building?"

Sam told him, and Morlef listened attentively while he slowly chewed on the bread and sipped the yuck.

"Could be done," he said when Sam had finished. "I once was a building super. Had hundreds of employees under me. Made big money, but I also spent big money. Even came to Mort once, as a tourist, and blew a year's savings at Pakovich's hotes and the Road to Hell. That's how I found out about the Valley. I earned a lot and spent a lot, and when the conglom decided I was worked out, I hadn't anything left. So I came here. There isn't much about the building tech that I haven't done myself. Sure, your building is possible."

Morlef paused for a gulp of yuck. He seemed to enjoy having an audience. "It's bothered me that I can't do anything here when there's so much to be done. Most of these buildings should come down, one at a time, and be replaced by buildings planned for the Valley. There's enough land space here to accommodate five times the population comfortably if it were used right. These old buildings weren't planned for occupancy by so many people."

"We understand that you'd need workers and tools and materials," Sam said. "The workers would have to be trained, and since there's no place on Mort that supplies building materials, the shipping costs would probably be enormous. But we need to get an idea of how large a problem we have to deal with."

"The labor might be a considerable problem. Hard to tell that until it's been tried. Most of these young mals have never done any real work. They seem to want jobs they can play at, and they're not willing to spend much time doing that. There are two retired mals and one fem who might be useful. We can teach, but whether the young mals will learn, and whether they'll use what they learn, are questions I wouldn't try to answer."

"The materials?" Caland suggested.

"That may be less of a problem than you'd expect. Shipping costs might even be reasonable if we were to give an exclusive contract to one ship. Mort exports an awful lot more than it imports. Maybe hundreds of times more. Most of those ore ships and the fertilizer ships make the return run almost empty. They'd welcome a bit of freight business. But there are plenty of materials available right here on Mort. Pakovich has a mill. Only operates it now and then for mining timbers, but it turns out lumber when he wants it to. He has a brick kiln—that's where the brick came from for the Houses of Fame and other Valley buildings. Probably he closed it down years ago when he decided to build Pak Enterprises installations of cement, but if it's still operable, we might be able to lease it and make our own brick. Pakovich also makes his own cement. Special grades, like stress cement, we'd have to import, but we should be able to buy the ordinary grades from him. He doesn't like the Valley, but he's also a businesser, and he has to pay his employees and maintain installations whether they produce or not. He should be willing to sell cement and lumber and brick and anything else he has available at reasonable prices."

"If materials are so readily available, why is the Valley so run down?" Caland asked.

"Dom. Dom is the problem. He's satisfied to leave things as they are. He's making lots of money that way. It's a pity, really it is. This could be a beautiful community with everyone comfortable. But Dom keeps it a junk heap because it's a profitable junk heap. Think he'll let you build this new building?"

"The Reverend is working on that," Caland said.

"If he lets you do it, I'll build it for you." Morlef spoke slowly, flexing his hands as he talked. "Never thought I'd want to work again when I retired, but when I see so much work to be done, I'd like to get back to building. As for your laborers—I've got a theory about that. Lots of these young Vals would enjoy working if there was something creative they could do with their hands. That's the problem with modern life. Machines do things. People sit. Give people a chance to build, and they'll work hard and be happy. It's a wonderful experience. You can see that you're accomplishing something important, something big, and can measure your progress day after day and even hour by hour."

He flexed his hands again—a gesture of regret that humans had created a civilization that destroyed their creativity.

"It's happened all over the galaxy," he said, his voice heavy with a deep sense of loss. "As soon as civilization arrives, machines take over. Used to be a mal could take a piece of metal and make something of it. Or a pile of lumber and build something. And then one day he's out of work because a machine presses a synthetic into a mold. There's nothing left for people to do but push buttons. They want to use their hands, but there's nothing for them to do."

"Bronlan uses his hands."

"Ah! But Bar is a genius. A genius will find a way even if it means spending his life building a spaceship that will never fly. Look at the dirt artists." He sent a shy smile in Tel's direction. "They've found a way to use their hands. Their art may start to crumble as soon as it dries out, but they've had the pleasure of making it. People with art talent usually find ways to use it. All the others can do is invent silly excuses to waste time. Sure, I'll build your building. Get Dom's permission and I'll build it."

"What about the cost?" Tel asked.

"How big is this building going to be? We can't talk about costs until we have plans drawn up."

The Reverend joined them. "Dom was in conference with

your friend Doctor Gormaz," he said. "Dom was talking and Gormaz was listening, poor mal. I deemed it unwise to wedge at a moment when Dom was so obviously enjoying himself with a victim too polite to escape."

"Gormaz isn't too polite to escape," Caland said. "Dom must be telling him something he wants to know. When we saw them, Gormaz was more than holding his own."

"Perhaps they deserve each other," the Reverend said. "All the better reason for not interrupting. How are you making out here?"

"Morlef has just pronounced the doom of civilization," Sam said.

Morlef grinned and repeated his comments on obsolete humans.

"He's right, you know," the Reverend said gravely. "The decline of civilization is really the decline of people, and it starts when the machines take over. Hands made humans different from animals and enabled them to develop their intelligence and become civilized. When they stop using their hands, both their intelligence and their civilization start to wither. I'm talking about average humans, not the geniuses who design our incredible machines and then devise ways of using them to build far more incredible machines. Average humans have been in decline for a long, long time. But it took millions and millions of years for humans to develop their intelligence and their civilization, so it shouldn't be surprising that they can push buttons for a long time without realizing that they're on their way to being animals again."

"I haven't noticed very many buttons to push in the Valley," Caland said, "so I refuse to worry about that sort of thing. Is there anyone here who could draw up plans for a community building?"

"Of course," the Reverend said. "The Valley has people who have failed in almost everything."

* * * * * *

Lying in the Valley's velvety darkness, body pressed closely against Tel's warm back, hand cupping her breast, Caland floated in dreamy quietude. A native night creature twitted plaintively outside their window; an upstairs tenant stumbled drunkenly up the steps to bed; refugees from a late beach fire passed by talking and laughing. Caland found such sounds soothing. Somehow they defined the world about him.

"Tel?"

She answered crossly. "Huh?"

"I love you."

She turned and embraced him. "And I love you. And even more, I love what you're becoming. You're like someone slowly awakening from a long sleep, and each day is a new revelation of what you are. I've been so happy watching you transform this stagnant Valley society that never got around to telling you that it's impossible. And you're doing it!"

Their lips met; their hands caressed each other. But he felt no passion, even though hers throbbed and pulsated under his touch. Later, as she lay drifting in relaxed euphoria, she murmured, "Still nothing?"

"A great deal," he said, "but not that."

"Strange. You never remember any problem before your accident?"

"I can't remember any."

"I mean—you've certainly had lovers, maybe been married—"

"I may have been married to the fem who was driving at the time of the accident. I was curious enough to try to find out about her afterward, since she died and I lived. She was an actress in the company I was working with. I found some publicity fotes of her—she was lovely. The report of the accident said she was my wife."

"But you don't remember?"

"I couldn't remember ever having seen her before."

"But if you've had lovers in the past—"

"Look," Caland said desperately. "I have a clear recollection of a perfectly normal sex life as far back as my memory can extend. The accident wipes out several years, so I don't remember this actress, and I don't remember the theatrical company—which I'd belonged to for a couple of years—and I don't remember anything at all about the world of Folamnin prior to regaining consciousness at the Institute. My ability to love isn't impaired. I have no uncertainty at all about loving you. But sex isn't involved. I have no desire at all. I don't miss it for myself, maybe because one can't miss something one has no desire for, but I miss it for you. If I love *without* sex, and you love *with* sex, that's an impossible equation and maybe it'd be best if—"

"Hush!" she said, pressing her fingers to his mouth. "We'll work it out. It'll be all right."

"Anyway, I never expected that you'd love me. When I first came here, someone said you were in love with Gary Dwand. I've wondered, ever since then, but I figured—"

"You figured wrong all around. Everyone in the Valley thinks in pairs. A fem without a mal isn't considered normal, and all the unattached mals—and a lot that are attached—take it as a challenge and consider it a matter of social duty to correct the imbalance. But a consuming passion for someone who isn't available is always an acceptable excuse, so I invented a passion for Gary, who certainly isn't available. Unfortunately, his passion for Melana is real. Now sleep."

Tel slept. Caland lay perspiring in the grip of an icy dread that had seized him.

Someone controlled him.

He was returning to normal because his brain hadn't been tampered with for so long. He had been left on this world of Mort unattended—left until called for, like luggage, just as he had been left at cheap hotes on world after world. But eventually those controlling him would collect him just as one collected a piece of left luggage suddenly remembered, and he would awake in a cheap hote on a world he'd never heard of.

Mort, and the Valley, would be wiped out of his mind as

though they'd never existed.

So would Tel.

The dread consumed him, and he tossed and could not sleep. He knew that he was going to lose Tel. One way or another, for one reason or another, their paths would separate. She needed a mal whose brain and body functioned normally, and eventually she would come to realize that.

Probably long before that happened, those who owned him would claim their property. He would leave Mort, and the time spent here would become another blank in a long procession of things forgotten. Somewhere down the convoluted avenue of time a fragment might slip through into his consciousness, a glimmer of worthwhile deeds attempted, of an afterglow of unexpected happiness, of things sensed but not remembered.

He could accept the pain of separation—one more pain among so many—if he could retain the memories. What he could not stand was the certainty that he would not even remember her.

In the morning Tel asked sympathetically, "Another nightmare?"

"The worst kind," Caland said gravely.

CHAPTER TWENTY

Valley time flowed. There were leisurely meals on the Prom; yuck and a putrebun from Hef's; and long sessions of yuck and conversation at Nello's with any Vals who chanced to join them. Caland listened absently, studied passing Vals as potential paras, thought about the prolonged negotiations with Dom over the use of a site for the proposed community building, worried about Sdissler and Nalce, and fretted over the meager results turned in by Louie Laggie's watchers.

They had maps to study. Just when they had begun to think that no one on the world of Mort except Sdissler and possibly Pakovich knew where Sdissler's labor camps were located, Melana chanced to catch a word of their oblique inquiries. She brought them copies of Pak Enterprises records that showed not only present camp locations but all of the past locations, plus a welter of information—in symbols and shadings—that summarized the geological and botanical information derived from each site. In was an embarrassing richness of data about a fabulously rich world, and none of it was helpful. They already knew that all of the camps except the one they had visited were accessible only by air, and discreet queries made by Chan Worntling of one of Pakovich's security officers concerning supply procedures established firmly that no stowaway on the small freight platforms could possibly escape notice. An accompanying relief map also scuttled another fanciful notion of Caland's—that of renting one of Bronlan's 'cabs and attempting the trip overland.

They were none the less grateful to Melana. She must have

been curious as to the reason for their curiosity, but she asked no questions. They reciprocated by asking her no questions as to how she had obtained the information.

"So sweet, so innocent, so beautiful," Tel murmured. "She could charm anyone out of anything. Still—she must have given them *some* explanation. I wonder what it was."

"She probably told them she needed the information for her book," Caland said. "Pakovich directed the library to give her anything she wanted."

"Yes," Tel agreed. "That must have been it. Useful thing, writing a book. I'll have to try it sometime."

Periodically Caland and Tel walked down to the Valley gate to inspect the team of paras. Zata managed them from a shelter she'd had built a few meters south of the gate. It was a smaller version of the shelter used by early Vals, and it provided refuge from sun and rain for the Reverend's paras and a place to rest between 'buses. There were comfortable seats, refreshments, and, in one corner, an improvised desk of boxes where Zata did her sums and kept records.

The afternoon was unusually hot for the Valley when Caland and Tel arrived on one of their routine visits. The unattended fire under the kettle of yuck had gone out, and the paras were sipping cold drinks generously supplied by Olgi. Zata, poised, crisply efficient, rejuvenated by a responsible job to perform, proudly showed them the day's figures. She had increased the size of the children's troop to eight.

"Many of the tourists feel that each child should be rewarded," she said. "We've more than doubled the take."

Moppy sprawled on a bench, a cold mug in his hand. Phem sat on the ground beside him and playfully tried to tip up the mug when he drank. She was dieting; she'd already lost considerable weight. A miracle had brought her a lover, but she'd adopted a thoroughly practical approach to holding onto him. She was a very different—and much prettier—young fem from the tortuously shy, lubberly creature Caland had first met.

"'Bus!" someone shouted.

Zata marshaled her troops, and Caland and Tel went along to watch. As the 'bus rolled to a halt, Zata sent the children into action. They began their welcoming song as the first tourists stepped down. Their songs and dances quickly attracted a crowd; the appeal of these charming little waifs in colorful long dresses, earnestly solemn in their performance, aroused squeals of delight, and set the tourists to digging for their money and stuffing it into the embroidered bags that the children carried.

When the tourists moved on, Hoppy was there on her crutches to smile her plea "for a new leg." Llabal accepted money in a container held with one foot. Moppy already had selected a victim; he donned the hat that Phem produced for him and set off in the wake of a group of tourists. Mac tried his soft-spoken line on individuals. Other paras joined in, and the show moved off along the Prom.

Caland and Tel returned to the shelter with the children, and Caland asked one of the young mothers who was helping Zata how she felt about the Valley's number one subject of conversation: the new community building and school.

"I thought we had a good school," the mother said. "Of course, if Dom wants to throw us out, then we'll have to find another place."

"Don't you think a building designed to function as a school would be much better for the children?"

"I don't think it matters," she said. "Teachers are what matters. Paradise has a nice school building with all kinds of fancy machines in it, but I don't think the children learn as well as our children. People get those things confused with education. So do teachers. But machines don't teach, and neither do buildings. Teachers teach, and they can do it in a new building or in an old one, and they can use machines or not use them. I think there can be too many trappings in a school room. The teachers start thinking that all the equipment is doing the teaching, so they stop. That's why Valley children get better educations than those in Pakovich's posh school."

"Surely you're not opposed to a community building," Caland

said, doubtfully.

"No. We need things like a medical clinic because we haven't got any. I'm just saying that a new building doesn't mean a better education. Even if we get this community building, I'd still want the same teachers."

"They're unpaid volunteers, aren't they?" Caland said. "They haven't been trained as teachers."

"They're teaching because they like to, and they like to because they're good at it. People who are naturally good at things don't need training, and some of them have better educations and more experience of life than the Paradise teachers. If we get this new building, I just hope the teachers don't stop teaching and expect the building to do it."

Caland was left wondering whether he'd done a wise thing.

The other paras returned with their takings, and Mac was chortling over a tourist who had been so convulsed by his appeal for money for one last fling that he offered to take him to Yda's.

"I told him the fems there are too young," Mac said. "When you go flinging at my age, you have to be a connoisseur about it. Same as with eating. A young cook gives you a lot of food to eat fast. The cook with years of experience doesn't try to stuff your stomach. She gives you food you want to take your time with because eating it is such a pleasure. Or maybe it's like that game of Zexit—"

"Better leave it at the food," Tel said. "If you have it like too many things, you won't have it like it is."

Mac cackled and turned over his take.

The children ran off to play at an improvised playground nearby, and Caland watched them and wondered whether Valley children really were deprived. He also wondered again about the morality of converting them into beggars or of building a new Valley society whose main economic support was a trained team of paras.

They drifted back along the Prom to Nello's where they joined Sam the Artist. While Caland watched the Prom traffic, Tel told Sam about Mac's culinary view of life.

Suddenly she exclaimed, "Look!"

Nalce was hurrying along the Prom. He moved through the crowds as swiftly as possible and without a backward glance.

"Interesting," Tel muttered. "A person walking that fast usually has a destination. What's his?"

Neither Caland nor Sam the Artist had any interest in speculating on Nalce's probable destination. Sam returned to the philosophy of viewing all life in terms of gastronomic experiences, which he found appealing. He thought the experience of painting a picture could be compared with the experience the gastronome achieved by carefully tasting a variety of foods, the contrasting brush strokes of color being similar to the strokes of food on the taste buds. He was enlarging on this theme when Tel leaped to her feet.

"Screet!"

"What's the matter?" Caland said.

"Who's supposed to be following Nalce?"

"Don't know." Sam said. "Maybe no one. We're only watching him now and then as a kind of check." He was still unaware of Louie Laggie's watchers.

"Let's see where he goes," Tel said to Caland.

They left their unfinished yuck and plunged into the milling Prom traffic. As they pressed forward they caught an occasional glimpse of Nalce far ahead of them still walking swiftly. It was obvious that he was giving no thought to being followed. By the time he reached the end of the Prom, where traffic thinned out, they were close behind him. He was headed for the Valley gate where a motley group was awaiting the arrival of the next 'bus: a few Vals bound for Paradise, returning tourists, and a hovering assortment of paras.

Caland and Tel turned off into the park and sat down on a bench.

"We can't follow him on the 'bus," Tel said.

Caland understood her frustration. She could not leave Caland alone while she looked for help, and if the two of them attempted to follow Nalce on the same 'bus, they would be ridiculously conspicuous. Far up the highway, Caland could see the grotesque outlines of one of Bronlan's ungainly vehicles approaching. It slowed its speed, swung into the rough turning circle, and whirred to a halt. Zata had emerged from the para shelter to send her charges into action. The tourists dismounted, and the children began their performance. When the bus was empty, Nalce climbed aboard with the other waiting passengers. It slowly completed its circle and began to roll away.

"Screet!" Tel exclaimed vehemently. "We've got to do something. Come on!"

She broke into a run.

A short distance along the Prom, they met Baris Bronlan taking a brief break from his labors on the spaceship or on one of the machines he was rebuilding. He still wore his eyeshade, and he walked along slowly, stiff arm held in front of him. To the tourists who brushed past this nondescript figure in patched clothing, he was one more nonentity in the Prom's drifting riff-raff. Nothing about him suggested that he was the true owner of the Valley—but he was, Caland thought. He had taken possession of the place because he loved it. No title deed could confer that kind of ownership.

Tel intercepted him and spoke in urgent, low tones.

Bar nodded. "Wait here," he said.

He started back along the Prom, moving at a trot.

Louie Laggie came hurrying up to them. "Where is he?" Louie gasped.

Tel pointed at the highway.

"He took the bus?" Louie exclaimed. "Screet!"

"What happened?" Tel asked.

"Fem brought him a message. He'd been watching Cal, and the three of you were in Nello's with yuck and obviously in no hurry to move, so I took a chance and followed the fem. Kept her in sight all the way to Fishstink Alley. Then she cut in behind a house and slipped me."

"Who was she?"

"Never saw her before."

"Valley fem?"

Louie hesitated. "Maybe. Newcomers often look that way—like they're trying awfully hard not to be newcomers."

Tel thoughtfully scrutinized both Louie and Caland. Louie was wearing his usual threadbare patches and no shoes. Caland wore stubs and a frayed wrapper he had become fond of.

Tel pointed at a nearby used clothing store. "Get yourselves over to Dudley's Duds," she told them. "Find something that will make you half presentable. Hurry."

Dudley quickly outfitted them in passably decent lounge clothing, and Louie picked out shoes for himself. Dudley was a worried-looking mal with a family, to whom every sale was important, but he smilingly acquiesced to Caland's assurance that they would return the clothing and settle with him later. Caland reflected that his monerating on the Prom probably exceeded the one tied to his father in Credit Centrex.

An electrocab was waiting outside the door for them with Baris Bronlan driving. Tel was seated inside, immodestly completing a change to her ludicrous tourist clothing, which she had reclaimed from Alz's wife at the Fig Stump.

They climbed in, and Louie gawked at Tel. "Zwingy! All of a sudden you're a tourist!"

"That doesn't take any special talent," Tel said. "All you need is money and bad taste."

"And time to waste," Caland suggested.

"True. Lots of time to waste."

Bronlan already had the 'cab in motion. They threaded their way out to the Valley gate, at which point he proceeded to demonstrate how fast one of his remodeled vehicles could travel. The motor's whirr became a high-pitched scream, and the bulky vehicle rocked and bounced over irregularities in the road that would have passed unnoticed at a normal speed.

"We'll catch 'em," Bronlan announced confidently.

"They've got a long start on us," Tel said.

"Doesn't matter. I told the driver to slow down."

Caland pondered this unexpected announcement while the

scenery flashed past. He had never thought about it, but of course the primitive Valley could not have functioned without secure communications with the modern world of Mort. The main Valley businesses—the houses of Fame, the restaurants, the transportation company—had to have telation facilities by which tourists could summon transportation and make reservations. And Bronlan, even if his transportation company had not needed it, would have contrived a workable communications network for his vehicles. Probably he built it himself from discards.

Halfway to Paradise the 'bus loomed ahead of them lumbering along slowly. Bronlan spoke curtly into a mic, and the 'bus picked up speed. They followed behind it until it pulled up in front of Pakovich's Merc Mart. Then Bronlan passed it and swung to the curb as though to discharge a passenger.

Tel turned and watched the passengers leaving the 'bus. "He's going into the park," she announced. "He may be meeting someone there. Louie—you wait here and follow him if he comes back this way. I'll see where he goes. Bar—take Cal to the hotes and wait there."

She flung the door open and headed for the park at a run.

"That doesn't make sense," Louie protested belatedly. "Why would he walk all the way across the park to the hotes when he could have stayed on the 'bus and ridden there?"

"Tel always has reasons," Bar said.

"Dressed like that she can't follow him closely, and if she hangs back she'll lose him."

Bar smiled. "No, she won't."

Louie shrugged and started toward the Merc Mart. The new clothing made him look almost respectable, but his long hair unmistakably branded him as a Val and drew disapproving looks from the Paradise residents.

Bronlan called him back. "Check with the 'buses," he said. "If there's a change, one of the drivers will have a message for you."

Bronlan put the 'cab in motion again, and they headed for

the hotes.

Pakovich's own public transportation system consisted of two enormous blue electrobusses that transported tourists between the space port and the hotes. Both of them were parked beside the Paradise Vista Inn, and Bronlan turned his 'cab around and backed in between them. He got out and went to the rear of the 'buses, and Caland followed him.

"We can watch from here," Bronlan said.

They waited.

The formal garden stretched between them and the shadowed dimness of the park. They saw nothing at all until Nalce's figure abruptly stepped through a gap in the hedge. Bronlan's stiff arm cautioned Caland, and the two of them backed out of sight between the 'buses. Nalce moved purposefully toward the hotes. A moment later Tel passed across their line of sight.

They continued to watch. Nalce approached a hote side entrance in a confident manner; either he had been there before or he knew he was expected. He opened the door and entered. The moment he disappeared, Bronlan stepped into the open and waved a hand. Tel waved a response and hurried toward the same door.

"I'll send word to Louie," Bronlan said. "Then we might as well sit down and relax. We could be here for hours."

He went back to his 'cab to send the message. Then he placed Caland on a comfortable seat on the front guard of one of the 'buses, and he went to watch from the rear. Caland, with an indeterminate wait ahead of him, suddenly realized that he was hungry. He had fallen into the usual habit of eating frequent, small meals, and he regretted the unfinished mug of yuck he'd left behind him.

Tel joined them. "He went into the room of a mal named Oplix. Name mean anything to you?"

Caland shook his head.

"Oplix has another visitor whose description very strongly resembles that of Granst."

"Who's Granst?" Bronlan wanted to know.

"Beefy vrump who contacted Nalce in the Valley. Oplix is expecting more guests. He's ordered an elaborate sup for six served in his room.

"How'd you find that out?" Caland asked.

"From one of the hote flunks. Oplix frequently entertains guests. He arranges with the flunks to have them come in a side entrance and be shown directly to his room. The flunks approve—if his kind of guests used the front door, they'd disgrace the establishment. They're scum from the Valley or the Port hote. But this is a special occasion. Usually Oplix has one guest at a time."

"It sounds like a silly, amateurish conspiracy," Bronlan said. "This Oplix ought to know that he can't bring that kind of people into a tourist hote without attracting attention to himself. I suppose if he had to meet the others at an uncomfortable place, it'd take the fun out of it."

"Something like that," Tel agreed. "It's possible that this is a reunion of old friends, and they'll eat and drink and go their separate ways. In the meantime Cal will have missed his para bit, and that'll cost money. Do you think we should stay?"

"What do you think?" Caland asked.

"I think they're up to something. The flunks will find out as much as they can for us, but my hunch is that we should wait. There has to be some reason for that sudden message to Nalce."

"Cal needs a vacation anyway," Bar said.

"A vacation from wasting time?" Caland asked with a smile.

"I've watched you. The way you do it, it's hard work."

Louie emerged from the formal garden and turned toward them. He was scowling when he reached them. "Nalce must be sprung," he said. "Why did he walk all that distance when he could have ridden the 'bus?"

"The same reason you did," Tel said. "He didn't want to use the hote's front entrance."

She described what was happening, and Louie said, "I suppose the idea is that we follow them when they leave. Or follow as many as we can. That may not be easy with only one 'cab."

"If they wait until after dark, it may be impossible. We can't make plans until we see what they do." Tel turned to Bronlan. "Can you have another 'cab waiting at the Merc Mart just in case we need it?"

Bronlan nodded.

"Right now there's nothing we can do except wait," Tel said.

"You watch," Bronlan said, "I'll listen."

He seated himself in the 'cab where he could remain in touch with his com network. Louie settled on the front guard of one of the 'buses, and Caland and Tel took the rear where they could watch the side entrance.

The wait quickly convinced Caland that he had no talent as a searcher, and his patience was not improved by the fact that he was not needed. Tel leaned back and half closed her eyes, intent on her own thoughts, but he knew that her most casual glance missed nothing at all. He had never felt more useless, and the tedium oppressed him. He had to contend with his growing hunger in silence; the others were at least as hungry as he was. The afternoon slowly stretched toward evening with nothing for him to do except watch an occasional marauding yodel bird and try to forget his empty stomach.

Then a 'cab arriving to pick up a hote guest swung over and delivered a package to Bronlan. It contained putrebuns and yuck for all four of them from Hef's Place. They slowly munched the putrebuns and sipped yuck while the afternoon waned.

Tel made another excursion to the hote and returned with the information that the elaborate sup for six had been served, and, as far as the hote flunks knew, all six were still there.

"Only two of the guests arrived by the side entrances," Tel said. "The other three were hote guests or entered some other way. One of the flunks will try to get descriptions for me."

They switched places with Louie to relieve the monotony, and Caland sat looking out at the bay as darkness set in. The last of the sail boats tacked to the pier, and the lovely colors of the water slowly faded into blackness. Fires sprung up on the distant Valley beach. The hotes were already ablaze with light, and for a time the traffic in front of them was heavy as groups of jovial tourists left for the Valley in 'cabs or 'buses, and a few extremely tired and dragging tourists returned. There was movement on the lighted veranda as hote guests finished supping and claimed their favorite chairs. A flurry of activity at the side entrance announced the arrival of the late shift hote employees.

Night set in and the traffic gradually thinned. Finally Bronlan leaned from the 'cab and said, "I think this is them. A 'cab for five people going from the hote to the hydroelectric plant."

"Hydroelectric plant?" Louie echoed incredulously. "And why only five?"

They continued to watch until Bronlan told them the 'cab was about to arrive. Then they climbed in, and he moved his own 'cab forward a short distance so they could watch both entrances.

The lights of the "'cab for five" approached, and the vehicle slowly coasted into the hote's loading circle. A group of guests hurried toward it from the now heavily-shadowed side entrance.

Bronlan handed Tel a pair of binoculars. She studied the figures for a moment. "Five," she said. "Where's the sixth? I recognize Granst and Nalce, but I don't know the others. I don't believe that bit about the hydroelectric plant."

The "'cab for five" rolled away. Bronlan waited until its lights had disappeared, and then he followed it.

"You'll lose it!" Louie protested.

"Nope," Bronlan said. "We know where they're going. At least, we know where they're starting out for. If there's a change, the driver will tell me. They'd soon know they were being followed if I stayed close. 'Cabs aren't often seen on that road."

They moved swiftly through the streets of Paradise, with Bronlan paralleling the route he knew the other 'cab was following. Then they were in open country, and Bronlan was constantly accelerating or slowing to a crawl as he maneuvered to keep one curve or one hill behind the other 'cab. The highway was negotiating the lower slopes of one of the Tin Mountains, and Bronlan pointed out the turnoff to Pakovich's mansion as they passed it. Caland would not have recognized it at night. They whirred on into the darkness and finally slowed and coasted to a stop on the shoulder of the road.

Bronlan turned. "They asked the driver to let them out. It's a nice night and they feel like walking—or so they said."

"Where are they?" Tel asked.

"A couple of kilometers past the turnoff to the mines."

"Ah." Tel thought a moment. "They're going to walk to the mines, of course."

"Or to the hydroelectric plant," Bronlan said.

"They'll walk there later. They'll have arranged an official appointment to visit the place to cover the fact that they've been to the mines."

The 'cab began to move forward again. "I'll let you out around this next curve," Bronlan said. "If you don't mind climbing, and you're fast about it, you can get over the hill to the mines entrance about as quickly as they'll make it back by road. I'll put the 'cab out of sight and wait there."

Tel spoke to Louie. "We'll post you at the top of the hill. You'll be able to carry messages quickly either way."

Bronlan brought the 'cab to a stop and backed it into some thick shrubs. He handed Tel the binoculars, and she and Caland and Louie climbed out.

As they started to push into the thick undergrowth of the forest that rose above them, Tel hesitated. "Sure you're up to it?" she asked Caland. "Climbing mountains is a special kind of exercise."

"I'll manage. If I can't make it, I'll go back and wait with Bar."

"Louie can take you back," she agreed. She laughed silently and looped her arm through his.

Caland made no comment. He was sobered by the thought that they still were not leaving him alone for a moment, whether in the crowded Valley or a lonely mountain forest.

He soon was puffing his way through his most realistic nightmare. The thick vegetation was his initiation to the native shrubs of Mort; he could see nothing at all, but he quickly learned that the bulging, drooping leaves had viciously sharp, serrated edges. He also experienced his first close encounter with Mort's native life forms. Clouds of mite-sized creatures bit furiously. Caland swore and tried to scratch and protect himself at the same time.

"Hush!" Tel whispered. "Just ignore them. They don't like humans."

"Is that why they bite? Because they don't like us?"

"They have to taste us first. Then they'll leave us alone."

"That's no help," Caland said bitterly. "There'll always be a whole forest of them that haven't sampled us yet."

Miraculously, the attack eased and then stopped altogether; or perhaps Caland became so intent on his laboring ascent that he no longer noticed it. The flow of recent days, the longest period in his fragmented memory without a lapse into unconsciousness, had enabled him to regain strength, and he'd thought that his strenuous para exertions had toughened him. He actually felt alive, felt an interest in life about him and an eagerness to participate in it; but the tremendous exertion of climbing quickly convinced him that his muscles were still flabby and his physical condition was not much better than that of the chronic invalid that he had been for so long.

Tel's arm steadied him; Louie, whose sinewy form had the deceptive strength of old tree roots, bounded along on the other side ever ready to lend a hand. They helped him around and over invisible obstacles, and eventually they got him to the crest. Through the trees they could catch an occasional glimpse of light far below.

"Don't talk," Tel whispered. "Sound travels further than you'd think."

She had a hurried, whispered conference with Louie, and then she and Caland began the descent. They quickly came to the edge of the trees, and the headquarters of Pakovich's tin empire lay just below them: the two square smelters, the ore ship landing field, ore storage piles, cranes, conveyors, work vehicles, buildings of indeterminate use, all crammed into a narrow valley between heights that contained the galaxy's richest tin deposits. No effort had been made to light the whole installation, nor was there any evidence of guards. There were no employees in sight and no signs of activity. The mines worked a double shift, but the second had long since gone home. The entire valley had a peculiarly mottled appearance, with bright patches of light shading to shadowed dimness in areas the illumination did not touch.

They paused while Tel studied the scene with binoculars.

Suddenly they were no longer alone. They heard voices nearby talking quietly. Tel gripped Caland's arm and drew him back into cover. Then shadowy figures left the trees a mere fifty meters from them and started down the slope. As they approached the lights of the valley below, Caland was able to see them more distinctly. There were five of them; two carried ladders, and the others had more compact loads.

Tel handed the binoculars to Caland. They were excellent night glasses, but he could see nothing but the mals' backs. He watched while they put a ladder against one side of the tall fence. One of them mounted, hauled a ladder up behind him, and let it down on the other side. As he turned at the top, Caland saw that his face was muffled. Four of the mals ascended and descended the ladders, one at a time; then, leaving a mal on watch on each side of the fence, three of them moved off toward the smelters and the loading equipment.

Minutes passed. The three mals came running back. Again Caland watched as the four inside the fence climbed and descended the ladders. The last one hauled the inside ladder up after him. Caland was still able to distinguish nothing but dark figures with muffled faces.

As they picked up the ladders and hurried away, the covering on one face slipped aside. Caland had only a fleeting glimpse, but he started and handed the binoculars to Tel. Before he could say anything, the night erupted in a blinding explosion that sent a column of flame skyward but produced almost no blast.

"Come on!" Tel hissed.

They labored back to the top of the hill, and Louie came to meet them in case Caland needed help. On the long climb from the road, Caland's one consolation had been the thought that the return would be much easier. It was not. He had to fight to keep from pitching headlong as Tel and Louie rushed him downward. He was panting as badly as he had been on the ascent when they found Bronlan's 'cab and hurried themselves into it.

Tel tersely told Bronlan what had happened, and he needed no instructions. "Better not take the highway back," he observed as he put the 'cab in motion. "We'd meet half of Paradise hurrying to investigate, and someone might think to wonder what we're doing out here."

He drove a short distance along the highway and then turned off on a narrow track. As a road, it looked impassable, but the 'cab had been cut down from a powerful truck, and it negotiated the steep rises and dips with ease, bouncing over ruts and even powering over tree limbs.

Not until they emerged near the space port and swung onto the Port's highway did they dare to relax. From that point they could drive to Paradise as though they were coming from the space port.

"Those characters will walk out to the hydroelectric plant and keep their appointment," Tel said. "Probably they've arranged for a special tour. When they've finished, they'll call a 'cab to take them back. If anyone checks up on their time, they'll claim they lost their way."

"There's a turnoff they can pretend they took by mistake." Bronlan said. "If the mine staff doesn't find the ladders, Pakovich will never know how it was done."

"We've settled one thing," Tel said. "The sabotage definitely is connected with Cal. I don't know how or why, but it definitely is connected. Otherwise, why would two of the mals involved come snooping on him in the Valley?" She turned to Caland. "There, at the end. Did you recognize someone?"

"Yes," Caland said. "I also recognized the explosion."

CHAPTER TWENTY-ONE

Regelz Arlu was scheduled back from Aravia on an early morning ship, and Tel—not willing to trust the privacy of hote communications—had one of Bronlan's 'cab drivers meet him at the Port with a message describing the night's events. Arlu responded by calling a full-scale meeting.

Hairy routed Caland and Tel from bed to deliver the summons. He also told them that there were strange rumors floating about the Valley—something about an accident at the mines. No one seemed to know much about it because no one in the Valley was much interested in what happened at Pakovich's mines.

Bronlan's 'cab and 'bus drivers reported that Paradise was rife with rumors about equipment damaged and workers injured and killed. There'd been no official statement, and all anyone knew for certain was that the first shifters on the loading detail had been sent home.

In the room above Fig Stump, they found Yda, the Reverend, Sam the Artist, and—a surprise addition—Baris Bronlan, who sat quietly in a corner. Bronlan had been plucked from atop his spaceship, and he still wore his eyeshade.

Calta Draning arrived attired in one of her voluptuous, slinky gowns. She announced irritably that she'd been in bed, and Sam the Artist congratulated her on her night attire and asked who the lucky mal was. In contrast the tiny, red-haired Yda, wearing a conventional light green daysuit, looked like an exceptionally well turned out schoolgirl.

Sam the Artist had claimed his usual place at the table, and he was steaming his whiskers in a mug of yuck with a plate of the Fig Stump's delicious break sweets at his elbow. Tel and Caland, who had not yet had their break, joined him.

Tel whispered to Caland, "Sam has changed his clothes."

Caland turned and scrutinized him. "How can you tell?" he demanded aloud. "He looks the same to me."

"Different paint spots in different places," Tel said.

Sam grinned and helped himself to another break sweet. The Reverend, solemn as ever in his black clothing, surveyed the scene with a gentle smile.

Regelz Arlu made his customary dramatic entrance. He had blossomed out in bright red, which did not suit him. Yda remarked that he looked like a flag, and all of them should take him outside and wave him.

He also looked ruffled and weary. He marched directly to the chair with the reclining support and dropped into it. His chins rippled, but there were no smiles. "I just had a talk with Pakovich," he announced. "I thought it was time that someone spoke to him. That mal is—" He sputtered for a word and failed to find it.

"One of the artists at the bazaar called him an unperson," Caland said.

"Something negative," Arlu agreed. "Since we finally have some hard evidence, I decided to spread it for him. The moment he heard that one of the saboteurs came from the Valley, he exploded. 'The Valley is responsible!' he shouted. 'People who call it a Garden of Eden should know that it's populated with snakes'." Arlu turned to the Reverend. "Coming from him that's a very strange remark. I'm certain he didn't read it. I doubt that he reads anything, so he must have heard it somewhere."

"A significant clue to his character is the fact that he refuses to provide religious facilities in Paradise," the Reverend said. "I agree that he didn't read it, but I'm also puzzled as to where he could have heard it."

"Anyway, he's going to do something about the Valley. The fact that the other saboteurs probably came from the tourist hotes or the Port is irrelevant. In the meantime, he doesn't want to talk about sabotage."

"The artist also called him a pipsqueak of a snob," Caland said. "In the Valley he's usually called an ass—though what that mythical beast ever did to deserve the comparison hasn't been explained to me."

"Fortunately, his mines super is no fool. I talked with him before I went to see Pakovich. He's already spaced an order for back-up loading equipment and surveillance gear, and he's added a security detail. Even he refuses to face up to the probability that employees have been involved in the sabotage, but at least no more saboteurs will get in over the fence."

Bronlan said quietly, "We've got to do something about Pakovich."

"You keep saying that," Sam the Artist complained. "All of us keep saying that, but no one does anything. Let's put our heads together and figure out something."

"Never mind Pakovich," Arlu said. "I came here to talk about Cal."

He paused. The rest of them waited expectantly.

"Of all the complicated problems I've encountered in a lifetime of complicated problems," he said finally, "I concede undisputed first place to this one. The more I find out, the less I seem to know, and what I know makes less and less sense. Let's get last night's friction out of the way first. Compared to the rest of it, that's fairly simple. Tell me everything that happened."

Caland and Tel alternately described their chase of Nalce and the scene at the mines. Arlu said nothing at all until Caland reached the point where the cloth slipped from one of the faces.

"That's all you saw?" Arlu exclaimed. "His nose?"
Caland nodded.
"And you can make a positive identification from his nose?"
Caland nodded again.
"Obviously it's a very distinctive nose," Tel said. "If Cal says he recognized him, that's enough for me. His memory is unpredictable, but there's nothing at all wrong with it when it func-

tions."

Arlu shrugged. "Very well. So we have Nalce and Granst, plus three other mals who went to the mines with them, plus one fem who delivered a verbal message to Nalce in the Valley. On the basis of the unusual nose, Cal identifies one of the other mals as belonging to the three couples 'for the Valley' he saw on the spaceship and in the Port after landing. From all of this we can safely deduce that there's a sabotage group on Mort consisting of Nalce, Granst, and those three couples. The fem who brought the message certainly belongs to the same group. Eight people—"

"Nine," Tel said. "At least nine. Oplix's lavish sup was ordered for six. This means that the group has a leader who didn't go to the mines. Search it."

"I've already started," Arlu said grimly. "The servers report that there were only five in the room when they brought the food, and there were still five when they cleared, but six places had been occupied. The sixth member of the party came late and left early, and none of the hote staff saw him."

"Only another guest of the hote could have slipped in and out like that," Tel said.

"Or someone who looked like a guest." Arlu turned to Caland again. "The explosion. You say it looked like the one that killed Wes Fulm?"

"Exactly like it."

"Mmmm. The thing fits. In veriest fact it fits perfectly. The saboteurs certainly don't have a monopoly on that particular explosive, but since Fulm had an interest in the sabotage, we'd be idiots not to connect him."

"Since Fulm and two of the saboteurs are linked with Cal, we'd also be idiots not to connect him," Tel said.

Arlu heaved a sigh. "That's the most confusing thing of all. Cal completes the circle. He has to be connected to the sabotage, but there's no possible way it could have anything at all to do with him. As I read it, this is an interworld conspiracy concerning the supply of tin for Aravia. The earlier efforts of sabotage, which almost certainly involved Pak Enterprises employees, were amateurish. The damage they did was relatively slight and easily repaired. That wasn't sufficient, so a group of professionals was brought in. Just to show how professional they are, the six 'for the Valley' made a fuss at customs to draw attention to their disguises and then vanished. Since then, with their appearances changed drastically except for one nose, they've been staying at the tourist hotes, or at the Port hote, or here in the Valley, or in all three places. They're supplied with explosives, and they know how to use them. Last night's explosion will halt the loading of ore for at least a term, and there aren't enough tin reserves on Aravia to make up the shortfall. The sabotage to Mort's tin production has suddenly become a critical factor in interworld commerce. But what could that possibly have to do with Cal, who had never heard of Mort until Fulm spoke to him on Rynaif, or of Aravia until he regained consciousness there? This is more than a problem. It's a dilemma."

He sat for a long time tapping his index fingers together and studying them with a scowl. Finally he turned to Caland. "Did you ever hear of a mal—or a fem—named Nurlas Ernst?"

"If I ever did I've forgotten it," Caland said.

"Mmmm—Nurlas Ernst was a very distinguished personage. I thought perhaps he—or she—might have been mentioned to patients at your Polyscience Institute. He—or she—founded the establishment. That was at least two hundred and fifty years ago, maybe more. Because the Polyscience Institute is an enormously wealthy institution on a world of small political subdivisions, it has a lot of clout, and facts about it aren't easily come by. You never heard Nurlas Ernst mentioned, or saw a statue or a portrait, or anything like that?"

Caland shook his head.

"Odd. Flourishing institutions usually honor their founders. What do you know, really, about this remarkable Institute that saved your life?"

"Very little," Caland said. "If I ever heard of it before I regained consciousness there, the accident wiped it out completely." He smiled ruefully. "I suppose I could have learned something while I was there, but I had too many problems of my own to be able to develop much curiosity about my benefactors."

"Did they hand you a bill for your medical treatment?"

"Yes," Caland said. "It looked like the decennial deficit of a whole sector of bankrupt worlds. It also was marked, 'Null.' The Institute's policy was to charge according to the patient's ability to pay, and it was thought at the time that I was without assets. As it happened, I did have a very modest monetary reserve on Folamnin, but I didn't find that out until after I was discharged, and the Institute didn't know about it."

"Did the Institute mention the possibility of billing your family?"

"No, it didn't." Caland scowled. "That would have disturbed me. But I don't think they knew who I was. They considered me an impoverished actor and told me so, and I had no reason to disbelieve them. The staff took up a collection to outfit me when I left. I've always considered the Institute's treatment of me remarkably generous."

"Mmmm—yes. That is indeed the Institute's policy—charges are based on the patient's ability to pay. Its prospectus claims that it sponsors research into all of the sciences, as well as medicine and surgery, but the only activity that's well known is that of its geriatrics department. In veriest fact the Institute is the most famous center in the galaxy for the treatment of medical problems of the elderly. People travel enormous distances for consultations, and miracles are achieved there regularly. The Institute is so famous that it doesn't even bother to publicize them. Word of mouth publicity brings it more business than it can handle. Virtually all of those patients are enormously wealthy, and they pay miraculous prices for the Institute's miracles. It could be the wealthiest medical foundation in the galaxy. Did it impress you that way?"

"It's a large institution," Caland said slowly. "There are a number of buildings, but I never thought to count them. I only saw the interior of one of them, and that didn't seem especially luxurious."

"The Institute occupies half of a province," Arlu said. "Five thousand square kilometers."

"Then I saw very little of it. The only oddity was that I was the only patient in the ward, and there did seem to be a lot of staff looking after me."

"You didn't meet any of the other patients?"

"Lots of them. I met them in the park and the game rooms and lounges while I was convalescing."

"Were they elderly?"

"I didn't think much about it at the time, but—yes. Many were elderly. I didn't really get acquainted with any of them."

"Mmm. The Institute once pioneered in some complicated forms of chemical research and even owns a few valuable patents. Recent activity is not known. It once had a celebrated electronic biologist, but he's dead. Perhaps his work lives after him. It's supposed to be an outstanding research center in some fields of physics, but it keeps its results to itself if it has any. The only thing I was able to search in any detail was its work in geriatrics, and even there its phenomenal record is mostly hearsay. There are rumors everywhere of its amazing successes, and no hint anywhere that it has ever treated a patient unsuccessfully—which makes it a remarkable institution indeed. But—" The pleated chins were set sternly. "—remarkable or not, your Institute definitely is not the place where one would take an accident victim. How'd you happen to end up there?"

"The accident happened less than a kilometer from the front gate," Caland said. "It was at least twenty kilometers to anywhere else, and farther than that to medical assistance. Institute employees heard the crash and investigated."

"It seems providential that you had a serious brain injury virtually on the doorstep of the one place on Folamnin that was able to help you. Apart from the Institute, there isn't a neurosurgical team on the entire planet that's equipped and competent to deal with an injury of that complexity. The interesting thing is that neurosurgery is one of perhaps many departments of the Institute that receive no publicity of any kind. They don't even brag about an amazing cure like yours. In retrospect your presence there seems more than providential. It seems downright suspicious."

His voice trailed away.

"Is that all you have?" Tel asked finally.

"No. That's just the beginning. Let's take another look at Nurlas Ernst, who probably was a 'he.' This is the most fascinating character I've ever turned up in all of my searches. He founded the Institute at some time in the dim past—and the Institute's past is as dim as the Institute chooses to make it. One of the many interesting things about Nurlas Ernst is that he still owns the institute and runs it."

"He must be mildly superannuated by this time," Sam the Artist remarked.

The others grinned; Arlu's chins did not. "I'm serious. Nurlas Ernst founded the institute, and Nurlas Ernst is still the owner and director."

"It must be a descendant," Tel said.

"One would assume so," Arlu agreed. "One would certainly assume so. But according to the documentary evidence, which I have had searched carefully, there's never been a change in ownership or in its professional accreditation, as would have been necessary if a different person had taken over the directorship. Everything points to the fact that the Institute is still being run by the person who founded it."

"That's impossible," Caland said.

"Precisely. But my search was as thorough as it was careful— tax and census records, registrations, title deeds, birth and death records. Everything that is in any way pertinent to the Institute or its personnel or its patients or its public records has been examined. No Nurlas Ernst left any official trace of marriage or offspring. If he had a descendant of the same name, that descendant would have had to leave some evidence of his existence even if he were born on another world. In order to claim an inheritance, he'd have to register, establish his identity, and so on, and there'd be a death record, and a testamentary filing, and a probate hearing. There isn't any of that. If a tradition has developed that the Director of the Polyscience Institute must be named Nurlas Ernst, to perpetuate the memory of the founder, and each new director assumes that name when elected—that kind of thing isn't common, but it does happen—then there'd have to be a legal record of a name change, records of property transfer, death records on the old Nurlas Ernst. Even on a backward world like Folamnin, there are certain strict formalities with regard to dead bodies, and property can't be left registered in the name of a person long dead. I've searched, and I've found no clue at all. According to the records, the head of the Institute today is the same man who founded it."

"Maybe he patronizes his own geriatrics department," Sam the Artist said. "If he's kept himself alive for more than two hundred and fifty years, he wouldn't need to advertise. He'd be his own best testimonial."

"Your assumptions of any kind about the law and legal records may not hold true on Folamnin," the Reverend suggested.

"I make no assumptions of any about facts," Arlu said testily. "The facts are as I have stated them. There can't be any doubt that there is something highly peculiar about the Polyscience Institute and Mal—or Doctor—Nurlas Ernst."

"What does that peculiarity have to do with Cal?" Tel asked.

"That's what we're trying to find out. Believe me, it has *something* to do with Cal." He heaved a ponderous sigh. "I have only two things to go on. One is factual speculation and the other is speculative fact. Neither makes sense, but they're all I have."

Yda said dryly to Calta Draning, "He does love to talk."

"I don't love to listen," Calta said. "Get on with it, Regelz."

"Mmmm—yes. Cal has an amazing configuration of metal in his head. That's a fact verified by doctors who have attempted to scan him. Another fact, amply verified by such literature as survives, is this: a long, long time ago there were so-called scientific experiments involving the placement of metal electrodes in the brain. These were connected to an amplifier which made it possible to send electromagnetic signals to selected parts of the brain."

"For what purpose?" the Reverend demanded.

"For the purpose of learning," Arlu said. "It was part of the unending quest for an understanding of the greatest human mystery—how the brain functions, or what the functions of different parts of the brain might be. Such experiments served a valuable purpose—they did advance human knowledge, and they laid the foundation for our present competence in supplying functional artificial organs. Artificial eyes couldn't have been devised without such experimental data. The technique also was used to study interactive behavior in animals. Electrical stimuli to different parts of the brain were found to affect hunger, maternal responses, sexual activity, and such things."

Tel exploded. "What was that? Sexual activity? You mean—by pressing a button and sending an electrical impulse, it's actually possible to—"

"Possible to do all of those things," Arlu said blandly. "But such experimentation was outlawed centuries ago. It even was outlawed for laboratory animals. Human knowledge had passed beyond such crude and inhumane experimentation. But when a thing is outlawed, it isn't necessarily abandoned. Here we have Cal with a lot of metal in his brain, and we have incredibly strange things happening with his mind. Someone takes control of him—there's no other way to describe it. This inevitably leads to the question of whether those strangely anonymous neurological experts at the Institute used him and are still using him in outlawed brain experiments. When he was brought to them, dead or dying, they might in good conscience have thought to advance their knowledge and technique by using him as a subject. If, in the process, they revived him—brought him back from the dead—they might have considered him their property and continued to use him for experimental purposes. It wouldn't be the first time in history that scientists have placed scientific ends above ethics or legalities."

"Even if those towers really did broadcast brain impulses, would it be possible to control a person's behavior that completely?" the Reverend asked.

"Primitive experiments concentrated on a few gross behavior factors," Arlu said. "Neurological science has advanced immeasurably since then. The amount of metal in Cal's brain—the multiplicity of electrodes—suggests an incalculable refinement of control over an experimental subject. As long as we're making speculative deductions, we aren't straining anything in deducing that. There's just one thing wrong with the proposition. If they were using Cal for that kind of experiment, why would they turn him loose and then chase their experimental subject completely across the galaxy? Why not keep him locked up like any proper laboratory subject and experiment as long as anything could be gained from it? If Cal somehow managed to escape, they could have captured him again by pushing a button. What, really, could they expect to accomplish by an expensive trek across the galaxy? This particular speculation fits the facts and makes no sense whatsoever. For my other speculations, I had to consult experts. Their speculative uses of facts make no more sense than my factual speculations." He turned to Caland. "Have you been aware of having memories or recollections that didn't seem to belong to you?"

"No," Caland said. "Never. My problem always has been in not having memories or recollections that should belong to me."

"Mmm. Since logic got us nowhere, my experts put their imaginations in free fall. They came up with two ideas, both related to another abandoned surgical procedure, the brain transplant. It once was thought that surgeons would be able to take a person with a dying brain and a healthy body and another person with a dying body and a healthy brain and produce one healthy individual. The notion eventually was abandoned for a variety of reasons. The ideal combination of subjects wasn't easily come by, and, as medical knowledge advanced, it became much easier and more economical to cure both the person with the sick brain and the person with the sick body than try to salvage part of each and thus waste an individual. Also brain transplants were fervently opposed by a lot of people on ethical and religious grounds. The final argument was that they never quite worked—perhaps because the other factors mitigated against them to such an extent that neurosurgeons never were able to acquire the practical experience they had to have to make such a complicated surgical procedure a success."

"That much is historical fact. The rest is imaginative speculation. Supposing the Polyscience Institute has devised a method of brain transfer other than brain transplantation—a method of transferring the mental content of the brain without physically transferring the brain itself. This might be done chemically or electrically or both—which would account for the electrodes in Cal's brain. On death of the legendary Nurlas Ernst, his brain's mental content was transferred to the brain of a younger mal. It would be a method of becoming immortal. His knowledge and memory could survive. When the second body died, the process could be repeated—over and over. Supposing that Nurlas Ernst's current aging body was due for replacement just as Cal's accident handed the institute a fresh, vigorous, young, highly intelligent body. Cal's brain may have been less damaged than later reports—which the Institute was responsible for—indicated."

"As far as we know, Cal may not have been seriously hurt," Tel said grimly.

"Mmmm. I doubt that. But whether he was or not, I also doubt that ethics figured in the selection of the Director's next body. They had the body; they used it. But this time, after maybe five or six successful transfers, something went wrong. In order to transfer the mental makeup of Nurlas Ernst, Cal's brain would have had to be wiped clean, just as the knowledge and memories of one computer can be wiped clean and replaced with those of another. It didn't work that way. As a result, his own mentality keeps breaking through and asserting itself. When he's blacked out, the Nurlas Ernst brain is dominant. Eventually one brain will prevail, and naturally the Institute's scientists are attempting to make certain that it will be the brain of Nurlas

Ernst. When that happens Cal will disappear, and the Director will return to Folamnin in Cal's body. In the meantime, the Institute officials are watching Cal closely to make certain that he doesn't run off with an irreplaceable mentality that isn't his."

"That's quite a fantasy." Sam the Artist said. "Is that what you call speculative fact? Where are the facts?"

Calta Draning had listened to Arlu's exposition with an expression of extreme distaste. Now she blew her nose with a honk of disdain and demanded, "Are we supposed to believe this nonsense? We should be discussing your brain instead of Cal's."

"It fits more of the facts than any other explanation," Arlu said.

The Reverend shook his head. "It doesn't fit the most important facts. It may account for a centuries-old Director of the Polyscience Institute and for the metal in Cal's head, but it still doesn't explain why they'd allow Cal to trek across the galaxy and finally settle in the Valley while carrying around this super valuable brain. Why didn't they lock him up until the Director's brain became dominant?"

"Is any of this scientifically possible?" Tel asked.

"It's scientific speculation," Arlu said. "Some scientific speculations are facts whose time hasn't come yet. The problem is in determining which are destined to become facts and which are merely nonsense."

"There is a second speculation that amplifies the first one. Supposing all of the background is true—Nurlas Ernst has achieved immortality through successive brain transfers into youthful bodies. How many elderly, extremely wealthy people are there in the galaxy that would trade fortunes for another lifetime? If Nurlas Ernst were able to mass-market this brain transfer procedure, he quickly would accumulate a significant percentage of the galaxy's material resources. In order to do that, he'd need a stockpile of young bodies for his clients to draw upon. In which case the Institute might be transporting Cal—and other bodies—about the galaxy in search of prospective customers. The metal in Cal's brain was put there to prepare him for a transfer when a sufficiently affluent customer has been found. Institute officials park these bodies where they can't get into trouble until negotiations are completed."

"That makes less sense than the first speculation," Tel said. "They'd also have to transport the equipment and personnel needed to perform this complicated brain transfer. Wouldn't it be much easier and indescribably cheaper to take the patients to Folamnin? And how do these two speculations account for catastrophes on the worlds of Cenaru, Olyndyt, and Skarlont, and where does the sabotage to Pak Enterprises fit in?"

Arlu said testily, "If we had a theory that fit *all* of the facts, we'd be well on our way to a solution. At least the catastrophes and the sabotage are extraneous to Cal. Concerning this second speculation, there is one more question worth pondering. Who, in this immediate neighborhood, is likely to have both the yearning for immortality and the enormous wealth to pay for it?"

Sam the Artist slapped the table and knocked the empty break sweet platter onto the floor. "Why—that screety, no-account unperson!"

Baris Bronlan, who had been listening to Arlu's scientific speculations with every indication of intense interest, now sat back in disgust. "We've got to do something about Pakovich," he announced.

"If there's any truth in that particular speculation," the Reverend said, "we've all got to do something about Pakovich."

CHAPTER TWENTY-TWO

Arlu descended to the Fig Stump with Yda and Calta for an early din. Bronlan returned to his spaceship. Caland and Tel, with Sam the Artist and the Reverend, retired to their favorite table in Nello's, and Sam brought yuck and a plate of dry rot, small, hard cakes that were inedible until moisture was applied to them. They dipped the cakes in the yuck; the result, as the Reverend said, was a kind of scrunchie sogginess in which each ingredient distracted from the bad taste of the other.

Caland became aware that Tel was looking at him strangely. "What's the matter?" he asked.

"How can I know which you is you?" she demanded.

"Ask me and I'll tell you. Right now, I'm the 'me' me."

"Somehow that method seems less than completely reliable."

"Perhaps we should rig a room that would be insulated against electromagnetic waves," the Reverend said. "Then Cal would be free from all those sinister controls."

"You can't confer freedom on him by putting him in prison," Tel said.

"Whoever is controlling Cal must have highly sophisticated equipment," the Reverend reflected. "I doubt that anyone could bring that sort of thing into the Valley without having it noticed. Have you seen someone following you around with a big traveling case, Cal?"

"For terms, maybe years, I knew someone was following me," Caland said. "I positively knew it. I could feel the eyes on me. I did everything I could think of to find out who it was, and nothing worked. Even when my sense of being watched was strongest, I never could catch anyone paying the slightest attention to me. After I came to the Valley, all of that gradually stopped. When it turned out that I actually was being watched by Nalce, it came as a complete surprise to me."

"Probably they realized after that first night on the beach that controlling your mind doesn't accomplish anything as long as we're able to restrain your body by force," Sam the Artist said.

"Force is the operative word," Tel said with deep feeling.

"Indeed it is," Sam the Artist said, grinning. "Tel was the only one who could handle you, Cal, so we gave her the job. When these other theoretical mysteries are cleared up, I'm going to try to find out where she learned her tricks."

"At least my tricks aren't theoretical," Tel said.

"They certainly aren't," Sam the Artist agreed. "You just casually knocked over three mals, Cal, and started to run, and Tel grabbed you and planted you on your back and kept you there. You broke away twice while we were trying to get you back to your apartment, and each time she did the same thing. If you found bruises afterward, ask her about them."

"Tel did that?" Caland asked, looking at her with surprised interest.

"Keeping a constant watch on Cal isn't a much better solution than locking him in a room," the Reverend said. "We need to do something. Arlu's latest lecture was a complete disappointment to me. I'd hoped for a solution by this time, but all he does is mystify the complications. His idea of Heaven would be a place where no one knew what was going on except him, and the Almighty had to come to him for information. Does his abandonment of global catastrophes mean that Mort is safe and Bar's spaceship is no longer a disguised tower?"

"Arlu hasn't abandoned anything," Sam the Artist said. "It's just that we have all these mysteries piling up, and we have Cal, who is the biggest mystery of all, and Cal is somehow mixed up with each and every one of them, and it's enough to make an undaunted mal like Arlu feel daunted. Nothing about Cal makes sense. Even small things that we know are true turn out to be preposterous." He turned to Tel. "What do you think?"

"I think," Tel said meditatively, "that I feel like a swim. In the ocean."

"I can think of a lot better things than that to do with the ocean," Sam the Artist said.

Tel and Caland went alone to the deserted ocean beach. They cavorted in the breakers for a time, and then, with Pakovich's net and cable as security in case Caland tired, they swam out to the narrow island in the bay mouth and routed the yodel birds. Later, after they dressed, they walked along the bay beach.

They found Sam the Artist sitting by himself in the shade and pensively looking out across the bay.

"What right do you have to look so beautified?" Tel demanded.

"I have a nobly stuffed stomach, a cool place to sit, something lovely to look at, and no problems," Sam announced. "Those are the essential steps to beautification, no matter what the Reverend says. I'm feeling especially beautified because Pakovich is up to his stupid head in problems and I haven't got any."

They joined him, and Tel, carrying water from the bay, began to make a dirt art sculpture that she said represented Pakovich. It was a sea monster of awesome visage and overwhelming dimensions.

Sam the Artist watched skeptically until it began to take shape. "You can't sculpt Pakovich," he protested finally. "You've never seen him."

"Artists work best when they're not inhibited by reality," Tel said.

"But it was such a nice beach, and now you're trying to use up all the sand."

"Why don't you non-artists shut up and talk," Tel suggested.

But neither Sam nor Caland had anything more to say. Tel continued to work; Caland leaned back drowsily and enjoyed the alternate pleasures of watching the lovely colors of the bay and its scudding sail boats and looking at Tel. She was wearing one of the roughly knit dresses she preferred, this time of dark green, and her long hair kept cascading down into her work. When she brushed it back the tenth time, by his count, he laughed at her, and she looked up with a scowl.

"I feel as though I've been away from the Valley for a sennite," Caland said. "I should have talked with Zata. How'd the Reverend's paras do last night?"

"Better than usual," Sam the Artist said. "The total take was up a bit because you weren't there to compete."

"What's the latest Valley scandal?" Tel asked.

"The latest? I suppose that would be Min and Mac."

Tel dropped a handful of moist sand. "What about them?"

"They came to a very noisy parting of the ways."

"But what happened?"

"You're a glutton for sordid detail," Sam the Artist chuckled. "I really don't know. Min wasn't happy with that para act Cal taught Mac—she didn't like his line about needing money for a last fling. She started hanging around the Prom and watching him, and she began to suspect that he was holding out some of the para money so he could start flinging the moment her back was turned. Evidently she was right, and she caught him at it. It made a frightful ruckus."

"We've got to look into this," Tel told Caland.

Caland agreed. He'd thought that the gentle, smiling, white-haired couple appeared to be as complacently happy as it was humanly possible to be at that age. He was both amazed and distressed that the harmless little act he'd taught to Mac could have had this result.

"They looked like a couple who'd been contentedly married for fifty years," he said bewilderedly.

"Actually, I don't think they've known each other for more than a few terms," Tel said. "They met here in the Valley."

"Really? They had the serenity of a couple who had weathered the storms of life together and finally found a peaceful harbor. They seemed to fit perfectly like the two sides of a coin. What possibly could have disrupted that?"

"Jealousy," Tel said, "usually is the fruit in the parasite."

They went to see Zata at the Prom gate, but Mac had not yet reported for duty, and Zata knew nothing about him. Walking back along the Prom, they met the Reverend and asked him what had happened.

"I'm a bit curious myself," he said. "All I know is that Min banished Mac from the cemetery shelter they were sharing. Well—'banished' is hardly an adequate word. She chased him halfway across the Valley screaming accusations and throwing anything she could lift. He must have done something dastardly, but neither of them wants to talk about it. Min seems to think Mac has taken up with Cleo."

"Cleo!" Tel and Caland exclaimed together.

They finally found Mac sunning himself at the north end of the park near the shelter the older Vals had built for themselves. He was watching a game of Zexit, and he did indeed seem to have all of the serenity of a person who weathered the storms of life and finally found a peaceful harbor. He greeted them with a soft smile.

The smile vanished when Tel asked him about the violent rupture with Min. "Ask her," he said.

"Look," Tel said. "If both of you refuse to talk about it, gossip will make it far worse than it was—whatever it was. We aren't interested in anything except helping you. Don't you want to make up?"

"Don't know," Mac said. "Min sure gave me a cold night and for no reason at all."

"Tell us what happened," Tel urged.

"I can't say that I know. But I do know there ain't no use at all in trying to reason with a fem who's screaming and throwing things. I found that out when I was a lot younger than I am now. Yesterday I took a little time off from begging. That's hard work for an old mal, and I needed some rest, so I went over to the beach to enjoy the sun. I've never in my life seen anything like the bay and its colors, and I used to sit there every afternoon before you put me to work. That warm sun makes me feel like I'm soaking up a little life. Makes me want to keep going for another day or two. So there I was, sunning myself and not thinking about anything at all except what a nice day it was and what a lovely place the Valley is, and that young hussy Cleo came along and sat down beside me. What was I supposed to do, get up and run? Wasn't no sense in that, she could have caught me in about three strides if she'd had a mind to it." He chuckled. "Anyway, I was there first. So we sat there, and she talked, and I didn't say much—I was mostly trying to ignore her and go on enjoying the sun and the bay. Then Min arrived, and she immediately began churning the sand in all directions, and I had to run away. Pity. I never did get to finish my sunning. Then last night Min wouldn't let it go. She kept throwing it at me until I saw that I'd have to leave if I wanted any sleep at all. Then she decided she didn't want me to leave. That was when she started chasing me."

He sighed deeply and closed his eyes. "Sun feels nice. I didn't get much sleep and that begging is hard work."

"What did Cleo want?" Tel asked.

"That I really couldn't figure out. What she said was clear enough, but I didn't believe her."

"We'll talk to Min if we see her," Tel promised.

"Do that," Mac said. "I slept under a bush last night, and there wasn't much sleep in it. Min may not generate any fires, but she has very comfortable warmth."

They circled around the cemetery where Min and Mac had been living, but Min wasn't home. A short time later they met Cleo, who was headed toward the Prom.

"What stupid tricks have you been pulling with Min and Mac?" Tel asked angrily.

Cleo snorted. "Why is everyone blaming me? All I did was talk with Mac on the beach. Just because I'm polite to an old mal—"

"It would take something more than politeness to set Min off," Tel said.

Cleo snorted again. "So what if I cuddled him a little? I

thought it'd be a kindness to remind him what a fem is like, since he's probably too old to remember, and I'm always ready for a new experience. I never tried it with an old mal. But he told me he didn't want to buy anything, he was just looking. The idea!"

They walked on. Tel said thoughtfully, "Someone better pass the word to Min that she had a gem and she'd better grab him back before someone else gets the idea. I know several older fems who'll be out looking for him as soon as they hear about this, and they're likely to be a lot more subtle about it than Cleo."

"Everyone is a lot more subtle about it than Cleo," Caland said.

They returned to the beach, where they found Sam the Artist still practicing his four stages of beatitude. He was alone, and he took advantage of the rare moment of privacy to pass along some information Arlu had handed to him after din.

Arlu's Mort watches were not going well; rather, they went with uneventful smoothness and produced no information of interest. Weflan Krann, Sam said, finally had left Mort after the dullest protracted vacation in any hote lackey's memory. He was Pakovich's ideal tourist; he rarely visited the Valley, but he took every tour that Pak Enterprises offered. Then he took all of them over again. Caland and Tel could have added a few private items of their own to this account of Krann's activities. Their watchers had caught him in two semi-surreptitious meetings with Sdissler, and there certainly had been more. Sdissler had the use of one of the fleet of small electrocars that Pakovich had imported for his top executives, and it frequently was difficult for the Valley watchers to keep up with him. Bronlan made 'cabs available on request, but the request often came too late when Sdissler unexpectedly hurried to his 'car and drove off.

Fellington Felroy and Gilrod Emson also had left Mort. Arlu had them followed when they transshipped on Aravia, but he refused to invest in a team of watchers for each mal when there seemed to be no connection between them and his main search, and both the veteran conspirators slipped their watches with ease.

Arlu refused to take Fremanz and his mathematical computations for controlled telepathic transmission seriously, since no one else did. If the towers had anything at all to do with Caland, he thought they were somehow used to transmit signals to the metal in Caland's head—though he had no explanation of why anyone would go to all that trouble and expense to send such signals.

"Does Arlu still think that the person who controls Cal is here on Mort?" Tel asked.

"Either he's here, or he comes and goes," Sam said. "When he's not here, he probably has an assistant or assistants acting for him, so it amounts to the same thing. As for who it is, Arlu thinks it's probably someone so inconspicuous that no one knows he's around. Arlu's not just being moody—he really can't make anything of this entire search. He still doesn't know what's going on or how Cal might be connected with it. That's why he's coming up with those wild speculations."

Sippy came running past. She halted when she saw Caland and flopped down beside him. She said apologetically, "I've been looking for you."

She wore an ornate, spectacularly flowered dress that almost certainly had been remodeled from something discarded by one of the girls at the Houses of Fame. She was breathing heavily, and her face was flushed from running. The bit of color in her thin cheeks made her look almost pretty.

"That's a nice-looking dress," Caland said. "It looks nice on you, too. I don't often see you with clothing on."

Tel looked up with a frown. "Really. Are you trying to start another Min and Mac act?"

"But it's true," Caland protested. "Around the beach fires she either wears a towel or nothing at all."

"You shouldn't make such remarks," Tel said. "In polite society, it would mean that you were trying to shock others. In Valley society, where no one cares anyway, it means that you're trying to shock yourself."

Sippy doubtfully smoothed down her dress as though she were uncertain as to whether she should remove it. Even with such a feminine adornment, her slight figure and tangled short hair gave her an oddly masculine look. Caland wondered if Moppy's defection from Sippy to the plump Phem had been a psychological reaction and if Phem might diet herself right out of her love affair.

"I've got a new mal," Sippy said. "His name is Gonger, but everyone calls him Ding Dong. Have you met him?"

"I don't think so," Caland said.

"He's nice. I mean—he's *really* nice, and I like him, but in some ways he's a bit odd."

"Odd!" Tel exclaimed. "He's completely and totally sprung."

"He's a whole lot worse than that," Sam the Artist said. "When a mal goes down to the beach every night and howls at the moon—on a world that doesn't have a moon—he's more than just sprung. He's fractured."

"He has a very expressive face," Sippy said with a pout. "I wondered if maybe you could find him something to do. Begging, you know. I'm sure he'd be a good para, and having something to do might make him less odd."

"I'll give some thought to it," Caland said. "A little later I'm going over to the gate to watch the paras. Have him look for me there."

Sippy thanked him and hurried away.

Caland said thoughtfully, "I wonder if all of this begging is a good idea."

Sam the Artist looked at him with interest. "You thought of it all by yourself. You've made a sensational success of it, and it's the best thing that's hit the Valley in the lifetime of anyone living here, by far. It means that we'll finally be able to accomplish something for ourselves. And now you're ready to exempt it?"

"There must be a better way."

"The moment you come up with one, tell me. The whole Valley will be waiting breathlessly to see what it is."

"I haven't been able to think of anything," Caland said glumly. "But there must be something. I'm just not sure that begging is good for the people."

"The Reverend would tell you that some religions esteem beggars because they make it possible for the pious to accumulate present or future blessings or eternal life credits of whatever it is the religion emphasizes. What you're really doing with the Reverend's paras is encourage the tourists to perform acts of charity. Since the tourists obviously need such opportunities if they aren't to be shut out of the Hereafter altogether, I don't think the morality of it can be challenged."

"That wasn't the question," Caland said. "I'm not worried about the effect on the tourists. They can spare the money, and if the act of giving is good for the conscience, no doubt they need it. I'm worried about the effect on the beggars. Is this little routine I've taught the children going to make them want to go through life begging? I see a serious moral question there."

"If that's what's worrying you," Sam the Artist said, "you can relax. All you're teaching the children is that if they get money by begging, someone will take it away from them and put it in a Valley Enterprises account with Dal Eddyer. They aren't likely to grow up thinking there's any future in that."

The news on the beach that night was that peace had been restored between Min and Mac. Caland already had forgotten the problem. His mind was occupied with Sippy and her new mal. Gonger was a gawky, wild-looking youth who had, as she had claimed, a wonderfully expressive face. He also seemed to be, in Tel's words, completely and totally sprung. Obviously anything Caland could think of that would give occupation and a sense of usefulness to him might be a turning point in his life; but thus far Caland had thought of nothing at all.

He described the Sippy and Gonger situation to the Reverend. "How would you explain that relationship?" he asked.

"Not logically," the Reverend said. "Not scientifically, either. Human relationships are like a chemical reaction where no one can figure out what elements and compounds are likely to be present. Even when I know the people well, I have no assurance whatsoever as to how a relationship will work out. When I have misgivings of a disaster, as often as not the pair will achieve a delightful association. If I expect serenity, the result ranges from the explosive to the totally inert. One can only wish the happy pair well, utter a few private prayers, and let nature sort the thing out."

"There's more involved than chemical elements," Tel said. "There's growth and change."

The Reverend nodded. "True. It's as though the chemical reaction remains the same, but the laboratory keeps changing. What gave off a steady, satisfactory warmth for a couple of years—or sennites—suddenly fails to heat the place at all because the room has been enlarged and the windows left permanently open. Or a tepid relationship may suddenly generate a consuming radiation because the room has contracted. That's why so few perfect marriages remain perfect and why imperfect marriages can improve."

"And how does one cope with a dilemma like that?" Tel asked. "One can't enter into the perfect relationship with the pessimistic certainty that it's bound to be ephemeral. And one can't endure a lousy relationship just because such marriages have been known to improve. I've wondered why the human race doesn't exempt the whole arrangement."

The Reverend favored her with his gentle smile. "Even in these advanced and cynical times, a perfect marriage still seems like life's highest blessing. It can sustain its partners through the most corrosive afflictions."

"What you're saying," Tel said dryly, "is that we suffering humans are incapable of learning from experience. As long as the ideal of a perfect marriage can be dangled as bait, we'll charge blindly into one disastrous mistake after another."

"Does the informal coupling we see in the Valley work for better or for worse?" Caland asked.

"Formal or informal are mere social labels," the Reverend said. "You can't alter the chemical reaction by labeling it. There still are long-term and short-term successes, and long-term and short-term failures, and brief or occasionally lasting happinesses, and bitternesses and resentments, and glowing satisfactions that may or may not endure, and all the rest. When one marries, formally or informally, one ought to be seeking a mate. If one is seeking happiness, or any of a long list of other things, one may be doomed to disappointment."

"What about marrying to make someone else happy?" Tel asked.

"That's the most foredoomed intention of all. Because there is no such thing as uninterrupted bliss, and if one marries to make the partner happy, each fluctuation of happiness is a testament to failure."

"You sound as if you aren't in favor of marriage," Caland said.

"But I am!"

"Have you ever married?"

The Reverend smiled and did not answer.

Sam the Artist changed the subject dramatically by announcing that the cider jug was empty. Tel got to her feet. "Cal and I will go," she announced.

Caland followed her obediently, but as soon as they were away from the fire, he asked, "Why this sudden craving for exercise?" He was in his usual state of exhaustion after his long stint of begging, and he'd been comfortably drowsy by the fire.

"To see if anyone will follow us," she said.

"Has anyone?"

"Not yet."

The shadowy Prom was still crowded at that late hour, but there were few tourists in evidence. Most of those who remained in the Valley were pursuing hedonism at the Houses of Fame or the restaurants, or testing the fallibility of their gods of luck at the Road to Hell. The character of the Prom traffic had changed. During the day, in addition to the throngs of tourists, there were endless streams of Vals wandering aimlessly back and forth. After dark most congregated in groups under the few dim lights to talk and eat. The restless moved from group to group, seeking but not finding, in the same way that some Vals on the beach moved from fire to fire. The eateries were as busy as ever, and all of the shops catering to Vals remained open, though few customers could be seen in their gloomy interiors.

Tel steered Caland along firmly, exchanging banter with the Vals as they passed but resisting invitations to stop and flap. For all of her seeming intentness on their errand, Caland knew that she continuously scrutinized the Prom behind them, and she saw and identified every indistinct figure whose course paralleled theirs.

"Is anyone following?" he asked.

"No," she said.

They garnered far more exercise than they had anticipated. The Prom shops were out of cider. All of them. Cider rivaled yuck as the Valley's staple drink, and it always had seemed ubiquitous to Caland—hundreds of jugs circulating around hundreds of fires every night. He never had given a thought to the source of supply.

The cider was a byproduct of one of Pakovich's sillier miscalculations, Tel explained. He started a winery to produce wines from native fruits. The wines were not even drinkable, but the cider, originally made from the winery's waste pulps, was excellent. Now the Valley's appetite for cider kept the winery in production so that Pakovich could inflict Mortian wines on his house guests. The hotes also offered them, but no visitor to Mort ever ordered a native wine twice.

Virtually every Valley shop catering to Vals had cider for sale. Normally one fell over displays of jugs everywhere one went, but suddenly, on this night, there was no cider.

"Delivery tomorrow," everyone told them.

They traveled the entire length of the Prom. "Louie Laggie usually keeps a few jugs in reserve," Tel said finally. "Maybe he'll let us have a couple."

They turned into a gap between the buildings. The faint lights of the Prom quickly faded, and they plunged into darkness with Tel leading boldly. A few scattered candles flickered in the windows on Primrose Lane; on Fishstink Alley, the power reception units were still functioning in several buildings, but only one house could have been called well-lit: Dombrily's mansion, which loomed off to the west.

Louie was at home, and he greeted them delightedly. After he'd lit an extra candle, they were able to pick their way through his room—an interior version of Bronlan's junk-cluttered yard—and find seats.

Louie's new career as a watcher had not interfered with his scavenging. He scaved as a cover while he was watching. He eagerly displayed for them a carton of scrap metal he had picked up while keeping one of Sdissler's barracks under surveillance.

"There's a fence around that dump, too," he said slyly. "Any time you want in, I'll show you how."

He had a dozen jugs of cider in reserve, and he presented one to each of them and refused payment. As they turned to go, Tel asked, "Louie—have you ever noticed someone watching the house next door?"

"That house?" Louie asked, pointing. "Sure. Lots of times. All of the time. Gary Dwand is always hanging around. Melana lives there."

"It figures," Tel said with a laugh. "Come on, Cal. People on the beach are dying of thirst."

Again they plunged into the Valley's darkness. Caland's eyes were slow to adjust after leaving Laggie's candle-lit room, and he could see nothing at all, but the few scattered gleams of light from windows seemed to be sufficient illumination for Tel. Caland followed on her heels, and only belatedly did he realize that they were veering off at an unlikely angle. Before he could say anything, she collided with someone. There was the resounding thump of bodies coming together, Tel staggered backward into Caland, and—directly ahead of them—someone toppled into a bush.

"I'm so sorry," Tel said. "I didn't see you. Are you all right?"

"Quite all right—I think," the voice said. Its owner was separating himself from the bush.

"Are you sure? Do you need help?" Tel sounded abjectly apologetic.

"No. I'm all right."

"I really am sorry. But if you're all right and as long as I didn't drop the jug—"

The voice chuckled, and Tel and Caland moved on.

"Did you recognize the voice?" Tel asked when they were safely out of hearing.

"Yes," Caland said. "It's Alexander the Second."

"I thought so. That really curdles the yuck!"

"Was he watching Melana's house?"

"Her apartment is on the second floor front. There are drapes in the window, but the light is on. I suppose he can see her shadow when she moves about."

"How'd you know it wasn't Gary?"

"I saw Gary at the Prom. Alexander the Second must have spotted Melana doing her research at the library. To see her is to love her, especially if one is very rich, and very much restricted by one's father, and very lonely, all of which Alexander the Second certainly is. As far as anyone knows, he's never been linked with a fem. Probably he's too shy. His father must have made the arrangement with the Aravian princess. In the meantime, he secretly watches Melana at the library, and when she skips an evening, he comes to the Valley and haunts Fishstink Alley."

"What does this bode for the Aravian princess?"

"It doesn't change a thing. Alexander the Second will marry the princess when his father tells him to. He wouldn't dare refuse. And then he'll go right on wistfully watching Melana as long as she's on Mort."

"At least that explains what he's doing in the Valley."

Tel laughed. "Poor Gary. Poor Alexander the Second. I wonder if each of them knows about the other. With both of them watching Melana, sooner or later they're bound to get acquainted."

"Poor Melana," Caland suggested.

"Melana is managing very well by ignoring them. She may not even be aware of Alexander the Second's existence."

The fire group was waiting impatiently for the cider. Morlef was there—he had stopped by to talk with the Reverend and Sam the Artist about the plans for the community building. Caland took a long slop from the new jug and composed himself to listen. Morlef had a work crew ready to begin clearing ground as soon as Dom and the Reverend reached an agreement. He talked at length about building dimensions and the utilization of interior space.

"Ground floor front is too valuable a place for the Rental Office," Morlef said. "Put it on the top floor rear."

Sam the Artist shook his head. "Dom wouldn't stand for that, and he'd be right. The Rental Office is the one place in the Valley everyone has to visit occasionally. Ground floor is where it belongs."

"Why not set up an organization that would lease the Valley from Dom, collect all the rents, and pay him a fixed income?" Caland asked.

All of them stared at him.

"Minus the cost of urgently needed repairs and payments into an escrow fund for capital improvements," Caland went on absently.

"You sound like your father's son," Sam the Artist said irritably. "Dom would never go along with that. Why should he?"

"Why shouldn't he? It would save him a lot of trouble, and it might even bring him more money. A lot of Valley residents must be terms in arrears."

"True, but your collecting organization won't be any more effective than Gus is at prying money out of people who don't have it—unless you also have a plan that provides income for everyone."

Caland lapsed into silence. His thoughts had turned again to his para children and the ethics of making beggars of them, but now even that seemed unreal. The previous night he had watched a violent act of sabotage; that morning he listened to Arlu's galactic speculations; in the evening he had been a vile Prom para; and now he was a party to planning a community's future. He wondered if he also would be the cause of its destruction.

Hairy lopped along the beach purposefully and suddenly turned toward them. Caland tensed when he saw him, but it was Sam the Artist who was wanted.

"Calta wants you right away," Hairy told him.

"Damn," Sam the Artist said good naturedly. "One jug hasn't been emptied yet and I have to walk off and leave the other untouched. It's times like this that I regret that Zareent died trying to prove that teleportation was possible."

"Not Zareent," the Reverend said patiently. "That was Odan, and as far as I know, his health wasn't affected. Zareent's specialty was time travel."

"Odan proved that teleportation was possible by teleporting himself onto the prophet's tomb?"

"Zareent tried to steal the prophet's bones. Teleportation wasn't involved. Odan merely proved mathematically that teleportation was theoretically possible."

"How can mathematics prove a thing like that?"

"Every point in the universe is contiguous to every other point. That can be proven mathematically. It's a rather elaborate, complicated proof, and it would occupy several volumes of calculations and take a great many lifetimes to perform them manually, but such proofs are easily constructed with a highly sophisticated modern computer. Once that has been done—"

"Never mind," Sam the Artist said. "All I want to know is how your theoretical proof can get me from here to the Prom without walking."

"It can't," Tel told him. "Unlike the proof, nothing about you is theoretical."

The night drifted along pleasantly. An occasional slop of cider fortified Caland's drowsiness. Tel finally escorted him to bed after twice preventing him from toppling into the fire. As they walked away, he glanced sleepily at those around the next fire. On this night, Nalce had his back turned to Caland. He was trying to practice what Louie Laggie called 'inconspicuosity.'

When they reached their apartment, Laggie was waiting for them. "Thought I'd better tell you right away," he said in a conspiratorial whisper. "I think we have a contact in Fish Town. We can get you a boat."

"That," Caland said, "makes a bright ending to an otherwise totally wasted day."

CHAPTER TWENTY-THREE

In the morning Caland and Tel went for a walk along the rickety fence that formed the Valley's eastern boundary. The flimsy barrier was virtually intact in the vicinity of the school's playground, where the boards of different ages defined the periodic repairs. Farther north, toward the Prom, there were frequent gaps. They found one where several boards had rotted away and stepped through.

"He probably comes and goes here," Tel said. "I don't see any sign of a path, but we know he only visits the Valley on the nights he can't stare at Melana in the library. Now let's find out where he comes from and goes to."

Pak Enterprises occasionally cut back the riotous growth of weed shrubs along the highway, but two meters from the road's edge these reared into a miniature jungle. They walked north past the boundary where the Valley's decrepit fence was replaced by the taut, shining metal strands of that of the fertilizer factory. The factory itself was invisible because of a low hill that rose between it and the highway, but the top of the distant chimney marked its location. Just beyond the hill was the factory service drive, and the fence bent inward along the drive to the distant gate.

A squawking arose in the thick shrubbery: native fauna challenging their passage, Caland thought; but it continued long after they had passed the point, so it probably had nothing to do with them. The human presence on Mort affected the world very little. The small clutter of eyesore buildings, the few smears of disfigurement, the invisible delving amounted to no more than a pimple on the globe's face.

"Here it is," Tel said suddenly.

Someone had repeatedly run a small 'car into the bushes and almost up to the fence. Tel stood with hands on hips and surveyed the location with a frown. "Alexander the Second has a reputation of being nice but rather silly—a mal with no will of his own and not much mind. But he has the mind. Anyone who chanced to wander out to the Valley gate and see him pull in here would think that he'd turned in at the factory drive. The same goes for anyone in Fish Town who happened to be looking in this direction. But no one at the fertilizer factory would see him at all because of the hill, and one of those tiny 'cars that Pak executives use would be completely hidden in that tangle as soon as he got off the road."

She turned to Caland. "We can write off Alexander the Second. He contemplates Melana at the library; when she doesn't show, he makes a clumsy attempt to disguise himself and drives out here to worship under her window. It's as simple as that."

"He really is rather silly," Caland agreed.

"'Infatuated' is the word. Different people react differently to it. Have you ever been infatuated?"

"If I have, I don't remember it."

"Clod! You're supposed to say that you're infatuated right now!"

"But I'm not," Caland said seriously. "The word 'infatuation' implies a temporary excess of feelings—a silliness that won't last. My feeling for you, silly or not, is permanent."

"It's silly enough," Tel pronounced firmly. "But I'll take it." She embraced him. "And," she added, casting a glance at the marks left by the 'car of Alexander the Second, "I'll venture a prediction of my own. Most of these mysteries that surround you are going to peel off just like this one and prove to be nothing at all—at least, nothing that concerns you. Including this mystery about Sdissler. The fact that he secretly met a mal who happened to travel to Mort on the same ship you did isn't much of a connection, you know. Finally we'll be left with the one mystery that matters, and we'll deal with it. Whatever it is."

They continued to walk southward following the road toward Fish Town.

As they approached the end of the fertilizer grounds, they turned aside and forced their way through the tall shrubs. At the corner of the factory's fence a mal stood waiting for them—tall, blond, but deeply tanned. He gave them a shy grin.

"Cal? Tel? I'm Quinotto."

He was a sailor by birth and a shipwright by training. Pakovich had brought him to Mort from Urdrurl to keep the fishing fleet in trim; but the fishers were a small, dark race from Grolaph, and they had ostracized Quinotto and his family. They preferred to do their own repairs, however badly, and Quinotto had little work to do. While waiting for Pakovich to find a replacement, come to some kind of settlement with him, and send him home, he had built a small fishing boat for himself, and he and his sons made short fishing runs along the coast.

Tel showed him a tracing she'd made from one of the maps Melana had provided. It showed the coastline but not Sdissler's camps. "This in the place," she said, pointing. "Could you put us ashore here?"

Quinotto pursed his lips, thoughtfully. "Big surf there," he said. "You could float in, but there'd be a problem taking you off again. But if you went in here—" He moved his finger a few kilometers down the coast where there were several small islands. "The islands shelter the coast, and it's quieter. Could put you in there anytime. And pick you up, too."

Tel looked questioningly at Caland. He said, "What's another few kilometers between sore feet?"

"Are a thousand chits enough?" Tel asked.

"Plenty. No problem."

"In case anyone asks you—"

"In case anyone asks me, I got nothing to say," Quinotto said grimly. "Pakovich reneged on almost everything his people promised me, and I know you Vals got no use for him either. Louie says you're up people, and that's enough for me. I'll take you any time you're ready."

"It may take us some time to get ready," Caland said.

"No problem. Just send word. Figure two days down there and two days back, leaving and arriving by dark each way, plus whatever time you'll need ashore."

They touched hands with him, and he turned and vanished into the shrubs.

Caland and Tel headed back toward the Valley.

It had been Tel who pounced on the fact that one of Sdissler's labor camps, an air journey of almost three hundred kilometers, was located a short distance from the coast. Unfortunately that short distance was all up and down, but she thought that they could negotiate it if a boat were available to land them there. One of Louie's scavs had contacted Quinotto.

"We'd have to figure on a sennite," Caland said regretfully.

Tel nodded. "This is your punishment for being such a notorious character. There's no way we can vanish for a sennite without causing an embarrassing amount of talk. Even those tourists you bilk every night will complain if you don't show up two nights in a row. They might even complain directly to Pakovich."

"I want to do it," Caland said.

"Of course," Tel said. "So do I. I want to exorcise Sdissler so we can get on with other things. We'll have to think of something. Are you ready for a break?"

They walked back to the Valley gate. Inside, at the para shelter, Zata was inspecting the troop of children. She had decided that they were losing money by ignoring the tourists who arrived in the morning. Admittedly there were fewer of them, but for that reason they might be more generous if they were welcomed warmly.

"It makes a long day for the children," Caland protested.

"They enjoy it," Zata said. "Lots of cold drinks, good food, plenty of rest between 'buses, and when they finish, they're invited to Olgi's for a special ice."

They reached the Prom just in time to watch the delivery of cider. Caland had expected a 'truck bearing a mountain of jugs; instead, there were four 'trucks heavily laden with large kegs. A crew of Vals delivered several kegs to each shop selling cider; when a 'truck was empty, it headed back to Pakovich's winery for another load.

"The jugs?" Caland asked bewilderedly.

The jugs were looked after by Soapy, the same Val who collected the Valley's empty yuck mugs. He gathered them up, cleaned them, and delivered them to the shops as they were needed.

At Nello's, the Reverend, and Sam the Artist were sharing their break with Duggal and Huggal. Huggal was pregnant, and Duggal was speculating on the best way to celebrate.

"Why don't you get married?" Caland suggested.

"We've been married six times," Duggal said. "Every time the Reverend thinks up a new ceremony, we let him practice on us."

Huggal turned on him indignantly. "I thought *we* were doing the practicing. Do you mean every one of those rigmaroles *counted*?"

"Not unless you wanted them to," the Reverend said. "Too many people confuse marriage with a legal contract. Actually, it's a state of mind."

"It's neither," Sam the Artist said. "Rather it's both, depending on one's perspective. Everything in life depends on one's perspective. Just sitting here and looking out at the Prom, I'm able to perceive that the great cider famine is over. Why would anyone want to celebrate anything else? Anyway, we Vals are no longer people. We're specimens. Specimens neither marry nor are given in marriage."

Tel set her yuck mug down with a thump. "What's going on now?"

"Haven't you heard?" Sam the Artist asked gloomily. "The Valley has been converted into a vast laboratory. Its inhabitants are to be subjects of a monumentally important scientific study. All of us. We can abandon our names. Henceforth we'll be known by laboratory numbers. Probably those on our cages."

Tel appealed to the Reverend for an explanation. "The great cider famine never touched Sam," she said. "I saw him last night taking two slops to everyone else's one. Something else must have sprung him."

"I suppose it is complicated," the Reverend said, "but like most complicated things, it has a simple explanation. Doctor Stran Gormaz, whom I believe you know, has worked out an arrangement with Dom. He's going to establish a sociological laboratory in the Valley using Dom's home as his headquarters. The exact function of a sociological laboratory is not clear to me."

"Even if you got the word directly from Gormaz, it still wouldn't be clear to you," Caland said.

"That's very true. In fact I did. I had a brief talk with him. He lost me somewhere between the macrocosm and the microcosm. Contrary to Sam's foreboding, the impact of this event on the Valley will be zero. If it isn't, the research will invalidate itself. However—" He addressed Duggal and Huggal. "Here's your opportunity. Ask Doctor Gormaz to marry you in his sociological laboratory. That would be a new experience for you."

"It might be a new experience," Huggal said, "but it certainly sounds like a lousy way to get married. Anyway, how could he marry us if we're specimens, and specimens don't marry or— how was that, Sam?"

"Don't worry," Sam the Artist said. "If specimens don't marry, neither do they divorce. At one stroke Gormaz is going to solve ninety-nine per cent of the Valley's problems."

"What's the other one per cent?" Caland asked.

"At least once every term we run out of cider."

* * * * * * *

Days passed and nothing happened. Caland and Tel, jointly

and separately, tried unsuccessfully to invent an excuse that would allow them to leave the Valley for a sennite without causing talk.

"I can't even pretend to be sick," Caland complained.

Tel agreed gloomily. "Half the Valley would line up to visit you."

Arlu left for Aravia or somewhere. His destinations were always vague. His assistants were continuing their check of visitors to Mort, and Sam the Artist was doing the same for residents of the Valley, where the search had taken on the dimensions of a complete census. It anything new had turned up, no one mentioned it to Caland.

Both Sam the Artist and Caland's watchers noted that Nalce seemed once again to have lost interest in Caland. "But that isn't the right way to put it," Sam the Artist observed thoughtfully. "He demonstrates abnormal curiosity whenever he sees you, but at least he doesn't prowl about the Valley looking for you, and he's given up following you."

One highly significant change for the world of Mort affected the Valley not at all. There was a drastic drop in ore ship traffic, and that would persist until the mines' new loading equipment arrived.

Caland, feeling himself at the vortex of a galactic conspiracy, brooding about world catastrophes that somehow impinged upon him, wondering when his controller might abruptly snatch his mind again, and pondering Sdissler's probable iniquities— Caland had to adhere to his prescribed role as bait and patiently move from one Valley triviality to another.

One of them concerned that unlikely couple Sippy and Gonger. Gonger had, as Sippy had claimed, an extremely expressive face. For several days Caland meditated his astonishing repertory of leers, sneers, grimaces, scowls, grins, swaggers, cringes, threats, pleadings, jubilations, despondencies, and insults. Then he consulted with Morlef, who improvised a gap between two Prom buildings. Gonger sat there, body concealed, expressive face sticking up through a hole in the canvas, and he tried to insult and cajole passing tourists into purchasing balls from Sippy to throw at him. Sippy quickly developed into an astute promoter. In slack moments she would hand a ball to a passing tourist and say, "Here—hit him one for me."

The project was not a huge success, but it consistently took in more than a hundred chits per day because an occasional tourist would develop such an uncontrollable wrath over Gonger's overly expressive insults that he would throw balls at him until his arm muscles failed him. All of the customers were mals; the fem tourists thought Gonger was cute. Sippy and Gonger were added to the para payroll, they were contributing to the Valley's future, they found better living quarters, and Gonger completely lost his urge to howl at a nonexistent moon. The occasional clout on the head did not bother him. The balls were soft, he said; and, anyway, most tourists missed.

The success with Gonger and Sippy did not ease Caland's problem. The spectacle of the children as paras still bothered him, and so did his entire para crew. Gonger seemed to symbolize what was wrong. The young mal deserved something better of life, Caland thought, than a job that utilized his head as a target.

After a night when Caland had been too restless to sleep, he and Tel went to Nello's for an early break. When they reached the Prom they found a work detail there with three trucks: Sdissler's garbage and trash collectors. Since this was one of the jobs so fervently despised by Vals, Caland paused to watch.

On this day there were no Vals in the crew. The young mals working the assignment did not seem in any way oppressed. They were husky and healthy, bare to the waist and burned almost black from work in the sun. They filled one truck at a time with waste set out by the Prom businesses and sent it off to the world dump. They finished by emptying two huge bins of accumulated waste brought by Vals from their dwellings. Then—to the accompaniment of hoots and jeers from passing Vals—they swung aboard the last truck and rode away.

"They certainly aren't riffraff," Caland told Tel. "It must cost

Sdissler plenty to import that quality of labor. We've got to see another labor camp."

The Reverend and Bronlan sought them out at Nello's. "We wanted to talk with you," the Reverend said apologetically. "I've had this idea ever since you started talking about how starved the tourists are for entertainment. Would it be possible to establish a regular theater in the Valley?"

Tel turned on him indignantly. "As if Cal didn't have enough to do now!"

"It'd provide a whole new industry for the Valley," the Reverend said. "It'd create employment for dozens of people who now have no prospect of it. It'd also bring prosperity to all the other businesses, because it'd give tourists—and also Paradise residents—a legitimate, respectable reason for visiting the Valley and spending money. It'd more than double the Valley's income—I'm sure of that. I've thought about this a great deal, and I agree with you absolutely—the tourists do need entertainment. If we could provide a theater, there would be nothing else on the world of Mort to compete with it." He smiled wistfully. "The Valley originally was supposed to be a cultural center, you know."

"I've thought about it, too," Caland said. "Unfortunately, it wouldn't be possible. Just to begin with, there are two problems. First, where would you put it?"

"I thought perhaps the park by the Valley fence—"

"It's a long, narrow strip of land," Caland said. "It'd give you a long, narrow theater. The worst kind."

"Not only that, but a theater by the Valley fence wouldn't bring people into the Valley," Tel said. "Tourists would arrive, see the plays, and leave without having set foot on the Prom at all. If you want a theater that will help Valley businesses, put it at the other end of the Prom."

"I see," the Reverend said. He looked crushed. "I thought the building wouldn't be too important in the beginning. I hoped maybe we could begin with some open air presentations."

Caland shook his head. "Valley weather is too unpredictable.

Tourists may be starved for entertainment, but they won't sit in the rain for a couple of hours to watch a play. Also, they won't come from the pampering luxury of Pakovich's hotes and pay admission to sit in a dump. Why do you think the Houses of Fame are so plushly furnished? No, you'd need a decent building, and the construction would be complicated and expensive. Your community building will be a simple partitioned box by comparison. A theater would need a competent professional designer to handle problems in acoustics and stage machinery and lighting. It'd have to be located near the Prom for 'truck deliveries and also for easy tourist access, and there's no space there big enough for even a small theater without tearing down some buildings. We don't have to inquire to know how Dom would react to that."

"That's only the first problem. The second concerns the actors. All of these tourists come from worlds with reasonably high levels of cultural activity. Since they're bored, they wouldn't insist on great acting, but they would expect reasonable standards. That means importing actors. It would take an enormous chunk of capital to build a theater building, and then it would take another big chunk to get the project started. You'd need a troop of actors—a repertory company. I can tell you, positively, that there's no acting talent in the Valley. Eventually actors or would-be actors might be attracted here if the theater was a success, but you'd have to start by importing the whole company. They'd insist on having their salaries placed in escrow for the entire engagement, plus traveling expenses, and they'd also insist on decent living quarters while they're here—and where in the Valley would you find them? There aren't any."

"I see," the Reverend said. He nodded gloomily. "Then the real answer is money. I'd hoped—the Valley so desperately needs a decent product, something it can sell in good conscience and which a large number of Vals can become involved with."

"I've thought about an automated puppet theater," Caland said. "The building could be small, and the puppets—if they could be built here—wouldn't require a huge investment, and they wouldn't present any problems of salary or housing."

A high-pitched hum sounded high over the Valley. The four of them went to the door of Nello's to look. An enormous cargo ship was slowly settling toward the fertilizer factory. Its huge shape momentarily enfolded the Prom in a vast shadow. The ship looked as though it could have crushed the entire Valley and enlarged Paradise Bay with a slight landing slippage.

"That's the *Porebus Seven*," Bronlan said. "Akonif's ship. He's switched from ore to fertilizer until the mess at the mines is straightened out. Means he'll come to din. Care to join us?"

"Glad to," Caland said. "Thanks."

"About those puppets. That's an interesting thought. I'd need to know exactly what sizes they'd be and what they'd have to do."

"There's a book about it," Caland said. "There ought to be a lot of books, but there's one that I know of. I'll ask Arlu to order a copy."

"It'd take a really small mechanism, wouldn't it?" Bronlan asked meditatively. "Been a long time since I worked on anything like that. Needs some thought. I'll see you two when the klaxon sounds."

He nodded absently and walked away.

"Would a puppet theater create any jobs?" the Reverend asked.

"Some," Caland said. "Sets of costumes would have to be designed and made and kept in repair. There'd be ticket sellers, cleaners, venders, maybe musicians, and people to operate the mechanism. Not as many as a live theater, but it'd have a worthwhile payroll. But let's not start calculating the economic impact. It's an intricate project, and it might be as long in the launching as Bar's spaceship."

Captain Akonif was delayed. He arrived late at Bronlan's din wearing a ruffled, perspiring look, as though he had just placed the monstrous spaceship on target with his bare hands. His morning's work had left him an appetite, and he ate hungrily and said little until the meal was almost finished. Bronlan had invited his usual mélange of guests, who included Kren Krent, the Reverend, an elderly fem called Viko—she had no teeth and had to laboriously masticate her food in a small, handle-driven machine before stuffing it into her mouth—Sippy and Gonger, and an assortment of the very young and the very old.

Gonger's success on the Prom had fired Sippy's imagination. She wanted to enlarge on it by offering the tourists a dance routine. She and Gonger had been practicing, and they were eager to try the result on a real audience.

They hardly needed an invitation, but Caland reluctantly gave them one, and they ran through their routine for Bronlan's din guests. The muscular Gonger tossed the slender Sippy about as though she were an object he was trying to juggle. He dropped her three times in the process, but he explained that he really didn't drop her, he had only let her slip.

Tel's eyes anxiously sought Caland's for guidance. "Perhaps a little more practice—" she suggested.

"No." Caland spoke firmly. These two were never going to be dancers, and he didn't want them coming back for a second audition. "If they keep practicing, Gonger will break Sippy's neck, and there won't be anyone to manage his Prom act. If he feels he's got to practice, he should get a mirror and work up new ways to insult the tourists."

They returned their attention to the food.

By that time Captain Akonif had quieted his hunger some-what. He accepted another serving of Bronlan's crisply toasted meat chunks, burped appreciatively, and waved for the jug.

"About this spaceship of yours," he said. "How soon do you expect to fly it?"

Bronlan was noncommittal. "When it's ready."

"But when will that be?" Akonif persisted.

Bronlan smiled. "Does it matter? I'm not under contract to anyone."

"Is the thing airtight?"

"Would be if I installed some gaskets," Bronlan said.

"Done any more work on the engine?"

"Work on it all the time."

"I want to see it again."

Bronlan jerked his head toward his shack, and the two mals strode away.

The Reverend smiled after them. "I don't know what's chewing Akonif, but there's one fact that I'm willing to guarantee: Bar's spaceship will never fly."

Caland tuned for a look at the gleaming silhouette. "What's wrong with it?"

"As far as I know, nothing," the Reverend said. "It's probably the most perfect one of its kind ever built."

"Then why won't it fly?"

"Bar won't let it. Why do you think it's taken him twenty years or more? He's not a slow worker, but his pleasure comes from fussing with the design and from figuring how to make do with salvage parts and materials. He tries something one way, then he tries it another way. Each change is a challenge for him. If that ship ever flies, it'll spoil all the fun he gets out of it even if it takes him with it. He's like a parent who won't let a child grow up and leave home. This engine easily could occupy him for another twenty years. While he's working on it, he'll continue to fuss with the ship's design. I'll guarantee it—that ship will never fly."

Eventually Bronlan and the captain returned bringing with them the end argument about Bronlan's proposed carburetor. The others had eaten to the point of satiety; they began to drift away. Sippy and Gonger hurried back to their booth on the Prom. Caland and Tel were waiting for a break in the conversation so they could take their leave of Bronlan.

Captain Akonif's mind was still on getting Bronlan's ship into space. "How long, really?"

"I work as I feel like it," Bronlan said. "I won't try to predict my feelings."

The captain looked up at the ship and scowled while he meditated that. "Look here," he said, finally. "Will you rent it to me?"

"Rent what?" Bronlan asked.

"The spaceship. Will you rent it?"

"What for?"

"It's like this," Captain Akonif said. "I met Willox on Aravia. Do you remember Willox? He came to look at the ship the last time he was here. He insisted that it'll never see space, and I insisted that it will, and it ended with our making a bet. Fifty gold Aravian pearls. There isn't any time limit on the bet. I don't know how Willox missed that, except that he was pretty drunk at the time. But I don't want that puffed-up vacuum sneering at me for the next twenty years and asking when your ship will finally get off the ground. So I'd like to rent it. I'll put it in orbit long enough to win my bet."

It was Bronlan's turn to look up at the ship. The thing had been growing in his back yard longer than some of the trees, and he seemed to be trying to envision the landscape without it.

"Mort's Port Control won't let you do that," he said. "Hazard to navigation."

"Well, now. I've worked out a deal with them. The Space Captain's Association has been after them to orbit a communication satellite. The supplier of the basic package goofed up the deal, and there's going to be a delay of several terms. Pakovich always orders from the lowest bidder, you know. They have the equipment sitting over there, waiting. The Association is threatening an embargo, and Pakovich has enough problems without that. Port Control would welcome my placing your ship in the com satellite's orbit if they can install their communication equipment. They're ready to do that right now. You give the word—they'll finish the job by evening."

Bronlan continued his grave study of his spaceship. "How would you put it in orbit?"

"When I pick up my load of fertilizer, I'll slip this way and pick your ship up as it stands. When Mort gets its satellite, I'll bring it back. It'll only be gone for a few terms, and you've got an awful lot of work to do on that engine."

"Won't putting it in orbit be a lot of trouble and expense?"

"No trouble. A little expense, but Port Control will reimburse me. They're getting panicky about that threatened embargo."

Bronlan kept his gaze on his spaceship and said nothing.

"Pakovich doesn't know anything about this," Akonif went on. "The Port people are afraid he'll find out about the delay on the satellite and remove someone's complexion. They think we can sneak your ship into orbit without him noticing it isn't the satellite he authorized. They're overlooking the fact that he'll devastate every complexion on the payroll if he ever finds out, but that's their worry. It'll be highly visible at night, and—once it's up there—you can tell Pakovich that his world's only moon is named Bronlan. The Association will make him keep it there until the other satellite is ready. But we'll have to do it now. By my next trip, Port Control will have had second and third thoughts about this."

Bronlan turned away and sat down by the fire pit. He picked up a chunk of bread and chewed on it. The Reverend caught Caland's eye and winked at him.

"All right," Bronlan said suddenly. "But I won't rent it. I'll lend it to you."

"What sort of gaskets do you need to make it airtight? The Port will have them. The air lock will have to work so Port Control can make maintenance visits to the com equipment."

"Come have a look," Bronlan said.

Bronlan led the way up the rickety ladder. The two mals disappeared into the ship. They left behind them a stunned, enlarging silence.

Finally the Reverend spoke. "I'm numbering this among the few occasions in my life when I'm truly astonished. Perhaps it would have been better if I'd never studied psychology. What made him agree—the moon named Bronlan and the opportunity to stew Pakovich?"

"Probably we'll never know," Tel said. "Bar seems to be a simple sort of person, but underneath he's the most complex mal I've ever met."

"Did he ever have a love affair?" Caland asked.

"Not that anyone ever found out about," the Reverend said.

"He's married to his work and his responsibilities. Whatever he does, and for whatever reason—whether it's wasting time on a spaceship or remaking the Valley with a transportation company—it consumes him completely."

The captain and Bronlan reappeared in the ship's hatch. They descended the ladder one at a time, and the captain waved a farewell and hurried away. Bronlan stood looking up at the spaceship.

"Thinking of Pakovich's face when he sees it in the night sky?" the Reverend asked.

"No." Bronlan said. "I'm thinking of my face when I look out in the morning and don't see it on the ground."

* * * * * * *

The entire Valley turned out for the ascension of Bronlan's spaceship. People crowded as close to the site as Bronlan would let them, and they filled every open space between the buildings that bordered on his backyard. Fifteen thousand faces, according to the Reverend's estimate, plus those of the fortunate tourists who happened to be visiting the Valley, watched apprehensively as the enormous ship hovered ponderously over Junk Vista Avenue with grapplers hanging limply like huge, relaxed claws.

But the operation proved to be ridiculously simple. The hold on Bronlan's ship was made secure, and the freighter rose slowly with the small, slender ship carried under it like its dead prey. Then the ascent quickened, and the pair diminished rapidly and vanished.

That night on the beach there was a celebration, with much of the Valley gathered to watch the first visible passage of Mort's new satellite named Bronlan. Bronlan himself was there as Guest of Honor, and as the bright new star moved quickly overhead, the Vals cheered it and him.

When it had passed from sight, they settled around the beach fires again and returned their attention to food and the jugs.

Sam the Artist took an enormous slop of cider and announced, "I hope that curls Pakovich's ears!"

"My friend," the Reverend said, with mock sternness, "I feel compelled to protest your uncharitable attitude toward a fellow mal. Never wish problems upon anyone. Life always provides a plethora of them unaided."

"I hope Pakovich's plethora keeps him awake nights," Sam the Artist said. "Then he can sit on his veranda and watch Mort's new moon named Bronlan and have a contest to see whether the satellite goes higher than his blood pressure."

"You're trying to apply universal laws of ethical conduct to the owners of worlds," Tel told the Reverend. "It won't work. Pakovich has nothing more than a few minor irritations to worry about. Because that's all he has, they seem like problems to him."

"Who knows what colossal burdens are borne by the owner of a world?" the Reverend intoned. "Fragile reeds that are lesser mals would break under them, but enormous responsibilities borne perpetually bring with them an endowment of strength."

"You're sprung," Sam the Artist said good-naturedly. "Better give it up and let Pakovich imagine his own burdens."

The Reverend got to his feet. "Off that way—" He pointed. "There, where the sky is dusty with stars, orbits a world called Hufflange. It's a bitch of a world, with stifling nights that foster revolutions and burning days that engender catastrophes. One day there appeared in the realm of one of the world's perennially contending monarchs a wizened old mal whose life was so pure, whose advice was so gentle and wise, whose religion was so holy, whose self-sacrifice was so noble, that he quickly attracted an enormous following."

The Reverend seated himself again. The Vals around the fire waited more in resignation than expectation for him to continue—except for Sam the Artist, who remarked, "This old mal certainly didn't have anything in common with Pakovich."

The Reverend ignored him. "The old mal's disciples sought to reward him, and he refused worldly goods; they sought to honor him, and he referred them to the infinite; they called him guru, and sage, and oracle, and master, and prophet, and mentor, and seer, and luminary, and he answered to none of these. He told them he was but one atom in the far-flung corporate mass of humanity, and no mal or fem could be more—or less. After that they began to call him The One despite his gentle reprimands. He taught them that every transient fleck of humanity was one; in afterlife it would become less or more, depending on the life's direction. Humanity was incapable of magnifying itself, and only by becoming one with the infinite could it achieve transcendence and Twoness.

"The monarch of the land heard of this new religious leader and of his enormous success, and she was troubled. Because of The One's popularity, she could not suppress him; because of his indifference to worldly things, The One was immune to bribery; because of his wisdom, he could not be exploited. Finally the monarch's scheming advisors devised a trap, and the monarch agreed and sent for The One.

"They brought him to her throne room where she ruled surrounded by opulent trappings and fawning servitors. The One remained upright in a place where failure to prostrate oneself could mean instant death, and he met the monarch's eyes calmly.

"'I seek guidance, oh wisest of the wise, the purest of the pure, and holiest of the holy,' the monarch said to him. 'Of all the gifts that the universe confers upon humans, what has the highest value? The universe itself? An entire galaxy? Few mortals would be so greedy as to project their desires beyond the world they stand upon, and surely a world contains the means of satisfying every human craving. If it were within my power to bestow a world upon you, to be your absolute property so that it and all who lived upon it were yours to do with as you chose, what would your first reaction be?'

"The One could not answer except honestly, and for the first time in many years he felt the corrosive force of temptation. A world that was his to own absolutely! He thought of abolishing poverty and strife and war, of teaching the populace of an entire planet to respect the universe's one law of love, of perfecting a world so that its very existence could be a monument to the infinite, and whose peoples would perform hymns of worship in their every action, of creating a blessed isle in a cosmos of evil from which would emanate the light that would guide all worlds to the true religion.

"Then he thought of the inevitable religious schisms, of the theological disputations, of the violent controversies that would die out only when replaced by decadent complacency; and he thought of government, and political favoritism, and bribery; and of economic cycles and depressions, and strikes, and worker and management jealousies; and he thought of relations with other worlds, and spies and espionage, and boycotts, and armies to defend or attack; and he thought of bureaucracies and proctors and petitions and corruptions of the franchise.

"'Come, oh wisest of the wise,' the monarch taunted. She beamed down on him triumphantly. 'Such a small favor I ask of you—the answer to a single question. If I could give you a world of your own, so that you absolutely possessed it and all those who lived upon it, what would your first action be?'

"The One bowed low, as he bowed to all he spoke to. 'Majesty,' he said, 'my first action would be to give it back'."

In the silence that followed, everyone turned expectantly to Sam the Artist. Sam did not hesitate. "That's the problem with Pakovich. He never gives anything back. We've simply got to do something about Pakovich."

But the last word was Bronlan's, and only Caland heard it. Bronlan was still gazing at the sky where his spaceship had lately been a fast-moving moon, and he said softly, "If Pakovich was planning on using my ship for a communications tower, that'll show him."

CHAPTER TWENTY-FOUR

Bronlan's spaceship was gone, and it seemed to Caland that the Valley had lost the one touch of man-made beauty that corrosive human hands had bestowed on it. There were few Vals who could remember a time when it had not been slowly growing toward completion in Bronlan's back yard, and most had taken its presence for granted. It was part of the landscape like an unusual geological formation. Its dramatic departure, and its emergence as an ornament to the night sky, gained for it far more attention in its absence that its uniquely lovely presence had ever received.

Its advent caused a sensation in Paradise. News of the ascension, brought back from the Valley by tourists who had happened to witness it, swept through both tourist hotes, and the guests and employees crowded balconies and verandas and spilled onto the beach to look at the new star. In the days that followed, those tourists who had missed seeing the spaceship on the ground inexplicably visited the Valley to view the place where it had been. Record crowds jammed the Prom for a sennite, with tourists lined up along the Valley Transportation Company fence as though expecting the ship to return as unexpectedly as it had departed. Paradise residents, most of whom had been no more than dimly aware of the spaceship's existence, regarded the sudden appearance of the new star as a portent, though no one could have said of what.

Those Vals who were eagerly awaiting word of Pakovich's reaction were disappointed. Pakovich did not react. Pakovich was not even on the world of Mort. He and Alexander the Second had left for Aravia three days before Bronlan's ship was launched. In a lavishly ornate ceremony, before an audience largely composed of Aravia's decadent aristocracy, Alexander the Second was to become officially and legally and socially betrothed to the impoverished Aravian princess.

"So much for infatuations," Caland remarked.

"Betrothals have nothing to do with infatuations," Tel said. "Neither do marriages, except that this particular princess may have cause for complaint about the number of evenings her husband works late."

On the day of the spaceship's departure, someone had seen Sdissler talking with Nalce on the fringe of the watching crowd. No one had been able to find out what they were talking about. This report caused instant speculation concerning a possible sinister connection, but Sam the Artist hooted at it.

"Sdissler talks with every Valley newcomer," he said. "Anyway, Sdissler is a dedicated Pakovich stooge, and stooges do not bite the shoes they lick."

"Neither do conspirators conspire in public," Tel told Caland afterward. "But we'll keep watching Nalce. It's his private connections that we need to know more about."

Valley life dropped back into its flowing pattern. The next morning Caland and Tel went to swim at the deserted ocean beach. Afterward they leaned against the boulders and relaxed in the sun.

"Daydreaming?" Tel asked Caland after a long period of silence.

"A bit."

"Tell me. I like your daydreams. Sometimes they have a wonderfully practical touch to them."

"I've never thought so," Caland said. "First I was thinking what a nice thing it would be if we had an eatery here. We could sit with our yuck and putrebuns and watch the ocean. Then I wondered if maybe some of the tourists might enjoy getting away from the bay. I changed the eatery to a restaurant just above the beach, with tables on a long veranda overlooking the ocean and Alz Hernl to manage the place. Then I decided that if any of those things ever happened, this beach would be completely ruined for us, and Bar probably would arrange with Captain Akonif to put me in orbit."

Tel nodded gravely. "That's what I mean. That's a wonderfully practical way to daydream. Everything completely under control—"

She broke off. Footsteps were approaching rapidly along the bay beach. Moppy and Phem burst into view, both of them panting from the exertion of a long run.

Tel pushed herself into a sitting position. "What's happened to Phem? She's the walking image of disaster."

The girl did, indeed, look as though her world had suddenly crashed about her in damp ruins. She was choking sobs, and her abject misery was reflected in Moppy's white-faced dejection.

"Screet!" Tel muttered. "The child's pregnant. We knew she was a pristine innocent; someone should have talked to her. Now you'll have to write another letter, First Academic Chancellor Caland. Do you have the proper format for explaining to her father that the child needs a larger allowance because the university has just granted her a pregnancy leave?"

Phem sank down beside them, still choking sobs, and tried to catch her breath. Moppy stood by loyally though he looked as if he would have preferred to keep on running.

"Nothing could be *that* bad," Tel said kindly. "Take your time and tell us about it."

Phem opened her fist. She was clutching the pink form of a spacegram, which she had crushed into a wad, and she began to smooth it out with trembling fingers.

"My father's coming!" she gasped.

Caland sat up with a jerk. "*What?*"

"He got Cal's letter and he was so pleased to hear about the university that he's coming to visit it, and—"

Her voice broke. The sobs became a torrent punctuated with howls.

Caland looked reproachfully at Tel, who was making choking sounds of her own. She was hugging herself and trying to contain her laughter.

"When is he coming?" Caland asked when he could make himself heard.

"Tomorrow!" Phem gasped. The sobs resumed.

Caland spoke with far more confidence than he felt. "Easy, now. We'll work it out, but crying isn't going to help. It isn't that kind of problem."

Tel was shaking with laughter. She began wiping her eyes, and Phem, thinking that the tears were a sympathetic echo of her own, threw herself into Tel's arms.

Tel finally brought her laughter under control. She said to Caland, "I've always wanted to ask some sophisticated mal-of-the-galaxy what kind of problem *can* be solved by tears."

Caland was examining the spacegram. "Tomorrow is rather short notice. I suppose he just happened to be in the neighborhood and decided to drop in."

Phem pointed a trembling finger at the arrival date. "It's been at the Port for more than a sennite. The people said they didn't know where or what Valley University is."

"You were lucky to receive it at all," Caland said.

Since Pakovich chose to pretend that the Valley didn't exist, the Port gave no precedence to Valley communications regardless of the priority rating. Bronlan's 'cab drivers picked up accumulated mail and messages regularly, and Bronlan sent a 'truck for freight whenever a ship landed, but handling delays of a sennite or more were not uncommon, and any kind of excuse to misfile a message was certain to be seized upon.

Partley hrv' Dasshalm explained that he was traveling on business, and an unexpected cancellation fortunately would allow time for a side trip to Mort. He furnished dates and times of arrival and departure, reprimanded Phem for not writing, congratulated her on her academic success, and asked her to arrange accommodation for his visit—all within the personal priority allowance. The terseness reminded Caland of his father's messages. His father had been psychologically incapable of wasting a syllable at space rates, and Dasshlam's bent was identical.

"It's too late to head him off," Tel said. She'd managed to suppress her laughter, but there still was an odd quaver in her voice. "Otherwise you could have told him that Phem has graduated and left for postgraduate study at the other end of the galaxy."

Caland said nothing. He was desperately trying to think.

"What are we going to *do*?" Phem sobbed.

"A sennite's notice would have been useful," Caland said ruefully.

"What could you have done in a sennite that you can't do in a day?" Tel asked. "If you're thinking of conjuring a university into existence—"

"Not a university. The illusion of a university."

"Excuse me. I didn't know that there were set construction times for illusions. Why don't we have Phem meet him at the Port and tell him the university's on holiday?"

"What holiday?" Caland asked.

"Surely it'd be easier to produce an illusion of a holiday than one of a university."

"He'd want to see the university anyway," Caland said. "The one encouraging thing about this is that he's arriving after dark and leaving after dark. Illusions always work better at night."

Tel was looking at the spacegram. "He's arriving and leaving after dark, but in between he'll be here for two full days. What are you going to do—produce the illusion of a two-day eclipse of the sun? I doubt that Mort's new artificial moon would be equal to it."

"Tel—be quiet," Caland said impatiently. "This is going to take work and cooperation from a lot of people. Just for a start—Sam, the Reverend, and Calta."

He sent Phem and Moppy to ask Alz for the loan of the room above the Fig Stump and to invite the others. They dashed away.

Caland turned and eyed Tel reprovingly. "You're snippy

today. What's the matter?"

"Matter? This thing is howlingly funny, and I can't laugh because you insist on taking it seriously."

Caland leaned back against the boulder and closed his eyes.

Tel said to him sternly, "This 'illusion of a university' thing is wildly impractical. It's very unlike you. Run it through again."

Caland made no response. He was wondering whether Partley hrv' Dasshlam's sudden visit portended anything more than a father's concern for his daughter's welfare.

Almost certainly it did. No doubt his friends and colleagues bragged about their children's achievements, and it had been acutely embarrassing to him to have a daughter who not only had no achievements but no whereabouts. When he received her message saying she was attending a university on a world he'd never heard of, followed by an official letter from First Academic Chancellor Caland, the renegade offspring suddenly became, "My daughter—only fifteen, you know and already a university student. Tuition subvented, too—won that all by herself by taking examinations."

Then skepticism had set in, perhaps prompted by the fact that no galactic educational directory extant had ever heard of Valley University or any other university on Mort. It also would occur to him—or be brought to his attention by friends—that a university admitting students of that age without prior educational distinctions was a marvel that should be believed only after he had seen it himself.

"Lies always have unstable orbits," Tel was saying, "and you can't keep one in motion just by launching another. What's wrong with telling Partley hrv' Dasshlam the truth? The worst he can do is cut off Phem's allowance. The youngster will survive. Valley youngsters always do. If you talk with him seriously, perhaps we can convince him that Phem is much happier here than she ever was at home, and he'll keep the allowance going."

Caland shook his head. A millionaire who had been bragging to friends about "my daughter—only fifteen and already a university student," could react no way except violently to a confession that he'd been hoaxed.

"This could be extremely serious," Caland said. "Dasshlam is rich enough, and important enough, to cause the Valley endless trouble if he was to take personal offense over this, and he certainly would. He might even join forces with Pakovich, and he probably has a much better legal staff. No. The only way out is to create an illusion."

"You can't be serious! Where on Mort can you show him anything that looks remotely like a university?"

"Nowhere. But I may be able to make him think he's seeing something like one. Let's go talk to the others."

* * * * * * *

Standing at the space port's observation windows with Phem and the Reverend, Caland felt like a novice playwright awaiting an opening night curtain. He'd had at least a dozen plays performed, several with considerable success; but this would be unlike any drama ever staged before anywhere. Not only would the visiting principal perform without a rehearsal, but—if all went well—he would be totally unaware that he had assumed a part in a carefully crafted illusion.

Phem's small face was pale and moist with apprehension. She wore trim dark green trousers and a lighter green wrap, and her hair was peeled back severely and pinned into a neat roll. Her clothing gave her an aura of poise and maturity that her father would find stupefying—if, indeed, he recognized her at all, for she had grown taller and lost considerable weight. The poise was genuine. For the first time in her life she had an emotionally satisfying relationship and a community of friends to sustain her. She might fear her father, but she wasn't going to run from him.

The Reverend was attired in a new black daysuit that Caland and Tel had forced upon him. It had been purchased in Paradise that morning and altered severely to match the Reverend's unnaturally angular dimensions. With his calm demeanor and his starkly ascetic appearance, he was the quintessence of rectitude. Caland was wearing the expensive suit he had bought on Aravia to invest him with respectability at the tourist hote. The three of them were, eminently, First Academic Chancellor, professor, and student of Valley University. Now all that was required was for Partley hrv' Dasshlam to step into the illusion and play the part Caland had written for him.

The ship settled ponderously to ground. The first descending passengers, after milling about uncertainly, began to board the 'bus.

"There he is!" Phem exclaimed.

Partley hrv' Dasshlam, traveling case in hand, was striding impatiently toward the terminal building. He was a robust man of medium height. Phem had described him as vain in appearance, and the elaboration of artificial curls in his hair and his stylishly modeled daysuit confirmed that. He had once been handsome, but his pulchritude was gradually losing ground to the bloat of affluence. Probably he resented the fact that Phem did not look the least bit like him.

They waited at one side until he had passed through a customs station. The illusion teetered momentarily when the official asked Dasshalm where he would be staying and Dasshalm answered, "At the university." But the official had been trained not to argue with Mort's conspicuously wealthy visitors.

Dasshalm claimed his unopened traveling case. As they stepped forward to intercept him, he halted and stared at them confoundedly. So intense was his astonishment that he did not move until Phem moved toward him with her arms extended.

Then he exclaimed, "Baby!" and enfolded her in his embrace.

Phem accepted it with cool nonchalance and spoke the first lines that Caland had written for her. "Please, Father. I'm not a baby any longer. Here they call me Phem."

She spelled it for him, P-H-E-M, with an aplomb grounded firmly in a long afternoon of rehearsals. Turning, she presented First Academic Chancellor Caland and the Reverend Professor.

As they moved in a group toward the exit, Dasshalm sidled toward Caland and muttered, "She looks great. But how'd you get her to dress up?"

Caland affected innocence. "But all of our students are required to wear uniform dress."

"Uniform?" Dasshlam echoed blankly.

He digested this information in silence until they reached their 'cab. Then he halted and scrutinized the ungainly vehicle with astonishment.

Caland gracefully handed Phem into it and turned to assist her father. "In many respects Mort is a primitive world," he explained as he climbed in behind them. "It's a world of simple people with simple pursuits. It's an ideal place for a university. Modern civilization is especially hard on its young people. They receive awards without work or achievement and freedom of action without ever having experienced discipline. The wrong environment can be destructive. We feel that young minds and characters develop best on a world that offers a minimum of distractions."

"To be sure, to be sure," Dasshlam murmured appreciatively. He turned and looked narrowly at Caland. "Are you by chance related to Jemler Caland?"

Caland bowed gravely. "My father."

Dasshlam bowed in turn. "Delighted to hear it. Very pleased to make your acquaintance. You're a credit to your father. It's a pleasure to see young mals with sound connections and a proper outlook on life taking positions in education and government. Drives out the riffraff and instills the right principles."

The 'cab was rolling swiftly along the road to Paradise. The dusk had deepened into darkness, and there was little to be seen, so Dasshlam turned his attention to Phem. "How's school?" he asked her.

"Like always," she said. "Some of it's stretchy and some of it's a tear." He gaped at her speechlessly. Before he could ask for a translation, she added, "Right now I have a pash for math."

"You always thought math was too difficult," he said

reproachfully.

"Some of it is." She tossed her head with superb indifference. Caland had worked on that gesture for all of a half hour, and he resented her wasting it in the dim interior of the 'cab. "This term I have a course in the Calculus of Imaginative Computer Functions," Phem went on. "It's utterly devastated my free time."

Before Dasshlam could ask another question, Phem gestured to the two tall buildings whose lights had just come into view. "The tourist hotes," she said. "Accommodations are fairly nice there, but it's a frightful crowd of stodgy people. Not your type at all, so I made a reservation for you at a place closer to the campus."

Dasshlam found this combination of flattery and daughterly concern overwhelming. He said, "Why, that's—that's—"

"But it's nothing fancy," Phem went on hurriedly. "If you don't like it, then it's the awful tourist places or nothing."

"I'm sure I'll manage all right," he murmured.

Caland interposed a comment. "Except for the tourists, Mort has few visitors. The university has almost none. Considering the urgent need for new buildings that a young institution always has to contend with, we couldn't in good conscience sacrifice classrooms to build accommodations for our few visitors."

"Of course not," Dasshlam said. "Certainly not."

They could have bypassed Paradise, but Caland had chosen a route through the city. He considered it a dreary place at any time of the day, and by night the dwellings were symmetrical concrete mounds punctuated by slashes of light, but the orderliness would appeal to Dasshlam. Soon they were humming past the lighted, bustling activity of the Merc Mart, with the buildings of the Government Mall looming behind it. On their right was Paradise Park, and the refreshing tang of the sea breeze became stronger.

Dasshlam leaned back contentedly. "Nice place," he murmured. Then he remembered his fatherly duties. "Your mother wants to know why you don't write. So do your brothers and sisters."

"But we have so little time!" Phem protested. She shrewdly changed the subject. "Are you hungry?"

"Oh, well," Dasshlam said. "I had a sup of sorts on the ship, but space meals—there's always something lacking about them. Maybe it's the low gravity."

"There are two very good restaurants near the campus," Phem said. "I've arranged for us to sup at one of them. Do you mind a second sup?"

"Certainly not. Not if it's good."

"Chancellor and the Reverend Professor will join us," Phem said. She turned to her father anxiously. "Is that all right?"

"Perfectly all right," Dasshlam said graciously. "That's why I'm here. Want to talk with your teachers and find out about this place. It's a father's duty to make certain a school isn't warping his daughter's character."

They left the geometric monotony of Paradise behind them. The smell of the sea became sharper, and its invisible presence enveloped them as they hummed along the bay road. Dasshlam, after several attempts to glimpse something through the window, lapsed into silence. Phem's nervousness seemed almost tangible to Caland, and he leaned forward and whispered into her ear.

"You're doing great. Just keep it up."

They negotiated a final curve, and the lights came into view ahead of them. The 'cab slowed as they approached the Valley gate. A 'bus had been waiting there, and it turned onto the Prom and preceded them, ostensibly headed for the Valley Transportation Company yard. It effectively scattered the tourists and also obscured Dasshlam's view of the Prom. The only impressions he could gain was one of poorly lit shops and a quite surprising number of decent-looking customers.

There were no scruddy Vals about. Caland had asked for the cooperation of the entire Valley, the first time in years that anyone had attempted such a thing. Sam the Artist, the Reverend, and Bronlan had made stern pronouncements, and the Vals had listened. Even the cloud of paras had been banished from the gate. The tourists on that night were deprived of their expected entertainment. The only Vals in sight were a few young people wearing clothing identical to Phem's.

Phem had missed a cue, and Caland surreptitiously trod on her foot to remind her. "This used to be a stylish street," she said to her father. "But for years it's been rumored that the university might take the land for expansion, so not many of the landlords make repairs."

Dasshlam nodded understandingly. "People are the same everywhere."

They rolled to a stop in front of the Fig Stump. Dasshlam stepped down and looked about him in obvious puzzlement. The Fig Stump's weathered and undistinguished looking exterior showed no promise of containing the excellent restaurant Phem had mentioned. A group of young mals wearing the university "uniform" stood a short distance away by the entrance to the Road to Hell, whose sign was mysteriously unlit at this particular moment. Before Dasshlam could savor his disappointment, they burst into song.

It was an old university song, and—according to Phem—a great favorite of her father's, a sentimental reminder of his own university days that he often hummed or sang in relaxed moments at home. Dasshlam's astonishment quickly gave way to nostalgic euphoria. He began to sing; the others joined in; the 'cab rolled off and disappeared before he suddenly remembered his traveling case. When he'd been assured that the Reverend Professor had taken charge of it, he listened raptly until the singers had finished. They started another song, and Phem's urgent tugs at his arm tore him away.

"Your hote is right next door," she said. "They'll put your case in your room."

The Valley restaurants were noted for a carefully cultivated atmosphere of relaxed informality that offered the tourists a welcome contrast to the stodginess of Pakovich's hotes. "Relaxed informality" did not fit the illusion that Caland was trying to create. At his insistence Alz Hernl had managed to borrow clothing from off-duty hote servers. Alz swept forward to meet them in a dazzling display of total dress. He escorted them to a partially screened table at the rear where a totally dressed server stood by to assist in their seating.

Dasshlam expansively announced that all of them were to be his guests.

"Thank you," the Reverend said graciously. "I took the liberty of ordering in advance so we could be served immediately. We want Phem to be able to finish her meal in a leisurely fashion before curfew."

"Curfew?" Dasshlam echoed in cracked tone. "How do you manage that? I never was able to get Baby—Phem—to observe reasonable hours at home."

"Discipline is an essential part of education," Caland said. "I'm sure you haven't forgotten your own student days. Young people will spend too much time socializing if we don't impose restrictions, so we require them to be in their rooms, studying, no later than the twenty-second hour. After all, their primary objective here is learning."

"To be sure," Dasshlam breathed.

Then he sampled the food that had been set before him, and his astonishment turned in another direction. He was enraptured. He began to devour the delicately toasted, stuffed tidbits of meat in ravenous fashion, proclaiming between mouthfuls that he'd never before tasted such a delicacy.

The others ate quietly. Phem, responding to another cue, asked the Reverend about philosophical attitudes toward the sensory pleasures of eating, and a carefully-rehearsed catechism followed that Dasshlam listened to open-mouthed.

"What is it that you are a professor of?" he asked the Reverend when they had finished.

"Philosophy," the Reverend said. "I teach courses in ethics and in the Philosophy of Religion as well as courses in general philosophy. Of course at a small university like ours, faculty members also have administrative responsibilities. I'm chairman of the Committee on Future Planning."

"What are you planning?"

"An expansion program."

"Just like business," Dasshlam said. "Everyone wants to be bigger and better."

"Not at all," the Reverend responded easily. "Our problem is that bigger almost invariably means the contrary of better in education. Expansion comes at the expense of educational standards. Our planning is to ensure that we maintain quality when we increase our size." Before Dasshlam could comment further, he changed the subject. "Phem is a very promising student, though right now she seems more inclined toward the mathematical than the philosophical. Did she demonstrate that talent at an early age?"

Dasshlam sputtered into his drink and then heroically asserted his self-control. He turned to Phem and began questioning her about her studies. The fact that she had enrolled in a course in interstellar trade interested him. Caland had had a considerable expertise in that subject inflicted upon him by his father, and he had drilled Phem carefully. Her memorized responses were clipped and mechanical, but Dasshlam was beyond noticing such nuances.

"The entire world of Wwilladzc doesn't have a restaurant that approaches this one," he announced as the server deftly placed the next dish in front of him. "Where does its odd name come from?"

Alz Hernl's father had in fact contrived the name because he wanted one that sounded just as stupidly incongruous as that of his rival, the Burned Wafer; but this was not the sort of fact that fostered illusions. The Reverend arched his eyebrows and appealed to Caland.

"In its original quarters, the restaurant had a courtyard," Caland explained. "There was a fig tree in the court yard, imported no one knew how long before or from where. Then the tree died. The proprietor kept the dead tree there as a sentimental memento—the figs it produced had inspired some of the restaurant's most popular dishes. And the place became known as the Fig Stump."

"Fascinating!" Dasshlam breathed.

By the time the meal was finished, Dasshlam had subsided to enraptured silence. He listened absently to the Reverend's account of ancient philosophers he'd never heard of while he slowly spooned a memorable dessert of nuts and fruits and ices. Alz Hernl had performed his part expertly. He screened the restaurant's tourist customers, placing only the more sedate types at tables visible to Dasshalm.

Finally three extremely attractive girls, all wearing clothing identical to Phem's, peeked around the screen. One whispered loudly, "Phem!"

The Reverend got to his feet. "I hate to separate you two after this long overdue reunion," he said, "but we don't want Phem to be collecting demerits. It would be unfortunate if Chancellor Caland felt compelled to take disciplinary action at the sup table."

Dasshalm scrambled to his feet, graciously permitted Phem to introduce her classmates, and then gave her a perfunctory good night kiss.

"I'll walk you back to your dorm, Phem," the Reverend said. "Have you arranged to see your father tomorrow?"

"I'll look in on you right after my morning classes," Phem told Dasshlam. "We can have din here."

"I'll look forward to it," Dasshlam said gallantly.

"If you would like to visit the campus tonight," the Reverend said, "there's a delightful lecture on the nighttime habits of Mort's sea creatures."

Before the appalled Dasshlam could react, Phem said sharply, "Don't be silly, professor. Father's had a long voyage, and even if he doesn't feel like sleeping, he'll want to relax."

"But of course," the Reverend said apologetically. "Please excuse me—I travel very little, myself. It's the price one pays in dedicating oneself to a contemplative life."

Phem waved a good by, and the Reverend departed with the four young fems.

Dasshlam seated himself again. "Those were Phem's class-mates?" he said dazedly to Caland.

"Of course."

"And—all of your students wear uniforms?"

"It's hardly a uniform. Regulations say 'uniform dress,' and we choose something that's comfortable, practical, inexpensive, and reasonably attractive."

"Amazing. I wouldn't have thought it could be done."

"About tomorrow," Caland said. "We're approaching examinations, and Phem really can't spare a lot of time from her studies."

Dasshlam gestured reassuringly. "I understand that. I wouldn't dream of disrupting her schedule."

"Of course she'll want to spend all of her free time with you, and when she's busy you can look around as much as you like by yourself. I've made arrangements with your hote. When you've finished your break tomorrow and you're ready to go sight-seeing, tell the desk super. She'll notify us, and we'll send you a guide. You can come back here to meet Phem for lunch, and then you can make arrangements to meet her again tomorrow evening and sup with her if you like."

"Excellent," Dasshlam said. He drained his goblet. "This drink is just as incredible as the food was."

Caland nodded at Alz Hernl, who was hovering, and Alz quickly produced a refill.

"Incredible," Dasshlam murmured as he raised the goblet again. "To think I'd never heard of this world."

"Haven't you heard of Pakovich?"

"Vaguely. Never paid much attention to him. No reason to. He's strictly a local operator. I suppose I should call on him."

"Unfortunately, he's on Aravia," Caland said. "He went there to attend his son's betrothal ceremony."

Dasshalm nodded; it seemed perfectly in order to him that the son of Jemler Caland would be privy to the social doings of a world's owner. "Maybe next time I come."

"I hope that will be soon," Caland said with a smile.

Dasshlam had another refill and then another. His eyes were taking on a slightly glazed appearance. Caland had totally exhausted his line of patter about the educational philosophy of Valley University.

He got to his feet. "I must apologize. You've had a long trip, and I'm keeping you up. Here—this way. There's a private entrance to the hote at the back of the lounge. Mal Hernl will guide you. It's been a delightful evening, Mal Dasshlam."

"Delightful for me," Dasshlam said.

"My own schedule is rather full for the next two days, so I may not be able to look in on you, but I will make it a point to escort you to the Port when you leave."

"Thank you," Dasshlam said. "Thank you very much."

Alz Hernl led him away.

As soon as they were gone, Tel materialized from behind the screen. She had refused emphatically to disguise herself as a university professor, and also refused to pretend to be a student. She'd had to entrust Caland to the Reverend for the trip to the Port to meet Dasshlam, but she insisted on watching the events closely from the moment of their return.

"Went pretty well," Tel said. "The uniforms were a great idea. They impressed him."

"They were a great piece of luck," Caland said.

One of the Prom clothing shops had made a speculative investment in forty pairs of dark green trousers and forty light green wrappers; but even when priced at 'fects the garments had been too expensive for the Valley trade. Dasshlam's visit had saved that particular Prom merchant from acute financial embarrassment. It had taken an all-day search to find Vals who could wear the available sizes; and under no circumstances would Valley University ever be able to assemble more than forty students.

Tel's arms encircled Caland affectionately. "You'll never stage a better performance. It went with a zing. Phem didn't bobble a line. But I'm very much afraid, dear one, that you can't possibly keep him fooled for two more days. There's nothing to show him in daylight except the chimney of the fertilizer factory, and the Prom is already back to normal."

"That chimney," Caland said sternly, "belongs to the university's power plant. Don't you forget that. Our fate is in Calta's hands, now, and they're very capable hands. Let's go have a peek."

They entered the Dolls' House by the connecting door to the Fig Stump and climbed the rear stairway's two steep flights to the top floor. Caland wondered how the unsteady Dasshlam had managed. Probably couldn't remember the last time he'd climbed that many steps. There'd been an argument as to whether he should be escorted up the sweeping grandeur of the front stairs, but there was business as usual at the Dolls' House, and Caland didn't want Dasshalm disconcerted by the bawdy banter between the dolls and their customers. On the basis of his long conversations with Phem, he had Dasshlam tabbed as spectacularly immoral in business matters and a prude about almost everything else.

On the top floor Caland opened a doorway. Sam the Artist was seated in a comfortable reclining chair watching Partley hrv' Dasshlam through a one-way transparent panel. Dasshlam hung up a few garments, tested his bed, and went through the commonplace motions of a seasoned traveler getting settled in a strange hote room. He inspected furnishings, he parted the drapes, and peered down at the darkened nothing that stretched behind the Prom buildings, and finally he dropped into a chair and began studying himself in the mirrors.

The room was lined with mirrors, and the transparency they were looking through was a mirror on Dasshlam's side. This section of the Dolls' House was infrequently used except by old customers who specified their irregular preferences in advance. Dasshlam's reaction was one of perplexity. He seemed overwhelmed by his multiple reflections and by the plushness of the surroundings that Phem had called "nothing fancy."

"You were right," Sam the Artist whispered to Caland. "This stodge is so innocent he doesn't even recognize a whorehouse when it's all around him. Is he related to Pakovich?"

"I don't see how he could be," Caland said.

"There always seems to be a resemblance between super rich people," Sam the Artist said. "They have the same bloat, they know the same dirty tricks, and they always expect someone else to chew their food for them. Did you get the drinks into him?"

"As prescribed."

Sam the Artist pursed his lips thoughtfully. "He just ordered another. I hope Calta hasn't miscalculated."

"Trust Calta," Caland said.

"We'll have to."

Phem had told Calta as much as she could about her father, and Calta produced a schedule for what she called programmed inebriation. She had calculated the amount of alcohol, taken in conjunction with a Fig Stump sup that would remove Dasshlam's inhibitions without impairing his libido. It seemed like a precarious calculation to Caland—a slight error either way could ruin them—but he knew that Calta could do it if anyone could.

Dasshlam was still gazing about him with studied disbelief. Ceiling and walls, between and around the mirrors, had the look of expensive cloth work. The furniture was of pastel shades with gilt trim splashed everywhere. The bed was enormous and circular, and in the adjoining sanctum there was a large, circular tub. The white carpet received Dasshlam's tread up to his ankles when he went to inspect the tub.

There was a discreet tap on the door. Dasshlam emerged from the sanctum and growled an irritated response.

The door opened. The fem who entered, a doll named Gildy, had long, flowing, golden hair, and she wore a clinging black gown that exposed a figure of startling voluptuousness.

She smiled sweetly and set down a tray that contained a carafe and goblets. "I'm one of the night supers, Mal Dasshlam," she said. "We want to do everything possible to make your stay here an enjoyable one."

She closed the door behind her.

And proceeded to do just that.

After the first twenty minutes, Sam the Artist muttered, "It's going to be a long monotonous night."

"Not for Dasshlam," Tel said. "And not for us. We were up most of last night getting ready for this. Cal needs his sleep. He has to be alert and rested tomorrow in case his illusion shatters and there are pieces to pick up."

"You might at least be sympathetic," Sam the Artist said.

They left him grumbling.

He was still grumbling the next morning when they stopped by for his report. The first doll, Gildy, had kept Partley hrv' Dasshlam almost excessively occupied for several hours. Just when he seemed about to fall asleep, in spite of her energetic attention, she announced that she was hungry, and Dasshlam considerately sent down for a five-course snack from the Fig Stump. The dolls received a percentage on restaurant orders, and they always encouraged their patrons to order food for them. Some dolls hastened their way into an early retirement by consuming several meals a night.

After eating, Gildy had taken a tender leave of Dasshlam; she had murmured that she was neglecting her duties. A short time later, a plump, cheerful, dark-haired creature called Zuza entered under the pretext of clearing away the remains of the snack. She stayed until morning. When Caland and Tel arrived, Zuza and Dasshlam were eating a seven-course break snack from the Fig Stump, with Zuza seeming to enjoy it far more than Dasshlam did. Dasshlam looked like a mal who had not been to bed for a sennite.

After Zuza left, the break had to be cleared away, and it was a tall, red-headed doll named Flame who undertook to do that. She was still with Dasshlam when Caland and Tel got up to leave, though both seemed to be sleeping.

"You need some sleep yourself," Caland told Sam the Artist. "Isn't someone coming to relieve you?"

"Moppy volunteered. I told him he was too young. I'll be all right. This job really doesn't require intense concentration."

They left him to it. Caland and Tel retired to Nello's, where the cast of characters scheduled to perform the first of Caland's Desperate Measures was waiting for them. These consisted of Phem, a group of carefully selected "students," and Sigley Varno, the artist. The "students" wore the university's uniform dress; Varno, spruced up unbelievably, his long beard carefully trimmed, wore a black drapery that Caland hoped would pass for a professorial gown.

Phem was to intercept her father the moment he left the Dolls' House, suggest an early din, and then invite him to accompany her on a field trip. A waiting 'bus would take them—along with Varno and the "students"—to the Art Bazaar, and Varno, with no preparation whatsoever, easily could extend his discussion of the hundreds of paintings there through the afternoon. Then they would invade Paradise Park and enjoy a beach sup among the sedate Paradise residents, and they would return to the Valley only when it would be much too late to visit the university or anything else.

But Dasshlam never left his room. At midday he managed to scribble a note to Phem telling her that he hadn't been feeling well, but he still planned to sup with her. Sam the Artist sent along an interim report of his own: Flame was still with Dasshlam and seemed likely to make a day of it. Caland placed his first Desperate Measure on standby.

The hour of sup brought another note. Sam wrote tersely but with a touch of awe: Flame was keeping Dasshlam so thoroughly occupied that he'd forgotten about supping with his daughter. Caland already dismissed the cast of his first Desperate Measure until the following morning. When Sam's next note arrived, Caland also dismissed the vocalists who were waiting to sing Dasshlam's favorite songs under his window when night fell. They were disappointed; they'd been rehearsing all day in the remoteness of the ocean beach. But exhaustion had finally seized Dasshlam. He was performing his own serenade of snores.

Sometime during the night, a youthful doll who was, for

obscure reasons, called the Zipper, awakened Dasshlam in the guise of another night sup. Dasshlam inquired about the time, and was immediately smitten with remorse for standing up his daughter. He wanted to send another note; the Zipper convinced him that there would be time enough in the morning, and soon diverted his attention to other matters.

"They keep flattering him," Sam the Artist said when Caland and Tel looked in on him on the second morning. "They tell him there aren't any real mals around a university town, just foggy professors and students who know nothing about life. Who invented that line? You?"

"Calta doesn't need any help in inventing lines for mals," Caland said.

"I've got two dolls he hasn't met yet standing by," Sam the Artist said. "If we can keep him going until midday, you can forget your Desperate Measures. He'll have to be carried down to the 'cab when he leaves."

"What about you?" Tel said.

"I'll keel where I am," Sam said grimly.

Caland and Tel went off to Nello's for their break. Caland took a few sips of yuck, then leaned back with his eyes closed. It actually seemed possible that he would not have to resort to a single one of his Desperate Measures—which was just as well, because none of them would have worked for very long. If Partley hrv' Dasshlam had walked out the door of the Dolls' House just once with the firm intention of visiting the campus of Valley University, there would have been no possible way to keep him from the discovery that it did not exist.

"Relax," Tel said. "The ordeal is over. If he finds out now, there's nothing at all that he can do about it."

"That's true," Caland said. He brightened and tore a chunk of bread from an O loaf. "That's very true. There's nothing at all that he can do about it now."

"What does the 'hrv' stand for?" Tel asked.

"The aristocracy. Means 'from the house of'."

"Dasshlam—an aristocrat?"

"Not really. His father had plenty of money and everything else a mal could desire, so he bought that."

Partley hrv' Dasshlam finally emerged from his room and from the Dolls' House with just time to make it to the spaceport for his return flight. To guard against encounters with passing tourists, the 'cab halted in the midst of a group of Valley University art students who were drawing Prom buildings in the fading daylight. Their professor—Sigley Varno, finally getting an opportunity to use his professorial robe—stepped over to be introduced to the groggy Dasshlam.

"Some of these buildings have a fine old architectural style," Varno announced cheerfully. "They're of considerable historical importance. Your hote, for example, is called the Dolls' House because it's actually a full-scale model of a real dolls' house built for a princess on the world of Nonulorsk. There are many instances of models made of real buildings, but it's a rarity to have a real building's design based on that of a model. Notice the relieving arches above the windows—"

Caland and the Reverend and Phem rescued Dasshlam and bundled him and his traveling case into the cab. He began to mutter an abject apology that his indisposition had prevented him from spending more time with his daughter.

"Oh, that's all right," Phem said. "It's a busy time for us, and I wasn't free much. I'm just sorry that you couldn't enjoy yourself more."

Dasshlam's reply was inaudible.

Later, just before he boarded the ship, he told Phem solemnly that he was glad to see her looking and doing so well, and that he'd tell her mother she was in good health and working hard at her studies. He also said he was raising her allowance and he'd visit her again at the first opportunity. With this endowment of mixed blessings, he turned to Caland and congratulated him on the splendid achievements of the Valley University. He could not commend the institution too highly, he said, but he tried at considerable length. Then he turned aside for a brief conversation with the Reverend.

The Reverend and Caland withdrew a few paces to permit Dasshlam to have a private word of farewell with Phem. He rode the 'bus out to the ship, and they watched him climb the ramp. He turned at the top for a final wave.

Tel had joined them, and the four of them watched until the ship lifted.

"My friend," the Reverend said to Caland when Partley hrv' Dasshlam had finally put the world of Mort behind him, "You are a genius in the psychology of millionaires. Do you know what he just handed me?"

"No idea," Caland said.

"It's a gift pledge for the university's Committee on Future Planning. It's in Wwilladzc monetary units, and I don't know how to translate it into chits, but it must amount to several million. We can go ahead with our community building *and* the theater. The two theaters, a real one and one for Bar's puppets. It frightens me to be standing here with so much credit in my pocket. Did you expect that?"

"I thought he might experience a belated twitch of generosity."

"It's really conscience money," the Reverend said thoughtfully.

"I suppose. Does that mean we have to give it back?"

The Reverend laughed. "Definitely not. It's his conscience, but now it's our money. Did he pay the girls?"

"Lavishly," Caland said. "He distributed hefty grats to everyone. Calta says any time we have a visiting millionaire to put up, the Dolls' House is available."

"But he's coming back," Phem said brokenly. "We'll have to do it all over again."

"No, we won't," Caland told her with a smile. "The next time he comes, he'll stay at one of Pakovich's hotes and arrange for his own entertainment. I promise you that."

Later, at a beach fire, Tel was speculating about Partley hrv' Dasshlam's future behavior. "He'll go home and brag insufferably about his daughter and her remarkable university. His friends will still be skeptical, and sooner or later he'll have to investigate further. How long will the optical illusion last before he realizes that he really saw nothing at all?"

"Too long for him to do anything about it," Caland said.

"We ought to take some of his money and start a real university," Sam the Artist said. "Cal can write him another letter thanking him for his generosity and informing him that the Board of Governors, or whatever it is that universities have, has voted to change the name from Valley University to Dasshlam University. The theater can be a part of the university. Make it the Partley hrv' Dasshlam Memorial Theater—being generous with names doesn't cost us a thing. Morlef can add a wing to it with university classrooms. Sooner or later Mort will have to have a university. If we beat Pakovich to it, the Paradise young people will have to come to the Valley for classes, and that will really burn him."

Tel nodded. "Since Dasshlam gave us the money for the university, I think we're obligated to use it for that. But— uniform dress, and curfews, and really tough classes?"

"Chancellor Caland will have to work that out," Sam the Artist said. "In any case, Phem has nothing more to worry about."

That was true. Phem had nothing at all to worry about ever. With a borrowed camera, Sam the Artist had foted a most detailed and revealing chronicle of Dasshlam's visit to Valley University, and thereby guaranteed his future behavior for all time.

But Caland doubted that they would ever have to mention fotes to him. Dasshlam's donation indicated that his conscience had begun to work on him even before he left Mort. By the time he reached home, it would be in a full ferment.

"The Partley hrv' Dasshlams," Caland mused aloud, "react to threats of blackmail with furious anger and counter-threats. Against a stricken conscience, they have no defense at all."

"That's true," Sam the Artist said. "But it's only because it happens to them so rarely."

CHAPTER TWENTY-FIVE

Caland awoke the next morning with a headache. It passed quickly, but it was a disquieting reminder of unnumbered tortured awakenings stretching into a past he had begun to forget.

"It gave me an idea," he said to Tel. "Everyone in the valley knows about this metal in my head. Would anyone think it odd if I went to the Paradise hospital for a sennite?"

She looked at him with alarm. "Are you feeling ill?"

"No. I'm looking for an excuse to disappear for a sennite. Supposing I was to tell everyone I'm entering the hospital under an assumed name so Pakovich won't know I'm there. Under those circumstances, I could ask the Vals not to visit me, couldn't I?"

"You wouldn't have to," Tel said. "They'd be thrown out if they tried to go near the place."

"Then I can 'disappear' any time I feel like it. I wonder why I didn't think of this before. Now all we need is an excuse for you."

"You'll be my excuse," Tel said. "I'll arrange to stay with a kindly Paradise family for a sennite so I can be near the hospital."

"Let's do it," Caland said. "We can go tomorrow."

They sent word to Fish Town; but Quinotto was at sea and not expected back for several days. Caland busied himself with two chores that had emerged in the wake of Partley hrv' Dasshlam's visit. He wrote a letter to Dasshlam, thanking him for the donation, and gave it to Sam the Artist for a voice-writer forgery. His next move was to close down Gonger's Prom act. Gonger had taken part in the chorus that greeted Dasshlam's arrival, and he led the rehearsals in preparation for the cancelled serenade. Somewhere in his unmentioned past, he had acquired an astonishing repertoire of popular songs. He knew all of the sentimental favorites. Caland appointed him the blind singer of the Prom, and assigned a young child to lead him by the hand and hold his collection basket. Gonger moved along slowly, eyes closed, concentrating on facial expressions that were esthetic rather than insulting, and singing, one after another, all of the favorite old songs that passing tourists requested. From a hundred chits a day his take shot up past the thousand mark, and his self-esteem underwent the same improvement. He was doing something instead of being done to.

Only two people were not satisfied with the change. One was Sippy, who suddenly found herself out of work. Caland sent her to Morlef. The builder needed someone to keep books and look after his paperwork.

The other was Caland. He wondered whether Gonger's elevation from target to phony blind singer really was an improvement.

Suddenly Caland had nothing to do. The Reverend's para acts were functioning well, and Caland deemed it unwise to clutter the Prom with more of them. His own act remained enormously successful. His performances needed neither further refinement nor any additional material except what came to him spontaneously when he was acting.

Quinotto returned, and they made their plans. Caland faked a sudden, disabling headache, and paid a genuine visit to the medical clinic under the name of Foma. The doctor there pondered his problem gravely, suggested a complicated electric nerve tracing that could not be performed anywhere nearer than Aravia, and finally prescribed a potent analgesic. Caland paid Pakovich's grossly inflated fee and left. News of this visit spread through the Valley at once accompanied by rumors of Caland's worsening physical condition.

Having informed a few Valley friends that Caland would be entering the hospital under an assumed name—but without telling anyone what the assumed name was—Caland and Tel left the Valley late the next afternoon in a 'cab. A sincerely concerned Knack, the driver, let them out at the Merc Mart and wished Caland a speedy recovery. As soon as he'd driven away, they crossed the highway to Paradise Park and waited there until dark.

Then they walked back to Fish Town, keeping well clear of the highway. The tromp was tedious and tiring, but is was good conditioning for the much worse trek they would have to undertake later, and they had a two-day sea voyage ahead of them in which to recover. They had already sent their packs to Quinotto with equipment, spare clothing, and the food they'd decided to carry. Quinotto had sailed that afternoon, but he turned back under the cover of darkness. One of his sons met Caland and Tel at a rendezvous near Fish Town, guided them to a quiet beach a kilometer south of town, and rafted out to Quinotto's fishing boat.

The trip was one that Caland preferred to forget even while he was having it. He was seasick. He was so ill that for a time he feared that his faked trip to the hospital had been prophetic. Tel nursed him patiently and assured him that people almost never died from sea sickness. Late the second day he was sufficiently recovered to have a careful look at Quinotto's smoothly powered fishing boat. What he saw made him resolve to confine his traveling to spaceships in the future. The craft was a mere twelve meters in length, and it tossed wildly on the gigantic waves of Mort's rampaging ocean.

The waves seemed gigantic and ocean rampaging to Caland. Quinotto remarked cheerfully that things were rather quiet for that time of year.

They held to a course frequently used by fishing boats until, after dark on the second day, Quinotto turned shoreward and steered the boat into the quiet strait between the islands and the mainland. Quinotto's son rafted them ashore. He would return for them two nights later, and again on the third, fourth, and fifth nights if they failed to appear. If there was no sign of them on the fifth night, Quinotto was to return to Fish Town and personally deliver a note—which Tel had written—to the Reverend or Sam the Artist.

Above the beach they selected an easily identified rock formation and buried a canister at its foot; in need, messages could be left there. Quinotto's son pushed off and vanished into the night, and Caland and Tel were on their own.

The first phase of their journey was easy. They walked north along the beach to the cape that had been opposite Sdissler's camp on the map. Tel reasoned that one unknown mountain was as difficult to climb as another, so they might as well start as close to their destination as possible. At midnight they were climbing upward and into another utterly forgettable nightmare.

Caland had gained strength since the sabotage raid on the mines. He and Tel had come equipped for this expedition— their clothing and footgear had been selected with care. They had made themselves chemically obnoxious to Mort's annoying native fauna. Each of them carried a plox, a special climbing tool that was a combination of pick and ax.

The difference was in the mountain they were trying to climb and in the forest that covered it. The slope near Pakovich's mines had been no more than a steep hill by comparison, and there had been no ground vines to snare their feet with every step.

They struggled and perspired, rested, clambered again. A thin wash of dawn found them still struggling—as well as they could tell in the thick forest—far below the crest. Grimly they toiled onward through the morning; they had abandoned all hope of reaching Sdissler's camp on the first day. Finally the ground began to slope downward, but there was no break in the crowded growth of trees and shrubs. They could not see into the valley below them, and they had no way of knowing whether they had gone astray during their long, zigzagging struggle through the thick forest or whether Sdissler's camp was anywhere near where they'd hoped to find it.

Noon passed. They paused to eat and watch, with sardonic enjoyment, the antics of forest midges that were simultaneously attracted to their food and repelled by their chemicals. They labored through the afternoon with no certainty that they were accomplishing anything at all except an exhausting descent. They were looking for a resting place, and talking about food, when suddenly the treetops far above them exploded.

They ducked and began to move laterally. The explosions continued. Shredded branches crashed down around them. A continuous thunder rolled through the forest above their heads. Tel—with hand motions, since the racket blanketed speech— urged Caland to greater speed. Just as they seemed to be putting the danger behind them, it erupted again directly overhead. They angled away from it, down the slope, and finally Tel permitted a brief rest. Behind them the thunder continued to roll.

Tel tried to prod the exhausted Caland into motion again, and he protested. "What is it?" he shouted in her ear.

"O projectiles," she said.

"What's that?"

"Vacuum gunfire. Military rifles. Someone's shooting at us, you clod!"

Dusk was approaching when the forest abruptly thinned out and they were able to see Sdissler's camp in the valley below. Because of the fading light they could make out little of the activity down there. They could only satisfy themselves that they had a suitable observation post for the morrow. They with- drew to a place of concealment and slept.

Dawn brought complete bewilderment. They looked down on an exact replica of the camp they'd spied on north of Paradise. As day came on, they also looked down on the same activities. There was a topological crew at work. Another crew was taking soil cores. Other workers, engaged in some kind of timber study, were ranging through the trees on the lower slopes. Caland's initial observations were of nothing more—or less—than a well-organized, efficient work force.

But as the morning wore on, other groups of mals appeared,

and their activity became increasingly perplexing. Tel suddenly nudged Caland and demanded, "Where are they coming from?"

"What do you mean?" he asked.

"How many can you count?"

When his count passed a hundred, he turned wonderingly.

"Right," she said. "There couldn't possibly be room for all of them in that camp. Where are they coming from?"

They moved across the valley in lines; they detached small groups that spread out and merged again; trailing squads wrestled utterly strange equipment along in the wake of the advance. None of it made sense to Caland.

"What are they doing?" he asked finally.

"Training," Tel said. "Military training. Sdissler is training an army."

There were tactical exercises. Later there were physical fitness exercises, drills in hand-to-hand combat, and finally, late in the afternoon, weapons training, and the treetops on the mountainside again exploded as one squad after another took a turn on the shooting range.

"At least they weren't shooting at us," Tel said. "We just happened to walk into the target area."

"That doesn't make me feel better about it," Caland said bitterly.

They had seen enough—far more than enough—but it was less than they wanted to know. That night they crossed the valley circuitously and edged their way along the mountain on the opposite side. They continued their movement through most of the following day, frequently pausing to watch the activity in the valley and taking cover when the maneuvers flowed in their direction. The next morning they stood looking down into a narrow, lateral valley. There, cleverly concealed among the trees on the mountain slopes and detectable only after protracted study with binoculars, were the cabins Tel was looking for—cabins of concealed military equipment.

"Now let's see if we can get out of this alive," Tel said. "I'm serious. My hunch is that these characters will kill us cheerfully to prevent us from taking this information back to Paradise."

They began the long, arduous backtrack.

They made their beach contact on the fifth and last night. They were exhausted, hungry—they'd carried only four days' food with them—and still sobered by what they had discovered. Quinotto looked at them curiously when they came aboard, but he asked only one question, echoing what Knack had asked them after their first excursion.

"Get what you wanted?"

"A great deal more than we wanted," Tel said.

They landed at night at the Fish Town dock. Caland, wracked by a second siege of seasickness, weakly made his way back to the apartment with Tel's firm assistance. They avoided the Prom, and no one recognized them. They collapsed into bed and slept until afternoon. Then Tel sent one of the neighbors for Hairy.

"Special emergency meeting," she told him. "Calta, Yda, Bar, the Reverend, and Sam. Also Chan Worntling. I don't care what they're doing. I want all of them. Right now."

All of them except Bronlan were there when Caland and Tel made their way up the outside stairway to the room above the Fig Stump. Bronlan had gone to the Port on an errand. Caland's appearance—he was still pale from his ordeal of seasickness—caused a stir.

Yda said disgustedly, "A hospital is no place for a sick person. Look what they did to him."

"Cal hasn't been near the hospital," Tel said. "Listen carefully, all of you, and save your questions."

She described Caland's instinctive reaction to Sdissler's act and the resultant expeditions to the forest labor camps. Their audience was first good-naturedly skeptical, and then perplexed, and then dumbfounded.

"The first question is obvious," Tel said when she had finished. "Is Sdissler double-crossing Pakovich, or is Pakovich using Sdissler to train a secret army? If the latter, Pakovich is a lot subtler than any of us could have suspected."

"Pakovich is the Galaxy's most unsubtle person," Calta said firmly. "If he had anything like an army on Mort, it'd be holding daily parades around the Government Mall. But I find it difficult to believe that Sdissler—"

"Believe it!" Tel snapped. "Sdissler has been building this conspiracy for years. First he took over Pakovich's dirty work, and did it so reliably and inexpensively because he has enormous financial backing, and you can believe that too. He's recruited quality mals on other worlds, smuggling them into Mort as Valley immigrants, so Pakovich won't know how large his force is, and given them extensive military training. His troops have to do occasional fatigue duty on the garbage details when there aren't enough willing Vals, but it probably doesn't happen often enough to be onerous. With six labor camps, Sdissler must have at least five hundred armed and trained mals on Mort. He may have as many as a thousand. Know what a private army like that means to this world? It means that Sdissler can take over Mort any time he chooses. The combined populations of Paradise and the Valley would be no match for trained and armed troops. What would we fight with?"

"If all of this is true," Sam the Artist said slowly, "what's Sdissler waiting for?"

"Those labor camps are widely scattered," the Reverend said. "He'd need transport to use his army effectively."

"He's got transport," Chan Worntling said. "Pakovich long since turned two freight platforms over to him for his own use. He needed them to ferry freight and personnel between his camps, he said. He can transport fifty mals at a time easily. Since no one is paying any attention to what he is doing, he can concentrate his army whenever he likes."

They considered the matter in silence. The Reverend's thin face had assumed a foreboding look; even Sam the Artist's bristling countenance was screwed into a troubled perplexity. Calta looked disgusted; Yda was furiously angry.

"The problem is this," Yda announced finally. "All of us despise Pakovich. If he were to lose control of his world tomorrow, we'd say it served him right. But there are worse things in this universe than Pakovich, and Sdissler is several of them. We don't want Sdissler gaining what Pakovich loses."

"That's not the problem," Calta said. "The problem is—what can be done about it."

"Our problem is—what can *we* do about it?" Sam the Artist said. "Offhand, I'd say nothing at all."

"Anything that we can do already has been done—thanks to Cal and Tel," Calta said. "Now the problem is in Arlu's league. I'll space a letter to him."

Tel and Caland retired to Nello's, where the Reverend and Sam undertook to bring them up to date on what had been happening in the Valley during their absence.

It had been a momentous sennite. Dom finally had succumbed to the argument that new buildings would enhance the value of the entire Valley. The Reverend had reached an agreement with him on the use of large tracts of open land on either side of the Prom for the community building and a theater, and they were discussing the basis upon which several obstructing buildings could be torn down when the need arose. Morlef's crew of Vals had started clearing brush and trees from the community building site. Money from the Reverend's Valley Enterprises account had begun to trickle through the Valley and feed people, to Baris Bronlan's delight.

Caland politely declined the Reverend's invitation to serve on a committee that had been set up to make decisions concerning the new buildings and consider the Valley's future. "That sounds too much like business," he said. "It's the sort of thing I left home to get away from."

Phem and Moppy rushed in to greet them elatedly. Phem had received another installment of her allowance, this time at the increased rate.

"We're sending Llabal to Aravia!" she exclaimed. "One more term, and we'll have enough money."

"Wonderful!" Caland said. "Wonderful for him, I mean. He'll get a new arm, but I'll lose one of mine. I'll have to find another para."

"Arms! Two of them! It doesn't cost as much as we'd thought." Phem looked at Caland tearfully. "You did it."

"No," Caland said soberly. "Your father did it. Don't forget that. He may have done it inadvertently, but *he* did it. Money has enormous powers for good and evil, and you've conferred the good on it. But your father supplied the money."

Tel looked narrowly at Caland. "You sound like the Reverend. Is that supposed to be a philosophy?"

"I don't know," Caland said. "It's the truth, though. Money isn't evil. What's done with it or for it or because of it can be horrendously bad or superlatively good."

"Then why did you reject it?"

"It wasn't the money I was rejecting. It was the obligations that came with it." He thought for a moment. "Why don't we advance whatever money Moppy and Phem need for Llabal? They could pay it back later."

"Good idea," Tel said. "If they have to wait another term, their good intentions will explode."

As word circulated that Tel and Caland had returned, a parade of Vals squeezed through Nello's to their table to welcome them back and inquire about Caland's health. Louie Laggie joined them, and Chan Worntling saw him and stopped to pursue a long-standing gag.

"We have complaints all the time that Louie is scaving things that haven't been discarded," Worntling said. "Just last sennite I caught him making off with old Bilkor's sole possession, his reclining chair. Louie said he found it discarded on the beach and scaved it. 'Then why is old Bilkor still sleeping in it?' I asked him."

Louie grinned. "One of these days I may scav old Bilkor—if I can figure out a use for him."

Gonger, led by his dutiful child assistant, came by with a crowd of tourists. When he heard that Caland and Tel were back, he abandoned the child and opened his eyes to greet them. Interestingly enough, he had a complaint about Sdissler. Several times—before Gonger had learned to recognize his voice and ignore him—Sdissler had requested songs without contributing so much as a token chit to Gonger's take.

Caland asked about Doctor Stran Gormaz. The sociologist had not been much in evidence in the Valley; he had been awaiting the arrival of his equipment and of some assistants he had hired.

"But he'll soon be able to go to work," Mucks Groilan announced. Mucks had been one of a group of Vals hired by Gormaz to transport a small mountain of shipping cartons from the end of the Prom's pavement, where a truck had deposited them, to Dom's mansion.

"What sort of equipment does a sociological laboratory use?" Tel asked.

"Office stuff," Mucks said. "A referencer, a comp filer, desks, stuff like that. We moved Dom's clutter of furniture out of that big back room and helped Gormaz get his unpacking started."

"When he's ready to study our sociology, will he give us notice?" Louie Laggie wanted to know. "Or will he sneak up on us and do it when we aren't looking? I've never had my sociology studied before. How am I supposed to behave? Do I keep looking over my shoulder to see how he's doing it, or do I pretend that I don't notice him?"

No one knew, but they all toasted Doctor Stran Gormaz in yuck. His money was good, and—Mucks reported with satisfaction—he paid well.

Time drifted pleasantly, and Caland luxuriated in loafing and in resting his aching muscles. He had begun to think vaguely of a sup at the Burned Wafer. The others were engrossed in their talk, and none of them paid any attention to the flowing Prom traffic until Moppy, on his way back to the Valley gate after a para stint, leaned through the glassless window and waved both arms excitedly.

"Something's flapping!" he shouted.

"What?" Louie Laggie shouted back.

"Don't know. Everyone's crowding around."

Caland and Tel were already on their feet. Even before they got outside, they knew that something was very wrong. The Prom looked and sounded different. Instead of the sustained babble of hundreds of simultaneous conversations, there was one distant, high-pitched voice that floated to them clearly on the fitful sea breeze. Traffic had thinned out as everyone gravitated toward the source of that unremitting voice. Those reluctant to join the compacted mass of spectators were watching curiously from a distance, and a number of Prom merchants had stepped outside to see what had happened to their customers. At Yda's and the Dolls' House, girls were staring down from windows and balconies. Odd as the gathering must have looked when viewed from above, from street level—when Caland and Tel came close enough to distinguish the words—it was extraordinary. The crowd was listening to a political speech.

"The people of the Valley have been exploited since the day the Valley was founded," the voice proclaimed. "Most of the electricity doesn't work. Sometimes the plumbing doesn't work. The houses are rotten and rotting. We live in an unhealthy and unsafe environment. Children don't receive balanced diets, and their education is neglected. There are no recreational facilities, no services of any kind. Why? Because the Valley is run by and for its owner. If the electricity doesn't work, Dom pays a smaller electric bill. Why should he bother to get it fixed? If the plumbing malfunctions, the tenants can use a sanctum down the street. If a roof leaks, Dom doesn't get wet. All he's concerned about is his own house. When was the last time his roof leaked? When has his power receiver ever malfunctioned? The fact that the Valley is one vast junk heap doesn't disturb him—there isn't any clutter around his house. The clutter that *you* live in isn't his concern, and he thinks it's not his responsibility.

"And then there's His Highness, the Pakovich, living up there on a mountain where the Valley's stink can't reach him. His Highness, the Pakovich, is wealthy beyond calculation, but has anyone ever tried to make the Pakovich meet his responsibilities to the people in the Valley? Never. The only one in a position to speak for us is Dom, and Pakovich finds it cheaper to pay Dom off than to supply the services that Valley people urgently need, like a medical clinic, and a library, and schools.

"What we need—what we've got to have—what we insist on having—is someone with the authority to represent all of us and the gumption to face up to the Pakovich and demand what should rightly be ours: someone who can be trusted to look after our interests without selling us out. The Valley needs an elected exek!"

The voice rolled on. It delivered an effective, rabble-roused speech, and it ended with call for an election. "The Valley needs an elected exek. No sane person would deny that; no honest person would oppose it; no one loyal to the Valley and its people would fail to support it."

As the crowd began to drift away, Caland and Tel pushed through to the center where the speaker was surrounded by a circle of Vals who seemed more curious than excited over what had been said. Caland got only a fleeting glimpse of his face as he swayed in animated speech with hands fluttering, answering questions, and countering objections.

The speaker was Nalce.

Tel nudged Caland, and they turned away.

"There's some profound mischief brewing," Caland remarked.

"Right," Tel agreed. "That vrump doesn't give a chit for the Valley. He's trying to involve it in some kind of attempt to sabotage Pak Enterprises."

"But will the Vals accept that business about an elected exek?"

"I don't know. Vals are likely to resent a newcomer trying to tell them what to do. On the other hand, Nalce obviously is experienced at this kind of thing. It'd be a mistake to underestimate him."

They returned to Nello's which was beginning to fill up again after losing its patrons to Nalce's oratory. Sam the Artist and the Reverend were still there. Tel and Caland joined them. Their abandoned yuck was cold, so Caland brought new mugs for Tel and himself and a plate of dry rot.

He passed the dry rot to Sam, who glommed a large handful. "I haven't considered making this a meal," Sam said, "but since you're imposing on my hospitality—"

Caland raised his mug. "To politics."

"I'm glad it's to something," Sam the Artist said. "Otherwise, getting you to spend a chit is like pulling nails out of that unbuilt theater."

Caland took a long draught of yuck and dropped some dry rot into the mug. "The longer I drink this stuff—"

"It's nourishing, it's filling, it refreshes and invigorates," Sam the Artist said. "Some claim it's even an aphrodisiac."

"I thought that was the stink of the fertilizer factory."

"That's another one. In the Valley you're surrounded by aphrodisiacs."

"Tell me about the others. I'd like to try them all."

"Probably you already have," Sam the Artist said. "Even Hef's putrebuns have a modest reputation, and I've heard a rumor that this dry rot is suspect. But don't worry. Tel will make certain that you don't miss any of them. What's this about politics besides an excuse for a yuck toast?"

Caland regarded him indignantly. "Do you mean to say that you sat in here stuffing your stomach when you could have been enjoying the speech?"

"Is that what was going on? The Reverend and I thought some tourist was cutting up."

"It was Nalce propounding wisdom about Valley affairs. According to Nalce, the Valley needs an elected exek who will face up to both Dom and Pakovich and protect the rights of Vals. He didn't say how this was to be done—hand to hand combat, perhaps. It was an extremely effective speech. Listening to it, I said to myself, 'There's really only one person with all of the qualifications a Valley exek has to have. That's my old friend Sam the Artist.' How'd you like to run for Valley exek?"

"The Valley doesn't need an elected exek, and it's not going to have one."

"Whether or not it needs one, it's going to have one," Tel said. "Nalce is going to agitate an election."

"How'd you like to run for the job?" Caland asked Sam the Artist.

"No form of torment could induce me to run for anything whatsoever. I haven't the figure for it. Anyway, contrary to the view inflicted on you by that idiot, the Valley doesn't need an exek, I wouldn't try for the job if it did, and if, through some irresponsible exercise of the franchise, such a position were created and I were elected, the one thing I would guarantee would be to never exek anything."

Caland looked at Tel, who nodded gravely. "That's the right line, I think."

"I agree," Caland said. "Whether or not the Valley needs an exek, Nalce will agitate until it elects one, so we'd better take pains to make certain that it elects someone pledged not to exek. Right?"

"Right," the Reverend agreed.

"The three of us will be your campaign managers," Caland promised.

Tel described the speech they'd heard. "He hasn't announced his candidacy yet," she said. "At least he didn't announce it in the part of the speech we heard, but it's obvious that he expects to be a candidate. He may be counting on being the only candidate, and the people deserve a choice."

"Who, me? A choice?" Sam the Artist asked, grinning.

"You're a choice between a trouble-making outsider and a long-term resident who understands the Valley's problems and has the sense to leave well enough alone when it is well enough," Caland said. "That's your platform."

"You two are serious!" Sam the Artist said wonderingly.

"It's serious business," Tel told him. She sounded extremely serious. "There may actually be things that a sincere and dedicated exek could accomplish, but Nalce isn't concerned with any of that. His objective is to make use of the Valley in whatever it is that's being plotted against Pakovich. That's something the

Valley absolutely must not get involved in. We need someone who can put this agitation in the proper prospective."

"I must say," Sam the Artist observed reflectively, "that our good friend Cal would make an ideal campaign manager. For what is politics but a form of begging? A politician is just another kind of para, going his crying way and working for votes the way our paras work the tourists for grats. I don't know anything about those things a sincere and dedicated exek could accomplish, but I suppose they could be given leisurely consideration after the election. If it's merely a question of giving people the right to vote for status quo, I don't mind, provided that I don't have to do anything about being elected."

"You'll have to make speeches promising not to do anything."

"I could do that, I suppose, as long as they're short speeches."

"Those are the best kind."

The Reverend had been listening to the conversation with a mildly incredulous look. Now he raised his mug and took a long gulp of yuck. "I've never heard of political power being dispensed in such an offhand manner," he remarked.

"Cal has undergone a personality switch," Sam the Artist said. "When he first came here, he wouldn't even speak unless spoken to at least three times. Now he makes himself chancellor of a mythical university, he builds a business organization of paras, he starts remodeling and refurbishing the entire Valley, and he plans a political campaign for a candidate pledged to do nothing at all. The next thing we know—"

He broke off because he had lost two-thirds of his audience. Tel and Caland were staring through Nello's glassless window at the traffic passing on the Prom. Fem Wobbons moved along leisurely in the escort of a good-looking young mal tourist. For once she was not muffled in an ineffectual disguise.

"Was it Arlu who said that her pursuit of young mals is notorious?" Caland asked.

"I thought you'd learned that from personal experience," Tel said. "But why should it be notorious? All through history elderly mals have chased young fems as a healthy pastime. An older fem ought to be able to chase young mals without being considered a pervert."

"Perhaps it isn't what she does, it's the way she does it," Caland suggested.

"Tel," Sam the Artist said, "is justifying her own future conduct. With regard to politics—"

"You're a candidate," Caland said. "We'll announce it right away."

"We'll put up posters," Tel said. "That'll jolt Nalce. We'll have you elected before he announces his campaign."

Caland and Tel went off to the ocean beach to relax, leaving Sam the Artist to contemplate his political future. They swam, and then they dozed in the late afternoon sun. Caland was wondering whether he should attempt his para act that evening. He had never felt less like performing anything. He felt shrouded in gloom, and he must have looked the same way. He opened his eyes and found Tel studying him with concern.

"Headache?" she asked anxiously.

"No." Caland said. "I'm just feeling bewildered about the way things pile up. So much happens and none of it means anything. For me, I mean. I was hopeful about Sdissler, but his army couldn't possibly have anything to do with me. Nothing seems to take me a millimeter closer to the person who's controlling my mind."

Tel patted his arm. "Never mind. I told you we'd peel away Sdissler and we have. We'll peel away these other things, too, until we have the one that matters. You need rest. Forget the para act tonight. The tourists won't be expecting you anyway."

They easily fell back into their Valley routine—apartment to Prom to beach, with Caland doing an exhausting para stint each evening. His headaches resumed the day after they returned, leading Tel to wonder whether something in the Valley air was causing them. Caland awoke in pain; when the agony eased a bit he frequently went back to sleep; and so it was, several days later, that Hairy found both of them in bed at mid-morning.

He awakened them with a discreet cough from the kitchen.

"Calta wants to see you," he said. "Back of the Fig Stump."

"What is it this time?" Caland called irritably. "Big crisis or little?"

Hairy grinned at them. "I don't know the size, but it must be complicated. Simple things Calta takes care of herself." He nodded cheerfully and bounded away on his next errand.

"The Valley couldn't exist without Hairy," Caland observed.

"It could, but everything would run a sennite late," Tel said.

When they reached the Fig Stump, Calta, Yda, the Reverend, and Sam the Artist were waiting for them. Calta wasted no time. "Do all of you know Doctor Welic Fulnry?" she asked.

"Not personally," Tel said. She told Caland, "A Pakovich satellite. Health Director of Pak Enterprises."

"He's been here for five years," Calta said. "Middle-aged, but looks a bit younger than that. Very competent—people say. Probably means he's a blundering ass who makes a good impression. Doesn't know how to laugh. Tell a joke in his presence, and you spend the next half hour trying to explain it. Word is that he likes his job, likes Mort, and despises Pakovich, but that could be said of most of Pakovich employees. His predecessor, Doctor Qreen, was able to grasp the fact that the Valley's health problems can't be segregated. If someone develops a wheeze on Fishstink Alley, it'll hit Paradise before it gets to Bay Unview Boulevard. Yda and I keep close check on the health and sanitation, but the girls working the Prom, or working for Sdissler, have no medical supervision at all. Doctor Qreen used to sneak one of the Pak doctors over here occasionally to give checkups to anyone who wanted one. Probably that was why he was fired."

"He was fired because he couldn't come up with a medical excuse for cancelling Bar's pension," Sam the Artist said. "Bar is crippled, but he isn't disabled. No one has ever been able to convince Pakovich that this is possible."

"In any case, he was fired," Calta went on. "Doctor Fulnry replaced him, and there were no more free checkups. To finally get to the point, Fulnry turned up here an hour ago and asked for a conference with the Valley's leading citizens. I reminded him that Valley telation was mostly by word of mouth, and he said he'd be eating an early din here anyway, and he'd be available whenever I had anyone for him to talk with. Now you know as much as I do."

"Could this visitation be occasioned by the fact that Pakovich is still on Aravia?" the Reverend wanted to know.

"I doubt it," Calta said. "Pakovich has been on Aravia for a long time. If Fulnry had been panting to dash over here the moment Pakovich turned his back, he'd have shown up before now."

"I've heard that Fulnry is in charge of these spies that Pak Enterprises keeps sneaking into the Valley," Yda said. "Deity knows there's nothing here for a spy to snoop out, and we usually spot them immediately, but someone keeps trying. Fulnry might be manipulating some new variation on that."

"Why would the Medical Director be in charge of Pakovich's spies?" Caland wanted to know.

"Not even the Deity could answer that," Yda said.

"I know why," Sam the Artist said. "Pakovich is still looking for evidence that Bar isn't crippled. He's tried one scheme after another for years. Let's get the critter up here and see what this one is about. He'll give us ten per cent truth and make all of his lies sound like divine proclamations."

"I'll bring him," Calta said.

If Doctor Welic Fulnry never laughed, it was because he was too preoccupied with cultivating his smile to see the humor in anything. He bathed the room with it while Calta was introducing him. He even continued to smile when Yda snapped, "Sit down, Fulnry. Tell us what deviltry you're up to."

He did look young, and he had a subdued handsomeness about him. The one thing obviously out of character was his dining at the Fig Stump. His slender figure suggested that food of any kind played a very small part in his existence.

They seated themselves around the large table, and Fulnry's pale eyes moved from face to face before he spoke. "I'm concerned about the health situation in the Valley," he said pleasantly. His broad smile seemed to contradict that concern.

"Screet," Calta said without emphasis. "Is Pakovich about to resurrect that old silliness about compulsory health and sanitary inspections in the Valley?"

"Pakovich is on Aravia," Fulnry said. "I'm taking advantage of his absence to do something that should have been done years ago. What do Valley residents do when they get sick?"

"They get well again," Calta said. "Or they don't."

"Precisely. And when they do get well, too often they have a long and painful time of it. Not many show up at the Paradise Clinic."

"Not many can afford to. Pakovich prices—"

"Are ridiculous. I know."

The red-headed Yda was leaning forward indignantly. The tension in her small body made Caland think of a fully wound spring about to launch itself. "So what's new?" she asked caustically. "We survive. We manage to get along. How does it happen that you're suddenly concerned about it?"

"Getting along and surviving means that a lot of people get along badly. Why am I concerned? I'm a doctor. My profession exists to help the sick. Everywhere."

"Excuse me while I vomit."

"Everywhere," Fulnry said firmly. "Both the company and the community health facilities have been shorthanded for some time, but now we're going to add new personnel. We just might be able to spare someone for a medical clinic in the Valley. On a part-time basis, of course. We ought to be able to handle serious illnesses and give some attention to the general state of health."

"Pakovich would never stand for it." Calta said.

"He would if no one told him about it." Fulnry flashed a smile. "Let me put it this way. I'm not taking this step without having potent ammunition in reserve. I've had a medical study made, and—as Mort's Medical Director—I'm taking the action recommended in it. Pakovich won't dare to make a fuss about that."

"What sort of medical study?" Calta asked.

"A study concerning Mort's vulnerability to epidemics. If one ever started here in the Valley without medical resources at hand to nip it quickly, it'd spread to the tourist hotes and Paradise almost at once."

"How did you ever figure that out?" Yda asked.

Fulnry's smile did not waver. "The planet would have to be quarantined, and that would cost Pakovich plenty. We're all crowded together in a small area, and Pakovich's attitude in denying medical attention to the Valley is stupid, if not criminal. I consider it my duty to do something about it." He paused. "On the other hand, it'll be much easier for me if we can launch this project without Pakovich finding out about it until we have a fair beginning."

Both Calta and Yda were scowling. It was the Reverend who finally spoke. "What do you have in mind?" he asked politely.

"I'd like to open a clinic here. Two days a week, afternoons and evenings. I think I can manipulate schedules to provide two doctors and a nurse."

"You can't keep a thing like that secret," Yda said. "Contrary to what Pakovich believes, the Valley has no secrets. He'll find out instantly and fire everyone concerned."

"It's none of Pakovich's business what doctors and nurses do on their afternoons off."

"If you say so," Yda said. "But you don't need our permission to open a clinic here."

"Maybe not your permission, but I do need your help. I can arrange for the doctors and the nurse, but that's only the beginning. We'll need decent quarters for the clinic. We'll need a local manager. We'll need some medical assistants—the doctors and the nurse can train them. We'll need someone to keep the place clean. We'll need money for medicines and other supplies. I can't cover everything with paperwork—there are such things as inventories. I can quietly raise some money, but you people will have to help. And the other personnel we need will have to come from here."

"Pakovich will skin you alive," Yda said. "Then he'll fire

you."

"I think I'm covering myself well. He wouldn't dare fire me for properly doing my job as World Medical Director. I'd sue him, and he's very shy about litigation. He's never won one. Before he does anything at all, he'll have to find out about it."

"Don't you know that Pakovich has spies in the Valley all the time?" Calta demanded.

"Yes. I also know the mal in charge of them."

Calta tilted back and uttered a deep, vibrant, throaty laugh. "I can't see that we've got that much to lose. We certainly need a medical clinic. The quarters will be a problem, because decent quarters are hard to find in these dumpy buildings. The personnel—were you planning to pay them?"

"I think we should. The doctors and nurses will volunteer their services, but they already have good salaries. The Valley personnel wouldn't."

"You're telling me. But it's that much more money to be raised."

"Even so, I think they should be paid. I'll figure out a budget for the medicines and supplies and essential equipment, and you figure out a payroll, and then we'll consider how to get the money."

"There's the rent for the building, too. When's this clinic supposed to open?"

"Not instantly. It'll take a bit of arranging."

"On this end it'll take a dratted miracle, but we'll see what we can do. Shall I let you know?"

"Better not," Fulnry said cautiously. "I'll come see you when I have something definite."

"Do that," Calta said.

Fulnry flashed his smile, politely touched hands with everyone, and left.

As the door closed behind him, Calta took a deep breath. "I don't believe a word of it, but it's worth gargling over."

"Beware of the hands of a Pakovich bearing gifts," Yda proclaimed.

"What do you think?" Calta asked the Reverend.

"I think this is something for Bar," the Reverend said. "I'll get him."

Bronlan had been working inside since he lost his spaceship. He'd found a new way to waste time—he was designing an elaborate, electromagnetically controlled cast for Caland's proposed puppet theater. He gave no overt indication of missing the towering monument to his ingenuity that had graced his back yard for so many years, but several times Caland and Tel had seen him seated on the ocean bench late at night watching the swiftly moving light that was Mort's moon named Bronlan.

He arrived minus his eyeshade, which seemed to give his weathered and tanned face a new dimension of complexity. He carried his stiff arm partially extended. Caland surmised that there were times when he was in pain, though he had never been known to complain about it. He listened solemnly while Calta described their conversation with Fulnry.

"What's the problem?" he asked. "We need the clinic."

"Of course we do. No one knows that better than Fulnry. But look here. No doubt Fulnry has all the proper medical credentials, but he's no doctor. He's an administrator. When he comes here prating about being dedicated to helping the sick, it's time to taste your yuck very carefully before you swallow it. He couldn't hold his job for five years without carefully dedicating himself to the Law according to Pakovich. This whole thing may be Pakovich's idea."

"When is Pakovich due back from Aravia?" the Reverend asked.

"I haven't heard it mentioned. It's not like someone being away who's missed."

"There's a strange sequence of events here," Sam the Artist said. "First Cal proposes a community building with a medical clinic. He gets the planning nicely underway and even works a miracle for us on the financing. Then this character Nalce, who certainly is no friend of Pakovich's, starts agitating on the Prom, among other things demanding that Pakovich furnish us with a medical clinic. Immediately afterward, Fulnry shows up with the medical clinic in his pocket. Are any of these things connected?"

Bronlan said slowly, "If Fulnry is only an administrator, that may be what it takes to get a clinic started. If he's really willing to establish one—"

"We'll let him," Calta said. "Of course. We have no choice. We were thinking of the building first and the doctors second, but it's doctors that make the clinic. Any ideas about a place to put it?"

"A couple of shops aren't doing well," the Reverend said. "Maybe we could talk them into merging."

"You do that," Sam the Artist said. "I'm going to try to figure out what Pakovich is after. Yda called it right—beware of the hands of a Pakovich bearing gifts. If we don't watch this carefully, Pakovich's free clinic could end up being awfully expensive."

CHAPTER TWENTY-SIX

Caland's morning headaches increased in severity. The day came when the sharply throbbing pain so immobilized him that he had to lie in bed with eyes closed while Tel applied moist cloths to his head and kept the yuck heated so that a steaming cup could be ready for him the moment he felt able to sit up and drink it. When finally he could walk, he made his way unsteadily to the Prom with Tel's sturdy arm supporting him whenever he faltered, and they finished their break at Nello's. The pain slowly eased, leaving him with a strangely heavy lethargy that persisted for another hour or so.

Then he felt miraculously like himself again. He was Cal, the resourceful promoter who could transform anyone's dreams to reality. Vals with ideas for para acts sought him out at Nello's, and Caland listened to them patiently, encouraged or discouraged them according to each case's merits, and arranged an audition for one Val whose idea seemed especially promising.

But he was an actor, and the Valley image of Cal, the miracle worker, was as much a fraud as the Valley image of Sdissler. Inwardly he felt shattered. He knew, with a numbing certainty, that the return of his headaches could have only one explanation. Someone controlled his mind. For some inexplicable reason Caland had been left unmolested since he first arrived in the Valley. Now his mind was being reclaimed—subtly, in sinister fashion, one touch at a time. He said nothing about this to anyone, not even Tel.

When they left Nello's both of them were curious to see how

Morlef's work was progressing, so they walked toward the site of the new buildings. Along the way they paused frequently to admire Sam the Artist's election posters. Each poster had been individually drawn by a Valley artist. Under the proclamation, "SAM THE ARTIST FOR VALLEY EXEK," a caricature showed that particular artist's conception of Sam—all of them hilarious. Sam the Artist pretended to be outraged. "I don't look like any of them," he protested indignantly. "Imagine—every one of those artists has drawn me with whiskers! It's sacrilege!"

In front of the Road to Hell they encountered the Reverend in conversation with Doctor Stran Gormaz. Caland and Tel had not seen the sociologist since he moved to the Valley, but presumably he now had his headquarters organized and was ready for work.

The Reverend motioned them over for introductions. "Cal and Tel, this is Doctor Gormaz, who's brought sociology to the Valley."

Gormaz's eyes flicked over them without a sign of recognition. He murmured a polite greeting and returned his attention to the Reverend.

"I had no idea," Gormaz said. "I'm shocked. No professional medical care at all?"

"Yda is a professionally trained nurse," the Reverend said. "She helps as much as she can. Really serious cases can be taken to the Paradise Clinic, but they won't be accepted without payment in advance, and there's a steep fee schedule."

"Preposterous! Pakovich has to be experienced to be believed. What pushes that mal?"

"That's a subject for daily speculation in the Valley," the Reverend said with a smile.

"In effect, you've been doctoring yourselves. Isn't that what it amounts to?"

"Exactly."

"For a community this size, that's incredible. I knew the Valley was a sociological phenomenon, but I never expected a twist like that. You must be an extraordinarily healthy people."

"But we're not," the Reverend said. "That's the problem. And now we have this offer, which frankly we don't understand, but even part-time professional health care is an enormous improvement."

Gormaz's attention was still fixed on the sociological implications of a community without professional health care. "I'm surprised that all of you aren't dead. Matters like sanitation—"

"We're able to take care of things like that. A lot of health care and disease prevention is simply applied common sense, and the fact that humans apparently are not susceptible to native microbes helps, but we have enough problems without that."

"Of course you do. What is it that you have to finance?"

"The building and non-professional help," the Reverend said. "Baris Bronlan has generously offered to pay the rent, but we still need money for a manager, a custodian, and medical trainees."

"For two afternoons and evenings a week? Valley wages? That isn't much. Here's what I can do for you. I've taken on the same custodial people Dom was using. Call on them for anything you need, either in getting the clinic building ready or afterward. They'll report their time to me, and I'll include it in their regular wages. When you've hired the other personnel, give Dal Eddyer a list of the names, functions, and wages. He's handling the finances for my Valley Sociological Laboratory. He'll put your medical clinic personnel on my salary list and pay them every sennite. You can work out the details with him."

The Reverend was startled. So were Caland and Tel.

"That's extremely generous of you," the Reverend murmured.

"Not at all. My stake in the good health of this community is at least as important as anyone else's, and I consider it an obligation. Anyway—once these people have been trained, I may have a use for them myself, and it'll simplify things if they're already on my payroll. See Eddyer, and he'll take care of it."

Doctor Gormaz gave them a smile and a bob of his head. He bustled away with tufts of hair flopping.

They stood watching his small, bouncing, energetic figure

until he was lost in the Prom traffic. "I completely misjudged that mal," the Reverend confessed. "In our previous conversations he seemed interested in the Valley only as something to study. I'm relieved to be able to pay the clinic personnel without tapping into our building fund. We're going to put the clinic next to Hef's Place where Gyppy has been trying to run an It shop. He's going partners with Light-Fingered Howard."

The Reverend moved on; Tel turned to Caland and asked, "Would you call that a coincidence, or is it merely fortuitous?"

"I'd call it downright suspicious," Caland said.

Tel studied him for a moment. Then she pulled him into a doorway of the down eatery called Jijn's Poison. Passersby had been looking at them curiously. Such was Caland's status as the Valley's benefactor that everything he and Tel did was a subject of inquisitive scrutiny and gossip. Only pretending to eat could they find a modicum of privacy on the Prom. They picked out a table, and Tel went to the trouble of buying yuck and an O loaf.

"Out with it," she commanded when they had got themselves settled. "Is Doctor Gormaz acting a part, too?"

"I doubt that I could tell a phony sociological act from a real one. It's just that I still think that everything is happening too quickly. Before one thing is settled there's something else to worry about. Things pile up. Time seems to move faster and faster."

Or perhaps Caland's own time was slowing down. The day was still young, but he suddenly felt very tired—not physically, but mentally.

Tel was nodding thoughtfully. "In a properly functioning universe, fate shouldn't dump more than one untoward event on us at a time. You have a kind of magnetism for such events. On the other hand, none of them seem to have the slightest connection with you. Sdissler's plot has been developing for years. As for Gormaz—what could be sinister about a sociological study? Though Gormaz may think we're sinister before he's finished."

"How's that?"

"He searched diligently over a large section of the galaxy

until he found a lovely, compact, stable society. Then he set up here at the precise moment that you started to turn things inside out. These projects of yours already have changed the place and they're going to keep changing it."

"Change is as valid a subject for study as stability."

"Of course. But change has to be compared with something, and Gormaz arrived too late. The old Valley doesn't exist any longer, and the new one hasn't come into being yet. When he figures that out, he won't like it."

"There's a difference between changes the Valley people make for themselves and changes inflicted on them by outsiders—including Gormaz," Caland said.

"You think Gormaz might change the Valley by studying it?"

"Gormaz by studying it, Sdissler by plotting, Doctor Fulnry by doing whatever he's doing, Nalce with his political sabotage—"

"We can't very well order Doctor Gormaz to not study us, and we can't turn down the medical clinic—just as we couldn't turn down the Reverend's para projects. It's silly to worry about changing the Valley. It's been changing for as long as it existed, and it's going to go right on changing—for better or for worse. The most we can hope for is to influence some of the changes toward the better."

"When you start to influence a change," Caland said, "how can you tell which direction is toward the better?"

Morlef led Caland through the overgrown land about the houses at the end of the Prom's business section, pacing off dimensions and asking him questions about theatrical architecture. Tel trailed after them patiently. She made no comment at all until they got back to the Prom. Then she suggested that the community building, on one side of the Prom, and the entrance to the theater building—which would house both the live and the puppet theaters—on the other, should be set back from the street far enough to enlarge the Prom into a wide plaza with a roof and lots of seats.

"The Vals would enjoy it," she said, "and any tourist who

walks here from the Valley gate will be in a mood to sit down."

Morlef had discussed the possibility of purchasing building supplies from Pak Enterprises with several of the supers. The brick and cement works weren't operating and hadn't for some time. Pakovich had no new buildings planned. His underlings doubted that he would start up operations just to produce materials for the Valley. On the other hand, the saw mill had cut lumber for the Valley in the past, and that super knew of no reason why he couldn't do so again. Morlef had talked to Captain Akonif, who was still on the fertilizer run, and the captain was agreeable. Morlef thought there might be a chance of salvaging building stone from the mines' waste heaps for the cost of hauling it away. He was satisfied that there would be no insurmountable problems with materials.

Plans had been drawn up for the community building, and Arlu had promised to find a bright young architect on Aravia who would enjoy taking on the special problem of building a theater for the Valley. The Reverend already was working on an inventory of jobs that would open up when the two theaters were ready for operations: vendors, ticket sellers, ushers, maintenance people, stage hands and technicians, scenery artists, costume designers and makers. He hoped wistfully that a few Vals could be trained for roles as bit players. His gleeful conclusion was that it took a very large payroll to run a theater.

"Your arrival was the best thing that's ever happened to the Valley," Morlef told Caland solemnly.

Caland thought of the worlds of Cenaru, Olyndyt, and Skarlont, and said nothing.

"It really will produce a large payroll," Tel observed afterward. "The Vals will be performing useful work for their money, which will please them. The tourists will get something of value for theirs, which ought to be more satisfying than grudgingly dispensing money to beggars. It'll make the Valley a much more attractive place to visit."

"No argument," Caland said. "But it's going to be a different kind of place, and I have a hunch that a lot of the Vals aren't going to like it."

That night his Prom performance left him too exhausted to eat. Tel dutifully produced ten chits for their usual beach party, but when the food arrived Caland claimed a jug for himself and Tel, and left the feasting to the others. The cider soothed his fatigue somewhat; or perhaps it left him too benumbed to notice it. He was able to listen with interest when the Reverend stopped by with a report on the clinic planning, and when Doctor Gormaz arrived shortly afterward, Caland felt almost in a conversational mood.

The sociologist came wandering along the line of fires like a gaping tourist. "I knew nothing about this, nothing at all," he complained to the Reverend. He seemed astonished at the revelation that sociology went on all night in the Valley. He swept the long row of fires with a bewildered gesture. "Is it like this every night? Amazing! Why, these fires are a regular institution, and the socializing is entirely different from what one observes during the day."

The he noticed Caland, and he plunked himself on the vacant stone beside him without waiting for an invitation. The flagrant social blunder brought scowls from the ring of faces around the fire, but no one said anything. There seemed to be an unspoken awareness that an expert sociologist might be a bit slow in grasping social nuances.

"You're Caland, aren't you?" he asked. "I didn't recognize you on the Prom this morning. Silly of me, but you look so different here, and I don't believe I've seen you since that day we called on Pakovich. I thought you'd left Mort. I've heard so many people talking about Cal, and suddenly I remembered who you are. They tell me you're doing remarkable things here."

"All the remarkable things are still on paper," Caland said with a smile. "Nothing has been done yet."

"But you've raised the money, you have popular support, and you have the plans. Certainly they will be carried out."

"I've been sitting here wondering what will happen if they are. It's a puzzle for a sociologist. This is the real Valley, you know—what you see now along the beach. Most of these people live in the worst kind of crowded, sordid hives. Most of them suffer various kinds of deprivation. Many don't get enough to eat. Here around the night fires none of those things matter. The Valley glows. The people come alive. My question—how much will these remarkable things we're planning change the Valley that you're seeing here?"

"Umph." Gormaz screwed his hairy face into a meditative scowl. "You're concerned that the people and their outlooks or philosophies may change, or that the changing circumstances in which they live may change them, or that an influx of outsiders might dilute Valley attitudes—or perhaps all of these things?"

"Something like that," Caland agreed.

"Umph. The Valley sociology is a sociology of failures. Surely you've noticed that. You're going to introduce the element of success. I've heard about your theater. Even if it isn't very good, it'll be successful. You can expect excellent support from the citizens of Paradise as well as from the tourists. Pakovich frowns on public entertainment the way an old-fashioned moralist denounces the pleasures of the flesh, but that won't keep his employees away. Your theater will be successful, but the people of the Valley—the Vals—will still be failures. Even the actors your theater attracts are likely to be failures. If they weren't, their success would keep them elsewhere. The money your theater brings to the Valley will result in a growth in the population, but that only means that there'll be more failures to support. Many Vals are almost untouched by the tourist trade, and they'll be similarly untouched by the theater. No, I don't think you're going to change the Valley significantly except perhaps to alleviate its harshness somewhat." He got to his feet and clapped Caland on the shoulder. "There is no such thing as a static society. Change is inevitable, and yours is a good change."

He strode away with his odd, bouncy gait.

Caland frowned after him until Tel asked anxiously, "What's wrong?"

"Most scientists see the gloomy side of things. In Gormaz's sociology, everything turns out for the best. Pleasant dreams come true and nightmares go pop when the light touches them. People live happily ever after. But life isn't like that, and I don't believe it."

"I thought what he said made sense. What did you expect him to do? Create some nightmares for you that would turn out to be real?"

Caland laughed. "I think we're neglecting this jug. I also think I'm not going to ask Doctor Gormaz any more questions about sociology. If his sociological laboratory ever gets around to publishing a description of Valley society, I wonder if any of us will recognize it."

Moppy came hurrying along the beach with Phem trailing him. He veered off when he saw Caland and Tel. "There's a stranger," he said. "He's acting like he's sprung. We couldn't find anyone, and we didn't know what to do."

"What kind of stranger?" Caland asked.

"Mal. Tall. Couldn't see much else about him, but he's stumbling around in the bushes swearing."

Tel caught the Reverend's eye. "We'd better have a look," she said.

The three of them followed Moppy. Phem hesitated and then hurried to catch up. As they left the beach, Mucks Groilan joined them, a redoubtable companion for a nighttime foray. When he understood their errand, he strode to the front and marched along the overgrown path as though intent on assaulting every shrub that impeded his progress.

"Where did you see him last?" Tel called to Moppy.

"Wandering around behind the Prom buildings," Moppy said.

"A drunken tourist?" Caland suggested.

"He's drunk all right. He must be. But he doesn't act like a tourist. Anyway, he's sprung."

They emerged in the open space behind the Dolls' House and found it deserted. Their procession turned west. Mucks continued to lead the way with the rest of them stumbling after him and having difficulty in keeping up. They cut through the Valley Transportation Company lot, with its spectral carcasses of long-dead machines, and Mucks suddenly veered to the north. He had seen something.

He happened onto a well-defined path and increased his pace. As they wound their way among Baris Bronlan's mountains of junk, Caland had a bemused impression of being surrounded by strange archeological ruins. The junk piles at night took on a dimly supernatural aspect like that of a lost civilization's enigmatic religious monuments.

"You, there!" Mucks bellowed suddenly.

The Reverend produced a hand light, and its small beam cut through the darkness. They had reached the clearing where Bronlan's spaceship had stood. The cement slab that had supported it was a smooth scar amidst a circle of tall weeds. The path to it that Bronlan had trod for so many years was still bare and moist, a black slash through a rampant growth of weeds that already were beginning to encroach on it.

Standing on the abandoned slab as though poised to take off himself was a menacing figure: Captain Willox. He faced them angrily, cheeks flushed with drink, eyes wild in the Reverend's piercing light.

"Where is it?" he thundered.

Tel choked and buried her laughter in Caland's back. The others, fractionally slower to grasp what had happened, stared only for a moment before they succumbed. They laughed until they gasped for breath. The Reverend tried to keep his light on the captain, but the beam had a palsied quaver.

"This is some filthy trick of Akonif's!" Captain Willox shouted. "I know that damned thing can't fly. Where is it?"

Only Caland was able to answer. "It's in orbit," he said. "Didn't you see it?"

"I saw it, but I don't believe it. I don't believe it. I won't believe it, dammit. Where did it go?"

"Up," Caland said. "The Port Authority needed a satellite for a navigation beacon, so Bronlan lent it to them."

"Sure. But it didn't fly up there by itself. How'd they get it up there?"

"But it did fly," Caland said politely.

"It couldn't have!"

"It's gone, isn't it?"

"That screety Akonif put it there!"

"As a matter of fact, he did," Caland said. "He flew it up there himself."

"I don't believe it! Are you trying to tell me that Bronlan's engine—that the baking soda—"

"Worked perfectly," Caland said. "It was a flawless takeoff. The whole Valley turned out to watch. Pity you weren't here. The only bad thing about it is that the whole place has reeked of baking soda ever since. Can't you smell it?"

They turned away, and so shaken were they by their paroxysms of laughter that they traveled all the way to Bay Unview Boulevard before the Reverend's wavering hand light could pick out a path for them. Behind them Captain Willox charged hither and yon through the layered darkness of Bronlan's back yard, stumbling about in mindless fury while he sniffed and snorted and tried to smell the baking soda.

The others returned to the beach with a tale to tell. Caland and Tel turned toward the apartment and bed. He was experiencing the unmistakable onset of a headache. *Who am I where am I why am I?*

* * * * * *

The building selected for the medical clinic was a long, narrow structure a short distance west of the Valley Transportation Company lot and on the opposite side of the Prom. On its east side, in a gap between the buildings, was Hef's Place, the canvas-roofed home of the gourmet putrebun. On the west was one of the Valley's omnipresent clutter shops, offering almost anything for sale that was cheap and no longer wanted by its previous owner. The clinic's building was as decrepit as most

Valley buildings, but after a thorough cleaning and a few superficial repairs, Doctor Fulnry gave it his resigned approval and chalked out the interior partitions needed to make it functional.

The partitions were fashioned of frames covered with salvage canvas; the Valley could provide nothing better on short notice. While Morlef was erecting them, the clinic's newly hired manager moved about the Valley, conducting advance interviews with prospective patients. The objective was to screen them and make certain that the most deserving cases received priority attention.

The clinic took the Valley by surprise, but the clinic's new manager induced a state of stupefaction. It was Melana, who applied for the post as soon as she heard about it. She was tired of art lessons, she said, and she easily could organize her research to be free on the evenings the clinic was open. Also, she needed the money. These illuminating facts abolished with one stroke all of the mystery that had surrounded her. She quickly made herself an immensely popular figure. She set up her station wherever Vals congregated, and she sweetly and patiently talked with anyone who felt the urge to discuss aches, pains, symptoms, complaints.

"It'd be so much easier with a computer," she told Caland wistfully as she sorted interview cards into a long row of priority piles. "But then—if Gus has been able to keep track of the rentals all these years without one, I ought to be able to process medical appointments by hand."

The day before the clinic opened, she posted appointment sheets and passed out individual appointment cards.

"The girl's a gem," Sam the Artist said as he and Caland and Tel stopped to study the list. "She listens sympathetically and asks questions so professionally that a lot of people who weren't very sick were cured by her interview. She's also organizing some practical health measures that should have been looked after years ago. Some of the old people would have their aches eased if they could enjoy a hot bath now and then, but there are only five buildings in the Valley that have the facilities—the restaurants, the Houses of Fame, and the Road to Hell. Maybe six counting Dom's house, I don't know about that. Melana twisted arms and got permission to set up a schedule for medicinal hot baths at convenient times, and she's onto Fulnry to supply the minerals for the bath water."

"Fulnry behaving himself?" Tel asked.

"Perfectly. Yda says too perfectly. She expected him to tear through the Valley trying to condemn everyone and everything as unsanitary, but thus far he's restrained himself."

Sam wandered off, and Tel and Caland bought putrebuns and yuck from Hef and then crossed to the benches by the Valley Transportation Company fence to eat them. They sat looking across the Prom at Hef's gaudy sign—"Hef's Place, the Valley's Most Putrid Putrebun," and the shabby building next door where the unadvertised clinic would open the next afternoon. Sam had reported that Pakovich was still on Aravia, and Fulnry really was establishing the clinic surreptitiously. Several spy reports had confirmed that no one around Paradise Government Mall knew anything about it. Caland was curious about Valley spies in Paradise, and Sam asked why not, and remarked that they were a lot more efficient than the idiots that Pakovich sent over to the Valley.

The Reverend stopped to talk to them. "Everything looks to be in order," he said. "At the same time, Yda thinks it'd be wise to keep an eye on the place when it opens."

"What could happen?" Caland said.

"No one has the faintest idea, but anything or anyone connected with Pak Enterprises has to be suspect. Melana and the others will keep a sharp watch inside, and I promised to organize an outside watch."

"To watch what?" Tel asked. "The door?"

"Front and back," the Reverend said good-naturedly. "Louie Laggie's arranging a watch for the back. I'm setting up shifts for the front."

Tel turned inquiringly to Caland.

"I don't mind as long as I can sit and watch it," he said. "The

Prom is always interesting."

When they took up their position the following afternoon—relieving the Reverend, who cheerfully waved to them and strolled away—the errand made no sense at all. The windowless opening in the front of the building had been screened above the eye level with canvas. The door also was covered. There were side windows under the canvas roof of Hef's Place, but these weren't visible from the Prom. Tourists ignored the building except for a large poster at one end that showed Sam the Artist, as Valley Exek, sweeping up Pakovich. Passing Vals sent curious glances at the new clinic but did not linger.

Caland and Tel bought putrebuns and yuck from Hef and stood near the entrance sipping and munching. Nothing happened except that patients emerged at regular intervals, some carefully carrying their packets of medicine, and patients with appointments arrived with clockwork precision. All of them had been warned about punctuality.

Caland privately thought that Yda's mind was stretched, if not actually sprung, where the works of Pakovich were concerned; but there were far worse chores than being condemned to watch the Prom for a couple of hours on a lovely afternoon. Since there was nothing at all to see in or about the medical clinic, he directed his attention where the action was—at Hef's place.

Hef, perspiring over the open charcoal pit behind the boxes that formed his service counter, was not visible from the street. All that could be seen were the backs of waiting customers and the fronts of customers who emerged in a regular procession, a couple of meters apart, with putrebun in one hand and mug of yuck in the other. These latter invariably paused before stepping onto the Prom, took a tentative nibble at the putrebun, and breathed deeply, savoring the inimitable flavor. Then came a sip of the yuck before they moved slowly away in search of a place to eat in uninterrupted comfort. The only exception was the rare tourist whose curiosity drew him into the crush of waiting Vals. Tourists regarded their putrebuns with an intense, puzzled skepticism until they finally nerved themselves to take a bite.

Hef's business had expanded far beyond the maximum capacity afforded by the narrow gap he occupied, but he resolutely refused to move. Since he was unwilling to accommodate his customers, the customers accommodated him. There was no mealtime crush at Hef's. There was a crush all day and a steady stream of candlelight business until after midnight, after which Hef was up most of the night preparing food for the next day.

Hef paid little attention to anything going on in the Valley that he could not observe through the narrow gap where his eatery opened on the Prom. He lived directly behind it in a small tent. He used the sanctum and the water tap in the handicrafts shop located on the side opposite the medical clinic, and he indulged in fragmentary conversation only with those delivering supplies. His one indulgence was a helper who came in before the day's rush of business began and assisted with the cleaning. Each morning they scrubbed down the eatery's walls, which were the exterior walls of the buildings on either side, and swabbed them with disinfectant. Then they swept the ground, sprinkled it with disinfectant, and turned the surface over with a rake before they tamped it down. It was said, in all seriousness, that Hef kept the cleanest dirt floor on Mort.

Close proximity with Hef's Place inevitably made one hungry. After an hour of watching, Caland said to Tel, "Putrebun?"

She nodded. "If this were an all-day job, I'd gain weight."

They took their places in line.

They had almost reached the counter when Sippy, in a traditional blue nurse's costume, suddenly appeared behind Hef. Hef did not notice her until a customer called her to his attention. The job with Morlef hadn't worked out for Sippy—she proved to have even less affinity for mathematics than Phem had—but she made an enthusiastic medical student.

She carried a large tray. "Eight putrebuns and eight yucks," she said. Hef frowned. The request for service from the wrong end of his eatery upset his routine, but he mechanically prepared the putrebuns and filled eight mugs of yuck. As he placed the last of these on her tray and accepted eight chits in payment, he eyed Sippy disapprovingly. "What are you?"

"I'm working in the clinic," Sippy said.

"What clinic?"

"The new med clinic. Next door." She jerked her head.

"Med clinic?" Hef echoed perplexedly.

"Didn't you hear them getting the building ready for it? We just opened today, but if you have any aches and pains, save them. We'll be working until midnight to handle what's already scheduled."

Expertly balancing the tray, she walked away and vanished around the rear corner of the building.

Hef looked up at the small open window just above his head. "I've been hearing funny noises," he said. "Is that what it was?"

"They cleaned the place and put up partitions," Tel told him.

"They were noisy about it. The Valley needs a med clinic, doesn't it?"

"Needs one badly," Tel said.

"Next time I'll give them free food."

Tel smiled. "But they're getting paid. Why shouldn't you?"

They bought putrebuns and yuck, and left Hef perplexedly pondering the ethical dilemma of rewards for people who already enjoyed the reward of wages.

They drifted diagonally across the Prom and seated themselves on a Valley Transportation Company bench. They could glimpse the clinic door only intermittently, through the moving crowd, but since nothing was happening, this seemed more than adequate. They talked and watched the crowd, and time passed. Sam the Artist was due to relieve them, and they were looking about for him when a flurry of excitement in front of Hef's Place caught their attention. They hurried to investigate.

Kren Krent, Bronlan's former helper, lay on the ground retching. His recently purchased putrebun was still clutched in his hand, but the mug of yuck had dropped and shattered. His face was turning a startlingly vivid shade of blue.

Someone asked, "What's wrong with Kren? Too much jug?"

Tel commandeered some Val passerby. "Get him in there,"

she said, pointing at the clinic door. "Quickly."

Krent's body was jerking with spasms, and the mal who picked him up seemed reluctant to touch him. Before they could hurry him away, two more people collapsed. Each one of them clutched a putrebun from which one bite had been taken. They lay on the rough Prom pavement like piles of discarded rags.

Suddenly people were collapsing all around them. "Screet!" Tel exclaimed. "Stop Hef! It must be his food!"

Caland forced his way through the waiting customers shouting, "Hef! Hold it!"

Eventually Hef stopped scooping putrebun fill and looked up at Caland in bleary confusion. The mechanically repeated motions of serving putrebuns and yuck and collecting money had mesmerized him, and for a long moment he was unable to comprehend what Caland was saying.

"People are getting sick," Caland said again. He pointed at the large iron kettle from which Hef had been filling the putrebuns. "How long have you been using that?"

"It's a new batch," Hef said protesting. "I just started it."

"How about the yuck? You'll have to stop selling food until we can find out what's going on."

"But it's good food!" Hef protested. "There's nothing wrong." He filled a putrebun with one deft motion, and, before Caland could protest, he took a bite and began to chew solemnly. The next instant Caland had to dive over the counter to keep Hef from collapsing into his cooking pit.

Tel was at his side immediately, and the waiting customers pressed forward to help. They sent Hef to the clinic by way of the rear door, and they turned to the indescribable confusion behind them. Tel already had ordered the most recent customers not to eat or drink, and she had recruited help to collect the food. Now there was a growing row of uneaten putrebuns at one end of the counter along with a row of mugs of yuck; at the other end, examples were accumulating of putrebuns with one bite removed. These had survived intact when their owners collapsed; the mugs of yuck were less fortunate. Most shattered.

Only one had been salvaged unspilled, but there were several more that contained dregs.

Calta Draning hurried up with Yda only a pace behind her. Tel explained tersely, and Yda, the former professional nurse, went at once to the clinic to see how the emergency was being handled. Calta halted a passerby and sent an urgent message, and Alz Hernl appeared a short time later followed by one of his cooks carrying a large tray laden with containers.

They worked as a group packaging and labeling all of the accumulated specimens along with samples taken from the kettle of putrebun filling and the kettle of yuck.

"Refrigerate them at once," Calta told Alz. "They'll have to be sent to Aravia for analysis. We can't trust Pakovich's lab."

Yda returned from her brief visit to the clinic.

"Are you thinking what I'm thinking?" Calta asked her.

"I'm thinking what I know," Yda said. "That was no kind of food poisoning that I've ever encountered. I've never seen symptoms like that. Doctor Fulnry is lost without his computer. Probably everyone will die."

Tel arched her eyebrows. "Doctor Fulnry is there?"

"Been there all afternoon helping to get the clinic started," Yda said. "Now he's confidently injecting what he says is the indicated antibac. Those people don't need an antibac—they need an antidote. Only a chemical poison causes symptoms like that. Let's exempt Fulnry."

"What I'm thinking is this," Calta said. "Hef is a professional. Some of the people selling food in the Valley are rank amateurs. Conceivably one of them could get careless or ignore what he's told about sanitation, but Hef is educated and experienced. He's also fanatically conscientious. So I don't believe it."

"Neither do I," Yda said.

"Neither do I," Tel said. "I don't believe that the first incidence of food poisoning the Valley has had in all of the years I've been here would happen right next door to the clinic on the day it opens without there being something more involved than coincidence."

"How are the victims getting along?" Calta asked.

"It's too soon to say," Yda said. "Doctor Fulnry is promising rapid recoveries due entirely to his foresight in bringing in a huge variety of medicines to stock the clinic and his astuteness in diagnosis. He just happened to include a large quantity of that rarely used antibac. That's another coincidence."

"You've overlook the biggest coincidence of all," Tel said. "Hef was simmering his putrebun fill right under a clinic window.

Calta turned quickly and looked up at the window. "So that's the add," she said grimly. "Let's get this setup foted before our esteemed Doctor Fulnry tries to exert his nonexistent authority and dismantle things. Yda—get back in there and make certain that our people observe as much as possible and remember what they've seen. Collect all the specimens you can. It just may be that we've finally got Pakovich right where we want him."

CHAPTER TWENTY-SEVEN

All of the victims of what became known as "Valley Plague" knew that they were dying. They lingered in agony for a day or two, and then, with disconcerting suddenness, they recovered completely. The only aftereffects were weakness and a ravaging hunger.

Doctor Fulnry diligently questioned the victims who were able to talk, and only a couple of hours after the plague struck, was able to trace the illness to Hef's Place. He inspected it while clucking his tongue with indignation with the thought of food being prepared for sale under such conditions.

"We must take action!" he announced.

Whereupon he brought in a labor force from Pak Enterprises, a thing unheard of in all of the Valley's history. Hef's Place was demolished and the rubble hauled away. Kettles and equipment were sterilized and stored at the medical clinic until the owner could arrange for their disposal. Unused food was handed to one of Sdissler's garbage details for precautionary burning. Finally the work force brought in a load of slab rock, paved the little opening where Hef had operated his eatery, and put in a row of benches for tired prominaders. In a flowery speech in which he praised himself fulsomely for the prompt action that saved the lives of the afflicted and stopped in its tracks the spread of a serious contagious illness that could have laid waste to the entire valley, Doctor Fulnry formally presented the tiny park to the Valley citizens. The Reverend accepting it in their behalf, delivered an answering speech of thanks that was one of the shortest on record anywhere.

"Never mind that," Calta said when they met to discuss these developments. "When Hef opens again he'll have a paved floor. How's he taking it?"

"He's disappeared," the Reverend said.

"Screet!" Tel exclaimed. "How could he manage that?"

"He just did it. No one has seen him anywhere. Believe me, I've had the whole Valley looking for him."

"It was such a stupid thing for Pakovich to do," Yda said. "Why victimize an insignificant little fellow like Hef? What's he trying to accomplish?"

"Excuse me." Regelz Arlu said. He had just arrived from Aravia, and he had listened to the entire account of Fulnry's iniquity with drooping eyes and hands folded comfortably across the bulging stomach of his brilliant orange suit. Now he stirred himself and moved the recliner into a sitting position.

"It seems clear that Fulnry premeditated and staged this epidemic," he said. "Once you get reports on the analysis, you'll have him nailed, but you may never find out why he did it. That's likely to be complicated."

"Pakovich—" Calta began.

Arlu shook his head. "Pakovich is still on Aravia. This was done without his knowledge. I'll guarantee it. Pakovich isn't above exercising his rights in a thoroughly petty fashion, but this is different. This is criminal. He'd be shocked if anyone were to suggest that he had a part in it. Even if he had the inclination, he'd be too cowardly to risk such a scandal. His son's future in-laws and all the rest of the Aravian nobility would ostracize him. No, Pakovich isn't responsible. If you can prove your case, he'll stomp hard on Fulnry."

"Nothing can be done anyway until we get the lab reports," Calta said.

"There are plenty of other things to talk about," Arlu said. "Especially Sdissler. Sdissler is real, and he's dangerous. Or— more likely—he's fronting for someone who's dangerous. Sdissler is part of a conspiracy, and Pakovich is virtually sponsoring it himself. If it weren't serious, it'd be hilarious."

"What's Sdissler's background?" Tel asked.

"Before he sold himself to Pakovich, he was part owner of a business enterprise on Aravia called Physcul. Probably still is. It's a semi-military recreational establishment where young people come to enjoy a few terms of vigorous outdoor exercise and recreation. According to its brochure, it's an interworld meeting place for physical culture enthusiasts. It's also an ideal place to recruit young mals with a bent for military training. I have five searchers trying to pick up information from present and past customers of Physcul, but my hunch is that Sdissler picked his recruits with care and they'll be fanatically loyal. In other words, no one will talk."

"But what's it all about?" Calta demanded. "What's he expect to gain? You can't grab a world by piracy these days."

"Mmmm—you can, but you have to give it back. Probably his intention is to grab Mort under circumstances where he won't have to give it back. The reason he hasn't moved is because the circumstances haven't been quite right. So he's waiting. With plenty of financial backing and a prize this large, he can afford to wait. My guess is that he's been training an army here for years, maybe gradually enlarging it as Pakovich approves more labor camps. He recruits young mals for a set period—say a couple of years; he gives them first-rate military training and lots of the outdoor living and exercise they crave; and he treats them well and pays them comparatively well. It's an ideal situation for young mals who want to play soldier, and all that Sdissler asks in return is a little work on the garbage details when he's shorthanded—say once a year or so, and Sdissler can give that duty a military slant by using it to familiarize his soldiers with all of the Pak Enterprises and with Paradise and the Valley. Not only does Sdissler have an army perpetually in training here, but he has a reserve army scattered about neighboring worlds—an army of former soldiers who have served their time and gone home. He can multiply the size of his present army three or four or five times just by chartering a few spaceships."

"But obviously the circumstances aren't right yet. There must be some compelling restraint."

"What's to be done?" the Reverend asked.

"The Aravian government will now take whatever action against Physcul that Aravian laws permit—which may be very little. Aravia is alarmed about Mort's tin production, and it doesn't want the sabotage topped off by a war. Unfortunately there's nothing it can do about the army that's already here or about the potential reinforcements on other worlds."

"Pakovich has a few capable supers, and they're highly concerned," Calta said. "They've already taken Sdissler's freight platforms away from him, and they'll watch him carefully from now on."

"For whatever that may be worth," Arlu said. "Sdissler has the financial backing to smuggle in all the transport he needs. But he's probably already done it. There's no kind of customs check on materials marked for his labor camps, and he's been able to bring in disassembled platforms or military equipment or anything else he needed. He won't miss Pakovich's platforms. So much for Sdissler. I'm afraid we're going to be hearing a lot more about him, and at the moment I haven't any idea what to do about it. I refuse to go back to Pakovich with information about another conspiracy."

"Let's talk about Doctor Stran Gormaz. I'm pleased to report that Doctor Gormaz is real and I've been able to find no hint of a conspiracy about him. At the time Cal was enjoying the hospitality of the Polyscience Institute, Doctor Gormaz was a faculty member at Planft University, which is half a galaxy away. Doctor Gormaz not only is real, but he's famous—among sociologists. He left the university on an extended leave of absence to study societies, which he has been doing. Until he got to Mort, he was methodically moving from world to world making sociological appraisals and looking for a place to locate his sociological laboratory."

"How'd he get to be a millionaire?" Sam the Artist growled. "There can't be that much money in sociology."

"He didn't. He's not. He's the author of a number of successful books, and he has moderate means."

"Moderate means wouldn't buy him the use of Dom's house," Sam the Artist persisted. "Moderate means wouldn't donate money for the clinic payroll."

"The success of his sociological research depends on the Vals' good will, and he probably thinks a donation or two would be a good investment. As for Dom's house—if Dom is a fellow sociologist, why not? Gormaz's 'moderate means' will certainly go a lot further in the Valley than it would anywhere else, and if he wants to blow all of it on sociological research, that's his affair. Some mals blow their moderate means at the Dolls' House or at Yda's. Who's to say they receive more plea-sure from their money than Gormaz does from his sociology? Do you have personal suspicions about Gormaz?"

"Not at all," Sam the Artist said. "I like the mal. He adds the one touch of preposterousness that the Valley has always needed."

"I'd like to comment on the pleasure mals receive for their moderate means," Calta said.

Arlu heaved a sigh. "Some other time. Next we have the saga of Alexander the Second and the charming Melana, and Deity be praised that no further comment is required. The same can be said for Nalce. We know Nalce, now. We know some of his colleagues. The Pak Enterprises people would like to grab him the next time he sets foot outside the Valley and throw him off the planet, but they'd also like to make certain that they've iden-tified all of his co-conspirators, so they're waiting. Are there any other odds and ends that I should touch on?"

"Weflan Krann has returned to Mort," Tel said.

"At least this time he didn't arrive on the same ship Cal did," Arlu drawled.

"There's something you should know about Krann," Tel said. She described the surreptitious meetings with Sdissler.

Arlu pursed his lips thoughtfully and tapped his index fingers together. "I don't remember much about Krann. Is he wealthy?"

"He gives every indication of being extremely wealthy," Tel said.

"You're suggesting that he's one of Sdissler's financial backers?"

"I'm proclaiming it."

Arlu heaved a sigh. "I'll search him." He sank back into his chair. "It's interesting. It may be extremely important, but I point out that as far as Cal is concerned the sum total of all of this is zero, because we haven't succeeded in linking him to any of these things. Not with Sdissler, not with Gormaz, not with Nalce, despite Nalce's interest in Cal, not with Doctor Fulnry's medical manipulations, not with anything at all. So I'd like to talk about the one thing we know is connected with Cal, the Polyscience Institute."

He heaved another and much deeper sigh. "In veriest fact this has been a convoluted search. I've succeeded in locating some former patients of the Institute, and my searchers have gleaned everything available from and about them, which turns out to be very little. It amounts to an impressive set of testimonials and one peculiar fact. To consider the testimonials first, we know that treatment at the institute is incredibly expensive, but we failed to find a former patient who didn't think it was worth it."

"I certainly got my money's worth," Caland said.

"Mmmm—yes. You were dead and the Institute revived you. Most of the geriatric patients were pretty far gone, if not actually dying, and the Institute revived them, too. I still haven't been able to discover that it ever lost a patient."

"Sounds commendable," Sam the Artist said.

"Mmmm—yes. But if that's the case, why does the Institute have its own crematorium? And an usually large one, too. It serves the entire principality, but why is it located there? The whole setup is exceedingly strange. The former patients have little to say about their treatment except to praise the results ecstatically, but conversations with friends and relatives turned up that peculiar fact I mentioned. All of the patients suffered a loss of memory after their treatment. All of them."

"Do their memories come and go the way Cal's does?" Tel wanted to know.

"The information isn't that detailed. I simply know that every patient we searched had memory problems after returning home. How that's to be interpreted is beyond me. It's entirely possible that some medicine in common use at the Institute has an effect on memory. If I could only figure out how the world of Mort comes into this—"

"Does it?" Tel asked.

"It must," Arlu said. His row of chins had a mournful droop. "It must, and I can't see how. Unrelated things like Sdissler and Gormaz and this food poisoning clutter up the search. I'll keep trying. Sooner or later I'll shake it loose."

He absently patted Caland on the shoulder and shuffled away.

"Screet!" Tel muttered.

"What's the matter?" Caland asked anxiously.

"I feel like one of Hef's putrebuns. Whether Pakovich is responsible or not, he has a lot to answer for. Where do you suppose Hef could be?"

There were rumors that he had been seen about the Valley after dark, an ungainly shadow that hung from the shrubbery along the beach to watch the fireside feast or that peered into the windows of the Fig Stump or the Burned Wafer. Caland found this almost credible because Hef always had liked to watch people eating. No one knew where he slept or what, if anything, he was eating himself.

It was Sam the Artist who found him. Sam came to one of Bronlan's dins marching Hef in front of him like a proctor escorting a prisoner.

"Plucked him out of the trash heap," Sam the Artist said cheerfully. "He was sleeping there. I don't believe he's eaten anything since he stopped cooking. I think I've convinced him that the plague wasn't his fault, and he needs nourishment. Got enough for one more?"

Bronlan grinned and nodded.

The meat was sizzling on the grill; the other guests were

gathered around expectantly: Caland and Tel; Moppy and Phem; Mucks Groilan; Thalm, the retired doll; a wizened little mal named Orlqwin Lincoz, who had a wife and three children and eked out a marginal existence by passing out leaflets to tourists for various Valley enterprises. Caland had watched Lincoz work: he had the deftness of a slight-of-hand magician. He placed the leaflet in the tourist's hand so swiftly that it seemed to materialize there. No tourist ever refused a leaflet presented by Lincoz; few of them detected where it came from.

Hef had lost weight, and his unhealthy pallor, acquired from the killing work schedule that kept him always under the shelter of his eatery, had been deepened by his bout with the Valley plague.

"When are you going to reopen?" Mucks Groilan asked him.

Hef shook his head.

"Why should he reopen?" Moppy asked. "He can sue Pakovich for enough money to last forever."

"He should reopen because he's a good cook," Mucks said. "The Valley has a lot of eateries, but Hef's Place was the only one with a cook." He appealed to Bronlan. "Where will the universe be if good cooks refuse to cook?"

Bronlan grinned but did not answer.

"The question isn't how well Hef cooks but how well he likes to cook," Sam the Artist said. "What if he hates it? Do we have the right to condemn him to spend the rest of his life doing something he hates merely because he does it well?"

"How could he cook well if he hates it?" Mucks wanted to know. "I now and then do a turn working on Sdissler's garbage detail when I need the money. I give Sdissler his money's worth, but no one would ever accuse me of doing the work well."

The food was ready; the chunks of bread were passed around. Hef accepted a piece, and Sam the Artist carefully selected pieces of meat for him and placed them on the bread, but Hef sat holding it and not eating it. Eventually Tel persuaded him to take a tentative mouthful, and he began to chew slowly.

Mucks and Sam the Artist continued their discussion about

work. "Could Bar have built a beautiful spaceship if he hadn't liked working on it?" Mucks asked. "Could Hef have built a beautiful putrebun if he hadn't liked doing it?"

"That doesn't count," Sam the Artist said. "For Hef, running the eatery was hard work for not much money. Building a spaceship was just a way to waste time for Bar. No one wastes time on something he doesn't enjoy doing. Maybe that's the answer. Let's dispense with work and let everyone waste time. If a job has to be done and no one wants to waste time doing it, change the job. Did you notice that Bar always had a volunteer helper when he was working on his ship? There was something about the beauty of it, or the idea of helping to build something that could fly to another world, or the sheer pleasure of seeing something like that take shape, that attracted volunteers. Bar never had to fetch a tool that he dropped. There was always someone there to hand it to him."

"What about this theater?" Mucks asked Caland. "People say it'll be the biggest employer in the Valley, and there'll be dozens of jobs. What will you do if no one wants to work on them?"

"Theaters are fascinating places," Caland said. "Most people would find them even more fun than building spaceships. There'll be far more applicants than there are jobs."

"Right," Sam the Artist said. "I'll be willing to take a job there myself. I wouldn't especially enjoy hauling cables around and fussing with electrical connections, or moving scenery, or any of the other sweat work, but I've loved the theater all of my life, and I'd do any of those things just to see the plays. Sometimes it isn't the job that's important, it's the extra things that come with the job. If Hef hates to cook, maybe he enjoys watching the people eat."

"That's true," Mucks said. "Ask Thalm. She never enjoyed her work at the Dolls' House—"

Thalm crackled.

"—but she loved all the extra things that came with the job. Food from the Fig Stump, pretty clothes—"

Thalm cackled again. She had lost her few remaining teeth

since Caland had first met her. Now she was mouthing bread and meat with toothless gums, but she showed no embarrassment at suddenly becoming the center of attention.

"You talk," she told Mucks. "But you don't know."

"Don't know what?" Mucks demanded.

"Anything. Ask someone who knows."

"It's a philosophical discussion," Sam the Artist said. "Perhaps we should ask the Reverend."

"No." Thalm shook her head emphatically. "The Reverend *thinks*. And you—" She turned scornfully to Sam the Artist. "You *talk*. But Bar *feels*. So Bar *knows*."

Baris Bronlan, thus eulogized, grinned, offered seconds on meat or tubers, and said nothing at all.

"Bar *knows*," Sam the Artist said, "but most of the time he keeps it to himself."

* * * * * * *

Valley time flowed again, but Caland felt himself less and less a part of it. The increasing severity of his headaches kept him late in bed in the morning with Tel fussing over him concernedly and sometimes sending someone to Olgi's for ice. He felt exhausted when the headaches finally subsided, and usually it was late morning or even after the klaxon when they finally reached the Prom. They enjoyed a leisurely din, after which they wandered from one eatery to another holding interminable discussions over yuck and poking fun at the day's crop of tourists. Nalce provided an occasional ripple with another political speech, but Sam the Artist's campaign posters seemed to have unnerved him. He had not yet got around to announcing his own candidacy.

Caland and Tel were walking leisurely toward the Valley gate when Caland caught a glimpse of a mixed group of tourists headed in the opposite direction. He wheeled immediately and followed them. Tel, left momentarily by herself, had to scramble to overtake him."

She grabbed his arm. "What is it?"

"That's her!"

"Who? Which one?"

"The one that isn't dressed like a tourist," Caland said.

He had recognized her instantly. It was the same severely dressed, business-like fem who had almost approached him in the Paradise View Hostelry's lounge, and who figured prominently in a dimly-remembered nightmare.

"Old memory or new?" Tel wanted to know.

Caland explained while they dodged Prom traffic and kept pace with the group of tourists.

"We'll need help," Tel said. "We'll have to have someone ready to follow her when she leaves the Valley."

She sent passing Vals to look for Louie and Sam the Artist; before either of them appeared, the tourists turned into the Burned Wafer.

"Now we can relax," Tel said. "They'll be there for a couple of hours. We'll have time to organize this properly and also to alert Arlu so he can have someone ready at the hotes."

Tel and Caland found a table in a crowded little down eatery—called the Bent Tooth—from which they could watch the Burned Wafer's entrance. Hairy was dispatched to summon reinforcements. Louie Laggie and two of his watchers joined them, and Sam and the Reverend arrived a short time later. One at a time Tel sent the others across to the Burned Wafer to have a good look at Caland's mystery fem. They had no problem identifying her. No other customer in the place could be called "severely dressed and business-like."

Finally she went herself. "No one at the Burned Wafer knows who she is," she told them when she returned. "Arlu's not available. There's nothing to do but wait and watch, I suppose."

They did both while the rich panorama of Prom traffic flowed past them. An occasional electrocab discharged passengers at the restaurants or the Houses of Fame and moved on to the Valley Transportation Company lot to turn around. Groups of tourists move back and forth, coming and going. Time passed.

Sam the Artist suddenly leaped to his feet and snapped his fingers. "I'll get a camera," he said. "I'll do the fote act—pretend I'm foting all the diners. If I can get a good fote of her, we'll soon find out who she is."

"Good belated thinking," Tel told him. "And," she added, as he strode away, "he's even moving relatively fast—for Sam."

He was back a short time later. He waved to them from the Prom and marched directly to the Burned Wafer entrance. He reappeared almost at once and recrossed the Prom to lean in at the Bent Tooth's open window.

"She's gone," he announced.

"Impossible," Tel said.

"Go look for yourself."

"Get back there. She just went to the sanctum."

Sam the Artist shrugged and returned to the Burned Wafer. This time he was inside for some minutes before he emerged. He shook his head at them. Tel motioned him to return.

It took another hour to find out what had happened. The mystery fem had interrupted her din to visit the private telation cabinet, where she either sent or received a message. She returned to her table but did not sit down. She spoke briefly to the tourists who had accompanied her, and then she left the restaurant. Traffic probably obscured the door at the moment she emerged. She turned west, walking away from the Bent Tooth instead of toward it as she normally would have done on leaving the Valley. She went directly to the Valley Transportation Company lot and told Gary Dwand that she needed a 'cab immediately. None was available at that moment, but Gary saw an off-duty driver walking past and hailed him. They put a 'cab in service, and the mystery fem was driven to the space port. She handed the driver a hefty grat and disappeared into the terminal building.

They were still discussing the matter around their table at the Bent Tooth when Regelz Arlu arrived. He descended from his 'cab in front of the Burned Wafer, sent it on its way, and stood looking about him.

They went outside to meet him. Because there was no down

eatery in the Valley whose tables were spaced far enough apart to admit Arlu's bulk, he took them to the Fig Stump, ordered yuck and freshly baked blobs, which were balls of dough stuffed with fruit, and sat back patiently. "Tell it," he ordered.

He made no comment at all until they had finished. Then he said wryly, "This is the first time I've ever had a subject slip past seven watchers by walking out the front door right under their noses. The lesson is this: when there are seven of you to watch, you don't all gather in the same place for yuck and conversation. One east, one west, one by the doors—or both the Burned Wafer and Yda's, there's an inside connection, you know—one in the rear and a couple of floaters. However, it happened. You didn't see her go out the door and head west, and I suppose you never thought to look at the passengers in any 'cab that didn't stop at the Burned Wafer. Never mind. If she's really interested in Cal, we'll see her again."

"You don't sound very interested in her," Tel said reproachfully.

"If she presents herself to me, I'll be glad to talk to her. I'm not interested enough to spend time searching for her. Look." He squirmed around to face Tel. "Either in a dream or a nightmare, Cal saw a fem who looked like this one. That may or may not mean that he has a memory of her. Later, at the hote, this fem—or another who looked like her—started across the room toward Cal and then seemed to shy off when Fem Wobbons intruded. She could have been walking toward a friend who happened to be standing behind Cal. Today she visited the Valley with a group of tourists, and for some reason she left suddenly. Her departure couldn't have had anything to do with Cal. As far as we know, she never saw him. There's nothing about her behavior in any of these instances to indicate that she has any interest in Cal." He turned to Caland. "What makes you suspicious of her?"

"It was the way she acted—the way she looked at me."

Arlu threw up his hands. "If you want to complain about a strange fem flirting with you, that's Tel's department."

"*Not* flirting," Caland said firmly.

"Never mind. If she's weaving a plot, she'll be back."

Tel said angrily, "The idea is to find out who she is and what her motives are so we can anticipate her plot. You'd prefer to assume that she's innocent until she blows something up."

"No." Arlu was brusque. "I assume nothing. I look for facts. We have enough serious problems without trying to construct one where none exists." He got to his feet. "Next time don't put all the watchers in the same place."

He left.

Sam the Artist said broodingly, "We should have hauled her off somewhere and applied the torture treatment until she confessed."

"What sort of torture?" Caland wanted to know.

"Make her drink yuck all day. To a tourist that would be the ultimate torment."

"She may not be a tourist," the Reverend said. "What do you think, Tel?"

"I think Arlu is right," Tel said. "We shouldn't have put all the watchers in the same place."

CHAPTER TWENTY-EIGHT

Valley time flowed, but Caland's personal time ran more and more slowly. He still was aware of a quickening of events about him, like a river's current slowly but steadily gathering speed for an ultimate plunge into an abyss, but the current no longer was carrying him with it. His headaches continued to devastate him for much of the morning, and he would emerge, weak and distracted, to face without appetite whatever din was placed before him.

Nalce finally responded to the challenge of Sam the Artist's election posters. He called for an election to choose a Valley exek, announced his own candidacy, and resoundingly vilified his opponent. Sam the Artist resignedly let it be known that the next time Nalce delivered a speech, he would be on hand to answer him.

The entire Valley turned out to listen. When Caland and Tel started up the Prom, they could get no further than Nello's without a struggle, and the Reverend reported that the Prom was jammed solidly between the restaurants and the Houses of Fame. Bewildered tourists stood in a group around the Valley gate and wondered what was happening and whether they should brave the crush.

But Sam the Artist did not appear.

Nalce now had a force of election workers made up entirely of the six "for the Valley" whom Caland remembered from his journey to Mort. Two of them, mal and fem, actually had been living in the Valley. The other four had recently moved there.

They had adopted less conspicuous dress and divested themselves of their excess hair, and they moved about in the crowd pretending to be long-term residents and trying to generate cheers or hoots of derision where appropriate.

Nalce, blond hair flying as he flaunted his indignation, soundly bereted the cowardly, non-appearing Sam and his associates as stooges of the Pakovich. "Who but paid vermin would oppose my demand that Pakovich honor his commitments, face up to his responsibilities, contribute his fair share, meet his obligations, and conduct himself honorably in his relations with the Valley?" Nalce demanded. His voice carried clearly to Caland and Tel over a hushed crowd, but only the taller Reverend could see the gyrating top of Nalce's head.

Except for his own followers, the crowd remained quiet. Nalce's most emphatic and vituperative points dropped into silence ruffled only by the yipping of the six "for the Valley." This prolonged stillness around him was actually one of hushed expectation. The crowd was waiting for Sam the Artist.

Sam appeared with dramatic suddenness on a lower balcony of the Dolls' House, and the cheer that went up drowned out Nalce's futile ranting. Sam signaled for silence and generously allowed Nalce to complete one more insult before he made his own announcement.

"Friends, these uncouth outsiders need to be taught manners," his voice boomed. "Our fellow citizens, the shopkeepers, are trying to earn an honest chit, and this uncivil blocking of the Prom interferes with business. Let's move our politics down to the park where it won't keep the tourists from spending money."

The crowd moved off the moment Sam disappeared, and Nalce was left standing in the center of the Prom shouting futile insults. Morlef had put up a makeshift platform in the park midway between the Prom and the bay, and the crowd reassembled there.

Sam mounted the platform confidently. "My speech will be brief," he announced. The crowd cheered. "After which my opponent can get up here and talk all afternoon if he likes. All

I ask is that I don't have to listen. I'm sure you feel the way I do about outsiders who have lived in the Valley for a few days or a few sennites and think that gives them the right to run it for us. I resent it." He paused until the cheers faded. "Nalce is advocating a lot of changes. I want to talk to you about changes."

He described the Reverend's Valley Enterprises Fund and the benefits it already was conferring on the Valley. Valley gossip had circulated such information vaguely, but Sam was dealing with facts and figures. He described Partley hrv' Dasshlam's contribution. "Note that our friend Cal has bestowed this enormous gift upon us without any thought of return for himself. He gives; he works hard for all of us; he takes nothing back. He is not a candidate for anything. He has made it possible to do for ourselves all the things that Nalce is demanding that Pakovich do for us."

"If Pakovich ever brings a generous hand to the Valley, he'll also put his foot in the door, and that foot will cost us. What Cal has given us is ours. Nalce wants change and reform; but the Valley is a wonderful place to live just the way it is. We don't need reforms. We don't need a government. We need a few simple improvements, and we're getting them: community building and school, some essential services, and the theater to bring money into the Valley and make more jobs possible. We want no changes except those we decide to make for ourselves. Our first problem is to protect and preserve the Valley the way we want it."

"If we let Pakovich in, we'll lose, not gain. If Nalce had been paying any attention to what goes on here, he'd know that. We recently had a demonstration. When Nalce started this nonsense, he was demanding that Pakovich give us a medical clinic. Since then Pakovich has done so, and you saw what happened. Half the Valley got sick. We want to take over the clinic for ourselves as soon as we can and get Pakovich out."

"I'm in favor of things that will improve our lives without changing them. We don't want the Valley remade into another town of Paradise, with Pakovich watching us with binoculars to make certain we don't misbehave and issuing orders that will tell us how to live. As your exek I promise that I'll never interfere with your lives, and I'll make damned certain that Pakovich doesn't either."

The crowd cheered.

"Now go ask Nalce why he knows so little about what's going on in the Valley, and why he's suddenly advocating that we beg Pakovich for all of these things that we're already doing for ourselves."

As Sam the Artist withdrew, Vals were already crowding around Nalce and shouting hostile questions.

"A good speech," Tel told Sam the Artist, "but Cal provided all of your ammunition. If Nalce had run his campaign a few terms ago, he could have caused trouble."

"I was thinking the same thing," Sam the Artist said.

"Did you see Doctor Gormaz?" Caland asked. "He was energetically taking notes."

"He energetically takes notes about everything," Sam the Artist said. "He also was energetically taking notes about Nalce's speech."

Sam took leave of them, and Caland and Tel strolled slowly along the Prom. At a small shop offering handmade jewelry, Caland took Tel inside and announced his intention of making her glamorous. He had a hilarious time trying different items on her, but, in the end, she pronounced her determination to remain unadorned.

Caland was determined to take her to the Merc Mart or the jewelry shop at the space port at the first opportunity and buy her something of value. He could not remember ever before wanting to spend money recklessly and lavishly to make a fem happy.

"I won't let you squander the Valley's resources," she said sternly. "Why this sudden urge to see me in jewels?"

"I want to give you something to remember me by."

"I have you to remember you by."

As they threaded their way through the Prom traffic, Caland

stopped once to scrutinize those around him, and several times he looked over his shoulder.

"Back again?" Tel asked finally.

"It seem as though it's never left," Caland said. "But of course it did, so it's back."

"Eyes watching you?"

"Yes."

"All of us searched, you know. Sam and the Reverend and several others spent an entire day following you around and checking. Except for Nalce, there's never been anyone watching you, and he's given it up."

"I only know what I feel," Caland said slowly. "Anyway—on the day they said no one was watching, *they* were watching."

"Screet!" Tel exclaimed. "I never thought of that!"

They encountered the Reverend, who walked along with them and discussed Nalce's latest speech. "He's very good. He's thoroughly professional. If Cal hadn't launched his projects when he did, the Valley just might have acquired an exek named Nalce."

"That's what I think myself," Tel said. "Has anyone figured out what Nalce's game is?"

"It must be some kind of scheme to use the Valley to embarrass Pakovich. He made his plans without paying any attention to what Cal was doing—which was fortunate for us. Otherwise it might have been a close election."

They paused for a time to watch Morlef's crew of mals and fems clearing the site of the future theater. Shrubs were being uprooted, trees felled, and the ground leveled. A machine or two would have saved immense amounts of time and labor, but the cost to import one would have been prohibitive. They had plenty of time and Valley labor was cheap. Pakovich owned every kind of machine, but no one suggested renting one from him.

On the other side of the Prom, another crew of workers was building forms for the pillars and beams that Morlef intended to cast of stress cement. It was an usually warm day, but the perspiring workers kept to their tasks with surprising diligence.

Caland mentioned this to Morlef.

"Sure they're working hard," Morlef said. "I made it clear to them at the start: this is a big project, there'll be jobs here for a long time—but only for those who work. We're paying well by Valley standards, and anyone needing money can sign up for a day's work, or two, or whatever he wants. But if he doesn't work, that day will be his last. I've only had to exempt two, the first day, and the rest got the message."

At the community building site, a maze of strings criss-crossed the area—Morlef's method of squaring a foundation. "It's a way to do it without instruments," he said cheerfully. "It's been used for as long as humans have been building. Sometimes the modern ways, with all the technology, are really crude short-cuts, and the early ways are better."

Caland watched him level one side of the foundation form to the other with a long hose filled with water and believed him.

"We get our first load of cement tomorrow," Morlef said with a note of elation in his voice. "Akonif will drop it off on his way in to the fertilizer factory. He's also bringing the one piece of equipment I'm buying, an acoustic mixer. Then things will start to happen. I'm going to begin by paving the plaza and adding an extension to the Prom. It'll make it easier to work."

Sam the Artist strolled by pursued by waves of congratulations on his campaign speech, and he sat with the Reverend and Morlef and discussed the construction project's greatest problem to date: the disposal of the dirt excavated for footings and foundations. Caland and Tel found seats nearby on one of the toppled tree trunks and listened. Tel had her sculpture board on her lap and a pail of damp sand beside her, and she was fashioning a dirt art model of her vision of the proposed theater. Occasionally she looked up anxiously at Caland.

They were trying to analyze his acute awareness of a pair of eyes watching him. Sometimes the feeling vanished for long periods; sometimes it was with him constantly. He did not have it now, and they were both waiting for it to return.

"Too bad we can't sell the dirt to Pakovich," Sam the Artist said. "He has a natural affinity for it. Why else would he want to own a whole world? Would he accept it as a gift?"

"The world dump buries trash and garbage with dirt," the Reverend said, "but there's plenty of dirt already there from the excavation they made to put the trash and garbage in. I really don't know. The Valley is such a small place when it comes to dumping things. I suppose we could level off the streets with it, but some of it would have to be hand-carried a long way."

"The theater is going to take a lot of excavating," Morlef said. "Bar is going to try to convert one of his 'cabs into a dozer for us. If we don't dig down, then we have to build higher. Unfortunately, we can't wish the stuff away. Hauling it outside the Valley, even if Pakovich will let us, would take a lot of trucks and a lot of work loading and unloading."

"I wonder, now," Sam the Artist mused. "Why can't we wish the stuff away? Who was the scientist who proved levitation was possible? Odan? Or was it Zareent?"

"Odan worked on teleportation," the Reverend said. "Zareent's work was on time travel. I haven't been able to remember who did levitation."

"Someone prove it could be done?"

"Someone developed the mathematics to prove it theoretically possible."

"Can it be done or can't it? All I want to do," Sam went on quickly before the Reverend could speak, "is levitate this excavated dirt as far as Pakovich's mansion and dump it on his garden. Get out your mathematics and let's have a try at it."

The Reverend smiled. "Mathematics doesn't show us how to do those things. It merely indicates that they are possible."

"Then mathematics doesn't prove anything at all. Odan and Zareent and your unnamed scientist are frauds."

"I don't think so," the Reverend said. "They're positives. They worked to show that something could be done. Too many scientists—social scientists, too—work to prove things can't be done. They're negatives. Down through history the negatives have proved conclusively that almost everything is mathematically impossible, economically unfeasible, sociologically impractical, medically unhealthy, ethnically reprehensible, theologically blasphemous, and scientifically irresponsible. Then they sat back and did nothing until a positive braved their scorn and accomplished the impossible, the unfeasible, the impractical, the unhealthy, the reprehensible, the blasphemous, and the irresponsible, upon which time the negatives stepped forward to claim the credit. This is called the march of human progress. The universe needs more positives."

"Sure," Sam the Artist said. "But I'm not interested in the hypocrisy of human thought. I just want to move a little dirt."

They went off with Morlef to see for themselves how high the Prom could be raised at its west end without becoming an obstacle. Caland and Tel remained where they were to enjoy the sun and watch work on the ground-clearing operations.

Doctor Gormaz wandered past with a portfolio under his arm. He saw Caland and Tel and came over to share their tree trunk with them. "The Valley is a confusing place," he announced.

Tel smiled. "That's because it's so simple."

Gormaz pondered that while he fretfully fingered his unruly whiskers. "You may be right. I'm trained to unravel complexities, and unraveling simplicity could actually be impossible." He opened the portfolio and took out a sheaf of papers. "I'm doing a preliminary sociological survey. I never realized that there were so many people here. I may have to bring in more assistants."

"Hire some Valley people," Caland suggested.

Gormaz shook his head. "It requires at least a basic sociological training."

"There are plenty of capable Valley people," Caland said. "They're instantly available, and they have the advantage of knowing their subjects and being familiar with Valley customs. Surely you could train them yourself. The evaluation will be your task no matter who does the survey."

"You may have a point," Gormaz agreed. He made the

concession sound generous. "Valley people rarely have occupations, but they do have some exceedingly strange avocations. What is—" He shuffled papers. "What is a screeter?"

Caland caught a glimpse of Tel's face and choked. He remained silent waiting for her to control her laughter.

"This subject calls himself Slim," Doctor Gormaz went on when neither of them spoke. "This seems strange because he's so excessively fat. He told me quite seriously that he performs labor when he's hungry enough; the remainder of the time he's a screeter. He definitely said that."

"A screeter," Tel said, fighting to control her voice, "is difficult to describe in polite terms. It refers to a person who spends his time contemplating his own digestive functions."

Doctor Gormaz gazed at her perplexedly. "I'm not quite certain that I understand. Could that really be an avocation?"

"It's an excellent way to describe a person who does nothing at all."

"Yes," Gormaz murmured, his voice heavy with uncertainty. "Yes, I suppose it could be that." He paused. "I agree. It might be a good idea to hire an assistant or two from the Valley. Have you any suggestions?"

"We'll find someone for you," Tel promised.

Caland knew that she would discuss the matter at length with the Reverend and Bronlan and a few others. Gormaz would obtain some capable assistants for which he would be grateful; a few Vals would obtain employment; and the Valley espionage system would have reliable observers inside Gormaz's laboratory. If nothing else, this would serve to reassure people. Suspicions as to what Gormaz might be up to were rampant in the Valley, where few people understood what sociology was or cared.

"Calta claims there isn't any such thing as a sociologist," Caland said as he watched Doctor Gormaz bounce away.

"I thought she said there isn't such a thing as an honest sociologist." Tel said. "Though what there could be for a sociologist to cheat about I have no idea. Maybe she meant 'unbiased.' In

Calta's profession sociologists are an occupational hazard."

"I don't even know what there is for a sociologist to be biased about," Caland said.

"There'd have to be something. It isn't an exact science like counting cells or particles." Tel gestured indifferently. "I can't imagine what use a sociological study of the Valley would be to anyone, but if Gormaz hires people and spends money here, then I say let him study as much sociology as he can find."

"I can't imagine how a sociological study could possibly have any connection with me," Caland said. "And that's reassuring. It makes me feel gratifyingly indifferent toward it."

The fat mal called Slim was one of their fire group that night. Caland asked him, "Why have you been making trouble for Doctor Gormaz?"

"Trouble?" Slim said resentfully. "I didn't make him any trouble, but he made me plenty. I thought he'd never stop asking questions."

"You told him your avocation was screeting."

"Maybe I did. I don't know what 'avocation' means, but that seemed like a good answer."

"It is," Caland assured him. "It's an excellent answer."

Much later, when all of their food had been eaten and the last jug was making the rounds, Mucks Groilan strolled purposefully along the line of fires. When he saw Caland he came over and dropped down beside him.

"Got something I want to talk to you about," Mucks said in a low voice. "Been working all day over in Paradise on one of Sdissler's stink details, and I just finished."

Tel, who was seated on the other side of Caland, leaned forward to listen. No one else was paying attention.

"Sdissler needed help in a hurry and offered double rates, so I signed on," Mucks went on. "One of Pakovich's pets was moving. When one of them is promoted, he also gets to move to a bigger house if one is available, and this pet had won himself one of those little mansions Pakovich had built at the foot of the mountains. He asked Sdissler to find him a detail to clean up the new house and move him into it, and we were all day at it. The interesting thing was another Pakovich pet who was moving into the old house—the one our pet was moving out of. He had a few friends helping him. The Paradise people say he hasn't been on Mort long, but he's moving up fast at Pak Enterprises. He goes by the name of Raul Elat."

"I don't think I've ever heard of him," Caland said. "Of course there's no reason why I would. Tel?"

She shook her head; the name meant nothing to her.

"I've never heard that name before, either," Mucks said. "But I do know this vrump, and I thought maybe I'd better talk to someone. The story Paradise people tell is that Raul Elat came to Mort as a tourist. He liked the place, so he applied for a job at Pak Enterprises. He had a pile of references and enough qualifications to make a Pak super's mouth drool, and he was obviously a high-quality mal, so Pakovich hired him. Now he's some kind of a sub-super over at the mines, and everyone thinks highly of him. Especially Pakovich. They say he has a big future with Pak Enterprises."

"Why not?" Caland asked indifferently. "Pakovich certainly needs all the quality people he can get. He has a world to develop."

"That may be," Mucks said grimly, "but he's not going to get much of it developed with this Raul Elat. I'm telling you—I know him. He's no management person no matter what his references say. He's no labor person either. He's a hell raiser for his own profit."

Caland and Tel exchanged glances. Caland let Tel ask the question, "Where did you meet him?" He knew where the conversation was headed, and he was experiencing a shrinking anticipation.

"On Verblanif. I was one of his pals—I thought. That's why I came to Mort. I just got away from Verblanif with my life, and if I ever poke my nose in that atmosphere again, they'll slice it off. That's what Raul Elat did for his pals on Verblanif."

"What was his angle?"

"Cash. That was his angle. He's worked the same thing on a lot of worlds. He stirs up the labor force. You wouldn't believe how he can stir up a labor force. Then he either takes over the management and loots everything he can lay his hands on or he lets the owners buy him off. The moment he folds his pretty fingers around the cash, he pulls out, leaving everyone else holding."

"You were a holder?"

"Right. When the owners and authorities get control again, they're bound to be seething mad about the whole thing and especially about the missing cash. They take it out on the poor boobs Elat leaves behind. I was lucky to get away. Some of my friends did a year, and it wasn't a pleasant year. This Raul Elat may be acting like a fair-haired management stooge right now, but that's just until he gets his claws in. Then the trouble starts. I know all about him."

"Would he be able to work the same thing here?" Tel asked. "Pakovich is an ass, but he's an ass who sometimes tries to do the right thing, and his workers have things pretty good. A lot of them might be loyal to him."

"Look," Mucks said grimly. "This Elat is an expert in making satisfied people dissatisfied and loyal people disloyal. If he walked in here and started talking about the Valley, you'd be ready to move out after ten minutes. He can talk up a revolution or a labor uprising anywhere. That's his business. He works at it all the time. I know that, but I don't know what to do about it or whether anyone in the Valley cares what happens to Pakovich. Maybe this is nothing to us, but it worries me. When Mort blows, and it's going to, the Valley's bound to go up with it. There won't be any tourists using the hotes, and there won't be any electricity. The sewage plant won't be operating. There won't be any deliveries from farms and the meat packing plant and the dairy and the winery, because there won't be anything to deliver. Pakovich is asking for it—has been for years. If the employees want to lop themselves, that's their own lookout. The Vals will suffer the most, and both sides may end up trying to dump on them. It'll be a shame. I like it here."

"We all like it here," Caland said soberly.

"So something ought to be done," Mucks went on. "The Reverend says Pakovich is due back from Aravia tomorrow. Would it be possible to slip the word to him?"

"Slipping the word wouldn't be enough," Tel said. "You'd have to knock him down with it. He has a knack for resenting advice. The better it is, the more he resents it. What did the Reverend think about this?"

"I didn't mention it to him," Mucks said. "The Reverend tries to see good in everyone. His reaction to a vrump like this Elat would be to try and convert him. The Reverend even stands up for Pakovich."

"This really puts the Valley in a squeeze, doesn't it?" Tel mused. "Either we sit tight and let Elat mess up the whole world of Mort, or we try to help Pakovich—and Pakovich will react to our help about the same way he'll react to Elat's labor shenanigans. He'll try to dump on both of us. This is going to take some careful figuring."

"What was Elat calling himself when you knew him on Verblanif?" Caland asked Mucks.

"Todd Gespers."

"All right, Mucks," Tel said. "Thanks for the information. We'll talk it over and see what can be done about it."

"My pleasure," Mucks said. "I hope you can figure out something."

"So!" Tel said softly. "We already know a few things about Raul Elat, don't we?"

Caland nodded glumly. He felt extremely tired. "Prency Tate has arrived on Mort. He seems to be living up to all of Fellington Felroy's expectations."

"And so does Pakovich," Tel said.

CHAPTER TWENTY-NINE

Caland floated in the darkness with Tel's warmth enveloping and caressing him. He loved to lie in dreamy half-wakefulness with her arms drawn firmly about him, awed by the miracle of her presence.

Then he started.

Tel was instantly awake. "What is it?"

"It's back."

"Watching?"

"Yes."

"I could check," Tel said slowly. "But there'd be no one there."

"I know."

"If you have the sensation of being watched when no one is watching, then it must be a sensation of something else. There's probably a simple answer if only we could figure it out."

"I know."

"Still watching?"

"Yes."

Caland continued to float, but the magic had vanished.

"Still watching?" Tel asked again after a long pause.

"No."

"No? You mean—just like that—"

"Probably you're right," Caland said patiently. "It's only a sensation. Suddenly I had it and then suddenly I didn't."

She said nothing.

"Tel?"

"Yes?"

"Do you think it would be better if I left Mort?"

"You're thinking of Cenaru, and Olyndyt, and Skarlont?"

"Yes. Something's going to happen here."

"Things do seem to be building up, but whatever is going to happen will happen whether you're here or not. Prency Tate, and Sdissler and his army, and Nalce and his saboteurs wouldn't leave just because you did. Pakovich wouldn't suddenly acquire wisdom just because you went away. You're being silly."

She slept, finally, and he lay in depressed wakefulness and thought again about the inevitable moment when his mind and his memory would slip beyond his control. He would forget Tel utterly, and when that happened he would lose something of himself—perhaps the last vital thing that he ever would possess. He would lose it and never know that he had lost it. He could understand and accept that he must lose Tel eventually. She was a normal fem, and he could not even guess at her frustration in being linked with a hopelessly impotent mal. He knew he would lose her, but he wanted to remember. *Who am I where am I why am I?*

After the sensational events of its first day of operation, the medical clinic achieved a smoothly functioning routine—in large measure due to the energetic efficiency of Melana, its manager. The only threat to the clinic's anonymity was posed by Gary Dwand, who hung on the Valley Transportation Company gate during every free moment hoping for a glimpse of her.

Calta remained apprehensive of another outbreak of plague or something worse, and she continued to have the building watched. When Caland and Tel received an urgent summons from her, they arrived in haste anticipating another catastrophe, but she greeted them jubilantly and waved a handful of laboratory reports that had just arrived from Aravia.

"We're finally grooving on this!" she announced.

Sam the Artist, who was there ahead of them, grumbled, "That's all she'll say. 'We're finally grooving on this.' She's as bad as Arlu. It's getting so no one wants to tell anyone anything."

"We're waiting for Yda and the Reverend," Caland explained.

"Yda's bringing a vital piece of the puzzle—I hope. It wouldn't do to unveil a puzzle with one piece missing."

"The only puzzle that worries me is what's happened to the Fig Stump's hospitality." Sam gestured disgustedly at the empty table. "No yuck. Not even a crumb of dry rot to sustain us. Surely Alf could offer us his leftover glop before he throws it to the scavs. After I'm elected Valley exek, I'm going to be severe with him about this."

"Stop worrying about your stomach," Calta said. "It's big enough to look after itself. They're busy downstairs and Alz is short-handed today. Surely you can survive for a few minutes without food."

"I can survive," Sam said, "but I can't function. A mind doesn't produce sagacious counsels when it's attached to a stomach that keeps sending distress signals. Why didn't you tell Alz we could wait on ourselves?"

The Reverend entered awkwardly carrying a tray laden with mugs and a steaming carafe of yuck. Sam was not appeased. He filled a mug for himself and sniffed disgustedly. "But not a crumb of anything to soak it up," he complained.

Yda burst in elatedly and threw her arms in the air. "Melana strikes again! We've got it!"

"The chemical?" Calta demanded.

"Well, no, not the chemical. Fulnry could have palmed that over at the mines without leaving a record. Probably he did. But the antidote is medicine, and for that there are records. Melana brought three copies of the pharmacy ledger." She dropped the papers onto the table and perched her tiny form on the edge of a chair.

"The girl's a genius," Calta proclaimed.

"She's beautiful," Yda said with a matter-of-fact shrug. "Mals fall for her just as hard over at the Government Mall as they do in the Valley. It's much to her credit that she refuses to exploit it except in a worthy cause. Is Olgi ready?"

"Are the pictures any good?"

"Mushy. The kind of thing Pakovich likes. Sigley Varno did

them."

Sam the Artist exploded. "If Zareent or somebody ever wants to prove that telepathy is possible, he won't have to do it mathematically. He can find all the proof he needs by listening to you two. If we aren't supposed to know what you're talking about, why did you invite us?"

"I'll explain it in words even you can understand," Calta said. "Some people got sick from eating Hef's putrebuns—"

"That I noticed," Sam the Artist said. "It was fairly conspicuous."

"Listen. Fulnry diagnosed it as a rare type of food poisoning that no one around here had ever heard of, and he preened himself on his foresight in having the necessary antibac on hand. But we have checked this kind of food poisoning through all the available medical records, and its symptoms are nothing like those exhibited by the people who got sick. Further, we stole some of his antibac and had it analyzed and identified, and then we checked *that* through medical records, and we found that it is not an antibac and it is not indicated for the medical condition that Fulnry diagnosed. It is contraindicative. Used on food poisoning patients, it would kill them. It has in fact only one medical use, and that's as an antidote for something called Antioxplus, which is the commercial strength of a common rust inhibitor used on heavy machinery in outdoor and mining operations. Pak Enterprises uses a lot of it, and for that reason, as a routine safety precaution, it keeps a quantity of antidote on hand. As far as anyone knows, the antidote has never been used on the world of Mort because there had never been a case of Antioxplus poisoning here—probably because the stuff has such a pungent odor and foul taste that no one could possibly mistake it for anything potable. Introduced into highly spiced foods, however, it can pass unnoticed—as is evidenced from the fact that all of the samples we sent to Aravia, including vomit from the victims, contained Antioxplus. Hef's putrebun filling is highly spiced. It that clear enough?"

"In other words," Sam the Artist said, "you've nailed the

screety vrump."

"We have indeed. For reasons best known to him, Fulnry came to the Valley with the intention of manufacturing an epidemic. He knew that Antioxplus would produce alarming symptoms that would pass in a couple of days with no great damage if the antidote were administered promptly. Melana managed to get copies of the medical ledger from the Mines Clinic that shows him drawing—how much antidote?"

"Two liters," Yda said. "An incredible amount. He had to go to the Mines Clinic for it because the Paradise Clinic doesn't keep it on hand. He drew two liters of it and repackaged it in small containers which he labeled as a rarely used antibac."

"We have the whole record, and we're going to make Pakovich eat it," Calta said. "Tel and Cal—we want you to come with us."

"When?" Tel asked.

"Whenever we can get an appointment. It may take a while—he's just back from Aravia, and he'll have a lot of loafing to catch up on. We want you to come because we need witnesses. It's difficult to make any kind of impression on a mind like Pakovich's, so we'll have to use somewhat unorthodox methods."

Later, when they had retired to Nello's with Sam the Artist and the Reverend, Tel said to Caland, "We could hardly refuse."

"No," Caland agreed. He felt depressed about this development. He had no desire to see Pakovich again, but there was no polite way to avoid it.

The Reverend had brought Hef with him. They put their heads together to talk confidentially, and Tel described for Hef the circumstances that had made his innocent eatery the source of the Valley Plague. Hef listened impassively. He had suffered his fifth defeat, and he seemed to have no interest at all in assessments of guilt or innocence.

The Reverend said gravely, "I'm confident that Pakovich had no personal involvement in the crime. That's not the sort of thing he would do, or have done, or permit anyone to do. We all of us have mind images of ourselves, and in Pakovich's mind image, Pakovich is a good mal, a just mal, and a fair mal. He's not consciously going to do anything, ever, that contradicts that mind image."

"In that case, he has to be held responsible for what he does unconsciously," Tel said. "His personal attitude toward the Valley has shaped his ethical basis for all of Pak Enterprises' dealings with the Valley and also his employees' attitudes. None of his employees are going to do anything that they have reason to believe Pakovich will disapprove of."

"I hope you're wrong," the Reverend said soberly. "We have to share this world with Pakovich, and I'm confident that he'll disassociate himself from such a dishonorable act, whatever its aim may have been."

Hairy tracked them down on the beach an hour later. Pakovich had generously granted them an appointment for the following morning. "Dress for it," Calta's message cautioned.

Calta and Yda dressed for it in gowns that were as impeccably conservative as they were grotesquely out of character. Caland and Tel resurrected their tourist hote garments. They needed only the totally dressed butler and Pakovich in his pajamas, Caland thought, to achieve the ultimate absurdity of a costume ball.

They joined Calta and Yda in front of the Dolls' House where an electrocab waited for them. Yda was carrying a package wrapped in tinseled fabric commonly used by Pakovich's posh shops at the space port.

"Did Pakovich act reluctant?" Tel asked Calta.

"Not at all. I think sometimes he gets lonely sitting up there all by himself with no one to talk with except that stupidly costumed servant. He welcomes company even if he knows that the interview isn't likely to be pleasant."

"Did you tell him what it was about?"

"No. I didn't tell him I was inviting Fulnry to join us, either. I just said it was a matter of important personal interest to him. He's learned from experience that when I call something important, it is."

"What did Fulnry say?" Yda asked.

"He wanted to know what it was about. I told him if he wanted to be present when we discussed him with his boss, he'd better walk in the door precisely on time. He'll arrive with his toenails shaking. I gave us fifteen minutes on him."

"That sounds about right," Yda said.

The drive up to Pakovich's mansion was as breathtakingly lovely as Caland remembered it. He and Tel discussed the unfolding panorama in whispers, pointing out things to each other. Calta and Yda maintained a brooding silence that boded no good for Pakovich. Their only comments concerned the weather. Calta asked if Yda had noticed the sudden wind during the night, and Yda asked in turn, with sweet sarcasm, whether Calta was having trouble keeping her mind on her work.

The totally dressed butler opened the massive door as they descended from the 'cab. His lank and gloomy figure towered over them as they filed past him. He looked as though he had neither eaten nor smiled since Caland last saw him.

Calta turned and eyed him severely. "Tell me," she said. "Do you undress Pakovich when he retires at night?"

For once the butler's impeccable calm was ruffled. He blushed.

"You're embarrassing him," Yda said.

"Why should undressing Pakovich embarrass him?" Calta wanted to know. "I've undressed thousands of mals, and I've never felt embarrassed about it."

The butler's blush deepened. When Calta informed him that Doctor Fulnry was joining them and should be brought in the moment he arrived, the butler averted his eyes as though she had imparted a ribald story.

He politely invited them to follow him. As they moved away, Tel whispered to Calta, "What was that all about?"

"Every mal should be put in his place," Calta whispered back. "I was trying to find out what his is."

When they reached the plastic bubble that served as Pakovich's veranda, the master himself stepped forward to greet them gruffly. He was wearing a flowered garment that hung halfway to his knees and almost concealed his trousers. The contrast with the formal dress worn by his visitors in no way disconcerted him. In this, as in everything else on Mort, he considered himself the standard by which all others were measured.

He indicated chairs, permitted them to seat themselves, and then dropped into his own favorite lounger. "Well?" he demanded.

The awkward silence that followed was broken tentatively when Caland made a fumbling remark about the scenic veranda and Yda responded tartly that the scenery was all right when it didn't interfere with the view.

Pakovich scowled and said again, "Well?"

"Doctor Fulnry is supposed to meet us here," Calta told him. "If you don't mind, we'll wait for him."

"Fulnry?" Pakovich echoed suspiciously. "Why?"

"If you don't mind," Calta said cheerfully, "or even if you do, we'll wait. Food is almost never improved by being digested twice."

Pakovich glared at Calta, glared at Yda, dismissed Caland and Tel with a scornful glance, and finally transferred his attention to the magnificent view. But he was not enjoying it. His curiosity had been piqued, and his fingers drummed impatiently on the arms of his lounger.

"I have better things to do than sit here waiting," he snapped finally.

"I doubt that," Calta drawled.

He was not appeased when the butler appeared escorting Fulnry. His curiosity had given way to resentment. "What does Fulnry have to do with this?" he demanded. "Sit down, Fulnry. What do you have to do with this?"

Fulnry sat down. His toenails probably were shaking. He had lost both his poise and his carefully arranged smile, and he was too befuddled to do more than stare blankly from one person to another.

"Doctor Fulnry is here because the Valley owes him a debt

of gratitude," Calta said. "We'll leave the explanation to him. Since we're indebted to him, and since you're his employer, we also feel indebted to you. We want to thank you both, and we thought a gesture of appreciation was in order."

Fulnry began to relax, but Pakovich was glaring at Calta in resentful disbelief.

Yda began unwrapping her package. "The Valley doesn't have extensive resources, but we've done the best we could," she said. "First of all, Olgi is bringing out a new kind of candy as a tribute to Mort and its owner. It's called 'Fruits of Paradise.' It consists of fruits of Mort candied by Olgi's original process and covered with a deliciously spicy, whipped confection. The box will be as unusual as the product. Each one will be ornamented with two scenes of Mort, one a drawing and the other a water color, and each picture will be hand-drawn or hand-painted. The candy box is designed to form a frame after the candy is eaten. Clever, eh?"

Pakovich ceased his impatient squirming and leaned forward curiously while Yda demonstrated the candy box. The pictures were on the top and underside of the lid, and the lid was reversible so that either scene could be displayed. The box Yda was demonstrating showed a water color of Paradise Bay and an ink drawing of the Tin Mountains. The candy looked luscious.

"Darn clever idea," Pakovich said grudgingly.

"Isn't it?" Calta said enthusiastically. "It's the best kind of advertising there is for two reasons. For one, it's the kind of thing people will hang onto because it comes disguised as art. It ought to go big with tourists, both in your hotes and at the Port, and Olgi expects it to be a popular export item. She has business connections on several worlds."

"I know," Pakovich said sourly.

"There's a second reason why it's the best kind of advertising. It isn't costing you a chit."

Pakovich opened his mouth to protest and decided not to. "The candy looks—ah—very tasty," he said weakly.

"'Very tasty' never sold anything," Yda said sternly. "Call it scrumptiously delicious. It's all of that. You know Olgi's products, and this is a special creation never before offered to the public. Try a piece."

Pakovich hesitated and then took a piece of the candy.

"You, Doctor Fulnry?"

Fulnry, his lost smile fully constructed, followed his employer's lead. The two men bit, chewed thoughtfully, made appreciative murmurs, and stuffed the remainder of the pieces into their mouths.

While they continued to chew, Yda assembled the box and returned it to its wrapping.

"That's only the beginning," Calta said. "Of course, there isn't really a lot the Valley can do for a wealthy mal like you, but the little that it can, it will. We've decided that Mort should have a Pakovich Week."

"Pakovich Week?" The owner of Mort muttered, speaking around the candy in his mouth.

"Don't talk, finish your candy," Calta said. "There's too little identification between the world of Mort and its owner. We've worked out a program. What we want is permission to use the land adjacent to the Valley. There isn't enough open space in the Valley to put on the kind of celebration that a Pakovich Week should have. The tourists will enjoy this, of course, but we're more concerned with offering a week of commemorative fun to Mort's permanent residents—those of Paradise as well as those of the Valley. We'll start off with—"

She had lost her audience. Pakovich slid to the floor and began to gasp and retch. Doctor Fulnry was still erect in his chair, but he was no longer listening. He was pointing an accusing finger and making choking noises.

Yda bent over Pakovich. "Look after Fulnry," she told Calta coldly. "He might hurt himself when he falls."

Calta caught him as he pitched forward. Caland scrambled to help her lower him to the floor.

"Now?" Calta asked.

"Not until they've turned a deep purple," Yda said. "We

won't get the proper sympathetic reaction if we cut the effects off too soon."

Caland was thoroughly alarmed and uncertain as to what should be done. When he tried to speak, Yda silenced him with a wave of hand.

"Everything's under control," she said. "We're using a method identical to the one Doctor Fulnry already has approved and demonstrated."

The two mals were alarmingly purple when Yda finally relented and aimed a hypo gun at Pakovich's bare arm. She pulled the trigger, and then she slipped the doctor's arm from his sleeve and expertly gave him the same treatment.

"Now let's break some records getting out of here!" she hissed.

Calta picked up the box of candy. "You, there," she called. "Where's the blushing butler?"

That worthy individual was no longer blushing; he was ashen. He must have been looking on, but his long career of formal responsibilities had not properly prepared him for the sudden collapse of Mort's owner and its medical director. He stepped forward uncertainly and stood staring down at the lividly purple faces on the floor.

"They were suddenly taken ill," Yda said. "Did you see it happen?"

The butler nodded.

"I'm a nurse," Yda went on. "I've given them first aid. They seem in distress, but it's nothing serious. They'll be all right in a day or two. I'd suggest that you call one of the company doctors and then get them into bed. Here." She handed him a folded slip of paper. "Give that to the doctor. It will tell him what happened and what I did."

They moved unescorted through the sprawling mansion and scrambled into the waiting electrocab. Yda and Calta dissolved in laughter as they rounded the first sharp curve in the long descent to Paradise. Caland was simply amazed that he'd remembered to keep breathing. He exchanged glances with Tel.

Tel said, "'Somewhat unorthodox methods,' is good."

Caland said doubtfully, "I'm really not sure—"

"We knew that you really wouldn't be sure," Calta said. "That's why we didn't tell you what we were going to do. We really *were* sure."

At the bottom of the looping drive, where it joined the main road to Paradise, they met a small electrocar tearing up the mountain with a screaming whine. They recognized the driver as one of the doctors who worked in the Valley clinic. He was intent on the road and did not glance in their direction.

"First thing we do," Yda said, "we totally destroy this candy. The stuff looks and tastes and smells delicious, and the spices perfectly mask the smell and taste of that dratted Antioxplus. If we accidently leave it lying around, we'll start another epidemic."

"Right," Tel said. "Be sure to do that first thing. The second thing is to start putting up barricades."

* * * * * * *

Nothing happened. If Mort had had an army, Caland would have expected full mobilization. In the absence of an army, at least one of the two shifts of miners should have been sent marching on the Valley.

But nothing happened. Valley life continued to flow placidly, and if there were smoldering eruptions in the mansion on the mountain, none of the smoke drifted westward.

Two days after the strange conference with Pakovich, Calta sent Hairy for them. "We're invited back," she said. "Feel like risking it?"

"How's Pakovich?" Caland asked.

"According to the butler, he's recovering. He's most eager to see us again, and he earnestly requests that we call on him."

"I'll bet," Tel said.

"That's the way the butler put it. Yda and I are going. If we refuse, it'll create the impression that we may have done something wrong, and we wouldn't want to do that."

"No," Tel agreed. "We definitely wouldn't want to do that. It's the one thing to be avoided at all cost. All right—we'll come along and offer moral support while the four of us are waiting for the firing squad."

"There are a couple of things about this that puzzle me," Caland said. "Where'd you get the Antioxplus, and where'd you get the antidote? Even Fulnry had to sign for his two liters."

"Melana," Calta said. "She's a gem. Her personality is as lovely as her appearance. She's well known in Paradise because of her library research, and probably half the mal employees of Pak Enterprises are in love with her. The other half haven't been lucky enough to see her. If she were to ask it as a small favor, any of them would be willing to bring her a few chemicals for the kids at the Valley school to perform experiments with. That's how she got the Antioxplus. The antidote was easier. It came from our own clinic. Fulnry couldn't very well remove the stuff immediately after it saved so many lives. What if another of our filthy eateries started a plague?"

"What did the other doctors at the clinic think about the plague?" Caland asked. "If it didn't fool Yda, it shouldn't have fooled them."

"Ah, that. Who argues with the boss? Whatever Fulnry said, the antidote he used was the right one, and it wasn't their job to figure out how the Antioxplus got into Valley putrebun filler. Nothing they could possibly find in Valley putrebun filler would surprise them. We'll meet in an hour in front of the Burned Wafer. Yda refuses to board a 'cab in front of the Dolls' House again. She's afraid her customers will think she's working both sides of the street."

Pakovich received them in his bedroom. He wore a flowery robe, and he was sitting up in bed with a food tray on his lap. The butler removed the tray, and Pakovich glared weakly at each of them in turn. His robe, of a glistening material, made his pallor far more unhealthy than it actually was.

"You might have killed me!" Pakovich snapped.

"Not a chance," Yda said. "You weren't in half the danger that your stooge's Valley victims were in."

Pakovich glared again. Then he said, "Tell me."

Calta told him in graphic terms.

"It sums up like this," she said when she had finished. "You opened a clinic in the Valley—"

"*I* didn't do it!" Pakovich protested. "I didn't know anything about it. I wouldn't have permitted it."

"Your stooge did it. It amounts to the same thing."

"But it doesn't! I can't be blamed for something I didn't know anything about. I wouldn't have let him open the clinic, and I certainly wouldn't have let him poison anyone."

"You'll have a tough time convincing a court of that. Fulnry is your agent, and you're responsible for what he does. He's not the type to go around opening clinics without your knowledge."

"Never mind that. I'll take care of Fulnry. I just wanted to know whether you can prove what you said."

"Everything except his access to the Antioxplus. He probably filched that at the mines. Your employees out there may know something about it."

"If I send my counsel to see you, will you show him your evidence and arrange for him to interview witnesses?"

"Of course. He also should interview your own medical people who were working in the clinic. They must have known that something suspicious was happening."

"Show him the evidence, and I'll take whatever action seems appropriate," Pakovich said. "Fulnry is an idiot. Doctors are supposed to cure people, not make them sick. Why didn't you just tell me about this? It wasn't necessary to poison me."

"You're a slow learner," Calta said. "We thought you'd be more sympathetic toward the victims if you shared their experience."

"I'm a lot older than they are."

"That's not true," Yda said. "Any Valley eatery serves people of all ages and of all physical conditions. Fulnry poisoned the food without knowing who would eat it, and he had very little control over the size of the dose in the portion served. All of us are lucky that he didn't kill everyone who ate it. You were in no danger at all. We carefully figured the amount of poison in each piece of candy."

"Get out," Pakovich said.

"Not so fast," Calta said. "One person in the Valley was permanently injured by this caper. Fulnry maliciously destroyed a mal's business and almost destroyed him. Then he had the nerve to announce that the eatery was responsible and tear it down."

"Tell my counsel. He'll do whatever is right."

The four of them got to their feet. "I don't know why you're questioning us about this," Calta said. "Your spies already have told you everything you need to know."

Pakovich's pallor vanished in a flush of anger. "If I have spies in the Valley, it's to find out the truth. You people are worse liars than Fulnry. Now get out!"

"But we do occasionally tell the truth," Yda protested cheerfully. "Olgi really is marketing that new candy in the special box. It's already selling well in the hotes. Just in case your unexpected illness blighted your appreciation of it, I brought you another box."

She placed it on the stand beside the bed: Fruits of Paradise with a different water color of Mort, this one showing the ocean in the full glory of its magical sunset. "Enjoy it as soon as you're able to eat," Yda said.

"Get out!"

They left Pakovich glaring at the box of candy.

As the 'cab began negotiating the steep curves down the mountainside, Calta remarked, "I wonder whether his eminence, the butler, will take kindly to demotion to food taster."

CHAPTER THIRTY

Pakovich's counsel called on Calta, foted copies of her evidence, and interviewed each and every one of the victims including Hefnan Troule. Then he proposed a settlement: a hundred chits outright payment to each of the victims, and a pension for Hef of ten chits per sennite.

"Don't be ridiculous," Calta snapped. "You know what a court would do with this, and so do I. You're wasting your time."

She demanded five hundred chits for each victim, a life pension of fifty chits per sennite for Hef, and continuation of the Valley clinic under Valley control. The settlement promised the largest financial bonanza in the history of the Valley, and most of the uninjured residents were wishing that they'd been lucky enough to be poisoned.

Doctor Fulnry was fired. Melana returned from Paradise to report that gossip was rampant in the Government Mall. It was said that Fulnry accused Pakovich of authorizing his action.

"Sam the Artist was right," Melana said. "Pakovich has been complaining about Bar for years. He thinks Bar's pension isn't justified because he isn't disabled."

"He really isn't *much* disabled," Tel conceded.

"That's what Pakovich thinks. The pension isn't for being crippled, it's for being disabled, and how could a disabled person overhaul vehicles and build spaceships? But Pakovich doesn't believe that Bar is crippled, either. He claims that Bar has trained himself to hold his arm like that, but when he goes to work on something, he uses it normally. Pakovich has been needling Fulnry ever since he hired him to produce the medical evidence that would justify terminating Bar's pension. Fulnry got nowhere with spies, so he had the bright idea of establishing the clinic and making a big hero of himself by stopping an epidemic—after which he thought everyone would trust him and he could get all the evidence about Bar that he wanted."

"Screet!" Tel exclaimed. "For once, Pakovich was right. Fulnry's an idiot. Twice an idiot—if he'd taken his time about it and had a plague originate somewhere other than next door to the clinic, we might not have tumbled."

"But what was there for him to find out even if he succeeded?" Caland asked. "Bar has a crippled arm, and he accomplishes miracles in spite of that."

"Pakovich doesn't understand miracles," Tel said. "Maybe Fulnry deserves our sympathy. Working for a petty tyrant must be a strain. It might even shatter a person's integrity."

"A person with integrity wouldn't take the job," Caland said.

On the beach that night, Caland found himself seated next to Orlqwin Lincoz, known to his Valley friends as Link, the little mal who passed out leaflets for Valley businesses. He had passable manners and speech, a well-groomed appearance, and a carefully maintained wardrobe of almost presentable garments assembled by diligent search among the Valley's clutter shops. He was sufficiently nondescript to go unnoticed in a crowd, and yet his appearance and manners were marginally respectable enough to pass scrutiny in a gathering of tourists. Occasionally he was able to penetrate the verandas of both the Paradise View Hostelry and the Paradise Vista Inn, and he moved freely about the hote gardens and beach as well as the space port shops and lounge.

As they sat watching the fire and taking their turns at the jug, Caland asked him about his strange occupation.

"The point is," Link said, "you don't give a leaflet to just anybody. Otherwise there's trouble."

"I thought you did it so deftly that no one noticed you," Caland said.

"They notice the leaflets, though. Give one to someone who isn't curious enough to look at it, he drops it. Hotes don't like clutter when there's no profit in it. Give one to someone who's offended by it, he complains. Either way you have all the servers and flunks on the lookout for you, and it makes it hard to operate. I try to give leaflets to those most likely to want them. If I'm working for Calta, for example, I look for two kinds of mals—those that are unattached, and those that are too much attached. The unattached naturally are interested, but the other kind, those that have been pinned down by a wife for years, they make the best customers. Hit them at the right moment with a leaflet that guarantees discretion and—and—"

"Unrestrained lasciviousness?" Caland suggested.

"Yeah. All that stuff. Calta's leaflet describes it so no one can mistake the meaning, but all in very proper language. Strong language frightens them off. The leaflet has detachable stubs for free electrocab fare to and from, and there's instantly a great temptation for the pinned-down mal to slip the wife for an afternoon and be wicked. Calta redeems the electrocab stubs and pays me a commission."

"Doesn't that cut into her profit?" Caland asked.

"Naw. She adds it to the customer's tab. It's nice for everyone, especially the customer, because he doesn't know about it."

Sam the Artist interrupted them. He had an artist with him, the genuine variety from Pakovich's Art Colony, attired in cape and turban—articles of apparel scorned in the Valley and therefore never seen there except when flaunted by visitors. Sam introduced his guest as Farlon Cerfis and asked for permission to join them. The two of them squatted down in the sand beside Caland and Tel.

"It's like this," Sam the Artist said. "We've really got to do something about Pakovich."

"We just did something about Pakovich," Caland protested.

"That 'liver for a liver' stuff is no good, especially when he's snatching yours first. You spend your life trying to catch up. We want to clobber him with something that will last long enough to be remembered."

"No more poison," Tel said firmly. "Not that it would ever work again, anyway."

"No more poison," Sam the Artist agreed. "The problem is that Pakovich owns everything a mal could want except happiness, and he's stupidly jealous of anyone who has that. It's one reason he hates the Valley—there are so many happy people here who own nothing at all, and he's unhappy while owning a whole world, and he can't understand that. It doesn't seem fair to him. Sabotage can't really hurt him because he's so rich. Also, we don't want to hand him an invitation to strike back. If he feels obligated to get even about something, he'll brood for years. Look at that nonsense about Bar's arm."

"That doesn't leave much to work on," Tel said.

"Just one thing," Sam the Artist said. "Pride. Pakovich figures that a mal who owns a world ought to be a lot more important than he obviously is, and he can't understand why he isn't. Instead of showing respect for him, people tend to laugh. It bothers him. He has pride and he's very sensitive. He won't accept the fact that he's just a nobody with bank accounts. He's so certain that he ought to be somebody. That's where he can be hurt. We're going to put a few nicks in his pride."

"How?" Caland wanted to know.

"Farl and I worked it out," Sam the Artist said.

The artist spoke for the first time. "I agree with Sam. Pakovich is a nobody with bank accounts. Nothing is smaller than a rich man who thinks his wealth makes him big."

"You artists are his guests, aren't you?" Caland asked politely.

"Not his guests," the artist protested. He had a thin face, a small, neatly trimmed beard, and an over-balancing, large mustache, but his most conspicuous features were his long, graceful hands. Periodically he fingered his mustache, which displayed one feature while directing attention to another.

"Not his guests. His captives. He shelters his artists generously for three years, but he also thinks he owns them. He writes the rules they must work under. He writes laws governing their personal conduct. He sent two of my friends home because they were found together under what he called suspicious circumstances. What under all suns of all the galaxies could possibly be suspicious about a mal artist and a fem artist sleeping together? He presumes to criticize our work. He said one of my paintings of Paradise Bay didn't look like the bay. I asked him, 'When did you look at it last?'"

"He has regulations for nature, too," Sam the Artist said. "The bay is supposed to look exactly the same to everyone, all the time."

"Right," Farlon Cerfis said bitterly. "I made an interesting abstract using the shapes of the Tin Mountains. That offended him. No one had any business abstracting his mountains without permission. I agree that something should be done about him. What we have planned is a very small thing, but it must be done."

"What exactly are you going to do?" Caland asked.

Cerfis took a piece of paper from the case he was carrying. He handed it to Caland, who held it so that Tel could share it with him. It contained a drawing of the space port's terminal building done almost with the precision of a fote, and showing the building as it looked to the new arrival descending a ship's ramp. It was exactly like the scene that Caland remembered with one startling difference. All across the building's façade, in glowing color and hideously ornate letters, was an enormous sign.

WELCOME TO MORT
THE WORLD THAT PAKOVICH MADE

"I don't understand" Caland said. "You're going to give him a drawing of the Port—"

"No, no. We're going to give him the sign. We'll paint it on the terminal building. Just like that. It's a special gift from the senior artists."

Caland and Tel exchanged bewildered glances. Caland did not know what he had expected, but this sign hardly seemed to fit Sam's bitterly announced intention to do something about Pakovich.

"Of course it's in grossly bad taste," he said slowly. "It's just the kind of thing he might think of himself if he had any imagination. On the other hand, he also might have just enough of a glimmer of protective common sense to see what an ass this makes him look like."

"He's just had a shattering experience," Tel said. "It's likely to make him examine any gift very carefully, from both ends, to make certain it doesn't go bang when he opens it."

"He does that, all right," Cerfis said with feeling. "I didn't know about this stunt you pulled on him. I should have guessed something was wrong when he received us in bed."

"You mean—you've already shown this to him?"

"We saw him this afternoon," Cerfis said. "A delegation of senior artists called on him to offer this as a memorial. He was more than suspicious. He was downright nasty. We'd asked for fifteen minutes of his time in which to make a presentation, and he acted as though we were trying to pick his pocket. I made the most touching speech I was capable of, all about the gratitude we seniors felt for his succoring us for three comfortable and productive years, and our enjoyment of the Attic's inspiring environment, and his generosity in granting us the fellowships that had made our stay here so educational and productive, and how we wanted to leave something behind us in token of our appreciation and as an apt tribute to a mal who had contributed so much to galactic art, a memorial that would instantly impress itself upon every visitor to the world of Mort. He listened with a sour look on his face. That stupidly dressed butler stood behind his bed eying us as though he were trying to decide which to throw out first. I finished my stirring speech, which I'd taken the trouble to memorize, and before I could hand Pakovich the drawing, he snarled, 'What's it going to cost me?' Imagine that. We offered him a memorial, and he wanted to know the price.

In a nasty tone of voice, yet. I felt like snatching it back and walking out."

Caland was still studying the drawing perplexedly. "He did eventually take a look at it, didn't he?"

"Eventually he did. Reluctantly and complaining about how everyone tries to take advantage of him."

"What did he think of it?"

"He started pounding the table by his bed and saying, over and over, 'By God, I like it! By God, I like it!'"

Tel said to Caland, "He told us he was interested in the truth. I suppose that sign would impress him as a truthful statement."

"A truthful statement told with glowing candor," Caland agreed. "I take it that he accepted your memorial."

"Accepted it and tried to pay us for our work. It got embarrassing. When we first arrived, he was resentful because he thought we were trying to sell him something. When he found out it was a gift, he positively insisted on paying for it. We finally compromised. He's to furnish the paint, and we'll furnish the labor—as a token of our gratitude for the inspiring environment of the Attic and all the rest. I had to give my speech a second time while we were arguing. He not only accepted it, he's guaranteed his full cooperation. Pak Enterprises will find the scaffolding for us. We'll cut stencils for the letters and tape them into place for his approval, and then we'll spray the letters with a kem-bond paint that forms a chemical bond with masonry and cement. The sign will literally become part of the building, and it'll memorialize the name of Pakovich for as long as the terminal stands. He liked that idea, too."

"But you're not putting nicks in his pride," Tel said. "You're inflating his ego."

"Only until the sign's up and he starts getting reactions," Sam the Artist said. "By the time he realizes what an absolute boorish thing he's done, it'll be much too late. The paint won't wear off, and it can't be painted over. The only way to get rid of it will be to put a new façade on the terminal."

"What if he doesn't get reactions?" Caland asked. "What if

no one dares to say anything about it? Won't he keep thinking he's done something great?"

"I suppose there is that possibility," Cerfis conceded.

"You're not going to put much of a nick in his pride with this."

"It's a small thing," Sam the Artist said. "But it's the only thing we could think of, and it's absolutely legal, and he'll have no basis for complaint afterward because we offered and he accepted it. It doesn't impress you?"

"To be honest about it, no," Caland said. "But that may be because we just witnessed Calta's and Yda's conception of 'doing something about Pakovich,' and it was awesome to watch and devastatingly effective. It'll have a cautionary effect on him for years to come. Your sign, now—"

"Seems pretty tame, doesn't it?" Sam the Artist said agreeably. "But we're going to do it anyway just for the hell of it. If Pakovich does decide that he's been had, the worst he can do is send the artists home. But all of them are seniors finishing their last year here, and they'll already be home."

Caland awoke that night with rain blowing in his face. Tel, on the sheltered side of the bed, sleepily told him to cover his head and forget it.

"One of the Prom shops sells shutters," Caland said. "Easy to install. Nail 'em on. Guards your privacy and protects you from the weather."

"Anyone who needs privacy that badly doesn't belong in the Valley," Tel said. "We don't get a driving rain like this twice a year. Go to sleep."

Caland covered his head and went to sleep. But as he did so, he had the disquieting feeling that on several recent nights he had felt rain on his face.

He awoke in the morning with the usual headache and lay long abed with Tel hovering about him concernedly. "Arlu wants to see us," she told him when he finally felt like stirring.

"Now?"

"He's coming to the Fig Stump for din. He specified that he

wants only the two of us. Any time after the klaxon. Do you feel like eating?"

Caland did not, but he idly spooned the glop she fixed for him and sipped the yuck. Eventually they made their way to the Prom and climbed the stairs behind the Fig Stump. Alz Hernl's wife promised to let Arlu know that they had arrived. She offered yuck and sweets, and Caland tiredly sat back with his eyes closed and left the refusal to Tel.

Arlu swept into the room, an optical illusion of green and white zigzags. He nodded at them, turned, and stepped aside to admit a companion. Afterward Caland had no recollection of getting to his feet, but he found himself there, staring.

It was the mystery fem, as severe-looking as Caland remembered her, and in fact wearing the same conservatively cut daysuit she had been wearing the last time he saw her.

"Fem Dorlana Ornal," Arlu said and introduced each of them in turn. For once Arlu forsook his reclining chair. The four of them seated themselves at the table.

"Fem Ornal is Aravia's Business Representative on Mort," Arlu said. "On other worlds she would be an ambassador. Since Mort doesn't maintain political relations with other worlds, her official status here has to be modified accordingly. Her office is in the space terminal, and she also lives there at the Port Hote. She already knows a great deal about Cal, but she was very much surprised to learn that Cal knows her well enough to pick her out of a crowd."

Fem Ornal learned forward. "You had only seen me twice that I was aware of—once in the park on Aravia and once at the hote."

"You made an impression on him," Arlu said. "Cal, Fem Ornal was a friend of Wes Fulm's. Perhaps it would simplify things if she told you about that."

Fem Ornal nodded. "Aravia has been deeply concerned about the sabotage to Mort's tin production and even more concerned that Pakovich refuses to take strong preventive measures. I determined quite early that the world of Rynaif was responsible for the sabotage. Rynaif is Aravia's principal industrial rival, and a tin shortage on Aravia would profit Rynaif immensely. Only one Pakovich employee seemed at all concerned about the sabotage—Fulm. He agitated for action in the Council of Supervisors and made a mild nuisance of himself about it. He was gradually gaining some support. Just when it looked as though he might accomplish something, he was suddenly sent to Rynaif for a training course."

"Cause and effect?" Arlu asked.

"I don't know. I searched the possibility as thoroughly as possible afterward, and I still don't know."

"Fulm gave me the impression that the Council of Supervisors wasn't concerned about the sabotage and refused to take action," Caland said.

"He was a strange little mal," Fem Ornal said thoughtfully. "He was totally without confidence, and he always deprecated himself and his achievements. His one positive trait was a fierce loyalty to Mort and Pak Enterprises. I met with him several times, and I could have helped him if he'd been willing to confide in me. But I was an outsider whose first loyalty belonged to another world."

"So he went to Dom instead," Caland said.

"So Mal Arlu has told me. It was an unwise move. Dom's loyalty is to himself. He would pretend to help Fulm on the chance that it would work to his own advantage."

"They conferred together several times," Arlu said. "Then Dom accompanied Fulm to Rynaif. At least they traveled on the same ship."

"I tried to keep Fulm from going," Fem Ornal said. "It was a Pak Enterprises assignment, so of course he considered it his duty. I felt certain that the world of Rynaif would be aware that Fulm was a potential danger to its sabotage operations, and I asked the embassy there to take whatever steps were necessary to protect him. A guard was to follow him everywhere and regularly report his movements."

"Then Fulm suddenly disappeared and so did the embassy

employee who was watching him. Obviously the Rynaif government was responsible, but the only clue the embassy has was contained in the employee's last report. He said that Fulm had sat beside a mal named Caland at din and later had visited Caland in his room."

"Then the employee managed to get off a report while I was talking with Fulm," Caland said. "I thought it was a cipher, but he did a very creditable job to identify me that quickly."

"When both mals vanished, I naturally pondered the significance of the visit to an unknown mal named Caland. I was on Aravia at the time, and when I began to search him, I was amazed to learn that he had just landed there. I sent someone to identify him and follow him, and when I received a report that he was sitting in a public park, I went to have a look for myself. His appearance seemed harmless enough. Then I checked his name through Credit Centrex, and I was certain that there'd been a mistake. When I learned that he'd gone on to Mort, I visited his hote to have another look at him."

"You were going to speak with me," Caland said. "What changed your mind?"

"I suddenly found you in familiar conversation with Fem Wobbons, who is in charge of Rynaif's espionage on Mort."

Caland said incredulously, "Fem Wobbons is—"

"Your association with Fulm on Rynaif, followed by your familiarity with Fem Wobbons on Mort, could only mean one thing. I immediately notified my world that you were an agent of the world of Rynaif. Before I could search further, you disappeared."

"Mmmm." Arlu grinned slyly. "You can safely change that entry now, I think. And we'll change our entry concerning you. One less mysterious fem unclutters things just a little."

"We could bring pressure to have Fem Wobbons and her assistants expelled from Mort," Fem Ornal said. "But she's rather stupid, and she's preoccupied with her ludicrous pursuit of young mals. Given her opportunities, she could have created a disaster here instead of an occasional interruption. We've been able to counter most of her moves. We'd rather keep her here than run the risk that her successor might be more competent. We don't underestimate her, though. Occasional interruptions to the tin production are serious enough for us."

"Mmmm." Arlu was ruminating again. "This is my fault. I should have consulted with Fem Ornal earlier. Now we'll pool our information. I've had some talks with Pakovich's counsel. Have you met him?"

"Calta talked with him," Tel said.

"Mmmm. Mal named Gilf. Since you know Pakovich, you ought to be able to predict Gilf. They look entirely different and think exactly alike. I've been discussing Prency Tate with him. He refuses to believe that Elat is Tate, refuses to accept evidence about Elat's activity on Verblanif, refuses to credit the conversation Cal overheard, loses his temper over the suggestion that anyone might presume to tell Pak Enterprises whom to hire and fire, and finally says Elat anyway has a contract and nothing can be done until it expires. This may be a more pressing problem than any of us realize. Fem Ornal and I will consider it while we finish our dins." He got to his feet. "Glad to have this item settled."

Tel burst into laughter. "I told you we'd peel these things away one at a time," she said to Caland. "This is a great day for it. We've rid ourselves not only of your mystery fem, but also Nalce and company, including Fem Wobbons. And we can scratch off Dombrily and Wes Fulm. Fulm's contact with Cal *was* accidental—but it fooled the world of Aravia, and it also fooled the world of Rynaif. There weren't just two people following Fulm that day. The world of Rynaif also had a watcher on him, and that watcher made the same report that Aravia's watcher made. So the world of Rynaif did a search on Cal, and when it found he was bound for Mort, it asked its agents here to continue it. As a result, Fem Wobbons tried to seduce him at the hote, thus mixing business and pleasure, and Nalce and friends have been watching him in the Valley. I'd love to read their reports! They still haven't figured him out. Because of that casual contact with Fulm, and because he moved to Dombrily's Valley, they're certain that he's involved in Fulm's anti-sabotage work. Because he's a Caland, they know he represents a colossal financial interest. But his behavior here can't make any sense at all to them. How could a Valley para be working against the saboteurs? They must be as confused now as they were in the beginning.

"As for Dombrily, it's easy enough to account for him. He thought he could manipulate the sabotage situation to his own advantage, and the explosion that killed Fulm scared him out of his wits. He suddenly realized that the saboteurs weren't playing games, and he wanted no part of what they were playing." She laughed again. "A great day for peeling!"

Fem Ornal nodded politely.

Arlu said, "In any case, it's reassuring to know that not all of Cal's dreams foretell doom."

"You're missing one point," Tel said severely. "If anything this proves how accurate Cal's dreams are. When one of them does foretell doom, we'd better pay attention to it."

"I suppose," Arlu said gloomily. "But before you get too excited about peeling away mysteries, I want to point out that this really hasn't cleared up a thing with our most important problems."

* * * * * * *

Tel was taking art lessons. A sculptor calling himself Olorn had an unusual studio in a small shop on the Prom. Olorn offered portraits to tourists. He modeled the subject's head in clay, made a mold, and then cast as many copies as the subject wanted in a light plastic material that he manufactured himself from his own secret formula. He sprayed the busts to simulate whatever metallic finish the customer preferred—gold, silver, bronze, aluminum, platinum. The finished bust was hollow and easy to transport, but it could be filled with a heavy material, such as sand, to give it the weight of a genuine metal bust.

Olorn was a bona fide artist, capable of doing splendid work, but he received very few commissions. For one thing, his fees were exorbitant. For another, he hated his subjects. He rudely rejected any applicant whose head did not appeal to him, and his insults drove some of his subjects away before the work was finished. The bust sometimes turned out to be a vicious caricature. He charged half down and the balance on satisfactory completion of the castings, and frequently he did not collect the second half of his fee.

But an occasional commission enabled him to live well in the Valley, so he worked on things that interested him and received potential customers fractiously. Visitors to Mort never bought his serious sculpture—he had to ship that to an art gallery on Aravia to dispose of it, a fact that he resented bitterly. He spent his free moments sitting in the door of his shop and glaring at the passing tourists. He felt every one of them was rejecting him and his art. He divided the universe into two types of people: his fellow artists, who were rivals; and everyone else, who was an enemy.

He accepted Tel as a disciple and tolerated Caland because they both needed a model. Caland sat in amused relaxation watching the Prom traffic and listening to Olorn's indignant comments on the shape of his ears or his untidy growth of eyebrows or on Tel's blundering efforts to model them.

The Reverend passed by, returned for a second, incredulous look at Caland in the modeling chair, and paused to remark, "Olorn's caught another rich tourist!"

Sam the Artist, following close behind, mimicked shocked consternation. "Beware!" he proclaimed. "All of Olorn's busts have two heads. He got double vision from trying to count his money twice."

"A bust of you," Olorn snarled, "would have no head and two stomachs." He shouted at Caland, "Sit still. Why do all models start to twitch the moment they're put in a pose? The only good model is a dead one." And to Tel, "No, *no!* The two sides of the same face are always different, but they're never convex and concave."

It would have reminded Caland of his pointless hours spent sitting in parks, except that this park was frequented by friends who waved or spoke or nodded as they passed. Caland, after Olorn's explosive reaction to his first attempt to respond, stoically maintained a rigid posture.

Whereupon Olorn began referring to him as "Stone Face."

Finally lethargy crept over him, and he closed his eyes. Tel shook him awake. "Olorn says that you twitch more when you're asleep than you do when you think you're modeling."

There was a flurry of excitement in the Prom. Moppy and Phem came bouncing along jubilantly on either side of Llabal, the armless old mal whom Phem's enlarged allowance had finally set to Aravia for prostheses. He was proudly exhibiting them to passersby, and they brought him into the studio, despite the menace of Olorn's fury, to present him to Caland.

"It really was Cal who did it," Phem said. "If it weren't for him, there wouldn't be any allowance."

"I'm touching hands with everyone in the Valley," Llabal announced triumphantly, waving an artificial arm.

Caland offered his hand.

"I'm touching *both* hands with everyone in the Valley," Llabal persisted. He touched Caland's hands and also those of Tel and Olorn, ignoring the fact that theirs were clay smeared.

"I can wash 'em," Llabal said jovially. "I'm pretty good at washing things now."

Llabal waved a farewell and continued his elated progress up the Prom. Olorn and Tel worked in silence for a time. Then Olorn asked, "What did he do before he lost his arms?"

"I don't know," Tel said. "He lost them long before he came to the Valley."

"The measure of a person's loss is not what he has lost," Olorn said. "The measure of the value of an arm or hand is what the arm or hand is used for. A machine operator uses his to push a button. The arm functions only as a link with a machine; the machine is able to perform regardless of what happens to the arm. The operator's foot could make contact with the button just as well. So could his chin. But for an artist, or a musician, or a sculptor, hands are a medium of expression. What could be more starkly tragic than the loss of an artist's hands or a singer's voice? If Llabal never used his hands for anything except his convenience, he lost nothing except his convenience, and now he's regained nothing except his convenience."

Caland dozed off again, and he dreamed that he heard Olorn ask Tel, "What did he do with his brain before he lost it?"

CHAPTER THIRTY-ONE

Caland's life continued to slow perceptibly. His devastating headaches continued. He began to sleep badly at night, and as a result, he dozed off unpredictably during the day. His para performances dropped to one or two an evening and occasionally he skipped them altogether. Much of the time he listened blankly while others talked. To discuss anything at all—even to answer a question—required a mental concentration that he shrank from.

Doctor Gormaz announced an open house to which the entire Valley was invited.

"People are resenting the way he and his assistants go around snooping into their private affairs," Sam the Artist explained. "He wants the Vals to know that he's one of them. He's only snooping in the name of science."

"I didn't know the Valley had any private affairs," Tel said.

"It hasn't—until someone starts to snoop. That's true of people anywhere. As long as they think no one is paying attention, they're totally uninhibited. Gormaz not only pays attention; he asks questions and takes notes."

Caland stirred himself. He had not yet encountered any antagonism for Doctor Gormaz. "Do they resent his snooping enough to boycott his open house?" he asked.

"What a question!" Sam the Artist exclaimed. "He's not only offering free food, but he's persuaded Hef to cook it for him. Even Pakovich could draw a crowd if he held an open house for Vals with free food. It's also a chance to do some reverse snooping. Few Vals have ever seen the inside of Dom's place. Everyone is going."

Everyone went. Tourists had the Prom to themselves for an entire afternoon. Even the Reverend's paras worked in shifts so they could take turns attending Gormaz's party. All of the Prom shops and eateries catering to Vals were closed.

A large canopy had been erected at one corner of the garden adjacent to the Valley fence. The tall fertilizer factory fence arched over it. There Hef labored and perspired over his iron kettles. He had ample time to enjoy the spectacle of people enjoying his food again because Gormaz had supplied him with a crew of assistants to serve the putrebuns and yuck. All Hef had to do was cook, and his putrebuns were as delicious as everyone remembered.

His performance made the party an overwhelming success despite the fact that those Vals hoping for a glimpse of the interior of Dom's house were disappointed. Gormaz wisely decided against opening his laboratory to the tread of thousands of Vals. He entertained his guests in the garden, and they packed it to capacity and overflowed into the tangled yards of the neighboring houses on either side and into Fishstink Alley on the front.

Tel, with a disinterested Caland following on her heels, wandered about the building's exterior looking unabashedly through windows.

"What did you see?" Caland asked finally.

"Offices," she said. "Disappointingly mundane. Sociology must be a bore."

"They're going to put fifteen thousand people on file," Caland said. "Let's eat."

They waited in line for putrebuns and yuck. Then they drifted with the crowd, and eventually they passed the veranda. Doctor Gormaz stood there overseeing everything and passing out instructions to the Vals he had hired. He seemed to be enjoying himself immensely. There was an aura of contentment about him that Caland had not noticed before—perhaps because his beard was longer and sleeker and presented less of an aspect of bristling menace. His assistants were attempting to move through the crowd and get acquainted with people. They kept colliding with Soapy's crew, which was gathering up mugs to wash so they could be used again, and picking up discarded putrebun wrappings.

Gormaz looked down and saw Caland and Tel. His chuckle was like a loud gurgle. "I'm surprised that so many people turned out for this," he said in his booming voice. "Have you noticed how little community activity there is in the Valley? Everything breaks down into small groups and cliques. Look at the nightly beach fires. Each of them is an independent unit organized against the world, no outsider admitted without an invitation. Night after night the same people gather around the same fire, and the few who circulate between fires are almost without status. This is amazing for a commonality that shares so many problems. One might suppose that the Valley's inhabitants have no communal awareness. And yet—" he gestured expansively. "—here they are. Here everyone is. I must perform more experiments like this."

"Vals have too much communal awareness," Tel said. "They're forced to share everything, all the time. When they have an opportunity at privacy or restrictiveness, they grab at it."

Doctor Gormaz cocked his head. "Perhaps. Perhaps."

"As for the number of people who turned out, don't forget that most of them would walk a lot further than Fishstink Alley for one of Hef's putrebuns."

"Ah! Hef is an artist. I offered to finance a restaurant for him, but he wasn't interested. He only consented to work here today because I convinced him that a lot of hungry people would be here. I invited the supers of the View and the Vista to come and sample his cooking, but they declined."

"If they came, Pakovich would fire them."

"Perhaps. It's unfortunate, it really is. They could make a splendidly popular thing of garden parties for their hote guests with Hef doing the cooking. We must do something about Hef. He's a Valley asset."

"Where's Dom?" Tel asked.

'He was here a little while ago watching from the veranda. Perhaps he got tired. Have you any idea what his age is?"

Tel shook her head.

"I asked him and he got coy about it," Doctor Gormaz said. "He may be as much as a hundred. He's remarkably active, all things considered, but he does tire easily. Has anyone given a thought to what will happen to the Valley when he dies? Does he have any heirs?"

"I don't think anyone knows very much about him," Tel said.

"That's something you Vals should be losing sleep over," Doctor Gormaz said bluntly. "What would happen if the heirs sold out to Pakovich?"

"That," Tel said, "I'd rather not think about."

Doctor Gormaz was scowling at the sky, which had suddenly clouded over. A few scattered drops of rain began to fall. The Vals, who rarely bothered to seek shelter for anything less than a deluge, did not even look up.

"I have never encountered such unpredictable weather," Gormaz said. "It's impossible to plan anything. These sudden wind storms are dangerous. I thought the one yesterday afternoon would capsize all the boats on the bay. Pakovich should have a meteorological office."

Caland half listened to their talk and watched the milling crowd. The Vals did indeed tend to coalesce into animated groups—cliques, to Doctor Gormaz—that talked for a time and then drifted apart. It seemed to him that Gormaz was grossly oversimplifying the complexities of Valley society, but the doctor was a newcomer and also a scientist. In one role he eschewed complexities; in the other he searched for essentials. Both processes involved oversimplification.

Caland, also, was a newcomer. He felt very tired and very much the outsider, and he had difficulty in interesting himself in anything.

He missed Sam the Artist. Sam always was entertaining to listen to whether Caland felt like listening or not. But Sam, to his own everlasting regret, was out at the space port with a group of artists painting, "WELCOME TO MORT THE WORLD THAT PAKOVICH MADE," on the terminal building.

Morlef stopped by to enthusiastically describe his progress, but Caland had no interest in that, either. Then the Reverend greeted them with a nod and a smile. He spoke briefly to Tel before he moved on.

Tel turned to Caland. "The Reverend thinks it's time for our nap."

"Nap?" Caland echoed as though such a thought had never occurred to him.

"You're almost asleep standing up. Come along. Back to Bay Unview Boulevard. The rarefied heights of Fishstink Alley are too much for us."

On the beach that night, Sam the Artist regaled them with his tales of sign painting for Pakovich. "Looked over our shoulders all the time we were cutting the stencils," Sam said. "Fussed about the letters' shapes. Fussed about the proportions. Fussed about their size. Then when we were taping them in place and testing the spacing, he was a good kilometer away out on the landing field trying to shout instructions to us. Cerfis finally convinced him that the project should be kept secret, with an unveiling ceremony after it's finished, so he let us rig a canvas. He's probably at home right now drawing up a list of guests for the unveiling."

"Aren't you rather conspicuous among Pakovich's artists?" Tel asked.

"Of course," Sam the Artist said, grinning. "But the artists told him I was a flunk they'd hired for the scratch work, and he insisted on paying me himself. So I'm collecting Pakovich's wages instead of working for nothing."

"Doesn't that bother your conscience?" Tel asked.

"Not at all. Pakovich wages aren't that much better than nothing."

"When will it be finished?"

"Couple of days. Maybe three. Those big letters take a lot of paint, and we want to do it right. Care to attend the ceremony? I might be able to filch a few invitations."

"To see Pakovich make an ass of himself?"

"It requires no making. He simply is. I thought today when he was trying to redesign our letters—he's more than just an ass. He's a harass, which is an ass on a galactic scale. But the ceremony is certain to have its diverting moments."

Tel nudged Caland. "Do you want to attend Pakovich's unveiling?"

"No," Caland said firmly.

Tel turned to him. "How are you feeling?"

"I feel fine," he said protestingly. "I had a nap this afternoon."

"Sure you don't feel tired?"

"Not at all."

But when the wind began to rise, blowing rain, he was glad enough to go home to bed.

* * * * * * *

Morlef already had transformed the end of the Prom. The plaza was paved, and pillars for its roof had been erected. Off to one side arose the skeletal structure of the community building. The young architect had arrived and was at work on the plans for the two theaters. Each day when Caland was finally able to make his unsteady way to the Prom, Tel asked him whether he wanted to watch the work, but the bustling activity depressed him. He had the feeling that he ought to be contributing something, and he knew that he was incapable of doing anything at all.

He much preferred the benches by the Valley Transportation Company yard. There was a restful relaxation about the lethargic, purposeless flow of Prom traffic. He sat there for several hours each day, considering without appetite the putrebuns and yuck that Tel had brought him.

On the day after Doctor Gormaz's open house, she sat beside him asking passersby, "Did you see Dom yesterday?" She got nothing but negative answers until she asked the Reverend.

"I didn't exactly see him at the open house," the Reverend said. "But I did see him watching from an upstairs window."

"How did he look?" Tel asked.

"He looked fine. He waved at me. Or to someone. I waved back. Why do you ask?"

"I thought it odd that he didn't turn up at a party held in his own back yard."

"Dom never has cared much for Valley gatherings," the Reverend said. "He ridicules Pakovich for putting on airs, but his own outlook is just as aristocratic. When the Valley people gather, an upstairs window is precisely where I would expect to find him."

He asked Caland, "How are you feeling today?"

"A little tired," Caland said.

"Headache?"

"Just a little."

Later Caland asked Tel," What's the mystery about Dom?"

"Maybe nothing," she said. "Dom certainly is old, and he certainly is a snob, and it wouldn't be unusual for him to avoid a crowd of Vals in his own yard. On the other hand, he's hardly been out at all since Doctor Gormaz moved in with him. I was wondering whether anyone had seen him face to face lately. A face in an upstairs window doesn't count."

"Is it another mystery to worry about?" Caland asked.

"Hardly that. The Vals who work for Gormaz probably know all about him. Head still aching?"

"A little."

"It wouldn't be the first headache that Dom has caused. How about a swim?"

They swam in the bay, and then they luxuriated in the caressing warmth of the sun until Caland dozed off and slept soundly. When he awoke, Tel was gone. An elderly, long-time Valley resident called the Knife was sitting in attendance on him. Two of Louie Laggie's scavs were lolling nearby—a body-guard, Caland supposed, in case whoever had stolen his mind should make another attempt to pilfer his body as well. All of their searching and watching had ended up in failure; perhaps this was the last resort, an attempt to catch someone trying to abduct him.

The Knife was a woodcarver. He fashioned figures and toys for the tourist trade. He lavished a remarkable ingenuity on them, producing detailed, finely traced figuration and moving parts.

"But it takes so long to make one," the Knife lamented. He was a sturdily built old mal, and when his great hands closed around one of his carvings, it looked as though he were about to smash it. "Hands are stiff," he went on. "Eyes aren't what they were even a year ago. Wearing out, that's what I am. Everything wears out, but it's a shame it has to happen to people."

Caland agreed that it was a great pity, though he thought that the Knife's nimble fingers seemed to perform with an ageless dexterity.

"Minds wear out, too," he said. "Or they get worn out."

The Knife chuckled. "I suppose."

He worked on, and Caland thought about Tel. He was seeing less and less of her. It wasn't unusual, now, for him to wake up and find someone else keeping an eye on him. He could not blame her. Life must be dull indeed for any active fem condemned to lead a faltering mal about and waste her days watching him sleep and her nights being kept awake while he twisted in pain. Perhaps it was time that she left him with his memories. He cherished his memories. Even during his sleep-less, pain-wracked nights, he could think with pleasure of the joyful, purposeful days when they trained and organized a troop of paras, presented Partley hrv' Dasshalm with the illusion of a university, planned new buildings and a revitalized Valley, and all the rest.

"Important thing," the Knife said, "is not to make any two carvings alike. If they're too much alike, the tourist looks at one, decides he's seen them all, and walks on. If each one is a little different, he gets curious as to *how* it's different. He starts making comparisons. He decides he likes one better than the other, and he looks for something he might still like better. If he finds it, he's almost a customer. But each one has got to be a little different."

"What use are they?" Caland asked.

The Knife chuckled gleefully. "No use. No use at all. But what in all the galaxy really has any use? Will this theater you're building be useful? It'll cog the tourists into spending money, and that's what my carvings do. That's what the whores in the Houses of Fame do. All the humans in the universe prey on each other, just like those sea creatures that are supposed to color Mort's oceans with their blood. On their own worlds these rich tourists cog the likes of us, and when they come here, we get something back. But we have to pay rent or buy food, and the money ultimately ends up with Dom or Pakovich, who get cogged when they visit other worlds. What possible use is the whole rigmarole to anyone?" He clucked his tongue and shook his head sadly. "Important thing is to make each one different. Now—let's see. The last one—"

Caland slept again.

* * * * * * *

The only outsiders who received invitations to Pakovich's unveiling ceremony were the artists who painted the sign. Sam the Artist, whose status as a scratch-work flunk had not entitled him to an invitation, borrowed one of them to show his incredulous friends in the Valley.

The invitation's text was a three-dimensional casting embedded in transparent paper. Caland examined it with astonishment; he hadn't seen the process since it had enjoyed a brief vogue when he was a child. "How did Pakovich ever manage this?" he asked.

"The Aravian aristocracy uses it," Sam the Artist said. "So

of course Pakovich has to use it. It's his way of bringing culture to Mort."

"But there can't be enough social functions on Mort to justify importing equipment for this!"

"What does cost matter to Pakovich if he can keep up with Aravian styles? Anyway, you're underestimating Mort's social activities. Occasionally one of the hotes sponsors what is called an 'occasion,' and all of the guests get invited along with a select list of Pak Enterprises employees. That's the measure of status on Mort. Being on the list. Pak Enterprises sponsors social functions all the time—like this unveiling ceremony—and every employee gets invited now and then. Pakovich also issues invitations like this to his private parties. His idea of getting his money's worth out of something is to make certain that an expensive but useless process is used as much as possible."

"I'm beginning to feel curious about this ceremony," Tel said. "Are all of the artists using their invitations?"

"All of them are using their invitations, but not for the ceremony. They're leaving Mort on tonight's ship. They're taking their invitations home as souvenirs."

"Sam!" Tel said sternly. "Just what mischief have you steamed up?"

"A sign," Sam the Artist said. "'WELCOME TO MORT THE WORLD THAT PAKOVICH MADE.' It looks handsome. I told you—Pakovich himself supervised spacing the letters."

"Are *you* attending the ceremony?"

"Of course. I'm in charge of the unveiling. I'm going to pull the rope myself."

"Then why are the artists clearing out?"

"They're seniors," Sam the Artist said. "Their terms here are expiring. After three years in Pakovich's art colony, they don't need any special motivation to be eager to leave."

"All right. But I'm going to watch this ceremony myself if I have to sneak in."

Sam the Artist shrugged. "You won't have to sneak in. The terminal is always open to the public, and you can look through the observation windows. You can't mingle with Pakovich's loyal workers or slurp refreshments without an invitation, but you can watch the crowd's reaction."

"We'll do it," Tel said. She nudged Caland. "Right? We'll do it. How many hours of oratory does it take to unveil a two-line sign?"

"This much I promise you," Sam the Artist said grimly. "The speeches will only last until I get tired of listening. Then the canvas is coming down. Ready or not."

* * * * * * *

Caland and Tel had the terminal's vast waiting room to themselves. There were no ships berthed at the moment, and the shops and lounge were closed—probably so that their employees could attend the ceremony. The landing field teemed with people.

"The clod has turned out the entire city of Paradise," Tel said as they stood watching the crowd. "Even the school children. To unveil a 'Welcome to Mort' sign. I'm glad I don't work for Pakovich. How does his labor force stand it?"

"It's an excuse for a celebration," Caland said. "Mort doesn't have many. Also, he's serving refreshments."

"Also, his supers are probably taking roll and docking the pay of anyone who doesn't show up," Tel said.

The loyal Pak Enterprises employees seemed to know what to expect from a Pakovich speech. They had brought chairs and blankets, and the crowd had arranged itself comfortably in groups of families and friends. Children raced about in highly controlled jubilation, and never seemed to wander far from the territory their parents had staked out. At the far end of the field was a row of refreshment tents.

Pakovich arrived in an excessively large, overly ornate limousine, and strode directly to the small platform that had been set up near the terminal building.

"Precisely on time," Tel murmured appreciatively.

He was in total dress and so were the Pak Enterprises supers who sat in two rows of chairs just in front of the platform. Caland and Tel had a choice between watching the supers' solemn faces or watching the back of Pakovich's neck. The neck proved to be more interesting. It underwent its own unveiling every time he leaned forward, and it became increasingly red as the speech progressed. They could hear nothing at all except for a faintly echoing blur of words. The amplifiers were turned toward the audience, and the building was sound-proofed against landing and take-off noises from the field.

Pakovich struck poses, he gesticulated, he paced, he made dramatic pauses, and through it all the reddening back of his neck came and went.

"Enough," Tel said finally. "Every world needs an identity of its own, and this peerless sign guarantees that no one arriving at this port will long remain ignorant of his destination. He must have said that twenty times over by now. Pull the rope, Sam."

Pakovich talked on. And on. Caland tensed himself expecting Sam the Artist to lose patience at any moment. He wondered whether the canvas would billow out as it fell and bury both Pakovich and the supers.

Abruptly Pakovich concluded. Hands made motions of applause that Pakovich's bobbing head acknowledged. Then he half turned and waited, looking upward. The signal, if there was one, did not come from him, but Sam the Artist performed his role with commendable efficiency. The enormous canvas, which had been covering the terminal's entire upper façade, dropped straight down the side of the building and crumpled neatly at its base.

They now had a full view of Pakovich's face as it registered, in rapid sequence, bewilderment, consternation, and outrage. He turned and began ranting at the top officials who quickly gathered about him. The vast audience in the field beyond seemed unaware that anything was wrong. Some of its members were applauding politely.

The strangeness of that tableau—calm audience, enraged Pakovich, thoroughly frightened supers—was so incomprehensible that Tel grabbed Caland's arm and said, "Come on. I've got to see what this is all about."

They hurried to the exit and followed a walk around the building. A vehicular gate to the field had been guarded when they arrived—entrance by invitation only—but now it stood opened and abandoned, its watchers having vacated their posts in order to enjoy the ceremony. Caland and Tel walked through it and made a wide circle so as to emerge well to the rear of the crowd of Pakovich employees.

No one challenged them. They headed across the field and halted the moment the enormous, glowing blue letters of the sign became visible to them.

It was a magnificent sign, brilliantly conceived and masterfully executed. It stretched the full length of the building's upper façade, and the bonding paint gave the letters an embossed appearance. At a single stroke the nondescript terminal building had been made memorable.

Sam the Artist was nowhere to be seen. He had pulled the rope and discreetly vanished. The vast audience was stirring curiously, but it was still unable to comprehend what was wrong. At the edge of the platform Pakovich continued to rant and gesticulate.

The enormous sign that now was a permanent part of the terminal's façade seemed to hover above him:

WELCOME TO MORT
THE WORLD THAT MADE PAKOVICH

CHAPTER THIRTY-TWO

Tel and Sam the Artist had several discussions in which they tried to decide which of the assembled supers had been Prency Tate. Their talks seemed portentous to Caland because neither of them thought to consult him.

He would have had no opinion if asked. The possibility had not even occurred to him.

The reality of the Valley and the Valley's problems no longer concerned him. He had given up his own para performances after an evening during which he fumbled his lines, kept forgetting what he was trying to do, and finally lost an audience that left a paltry twenty-two chits in the dust behind it. The Valley activity that he had once been a part of now drifted by without touching him. His friends greeted him and accepted his mechanical responses with a smile as they moved along. Only when Tel was stationed loyally beside him did they pause, but it was her that they talked quietly with.

Phem, with two of Louie Laggie's scavs in reserve, spent an entire afternoon with him while Tel hurried about taking care of some undefined business that had come up unexpectedly. Phem sprayed his face and wiped off his untidy growth of beard, and then she insisted that he put on clean clothing—joking, as she did so, that Tel was neglecting him because she no longer loved him. The suggestion was a painful one to Caland.

Later, sitting on the bay beach, Phem prated enthusiastically about helping the Valley's blind child. She wanted to know whether there were artificial eyes that could be bought the way they had bought artificial arms for Llabal. Caland tried to focus his thoughts. He could not remember, but he supposed it possible. A mal with a brain that had been torn apart and wired together again was likely to suppose anything possible, but he could give her no information about it. After a time she stopped questioning him, and he slept.

His headaches continued to intensify; some days they were unrelenting.

"Beach?" Tel would ask cautiously in the evening, and he would assent even though he would have preferred to go to bed early. He liked to watch Tel at the fireside, liked to study the play of the firelight on her sturdy femininity, liked to dream of untangling the knot that caught up her long, dark hair and burying his face in her breasts and engulfing her in his long dormant passion miraculously revived.

But he never watched her for long. He dozed off and had to be awakened long enough to totter home and collapse in bed.

For all of his lethargy and persistent sleepiness, he continued to sleep badly. He kept awakening to the sensation of watching eyes. Sometimes Tel would patiently let him get out of bed and look about, and he would stare from the empty windows into the blacker night outside.

Or into a storm. Lately it seemed that every night there was a storm whipping about.

Once he awakened to find Tel gone. He wondered whether she too, had an awareness of someone watching and had gone to investigate. The shock of her absence kept him wakeful for a time, but he fell asleep before she returned, and the next morning forgot to ask her about it. The severity of his headache drove the incident from his mind.

Abruptly the course of events quickened into a crisis. It began harmlessly enough with the Valley running out of cider. This happened regularly, but each occurrence took the entire Valley by surprise, and inspired Sam to new heights of invective in condemning such an iniquity.

Now it happened again, and they sat around a beach fire, ate a sumptuous feast, and drank—yuck. The Knife, who carried a bit of carving to work on, bent low to catch the firelight on it and announced cheerfully that things weren't as bad as they might be. He could remember an occasion when the water line had broken, and there'd been nothing at all to drink in the valley for two days except cider.

"Are you trying to cheer us up?" Sam the Artist demanded. "What are the odds against *that* ever happening again?"

Knack, one of Bronlan's drivers, had picked up an odd bit of gossip from a tourist just in from Aravia. According to the tourist, the impoverished Aravian princess who had been betrothed to Alexander the Second—in a ceremony that would long be notorious on Aravia for its extravagance and bad taste—had eloped with a former lover. Her family had gone into mourning because of the humiliation and disgrace. The tourist didn't know how the two Pakoviches were taking it or even if they knew.

"If there were anything but yuck to drink it in, I'd suggest a toast to the princess," Sam the Artist said.

Louie Laggie protested. "That's tough on Alexander the Second. He's really an up person. Once when they caught me sneaking into the mines dump, he happened by and told them to let me scav as much as I liked. They were only going to bury the stuff anyway, and he wanted to know what possible harm it would do if I shagged a little metal out of the discard first. The answer was absolutely none, but old Pakovich never looks at things that way."

The Reverend pursed his lips thoughtfully. "If she's a lively enough young fem to have a former lover, she probably would have been the wrong wife for Alexander the Second. He's a quiet type, and she'd have been held firmly under the older Pakovich's scrutiny, not to mention the fact that the entire population of Paradise would have expected her to be almost excessively endowed with rectitude."

"What does Alexander the Second think about it?" Phem asked. "There's no reason for us to go into mourning if he hasn't."

Tel caught Caland's eye and winked. "Alexander the Second will be pleased. He won't have to explain to the princess why he stays out so late. Has anyone seen him in the Valley lately?"

"I have no interest in his Valley visits unless he's delivering cider," Sam the Artist said. "Is it really due tomorrow?"

"Bar says the trucks have been ordered," Louie Laggie said. "Mucks says the work crews have been hired."

"Why, by all principles of unreason, does Pakovich insist on his winery doing business according to the calendar instead of according to the amount of cider we drink?" Sam the Artist demanded. "Does he resent the fact that we buy cider from him?"

"Actually he does," Tel said. "If he didn't, he'd deliver it himself instead of making us go after it."

"As long as it gets delivered—" Sam the Artist said.

This time it did not get delivered. The news crashed about the Valley like a tidal wave the following morning: Trucks dispatched to the winery returned empty. Winery workers were refusing to work.

Sam the Artist headed for the Prom at a most uncharacteristic frantic run the moment he heard about it, and he stood staring incredulously at the empty trucks.

"Do you suppose that Tate is responsible?" Tel asked him.

"If he is, I'll tear out his most conspicuous glands with my two hands. How did he do it? It isn't possible. It shouldn't be possible."

No one knew anything about it; but the next day there was no meat delivery, and the following day milk deliveries from the farms failed, and left Olgi highly concerned about her supply.

An extremely troubled Regelz Arlu called all of them to a meeting. He made himself comfortable in the chair with the reclining back, a mound of crinkly yellow topped by a multiple scowling face. The rest of them turned their chairs in his direction and waited for him to speak. For once he abstained from mystifications; the facts were bewildering enough.

"Tate unerringly picked out Pakovich's weaknesses," he said. "The winery only employs ten or twelve people, but they're highly skilled, and they were brought here to establish the foundations of a great wine industry. Pakovich's ambition was to take a group of his aristocratic friends into a posh restaurant on Aravia, order a Mort wine, and say, 'Mine!' But it didn't work out because Pakovich kept meddling in the winery management and telling the expert workers what kinds of wine to produce and how to make them. There's no demand for his wines. The sale of cider to the Valley barely meets the overhead and keeps the place operating about one sennite in four, but he's too stubborn to close the operation."

"Praise fate for that," Sam the Artist muttered.

"The labor problem arose from the fact that Pakovich has these skilled workers there with very little to do. So they're assigned to regular farm labor when they're not running the winery. Naturally they resent that. Their only recourse would be to quit, in which case they'd have to pull up roots and pay out their savings in order to transport their families to another world where they'd start from zero. Tate played on their bitterness by telling them Pakovich was about to reduce their wages to those of regular farm laborers when they weren't working the winery. They struck. From that point it was easy for Tate to bring other specialists into it in support of the winery workers. What Pakovich does to one group threatens all of them. Only a couple of sennites ago, a salesman was here discussing with Pakovich and his supers the possibility that it might be cheaper for Pakovich to import food than produce it himself. Tate made certain that all the farm and dairy and meat packing workers knew about that. I'm positive that the salesman was an imposter brought here by Tate, and Pakovich fell into a trap. Tate has the labor pot boiling, and it's not going to be easy to turn it off. All of the food producers are in full revolt. Next he'll convince the other specialists, like power plant workers, that their futures are threatened."

"Is Tate still considered a promising Pak Enterprises super?"

Tel asked.

"He is not. Pakovich's counsel rejected my advice, but he slyly had Tate watched just to see whether there was anything in it. As soon as he discovered the connection between Tate and the winery workers, he took the story to Pakovich. Pakovich fired Tate in a rage, contract or no contract. Probably Tate planned it that way. He went back to the food producers and said, 'I spoke for you. I insisted that Pakovich listen to your grievances and treat you fairly, and look what happened. We're all in this together.' With one deft move he went from management to labor, and now he's openly leading the strikers. If he isn't stopped, he'll have this world shut down completely within a sennite."

"But how does he do it?" Sam the Artist asked bewilderedly.

"He's good. He's extremely good. The farm workers have a lot of grievances. Their housing and working conditions don't compare with those of workers living in Paradise, and they don't enjoy anything like the same services. Their children have to come all the way to Paradise to school. They have no medical clinic—they have to go to the mines or the Government Mall, and transportation is uncertain. An expert like Tate can do a lot with material like that."

Arlu turned to Caland. "Your friends Emson and Felroy arrived on Mort yesterday. Officially they're tourists returning for another enjoyable stay at the Paradise View. Actually they're here for the kill, and they timed their trip to arrive before the Port is closed—which it will be in another day or two."

"So what can be done about it?" Sam the Artist demanded.

Arlu sighed. "It's complicated. There are several factions, and we still don't know which is the more dangerous. Tate and associates want to brew up as much turmoil as possible, and wreck things as much as possible, until Pakovich is willing to pay them off to get rid of them. Tate will sell out his labor movement the moment the price is right. He has no further interest. Then there are the saboteurs."

"Nalce and his friends have disappeared from the Valley,"

the Reverend said. "He dropped his election campaign several days ago."

"I know," Arlu said. "It wasn't accomplishing anything, and there'll be plenty of employment for him elsewhere. As agents of Rynaif, Fem Wobbons and her crew want to sabotage the mining industry as thoroughly and as permanently as possible. They'll be in sympathy with Tate to whatever extent he disrupts the mines and smelters and loading equipment. They'll even give him a hand. We can expect some timely explosions as soon as the miners go on strike, which they will. But the moment Tate tries to call everything off and run with the loot, Fem Wobbons will start working to keep the strikes going.

"Then there's Sdissler. Only Sdissler knows how many troops he has on Mort. He may attempt to bring in reinforcements—Fem Ornal spaced a warning about that to Aravia two days ago. If Sdissler has been waiting for an opportunity, this certainly should be it."

"Has he actually done anything?" Tel asked.

"Yes. He had a meeting with Pakovich and his supers this morning. He told them he was alarmed by some of the talk going on in Pakovich's labor force. He suggested that he transfer personnel from the forest labor camps to Paradise. Sdissler's employees have no contact with the subversive forces at work, here—the Pak Enterprises people regard them with contempt—and he could guarantee their loyalty. He suggested that his mals be placed in key installations—at the Port, the power plant, the sewage and water plants, and so on—camouflaged as special cleaning details. If necessary, even in the mines. If Pakovich's workers strike those places, Sdissler could take over and perhaps keep them operating with help from the supers. At a minimum he could prevent sabotage. Pakovich told him to go ahead, and he told his supers to give Sdissler all the transport they can spare and furnish him with everything else he needs.

"Thus far Sdissler is on Pakovich's side. If his objective is the world of Mort, he doesn't want it wrecked by a labor agitator. He also doesn't want the mines sabotaged. He'll have nothing to do with Rynaif and its agents. Aravia is always going to be Mort's best customer regardless of who owns the planet, and no usurper could hope to succeed against Aravian opposition. Sdissler wants to be able to say to Aravia, 'See—I restored order here and saw that your essential supplies of tin weren't interrupted.' He desperately needs Aravian recognition and support. So he'll bitterly oppose both Tate and the saboteurs, and he'll pretend loyalty to Pakovich until everyone else is beaten into submission. Then his will be the only force left."

The Reverend spoke quietly. "What we have building up here is a small scale war."

"I hope you're right," Arlu said. "I hope it's only a small scale war. Pakovich keeps doing one stupid thing after another. Bringing in Sdissler's mals to take the jobs of Pakovich's workers will arouse unimaginable bitterness. Whatever the size of the war, it's going to be bloody."

"Is there anything we can do?" the Reverend asked.

Arlu raised both hands. "In this tangled mess, whom would you try to help?"

"A better question is how we can help ourselves." Calta said. "Let's talk about ways and means to keep this small war out of the Valley."

"Mmmm—yes, we can talk about that," Arlu said. "But first, we should talk about one force on Mort that all others are overlooking—us—and the one unknown factor that even we haven't been able to figure out—Cal. Because Cal must have some connection to all of this. He simply must."

* * * * * * *

Morlef had no labor problems. The community building was taking shape before the Vals' startled eyes, and no one seemed more gratified about that than those who were working on it. The entire shell of the lower story was in place, a large T with its base just south of the completed plaza. The interior was already being divided into rooms, and Morlef was getting ready to roof the second story.

Caland paid no attention at all to the construction. There were comfortable benches on the plaza now, and a high roof over it, and it was as pleasant to sit there in the shade, with a putrebun and yuck beside him and eyes closed, as it sometimes was to sit on the beach in the sun. The tourists seemed oblivious to the momentous events on Mort, and they visited the Valley in their usual numbers. The Vals, also, went about their customary activities, but now they paused frequently to ask or relate the latest rumors. On the afternoon after Arlu's meeting, Caland heard that the winery, dairy, and meat packing plants were on strike; that the farms were on strike; that there were no government services in Paradise; that the Merc Mart was closed; that the hotes were about to shut down; that water would be cut off the next day. Rumors spread and became bloated, feeding on themselves, and the incredible thing about them was that some of them were true. Calta called a high level meeting of her own, and Caland went and paid very little attention to what was said because none of it seemed to concern him. There was much discussion about stocks of food, and how to best utilize them, and a possible shortage of drinking water, about what would happen to refrigeration units in the Valley if the broadcast power failed, and so on through a long list of premonitions.

On the beach that night they sat staring through the darkness at the Tin Mountains northeast of Paradise. Flames leaped up sporadically, and they tried to identify the place.

"Sdissler has a large barracks over that way," Sam the Artist said. "That's where the mals on his cleanup detail stay. He has another out by the world dump."

"Why would anyone be burning Sdissler's barracks?" the Reverend asked.

"If it isn't that, it's the mines. And what's there to burn at the mines?"

"Timbers, perhaps. There's always a stack of them there curing."

"I don't think we could see the flames from here. The mines' buildings are set back in a valley."

"The timber isn't," the Reverend said. "It's stacked along the highway."

"Tomorrow we'll know all about it," Sam the Artist said. "All we'll have to do is figure out which rumor to believe."

Doctor Gormaz came wandering past. He nodded in their direction, and on his return trip he veered over to join them. He had mastered Valley etiquette sufficiently to ask their permission before he sat down. "What *is* going on?" he demanded.

"It's complicated," Sam the Artist said. "Several illicit organizations are trying to take over the world of Mort, and Pakovich blunders about helping them twice over every time he tries to hinder them."

"What sort of organizations?"

"Let's see—we have saboteurs, and we have labor agitators, and we have a long-term conspiracy of some kind. Those are the main ones."

Gormaz glared at him incredulously. "Do you mean to say that Mort is in danger?"

"I'd say that it's in considerable danger. I don't know about the Valley, though what happens on Mort certainly will affect us."

"That idiot Pakovich!" Gormaz said bitterly. "I never should have come here. When is it going to happen?"

"No one is consulting us about this," Sam the Artist said. "It's been slowly building for some time, but now it's picking up momentum hourly. Give it another two or three days and things should get very interesting."

"Is Pakovich doing anything about it at all?"

"Nothing that's likely to help."

"Is there anything that anyone can do?" Doctor Gormaz asked.

"We've been talking about that. Even if we do something, whom do we help? Because when the dust settles, there'll be just one of the contenders left. I don't care much for Pakovich, but I'm sure I wouldn't like the others any better. It's like inventing a new game—'pick an evil'. I'd rather not."

"I see," Doctor Gormaz said. "There's nothing to do but wait it out and see what happens."

"Something like that."

"I see. If there are any sudden developments, will you let me know?"

Sam the Artist shrugged. "Why not? But you'll probably hear about them as soon as I will. Valley gossip and the speed of light are virtually synonymous."

"There are worlds where I have a modicum of influence," Doctor Gormaz said reflectively. "If anything like this were to happen on one of them, I could do something. Here, I'm completely helpless."

"Get in line with the rest of us," Sam the Artist said. "Practice patience. Ninety per cent of the universe's problems vanish if no one meddles with them."

"The other ten per cent worsen by geometric progression."

"Dom's house still has its shutters," Sam the Artist said grinning. "All you have to do it close them."

Doctor Gormaz got to his feet. "It also has electricity, though not much. If I close the shutters, how will I see to work?" He bounded away.

"Lucky mal," the Reverend said. "He has work to do."

For another day little seemed to happen. There were the usual contingent of tourists in the Valley, and the Valley's food reserves were holding up despite the failure of deliveries, but the proprietors of eateries were becoming worried. Few of them had food storage facilities. They bought their meat daily from the Valley's one outlet for Pakovich's packing plant, and stock there was getting low.

That night the power failed twice. The tourists began to grasp some of the flavor of the rumors, and the first failure sent them scurrying for the 'bus stop or frantically trying to waylay 'cabs. There were more flashes around Paradise, and by midnight it seemed ringed by fires.

Early the following morning the blow fell. Sam the Artist

hastily convoked a meeting. The twenty or so Vals invited gathered in a compact, sleepy group in one corner of the new plaza. Many of them had been rooted out of bed. They listened soberly to the 'bus driver's report.

"The road is blocked," he said. "Someone has cut down trees in that hollow just beyond where the road into Paradise meets the highway. They're lying across the road. There are mals with weapons, and Sdissler is in charge of them. He's in charge. He said everything is under control and he expects the trouble to be over in another day or two. In the meantime everyone should stay here. If we're critically short of anything, we should let him know."

"It sounds almost excessively cooperative for Sdissler," the Reverend mused.

"Probably he doesn't want us to start a war at his back until he gets the one in front of him settled." Sam the Artist grabbed Hairy. "Get over to the Fig Stump. See if telation is still working."

It was not. The Valley was cut off and isolated. The Vals exchanged anxious glances and shuffled feet uncertainly.

"Life's most challenging problem," the Reverend said finally, "is figuring out what to do when there's nothing that can be done."

"There's plenty that can be done," Sam the Artist said. "The problem is that no one has any responsibility for it. We really should have held the election."

"Let's pretend we did," Mucks Groilan said. "If the Valley ever needed an exek, it's now. Go ahead and start exeking."

Sam thought for a moment. "The fertilizer factory's fence protects us on the south, and no one is likely to try to land a boat on the ocean beach. We're vulnerable all along the bay, and the east fence won't keep out anyone who has shoes and can kick. I want the bay patrolled, and I want the east fence patrolled, and I want a watch on the Valley gate. To back it up, I want a defense force that's ready to go where it's needed. Mucks, grab all the Vals you can find who're able-bodied enough to fight, and take them over to Bar's junk piles to look for weapons. We won't need fighters for the patrols—just people who can run fast."

Caland quietly withdrew to one of the plaza benches. Hairy had brought the tale about the roadblock long before his usual time of waking, and his head throbbed furiously. He watched the coming and going with little interest, paid no attention to such reports and rumors as he chanced to overhear, and could not even stir himself to eat the putrebun that Tel placed beside him.

By late afternoon the power had gone off again, and it had begun to rain heavily. Sam the Artist's executive council had been continuously in session all day. It included the Reverend, Bronlan, Hairy, Morlef, Zata, and Tel. Others—Calta and Yda, the enforcers from the Houses of Fame, Louie Laggie and his scavs—came and went. Morlef considered a revolution no justification for abandoning work on the community building, but he had lost most of his work force to Mucks Groilan's army. The Reverend appropriated everyone else who could walk and carry to begin storing cider jugs full of water in the community building's enclosed lower level. Caland watched and listened until he tired, and then he stretched out on a bench and slept. When he awoke, the desultory discussion was still continuing. It seemed remarkably futile to him. Obviously, when there was nothing that could be done, there was very little that anyone could do.

Restrictions had been placed on food, and most of the eateries and almost all of the other shops were closed. By mid-afternoon the Prom was so deserted that when Mucks Groilan returned from a scouting expedition, those in the plaza saw him the moment he entered the Valley gate. Conversation ceased, heads turned, and everyone watched his limping progress.

He reached the plaza and wearily dropped onto a bench. When he did not speak immediately, Sam the Artist demanded, "Well?"

"I made a big circle around Paradise and got all the way to the Attic," Mucks said. "Talked with some of the artists. They don't know any more about it than we do. No one knows anything at all except that the tourists have been asked not to leave their hotes and the artists have been asked—some say ordered—to stay home. I went up in that silly cupola atop the Art Bazaar and had a good look at Paradise. I counted three bodies lying in the road by the Merc Mart. The streets are deserted. Everyone is staying indoors."

"Did you see anything that looked like an army?" Sam asked.

Mucks shook his head. "I avoided the road, of course. Even an army keeps under cover when people are getting killed, so the fact that I didn't see one doesn't mean it isn't there." He added, almost as an afterthought, "Pakovich's mansion was blown up last night."

"Is that so?" Sam the Artist remarked without showing any emotion at all. "That would be Nalce using up his stock of explosives. I'm surprised no one here has missed it. Even on a dark day, it's fairly conspicuous."

"With so many other things going on, maybe no one thought to look in that direction," Mucks said. "There's just a black smear on the mountain where it used to be. I didn't notice it myself until one of the artists mentioned it. Pakovich is said to be either dead or a prisoner."

"Whose prisoner?" Tel demanded.

"If the artists knew, they didn't say, and I didn't think to ask."

"Is there any kind of government functioning in the Government Mall?" Sam the Artist asked.

"I don't know. It didn't look as though anything is functioning there."

"I want to find out," Sam said. "Is it possible to get into Paradise?"

"I suppose. I'd rather not try during daylight."

"We could rig a raft with a sail," Bronlan said. "Ride across the bay instead of walking. Land at the park. Then it'd just be a short walk over to the Mall."

"Great idea," Mucks said. He had slipped off a mok, and he was rubbing his foot tenderly.

"They could carry a com unit from one of the 'buses,"

Bronlan went on. "Leave it there. Then we'd be in touch with what's going on."

"Is there one really competent person among Pakovich's fools?" Sam the Artist asked. "We need a reliable contact."

"Melana would know," the Reverend said.

"Where's Melana? I haven't seen her all day."

"Gary Dwand was looking for her a while ago," Tel said.

Hairy was dispatched to search the Valley for Melana, and Tel went to look for her at her apartment. An hour later, with darkness upon them and the sea wind whipping the rain across the plaza so that all of them huddled together on the east side, they were confronted with the certainty that Melana had disappeared.

"Do you suppose that Sdissler took advantage of the confusion to abduct her?" Sam the Artist wondered.

"It's much more likely that Melana took advantage of the confusion," Tel said. "If she's been spying for someone, her work here is probably finished. She's slipped away to help out somewhere else."

"I don't believe it," the Reverend said.

"Neither do I," Tel said. "But we have to face up to the fact that anything at all is possible."

"In any case, she's gone," Sam the Artist said. "Mucks, do you feel like going to Paradise?"

Mucks groaned. "No, but I'll do it."

"Pick a couple of people to go with you. Get some sleep. Bar will fix the raft for you."

"Sleep sounds good," Mucks said.

A gust swept a sheet of rain across the plaza. "Home," Tel said to Caland. "There'll be no beach fires tonight, and we've all had a long day. Let's sleep while we can."

A runner from the beach patrol darted panting from the shelter of a building to the shelter of the plaza roof. He gasped his message. There were flashes all around Paradise, with rumbling noises. The flashes looked like weaponry.

Before anyone could comment, lights pinioned them. One

of Pakovich's small executive 'cars was approaching along the Prom. "So much for the guards at the gate," Sam the Artist said bitterly.

As the 'car came closer, they saw that armed mals walked on either side and behind it. It made a looping half-turn and came to a stop by the plaza.

Sdissler got out and strode toward them. Hand lights held by the armed mals flooded the plaza with light.

"Glad to see everything under control, here," Sdissler said.

He was no longer acting. He had shed his ludicrous clothing along with his affected speech. He wore a very practical weather suit, and he spoke with clipped precision.

"See that things remain that way. I'm going to place my own guard out at the highway. No one is to leave the Valley. I hope to have everything back to normal by tomorrow evening."

"Who are you speaking for?" the Reverend asked.

"Myself," Sdissler said. "I've taken over the world of Mort. I expect to have a government functioning in another day or two."

He returned to the 'car and drove away. The armed mals pivoted without a word and followed him. Behind them they left a wake of stunned silence torn by the whipping wind.

CHAPTER THIRTY-THREE

In the beginning there was agony.

Thunderous pulsations wracked him, points of light blinded him, and the rapier of pain cut cruelly through his mind.

All of that was familiar; but when Caland slipped into a nightmare, he found it turned inward upon itself. He was no longer an observer; he was entrapped in it. He staggered with panting sobs through a wind-ravished, rain-swept night. Venerable, gigantic trees pressed in on the narrow path he followed, their trunks bulging with the tumid growths of age. His thin, water-soaked garments clung to him and chaffed with every faltering step. The shrieking wind whipped the distant tree tops, and lightning transfixed the surreal scene through which he wandered following a muddy, meandering forest trail with slopping feet.

He could not distinguish the external nightmare from the inner one.

Again the lightning flashed, silhouetting the brittle, uplifted bones of towering trees; the instant it faded, blinding points of light surged across his retinas and outlined the fragile web of his capillaries or perhaps the universe.

Caland's hands clawed at the pain that seared his brain. He tried to focus his thoughts, to ask himself why he was struggling through a nightmarish forest in the dark, in a driving rain, and what he was fleeing from or to, but he could not think. Each swollen throb of his head was a new thrust of agony, dragging with it the counterpoint of flashing lights, aching explosions of sound, and raw spasms of a brain crucified. He tightened the clutch on his head and expected to lose consciousness at any moment.

There were other agonies. His muscles tormented him with each lurching step; his hands and feet felt raw and bruised.

The wind continued to shred the treetops. Crinkly old fronds, torn loose in the gale, dropped out of the night to stick clingingly to his body and clothing. Lightning flashed; an odd, rattling thunder raked the dark sky; the rain intensified.

Another lightning flash catapulted Caland into reality. Just ahead of him the path widened into a clearing. A shelter stood there. For a moment its door resisted his fumbling fingers; then he was able to open it and enter.

The interior was warm and dry, but there was no light. He took a few steps forward, bumped into furniture, and identified a chair. He dropped his exhausted body into it and clutched his head again.

The shrieking wind drove the rain against the shelter's metal roof with an incessant clatter that drowned out the thunder. An occasional lightning flash could be glimpsed through small windows; it unfolded shadows in the shelter's interior without disturbing the darkness. Caland relaxed and breathed deeply. He must have slipped into a prostrated slumber, for he awoke with a start and found himself slumped uncomfortably sideways in his sopping clothing. He stared bewilderedly into the darkness and tried to remember what had happened and how he came there.

He got to his feet and stepped forward, feeling about him. His hand encountered something he had only half seen in a flicker of lightning, a dangling cord. He grabbed it and jerked sharply.

A lantern flickered on. It was suspended from a rafter, and it swayed wildly, scattering shadows that elongated and shrank with the pulse of its swing. Caland dropped into the chair again, and his eyes took in the shelter's sparse furnishings without really seeing them: two chairs, a rough table, a spherical stove, shelves laden with boxes.

The stove stood in the far corner of the room on a brick platform. Caland crossed to it and found its fire burned down to a few glowing coals. He took blocks of compressed fuel from a box and carefully placed them in the stove. When they began to flame, he closed the stove's door and leaned over it, body arched to its contour, to absorb the warmth. Despite the shelter's cozy atmosphere, he was still shivering, and his wet garments were dripping cold water onto the floor.

"I must have walked a long way to get this chilled and wet," he told himself. "Why? Where did I come from? Where am I?" After a long pause, he added, "Who am I?"

He turned his back to the fire to toast the unwarmed part of his body. As he did so, a stack of crates along the wall caught his eye. They had an address stenciled onto them: "Pak Enterprises, Forestry Department, Sec 49, Mort...."

Suddenly he knew where and who he was.

And he knew what was happening.

He stood motionless, arms at his sides, hands extended tensely while he focused his thoughts in the most fervid concentration his exhausted mind could achieve. His fingers were tingling faintly, as though circulation had recently been restored to them. So was his brain.

He leaped to the door of the shelter and flung it open. A deluge of rain swept in on him, but he did not hesitate. He sprang into the storm and ran frantically down the trail, feet churning and splashing in the muddied path. He held an arm extended in front of him, but the precaution was unnecessary because of the frequent lightning flashes. The path wound among the huge trees and occasionally took a sharp turning, and Caland frequently slipped in the mud and lost his balance. He staggered sideways, bounced off trees, and continued to run.

Abruptly the sheltered forest ended. Caland ran headlong into the full force of the wind and was hurled back. He stood at the edge of a meadowed mountain slope clinging to a tree and peering downward into the lightning-lashed night while the vicious, driving force of the wind tore at him. It had twisted and toppled outlying trees and flattened the long mountain grass.

The coastal plain lay far below him in a darkness that was

just perceptibly thinning with the first touches of dawn. The lightning gave him only random glimpses of the devastation being wrought there by this unrelenting fury, but he knew its impact without seeing it.

A world was being ravaged.

He remembered—*now* he remembered—and he knew that he'd seen it happen three times before. Three worlds, or parts of worlds, had been devastated before his eyes. Peaceful, prosperous lands had been smeared with destruction. Human bodies lay in the fields when the storm had passed, toppled like the mountain grass in the meadow just below him. Or they lay crushed in their smashed homes, or they floated—bloated carrion—in canals and rivers and harbors and on the open sea.

And now the fourth—the world of Mort.

But Mort was a world with a difference. Caland was not merely a passenger on this planet. He had lived here, and he knew many of the people well. Among them were friends he cherished and one person he loved, and all of them were down there in the storm-shredded darkness. He could only watch helplessly while the lightning sketched a landscape dissolving under an enraged wind's pounding. When daylight came, and the storm passed, he could go down and search for his dead.

"This time," he said fiercely through clenched teeth, "this time I'm going to find out who's doing it. This time, for certain, I'm going to find out. And when I do, I'll kill him."

* * * * * * *

As soon as the wind began to fade, Caland began his cautious descent. He knew approximately where he was. South of the fertilizer factory, the Tin Mountains swung close to the coast, and the Pak Enterprises highway, which turned south at the Valley, ran along the coast for a short distance south of Fish Town, shrank to a narrow, unimproved road, and then vanished altogether, a memento of some project in which Pakovich had lost interest.

The storm had passed and dawn lay tenuously on the sogged and battered landscape when Caland reached the highway. He turned north and traveled as rapidly as he could force his aching, exhausted body to move—and walked into an ambush. Armed mals in dusky green uniforms poured from the concealment of fallen trees and seized him roughly.

An officer stepped into view at the top of an embankment. "Twelve aren't needed to handle one," he called caustically. "Release him."

As Caland stepped free, the officer called, "Where are you going?"

"To the Valley," Caland said.

"Why?"

"I live there."

The officer studied him for a moment. "No one lives there now," he said. "But if you want to go—"

He waved a hand. The uniformed mals stepped back. Caland hunched his shoulders at though he were still fighting the storm and began to move at a faltering pace along the highway.

He passed Fish Town. Except for broken windows, Pakovich's cement houses seemed undamaged. The fertilizer factory showed no discernible damage except for the fishing fleet. Towering waves had tossed the ships far inland and smashed them.

Then he topped the last rise and turned to look into the Valley.

The officer had been right. No one lived there. The ramshackle fence was gone, blown across the Mort countryside along with bits and pieces of Valley buildings: sections of roofs or walls, ornate trim, cupolas that once had been distinctive ornaments on the old vacation homes, porches. But most of the buildings had not blown away. They simply had collapsed where they stood. Here and there a pile of rubble reared higher than the others, with intact walls leaning crazily against each other. The Prom was rendered almost impassable by the buildings that had toppled into it.

The brick buildings appeared undamaged except for the loss

of windows. Only a few well-built and well-maintained wood structures survived with minor damage. Olgi's red-and-white-striped Cloy shop had stout pieces of canvas nailed where its windows had been, and an employee was sweeping shards into the street. The Valley hote had lost its balcony, which had crashed down onto the outside tables below, and the building looked crazily askew. All of the trees were down, and it was possible for the first time to see from one end of the Valley to the other. Here and there a house still stood. Over on Fishstink Alley, several buildings apparently had been sheltered from the worst force of the storm by the massive fertilizer factory buildings. Dominating the scene was the sprawling form of the new community building, which seemed to be intact.

Caland turned into the Prom and began picking his way through the debris. He paused for a moment to look at the splintered wreckage that had been Nello's. He was feeling deathly tired. Wet clothing had chaffed his body to a searing rawness. He had worn holes in his moks, and his feet pained him severely. His hands were abraded and lacerated. He staggered on because he had to.

Then he became aware that there were scattered groups of people at work on the wreckage. Just ahead of him, several Vals were pulling blankets from a collapsed shop. He quickened his pace.

A fem, ragged-looking in torn clothing, straightened up clutching an armload of blankets. It was Phem. She started when she saw Caland.

"It's Cal! Where have you been?"

"Where's Tel?" he asked.

"Don't know. Haven't seen her since last night. She was looking for you. Didn't she find you?"

"Where is everyone?"

Phem gestured with her head. "Over there. Across the highway—we're setting up a camp."

"Anyone hurt?"

"Lots. Hurt and killed. I don't know how many. We moved

out when it started to get bad. The whole Valley moved except some that wouldn't go. Wasn't that a whump of a storm? We're setting up hospitals, and I'm collecting blankets and rags for bandages. I've got to run.

She hurried away.

Caland limped slowly and painfully after her.

One of the Dolls' House balconies lay in the street. Its metal supports had rusted away, and the storm had vibrated it loose. Caland instinctively looked up to see whether others were likely to follow it.

"Cal! Tel was looking for you."

Caland turned. Olorn, the sculptor of fake metal busts, stood by the ruins of his collapsed studio.

"Where is she?" Caland demanded.

"Haven't seen her for—oh, for hours."

Caland walked on. From the open door of the Road to Hell came a familiar voice booming instructions. The building evidently had been converted into a makeshift hospital; a patient had arrived on an improvised stretcher, and Doctor Gormaz, his tufts of hair pinned down by a bandage, was inflicting efficiency and order with waving arms.

The Valley Transportation Company fence had vanished. Caland turned and tried to find a familiar path amidst the debris that littered its lot. All of the operable vehicles were gone. Gary Dwand's shack had blown down. The cannibalized vehicles remained, and—further back—Baris Bronlan's towering junk piles had survived unscathed, but his shack was a low mound of rubble. Caland moved in that direction, stepping around or climbing over the fallen trees. When he reached the remains of Bronlan's shack, he sagged tiredly against a tree trunk. He was too exhausted to go further, too weary even to think.

"Cal!"

Sam the Artist came trotting toward him, shirt flapping, stomach bobbing. "Are you all right?" He grabbed Caland's arm anxiously. "Tel was looking for you."

"Where is she?"

"Haven't seen her since the exodus started. How'd you two get separated?"

Caland shook his head. "I've got to find her."

"Of course. Where are you going? To your apartment?"

Caland nodded.

"All of those buildings are down. Why don't you go back to the Prom? Go to the plaza and sit down and rest—you look as though you could use it. There's hot yuck there, and you look as though you could use that, too. I'll find Tel for you and send her there."

Caland pointed at Bronlan's shack. "Bar?"

"Hurt," Sam the Artist said. "A bad whack on the head and some broken bones. We had to pull his roof apart to get him out. Probably slept through the whole thing until the house fell on him. He has an unblemished mind. I'll find Tel for you."

Sam looked as though he had survived a sizable war of his own. One sleeve was ripped from his shirt and a trouser leg flapped loosely. He grinned at Caland and hurried away. Caland paused momentarily before he got to his feet and stumbled on— toward Bay Unview Boulevard.

He met Louie Laggie and Kren Krent, who were assisting Thalm, the retired prostitute. She had an improvised bandage on her leg, and she was limping badly. Her eyes were all but swollen shut from an ugly bruise. The two mals nodded at Caland but did not speak; keeping Thalm's bulky figure in motion required all of their concentration.

Caland now became aware that theirs was only one of numerous rescue missions going on all over the Valley. Looking down on Junk Vista Avenue toward the ocean, he saw groups of people at work on every collapsed building, and a pair of stretcher bearers passed him on their way to the Prom with another victim. Caland stepped over a tree trunk, skirted debris from a roof that had blown off, and doggedly continued toward Bay Unview Boulevard. Finally he threaded his way between two partially collapsed buildings and looked toward the end of the street where his apartment had been.

There were no houses there—just mounds of rubble scattered about with trees lying across them. The full force of the storm, raging in off the ocean, had struck these buildings first, and waves had crashed far inland.

He almost turned back. He desperately needed rest, and each unsteady step felt as though it had to be his last. He had hoped Tel might be waiting for him here, but there was no place for her to wait.

He continued to move haltingly toward the smashed building. He had nowhere else to go. A few people were sifting through the ruins—looking for belongings, he supposed. He almost turned back a second time; he did not care about his belongings. Zooie, the fellow resident who had once given him mopping lessons, saw him coming and waved.

"No house!" he shouted. He sounded almost jubilant.

With several others Zooie was prying loose sections of wall and roof to see what could be salvaged.

The building seemed to have collapsed inward while being blown over. It had taken one tree down with it, and another had fallen atop the debris. Caland thought it impossible to look at the wreckage and decide which apartment might be where, but Zooie and the others were attempting to do so.

"Looking for something?" Zooie asked Caland.

Caland now wanted nothing more than a place to lie down. He stood teetering uncertainly while he tried to focus his thoughts on what he should do next. Zooie and the others nudged another slab of wall aside and began tugging at a piece of roof.

Then Caland saw a leg.

His fatigue dropped away from him, and he began clawing frantically at the wreckage. The moment the others saw what he was doing, they scrambled to help. Everyone came. In an instant there were a dozen people there, and Caland left off his own ineffectual fumbling and watched helplessly.

The piece of roof came aside, and then another wall slab, and Tel lay at his feet. She had been outside the house, just leaving or just returning, when the storm brought the building down on her. Her body was almost untouched. She was wearing one of the coarsely knit dresses she always preferred, and her long black hair was spread loosely under her. When they attempted to move her, the hair caught on a board and had to be carefully loosened. The fallen tree had kept much of the ruins from crashing down on her, but something had crushed the back of her skull. Her head lay at an unlikely angle, her neck broken, and when they shifted the body, her head dangled crazily.

She was dead, of course.

Caland picked her up and staggered away. Her body felt icy to his touch, and he cradled her to him to warm her and supported her head with his arm so that she looked almost normal. He stubbornly shook off efforts to take her from him or even to help support her weight. He staggered through and around the storm's devastation with a silent group following to help him when, inevitably, he had to collapse.

But he kept going, moving one foot haltingly after another, walking a treadmill into his worst nightmare, where all patterns of his existence had come unglued and flopped crazily askew, and all of the familiar faces belonged to strangers. Only Tel remained real, Tel in his arms, and it was not possible that she was dead. In all of his tormented worry about not remembering her, he had never thought of the possibility of having to remember her dead. He staggered on, still shaking off all attempts to help him, until finally he stumbled onto the Prom.

There he found himself face to face with the bandaged Doctor Gormaz, who was still booming confident instructions and imposing order on chaos. Gormaz paused in mid-sentence when he saw Caland, stared searchingly into his face for a moment, and then turned to the others.

"This mal is exhausted. Why didn't some of you help him?"

"She's dead," Caland said dully.

"Surely not." Gormaz motioned to the others to help, and finally they persuaded Caland to let them lower Tel's cold body onto the patchwork pavement of the Prom. Doctor Gormaz bent over her, straightened her head with one hand, cocked his own head thoughtfully when the broken neck allowed it to roll to one side the moment he released it.

"Dead," Caland muttered.

"Nonsense," Doctor Gormaz said. He straightened up and patted Caland's arm compassionately. "Nonsense. She's not dead, she's unconscious. She's totally relaxed. But she needs a doctor quickly. So do you." He turned. "Where's a stretcher?"

One was brought. Doctor Gormaz superintended the careful transfer of Tel's body to a piece of canvas mounted over a section of window frame. "Take her to Dom's house," he said. "There's a doctor working there. Hurry. Tell him I said to start resuscitation at once. I'll be along in a moment. And you—"

He grabbed Moppy, who was passing by and had stopped to stare, face aghast, at Tel's body. "You take Cal with them. Tell the doctor to give him a sedative."

Caland clung determinedly to the treadmill of his nightmare, but only Moppy's sturdy arm kept him erect going over obstacles. Some of the strange faces that gathered around them must have belonged to friends. They spoke to Caland as though they knew him; they seemed kindly and sympathetic; but he recognized none of them. The procession, the funeral procession, with Tel's dead body on the improvised stretcher, one bit of the storm's debris carried on another, wound slowly through the devastated Valley to Fishstink Alley, where Dom's house now stood like a beacon. The lesser buildings that had surrounded it had been cleared away by the storm.

Another stranger—they called him "Doctor," though he wore work clothing like that of Doctor Gormaz—came down the steps of Dom's house to meet them. He bent over Tel, heard Doctor Gormaz's message relayed by several tongues at once, moved Tel's lolling head back into place, and nodded.

"All right. I'll take care of her."

The stretcher moved toward the steps.

Then Caland saw the row of bodies in the yard beyond. They had brought Tel to a morgue, and he was not ready to surrender her to the dead. He shouted, "No!" and tried to fight his way to the stretcher.

It seemed that a multitude of hands restrained him. His arm was bared, an instrument pointed, a trigger pulled. He felt nothing at all. Somewhere in the background he heard Sam the Artist's voice. "Tel? Dead? No—she can't be! Where's Cal? Dear God, no! Not Tel!"

Then Sam was there, with an arm about Caland, and the Reverend joined him. The sedative began to take effect, and Caland slipped from the reality of a waking nightmare into the equally intense agony of an unconscious one.

CHAPTER THIRTY-FOUR

Caland dreamed that Tel was dead. His awakening was a return to a nightmarish reality where she actually was dead. He should have remembered her laughter, her warmth, her endearing honesty, but all of his visions of her were blocked by the one that showed him her crushed head dangling with a broken neck and her long hair caught in the debris. She had died in a violent storm while searching for him.

It was a storm that someone had caused.

He sat up. It was dawn; he must have slept through the day and the following night. His bed was a blanket on the lawn of Dom's house with another blanket to cover him. Other sleepers were lying near him, many of them bandaged. The Valley and its people had been hurt cruelly.

But he was not one of them. Tel was gone, and he no longer belonged.

He got to his feet and walked away slowly, following the Fishstink Alley path toward the ocean—now visible over flattened buildings and fallen trees and shrubbery.

A hand clasped his shoulder. The Reverend had overtaken him. Their eyes met briefly, and then they continued to plod along side by side. There was nothing that either of them needed to say.

They walked along the ocean beach to the boulders where Baris Bronlan had sat each sunset and many dawns fathoming the secrets of the ocean. Even the ocean had been marked by the storm; its breakers still ran unusually high. Caland hunched himself onto one of the stones, and the Reverend took the other. For a time they watched the long lines of waves move inexorably toward the beach to crash in ruins almost at their feet.

Finally the Reverend spoke. "The ways of divine providence, my friend, have never been discernible to mere humans. Perhaps it is better that way. Tel was a lovely light in all of our lives. Now the light is extinguished, and our lives are darkened. I don't think she would want us to grieve. It's enough if we remember."

"She was so real," Caland said brokenly. "Everything else in my life was like the scenery in a play—something painted on a backdrop and rolled up and forgotten when the scene was finished. Backdrops can be replaced by other backdrops, but when something real is taken away, it leaves emptiness." He brushed his eyes fiercely.

"She was indeed real," the Reverend agreed. "Perhaps it will be a help to you that your life lacks a religious inclination. Those accustomed to facing life's vicissitudes without divine consolation develop their own special resiliency. I've noticed that tragedies often have the harshest impact on devout people who should be the best prepared for them. No religion insures against tragedy. The most any of them can offer is strength to endure, and consolation for doing so. This is supposed to sustain the bereaved, but those who have devoutly and confidently placed the dimensions of their lives in the hands of their God too often turn bitterly on Him for permitting the tragedy to happen. They demand an accounting. Their lifetimes of piety are paraded as though they were due bills that God is liable to pay ten days after presentation. But providence proceeds in ways obscure to humans. It cuts the good life short and spares the sinner, and it never explains. Tel's was a good life. She sustained so many here who were less fortunate." His resonant voice had the misty quality of tears. "She will indeed be missed. We of the Valley are of small account in the galaxy's halls of commerce and politics and culture, but we confer our own form of immortality. We remember. We'll long remember Tel."

The Reverend turned suddenly and looked at Caland with

concern. "I don't think she would want us to grieve," he said again.

Caland felt ashamed of himself. There was work to be done; there were survivors who needed help. He had terms or even years ahead of him in which to unsuccessfully attempt to assuage his grief. He could postpone mourning until the crisis of the moment was resolved. He slipped down from the stone and fell into step beside the Reverend.

"What's been happening?" he asked.

"The Valley—you've seen the Valley. How much of the storm do you remember?" The Reverend took it for granted that Caland had suffered another mental blackout.

"I remember Sdissler announcing that he'd taken over the world of Mort. I remember going to bed. I woke up in a mountain forest south of Fish Town."

"You may have missed the worst of the storm. It hit heavily all along the coastal plain, but the Valley got the center of it. Pakovich's communities are well constructed, so there was little damage to their buildings, and the city of Paradise didn't even have its trees blown down. But it's been wracked by different kinds of violence. One war after another. In the process, the villains very effectively eliminated each other. Tate's strikers caught Nalce and his minions trying to blow up something and dealt with them emphatically. Then Sdissler's army dealt with the strikers. A fair number of them were killed, including Tate. That left Sdissler very effectively in control of the world of Mort, but it only lasted a few hours. An Aravian army had already landed—on invitation of the government of Mort, it's said, but the rumor doesn't explain who did the inviting and how the invasion happened to be so timely. The Aravians settled Sdissler even more emphatically than Sdissler did Tate. Now Government Mall is in charge of things again, and the Aravians are taking orders from Pakovich. Or so the rumors say."

"Pakovich? I thought he was—" Caland couldn't remember what it was that Pakovich was supposed to be.

"He was injured. He was Sdissler's prisoner for a time, which probably hurt him more than his injuries. Now he's functioning with his usual bungling efficiency, and he's angry enough at everyone else to feel almost kindly toward the Valley. He sent us several 'truckloads of tents yesterday. He also agreed to let Paradise volunteers help us clean up the Valley if any want to. We're trying to translate that into skilled people with machines. We have all the manual labor we need. We're keeping out sight-seers—the 'buses and 'cabs aren't running except between Paradise and the Port. Most of the tourists will be leaving on the first ship anyway. They've had their fill of this peaceful world of Mort where nothing happens."

"How's Bar?"

"In good shape. Experiencing a kind of remorseful glee. If he hadn't parked his spaceship in outer space, it would have been blown over and wrecked."

They were threading their way back along Junk Vista Alley, and Caland stepped on a sharp object and winced. "Is there anywhere I can get a new pair of moks?"

The Reverend stooped to examine Caland's foot. "You've worn the bottom right out of it," he said perplexedly. "Let's go over to the Prom. Everything in the shops is thoroughly water-soaked, but we should be able to salvage something for you."

Caland found a heavy pair of shoes for himself; they seemed ideal for climbing through the Valley's wreckage. At the plaza a communal break was being served to those who were without food. Caland took his turn in line, emerged with generous portions of yuck and glop, and then—he hadn't eaten for a day and a half—went back for another serving.

When he finished eating, he crossed the highway for a look at the encampment of displaced Vals. Sam the Artist's most brilliant stroke of leadership had occurred when he gazed into the intensifying storm and foresaw that the Valley buildings were about to become death traps; whereas this open country, with sheltering dunes, offered a chance for safety. Some Vals refused to leave; many waited too long. There were no injuries or deaths among those who sought refuge here.

Now a village of tents had grown up between the dunes. Sam had ordered the Valley kept clear of spectators during the dangerous salvage operations, and the children, the elderly, the sick, and the injured remained in camp. Caland wandered among them greeting friends and asking about casualties. Then he went looking for Gary Dwand. All of the Valley Transportation Company's operable vehicles had been moved to safety before the storm reached its height, and it now was impossible for any vehicle to enter the Valley because of the condition of the Prom. But Dwand assured Caland that the road to Paradise was clear, and, when Caland explained what he wanted, Dwand immediately agreed to supply as many 'buses as needed.

Caland returned to the encampment to do the one thing he was best qualified for: he recruited a troop of paras. He wanted people with superficial injuries that appeared to be much worse than they were. He assembled this selection of battered-looking Vals by the road and ordered them to remove all neat-looking bandages and replace them with wrappings improvised from rags. While they were doing that, a pair of artists hastily lettered signs for them on pieces of wreckage.

Calta Draning happened by and demanded to know what wild scheme Caland was working on now.

"They're going to Paradise," Caland explained. "They'll collect money for homeless and injured Vals."

"We have plenty of money," Calta protested. "The problem is in finding medicines and bandages and blankets and clothing and food to spend it on."

"They'll collect those things, too," Caland said. "The storm dealt lightly with the Paradise residents and the tourists. While they're sitting there gloating on their good fortune, they might as well help pay for what we need. It'll give them a purpose in life."

Calta's body shook with laughter. "Dear Cal!" she exclaimed. "That's a noble philosophy—a purpose for every life." She came over and crushed him against her ample bosom. "Poor boy. I heard about Tel." She sniffed, muttered something that sounded like, "Oh, hell and dammit," and stomped away angrily.

Caland sent two 'busloads of paras off to Paradise to haunt the hotes, the Merc Mart, and the Government Mall, and to confront the more fortunate Morticians wherever they were to be found. Then he went back to the Valley in search of something else to do. He was picking his way through the Prom debris when he encountered Sam the Artist.

The haggard-looking Sam gazed at him wearily with bloodshot eyes; he still wore the clothing that had been ripped and torn in the storm's fury. He muttered to Caland, "Damn you! I know what you're going through, but how do you manage to look so good? Is it being an actor that does it?"

"They gave me a sedative," Caland said. "I slept a day and a night."

"That's what I need. But there's so damned much to do. Do you know what they did with Tel's body?"

"Doctor Gormaz took her."

"We're going to have a mass funeral. It's the only way. Morlef is considering whether we can make some kind of memorial grave around the plaza."

"*Don't* put it near the plaza," Caland said firmly. "No one wants to mourn the dead surrounded by tourists and putrebun hawkers. Find an out-of-the-way place where there's some privacy."

"Yes...I see what you mean."

"I don't want Tel in a mass grave, anyway. I'll have to think about it."

He wanted her by the ocean, where the eternally pounding sea could echo the vibrant rhythms so tragically vanished from her. Probably they wouldn't let him, but he decided to ask someone about it.

Phem came by with a tray and handed Caland a putrebun. Sam also accepted one, munched solemnly on it, then shuffled away.

Caland continued to search for something to do.

He found the Reverend and mentioned his idea for Tel's grave.

"It wouldn't be possible to dig there," the Reverend said. "You'd have to build a tomb above ground, and there'd always be the risk of a storm destroying it. Don't you think Tel would rather be with the others?"

"Maybe. But I'd like to have her where I could be alone with her."

"Of course. I'll see."

"Where's Arlu?"

"He sent his apologies and said our immediate problems aren't compatible with his talents. He thought he could help us more by staying in Paradise. He's right, of course. Right now we need strong arms and backs. The mystery of what happened will have to be left for later. Arlu is helping out with Mort's political mess, and he'll do whatever he can for us over there."

Caland made no comment, but he was doubtful that anything could be more urgent than discovering what had happened. The mystery had to be faced, just as he had to face the fact that he had brought death to Mort as surely as he had brought death to Cenaru, Olyndyt, and Skarlont. He should have followed his own instinct and tried to leave when he could.

In the meantime he needed work. He joined the cleanup crews that were clearing the Prom. The search for bodies trapped in the wreckage had first priority, but as fast as Vals were released from that, Sam the Artist put them to work opening up the one Valley street that could be used by vehicles.

"We have to start somewhere," he told Caland. "If we don't get the businesses going again, we'll all starve. We've asked Aravia to send special tents to replace the smashed buildings."

Moppy was hovering at Sam's elbow. Sam snapped an order at him, and he rushed away. "I like being Valley exek," Sam the Artist said. "I say, 'Do this! Do that!' Everyone smiles and hurries off. Of course no one does anything, but there's an illusion of progress."

There was a brief diversion when a small government 'car showed up from Paradise with three tourists in it. They explained that they'd heard about the catastrophe, and they wanted to see the damage themselves so they could organize relief efforts on their own worlds when they returned home. They answered vaguely when asked how they'd obtained the use of a 'car. Sam scrutinized their credentials carefully and permitted them to see as much as they could from the Valley gate. Then he sent them over to the encampment under Hairy's expert guidance to interview the injured.

One of the tourists was Weflan Krann.

"I wonder if they're all Sdissler's backers." Sam the Artist mused after they'd left. "Government Mall is rationing news, and they're probably trying to find out what happened to him. I told Hairy to make certain the only thing they learn here is how much we Vals are suffering."

"Something should be done about Sdissler's backers," Caland said.

Sam the Artist shrugged. "I'll give their names to Arlu. It's his kind of problem."

The Prom workers were gathering rubble and loading it into 'trucks supplied by the Valley Transportation Company. As soon as one was loaded, it rolled away toward the world dump. Morlef drifted along behind the cleanup, studying the damaged buildings, deciding what was worth repairing and what had to come down at once, and marking things he wanted for salvage. Few of the wood structures were worth saving.

Calta, Yda, and all of the girls were out helping with cleanup. "We'll have no work until it's done," Yda said cheerfully, "so we might as well work here."

Caland joined some Vals who were clearing the wreckage of the collapsed clutter shop. The owner hovered around the operation and anxiously claimed anything remotely salvageable. The ridiculous conglomeration of second-to-tenth-hand odds and ends was his life's accumulation of wealth. He wanted to open another shop, perhaps merging what remained of his stock with that of another clutter shop owner.

When the last of the clutter had been salvaged, and the last of the shop's rubble had been loaded, Caland straightened up wearily. An Electrocab had wheeled into the distant end of the Prom and stopped where the cleanup operation still barred the way. A couple descended. There was a chorus of muted gasps, and everyone in the work crew stood staring.

The girl was Melana—neatly and conservatively dressed, spectacularly beautiful. As for the non-distinctive-looking mal who accompanied her....

Sam the Artist uttered a peculiarly strange sound. "As I live and digest! Melana—with Alexander the Second!"

The two moved along slowly, scrutinizing everything with grave concern. They seemed completely unaware that they had become the center of everyone else's attention, and that work, talk, and movement along the Prom had halted. Melana smiled and spoke to the occasional Val whom she knew well.

As they approached Caland and Sam, she halted her companion with a touch of her hand. "'O, Sam. 'O, Cal. Have you met my husband? I call him 'Lex."

Caland tried to say, "Yes, I once had the pleasure," but no words came out. Being speechless, he reflected, was more likely to result from being able to say nothing than from having nothing to say. He found himself touching hands with Alexander Pakovich the Second and producing inarticulate murmurs.

"I've heard a great deal about both of you," Alexander the Second said. "We're going to work to make this a turning point—both for the Valley and for Mort."

Melana said to Cal, "I heard about Tel. I admired her and loved her. Everyone who knew her did. If having a sorrow shared will ease it in any way, everyone in the Valley will be trying to ease yours."

They moved on. Caland found that he could breathe again, and he turned to Sam the Artist. He wanted to ask, "What about that Aravian princess?" But he did not. Sam was stricken speechless; probably he would not have heard. He stared after Melana and her husband for a moment. Then he turned, grabbed an armful of rubble, and strode to the 'truck with it. Caland joined him, and they worked silently side by side. Work seemed to be balm for every physical pain and every mental perplexity. Caland focused his mind on his hands, concentrating on moving the next piece of debris to the 'truck, and for a time he even forgot Tel. The laden 'truck moved away and was replaced with an empty one. Time passed. Finally Sam the Artist gripped Caland's arm firmly and announced, "You need a rest." He escorted Caland to one of the surviving benches by the Valley Transportation Company yard.

The Reverend found him there. He was carrying a tray of putrebuns and yuck. Caland protested that he'd eaten. The Reverend asked him when, and Caland couldn't remember, so the Reverend placed a mug and a putrebun on the bench beside him.

"I talked with Bar about your idea for burying Tel," he said. "Bar thinks it's wonderful. When he dies, which we all hope is an event belonging to the remote future, he'd like to be buried there himself just beside that boulder he's so fond of sitting on. If you wouldn't object to his being buried near Tel, that is. So I talked to Morlef, and he went and had a look. Morlef thinks it's feasible if the graves are moved back a bit to where the ground is higher. He's going to dig a couple of test holes. And Melana and her husband—I can't quite accustom myself to calling him 'Lex—they've promised us all the cement that Pak Enterprises has in stock, so we'll be able to give Tel the most durable grave possible."

Caland asked, "How, in the midst of all of this turmoil, did they manage to get married?"

The Reverend smiled. "They've been married for more than three years. Why they kept it a secret for so long, and why they suddenly revealed it now, and where that fuss about the Aravian princess figures into it, certainly will make an interesting story when they're ready to tell it. One would expect this marriage to shake Pakovich in the same way that the storm shook the Valley, but perhaps after so many blows he hardly noticed it."

The Reverend smiled and went off with his tray.

Caland had no appetite, and the putrebun seemed tasteless.

He ate hurriedly. Then he slipped away from the dust and noise of the Prom cleanup and cut through the Valley Transportation Company yard and Baris Bronlan's junk piles to Junk Vista Avenue. He turned there as he had so many times with Tel at his side and headed for the sea.

He sat for a long time on one of the boulders thinking of that distant evening when he had slipped away from Tel and experienced Mort's sunset for the first time. That had been the real beginning of his relationship with Tel. She had filled his life and given it direction and meaning, and now she had left it. The direction and meaning had vanished with her.

He would have to leave Mort. He could not remain here with memories of her lingering in every turning he took and fueling his yearning for her. So the privacy of her grave did not really matter.

But he did want her at rest in a place as uniquely beautiful as she was, and the Valley offered no better one than this. He slipped from the boulder and prowled along the high ground behind the bench until he found the test holes that Morlef had dug. He stood there looking out to sea, watching the shoreward march of the waves and the heaving water beyond them where the sun would work its magical transformation every clear evening, and he thought—yes. This was the place. This was for Tel, whose personality underwent the same breathtaking transformations. This was where she should rest eternally or for however long the world of Mort would spin.

He returned to the boulder.

Hairy found him there. "The Reverend wants you," he said.

Caland scowled at him irritably. "What about?"

"Don't know. He's at Dom's house. They're planning funerals, and he said to fetch you."

"All right," Caland said. Obediently he jumped down and set out for Dom's house.

The outdoor hospital had diminished considerably since Caland left it that morning. The bodies still lay in a row at one side of the house, but most of them were covered. A group of

Vals, Phem among them, were sewing shrouds of whatever rough cloth Valley stocks could provide. Nearby was a stack of lumber, and Morlef was supervising another group that was quickly assembling coffins.

The Reverend detached himself when Caland approached. He had a list of names in his hand. He frowned at it and then at Caland. "Do you know where Tel's body was taken? I can't find her."

"We brought her here," Caland said. "They took her into the house."

"Then she's still there. The original morgue was established inside, but it quickly overflowed."

The Reverend spoke to two of the mals helping him and led them away. Caland turned in the opposite direction. Suddenly he did not want to see Tel's body again. He had seen her dead, but now he was remembering her alive, and he did not want that image shattered.

Doctor Gormaz blocked his path. "I've been looking for you," he said. "We need you."

He led Caland toward the house.

The entrance hall was wide and ornate, with a large mirror at the end and heavily carved portals. Caland hardly noticed them. In the long room at the right, bodies lay side by side and head to foot. The Reverend was already there, tiptoeing over the dead and checking off names on his list. The two mals who were helping him stood by the door waiting. Caland stared dumbly into the room. He recognized faces: Old Gus; Marto, a clothing shop proprietor; Dave, the wiry little para who had entertained tourists by walking on his hands; Duggal and Huggal, who had been so elated over Huggal's pregnancy. Some of the faces were covered. The Reverend stopped over every body, raised a cloth, dropped it, and moved on.

Doctor Gormaz plucked at Caland's arm. "This way."

They turned left and stood in the doorway of a room crowded with makeshift beds. On the bed in the far corner, Tel lay. She looked very lifelike.

Then she sat up. "Why doesn't anyone answer?" she demanded. "When can I get out of this screety place?"

Her long hair had been cut. She wore an elaborate cervical collar that immobilized her head and kept her facing forward. The entire back of her head had been wiped clean of hair, and a bulging bandage concealed her injury.

Caland took a step forward. "Tel!" he exclaimed. His voice broke, and he reeled uncertainly.

She had to twist her body in order to see him. She scrutinized him with evident interest. "Who are you?" she asked.

CHAPTER THIRTY-FIVE

The ocean beach had become a place of refuge, and Caland fled to it with Tel's words ringing ominously behind him.

She had been politely indifferent to him. "Have we met before?" she asked brightly. "I'm sure it must have been a pleasure, but I don't remember it."

She did not remember. She had received a crushing blow on the head, and she'd lost her memory. Of all the benighted souls in the universe, surely Caland was best prepared to extend sympathetic understanding over a loss of memory.

But Tel's words to Doctor Gormaz had shattered him. First she had been caustic; then she burst into rage. "Look, pipsqueak. No doubt you mean well, but this alleged doctor of yours graduated from a meat processing plant. Keep him away from me and bring me some shoes. I want out."

"You've been very ill," Gormaz murmured. "We're concerned about your mental adjustment—"

"This whole place is going to need adjustments if you don't turn me loose immediately. I'm a prober, I tell you. I'm on assignment."

Caland had turned silently and walked away. Behind him he heard Tel's voice rising and falling stridently, but he did not look back. This was not the Tel he knew—thought he knew.

But the Tel he thought he knew had never existed. She was a prober, one of the galaxy's legendary searchers. Of course she was. He had known that she was no ordinary person from the manner in which she took charge of everyone and everything whenever the need arose. He had never met a more capable person.

But the word had cast a portentous shadow over all of his memories. She was a prober. She was on assignment, and he had been part of that assignment. When her memory returned to her, that was how she would remember him. Like Arlu, she had considered him an unwitting key to a mystery.

Baris Bronlan was seated on his favorite boulder. They had not met since the storm, and he greeted Caland with a shy smile. He did not offer to touch hands. His left arm, the stiff one, was in a cast, and he had another cast on his right hand. A patch covered his forehead, his face was deeply marked with scratches, and the bandage on his lower left leg could be seen below his trousers. Caland remembered the mound of rubble that had been his shack and wondered how he survived.

"Sad days for the Valley," Bronlan said quietly.

"Sad days," Caland agreed.

For a time the two of them watched the waves roll shoreward. Then Bronlan asked awkwardly, "You're going to bury Tel here?"

"Tel isn't dead," Caland said.

Another long silence followed. Caland turned and found Bronlan staring at him. It was the first time Caland had ever seen him overtly emotional. He was astonished. "They said she was dead!" he exclaimed.

"They thought she was. I thought she was."

"Those that found her said her neck was broken and she'd been dead for hours. Her body was cold, they said. Are you sure?"

"I found her," Caland said. "I thought she was dead, but she was only unconscious. I just came from talking with her. She got a bad whack on the head, and her neck was injured, and she's lost her memory."

"I see," Bronlan said.

"We all thought she was dead, so no one asked about her," Caland said. "No one realized she was on the wrong list of names until the Reverend started matching names with bodies."

"I see," Bronlan said again. His face wore a perplexed expression. He seemed to be contending with mixed emotions—pleasure that Tel was alive and regret that she was not being buried by the ocean. He wanted to reserve a place in the tomb for himself.

Caland remembered all of the mornings and evenings he'd seen Bronlan raptly watching the ocean and the rising and setting sun, and he thought he understood. "It would be a good place to be buried," he said slowly.

"Yes. That was what I thought when I heard you wanted to put Tel here." Suddenly Bronlan grinned. "But there's no hurry about a tomb if she's not dead."

"She would agree with that," Caland said, and he experienced a cruel wrench of loss as he spoke. He had no idea what the new Tel would think about anything.

"Maybe later we can give some thought to a burial place, here," Bronlan said. "Other things are more important right now. One of them is to grab the person responsible for this. I don't understand how it was done, but Arlu thinks someone did it."

"So do I," Caland said. His exhaustion, and the blow of Tel's apparent death, had momentarily put the thought of vengeance from his mind. He also had forgotten his own guilt: Cenaru, Olyndyt, Skarlont, and now Mort.

"It's my fault," he told Bronlan

"How do you figure that?" Bronlan asked

Caland told him.

Bronlan was silent for a time. Then he said, "Arlu thinks these things are somehow connected with you, but he's never suggested that you might be responsible for them. He thinks that the same person who's controlling you caused the disasters. This feeling you have of someone watching you must have something to do with your being controlled, doesn't it?"

"I don't know. I only know that I have the sensation of being watched."

"Do you have it all the time?"

"No. Not all the time. Frequently enough so that I'm always looking for it and expecting it, so it seems as though it goes on all the time."

"After you moved to the Valley, was it just the same as before?"

Caland hesitated. "No. It stopped. At least I stopped being aware of it. Then it started up again."

"Tel said someone was controlling you when you arrived here, but you seemed to give them the slip. And then she had the impression that they were trying to grab you again. When you complained about being watched, some of your friends investigated. They stayed up all night and made certain that no one went near you. But you kept right on complaining."

"I *was* being watched," Caland said stubbornly.

Bronlan smiled. "It must have seemed that way to you. This business about controlling your mind. Do you know how it works?"

Caland shook his head. "I'm unconscious when it happens. All I know is that when I regain consciousness, time will have passed—sometimes days, sometimes even sennites—and I may be worlds away from the last place I remember."

"Anyone able to control you that well must be wired into your senses. He sees what you see and hears what you hear. It's the only way he could do it without watching you all the time. Arlu brought in special equipment to see whether anyone was sending signals to all of that metal you have in your head. He couldn't detect any. Of course, electromagnetic waves cover a broad band, and he may not have tried the right frequency at the right time. If that's the way someone controls you, that's also the way someone watches you."

Caland gazed at him perplexedly. "I don't quite—"

"The eyes that are watching you are your own." Bronlan said impatiently. "Rather, the person that controls you watches you with your eyes. How else could he do it? As for the storm being you fault, consider this: you're the only link with the person responsible. Your being here didn't cause the storm, but it gives us a chance to catch the person who did. The only way to get at him is through you. If you leave, we lose our link, and we may never catch him. There'll be more storms here and on other worlds. Personally I hope you'll stay. I want him caught."

They walked back to the Prom together. There they encountered a spectral black figure that was standing in front of the teetering Valley Hote watching the Prom cleanup: Dom.

He greeted them with a wave of his bony hand. The gaunt, fleshless face peered slyly from under the black hood and grinned at them.

"Bad business," Dom announced in his raspy, thin, dry voice. "Bad happenings—all these people hurt and killed. But we'll have a better Valley because of it. That's the only attitude to take toward a thing like this. I've been talking with Morlef. We'll rebuild the Prom shops first. With the new theater, we'll attract more tourists than ever before. Then we'll start replacing the housing."

He looked intently at them. Caland met his eyes and was surprised at such a concentration of brightness and energy in the skeletal caricature of a face.

"You're Cal, aren't you?" Dom asked. "I don't remember meeting you."

"We almost met on Rynaif," Caland said. "I saw you running away after the explosion."

The bright eyes remained fixed on him. "I've never been to Rynaif. You must have confused me with someone else."

"Perhaps so," Caland said with a smile. "I would have been easy to counterfeit Dom's clothing, but no makeup could have simulated the bony hands and face."

"You're the one that promoted the theater and the community building," Dom went on. "I've never had an opportunity to thank you. If the Valley is transformed, as I expect it to be, you'll be more responsible for that than anyone else. I hope you'll stay here and enjoy it with us."

"I haven't decided," Caland said evasively.

The bright eyes narrowed just perceptively. "Surely you'll stay and get the theater launched. You're the only one in the Valley who knows anything about that."

Caland answered noncommittally, and Dom walked on.

Caland said, "He looks as old as I thought he was, but he acts a lot younger. Certainly his age hasn't affected his mind."

"He's always been spry and mentally alert," Bronlan said. "There's nothing odd about that. The peculiar thing is that he's acting friendly. He hasn't done that for years."

"Could the storm have changed him?"

"I suppose that's possible. A lot of people who'd never lifted a finger to help their fellow humans are suddenly dedicating themselves to the welfare of the community. I'm glad to see it happen. I suppose we shouldn't worry about why it's happened."

"Perhaps Doctor Gormaz could tell you."

"He's another who changed. When he came here, he seemed to want all of us pinned under glass so he could study us without having to chase us around. But when the storm came, he was one of us. No one has done any better work."

The Prom now was passable as far as the Valley Transportation Company, and the vehicles that had been removed for safety during the storm had returned. A tent had taken the place of the shack that Gary Dwand had used for an office.

"I'm staying here with Gary," Bronlan said.

"Has he heard the news about Melana?"

"Yes. Odd thing, that. The moment he found out she was married, he seemed to lose interest. Can you account for it?"

"Perhaps it was because she always seemed totally unattainable. Now that she's actually been attained, she's not unattainable anymore."

Bronlan looked at him with interest. "Is that so? I wouldn't have thought of it that way. I just assumed that the storm maybe shook some sense into him."

They separated, and Caland walked alone. It was late afternoon, and he had not given any thought at all to a place to sleep. He postponed the problem again because he preferred the contemplation of past memories to present problems. He returned to the ocean beach and slowly walked to the end, where the fertilizer factory's high metal fence reached almost to the water's edge. There he sat down to watch the ocean.

The light was failing when Sam the Artist found him. Sam plunked down beside him breathing heavily. "How was the sunset?"

"There wasn't any color. The sky's too overcast."

"Still counting waves?"

"Not exactly counting. Just letting my mind float freely. And enjoying being alone. Do you realize that from my first day in the Valley, I never was allowed to be alone until now?"

"We were afraid that someone would steal your mind and spirit you away."

"But that happened anyway," Caland said. "Now I suppose it no longer matters."

"I wouldn't say that. It's just that we've had so many other things to worry about. I went to see Tel. Now I'm as upset about her being alive as I was about her being dead."

"Did you talk with her?"

"Screet, yes! She didn't know me. I heard that she didn't know you. The doctor says she's had a serious concussion, and she may get her memory back any minute, or in a few days, or a few sennites. In other words, he doesn't know. He wants her to stay in bed for another day. She says screet; she's got work to do. She still hasn't comprehended where she is or what year it is."

"Who's the doctor?" Caland asked.

"Kalff. The one that's been running our clinic since Fulnry was fired. We had so many casualties at first that anyone who could tie a bandage automatically became a doctor. One of Gormaz's assistants is a medical sociologist, whatever that is, and he did great work until we could get help from Paradise. Kalff has everything regulated. He's moved all the seriously hurt people across the highway. They were scattered all over the Valley from the Houses of Fame to Dom's. He found a big tent to use as a hospital, and he'll be able to take care of them better with them all in one place. He's transferring Tel over there, too. She insists that she's able to be up and about, and she's keeping Gormaz's sociological laboratory in an uproar. It's disrupting his packing."

"Packing?" Caland echoed. "Is Gormaz leaving?"

"Getting ready to. The storm blew away the society he was supposed to be studying. He thinks it'd be quicker to find another than to wait for us to put it together again. Have you eaten recently?"

"I don't know. I don't feel hungry."

"Do you have a place to sleep?"

"I'm thinking about sleeping here."

"Don't be silly," Sam the Artist said. "We've got to get things regulated again, and you can help. Don't try to resign from the human race while the game's still in progress. What happened to upset you so?"

"Tel is a prober."

"She let that slip, did she? So what? Surely you don't think—" Sam turned on him indignantly. "As I live and digest! Surely you don't think she was probing you! Probers deal with inter-world crime and conspiracy. You don't qualify. Whatever Tel was working on started long before you had your brain rear-ranged. It couldn't possibly have anything to do with your rela-tionship. That was whatever the two of you made it. Tel's knock on the head shouldn't affect it at all once she gets her memory back. Now come along and make yourself useful."

The beach was crowded that night. Every ring had a fire, and every fireside circle was complete except for one where Willen Blens had several stones reserved for latecomers. Sam the Artist firmly escorted Caland there, and Caland allowed himself to be persuaded to stay; as in the early days in the Valley, he had nothing else to do.

He sat surrounded by long-time friends and felt like a stranger. Min and Mac were there, and their gentle affection was as warming as the fire. Sippy and her mal Gonger were just as affectionate but in a much less demonstrative manner, as though each were unwilling to be connected publically with a person as obviously sprung as the other was. Louie Laggie was there, and Sigley Varno, and Hefnan Troule, who was taking a gentle ribbing over the fact that he'd gone out of business just in time to avoid having his makeshift eatery blown away. There were three empty stones that presently were occupied by Phem and Moppy, who were escorting Tel.

It was a kindly conspiracy. These friends had met that afternoon and told each other, "Something has got to be done," and this was the something they had settled on; but the problem was not one to be resolved by a casual meeting. Tel had a monstrous chasm in her memory. The blow on her head had wiped out more than five years of recollections, including all of her memory of Mort, and she was bitterly suspicious of everyone connected with an episode in her life that no longer existed for her. She still wore the elaborate cervical collar, though her head bandage had been replaced by a smaller one. Watching her across the fire, Caland knew exactly how she felt, but he could not help her. The fire between them symbolized a chasm as deep as the one in her memory. They had been close enough to share minds and bodies; he had been restored to as much life as he ever would be capable of experiencing by her healing warmth, and for that very reason she would resent him more bitterly than the others. He remembered, and she did not. He possessed something that had been a part of her, and she could not reclaim it.

Turning stiffly, Tel glanced from one person to another, and from time to time she and Phem exchanged whispers. Phem was being touchingly eager and sympathetic. She wanted to clear away this incredible barrier that had put asunder the lives of two people she had liked and admired and who had been so helpful to her. She spoke to Tel. Tel glanced at Caland, frowned, asked a question, listened with deepening frown to Phem's reply, glanced at Caland again.

Caland submitted patiently, but he would have liked to explain to his friends that a gaping hole in the memory could not be healed by a few casual explanations and assurances. It had to be lived with, and time's mocking hand had to wall it off and make tenuous essays at filling it with scaffolding before the owner could be at ease with it. Until then it was a personal abyss, and its owner always had the dizzying sensation of being about to fall into it. Tel would need time and such help as she could find.

But the help could not come from Caland. He was already on the far side of the abyss, and any attempt on his part to bridge the gap would be painful for both of them.

Sam the Artist sensed something of what he was thinking. "Where can a memory go?" he muttered. "The mind doesn't accidently erase things like a mishandled computer. Ten to one it'll all snap back while she's asleep, and she'll wake up and be thoroughly alarmed because you aren't sleeping beside her."

Caland smiled and said nothing. Life without memory was the one subject he could claim to be an expert in, but he knew next to nothing about the restoration of memory.

Mucks Groilan and Kren Krent walked along the beach with a crew of assistants, leaving a carton at every fire: food and jugs of cider, compliments of an anonymous donor. Hefnan Troule expertly took charge of the cooking, and it touched Caland to see Phem instructing Tel as the most effective way to hold he stick over the fire so as to cook the meat impaled on it and at the same time bake the strange Valley concoction of dough that was wrapped around it.

Sam the Artist tilted a jug, took a generous slop, and passed it to Caland. "I'm reminded," he said, "of the last time I starved to death."

Sigley Varno, by far the thinnest member of their group, turned to Sam wickedly. "That must be brain memory," he said. "Obviously your stomach has forgotten all about it."

"My stomach would never forget an affront like that," Sam the Artist said. "Some people claim that nutrition is a science, and others maintain that it's an art. It's neither. It's a religion."

"I suppose that's why the place of ultimate digestion is called a sanctum," Sigley Varno said.

"Spoken like a true non-believer. No one would ever accuse a malnourished specimen like you of being devout."

"All these years I've been thinking you were afflicted with unusually loud stomach noises," Varno said. "I never suspected that you were praying."

The Vals listened to this banter with studious attention, but there were few smiles. On the morrow the Valley would hold a mass funeral. Thirty-six Vals, seven of them children, would be laid to rest in what was to become a memorial park in an angle formed by wings of the community building. The low death toll seemed miraculous, but there was grief enough to go around.

They had finished their food and were enjoying their final slops of cider when Louie Laggie whistled and exclaimed, "Behold—the anonymous donor!"

Melana, leading Alexander the Second by the hand, came walking slowly along the beach. The Reverend accompanied them. They stopped at every fire, talked briefly, and touched hands with anyone who felt inclined to do so.

"It was very nice of them," Phem said. "There's plenty of glop about, so I suppose no one is starving, but real food tastes good."

At Caland's fire the trio greeted everyone warmly. "We have news for you," the Reverend said. "I've just come from a conference with Dom. He's agreed to cede ownership of the Valley to its inhabitants in return for a guaranteed life income."

Sam the Artist was on his feet instantly, bristling with suspicion. "How'd Dom happen to agree to that?"

"I don't know," the Reverend said. "I was a bit surprised myself. It was his suggestion."

"He's never in his life done anything benevolent. Not in my memory. Not in anyone's memory."

The Reverend smiled tolerantly, which was his usual reproach for an uncharitable thought. "Surely we can be more generous than that toward him. He's always been very lenient in the matter of arrears of rentals and such things. Maybe he's suddenly realized how old he is, and he wants to arrange the

Valley's fate while he's still able to do so."

"I saw him today," Sam the Artist said. "He looks a zillion years old, but he always has. I don't think he's aged a moment in all the time I've known him. I told him he was going to live forever, and he grinned as though he believed me."

"Perhaps he doesn't want to be bothered with all of the problems and decisions involved in rebuilding the Valley," the Reverend suggested.

"More likely he doesn't want to invest any of his money in it. This afternoon he was enthusiastic about rebuilding the Valley."

"Then he's changed his mind since then," the Reverend said. "Does it matter why he's doing it? It's good news for everyone. The Valley will be ours!"

"It's not good news for the Pakovich family," Sam the Artist said, turning to Alexander the Second and Melana. "It means that you'll never own all of Mort."

"There'll be enough left to satisfy us," Melana said. "We both love the Valley. We'd like to see the squalor eliminated, but the spirit of the place is unique, and we want that kept exactly as it is."

"*Both* of you love the Valley?"

Sam's skepticism sent them into peals of laughter. "Melana has been living here for two years," Alexander the Second said. "I've been visiting the Valley ever since I was a child."

"You *what*?"

"How could my father keep me away? He made the place seem so forbidden. For a time I had a tutor who was in love with a Valley fem, and he brought me with him and sent me to play with Valley children while he visited her. When I was older, I disguised myself and came alone. Old Gus was a dear friend of mine. He was the only person on Mort who knew that Melana and I were married. When I asked him to find an apartment for her, he gave her the best one in the Valley. We'll miss old Gus."

Sam the Artist said accusingly to Melana, "You love the Valley, but you ran out when the trouble started."

"The trouble wasn't here when I left. It was in Paradise. I

wanted to be where my husband was and help him if I could."

"How does your father feel about all of this?" Caland asked.

"Father is retiring," Alexander the Second said complacently. "That fall down the mountain shook him up. It made him wonder why he was spending his life alone on a mountain top. He enjoyed himself so much on Aravia during our recent visit, and he got on so well with the aristocrats, that he's decided to live there."

"Poor Father Pakovich," Melana said, sounding genuinely sympathetic. "It's been awfully frustrating for him—owning a world and not being able to get anyone on it to do things the way he wants them done."

"Just a moment," Sam the Artist said. "I've never heard of anything that sounded quite this complicated. Your husband, Melana, was supposed to have been betrothed to an Aravian princess in one of those disgustingly posh ceremonies that only an aristocrat can love. Later we heard that she'd jilted him, but you two have been married for years, and he couldn't have married her anyway. Now you're saying that old Pakovich gets along well with the princess's relatives in spite of all this, and he's moving to Aravia to spend more time with them. I'm surprised that they aren't challenging each other to duels."

Again the two burst into peals of laughter. "It's a long and complicated story," Melana said.

"Sit down and tell us about it," Sam the Artist said. "An authentic scandal is just what the Vals need to take their minds off their own troubles."

Alexander the Second and Melana good-naturedly sat down on the sand and described the tribulations of their marriage. "Princess Arnta is a good friend of ours," she said. "So is her husband. We were students together at Aravia University, and we were secretly married at the same time in a double wedding. Then 'Lex graduated, and we came to Mort. Princess Arnta's husband had another year of medical training on Aravia, and then he was to go to Klompf for advanced training. He's going to be a great electrosurgeon, and someday Arnta's family will be proud of him, but that will take time. The problem was with Aravian law. There are two codes of law there, one for commoners and one for aristocracy. The aristocratic code is ignored by most families, but Arnta's family is severely old-fashioned. They're especially old-fashioned concerning the restrictions on fems. When it came time for her husband to leave for Klompf, she tried to slip away with him. Her family caught them. The family didn't know they were married—that would have made it worse. She was literally put in prison. The family wanted to put her husband in prison, too, but he's not an aristocrat, so the Aravian government refused to impose the aristocratic code on him. That was a year ago. When we heard that Arnta's family was trying to marry her off to a decrepit creature of a cousin, we decided to help her. So 'Lex told his father he wanted to marry a princess."

"And his father was delighted," Sam the Artist murmured.

"Actually he was. He made all the arrangements. Arnta's family wouldn't have considered a suit by an impoverished commoner, which her husband is, but a rich suitor had to be taken seriously. A fabulously rich suitor like 'Lex couldn't be resisted. All we wanted to do was create an excuse for Arnta to visit Mort. We would have sent her on to Klompf, and her family would have been powerless to interfere. No other world in the galaxy recognizes that stupid aristocratic legal code. But her family was suspicious—not of 'Lex, but of Arnta. They kept her locked up. There was no way out but to go through with the betrothal ceremony. Once the ceremony was over, she was granted a token of freedom, and 'Lex was able to smuggle her away from Aravia. Now she's joined her husband, and they're very happy. It's worked out well for everyone."

"Father was furious," Alexander the Second said. "He couldn't tolerate the notion that any fem would jilt a Pakovich. If he'd had an army, he would have declared war on Aravia. I took advantage of the indignation to confess that actually I'd already jilted the princess but hadn't quite known how to break the news to her. That pleased him. And once he met Melana, all the problems were resolved instantly. Everyone loves Melana."

"That still doesn't explain why your father wants to live on Aravia," Sam the Artist pointed out. "He and the aristocrats ought to be bitter enemies."

"Actually, he hit it off very well with Princess Arnta's relatives," Alexander the Second said. "Now that she's humiliated them by breaching her marriage contract, they'll be forever obligated to father. The only way they could extinguish that debt would be to offer me another daughter, and they haven't got one. It's that stupid aristocratic code. They have to treat him with the utmost hospitality as long as the debt lasts, which means treating him like a fellow aristocrat. He enjoys that very much. He'll probably be quite happy there. He feels that no one on Mort respects him."

"How can a multi-billionaire hit it off well with an impoverished nobility?" Sam the Artist demanded.

"They have identical views of the class structure and the role of the average citizen."

"It figures," Sam the Artist muttered.

"I'm trying to get father to visit the Valley just once before he leaves," Alexander the Second said. "I told him it would mean a great deal to the people here to know that he supported them in a time of need. But I'm afraid he won't do it."

"I've met your father," Caland said to Alexander the Second. "I really don't understand this sudden decision to leave Mort, no matter how well he may get along with Aravian aristocracy. I know he's had plenty of problems—labor unrest, espionage, and a couple of armed invasions, not to mention his home being blown up—but he impressed me as a stubborn person who'd never yield a position he thought was right. He also has an understandably possessive attitude toward Mort. Why did he suddenly decide to retire and move to Aravia?"

"I think it was the storm," Alexander the Second said.

"The storm? Pak Enterprises wasn't hurt much by the storm."

"No, but it blew the paneling down."

"What paneling?"

"It's like this." Alexander the Second sounded embarrassed. "Sam and those artists painted a sign on the terminal building, and father was so angry about the word switch that he ordered paneling installed over it. Permanently. He was going to have another sign painted on it. The storm blew it down. I think that was when he decided fate was against him and he'd be happier on Aravia."

CHAPTER THIRTY-SIX

Sam the Artist had remarked that the Vals needed an authentic scandal to take their minds off their own troubles. Scandalous or not, for several days the Vals were agog with the tale of two years of furtive marriage on Mort and the romance of the imprisoned princess Arnta.

"Myself, I don't think much of it," Sam the Artist told Caland sourly. "If Alexander the Second had been created with a normally structured backbone, he would have informed his father of his marriage when it happened. Why not? As he said, to see Melana is to love her. His father could have loved her just as much three years ago."

Caland was amused. "But if he'd done that, they couldn't have rescued the princess with a fake betrothal. Melana was right. Things worked out well for everyone."

"The way I see it, all Alexander the Second accomplished during three years of marriage was to demonstrate to his wife how spineless he is."

"But wasn't it brave of him to sneak into the Valley to see her? And what could better sustain matrimonial romance than two whole years of clandestine meetings, her seeing him by stealth when she was supposed to be working in the library, him braving local gossip and paternal wrath by ineptly disguising himself and sneaking off to her apartment in the Valley. And look how bravely he seized the opportunity to tell his father when one finally arrived. Alexander the Second knows Old Pakovich far better than we do, and we have no business faulting his timing.

Certainly it worked out well for everyone. You couldn't pick a nicer young couple to hand a world to. I heard someone call him an up person, and Melana certainly is. This is going to be great for the whole world of Mort."

Sam grumbled and went his way. Caland alternated long periods of cleanup work with intervals of aimless wandering. He even explored the ocean shore south of Fish Town. He was experiencing a belated surge of sympathy for Gary Dwand, who no longer needed it. Gary had left off bleating, "Have you seen Melana?" because he knew where she was—home with her husband. Caland had to resist the temptation to start asking, "Have you seen Tel?" If anyone could have invented an excuse for visiting the encampment across the highway, where she was staying, he would have done so. He could not, so he had to wait for her to appear.

Caland worked and wandered until one morning he cast up like a piece of driftwood at the plaza where Sam the Artist, the Reverend, Morlef, Bronlan, Zata, and Calta Draning were contending good-naturedly over plans for rebuilding the Valley. Partley hrv' Dasshlam's generous donation was being stretched to the utmost. Caland found himself listening to the merits of cement as opposed to stone-faced buildings, and of exterior gardens as opposed to interior courts lined with shops.

"We don't want to rush this," Calta said. "There's a great temptation to build quickly and get back to business as usual, but doing it right is more important than doing it fast. We need someone with experience in city planning, but I don't think anyone on Mort has any."

"Doctor Gormaz might know something about it," the Reverend suggested.

"The very person," Calta agreed. "Send Hairy."

Doctor Gormaz generously left off packing his equipment and records to share his city planning experience with them. He already had apologized for the abrupt decision to leave, but the storm had effectively disrupted the society he was attempting to study. A society under duress and in transition could well have provided the basis for fascinating sociological observation, he said, but this was not the kind of study his sociological laboratory was designed to deal with.

He was in no rush to leave because he had not yet decided where he would go. While he was making up his mind, he obviously was enjoying the sociological spectacle about him. He had packed his gloomy countenance along with his records. Not only did he seem in good spirits, but his scraggly beard even showed signs of brushing.

As for planning the Valley's reconstruction, any knowledge he had was at their disposal. He listened to the contending arguments, and he watched Morlef sketch plans on the plaza's cement with chalk.

"You people should stop drawing lines and start thinking of function," he said finally. "Consider this community building that's half-finished. You've put your medical clinic in a prime front location. That's silly. There'll always be a throng of tourists crowding this plaza and resting from the walk up the Prom, or waiting for the theater to open. Why should everyone in the Valley who feels sick have to push through that? And if any of the sick people turn out to be really sick, you'll have to get a vehicle through this mess in order to send them to the hospital. Finally, the only hospital available to them is in Paradise. All of that is worse than silly. It's ludicrous."

Bronlan was curiously polite. "What do you suggest?"

"Think about function. Think about how things are actually going to be used. For example, the courts off the Prom. There are a lot of Prom shops that are patronized only by Vals. Why do they have to be on the Prom at all? If you make some of these courts extend through to the next street, you'll be able to locate clutter shops and cheap eateries and things of that ilk away from the Prom. Tourists don't patronize them anyway, and an off-Prom location would be much more convenient for Vals."

"The clutter shops are a part of the Valley's color," Caland objected. "The tourists may not patronize them, but—in a distasteful way—they find them fascinating. They'll spend more time studying shoddy merchandise in a cheap clutter shop than they will that of a stylish shop catering to tourists. Tourists also are curious about Valley residents. The Prom would be much less interesting to them if the Vals stayed away."

Doctor Gormaz shrugged. "Perhaps. Perhaps. But none of that applies to the medical situation. There should be two medical clinics in a community of this size—one north of the Prom and one south of it, and one of them ought to have a hospital attached. In any case, function is the answer to your planning problems. For each structure, consider who will use it, and where the users will come from, and where they'll go when they leave it. When you get some actual plans drawn, I'll be glad to look at them."

They watched him bounce away.

"What was so expert about that?" Sam the Artist wanted to know.

"But those actually are good ideas," the Reverend said. "Why *are* we putting the medical clinic in the community building? When we planned the building, that was the only place we could put it. Now things have changed drastically. He's right. We need to consider function, and we need to establish priorities. The school, for example. It's important, but right now the children are homeless. Maybe we should convert the community building to temporary housing."

"You tell me what to build," Morlef said. "And I'll build it. If we make all these Prom buildings two stories, we can put a lot of apartments on the second floors. We also could put some at the rear of the shops."

"We need to think more about important businesses like Olgi's," the Reverend said. "She should have a new, much larger building for a factory, but that doesn't have to be on the Prom. Perhaps we should offer her a new Prom shop to serve her ices and confections, and a factory somewhere else to make them."

"'Function' also applies to the factory," Baris Bronlan said. "If we put the factory somewhere else, we'll have to build a street there so 'trucks can get to it."

The discussion began to meander; Caland tired of it long before he nerved himself to slip away and return to the Prom cleanup crews.

Eventually Hairy found him there—an acutely harassed Hairy trying to maintain Valley communications in troubled times. He had lost his confident mastery of the Valley population. In the old Valley, the apparent chaos overlaid an orderly arrangement of currents and counterparts and immoveable loci. Hairy's finely tuned memory had kept the entire Valley population tabbed in terms of fixed locations and movement to or from them. Suddenly most of the points of reference had vanished and currents swirled without direction. No one knew where anyone was supposed to be, and anyone was likely to be anywhere. Whenever Hairy finally located his quarry, his face assumed an expression of incredulity.

"Arlu is coming," he told Caland. "The Fig Stump."

"All right," Caland said. "I'll head that way when I see him arrive."

The response troubled Hairy. When Arlu convoked a meeting, Hairy took it as a point of honor to have everyone assembled and waiting for him. "There's yuck and glop there," Hairy said.

The promise of food did not tempt Caland. He returned to his work, and Hairy loped away. Not until Caland saw Arlu's 'cab threading its way past the 'trucks that were still being loaded with Prom debris did he desist and head toward the Fig Stump.

The others were already assembled: Calta, Yda, the Reverend, and Sam the Artist. Sam was busily engaged with the yuck and glop; the others were waiting silently.

As Caland entered, Calta turned on Sam the Artist with a snarl. "That's right. Go ahead and stuff yourself while we sit and waste time."

"She says, having stuffed herself in private," Sam the Artist responded complacently. "What are we keeping you from? A houseful of customers?"

Calta glared at him.

"How's Tel?" Yda asked the Reverend.

"Fine," the Reverend said. "Never looked better. The doctor has let her remove her cervical collar. She's restless, of course. She thinks she ought to be doing something, but she hasn't been able to remember what it is."

"Has her memory improved any?"

The Reverend shook his head. "So of course nothing makes sense to her."

For once Arlu made a nondescript entrance. He was attired in a drab, weather-proofed garment, and he looked as though he expected the storm to break out again at any moment. He halted and glanced around the room. "Tel?"

"There was no point in inviting her," the Reverend said.

Arlu sat down heavily and turned to Caland. "Any sensation of watching eyes, lately?"

"Yes," Caland said.

"And?"

"Just that. A fleeting sensation. It happens two or three times a day."

Arlu sank back on the recliner and closed his eyes.

"If you've come here to sleep—" Calta began caustically.

Arlu stirred himself. "I thought we had everything regulated." he said pensively. "I really thought we were about to lay it out. Suddenly the whole thing has blown and we're nowhere. Would it help if I talked with Tel?"

"If you knew her long ago, she'd probably greet you like an old friend," the Reverend said. "Her memory seems to be intact up to about five and a half years ago. After that—nothing."

"Did you know Tel is a prober?" Caland asked Arlu.

"Of course. I don't know what she was doing on Mort, though. Probers don't talk about their assignments. Evidently she thought Cal's problem touched on her own because she identified herself to me and offered to take over the Mort end of my search. That seemed like an ideal arrangement. She was here, and she knew the scene. She already had contacts. There was plenty of work for me to do elsewhere on a case that has tangled threads all over the galaxy. So she went to work. I know she had every possible suspect tabbed and watched. In veriest fact, I thought we were ready to break the case. Suddenly we're back where we started, and we have the added mystery of what happened to Tel. Was she bashed accidently when the building collapsed, or was it done intentionally by someone she had in focus? It's important that we know, and I have no notion of how to find out. Does anyone know anything at all about this accident of hers?"

"I'm afraid not," the Reverend said.

Arlu shot an anguished glance at him. "Tel is a highly competent person."

"She is that," the Reverend agreed.

"She had the Valley and everything connected with it regulated. I left it all to her. Now I don't know where to start. Do any of you know who was working for her?"

"Everyone worked for Tel," Sam the Artist said. "A lot of people worked for her who didn't even know they were doing it. She would say to me, 'Watch for the next hour and see who pays attention to Cal.' so I would. She'd grab someone who wasn't doing anything and say, 'Follow so and so,' and he would. But she never explained what she was after. We did what she told us and brought back the result, and if there was an add, she was the one who made it."

"Did she have any regular employees?"

"She may have. I wouldn't know who they are."

Arlu heaved a sigh. "In veriest fact, I thought Tel had the case skewered."

"What's been happening over in Paradise?" Sam the Artist asked.

"As far as the problem is concerned, a lot of loose ends and irrelevancies have been tied up and eliminated. Tate is dead, and the probers have Felroy and Emson in custody. Those two are wanted a lot of places for a lot of iniquities. The Pak Enterprises employees are back at work mourning their dead, and feeling chagrinned over being had by a jobber like Tate. Alexander the Second has talked with each and every one of them personally, and they now know that they don't have to revolt when they have a grievance. Fem Wobbons and the saboteurs—those that survived—have been sent to Aravia. They, and the world of Rynaif, will be charged in the interworld court there for their espionage. Sdissler is dead, and his troops are dead or captured. Alexander the Second listened to reason when his father wouldn't, and took responsibility for inviting in the Aravian army—just in time. Aravia will keep troops here until Mort is able to protect itself. It's been costly to everyone concerned, but the wipe-up is highly satisfactory. Alexander the Second has taken over very capably. The only thing that's uncertain is whether any of those conspiracies were connected with Cal. That was Tel's department."

"There must have been some kind of connection," Calta Draning said. "Everything started happening when he arrived here."

Arlu shook his head. "The beginning came long, long before that. Cal's friend Fellington Felroy put his finger on the situation in that conversation Cal overheard. He was talking about the world of Mort being ripe for the plucking, and he wondered why someone else hadn't thought of it. But a lot of people *had* thought of it. The world of Mort is enormously wealthy, with a potential far beyond anyone's ability to calculate, and Pakovich's guardianship of that wealth has been unbelievably inept. He was so conspicuously vulnerable. The situation was made to order for conspirators. Sdissler is a prime example. He worked patiently for years, waiting for the right moment. His backers gambled a substantial investment, but the payoff would have been enormous if they'd won. We didn't know how many other conspiracies there may have been. We can be certain that there were enough to justify the permanent assignment of a prober to Mort. Felroy was a latecomer."

"Why did Sdissler wait so long?" Sam the Artist asked.

"Because Pakovich's ownership has no cracks in it. None at all. He has old Mort Pakovich to thank for that. Sdissler could have taken over Mort at any time, but he never could have gotten his ownership validated in the interworld courts. He would have been boycotted and isolated, and eventually the neighboring worlds would have taken direct action. He was waiting for a loophole, and he thought Tate and the sabotage had given him one. But I'm certain that none of those things had anything to do with Cal. The storm is another matter. Was it part of the pattern of natural upheavals on worlds Cal has visited, or was it just a storm? Tel may have known, but now she knows nothing at all. I don't know what to do except start over."

"She may get her memory back," the Reverend said. "It hasn't been very long."

"Is there likely to be another storm?" Sam the Artist asked.

Arlu heaved himself to his feet. "That's a critical question, and I have no idea what the answer is. I'll be sending one of my searchers to try and pick up the pieces. A young fem named Jinli. Help her if you can."

He waddled out.

"Now that was a cheerful conversation," Sam the Artist said. "I haven't heard such gloomy pronouncements since all of the sanctums on Primrose Lane got plugged up at the same time."

"I thought he was more cheerful than usual," Yda said. "Up until now he's been complaining that the clues are scattered from one end of the galaxy to the other. At least he's finally got the trouble concentrated in one place."

Calta got up languorously. "If that's progress, please take it somewhere else. Going to hang around here all morning, dearie?"

"I'd like to," Yda said. "But if all of us don't get to work and get the Prom cleared, there never will be a houseful of customers. You able-bodied types are cordially invited to come down and help us."

"Just as soon as we finish the yuck," Sam the Artist promised.

The two fems left. Caland was about to follow them when the Reverend stopped him and asked, "Do *you* think the storm had some connection with you?"

"I know it did because of what happened to me. The same thing has happened before—on Cenaru, Olyndyt, and Skarlont. And I know that it'll happen again—here or somewhere else—if the person responsible isn't stopped."

"Then we'll have to stop him," the Reverend said. "Any suggestions?"

"None at all. But I agree with Arlu that the person is still on Mort. Otherwise, how could he be watching me?"

Sam the Artist drained his yuck mug and set it back down with a crash. "I'm sorry to say it, but it would have been a lot better for everyone concerned if Tel had broken her arms and legs and protected her skull. We might as well go down and labor manually for a few hours. We don't make much progress when we use our heads."

The laboring hours lengthened into days. The Prom wreckage was cleared away along with everything left standing that was structurally unsound. The Valley Hote fell with a crash, scientifically brought down by Morlef. Alexander the Second sent in machinery from Pak Enterprises to carve the Valley streets into a condition that would support vehicular traffic. Nothing could be done about clearing away wreckage located away from the paved section of the Prom until 'trucks could reach it.

Doctor Gormaz had proceeded with his packing in leisurely fashion. Cartons containing his records and equipment were stacked on the veranda of Dom's house ready to be carried to the Prom for transport to the Port. He had picked his destination, and he was awaiting a reply to a query he had spaced there. While he waited, he spent hours pacing the Valley with Morlef, examining the growing plans, offering comments and suggestions, and in every way making himself invaluable.

Dom, having signed—in the presence of a parade of witnesses—a legal document carefully roughed out by the best minds in the Valley and scrutinized for loopholes and set in proper format by the Pak Enterprises counsel, departed for Aravia, his ultimate destination unknown. His manner had changed since Caland had talked with him shortly after the storm. Then he had been cheerful and confident about building a new Valley; now he seemed furtive and eager to get away as quickly as possible.

Sam the Artist noticed. He muttered to Caland, "Do you suppose he knows something we don't?"

The elder Pakovich left Mort for a new life among companionable Aravian aristocrats. Rumor had it that he was even more eager to depart than Dom had been. Unlike Dom's departure, Pakovich's was without ceremony—though, as Sam the Artist suggested, the Valley's entire population would have been pleased to celebrate it.

The final Valley plans called for widening the Prom except where the buildings housing the Road to Hell, the restaurants, and the Houses of Fame constricted it. But the new Prom was to be closed to vehicular traffic. At the east end there would be a central mall where artists could offer pictures for sale, create art works to order, or do portraits of willing patrons, and where individual Vals could sell their own handicrafts. There would be room for floral displays, statuary, and whatever else might offer beauty, interest, color, or entertainment to visitors. The new buildings were to be large rectangles with shops arranged around a skylighted court. Protruding roofs would shelter walkways against the uncertain Valley weather. The park along the east boundary was to become a roadway connecting with each of the Valley streets, all of which were being leveled and graveled. In addition, a service drive was to be constructed behind the buildings on either side of the Prom for 'truck deliveries, trash pickup, and the use of 'cabs taking patrons to the restaurants, the Houses of Fame, or the Road to Hell. Eventually the north service drive would carry 'cab and 'bus traffic to a vehicular plaza at the theaters.

The Valley Transportation Company had yielded its prime Prom location in favor of a new yard at the extreme south of the Valley along the Fertilizer Factory fence. The new roadway and streets would make the move possible. Adjacent to it, also along the fence, was to be a fine new building where Olgi would manufacture her ices and confections. She would be able to expand her export business—and her payroll.

The tents arrived from Aravia, and as fast as the ground was made ready for them, they were put up on both sides of the Prom. Morlef, having performed his measurements and buried survey stakes where he thought he would need them, reserved only the site of the first new building—south of the Prom, next to Yda's.

No decision had been made concerning the location of the new medical clinic or clinics, or the feasibility of erecting a hote building to replace the demolished Valley Hote. If a hote were to be built, some thought it belonged on the Prom. Others favored moving it to a site overlooking the bay and letting it compete with the two Paradise hotes. Caland offered no opinion; he didn't care where they put it as long as it was not on the ocean beach.

The Valley reopened in tents. The tourists who had been frightened away by the storm and the several small wars that had erupted about them had been replaced by others who knew nothing of Mort's crises, and were eagerly awaiting an opportunity to sample the Valley's celebrated hedonism. They arrived in large numbers the morning the Valley reopened. Sam the Artist and Caland sat in the tent in which Nello had re-established his eatery and sipped yuck and watched the passing crowds, and Sam remarked that things were back to normal and getting better.

Caland said nothing. The Valley had not been normal for him without Tel, and her condition was unchanged. She had a visitor, however—a mal out of her past named Edlan. Caland saw the two of them strolling along the Prom together—she in a different knit dress from the one she'd been wearing at the time of the storm, probably salvaged from the demolished house, he in a casually tasteful daysuit. He was tall, well-built, blond; she was sturdy, shapely, dark. She'd replaced the head bandage with a hat that concealed the patch where her hair had not grown out. Probably the entire Valley thought they made a handsome couple, but no one was so tactless as to mention that to Caland. During the course of a couple of days they were seen together frequently as they moved about the Valley, or talked quietly together over yuck in a down eatery. Then he left, and Phem resumed her function as Tel's chaperon.

Alexander the Second and Melana had been furiously busy with their new position and responsibilities, but occasionally they looked in on their friends in the Valley. They delighted in reminiscing about Melana's two years in the Valley and Sdissler's bungling pursuit of her.

Watching them strolling hand in hand along the Prom, Sam the Artist remarked, "They don't look the part."

"What part should they look?" Caland asked.

"They look like a couple of naïve tourists. Owners of a world ought to look like owners of a world."

"What should owners of a world look like?"

"What Mort needs," Sam the Artist said thoughtfully, "is a king and a queen."

"You're the one who was outraged at the thought of Alexander the Second marrying a princess."

"I don't want a royal Pakovich family. What these two should do is hire a couple of actors to play the parts of king and queen. Then they could go about like commoners, which obviously they enjoy, and the actors could make like royalty. There's a world somewhere that's actually done that. Any royal family that remains in power very long, anywhere, achieves nothing but a long history of villainous ancestors and horrendous misdeeds. Even when a king is a common, tolerable run-of-the-mill scoundrel, his relatives go out of their way to keep up the family tradition of arrogant, self-indulgent wickedness, and the cost of maintaining such an establishment is preposterous. This world I mentioned got rid of the whole degenerate mess and made up a fictitious royal family by hiring actors. The king always looked and behaved kingly. The royal family always behaved itself. When it had no official functions, it ceased to exist, and the government was never embarrassed by royal scandals. On the other hand, king or queen or princes or princesses were always available at guild rates whenever anyone wanted royalty to lay a cornerstone or grace a country fair. It satisfied everyone, and it was fantastically less expensive that maintaining an utterly worthless full time royalty. Let's suggest it to Alexander the Second and Melana."

Caland shook his head. "Speaking as an actor, I'd say that Mort couldn't provide enough work to justify having a king on any basis."

Zata had the regular group of paras functioning again; and while Caland made no attempt to resume his own para role, he did inspect performances regularly, suggest improvements, and audition the acts of would-be paras.

One bright afternoon when both the Valley and Mort had sufficiently returned to normal to make it possible to steal a few hours of relaxation in good conscience, Alexander the Second and Melana hosted a small picnic on the bay beach. Sam the Artist, the Reverend, Caland, and Baris Bronlan attended. Tel and Phem had been invited—Melana was supporting the Val's efforts to bring Caland and Tel together—but talk about the immediate past still distressed Tel, and Phem thought it wise to politely refuse for both of them.

The Reverend was entertaining the group with his own description of Caland's efforts to recruit a troop of paras when Hairy loped into view. "People here to see you," he panted. "I'll bring them."

"People to see whom?" Sam the Artist called after him. Hairy made no response. He darted away in the direction of the Prom.

"It can't be anyone important," Alexander the Second said cheerfully, "or we would have been summoned to see them."

Hairy returned with a dozen people in file behind him, and their variety of dress gave Caland the startled impression that someone had assembled a comic para act. There were robes of various colors and persuasions; there were academic garbs and work garbs and flamboyant tourist costumes. It was only when the introductions were performed that they realized how wrong

Alexander the Second had been. This was an assemblage of quite preposterous importance.

The spokesman, a lank mal in full purple legal regalia, introduced himself as an administrator of the Aravian Interworld Court. "Administrator Quaslef, serving justice on all of our member worlds," he murmured. He introduced in turn the court clerk, assistants, and an amorphous group of mals and fems described as "legally qualified experts."

"To what do we owe this entirely unexpected pleasure?" Alexander the Second murmured politely.

"The court has been petitioned formally for a review of a verdict handed down more than eighty years ago," Administrator Quaslef said. "It's a highly unusual request, but inasmuch as it is accompanied by evidence that strongly suggests that the original verdict was in error, the Court has no choice but to test the claim with utmost stringency."

"I see," Alexander the Second said.

"I don't see at all," Melana said impatiently. "What is it that you expect to test on Mort?"

"Evidence filed against the claim in which the Court awarded ownership of the world of Mort to one Mort Pakovich eighty-four years ago. The petition alleges that this verdict was in error, and the petition furnishes detailed evidence to support a legal claim to the world of Mort that antedates the discovery upon which Mort Pakovich's claim was based by one hundred and seven years."

Whereupon the administrator, in an abrupt outburst of ceremony and stilted language, served an embossed and embellished legal document on Alexander the Second. The younger Pakovich, like his wife and all of the Vals present, lapsed into speechlessness.

"Evidence, of course, must be substantiated," Administrator Quaslef proclaimed. "We have been supplied with maps, but a map can be feloniously misdated with ease. The maps show the locations of bench marks from an onsite survey alleged to have taken place two hundred and eleven years ago—but bench marks do not by necessity always bear the date of their planting. The new claim would have been rejected on both qualitative and quantitative grounds—a layman might say, 'too little, too late'—were it not for the curious fact that these bench marks are alleged to contain radium chronographs."

The administrator talked on, and Caland's mind attempted to sift a morsel of meaning from the outpouring of words: maps could be forged; bench marks could be fraudulently planted long after their engraved dates; only rarely could fotes of a planet be dated from internal evidence. Ordinarily, the Court would not have deigned to acknowledge the existence of a counterclaim filed more than eighty years after a verdict with a basis so susceptible to fraud. But bench marks containing radium chronographs were another matter entirely. If discovered and removed and validated under the supervision of the Court's scientific experts, they constituted infallible evidence. The Court's scientists could quickly determine how much time had elapsed since the marks were planted.

"Assuming that there are such marks to be discovered," Alexander the Second suggested.

The administrator bowed. "Naturally assuming that. The map shows precise locations. Of course, if there are no marks there, there will be no evidence. Would you kindly appoint someone to accompany us and represent your interests?"

"I'll represent my own interests," Alexander the Second said.

"Very good." The administrator turned to his entourage. "How do you wish to proceed?"

"One site is nearby," an assistant announced.

"As a preliminary check, let's try to find it," the administrator said.

Instruments were brought from the 'cab waiting on the Prom. All of them moved in solemn procession along the bay beach to the spit of land that arched out into the bay's mouth. They turned left. At the point of higher ground midway between the ocean and the bay beaches, a surveyor unlimbered his instrument, and a scientist—the one in the most outrageous tourist costume—began pointing a detector at the ground.

"I make it here," the surveyor said, planting a red stake. "The contour of the bay could have changed, of course."

"Must have changed," the scientist said scowling at his detector.

He took a few strides toward the ocean and swung back. The detector beeped.

The surveyor planted another stake.

Digging quickly revealed a bench mark, which consisted of a heavily corroded metal disc embedded in cement.

"The chronograph capsule will be under it," the scientist remarked happily. "We'll have to remove the entire base, plus soil samples, for scientific study. Then we'll find the other marks and start looking for supplementary evidence."

"What supplementary evidence?" Alexander the Second wanted to know.

"The map shows the site of the explorers' encampment. We'll look for relics there. The exploration diary notes the sinking of a boat off the northeast shore of the bay. Those things wouldn't be conclusive evidence in themselves—but as supplementary evidence to the radium chronographs, they're valuable."

"Will you accompany us, Mal Pakovich?" the administrator asked politely.

"Oh, yes." Alexander the Second looked grim. "I'll accompany you."

"We'll need assistance in removing the marks, and we would appreciate lab accommodation. The scientists would prefer to do their preliminary testing and analysis here."

"Of course," Alexander the Second said. "I'll make arrangements now."

He turned away stonily.

Melana and the Vals followed him, leaving the strange assemblage of visitors looking admiringly at the bench mark.

Suddenly Melana laughed merrily. Alexander the Second halted and looked at her perplexedly.

"Don't be so glum!" she told him. "What's a world, more or

less? If they evict us, we can move to the Valley."

"If that so-called evidence proves to be valid," Alexander the Second said, "and I have a presentiment that it will, we'll be moving completely away from Mort. Everyone will be moving. If the Pakovich claim is ruled invalid, all subsequent transfers of property will be equally invalid—including Dom's claim to the Valley. The entire world of Mort will belong to someone else."

CHAPTER THIRTY-SEVEN

The investigators worked for a sennite discovering and assembling evidence and completing their preliminary testing. They politely handed a copy of the results to Alexander the Second.

They had discovered four bench marks at approximately the locations indicated on their maps. These were standard survey marks of a type in use two hundred years before, and they had been cast with the expedition's insignia. They recorded the explorers' formal claim to the planet, and indicated that a survey had been planned and commenced. For some unknown reason it had been interrupted—the explorers had not bothered to record elevations—but the exploration diary indicated that they expected to return to Mort at a later date to extend and complete the survey. There was no evidence that they had done so.

All of the chronographs showed an elapsed time of two hundred and eleven years. Corrosion of the metal was consistent with that age. A hole digger of a type known to have been in use two hundred years before had been found near one of the marks. The indicated camp site, located in Paradise Park, had yielded debris and a few tools of similar age. The sunken boat's synthetic hull was presumed to have dissolved long before in Mort's mildly acidic sea water, but the scientists had brought to the surface a two-hundred-year-old electric boat motor.

Scientists and court officials were elated with their prompt and decisive resolution of what could have been a vexing problem. They returned to Aravia in an effusion of mutual congratulations on a job well done. With them went Gilf, the Pak Enterprises Counsel, girded for the legal battle of his life.

The Valley mood changed abruptly from optimism to indifference. Vals began wondering who would benefit from their labor, and it became difficult to find volunteers for work details.

Sam the Artist asked gloomily, "What are the odds that the whole business was faked?"

"Most of it could have been," the Reverend said. "But not the chronographs. Of course, if someone had had the foresight two hundred and eleven years ago to attach the radium chronograph capsules to those particular bench marks and enclose them in cement and bury them somewhere for aging, *then* they could have been planted here as fake evidence. Even so, the soil they were buried in would have had to be virtually identical to the soil they were found in, or the scientists would have started asking themselves puzzled questions. Obviously, nothing like that could have happened. I'd say there's absolutely no possibility that those bench marks weren't planted where they were found and at the time the chronographs indicated."

"Who filed the petition for a rehearing?" Caland asked.

"An old, eminently respectable family from the world of Galeria. It has a prospecting spacer for an ancestor. The story told is that he was extremely thorough with his explorations, but a bit absent-minded when it came to filing his just claims with the proper authorities. There'll be a hot legal contest on that issue alone. The Pakovich claim is based on an exploration that was filed promptly. The Galeria family will contend that there was no Office of Interworld Affairs with which a filing could be made two hundred years ago. That was no excuse for not making a local filing of record, of course. Actually, the prospector may have done so, almost anywhere, and it just hasn't turned up yet."

Caland said slowly, "If the prospecting ancestor was meticulous enough to use bench marks with radium chronographs to establish his claim, one would expect him to be meticulous enough to file it."

"That's true," the Reverend said. "Those particular chronographs were developed for that purpose, but very few explorers used them. Explorers usually settled on the world they found and reaped the benefits of their exploration immediately. Filing was a legal formality to put their occupation on record so usurpers couldn't come along later and pull the world from under them."

"In other words," Caland mused, "the chronographs serve no useful purpose for an exploration unless it's suspected that they might be needed to resolve a legal claim two hundred years later."

Sam the Artist thumbed the table. "I say it's fraudulent. I also say that Arlu is sprung. All of these things *have* to be connected. This is just one more attempt to grab the world of Mort. It's Sdissler all over again with a bit more subtlety. We ought to tell the Court that."

"I gravely fear that the Court will prefer to credit the scientific evidence," the Reverend murmured.

Baris Bronlan had been listening to the conversation with a look of intense puzzlement. He said, "I think maybe the problem from the beginning was paying too much attention to all of those other things and not enough to Cal." He turned to Caland. "Are you still being watched?"

"Just once in a while. Maybe a couple of times a day."

"I've been thinking about that," Bronlan said. "If Cal is connected with all of these things, then his being watched is connected with them, too. Controlling him through wires in his brain has to be connected with them. So I thought about the things that have happened to Cal, and I asked myself how they must have looked to the person controlling him." He turned to Caland again. "You said you always stayed in cheap gen hotes before you came to Mort."

"Always," Caland agreed.

"In other words," Bronlan said to the others, "he stayed with transients and strangers who mostly paid very little attention to each other. When he came to Mort, he had to stay at a different kind of hote. Tourists get to know each other and even get down-right snoopy about what the others are doing and how they pass their time. Since Cal is a good-looking young mal, a lot of the fems would take a special interest in him. The person controlling him didn't like that, so he let Cal move to the Valley, or perhaps he made him move here. Then right away Cal seemed to be making a lot of new friends, and the controller tried to make him leave."

"At which point Tel took charge and made him stay," Sam the Artist said.

"Right. I'm still thinking about how it looked to the person controlling Cal. Obviously, he was new to Mort and didn't understand the Valley. We kept Cal here, and this controller kept watching, and eventually he decided that we Vals were harmless. He wanted to put Cal in a safe place for a time, and this seemed as good as any. Probably he had other business to look after, and he checked up on Cal less and less frequently. As a result, Cal slowly came out of the fog that he'd been in through having his brain controlled, and he became a different person. Suddenly he was a leader everyone looked up to, and he invented a lot of things that were helpful to all of us. The controller must have been aware of this, but he didn't mind. Otherwise he would have stopped it. Finally he decided he'd let Cal go too far, or maybe he wanted to use him for something, and he began to clamp down again. The more he meddled with Cal's mind, the more Cal changed. He slipped back to what he'd been when he came to the Valley. He lost interest in things." Bronlan turned to the Reverend. "Does it look that way to you?"

"Exactly that way," the Reverend said. "Life kept flowing along, and Cal wanted to get off."

"I don't think Arlu understands this, because he hasn't been constantly in touch with Cal the way we have. Also, Arlu spends too much time trying to figure out the how and why of things. If you catch someone making off with another person's property, you don't sit down and meditate and try to understand how he got it and why he wants it. You grab the person and put a stop to it. There's always time afterward to figure out how and why. It's the same with Cal. Someone is stealing his brain. Let's put a stop to it. The hows and whys about underworld conspiracies can be worked out later."

"Great idea," Sam the Artist said. "How do we go about grabbing and stopping when we have no idea who it is?"

"My notion is that when Cal has the sensation of someone watching him, what actually is happening is that the person controlling him is taking over his mind momentarily. He's looking at the world through Cal's eyes and hearing through Cal's ears and maybe feeling with Cal's sense of touch and all the rest. He's checking to make certain that Cal isn't getting into mischief, or maybe he's just testing his equipment, but the important thing is that he does check. So I suggest that we blind-fold Cal, and plug his ears and maybe wrap him in some kind of restraint and hide him somewhere and have him think blank thoughts. This will be a bit of an ordeal for Cal if his controller doesn't think to check him for a couple of days, but we can help that by spreading the rumor that he's disappeared. We'll say he's been despondent because Tel doesn't remember him, and all of us are worried about him. If someone really is controlling Cal, that'll send him to his instruments to find out what's happening. If his instruments tell him that Cal isn't seeing anything, isn't hearing anything, is under some kind of restraint, and has blank thoughts, this controller ought to be sufficiently alarmed to investigate. When he comes snooping around, we'll grab him."

"You're assuming that he receives some kind of signal from Cal and can trace it," the Reverend said.

"I'm not assuming anything at all. You're trying to make us worry about how it's done. That comes afterward. First, let's put a stop to it."

"What do you think?" Sam the Artist asked Caland.

"Bar is a practical mal. It sounds like a wonderfully practical plan."

"An admirable plan," the Reverend said. "It's simple, it costs nothing except a little inconvenience, and if it doesn't work, we're surely no worse off than we are now. When can we do it?"

"The problem is where to do it," Bronlan said. "There aren't many places left in the Valley where we could hide Cal."

"We won't exactly be hiding him," Sam the Artist said. "We'll be setting a trap with him as the bait. It won't work unless we're able to watch the trap without being seen. One of the wrecked houses might do. Let's go look."

"That doesn't sound like a very comfortable place for Cal," the Reverend said.

"Never mind comfort," Caland told him. "It'll be a relief just to have something to do. All I ask is that you tie me loosely enough so I can get my hands on this controller if he does show up."

* * * * * * *

Caland lay in a rope hammock and tried to make his mind blank.

He was blindfolded, his ears were plugged with wax, and his hands and feet were loosely bound. His mouth was gagged. He could see nothing; he could hear nothing; he could feel nothing but his restraints and the pressure of the hammock strands.

The trap was set.

Caland feared that it was already sprung. The eyes had watched him intermittently; probably there were ears that listened, and a mind that probed his thoughts. He had mentioned this to the others, and they promptly chased him off the beach and told him to count ocean waves and otherwise keep his mind blank until they finished the preparations, but this precaution could have come too late.

Because they had brought him to the trap blindfolded, he had no idea where he was. Now there was nothing for him to do but wait.

A few minutes of effort convinced him that it was impossible to keep his mind blank. For a time he counted imaginary ocean waves, and then he concentrated on creating images that would dumbfound anyone eavesdropping on his thoughts. First he climbed stairs. He went slowly, one shuffling step at a time, up an enormously long flight. Then he turned and shuffled up another, counting the steps. When the count reached sixty, he turned again and continued to climb. At the end of ten flights he gained the top of the tower and looked over a barren desert land-scape. For a time he allowed his mind to dwell on the intense heat. He looked down on the rippling sand far below. It was kept constantly in motion by a whistling wind that shifted it into grotesque patterns. The wind drove stinging particles into his face with painful force. When he could no longer keep his mind occupied with the desert, he turned and climbed down again, counting every step on the ten sixty-step flights.

Then he concentrated on digging. He dug an endless ditch as deep as his shoulders. As the sun arched overhead and the day became hotter, he perspired profusely. His pace slowed. Each scoop of his gigantic shovel required monstrous effort. The whistling wind increased its force and became a shrieking sandstorm. The ditch began to fill up as the shifting sands he had seen from the tower swirled around him. He turned and worked his shovel frantically to keep from being buried, but the sand rose steadily—to his knees, to his waist, to his shoulders....

He turned off the storm. The shoveling had made him tired; the imagined heat and sand gave him a tormenting thirst. He was on a raft lost at sea. He had been without food and water for days. Lying on hard planks under a sweltering sun, floating on water he could not drink even in his imagination, he created images of billowy mattresses and cool, gurgling springs.

It was difficult to keep his mind away from the world of Mort. The indefatigable Hairy was at work with some care-fully recruited assistants pretending to search for Caland and spreading the rumor of his disappearance. Throughout the Valley, at the Merc Mart, at the Government Mall, at the hotes, and the Attic at the Por,; passersby were being confronted with his description: known as Cal...age...height...general appear-ance...last seen wearing...please notify immediately....

Word surely would have reached Tel by this time. Caland wondered how she would react to it. She was occupying herself with menial tasks, Sam the Artist had told him, while she grasped for mental equilibrium. She nursed the sick, she worked in a co-op laundry, and in her idle moments she asked puzzled questions about the Valley and its inhabitants. None of the answers had piqued her memory in any way. Caland had gone to see her once as one of a group of well-wishers who politely asked how she was feeling, told her she was looking well, assured her that a little more time was all that her mind required, and came away. Caland had said nothing. He knew about the abyss, knew that such a gulf could not be bridged by words.

He wrenched his thoughts away. He was pursued. A grotesque beast, of hallucinatory shape and proportions, was sniffing on his heels, and he fled from open country into a tangle of prickly vegetation. As he forced his way forward, the ground suddenly became soggy. He turned back and found the beast crouched behind him waiting to spring. The quagmire began to engulf him. Each time he struggled to lift a foot, the other was forced deeper. He threw himself backward and attempted to swim through the muck, but his body was sucked downward, ever downward....

He felt increasingly thirsty. This thirst was not imaginary, and he thought ruefully that he should have drunk something before he allowed them to tie him up. How much time had passed? Certainly no more than an hour. Again he wearily climbed the ten flights of sixty steps each, looked out on the harsh desert landscape and descended. He left the tower and dashed dementedly into the blowing sand.

He switched the image to a forest on a wind-blown night, with rain-drenched trees moaning in the gale and crashing down around him. He took refuge in a forest hut of evil memory. Then he headed back into the storm and looked down on the ravished world of Mort as dawn faintly penetrated the dark clouds.

Next he was pawing through the rubble and lifting out Tel's limp body.

"Don't think about Tel!" he commanded himself. He began to climb the steps again. Enforced relaxation with his senses sealed off made him drowsy, and eventually he dozed off. He awoke in a panic. For a moment he could not remember where he was, and the bindings frightened him. Then he began to count steps again. He ascended; he descended into a dungeon, was overwhelmed by enemies, tied up, and left lying on the stone floor in murky dampness with water dripping onto his face.

He wondered if two hours had passed, and how long it would take for Sam the Artist and the Reverend to realize that the trap had been sprung. "Don't think about the Valley!" he ordered himself irritably. "Don't think about Tel!" That was the worst of his tribulations. He enjoyed thinking about Tel and reliving their days together. After his fear that he would not remember, the bitter irony of her forgetfulness overmatched all of the agonies of his nightmares.

He concentrated on his nightmares: the spaceship corridors unfolding into a maze; the pursuit of Wes Fulm down the Avenue of Fountains; the waterless streams choked with the dead. His thoughts circled back to Tel. He had lifted her from the wreckage with crushed skull and broken neck. She had been dead. Her body was cold.

He started. "That's it!" he mumbled into the gag. "She was dead. She *was* dead. Everyone there knew it. Her skull was crushed, her neck broken, her body was cold. If she was dead, she is dead, and the person who's alive must be someone pretending to be Tel. That's why she can't remember. *That's* the answer!"

If it had not been for the gag, he would have cried out. He struggled briefly with his bounds. They were loose, but not loose enough for him to remove them by himself without a prolonged struggle. Finally he relaxed. His ordeal could not last much longer, and then he would show the Reverend and Sam the Artist how Tel was the mystery's critical clue.

He began to climb steps again.

Suddenly someone was fumbling with the cloth tied around

his head. It came free, and he looked up into Regelz Arlu's perplexed face.

Arlu was clothed in white, but on this day his clothing was not immaculate. His suit bore smudges from the wreckage he had just clambered over. His bulky figure arched over Caland; he was talking excitedly, but Caland heard nothing at all. When Arlu freed his hands, he reached up and pried the wax out of one ear.

"Your ears were plugged, too?" Arlu demanded incredulously. "What *is* going on here?"

He bent over and slipped the bounds from Caland's ankles.

Sam the Artist and the Reverend had arrived. They were looking through the cramped opening. Behind them stood Mucks Groilan and Sigley Varno.

Arlu's puzzlement had changed to anger. "What kind of skullduggery—who did this?"

Sam and the Reverend were as stunned as Caland was. They were unable to speak. Finally Sam stammered, "Arlu? You mean all this time—"

The Reverend said, "Sometimes the problem with a trap is to figure out what's been caught."

"What trap?" Arlu demanded. "You mean Cal was caught in a trap? Did you see him? He was blindfolded and gagged, his ears were plugged, and his hands and feet were tied. Why would anyone—?"

"Cal wasn't caught in the trap," the Reverend said. "He was the bait."

Arlu's perplexity had deepened. "Is this whole Valley sprung?"

"It was a trap," the Reverend said, "and it caught you. If we don't figure this out quickly, we may waste an opportunity that won't come again. What are you doing in the Valley?"

"I came for a meeting. I sent word to Calta a couple of hours ago—didn't she tell you? I'm leaving for Aravia tomorrow, and I wanted to see all of you before I go."

"All of us have been busy," the Reverend said. "How'd you

happen to be snooping through a wrecked building?'"

Arlu took a deep breath. He was controlling his temper. "I got out of my 'cab at the Fig Stump. I was about to go in when I heard someone say, 'Cal is missing. We're going to help look for him'."

"Hairy overdid that part of it," Sam the Artist muttered.

"So I went with them," Arlu said. "Naturally, I was extremely alarmed. There were fifteen or twenty of us before we split into small groups. The group I was with began looking through the remains of houses along Junk Vista Avenue. Someone said, 'Check that one—no one has looked there.' So I did, I saw something inside, and it turned out to be Cal. Understand, I'm being patient. Maybe I could help more if I knew what this was about."

"Who told you to look there?" the Reverend asked.

Arlu hesitated. "It was anything but an organized search, and people were scattered all around and coming and going. I don't know. I didn't look to see who it was. Someone said check here, and I did. Does it matter?"

"It might be crucially important. Would you know the voice if you heard it again?"

"Probably. It wasn't a voice that I'm familiar with, but I don't know very many Vals."

Sam the Artist said softly, "Maybe he hung around to watch. Let's spread out quickly and try to grab him."

Sam and the Reverend backed away from the opening. Arlu eased himself under a fallen beam and clambered over a section of roof. Caland followed him. There was nothing to be seen outside except a number of Vals, mals and fems, who were wandering aimlessly and peering into the Valley's wreckage.

Sam whispered to Mucks Groilan, who attached himself to Arlu and remained by his elbow. Arlu seemed not to notice. He was exacerbated over the fact that he'd been confronted with a mystery and no one would explain it to him.

They drifted slowly toward the Prom, with Sam and the Reverend ranging about widely in search of a hidden watcher.

It seemed that much of the Valley had been looking for Caland. Off to the east, Calta Draning and several of her dolls were prowling about with a large group of Vals. Yda's voice drifted to them from a group searching south of the Prom. West of the plaza was another group with Doctor Gormaz. Even Dal Eddyer and Alz Hernl were poking through the wreckage of a shack behind their buildings.

Caland had outdistanced Arlu and Mucks Groilan. Sam and the Reverend joined him, and Sam remarked, "We shouldn't have spread that rumor about Cal disappearing. I know everyone in the Valley feels responsible for him, but I didn't expect the whole Valley to drop what it was doing and start looking. You'd think he'd vanished with the only key to the Valley's sanctum." He added softly, "Could it be Arlu?"

"If it isn't, then someone used him," the Reverend said.

Sam the Artist nodded. "Someone got suspicious, didn't want to go himself, and said to Arlu, 'Check over there.' Maybe he saw us watching the place."

"What do we do now?" Caland asked.

"I don't know," Sam the Artist said. "It was a great idea, and we wasted it. There'd be no point in trying it again."

All of the groups seemed to be converging on the Prom at the same moment. Yda was the first to notice Caland. She called excitedly, "There he is!" The others quickened their paces. Doctor Gormaz, arriving at the head of his group, demanded, "Where was he?" He turned to someone behind him and in the same breath said, "We've found him!"

Arlu came up behind Caland. He stiffened and pointed a finger at Gormaz. "He's the one! *He* said, 'Check that one!'"

Mucks Groilan's instinctive reaction was to grip Gormaz's shoulder with a powerful hand. Gormaz jerked loose and wheeled about, his face a panicky mask. Like a cornered animal making a frenzied dash toward an escape hole, he scurried through the only opening left in the almost complete circle formed by the assembling Vals. He ran westward toward the sea.

For a long moment everyone stared after him uncomprehendingly. Then Mucks Groilan unleashed an angry bellow and raced in pursuit with long, churning strides. In an instant twenty Vals were following; in another instant, fifty. What Gormaz hoped to accomplish was not clear to anyone, then or later. Probably he had no objective except blind flight. His only place of refuge was Dom's house, two streets to the south, and he was actually running away from it. He could not have outdistanced a crowd of young and energetic Vals.

He ran, but his pursuers gained on him easily.

Suddenly he collapsed. He fell like a rag doll that had lost its stuffing. Mucks Groilan, still in the lead, warily approached the untidy object sprawled on the ground and gingerly turned it over. All of them gathered to stare down at it.

It looked like a leathery mummy that belonged in a museum's display case—a relic of antiquity that had survived time's vicissitudes but bore every mark of its passing. The lips peeled back tautly; the teeth were laid bare; the fleshless hands were claws clenched as though clutching an invisible object.

The head was tilted to one side. When the Reverend reached out tentatively to straighten it and make certain that Gormaz was really dead, his hair and scraggly beard brushed away.

All of them drew back, but they continued to stare disbelievingly at the body. "I wonder," Sam the Artist mused, "whether anyone has proved mathematically that whatever it is we're looking at is theoretically possible."

Regelz Arlu, slowest of the pursuers, arrived puffing and demanded, "What happened to him?"

"None of us know," the Reverend said. "Why don't you search it? If you can find the answer, you'll probably have all the answers."

They placed Gormaz's body on an improvised stretcher. The entire group headed for Dom's house, grimly determined to extract information from his assistants until all of the mysteries were dispelled. Caland watched them go. Then he walked slowly to the ocean beach and hunched himself onto one of the boulders. For the moment, at least, the solution of mysteries held no interest for him, not even his own. He felt mentally exhausted, and the ocean's unrelenting rhythms had the blessed, relaxing quality of stretching a mind out to infinity.

He was not even aware of the passing time until he suddenly noticed that the sun was low on the horizon. The sky was brilliantly clear; the ocean seemed murkier than usual—clear forecast of a spectacular sunset. Baris Bronlan had arrived unbeknownst to him and taken a seat on the other boulder.

Sam the Artist came plodding down the beach. "It's all over with," he announced. His voice sounded peculiarly flat and disinterested. He was as exhausted as Caland. The strain of the afternoon's events had worn out all of them. "Finished, do you understand?" Sam went on. "Arlu's getting everything he wants."

"I thought probably he would," Caland said.

"Don't you even want to know who Gormaz was?"

"He looked awfully old," Caland said indifferently. "I suppose he was the legendary Nurlas Ernst, who founded the Polyscience Institute—was it three hundred years ago?"

Sam the Artist stared. "Actually, you're right. But it's a lot more peculiar than that. Do you remember the tales I kept joshing the Reverend about—a scientist named Odan proved that teleportation was theoretically possible, and Zareent proved that time travel was theoretically possible, and someone—was it Fremanz?—proved that systematic telepathy was theoretically possible, and so on?"

Caland nodded. "What did Gormaz prove is theoretically possible?"

"Gormaz," Sam the Artist said, "was Zareent."

CHAPTER THIRTY-EIGHT

Arlu called it their last meeting. Then he corrected himself with a flash of multiple smiles. "Last *official* meeting. I hope we'll all meet many times in the future under far happier circumstances than those that have occasioned these past meetings."

"If you've actually got this mess figured out," Yda said, "what circumstance could be happier than that?"

The Reverend said politely, "Perhaps if we dispense with the philosophical irrelevancies—"

"That's telling him," Calta Draning said. "Keep him on the subject, or Alz will be serving us an early break right here."

Outside it was another brilliant Valley afternoon, and all of them except Arlu would have preferred to be there enjoying it. Off to the west, and visible through the room's west window, the entire population of the Valley plus colorful alien clusters of tourists had gathered around a slab of cement where a park was projected near the ocean end of the Prom. An enormous cargo ship hovered over them—Captain Akonif was returning Baris Bronlan's borrowed spaceship. Bronlan unexpectedly had decided that he didn't want it back. He had solved all of the problems, including those of an engine run on baking soda, and he had other things to do. Sam the Artist had suggested a park with a spaceship as a memorial. When asked, "A memorial to what?" he had grinned and answered, "Us."

Arlu, whose projected trip to Aravia had been deranged by the unexpected disclosures concerning Doctor Gormaz, was determined to catch the next ship. Hence his insistence on the meeting, but he lost his audience when those present turned to the window to watch Akonif skillfully plant the gleaming spaceship squarely on the slab. The spectators cheered. In the room above the Fig Stump, Arlu sounded an impatient snort.

The Reverend, Sam the Artist, Calta, Yda, Bronlan, and Caland gave him their reluctant attention. Off to one side, present but not really part of the group, were Tel and her new—or old—mal, Edlan.

"By now, all of you know that Doctor Stran Gormaz was really Nurlas Ernst, who was really Zareent," Arlu said. "Since Zareent would seem to be the only name that he was legally entitled to, I'm going to call him that. Much of his history will never be known, and much of what is known will never be explained, but the rough outline goes like this."

His voice droned on. Caland leaned back and closed his eyes. He was attending out of politeness; he really had little interest in Arlu's interminable explanations. He had lost Tel, and he still had a weight of metal in his brain, and no solution promised to alter either of those facts.

"As a young physicist," Arlu intoned, "Zareent had evolved a magnificently imaginative and ingenious mathematical theory concerning space and time. When his work brought him no plaudits at all—only insults—he offered to remove the word 'theoretical' from his speculations the moment anyone provided funding for the necessary apparatus. He was laughed out of his profession. The legend of his assassination by religious fanatics had no basis in fact. Zareent had only mentioned in passing, in a lecture, the possibility of restoring a prophet to life. Religious indignation was nothing compared with the scientific scorn he aroused, and what happened to him professionally was almost worse than assassination.

"He languished in poverty for a time while he continued to work on his theory. Since he failed to interest anyone in its scientific potential, he concentrated his efforts on the possibility of using it to make money. Somehow he raised the necessary capital. His theory worked, and—as he had calculated—it made him rich.

"He set up his headquarters on the remote world of Folamnin and founded the Polyscience Institute, where he built what was probably the galaxy's greatest fortune by restoring the elderly rich to youth and good health. Using their decrepit and dying bodies as temporal fulcrums, he pulled their more youthful and healthy selves from the past. Patients who entered his hospital as wasted hundred-year-olds about to expire emerged at the relatively youthful and healthy age of seventy. Whereupon Zareent told them to go and sin no more and avoid whatever it was that had been killing them at one hundred. In most cases this was literally possible; anyone knowing at age seventy all of the medical details about the disease fated to kill him thirty years later was able to take countermeasures while there was still time. In any case, the patient was given back thirty years of his life to live over again, and who could say that the fortune Zareent charged for the treatment was excessive? The Polyscience Institute was immensely successful. Zareent's wealth was virtually unlimited, and—since he periodically applied his treatment to himself—he also possessed eternal life."

Caland, listening absently, suddenly perceived a paradox that jarred him to alertness. "What about memory?"

Arlu smiled. "Ah! The scheme's most dramatic weakness! But of course you know about that from personal experience. When a hundred-year-old patient's seventy-year-old self was plucked out of the past, naturally he had no knowledge of those last thirty years the older self had lived. The focus of the Institute's treatment centered on this problem. All of his patients lost memories. The Institute dealt with this by requiring patients to spend a considerable amount of time before their rejuvenations in compiling records, albums of fotes, dictated memoirs, and whatever else might be useful to their more youthful selves. After the rejuvenation, the younger patient was required to study this material and submit to long lectures from his elder self before the Institute would release him. This didn't wholly replace the lost memory, but in most cases it proved adequate. The Institute glossed over the blanks by cautioning family and friends that one of the side effects of the miraculous cure the Institute achieved was a slight blurring of memory."

"What happened to the older self when the younger self replaced it?" the Reverend asked.

Arlu's chins folded into multiple frowns. "That's another dramatic weakness, and one that is glossed over by Zareent's assistants. No doubt this problem was discussed in detail with the patient, and the patient willingly accepted the solution. The Polyscience Institute has a highly efficient crematorium in its central complex of buildings—used for disposal of experimental animals, the assistants claim. I have two theories about this. One is that when the youthful self is pulled out of the past, the elder self is propelled into the future, and when that future arrives, there's a body to dispose of. Whether it's a living body or a dead body, and where it has been in the meantime, are better left unanswered. In my theory, the temporal fulcrum, the older self, remains in the present, dead or alive. Either way, there would be a body to dispose of. The older self could not be permitted to co-exist with the younger self. Cal was an exceptional patient. His older self was already dead when he arrived at the Institute."

"Just a moment," Caland said. "They wired my brain together and restored me to life."

Arlu shook his head gently. "No. What really happened was that they plucked your younger—and living—self out of the past, using your dead body as the necessary fulcrum, just as they did with all the other patients."

"But—the metal in my head—"

"Having reclaimed your younger and living self, they then performed a most ingenious surgical procedure, and filled your brain with wire. I suspect that they'd been making preparatory experiments for years, and that they had many failures before they finally succeeded with you. I also suspect that they experimented extensively on their elderly patients—who were going to be cremated anyway—before or after they replaced them with their younger selves. Naturally the assistants deny that."

"But why did they fuss with Cal's brain?" Sam the Artist asked.

"Because they had a use for him."

"But why me?" Caland asked. "And why didn't they rejuvenate the fem who was killed with me?"

"Because it was the mal that they needed—a young, healthy, active mal. You—or your body—happened along at precisely the right time. It would seem providential if we didn't already have evidence that the Institute was dedicated to arranging providence to suit itself. An accident so conveniently near the Institute's grounds, with Institute personnel so conveniently on hand, sounds peculiar even in the official report, but of course we'll never know what really happened."

"But what did they want of me with metal in my head?" Caland persisted.

Arlu leaned back and tapped his index fingers together. "Consider the plight of Zareent, now Nurlas Ernst. He's achieved eternal life—apparently. He has, over the centuries, accumulated fabulous wealth. He's able to indulge his interest in *outré* scientific experiments and any other interest he may have. He lives as he chooses, and on his own grounds he is an absolute monarch.

"But his own grounds, extensive as they are, are still part of a district, which is part of a province, which is part of a fiefdom, which is part of a continental federation, which is part of a global league. All of those political entities have governments, and are infested with bumptious, arrogant politicians. The politicians know that the Polyscience Institute is immensely wealthy, and they maneuver to extract whatever they consider to be their fair shares. The governments lavish their creative energy on the structuring of tax laws that will apply almost exclusively to the Institute. They also fabricate restrictive laws, and demand that the Institute pay bribes to avoid their enforcement. Naturally, such harassment infuriates Zareent. He easily could move to another world—he already owns potential sites on hundreds of worlds—but if he did so, he'd merely acquire a new set of governments and a new set of obnoxious politicians to deal with.

"What he wants and needs is a political entity of his own where he can make his own laws. It's a natural ambition—he has everything else. As the years pass, this desire swells until it consumes all of his energy. Nothing less than the absolute ownership of a world or a nation will satisfy him. But even unlimited wealth can't buy title to a world. Geographic and political entities have been owned by individuals with some frequency, but one has to discover them first and claim them. Success is a matter of timing and luck. Zareent has neither the patience nor the adventurousness to launch himself as an explorer, but he does possess a different sort of weapon—his mastery of time. He reasons that it should be possible to find a world, or a political entity on a world, whereby his mastery of time can enable him to claim lawful ownership."

Sam the Artist exploded. "You mean those bench marks and the rest of the two-hundred-year-old junk were fakes?"

"Certainly not. They were planted two hundred years in the past and left there to age naturally. They looked genuine—they *were* genuine. They actually had been there two hundred and eleven years. But they were planted there the night of the storm."

"What did the storm have to do with it?" the Reverend asked.

"Ah! The storm on Mort, and the natural upheavals on other worlds, were complications that Zareent didn't anticipate when he formulated his plans. His mastery of time was limited in scope, since it involved only the plucking of younger selves of patients from twenty to thirty years in the past. His technique wasn't adequate for the vastly more complicated process of sending a living person a considerable distance into the past, and having him survive to plant the necessary evidence of exploration. Time is the most potent force in the universe, and it's a fearful thing to unleash. Mishandled, it could completely destroy a world. Zareent's early attempts all but devastated the lands he was trying to claim."

"Is that what he wanted me for?" Caland asked. "To plant evidence in the past?"

"That was his plan, and it worked."

"He was able to control me two hundred and eleven years in the past?"

"I don't know. The assistants don't know. Zareent handled that part of the operation himself. Either he was able to control you through time, or his control over you was such that he could give you detailed instructions that you would carry out automatically once you arrived in the past. What he had to have was a messenger who could be controlled absolutely without knowing what he was doing. No hint of this could come out. His well-laid plans would miscarry on the first faint suspicion of skullduggery. Originally he tried to hire someone for the task—an adventurer who declared himself willing to do anything for a price. Then the adventurer caught a hint of what was going to happen to him and changed his mind. He already knew too much; probably he ended in the crematorium. A robot was experimented with and found inadequate for a number of reasons—for one, such a technologically advanced messenger couldn't be left in the past without risking the potentially embarrassing scientific inquiry. Because that was the plan. The messenger was to be left in the past. It was difficult enough to project him there, and Zareent saw no point in heightening the complications by attempting to bring him back."

The Reverend said indignantly, "Do you mean Cal—?"

"Was to be left two hundred and eleven years in the past. Yes. The moment Cal's surgery had succeeded, and Zareent had that absolute control over him that he required, he and a small staff began a galactic search for the world or political entity that would best serve their purpose. Cal was so completely under control that they could park him in safe places while they ranged widely looking for a place where a claim of prior exploration could be pressed with reasonable chance of success. Zareent and his assistants traveled under a number of aliases and disguises, but the uncertainties of Cal's mental processes made it necessary for him to retain the same identity. This is why he was the only identified traveler who was present on all three of those worlds when catastrophes struck.

"On Cenaru, Olyndyt, and Skarlont, Zareent thought he'd found the world he was looking for, but his technique was still inadequate. Once he almost got Cal and his entire staff killed, including himself. But he persisted. He had plenty of time, the money was a triviality, and the objective was overwhelmingly important to him. He had everything else he wanted, and he expected to live forever—or for many more centuries, at least, in a series of rejuvenations.

"He made three major attempts, and I suspect that minor disasters on at least a dozen worlds represent lesser experiments that he made along the way. I haven't been able to identify the precise point where Zareent became Doctor Stran Gormaz. Probably the real Doctor Gormaz figured in some kind of experiment, after which his name and professional reputation were extremely useful to Zareent.

"An assistant traveled to Mort on the same ship that Cal did. Of course he paid no attention to him except in private, with his apparatus, so neither Cal nor my assistant saw any sign of his being watched. Zareent reached Mort several days later, coming from a different direction and traveling as Gormaz. He immediately sent his assistant to check out another world. Other assistants came and went, all of them effectively disguised as tourists, which completely defeated my attempts to connect someone with Cal. They parked Cal again—this time in the Valley—while they investigated the world of Mort. It was such an ideal world for Zareent. It had only one owner, who was an ass, and the ownership claim was based on an exploration that was less than a century in the past. All Zareent had to do was find records of a prior exploration in this sector, establish a fictitious family of descendants through which he could claim ownership on the basis of a fabricated discovery of Mort, and send Cal back through time to plant the claim marks.

"But Mort had a serious disadvantage. Zareent needed to secure a base of operations, and that seemed such an impossibility that he was about to leave. Then he met Dom, who knew all about the Polyscience Institute, and he propositioned him. Dom enthusiastically agreed to allow Zareent to use his house for a sociological survey in return for a rejuvenation treatment. Zareent's first Mort experiment was to pull a younger Dom out of the past—with the necessary memory conditioning.

"Everything seemed to be working perfectly for Zareent. He was conducting regular experiments and sending innocuous articles into the past—and messing up the weather in this area while doing so. Given enough time, he might have perfected his technique sufficiently to be able to send Cal into the past without causing a catastrophe, but he hadn't counted on the other conspiracies that were maturing here. If Sdissler, or the world of Aravia, or any other entity, had taken over Mort in an extra-legal maneuver, than Zareent's prior exploration claim would have been as futile as Pakovich's. He had to rush his experiments. He also had to take time away from them to act the part of a sociologist, because he wanted no one, then or later, to suspect that he was a fake. Finally, he was forced to push Cal into the past before he finished modifying his technique, and he almost destroyed the Valley."

"What about the towers?" Caland asked.

"Ah! He needed a tower, if not towers. That was essential."

"The spaceship was gone."

"He had something better—a horizontal tower. That long metal fence around the fertilizer factory. It's conveniently located right behind Dom's back yard, and it worked even better than a vertical tower. It worked—that was the point—and Zareent was in a hurry. So he took over Cal's mind during the confusion the storm caused, and sent him back through time two hundred and eleven years. Cal was gone for only a few hours, but he may have spent more time than that in the past. He had to visit three places around the bay and plant bench marks in a cement base, simulate a camp site, sink a boat motor in a predetermined place, and then trek up one of the Tin Mountains to plant a bench mark there. Once all of that had been done, Zareent's mission on Mort was accomplished. He cut his temporal connection, leaving Cal two hundred and eleven years in the past. If the Court's investigators turned up a two-hundred-year-old skeleton in addition to the other relics, that was already provided for. Reference is made in the exploration diary to a missing explorer.

"So Zareent forgot all about Cal. He had plenty of other things to worry about, one of them being whether Dom's house was going to survive the storm. If it had collapsed, the equipment exposed there could have inspired embarrassing questions. He forgot about Cal, and that was a serious miscalculation. Time is tricky stuff to mess with. Cal was left two hundred and eleven years in the past, and apparently he snapped back into the present the moment Zareent turned off his apparatus. Cal regained consciousness in the present at approximately the same place where he finished his labors in the past—physically battered and exhausted, but with mind and body intact."

"What about me?" Tel asked suddenly.

Arlu flashed his smiles for her. "You were Zareent's second miscalculation. But let me finish with Cal. Put yourselves in Zareent's mind—he left Cal two hundred and eleven years in the past, he closed down his apparatus with mission accomplished, and he hurried out to be a helpful good citizen in assisting the unfortunate victims of the storm he had caused. And a few hours later he suddenly found Cal confronting him face to face. Two Vals who chanced to be looking at Zareent when that happened say he turned deathly white and tottered unsteadily. But he quickly recovered. Had any memories of what had happened slipped into Cal's consciousness? He had to find out before Cal or anyone else became suspicious. In the meantime, he couldn't very well dispose of Cal in the intimate surroundings of the Valley. He suspected that Cal's friends would be watching him closely. The important thing was to see that he was kept occupied and unruffled—that he had no emotional disturbances that might stir up recollections better kept buried.

"Tel's death was precisely the kind of emotional experience Zareent wanted Caland to avoid. So he restored her to Cal—he had the dead Tel's younger self plucked out of the past. He maybe plucked her from a bit further in the past than he intended, since it wiped out her memory of Mort completely, but time is tricky stuff, and Zareent wasn't accustomed to rejuvenating young people.

"Then came the next shock. Tel was a prober, and she'd been living in intimate association with Cal. What was she probing? What had she learned from Cal? Had she reported to her superiors? Zareent couldn't undo what he had done; he could only wait and see what would happen. The tension became enormous, and even the apparently favorable visit of the deputation from the Interworld Court didn't ease it. He continued to wait and to check Cal's mind regularly.

"That was the condition he was in when the rumor reached him that Cal had disappeared. It put him in a mental and emotional turmoil. He immediately did a control check on Cal, and what his instruments told him made no sense at all. He suspected a trap, but he had to find out what was happening. He attached himself to a search party and managed to send me to check the suspected location. As it happened, he spoke out of the crowd, and because I'd never spoken to him, I didn't recognize the voice."

"All of that is clear enough," the Reverend said. "He was under extreme tension, and when you suddenly identified him and Mucks grabbed him, he lost his head and tried to escape. But what happened to him?"

"No one knows. Even his assistants refuse to guess. Time is tricky stuff, and he'd fussed with it once too often. We don't know how many times he'd had himself rejuvenated. Each time he reached further into the past for a younger self. There were a number of extremely elderly Zareents strung out along the portals of time. All his assistants can suggest is that the unusual strain and exertion of recent events, plus his attempt to escape, made something snap, and time reasserted itself."

"Is that the future Tel and I have to look forward to?" Caland asked. "Reverting to our older dead selves at any moment?"

Arlu answered gravely. "No one knows that, either. The assistants say that such a thing has never happened before, but no one keeps records on all of the Institute's patients. Only Zareent and his assistants have been rejuvenated more than once. You'll simply have to live your lives and find out. We're going to take the most forceful action possible against the Institute. The great wealth controlled by it and its late owner will have to be used to compensate for the damages caused by these time experiments. We'll also have to slap controls on this practice of pulling younger selves out of the past. I don't think humanity will ever be ready for that. It poses too many problems."

"Mightn't it be possible to use the practice to benefit humanity?" the Reverend asked.

"The problem would be to control it and prevent the operators from abusing it. Zareent wasn't interested in benefiting anyone but himself. But who *could* be trusted with that kind of power?"

"Who needs rejuvenating anyway?" Yda asked. "Being young and foolish again may have its attractions for some, but not for me."

"Why should it?" Calta asked. "You have too much fun being old and foolish."

"At least it's not old and fat and foolish."

"Now see here, putreface!"

Caland quietly slipped away. As he descended the outside staircase, the argument, with a background of laughter, swelled in volume behind him.

CHAPTER THIRTY-NINE

A cluster of tourists still stood admiringly around Baris Bronlan's returned spaceship, but the Valley had gone back to work. Morlef no longer had a problem in finding workers. The demise of Doctor Gormaz and the collapse of his fabricated claim to the world of Mort had revitalized the Valley, and Morlef was pushing his building projects enthusiastically.

Caland paused to watch a grading machine from Pak Enterprises that was transforming the meandering path on Bay Unview Boulevard into a street. As soon as the building plots had been determined, there would be surfaced walks crossing the Valley from north to south, in addition to a vehicular road situated somewhere west of the theater. Caland remembered his first day as a Valley resident, when he had perplexedly watched the beach-bound Vals pop out of the concealed and overgrown pathways that had threaded between Valley buildings, and he wondered if something priceless had been lost forever.

There was a great deal to be said for a mode of living in which people and ideas and principles were so highly prized above material things. It was inevitable in a society where material things were junk; but now the Valley would have new buildings and streets and pathways. People would respond by wanting better furnishings for their homes, and labor and money would be invested in their upkeep. The balance between the material and the immaterial would change, and that change, once set in motion, would be as inexorable as time. Caland wore a troubled frown as he slowly made his way down to the ocean beach.

He sat on a boulder watching the waves sweep relentlessly shoreward, and he thought of his own future. Arlu's final resolution of his problem made his prospects seem worse than before. His head was still stuffed with metal; in addition, he was a fugitive from time, which might reclaim him at any moment. There was nothing he could do about that except make as effective use of his life as he could while it lasted—but that was all that anyone could do. He was free to leave the Valley and Mort any time he chose, but there was nowhere else that he wanted to go. So he would stay here, among the only friends that he knew, and work on the theater as effectively as he could, and hope that the changing Valley would retain some of the values that made him cherish it.

Having laboriously advanced his reasoning one step at a time until he arrived at that inevitable decision, he began to think that it was time for him to return to work.

Footsteps crunched on the sand behind him. He turned; it was still a bit early, but he expected to see Baris Bronlan arriving for his daily attendance on the sunset.

It was Tel. She hoisted herself onto the boulder adjoining his, and, avoiding his eyes, sat and looked at the ocean.

"Phem tells me that you and I spent a lot of time here," she said finally.

"We did," Caland agreed.

"Why?"

"It's private. Before the storm put everyone to work, the bay beach was a clutter of people day and night. Hardly anyone came here. And this is different. The open ocean gives one a glimpse of an uncorrupted and untamed eternity. An ocean squeezed into a bay loses its character."

She nodded. "Yes. I think I see what you mean. We need to talk, don't we? This seems like a good place for it."

Caland smiled wistfully. "The best of all places. In a way, we started here. I woke up and found you asleep in the kitchen when you were supposed to be watching me, and I slipped away. You found me here, talking with Bar. You said, 'Don't ever do that again.' Almost the first words you spoke to me. So it really started here, and it's only appropriate that it should end here. I knew from the beginning that this would happen."

She was frowning perplexedly. "Knew what would happen?"

"That you would find another interest. I didn't know that you already had one, but it amounts to the same thing."

"Another interest? What are you talking about?" she asked blankly.

"Edlan. Who else?"

"Edlan is a prober," she said, still looking blank. "He's taking over my assignment, and I brought him to the meeting so he could be up-to-date on what's going on. My assignment—about which I remember nothing at all—was to hold down the Mort end of a search aimed at preventing criminal elements from taking over this world. Such a development would have produced unthinkable complications for galactic law and order, and several conspiracies were in motion. The ones recently uncovered—by Prency Tate, and Sdissler, and even Doctor Gormaz—were child's games compared with a couple of long-term plots the probers had identified. As Arlu said, the world is so wealthy, and Pakovich left himself so vulnerable that something was bound to happen. My assignment was to lay the groundwork here on Mort for preventing that. Now that I'm incapacitated, Edlan has taken over the job. But we both agree that Mort is no longer in danger, and there's no further need for a prober here. He'll return to Aravia tomorrow morning with Arlu."

"Leaving the loose ends for you to gather up?" Caland suggested.

"Screet! Are you trying to be insulting? I'm no longer a prober. Prober qualifications are stringent, and memory failure is an incompatible defect. I sent in my resignation as soon as I was able to understand what had happened."

"I see." Caland hesitated. "You're staying here?"

"Why not? I have nowhere else to go, and Alexander the Second has offered me a job. I'm going to organize a force of proctors for him with a civilian reserve for emergencies."

"Of course," Caland murmured. He had vivid memories of the efficiency and decisiveness with which Tel could act. She would make a highly capable World Proctor Super.

"What do you mean by that?"

"It's a good choice. I'm glad you'll be staying on Mort. A lot of us would miss you if you left."

"Would you really?"

"Really," Caland said and wondered whether he was lying. He had expected her to leave Mort soon, and he already decided to see as little of her as possible until then. He cherished his warm memories of her, but in her physical presence they were blotted out by his overwhelming sense of loss.

She had turned to watch the long lines of waves surging shoreward. "They mark off time like a clock," she said finally. "I never realized how important time is, and I never expected to owe my life to it. But it is difficult not being able to remember."

"I know," Caland said.

"You know, and I know, but no one else understands. And we both know that time may suddenly swallow us up and spit us out again in some guise that all of these good friends would rather not recognize. You're staying here?"

"This is the only place in the galaxy where I seem to belong."

"That's because it's the place where that fiend Zareent let you come alive for the first time in years. My case is different. Probers rarely have a chance to put down roots. My Mort assignment was unusual because it lasted so long, but I don't remember any of it. I'm staying because I happen to be here, and because there's nowhere else that I want to go."

"You loved the place once," Caland said. "You'll love it again when it's rebuilt a bit and life gets back to normal."

"Maybe. I'll tell you, though, that a smashed Valley is a peculiar place to regain consciousness in with a lost memory. It's an entirely different experience from the one you had."

"Yes," Caland mused. "Yes, I suppose it would be."

"I'm glad you think so, because no one else seems to understand. All of our friends are saying, 'How charming! You've lost your memory! Now you and Caland have everything in common!' I either want to slug them or vomit. *You* woke up in a hospital, but even then you had a problem accepting it, didn't you?"

"Of course."

"I woke up in that absurdly ornate front room of Dom's house with a character in sloppy work clothing bending over me. The glass was broken in the window, and a fallen tree lay across the yard with the end of a branch sticking inside. Another window showed nothing but devastation as far as I could see. The place was infested with Vals, who are as improbable-looking as anything any newly conscious patient has ever been exposed to. The character in work clothing, who was one of Gormaz's assistants, introduced himself to me as a doctor and informed me that his remarkable skill had cured me. All I needed was a little rest, he said. I said, 'Where the hell am I?' And he laughed and told me someone wanted to see me. After a while they brought you in. And nothing meant anything at all to me—not you, not the Valley, not the world of Mort. If it was hard for you in a hospital, think how it was for me."

"The Polyscience Institute was a rather odd hospital," Caland said reflectively.

Tel stared at him. The she burst into laughter. "I was going to insist that I had a rougher time than you did, but when you shake your head at me, I have to remember that it's loaded with metal. At least I was spared that. Our friends are saying that nothing but good has come out of this mess. All the conspirators are wiped out. Pakovich has retired and gone to Aravia to put on social airs that he doesn't have. Everyone predicts great things for Alexander the Second, but I know better. I'm predicting great things for Melana. She must have been priceless in her role of a forsaken waif studying art and writing a book and being pursued by half the mals on the planet. I had a couple of glimpses of Dom while I was in that makeshift hospital, and I have him tabbed too. No one in the Valley seems to comprehend why he suddenly was smitten with generosity and let this place go in return for an enormous income, but I know now. He had the Polyscience Institute's youth treatment without really comprehending what Gormaz—or Zareent—was up to. When he suddenly realized that Gormaz was responsible for tearing up Mort and killing and injuring a lot of people, he got to thinking that maybe he was responsible, too, for giving Gormaz a place to work. He decided to cut and run before people found out and started a flock of lawsuits."

Caland had suspected as much, but he said nothing.

Tel turned and scrutinized him. "You don't talk much, do you?"

"I'm still recovering from the last time they took over my mind. I did a lot of talking when they left me alone for a while. When I look back on it, it seems like an enormous amount of talking. I even made you listen."

She burst into laughter. "All right. We're two people without pasts and with questionable futures. How does the present look to you?"

"I'll have work to do," Caland said. "The theater is going to be important, but only if I can make it good."

"My proctors are going to be important," Tel said. "It's a miracle that Mort survived for so long without any. I intend to make them good."

Again they sat in silence, watching the waves.

Suddenly she threw herself into his arms. "All right, dammit. They told me you'd be ridiculously polite and unwilling to presume on my defective memory. But I've been told in such intriguing detail about what I lost that I want to find it again."

It was the same Tel, enfolding him in the warmth that he'd thought was gone forever, but he struggled and turned his face away from her. "Tel. You've forgotten all about it, but we talked it over again and again. When they put that metal in my head—"

She pressed her lips to his, and his love for her overwhelmed him. Love and desire. The desire was such a stranger to him that he resisted it in astonishment but only momentarily. It swelled like the shoreward-bound ocean waves and moved just as inevitably.

They lay in the sand, closely embraced, with the deep rhythm of the ocean marking off the measures of Caland's racing pulse. He raised up his elbows and looked down at Tel wonderingly.

"Right!" she said. Her deep laughter held a note of elation that he'd never heard before. "I told Gormaz's scrutty assistant that he'd better push the right button and leave it pushed, or I'd come back and scratch his eyes out."

ABOUT THE AUTHOR

LLOYD BIGGLE, JR., science fiction and mystery author and musicologist, was born in Waterloo, Iowa in 1923. Relocating to Michigan, he received degrees from Wayne State University and the University of Michigan. With the publication of his first novel, *All the Colors of Darkness*, he became a full-time author, a profession he continued until his death in 2002.

Biggle introduced aesthetics into science fiction, utilizing his musical background and his interest in artistic themes. His mystery stories include the Grandfather Rastin and Lady Sarah Varnley short stories, two Sherlock Holmes novels, and the J. Pletcher/Raina Lambert series.

He was the founding Secretary Treasurer of Science Fiction Writers of America and served as Chairman of its trustees for many years. Biggle also founded the Science Fiction Oral History Association to preserve a record of science fiction notables' speeches and interviews.

He died after a courageous twenty-year battle with leukemia and cancer.

www.ingramcontent.com/pod-product-compliance
Lightning Source LLC
Chambersburg PA
CBHW032251020726
47495CB00001B/52